Edward Heron-Allen (1861-1943) was an English polymath, writer, scientist and scholar. Writing under a number of pseudonyms, as well as his own name, his works cover numerous forms of literature and fields, including those of Persian poetry, violins, chiromancy, and foraminifera, though he is probably best remembered today for his forays into fantastic fiction under the pseudonym of Christopher Blayre. His publications include *Chiromancy, or the science of palmistry* (1883), *Violin-Making, as it was and is* (1884), the volume of poetry *The Love-Letters of a Vagabond* (1889), a translation from the Persian of *The Lament of Bābā Tāhir* (1902), *Barnacles in Nature and in Myth* (1928), *The Strange Papers of Dr. Blayre* (1932), and *Asparagus as a Hobby for Amateurs* (1934).

SNUGGLY BOOKS

EDWARD HERON-ALLEN

THE COMPLETE SHORTER FICTION

THIS IS A SNUGGLY BOOK

ISBN: 978-1-64525-017-3

The publishers would like to thank Timothy McCann and the Heron-Allen Society, for providing the cover image for this book, and for their important work in promoting the study and appreciation of the life, interests and writings of Edward Heron-Allen.

CONTENTS.

A NOTE ON THE TEXTS.

MUCH of the material contained herein originally was printed in the United States and, therefore, in the breadth of the original texts there is a mixture of American and British spellings. We have chosen to, in most places, adopt British spellings for consistency, while occasionally using American spellings or punctuation where it appears to have been the Heron-Allen's preference.

Most of the stories were originally published by small publishers, or self-published, and there is ample evidence of a lack of editing on the part of the publishers. The problem is exasperated by numerous occasions where the typesetter clearly blunders, leaving occasion for interpretation or uncertainty. We have, therefore, made corrections where necessary, but on occasion, when we have felt that we could not proceed with absolute certainty, we have left what may or may not be typos in place, in the theory that it is better to leave a possible error than to possibly introduce a new error. Spellings of words are also often peculiar, and irregular, with different spellings of the same word, without any discernible reason, present even in the same story. We have for the most part left the spellings intact, while trying to make them uniform, and, very rarely, adopting more standardized spellings.

Two of the stories from *A Fatal Fiddle*, "On a Roman Balcony" and "The Heresy of Spencer Carlyon," were reprinted in *The Strange Papers of Dr. Blayre*, as "Mano Pantea" and "The Book," the reprinted versions differing mainly from the originals in that the framing stories are different. The texts themselves, though having numerous small changes, do tell the same stories. Due to the length of the current volume, it has therefore been decided to only retain one of these, "The Heresy of Spencer Carlyon," in its original form as well as its reprinted form, so that the reader can see how Heron-Allen readapted it to a new context.

The material has been arranged chronologically, aside from *The Cheetah Girl*, which, though technically appearing before *The Strange Papers of Dr. Blayre*, was written during or after the composition of much of the material in that volume (which had been previously presented as *The Purple Sapphire and Other Posthumous Papers*), and therefore makes best sense in its current location.

As with any collection that claims to be "complete," there is room for error. This is especially true with Edward Heron-Allen, an author who used numerous pseudonyms and who seemed to find no urgency in having his name linked to these. As the present volume neared completion and was being readied for print, it became increasingly obvious that we had overlooked material, some in the form of unpublished stories, and other pieces which had been printed under pseudonyms very likely to be those of Heron-Allen. Therefore, with more time and research, further work might well be presented to the public.

A CHRONOLOGY OF THE STORIES.

A complete chronology of the stories in this volume would be rather complicated, as many were first (and sometimes later!) published in journals under various pseudonyms. The following list, therefore, confines itself to the material's publishing history in book form, during the author's lifetime:

1888.
The Suicide of Sylvester Gray; published by Belford, Clarke & Co. (U.S.A.) as a standalone book, with the subheading "Ashes of the future (A study of mere human nature)" and bearing a copyright date of 1887. It is certainly possible that the publication date of 1888 is incorrect and the volume was, in fact, published in 1887.

1888.
Kisses of Fate; published by Belford, Clarke & Co. (U.S.A.), having as its contents *The Suicide of Sylvester Gray*, as well as the other two stories under that heading in the present volume.

1889.
A Fatal Fiddle; published by Belford, Clarke & Co. (U.S.A.), containing all the material under that heading in the present volume except "On a Roman Balcony", which was reprinted in a slightly different form, as "Mano Pantea", in *The Purple Sapphire and Other Posthumous Papers*.

1921.

The Purple Sapphire and Other Posthumous Papers; published under the pseudonym of Christopher Blayre by Philip Allan & Co. (U.K.). The book contained the following eight stories: "The Purple Sapphire;" "Aalila;" "Purpura Lapillus;" "The Thing That Smelt;" "The Blue Cockroach;" "The Demon;" "The Book;" and "The Cosmic Dust."

1923.

The Cheetah-Girl; published for private circulation under the pseudonym of Christopher Blayre in the U.K., in an edition of 20 copies.

1932.

The Strange Papers of Dr. Blayre; published under the pseudonym of Christopher Blayre by Philip Allan (U.K.). The book contained all the material in *The Purple Sapphire and Other Posthumous Papers*, along with the following four stories: "The House on the Way to Hell;" "The Mirror that Remembered;" "Mano Pantea;" and "The Man Who Killed the Jew."

1934.

Some Women of the University; published under the pseudonym of Christopher Blayre by Nubiana: Tip. Sorelle Nessuno [i.e. U.K.: Robert Stockwell], in an edition of 100 copies. The book contained all the stories under that heading of the present volume.

THE COMPLETE
SHORTER FICTION

KISSES OF FATE

(A Study of mere Human Nature)

It is Life's Law, that when Fate comes with kisses
She gives them on the eyes, so binding us;
And we look up again, but just in time
To catch the glint o' th' blade she stabs us with,
Not to prevent it——

—Amélie Rives.

DEDICATION

IN MEMORIAM

TO THEE,—dear Friend of mine,—I dedicate
This little Book that has been wholly Thine
Since long before 'twas written, for these Tales
Were told to Thee, invented for Thine ear
Alone. If aught of Purity there be,
Or any Truths be found, amid my Lines,
'Tis Thine alone the Glory of their Good,
For,—telling them, through the long Winter nights,—
I watched Thine Eyes, all-fearful lest a sign
Of Thy Displeasure should shine out from them
At aught I said. And when I took the Pen
In hand to tell these Tales of mine once more,
Mine only thought was of the moment when
Thine Eyes should con my little Book and learn,
—Taught by whatever Good there be in it,—
That, writing it, I laboured but for Thee.

E. H-A.

New York, 1887.

TO THEE once more I dedicate these Tales
Of mine,—more worthy now, since more complete;
And, blazoning anew Thy Name upon
The fore-front of my Book, men's eyes to greet,
I lay a perfect—yet imperfect—whole
                            At Thy dear feet.
Yet there are those who have declared it all
Unworthy Thine acceptance.—Ah, my Sweet!
Could I but make a Story worthy Thee,
None then would dare my page to criticise,
For then my Tale would be so pure, and free
From any blemish, ev'n in Thy dear eyes,—
That none less lovely could condemn, nor see
The merest shadow of a thought ill-said
In all Thy book:—[for surely it would be
                            Not mine, but Thine!]
                                        E. H-A.

New York, 1888.

FOREWORD BY WAY OF EXPLANATION.

A T the moment that these sheets are ready to leave the printer's hands, I am told that my title, like that under which these stories were announced, and "Sylvester Gray" was published, requires a word of explanation.

A recent writer has said: "The roses fade fastest when the sun is brightest, and when, on returning to the garden at evening, we find their fallen petals strewn upon the ground, we shall be sorry that we did not gather more of them at midday." The fallen petals of the Roses that promised such a wealth of fragrance for the morrow—the broken promises of Youth which heralded such brilliancy in Age, may be called "The Kisses of Fate." The Love of To-day becomes too often the Memory—the Regret—of To-morrow. Happy the man who can say "The Future for which I strove has become the Present in which I exult! to such this Cycle of Stories is not addressed, but to the infinitely larger section of humanity who have plucked the Dead-Sea Fruit of Hope. The reader is referred to Mr. Edgar Saltus' *Philosophy of Disenchantment.*

EDWARD HERON-ALLEN,
New York, U.S.A.

May, 1888.

**"The arrow which is shot
comes not back."**

*The worldly Hope men set their hearts upon
Turns ASHES, or it prospers, and anon
    (Like Snow upon the Desert's dusty face),
Lighting a little hour or two—is gone!*

*Ah! Love, could You and I with Him conspire,
To grasp this sorry Scheme of Things—entire,
    Would we not shatter it to bits, and then
Remould it nearer to the Heart's Desire?*
                        —OMAR-i-KHAYYĀM

THE SUICIDE OF SYLVESTER GRAY.

PART I.

False? Ah! no—hardly that. Dear heart, you are not to blame.
      (Who carps at the sun, or the fleeting rain,
           or the transient evening dew?)
And I cavil not at your fair young soul that would fain—but
           could not—be true.
           And I love you, aye, the same!

I.

WE were at Harrow together. I remember so well the first time I ever saw, or spoke to him! It seems like yester-year instead of a quarter of a century ago. The summer term of the year of grace 18— was two days old. For two days past the historic hill wheron "Lyon of Preston, yeoman John, full many a year ago," built his school, had been alive with a merry swarm of boys ranging in age from fourteen years upwards, clad in the jacket of the lower, or the swallowtails of the upper school, and all hatted alike with the shallow, broad-brimmed straw, kept securely in its place by an elastic behind the head,—the whole constituting the quaint costume in which the authorities and scholars of Harrow-on-the-Hill see nothing ridiculous. The whole place seemed to laugh, as it always did in the early days of a new term, as if amused at its sudden awakening from the quiet weeks of the holidays; and the heat of the young spring sun striking the red brick of the old schools, of the Fourth Form Room, where malefactors received condign punishment, and of "Speecher" (the new speechroom had not then been built), was reflected upon the asphalt of the "school-yard," causing it to bubble up and stick to the feet of the enthusiasts who followed one another in a long *queue*, bowling "yard-balls" at some champion of the school-yard cricket wicket.

I had walked up the hill, past "Sam's," to the school-yard, with my hands in my pockets—a Harrow boy never under any circumstances takes his hands out of his pockets;—I had read the first notice-slips of the term fluttering upon the notice-board at the gates; had peered into the cloisters under the old speech-room, and had wandered away to the low wall at the top of the steps leading to the gymnasium, leaning upon which one looks over the disused "Milling-ground" and the racquet-courts, and away, away, away over the fields, past Harrow Weald to Pinner, and Oxhey, and Bushey, and Watford, twenty miles into the blue distance towards great cities in which many of us were destined to play our parts in the drama of life, and towards vast oceans which we should many of us cross before long in search of wealth and fame. And whilst I leaned upon the wall and fidgeted with the leaves that peeped inquisitively over the coping, deliberating whether it was worth while to walk down the steps to the gymnasium or no, I became aware of the presence, a few paces distant, of a small boy.

When I say a "small boy" I do not mean that his stature was less than mine; he was about my height. Nor do I mean that he was younger than I; indeed, I subsequently knew that we were of an equal age. I say a "small" boy because I had been a "Harrovian" for two terms already, and felt a veteran—and a gigantic one to boot—by the side of the "new fellow" who stood at my side. He was of the ordinary height of a boy of his age, neither stunted nor run to seed, as is so frequently the case among school-boys of fourteen. Boy as he was, I remember that he was beautifully made, thin in the flank, deep in the chest, flat in the back, and straight and erect from the lines of the legs to the carriage of the head. He was very decidedly a juvenile "swell." His clothes fitted him with a perfection rare among children at the age when they "grow visibly;" they were cut after the latest fashion for boys; and I remember that I, who was always an outrageously slovenly person, felt for his attire a mixture of envy and contempt; but his face conquered me—it was beautiful. His broad, white forehead and deep, violet eyes were thrown into shadow by the broad brim of his Harrow hat, from beneath which there escaped the wavy masses of his hair, whose glossy blackness had a tinge of deep purple brown in it which gave to it an effect of wonderful warmth and life. A straight, Greek nose and finely-cut mouth completed the face, which was of a yellowish delicate tint—a perfect "*blanc mat*" complexion. Young as I was, I was charmed by this juvenile Adonis; and edging along the low, red-brick wall so as to get close up to him, I said:

"Are you a new fellow?"

"Yes."

"What's your name?"

"Sylvester Gray."

"Sylvester Gray," thought I, "what a delightful name!" All my life I had longed for such an one, and had envied the "Ronceval de Courcy's," the "Plantagenet Fitzjames's," and the other high-sounding sponsorials and patronymics owned by the heroes of inexpensive fiction. My father's name was Tompkins, and my godfathers and godmothers in my baptism had prefixed thereto the unassuming prenomen of "John," an insult which I felt that death alone—my death—could wipe out. I hold firmly to a theory that a man is heavily handicapped, as regards his individuality, by his Christian name. Thus, all the Toms I have known have been good-natured, and rather commonplace. All the Charlies have been delightful "bad lots," all the Freds have been rowdy, all the Georges practical, all the Franks prigs, all the Archies good, all the Edwards artistic, and so on. Therefore, to give a boy one of these characteristic names weights him from the start with a certain prescribed individuality. But call a boy Sylvester, or some name of that kind, he has the chance of moulding himself on an unique pattern;—and his mother has a chance of helping him.

Thus everything about him, save the fact that he had taken on entering the school a form above the one I had reached after two terms' work, attracted me to Sylvester Gray; and just as the most dissimilar persons often voluntarily cast in their lots in life together, so Sylvester and I swore an eternal friendship in the old school-yard on this sunny afternoon, and strolled oft, arm-in-arm, down the zig-zag pathway of our lives.

Nobody liked me when I was a boy; and looking back at myself after the lapse of never-mind-how-many years, I am really not surprised. In the first place, I was very ugly, and that makes a great deal of difference in the life of a boy; secondly, I was rather a fiend; I was quiet, morose, taciturn; I hated people of my own age, and got on much better with the masters than with the fellows at school. I didn't care about games. The hideous combination of colours worn by the Football Team had no attraction for me; the dark-coloured hat of the Cricket Eleven, the badge of the Rifle Team, and the certificate of gymnastic proficiency were not, for me, objects of envy. On half-holidays I preferred the cool and quiet of the Vaughan library to the tumult of the cricket-fields and the racquet-courts, or better still—as I could always get a master to "sign me for bill" (i.e., to excuse my attendance at the four o'clock calling-over of the school-list), I loved to wander far afield, to Pinner, and Oxhey, and Sudbury, and Wembley, to Stanmore and Elstree, in search of flowers and ferns, and butterflies, and solitude; and oftentimes Sylvester Gray would give up the joys of the courts and playing-fields, where he soon became a welcome *habitué*, to accompany me, and then we would talk of home, and of the past and the future.

I was to be a doctor, like my father before me. Sylvester was the orphan son of an officer, who had been an old Harrovian, and who had fallen for his queen and country at Balaclava. I remember Sylvester Gray bursting into tears one day in the school-chapel, as, for the first time, he read his father's name on the tablets in the south aisle, erected in commemoration of the Harrow boys who had fallen in the Crimea. His future would be one of dignified ease, and his mind was divided between going into the army, on the one hand, and being called to the bar and

26

then spending his life travelling about and seeing the world, on the other.

Bright hopes! Happy future! Sylvester Gray killed himself one warm spring night in Rome, when he was only thirty; and I alone, of his countless friends, have ever known the sequence of events that led to this catastrophe, which has been one of the profoundest sorrows of my life.

II.

Sylvester Gray and I began at Harrow a friendship that lasted all his life. He became, at school, the periodical companion of my youthful solitude, and took a kind of half-timorous, half-contemptuous interest in my scientific and quasi-scientific manias. He would sit in the reclining-chair in my room, his hands nervously grasping its arms, and watch me with grave, deep eyes whilst I mixed strange chemicals in a glass mortar or graduated measure, preparatory to the production of some perfume or explosion, destined to surpass all previous efforts in virulence and destructiveness. He would take a queer, puzzled pleasure in looking over my butterflies and dried flowers. He would even bring himself to poke my imprisoned snakes, through the bars of their cage, with a penholder; and, as a result, I confess that, over and above my personal adoration of him, I was flattered by his interest in my pursuits, for he was popular and "a swell" in the school, whilst I was distinctly the reverse. After school hours it was, as I have said, far more delightful for me to hide myself in the Vaughan library, or in my own room, to explore the mysteries of Rees' Encyclopaedia, or to concoct the experiments aforesaid, than to mix with my fellow-creatures; and this kind of thing does not tend to increase a fellow's popularity, even if he *is* a member of the Upper School, ready to give "cons" (Anglice: translations) to indolent athletes of the Shells and Fourth Form; and such appreciation of my schoolfellows as I enjoyed at Harrow was due practically in its entirety to the efforts of Sylvester.

He would carry about in his pockets, and exhibit, the successful results of my more showy experiments; he would appeal to me as to an authority on matters recondite and abstruse, and would ask my advice on any matters deeper than the ordinary problems of a schoolboy's existence, that might arise in conversation with "his set" and in this way I became an object of a certain respect, and went through life rejoicing in the nickname of "Professor." I was naturally impressed with a kind of gratitude—the gratitude of the physically superior "beast," for the fragile but more popular "beauty," and I did my best to share such joys as life possessed for me with young Gray, whom I was inclined to envy and admire in a public, and patronize in a private, capacity.

I have said that I was more popular with the masters than with the fellows. I had also many acquaintances among the residents of Harrow, whom I had met at the masters' houses, and none were greater friends of mine than the Woosters. In my first conversation with Mrs. Wooster I found that we were in some abstruse way connected with one another; and whether it was that I adored Mrs. Wooster, or whether it was that I loved to sit and talk to her golden-haired daughter Evelyn, I used to look forward with the liveliest anticipation to tea-time on Thursdays, when, as a regular thing, I used to find my way to their pretty little house, which looked out over the southern slope of the hill towards Edgware and London.

I made their acquaintance during my second term at Harrow, and never knew till many years afterwards why, after my last term at school, our friendship cooled off, and practically ceased. It is a terrible story, I am afraid, but it is very necessary to the development of this narrative that I should sketch in the main outlines, which outlines it is equally necessary that I should leave my readers to fill in.

When first I knew her, Evelyn Wooster was a blue-eyed child of fourteen, rather old for her age, as only-children are apt to be, with a glory of sunny hair that fell in a tangled mass far below her waist; and I suppose she holds in my life the elevated position of my first love. That she should care about *me* was, I knew, a ridiculous idea; but the joy of finding a white example of the *fritillaria meleagris* in a field near Pinner, and the delight of catching a humming-bird hawk-moth on the terrace behind the Chapel and the Vaughan, were increased a thousand-fold by her appreciation of my *trouvailles*, and by her borrowing them for a week to show to her "greatest girl-friend" (how my heart leapt at that qualification, "girl-friend"), and by her repeated subsequent allusions to these feats of prowess in the collecting line. But I never felt so proud of any specimen that I had submitted to her for inspection and approval as I did of Sylvester Gray, whom I took up there to tea one sunny afternoon of his first term at Harrow.

He cut me out completely. When it was a question of what has been justly called the softer, and unjustly the weaker, sex, he always cut everybody out. But I did not mind; I never thought anything could be too good for either him or her, and I gave them to one another without a murmur, and was quite content to sit and talk to Mrs. Wooster, or help her to tend her flowers, whilst Sylvester and Evelyn sat together and talked on the verandah that ran round the house, or, in winter, at the piano in their cosy little drawing-room.

And so the best part of five years crept by. It was our last term at Harrow. We were both in the Sixth Form, and I was a monitor. Sylvester wasn't, but he was in the Cricket Eleven and the Shooting Team, and he played racquets for the school, and helped us materially to beat Eton at Lord's cricket ground, and to win the Ashburton Shield and the Racquet Cup at Wimbledon and Prince's. Evelyn Wooster was a lovely young woman of eighteen, and she and Sylvester Gray were reciprocally "hard hit." Well, well! he was eminently "eligible," and my nineteen-year-old experience enabled me to detect a distinct satisfaction in the glances which Mrs. Wooster occasionally directed at the handsome pair, whilst we—she and I—walked about the garden as we had done for four years past, and talked horticulture and home.

I? Ah, what of that? So long as Sylvester and Evelyn were happy, what did *my* feelings on the subject matter? Nothing to anybody but myself, did they? Very well, then! They are both dead now, and I am still a miserable, buttonless bachelor!

Nearly five years! And during that time we had seen a good deal of one another—Sylvester, Evelyn, and I. Sylvester had been a beautiful boy—now he was a superlatively handsome young man. A silky, sable moustache decorated his upper lip, and his whole bearing was full of that graceful strength which signalizes the healthy, pure-bred gentleman. The more hypercritical used to object that his face was somewhat too delicately formed; that it was too womanish in the softness of its outlines, with its languorous violet eyes and long lashes. To me, as to all men who were not envious, he was always an object of unquestioning admiration; whilst among women he was always a kind of Admirable Crichton. Almost without exception they fell in love with him, and he would accept their homage quite as though it were a matter of course. "Entre deux amants, il y a toujours l'un qui baise et l'autre qui tend la joue;" and Sylvester was always the one "qui tendait la joue." The only woman I ever knew him to worry himself about was Evelyn Wooster, and her he simply adored.

His friendship for the Woosters had communicated itself to his sole relations, an aunt and a sister, who lived in a beautiful old Tudor mansion belonging to Sylvester by inheritance, near Staplehurst, in the County of Kent. During the summer of the year 18— Mrs. Wooster, Evelyn, and I were all spending a few weeks with them at his beautiful old home before we should severally part to pursue our ways along the different paths marked out for us in life. Sylvester and I had left Harrow a few weeks before, and on the last Thursday before the school broke up we had met as usual at the little cottage on the hill; and, as it had been a rather affecting little meeting, we had to get up our spirits by projecting this visit to Idlesse—such was the old-world name of Sylvester's Kentish home.

I had been there more than once during the five years of our school days, but I thought it had never looked so pretty as it did when, at the close of a summer afternoon, I drove up to the house through the winding grounds that hid it from the Staplehurst road, and saw it bathed in the splendour of an August sunset, with Sylvester, in the most *negligé* of attitudes and costumes, and Evelyn, in the freshest and prettiest of frocks, standing in the porch to welcome me. Sylvester's fox terrier, who sat in front of them, making good practice at the flies that investigated him—a grave dog, who rejoiced in the fascinating name of "Mr. Smith"—gave me one searching glance to satisfy himself of my identity, and then went into hysterics over me as I sprang from the dog-cart. The air was heavy with the perfume of the evening primroses that grew round the porch, and the Maréchale Niel roses that straggled all over it; and as I shook Sylvester and Evelyn by the hand I was overwhelmed by a sensation which I could not understand at the time, but which, looking back at that August evening, I know now was simply pure happiness.

Then there followed three perfect weeks spent among the orchards and the hop-gardens of the neighbourhood. The five years that had passed since my story had opened had not altered my disposition very materially, and I was still disposed to be quiet. Besides, I had my preliminary medical examination to look forward to; and with the enthusiasm that we all of us feel, when first we leave school, to reach as quickly as possible the dignity of a "profession," I had brought down with me some of my bran-new medical books to read up. They were not much read, but they lay about a good deal, and when one day Sylvester's aunt looked into one of them and nearly frightened herself into fits, I felt that the troubles of transportation were, in a measure, compensated for. At any rate, I studied botany with Sybil Gray, Sylvester's pretty sister, and really we gathered a lot of flowers together, and I dried some of them—that *she* found; but when I congratulated her, and indirectly myself, on the progress of our botanical studies, it was horrid of her to ask me what were the toxicological properties of Maréchale Niel roses, and what was the active alkaloid principle of the forget-me-not.

Meanwhile Sylvester and Evelyn lived in a fool's paradise of their own. They disappeared usually after breakfast, and turned up at lunch, with an appearance of unconscious virtue, to talk volubly of plans for the afternoon, embracing the entire party. After lunch they disappeared again, to return in time to dress for dinner, looking supremely foolish, but assuring us all that they had not been outside the grounds, and—Heaven forgive them!—that they had been looking for us everywhere. We used to laugh at them—it was "an understood thing"—but they were both young enough in all conscience. The future before them was as bright as it was long. Sometimes Sylvester would allude to it vaguely in the smoking-room before we went to bed. What a future it would be!

Well, well! She died long ago, and Sylvester Gray killed himself in Rome ten years later. Ah—yi!

III.

The three weeks ran by like a summer afternoon. The Woosters were to leave in two days, and Evelyn and Sylvester seemed to forget that we others even existed. They ran about together, or walked up and down the terrace arm-in-arm nearly all the time. The last but one was one of those frightfully hot days that we have sometimes in England at the end of August. It had been sultry and oppressive since early morning; the lovers had been away all day, wandering in the woods at the back of the house, and had arrived home at tea-time, flushed, silent, preoccupied, it seemed to me. During the interval before dinner and during the meal they scarcely took their eyes off one another, and I confess that their silent, constrained manner gave me an undefined sensation of uneasiness, which I could not have accounted for even to myself.

After dinner we—that is, Sybil and I, and Evelyn and Sylvester—went out on to the terrace, and wandered up and down in the stifling heat, which even the dew had been powerless to moderate. At intervals we would stop and stand at the terrace wall to watch the summer lightning in the horizon—lightning which was almost incessant, and more vivid than I ever remember to have seen it before or since. Sybil and I kept up a continual chatter, as we always did; but the other two were strangely silent, and would stand for ten minutes at a time against the wall, looking into the distance without saying a word, their fingers closely intertwined as their hands hung listlessly by their sides. There was, after all, something peculiarly unrefreshing in the air of this summer night, and presently, Evelyn's white frock having turned a corner at the end of the terrace and disappeared in the direction of the rose garden, Sybil and I turned to enter the house. As we did so she turned to me suddenly, and said:

"Jack, I don't know why, but I feel so uneasy about those two. It's a dreadful idea to have, but you have been our best friend for so long that you're the only person I can talk to about it. Sylvester is so impulsive and wild-hearted, and Evelyn adores him so absolutely, that I'm dreadfully frightened. Do go down to the rosery and tell them to come in and have some music."

She had noticed it too! I walked rapidly down the gravelled terrace, and turned off on to the soft grass walks of the rose garden. I could not see the lovers anywhere, and started to walk rapidly round the beds in search of them. I found them suddenly— too suddenly—as I turned a corner, beneath a trellised archway. They were standing motionless, locked in one another's arms. Her head lay upon his shoulder, and she seemed to have lost consciousness of the whole world beneath the spell of his kiss. I sprang back and retraced my steps some twenty yards, and then advanced once more, whistling to apprise them of my approach. They turned the corner arm-in-arm and advanced to meet me. I delivered my message, and we regained the house in silence.

The ladies retired early, and as Sylvester did not want to smoke, we went to our rooms also. I looked in on Sylvester on my way to mine, and talked with him for a few minutes—no longer, for he evidently did not want me to remain. His face was whiter than usual, but his hand, as we said "Good-night" was burning hot. I looked into his eyes, and said:

"Syl, old fellow, there's something wrong. What is it?"

"Wrong!" he exclaimed, "wrong! How can anything be wrong with a man who is loved as I am, and by such a woman? Why Jack, old man, I am so deliriously happy that I don't know what to do. We love one another so passionately that it is almost more than we can bear. Don't be uneasy on my account; if anything is

33

wrong it is a case of extremes meeting, of my being so happy that I don't know what to do with myself."

"Sylvester," I cried, "for God's sake, take care! You are not going to marry for a couple of years at least. Is it right for you two to be so much alone together as you have been?—to separate yourselves so entirely from the world as you do? Surely not."

"My dear Jack, don't worry yourself about me—or us; we can take care of ourselves. And now———good-night!"

And with that I left him.

✳

What a night it was! I felt suffocated, though I had opened all my windows. At last I got up and opened my door, and, cooled a little by the draught, fell into an uneasy slumber. Suddenly I woke. Surely I heard a footstep passing my open door—a stealthy, gliding footstep, like that of a robber; and the idea of burglars instantly occurred to my city-bred mind, as I thought of the massive Queen Anne plate which lay about on the sideboard in the dining-room, day and night. I lay still for a few moments, and then quietly rising and putting on a dressing-gown, felt my way down the corridor to Sylvester's room. The moon had hidden herself behind a cloud, and it was pitch dark. As I crept along, the clock in the hall struck half past two; I turned the handle of Sylvester's door, and went in.

He was out of bed, standing at the window, also in a dressing-gown. He turned upon me and said, in a voice which seemed to me to be choking with suppressed fury: "In God's name, what are you prowling about the place for?"

"Sylvester," I replied, "I heard footsteps in the house, and thought you were being robbed, and might not have been wakened up. I see you were, though. Is everything all right?"

His face was in the shadow, but his voice was natural again as he replied,

"Yes, yes, all right! I heard footsteps myself, or fancied I did, and went out to investigate. I found everything safe; if I hadn't I should have come to rouse you. It was probably me that you heard coming back to my room."

Undoubtedly that was it. I regained my room and went back to bed to fall into a feverish, confused sleep, in which I dreamed a ghastly dream, wherein Sylvester and Evelyn were engaged struggling with a loathsome monster, which crushed her in its iron jaws, despite the efforts of Sylvester to save her, whilst I was paralysed a few paces off, powerless to raise a finger in his assistance. When I awoke it was broad daylight.

Evelyn did not come down to breakfast. Mrs. Wooster said that her daughter had passed a bad night and was feverish; the frightful heat of the day before had been too much for her. Sylvester was in despair; it seemed so hard that she should be unwell her last day at Idlesse, and after breakfast he fidgeted around the house waiting for her to come down. We were sitting together on the terrace when she made her appearance at the drawing-room window, looking very pale and fragile in her white morning wrapper. We rose to go to her at once, and it seemed to me that there was something singularly subdued in her manner as she answered our anxious enquiries. She was still suffering a little; she had a headache, and was generally not "up to the mark;" but she had made a point of coming down for her last day in the country.

I left them together and trotted off to find Sybil and Mrs. Wooster, and the two lovers spent the morning together as usual. I saw them walking up and down the terrace, always in sight of the house, and from the gravity with which they conversed I knew that the all-important "future" was the subject of their conversation. Lunch was rather a silent meal—the last meals together of a country house party are always rather dismal functions, I think—and after lunch we all sat together on the grass in the rose-garden, and read and talked quietly.

Evelyn had recovered from her indisposition entirely, and was the most chirpy of us all; Sylvester, on the other hand, seemed, as the Americans say, "all broken up" by his impending separation, and hardly opened his lips, or took his eyes off Evelyn's face. It made me unhappy to see him suffer so, and I made many efforts to leave them together, which Evelyn, for some reason or other, quietly frustrated.

They disappeared after dinner, however, "to say good-bye with variations," as Sybil said laughingly. She and I went down the terrace and sat on the rustic seat at the end, and were mildly sentimental, when she gave me a dreadful fright. I had taken her hand in mine, and was playing with her fingers, when suddenly I said to her: "What fun it would be if you and I were to fall as badly in love with one another as those two simple things walking up and down there."

She shuddered, and said in the most terror-stricken voice I have ever heard,

"Oh Jack, Jack! Don't think me an utter fool, but unless I tell somebody I shall die, I think. I'm so awfully frightened about Syl and Eva; they've had a quarrel or something, and whenever I look at her, though she's just the same as she always was. I've the most dreadful feeling here;" and she pressed her left hand to her throat. The one I held trembled violently.

A kind of pall seemed to fall over the whole world. An icy feeling of horror crept over me. Heaven only knows why, for, after all, what is there so serious about a lover's tiff? I rose and said:

"It's getting chilly, Syb; let's go in."

As we passed them on the terrace, they were walking silently side-by-side. He was playing with his moustache, and she had her eyes fixed on the gravel in front of her.

That night, in the smoking-room, I said to Sylvester: "Have you and Eva had a row?"

"Good gracious, no! What an idea! We're the best friends in the world. I am awfully sorry they're leaving to-morrow. The place will seem so dull by comparison for Aunty and Sybil when we're all gone."

"All gone? How do you mean? You are not going away, are you?"

"Why, haven't I told you?" said he; "I'm going to Bellagio next week, and then I shall spend the winter in Rome, *en route,* as it were, for Constantinople and the East. I've always wanted to travel, and I think a couple of years of it will amuse me."

"And then you'll return and marry Eva, I suppose."

"I don't know; I hope so. For God's sake don't talk to me about it, old man; I can't bear it."

The same feeling of horror took possession of me again, and we said little more before we took our candles and made our way upstairs to bed.

The Woosters left next morning by the ten o'clock train from Staplehurst. The carriage which took them took my luggage to the station, and in the cool of the afternoon Sylvester and I walked over, that I might take the 6.30 train to town. We talked by the way of indifferent matters. He never mentioned the Woosters, and it was only when we were at the station, waiting for the train, that he referred to his own approaching departure. The train was in sight when I said to him:

"I can't see why you, who have all that can make life lovely here in England, should go and bury yourself in Palestine, and Syria, and Persia."

"Can't you?" he replied, in a dry, cut voice; "then I'll tell you. I am going away because I'm not fit to remain with decent people. I'm a thing so loathsome, so contemptible, that I shudder at the sight of myself in a looking-glass. You say I'm rich. Well, my money has been my curse. Good-looking? Yes. The beauty of some painted, venomous insect, which an humanitarian would crush beneath his heel! Don't pity me, old fellow; I deserve all my misery; and I *am* miserable, God knows! Good-bye, Jack! When we meet again I shall feel better, I hope."

The guard whistled, and the train bore me away. "Goodness me!" thought I; "he has indeed had a tiff with Eva. Just fancy the *debonnair* Sylvester taking anything so to heart, and admitting that he is in the wrong."

And so I reached London, and Guy's Hospital, and the College of Surgeons, and my work; and my life became full of distractions. But I often wondered what Sylvester could have said to Eva that had made such a breach between them, and had produced such an effect upon one of them at least.

PART II.

I.

Eleven years have passed, and the scene has changed. The lives of the actors in the drama, of which we have read the prologue, have developed with the years; people have married and died, and we two, Sylvester Gray and I, have remained. I have been sufficiently attached to my profession to succeed in it, and John Tompkins, M.D., has become one of the fortunate medicos who can afford to take a well-earned holiday after ten years of hard work. He is taking it at the moment when his story reopens.

I was in Rome, and it was the spring of the year of grace, 18—. In the autumn of the year before, having returned to Park Lane from a medical Congress held at Vienna, I was busily engaged re-writing the concluding chapters of my work upon the Conario-hypophysial tract, when, one day, meeting an old friend in the park, I could not for the life of me remember his name. An hour later I had to look in my address-book for the direction of a letter to an old patient, and that evening I fell fast asleep over my manuscript. I was a little alarmed, but fought against my fears, until one day, in the middle of a lecture at St. Augustine's Hospital, I suddenly found that my mind was a blank, and pleading illness, had been obliged to dismiss the students and leave the lecture-theatre. Dr. George Ayers, the principal consulting physician to the hospital, sent for me in the afternoon, and after a few questions said to me:

"Tompkins, you're overdoing it; you're playing the fool with yourself, and this hospital can't afford it. If you belonged to Guy's or St. Bartholomew's I shouldn't have the least objection to your killing yourself, but you're on my staff, and I can't allow it. You will finish the notes for your new book, and you will cart them off to Rome with you; you will return here in April next, and between this and then I forbid you officially to do any other work."

And so, after a short discussion, it was decided; and the end of November saw me installed in the prettiest of rooms in the Tempietta, at the top of the steps of the Trinita de Monti. From my windows I looked down upon the Piazza di Spagna and the steps of the Trinita, where artists' models do congregate. A little further on I caught a glimpse of the Piazza, and the Porta del Popolo, with the Borghese and the Monte Parioli beyond them, and beyond that, the Campagna and the yellow Tiber stretching to the sea.

I am of opinion that my rooms commanded the most beautiful view in Rome, and in this opinion the majority of my acquaintances, who climbed the Via Sistina to call upon me, cordially agreed.

So much for myself. What about the others? Sylvester Gray seemed absolutely to have disappeared out of my life. I heard sometimes from his sister, who seldom knew anything definite about his movements, and I kept up a desultory correspondence with Mrs. Wooster. About two years after our last meeting at Idlesse, Evelyn, to our intense astonishment, married a commonplace young man, a local lawyer of Harrow; and a year after died in childbirth. I went down to see her grief-stricken mother, but could learn but little from her. From the day that Evelyn had parted from Sylvester Gray she had never mentioned his name of her own accord, and she had never prolonged any conversation of which Mrs. Wooster made him the subject. Her mother had never penetrated the mystery that shrouded their estrangement. All that Evelyn had said was that they quite understood one another, and that she had quite made up her mind that it would be a grave mistake for them to marry one another. A few days after they had left Idlesse, Sylvester had written her a long, imploring letter, begging her to reconsider her decision, and this letter Mrs. Wooster had only found after Evelyn's death. What her answer had been, if she had ever answered it, her mother did not know.

That was all.

Of Sylvester himself our news was scanty and vague. I heard from him once, about six months after he left England. He wrote from Constantinople, and sent me his will to take care of, preparatory to his departure for Syria, Palestine, and Persia; and in the letter that accompanied the document he told me that he might not return for a long, long time. From his bankers I heard that he had communicated with them from Jerusalem and from Mecca, and this was all we heard of him for five years. At the end of that time I came across him suddenly in the court-yard of the Hotel Continental in Paris.

I was sitting, wondering vaguely whether the indigenous Parisian could find anything interesting in the pages of *La Vie Parisienne*, when the quiet, musical voice I knew so well said suddenly behind me,

"Tompkins, if I mistake not! How are you?"

I started to my feet as if I had been electrified—to find the old Sylvester standing at my side, holding out his hand with an amused look on his handsome face. It was undoubtedly the same old Sylvester, looking not a day older than he had looked the afternoon I shook him by the hand for the last time at Staplehurst station. He was as calm and quiet as he always had been, a little harder, perhaps, in his manner, and tanned to a rich olive pallor that made him, if possible, handsomer than ever; but beyond that, absolutely unchanged.

He sat down by my side and gave me a short outline of his doings. He had spent the winter of 18— in Rome, as he had intended, and had gone to Istamboul in the spring; there he had studied the languages and customs of the East, and had set out on a comprehensive tour of the Orient. He had joined a caravan, and in the guise of a "renegade" had performed as much of the Hadjj Pilgrimage to Mecca as a renegade is ever allowed to perform. He had wandered through the Holy Land to Damascus, and had spent rich, lazy months in the hanging-gardens of Baghdad. He had lived the luxurious life of an Eastern Pacha, and had made himself familiar with Asia Minor; he knew Samsoun and Sinope and Batoum and Erzeroum and Kars as well as he knew London or Paris or Rome, and had he taken any interest in anything so dry as politics he would have been an authority on the Eastern Question.

From there he had traversed the deserts of Persia, and had been a familiar figure in the streets of Teheran and Ispahan. From his button-hole hung a little bunch of microscopic decorations, among which I could distinguish the Annunziata, the San Lazaro, the Redeemer of Greece, the Medjidieh, the Osmanieh, and the Portrait of the Shah. In a word, Sylvester Gray had become the most fascinatingly interesting and accomplished vagabond in Europe. He spoke of his wanderings with the *insouciance* of a gypsy. He looked upon our meeting as a matter of course, though he had only arrived in Paris by the Orient Express three days before. He had no plans in particular—he never had; he would probably remain in Paris a few weeks and then return to London. He was not in a particular hurry to go anywhere or to do anything.

I spoke to him of England, and he looked bored; of Idlesse, and he changed the subject. He had heard of his aunt's death, and of his sister's marriage; he had sent her from Smyrna a bale of Oriental curiosities worth many thousands of piastres; he had heard of Evelyn's marriage and death, which he regretted sincerely but conventionally. He had but one object in life—to amuse himself; and his efforts in that direction met, apparently, with the completest success; and I congratulated him upon the attainment of his desires and his freedom from care. As I did so, a queer, cynical look came into his face, and he said, in his soft, languorous voice:

"You congratulate me, old fellow?—envy me, perhaps? Don't do it. Don't do it. I've got everything a man can want on the material plane; everyone I come across wishes he were me, whilst I!—do you see that young mechanic, standing looking in on this courtyard, with his honest face and careless eyes?—I'd give twenty years of my life and my right hand to change places with him. Hush! no answer required! What are you doing tonight? Dine with me at the Café Anglais, and we'll go to the Princesse de Cziquemine's together afterwards. I'll take you; she is one of my greatest friends. I helped her to buy some embroideries for less than ten times their value in the Bezesten at Istamboul two years ago."

And so, during the fortnight that I remained in Paris, I saw a good deal of Sylvester Gray, and had ample opportunities of studying the life he led. What a life it was! Never was there such a butterfly in this world; he was here, there, and everywhere. Everyone, save only the married man, was in love with him; his approval was the hallmark of excellence, whether it were stamped upon a horse, a cravat, or a woman. At receptions he might always be found in the nookiest nook available, with the most beautiful woman in the room; and the stories of Sylvester's *affaires* and of his *belles fortunes*, of his prowess in the Camp of Mars and the Court of Venus, were, as the sand on the seashore, innumerable.

"*Quel garçon!*" said the old men. "*Quel pschutt!*" said the young ones. "*Quel adorable enfant!*" said the young women. "*Quel frileux!*" said the old ones. "*Quel brute!*" said the husbands; but these last kept their opinions to themselves.

"One of these days," said I to him, "you'll burn your fingers, and fall in love or get into trouble."

"The good Lord forbid!" he replied, with holy fervour. "My mental fingers are made of asbestos; I haven't the capacity to fall in love, and I can't get into trouble because my memory is good and I keep my wits about me. *Vogue la galère!*" and he skipped off to keep some assignation or other, croodling a fragment of some song of the Ambassadeurs, some echo of the Éden or of the Folies Bergères.

There was no doubt about the fact that he led a gay life of it. He was the veriest Bohemian that ever walked this earth, and a Bohemian of the best sort. He never drank, or gambled, or affected any of the lower vices of the Quartier Latin; and whilst he was a little tin god on wheels in the Faubourg and the Champs Élysées, he was adored by hordes of impecunious artists whom he mainly supported by his purchases of works of art that he did not want, and by other delicate and indirect forms of a practically boundless charity.

My time was up, and I returned to London. Sylvester Gray saw me off at the Gare du Nord, and we made an appointment to meet again at my rooms in Park Street before the London season should have come to its timely end.

II.

Sylvester Gray came to London, and his rooms in Jermyn Street, St. James, were the envy of half the men in town. A man more eminently "clubbable" never looked out of a bay-window in Piccadilly; a man more eminently companionable never walked down "the Row" with "the beauty of the year;" a more charming conversationalist never suffered from an *embarras de choix* among his invitations to the smartest dinners in town, or to the most delightful country-houses in the kingdom. It therefore caused me the same sort of feeling of appreciation as I had experienced when he "took me up" at Harrow, to know that, with a fortnight's previous notice, I could always count upon him to dine with me, either *tête-à-tête* or otherwise.

He took an intense interest in a little book I was preparing at the time, a *Practical Handbook of the Vegetable Poisons*; and his intimate knowledge of Oriental toxicology was often of the greatest service to me in making my notes and experiments upon the lesser known Oriental alkaloids. His love for abstruse information of this kind, and his store thereof, were infinite and extraordinary. He had brought with him from the East a collection of drugs and plants that he had made over there with a view to giving them to me; and their value, with his notes upon them, was, to me, inestimable; and he often startled me with the Borgia-like *nonchalance* with which he would discuss the effects of, and experiment on himself with, the most deadly drugs.

He would sit with me far into the early hours of the morning, working with me at my manuscripts and my analyses; and the *Medical Times*, in subsequently reviewing my book, remarked that "Dr. Tompkins's data upon Asiatic drugs are the most minute and valuable to be found in medical literature." But he never referred to the past. It was only after our companionship had lasted thus for a couple of years that one day, our conversation having turned upon conscience and remorse and so on, he startled me again by suddenly saying:

"I tell you, Jack, now, as I told you when we first met in Paris, I hardly ever see an artizan or a careless clerk strolling in the park on Sunday but I envy him with my whole soul. You are quite right when you say that nobody knows anything about my past life, either in England or abroad. Well, old man. I'll tell you this. There *is* something in my life so horrible to remember, that it clouds my enjoyment of every moment of my existence. I *can't* tell you what it is, but it closes the doors of happiness upon me, and I can never hope to offer a thing so vile as myself to any woman who may honour me with her love. No matter where the events to which I refer took place, whether here or abroad, whether in the east or in the west! They hang like a pall over my whole existence, and not only do they prevent my allowing myself to lay my worship at the feet of a pure woman, not only do they condemn me to fritter away the sterling coinage of my love in the small change of flirtation, as somebody says in a play somewhere, but my past horror has actually rendered me incapable of loving. I shudder at the very thought of a deep passion; my heart is dry and sterile, and no woman may ever quicken it into life by the magic of her touch."

"But, my dear Syl, this is dreadful. I guessed that there might be something of this sort on your mind; now I am a medical man, and though a young one, I am admitted to have had some experience with mental troubles—can't you bring yourself to tell any one about it? Surely it would ease your mind."

"No," he replied, it is at the same time my curse and my safeguard. If ever, by any horrible chance, I *should* fall really in love, I should lay my past bare before the woman I cared about, to prevent her, if possible, from loving me; at any rate to show her the real Sylvester Gray that lies hidden under an exterior which, fortunately, is not disagreeable to people."

I thought over the matter for some time in silence, and when next I spoke it was to deliver to him what, in after times, he always would laughingly refer to as my celebrated oration

"On the Advantages of Confessional Familiarity."

"I believe that the name of the philosopher who first formulated the axiom that 'Familiarity breeds contempt' is lost in the roll-call of the crowd that populates the Walhalla of forgotten dogmatists and proverb-makers.

"When we were boys at Harrow together, you remember that there was a dear old gentleman, one of the masters of the fourth form—he is dead long ago, God rest his soul!—who used quaintly to observe, when there occurred in the day's portion of Homer or Virgil a passage of which the meaning was obscure to a depth beyond the reach of even his profound scholarship, 'Never mind, laddie; if I ever meet the author in the future life, I'll ask him what he meant; never mind about it now.' I have always felt much the same with regard to this unknown proverbial philosopher. What did he mean? Did he mean that to be familiar with a subject or object, whether on the physical or on the mental plane, leads one to despise it? Undoubtedly he did—we may start by admitting thus much. But I would have him tell me the nature of this despite upon which he spoke so oracularly.

"Was it the despite that the gladiator in the Colosseum felt for the pampered, plethoric potentate who sat above him on his chryselephantine throne, surrounded by his sycophants and concubines, to laugh when the blood flowed from the wounds torn in his quivering flesh by the savage beasts trained to rend him for the amusement of a Roman emperor? Or was it the despite he felt for the brute that had wounded him, when it lay writhing in its death agony at his feet, ploughing up the gold dust and cinnabar of the arena, whilst the sweating, brutal mob upon the benches rent the air with their shrieks of '*Habet! Habet?*' Was it the contempt that the circus gymnast feels for the danger that he courts for a livelihood, or that which he feels for *himself* as he prostitutes his manhood in making an exhibition of its power? On what plane must we seek the sentiment that the dogmatist wished to express? Who can tell? Shall we not rest content in accepting the proverb as it stands, and let each take from it for himself the meaning that suggests itself to him, and then, when we have interpreted it for ourselves metaphysically, or rather (if I may be allowed the polysyllable) met-egotistico-physically, and we ask ourselves what it all comes to, we have only to repeat, *but* to repeat with an inflection of voice which conveys its significance only to ourselves, 'Familiarity breeds contempt!'

"By this time you will be wondering what I am leading up to. My own interpretation of the axiom, of course; but what is that? Do not say my '*interpretation*,' say, rather, my '*application*' thereof; and that is as follows—if you will allow me an illustration, instead of the more difficult 'definition.'

"I am a person who never confides in anybody. I presume that this is the reason why people continually confide in me. Without this tendency, however, on the part of my fellow-men, there is no doubt that I should never have arrived at *my* application of our axiom, and I arrived at it as follows:

"Can anything be more terrible than remorse, if the remorse is genuine? Sometimes we know it to be purely theatrical, and then it excites contempt rather than sympathy; but when it is *real*, those who have seen it are not likely soon to forget the impression that it made upon them. I have seen it—once. And its victim was a woman.

"She was the whole world to a friend of mine; he had no thought that was not hers alone; the air was purer for him because she breathed it, the sun was brighter for him because it shone upon her—in a word he loved her with that absolute all-absorbing worship that comes to some men once, and to most men never. I had seen a good deal of the girl from her childhood, and she did me the honour of creating me her chief confidant. When, therefore, I realized that she was, for some inexplicable reason, making herself and the man to whom I have alluded as my friend, miserable beyond all reasonable limits, by her steadfast refusal to listen to his supplications on his own behalf, I took it upon myself to ask her why she pursued this course with such unbending relentlessness. She answered me that she loved the man from the bottom of her soul, but that her whole life was stained by a past history so black that she would account herself a vile gift to be laid at the feet of the man that she held to be the king among human beings.

46

"Now, if a counterbalancing axiom were required to go with the proverb we have been discussing, we might take for it, 'Confession eases the soul.' That the two accompany, and are inseparable from one another, I propose at this present to show; and it was following the line of argument that I am now laying down that I asked my girl-friend to follow her established precedent and 'tell me all about it.'

"'No,' said she, 'the crime, the horror which overshadows my life is too ghastly, too terrible for me to be able to whisper a word of it to a living soul.'

"Now, this was absurd; or at any rate there was a strong presumption that it was absurd. I would not for one moment admit the possibility of the literal, actual truth of her statement in her own case—she, a girl of nineteen, the carefully nurtured and only daughter of one of the noblest families in England! Therefore, there were two explanations for this statement of hers, which was made in all good faith, with pale face, wide-stricken eyes, and white lips, which gave testimony to the genuineness of her words, from her own mental standpoint at any rate.

"In the first place, let us admit—let us suppose, for the sake of argument,—that there had been in her life some boy-and-girl 'affair'; let us suppose it had terminated in a manner which to a highly-strung, sensitive girl had seemed highly tragic, whereas it had probably ended after a fashion merely moderately dramatic. Supposing, I say, for the sake of argument, this to have been the case, we have to allow for natural exaggeration. The Turks have a proverb to the effect that 'A little hill in a low place fancies itself a mountain'; it is a saying which, like much of the Turkish proverbial philosophy, is founded on a keen appreciation of human nature, and it probably explains my young friend's magnified opinion on the subject of her Past (with a capital 'P'). It reminds one of the gigantic helmet that creates such an excitement in Dryden's 'Battle of the Books,' in the remotest corner of which, on calm examination, there turns out to be concealed an atrophied head no bigger than a walnut! It need hardly be said that I did not suggest these ideas to her by way of an invitation of confidence.

"Again, we have to consider the element of *hysteria*; and here we tread on the most delicate ground in dealing with an impressionable girl of nineteen! Excepting to the severely pathological mind, there is something intensely insulting about the idea of events which have profoundly impressed us, never having happened at all! Once, when I was very much younger, I was nearly garrotted on Chelsea Embankment, opposite Cheyne Walk, on my return from an evening at Carlyle's. I escaped with difficulty, and only by means of the prompt use of a weapon which I habitually carry. A few weeks later, at a dinner-party in the same neighbourhood, a medical man was expatiating on the absurdity of stigmatizing the Thames Embankment after nightfall as 'dangerous,' and by way of counter-argument I cited my own experience with the Chelsea desperado. The doctor looked across the table and remarked, 'I hope you will not misunderstand me if I say that I don't believe that the incident you relate ever happened. Your studies in psychology, my dear Mr. Tompkins, show you to be endowed with a vivid, analytical imagination. Now, I think—as a medical man—that this experience of yours exists only in that imagination, and its reality to yourself results from an hysterical tendency to which I should think you were, like most analytical psychologists, singularly subject. It is on the same principle that half-a-dozen innocent persons surrender themselves to justice as the perpetrators of every murder whose real author remains undiscovered.'

"I am free to confess that I felt extremely annoyed; and the remembrance of that annoyance was sufficiently strong to prevent my suggesting the same explanation of her Past (with a capital 'P') to the young person whose case I am discussing.

"I therefore urged her to confide to me the story which blackened her soul in her own estimation with such a Cimmerian sable—on the unexpressed principle that, firstly: Confession eases the soul; and secondly: Familiarity (brought about by such confession) breeds contempt—contempt for the circumstances which it is advisable to forget; for we can never forget anything for which we do not feel that unexpressed contempt which prevents our taking the trouble to impress it on our memories. And *this* is the despite which the gladiator feels for the dying animal at his feet, a despite born of an appreciation of our own physical or mental superiority over the circumstances which, before we encountered and conquered them, inspired us with an uneasy apprehension, if not with a positive alarm.

"We have now arrived back once more at the point whence we originally started, and are in a position to 'start fresh,' as it were, with the continuation of the same story.

"The young person, whose name I have omitted to mention, having therefore refused absolutely to share her trouble with me by way of confession, I changed the subject of conversation, and presently left her. I took counsel on her case from the ever-ready-to-advise pages of the Emperor Marcus Aurelius Antoninus and from the herb nicotian, and as a result wrote her that evening the following letter:

"I asked you to-day to tell me of your trouble; I asked you to confide to my ear the story which, blackening your whole life which is past, stands, as you say, an insurmountable barrier in the way of your happiness in the future. You refused, and no doubt your reasons for doing so were just; but my reasons for inviting your confidence were none the less cogent, and it is because I wish to suggest to you a substitute for that confidence that I write to you now. I said to you, in inviting the recital, that 'Confession eases the soul.' I should rather have said, 'Familiarity breeds contempt.' In your case the two proverbs have the same significance and application. I suggest—and I trust that you will act upon my suggestion—that you should *write out* your story—your confession—call it what you will, for your own eyes alone: that you should, in this written narrative, pay the closest attention to the minute details of your case, and that you should give as much literary completeness thereto as possible; that you should endeavour to make your story a model of literary 'form;' in a phrase, that it should be complete as a 'word-picture,' as a faithful verbal representation of your Past. Nothing extenuate, nothing hide; if any points of your relation redound to your discredit, if any of its circumstances put you to shame, elaborate them to the fullest point. My object in advising this course is as follows: 'Familiarity breeds contempt;' conversely 'Mystery inspires respect;' the unknown is always alarming; but the most awful thoughts, stated in bald English, lose half their terror. So long as you brood upon the events of your Past they will hold you with a morbid, unspeakable interest. You will be a problem to yourself, and you will be continually picturing to yourself the supreme moment when, to some chosen individual, you will lay bare, willingly or unwillingly (either mode is equally dramatic), this cherished secret of your soul.

"But follow my advice. Degrade your Past from its altitude as a great dramatico-psychological study to the level of an ordinary word-picture, a vulgar romance, a novelette in fact. You will then find yourself in a position to criticise it from the ordinary artistic point of view; you will find yourself noting inartistic touches in the relation; you will find places where your *esprit de l'escalier* will suggest that you might have adopted a course far superior to the one you actually *did* adopt; in fact you will find that your drama was in many respects contemptible. In a word, in familiarizing yourself with this story of yours, which, as it stands at present, is panoplied in the dim magnificence of the unexpressed, you will awaken in your mind a certain contempt for the picture you are criticising; and when once we become critical, illusion is necessarily at an end. Such is man: so long as he admires from a distance he is awed; the moment he touches he is in a position to insult. The beneficial effect of this course in your own case hardly needs, I think, to be pointed out. Your own history, viewed and criticised merely as a work of art, will lose its importance, its horrors, for you; and when this end has been attained, the remaining gradient—the one which leads to peace of mind—will be easily climbed, and you will reach the broad table-land of contentment, where your life may once more run smoothly and in quiet places.

"I ceased there. I do not know whether she took my advice or no. From the fact that she never referred to my letter I concluded that she did; at least she subsequently married the friend in whose behalf I had pleaded.

"Than the illustration which I have introduced by the above story, I hardly think that I can give a more complete exposition of my meaning in coupling together the two proverbs which stand as the text of my sermon. What I have endeavoured to emphasize is the psychological *fact* that, *to express* a thought familiarizes it, and that to familiarize ourselves with a subject which has had any terrors for us, inspires us with a contempt for those terrors. Therefore, though I should be very loath to have it quoted as my advice that people should confide in one another the darker chapters of their life's histories, still, if such gloomy periods of life stand out with undue prominence in the scheme of one's existence, and throw into shadow the brighter passages, why, then I say that to state the case pictorially robs it of half its solemnity, that familiarity with the subject breeds in us a contempt for it, and that, in this manner, confession—even though it be made only to yourself—eases the soul."

I ceased, rather astonished at my own volubility and earnestness. Sylvester was lying in the position he had taken up on my sofa when I began, and I was relieved to observe by the regularity with which the smoke from his cigar rose into the air that he had not gone to sleep. When he found that I had really stopped haranguing him, he looked up at me and said seriously:

"Do you know, old man, you've quite astonished me; I didn't think you were such a philosopher. I'll say this for your sermon, that I quite understand and appreciate your point; but I can't take your advice. My horror of myself for what is past is due to neither exaggeration nor imagination. Thank God, I have sufficient control over my mind to prevent myself brooding over my story; but I verily believe that, if I were to concentrate my mind upon it as you suggest, and go over it all again minutely, I should go mad! No, no, Jack; let It lie, let it lie. I don't suppose for a moment that the occasion will ever arise for me to say anything to anybody about it. Let it die with me when I die, old man. Believe me that, in this case, no amount of familiarity could ever breed contempt, and no amount of confession could ever ease the soul. Now let's change the subject."

We did so, and I never broached the matter to him again.

III.

When first, on looking from my window in Rome, this year, I saw the trees on the Monte Pincio bursting into leaf, and the landscape beyond taking a shade of green where before all had been grey and black, I shut up my books, and, rolling up my proof-slips, went out into the warm spring afternoon for my first drive of the year in the Borghese. I found that this happy thought of mine was hardly unique; the *allées*, tho' not by any means crowded, were very fairly lined with carriages; and I had not been in the gardens long, before the startling crimson of the Royal liveries, seen in the distance, warned me to be ready to uncover to the beautiful Queen Margherita, and a few moments later the same ceremony had to be gone through for His Majesty Umberto I°, as he drove his four-in-hand round the villa paths, with the little Prince of Naples, Vittorio Emmanuele, at his side on the box seat. And I lazily wondered, as hundreds have done before me, how the king ever acquired the amazing art of holding the reins of his team in one hand, and his hat, which oscillated in incessant salutation, in the other.

Though I had only been in Rome a little over three months, my acquaintance in the Eternal City had become promiscuous and extensive; and finding that almost every one I knew was in the Burghese, I directed the coachman to seek the less-frequented *allées*, and the comparatively deserted outskirts of the park. I had been driving in solitary state for a few moments, when suddenly a victoria met mine in which reclined a singularly beautiful, golden-haired woman, who was laughing and chattering gaily with her attendant cavalier. I looked to see who this favoured individual might be; it was, of course, Sylvester Gray, handsome, *insouçiant*, calm as ever. He had been in Rome three days, having arrived, bored with himself and everything else, from the Riviera. He saw me, and without the least hesitation or shame hailed me to stop. I did so, and he jumped out and brought me to be presented to his companion, who proved to be an American lady, the wife of a prominent member of the American colony in Rome. We chatted and congratulated ourselves for a few moments, and then drove on our respective ways, having noted our respective addresses with a view to a proximate re-ëncounter.

After that, for about a fortnight, I saw a good deal of Sylvester, who was still, at the age of thirty, the same incorrigible butterfly that he had always been. Never a reception in the city but he was there, never was a party complete without him; and certainly a more delightful companion it was impossible to conceive; he knew everything and everybody. From the Colosseum by way of the Capitoline to the Vatican, and from San Paolo fuori dei Porti to the Catacombs of St. Calixtus, he seemed to know the history of every stone in Rome; and so Sylvester never suffered for want of companionship. His life, aimless as it was, was not without its charms, an ideal existence of *laissez aller*, as Anthony Trollope used to say of his brother Thomas, "a life of active indolence."

An afternoon that shall ever be marked with a crimson stone in the calendar of my life was that on which our ambassador, Sir John Savile Lumley, gave one of the most charming receptions of the year 18—. I had picked up Sylvester Gray at the Hotel Quirinale, where he had a charming suite of rooms "in perpetuity," and had strolled up with him to the Embassy, where the *fine fleur* of Roman society, aboriginal, colonial, and *passagère*, was assembled under the trees on Sir John's finely-kept lawns. It was a lovely afternoon, and Dame Nature was engaged in an active competition with her handmaid, Art, to make the scene as bright and beautiful as it was possible for it to be; and that is saying a good deal in the full glory of a Roman spring.

Sylvester and I had been strolling from group to group, and, as of yore, I had felt absolutely proud of him as I noted the smiles with which he was greeted by every knot of people whom he approached. We had made the complete round of the garden, when suddenly we came face-to-face with a woman. And Sylvester did a thing I never knew him to do before; he stopped dead and looked at her.

She was just stepping out into the garden, the fingers of her left hand lightly resting on the arm of one of the Secretaries of

Legation. There is only one word that in any adequate manner describes her,—she was superb.

She was of medium height, but the magnificent dignity of her carriage was such that she gave one the impression of a tall woman. Her dress, an arrangement in black *moiré* and beads, hung in straight lines about her supple figure, and showed all its perfections with a fidelity that only such perfection could bear with impunity. Her small, arched foot, in its low slipper, and black silk stocking, arrested the eye as it advanced from beneath her swaying skirts to step down into the garden, for it seemed ablaze with light as the sun struck the beaded embroidery of the slipper; a broad sash of soft, watered silk seemed, as it were, wrapped round her exquisite waist, and appeared reluctant to allow the curves of her figure to escape from its folds. One of her gloves, whose buff *peau de suéde* formed the one point of colour about her, was tucked under this sash with her handkerchief, and revealed by its absence the beauty of the wax-white hand that at the moment was raised to her throat. Her face was almost indescribable, but my first impression was of a hard, almost repellent beauty, and of a complexion absolutely colourless, of the most perfect *blanc-mat* hue. The jaw was rather square, and the mouth (accentuated perhaps—but of this a *man* cannot be sure—by a touch of crimson lip-salve) was straight, calm, and cold. The nose perfectly Greek, the eyes full, but rather deeply set, of a profound brown that most people called black. These were overshadowed by a pair of straight, fine eyebrows, forming, as it were, the southern boundary of a high, pale forehead, which was surrounded by the tiny curls of her raven black hair, curls that framed her pretty, white ears, as they escaped from beneath the broad brim of a hat turned up on one side *à la* Gainsborough. She paused on the steps to finish a remark that she was making to the Secretary, and as she stepped into the garden she looked up and caught Sylvester's eyes fixed upon her.

A great wave of crimson surged up from the beautiful throat to the marble brow, and as instantly died away, leaving the dead white of her complexion as it had been before.

The Secretary looked up, and, seeing Sylvester, exclaimed:

"Ah! Gray!" and then, turning to his companion, he said in Italian: "Princesse, I beg your permission to present to you a great friend of ours." And then, indicating Sylvester, who stood bareheaded in the sunshine, he made the presentation in form: "Mr. Sylvester Gray—Madame la Princesse Pamphila-Severi."

There is an hour in the life of man that strikes his fate, says someone in an old play; and Sylvester Gray's struck at five o'clock on this beautiful March afternoon.

"It's not only a hit, it's a bull's-eye," said the Secretary to me, half an hour later, as we passed Sylvester and the Princess Pamphila-Severi walking slowly round the lawn. They were conversing in Italian. He was talking volubly, with his little conquering air, and she, her eyes fixed on the ground before her, listened to him, the hardness of her expression softened by the half-smile that flickered round her mouth, and by the little spark which illuminated her eyes beneath their long lashes.

"Who is she?" I asked.

"Great Heaven! fancy a man asking who *she* is! Ah! but you're a stranger, and, in a manner, a recluse. Well, here is her whole history for you. She was the only daughter of the beautiful Marchesa di Santo-Moriani, and on the death of her mother, six years ago, finding herself alone in the world and a beautiful heiress of nineteen, married the young Prince Pamphila-Severi. He was a charming fellow, but jealous as the Moor of Venice, and one day was idiotic enough to grossly insult Vicomte de Brissac, second secretary of the French Embassy, because he had laughingly remarked, before a room-full of people at Prince Torlonia's, that he would sooner wear in his *boutonnière* a gardenia given him by the princess than the highest grade of the Legion of Honour; and as the princess accepted the challenge and held out to him a gardenia from her bouquet, he took the rosette of the Legion from his buttonhole and threw it in her lap. Five minutes afterward Pamphila-Severi stamped on his toe, and when the Frenchman expostulated he struck him across the face with his glove. De Brissac killed him next morning in the Borghese, and was transferred to St. Petersburg; and the princess, six months only after her marriage, became the coldest and most beautiful widow in Rome. But she's badly hit at last, if I mistake not, and you and I are lucky in being here to see the fun, my dear doctor."

I made up my mind that I had better find my way home alone, and so I took leave of our amiable host and left the Embassy.

Sylvester, at the door, was putting the beautiful Italian into her victoria, and as he did so I heard him say, interrogatively:

"*A rivederla, principina?*"

"*A rivederla, signore; si faccia vedere presto di nuovo.*"

"*La ringrazio, principina, non manchero. Andate 'stasera al palazzo?*"

A moment's hesitation and a quick blush; then shortly:

"*Sì.*"

And the victoria whirled off over the Roman pavement. I took Sylvester by the arm, and said:

"Come and dine with me,"

"Dine?" he replied; "not exactly!" But he came all the same.

"Are you going to the ball at the Quirinal tonight?" said he, during the dinner.

"No," I replied.

"I must," said he; "she will be there."

Until this moment he had not referred to the beautiful princess, and I knew him too well to broach the subject.

"Is she pleasant?" I asked, unconcernedly.

"Pleasant! She's the most superlatively beautiful, the most maddeningly fascinating woman I ever met!"

I had heard Sylvester say this of fifty other women, but I never saw such serious symptoms developed in him before. His silence and evident preöccupation were ominous, and I caught myself wondering, after he had left me to dress for the ball at the palace, whether the butterfly had been snared at last. Upon my soul, I hoped so; but as I lay back in my chair and pushed away my neglected proof-sheets, I found that my mind had wandered back to Harrow and to the little cottage that looked towards

London, to Idlesse, to its terraces and rose garden, and a sharp pain flew across my chest and seemed to settle on my throat as, in my mind's eye, the Princess Stella Pamphila-Severi stood before me, and by her side, radiant in the holy purity of her girlish beauty, there came and stood the wraith of Evelyn Wooster.

IV.

Of the progress of this narrative to its terrible termination, I know by personal observation next to nothing. Until the last leaf of this chapter of life had been turned, I counted for nothing in the pages of the story; indeed, I never knew the Princess Pamphila-Severi save by sight and from hearsay, until I had played my part in the last act of the drama whose *dénouement* was so rapidly approaching when Sylvester left my rooms in that cool March evening to dress for the State Ball at the Quirinal. But he frequently spoke to me of his love, of his happiness, and of his misery; and from these confessions, joined to those of the princess, whose intimate friend I had afterward the honour of becoming, and with whom I frequently held long, long conversations on the subject of our dear Sylvester, I have collected, and in a manner compiled, this section of my story—a section which is, in fact, my story itself.

Sylvester was not by any means a "dandy," but he dressed always with an attention to detail which, to a keen observer, revealed the real man to a very great extent, and was infinitely pleasing. He had a theory on the subject which always struck me, careless though *I* always was in such matters, as excellent.

"A man or a woman can only appear at his best intellectually, when he knows that his appearance is beyond criticism," he used to say. "I have seen a charming man and a brilliant conversationalist put absolutely *hors de combat* by the knowledge that he had been splashed with mud on his way to a reception. I have seen a woman entirely lose her sense of dignity and repose by a terrible fear that her hair was coming down; and I have seen a lecturer lose the whole thread of his discourse in consequence of his cravat becoming disarranged. It is therefore one's duty to oneself and to the world at large to be perfectly 'turned out' at all points."

Sylvester's court dress was a sartorial triumph. His coat and breeches were of the darkest blue velvet, and innocent of the slightest wrinkle; his buttons and the hilt of his sword were of the most exquisite workmanship; and as he entered the ball-room of the Palazzo on this eventful evening, dressed with the supremest care, and with the Order of the Annunziata hanging below his cravat, he was well worthy of the silent homage that was paid him in the admiring scrutiny of the throng that circulated in all directions. Indeed, it would have been difficult to have found a more perfect specimen of the genus *homo* as he stood out from the crowd in answer to a summons from one of the Queen's gentlemen-in-waiting, to engage in a short conversation with her Majesty, to whom, as an old *habitué* of the Eternal City, he was well known.

The ball was at its height when, leaning on the arm of her uncle, the old Prince Marcellini, the Princess Stella Pamphila-Severi made her appearance. There was a slight movement at the principal entry as she stepped into the room, dressed, as usual, in swaying black, embroidered in jet, her sole ornaments a band of diamonds encircling her wrist, and a diamond crescent set amid the raven masses of her hair. As she made her obeisance to Queen Margherita, no eyes were more fascinated by the dignity and beauty of her presence than those of Sylvester Gray, as he stood against a pillar at the end of the room, waiting for the signal that should call him to her side.

It came at length, when she had dismissed the last of the more eager candidates for recognition, and Sylvester advanced and took his place at her side with the little imperious and almost proprietary air that was natural to him and seemed offensive to no one. A moment later an aide-de-camp spoke a few words to Prince Marcellini, and, having smilingly dismissed her escort with a little inclination of the head, the Princess Stella found herself alone in the crowd with Sylvester Gray.

"And how have you spent the time since we met this afternoon, Signor Gray?" asked she, turning her eyes full upon him.

"I have been with my friend, the English Dr. Tompkins, Princesse. He had not the honour of an introduction to you at Sir John's, and so I had an eager listener, for whose benefit I could put my thoughts continuously into words."

"Ah?"—this with a little ironical inflection—"they were pleasant ones, I hope."

"They were exclusively of you, Princesse."

"Of course! And of what else?"

"Of myself, naturally."

"Yes, naturally. At that point of the conversation, or rather of the monologue, you must have been really interesting and eloquent, Signor Gray."

"You are pleased to be sarcastic, Princesse. I wish I could flatter myself that the most eloquent recital of the doings and sayings of Sylvester Gray could awaken an interest, however slight, in the mind of the Princess Pamphila-Severi."

"Do you really? See, is it not close and crowded here? Let us be seated a few moments in this ante-room. Do I keep you from your friends?"

"I have no friends, Princesse, when I am with you. Indeed, I have no interest in life, nothing, save to be by your side, to hear you speak, and when I dare, to answer you."

"Ah?" as before.

All this had been said on either side half-laughingly, half-seriously. Sylvester was conscious of a nervous curl at the corners of his mouth, and felt himself growing more and more grave, as the Princess Stella, in smiling, displayed her exquisite, snowy teeth, and her eyes blazed with the genuine amusement of a beautiful woman who knows her power and uses it boldly, half fearful the while of its effects, and of its possible "boomerang" qualities.

They had taken a couple of arm-chairs in the little ante-room. In one of them the Princess Stella had thrown herself in a graceful, easy pose, and shading her eyes from the light with her black feather fan, was looking out from underneath it with an amused expression at Sylvester, who, seated opposite her, with his elbows on his knees, and playing nervously—for him—with the lace of his cocked hat, was looking back at her, his eyebrows slightly contracted, as if he hardly knew what to make of the beautiful woman before him. Hitherto he had found them all the same, varying only in rapidity and degree of conquest; this was a new variety. There was something infinitely alluring in the parted, crimson lips and exquisite teeth, that was strangely modified by the baffling, almost repellent, look which shone out of the deep-brown eyes, even when they sparkled with the intensest amusement.

"Here is a woman," thought he, "who would lure a man to the verge of destruction and leave him there, and be as cold as ice through it all. And yet, only to look at her makes my heart beat as if I were a boy of sixteen."

"Well," said the Princess, breaking the silence at length, "you were going to tell me about yourself."

"Was I?"

"You as good as said you were; and I want you to. There's a confession to lead off with. Now, be equally frank with me. Come! *Avanti!*"

"Really, Princesse, you are flattering indeed. What do you want to know about me?"

"Everything—from the beginning." Still the same little mocking smile.

"Well, I was born of poor but honest parents, not a hundred miles from——"

"What! I was being serious, for once in a while, Signore."

"And I also."

"Very well, then; it is quite obvious that we are both out of our element at a ball. Will you take me back? I must find my good uncle, who will be wanting to leave."

"Ah! do not go, I beg of you. Come, be seated, Princesse, and I will tell you everything that I have ever done that is likely to interest you."

"*Cielo!* Signor Gray. Why, I am sure I should be here until next year if I were to yield to the maddening temptation which I feel to accept your offer. Come, it is late, and I must *fly*. Ah! how can you utter such a *banalité?* The word 'angel' would have risen to the lips of every other man in the room; I did not expect it of you. Do you know," she added, as Sylvester rose reluctantly to escort her back to the ball-room, "you are very different from most Englishmen I have met. In fact, you are really interesting to me, and I am hard to interest. I checked your confidences just now; you shall make them to me to-morrow, at four, if you will. Ah! Prince, I was looking for you."

And transferring her hand from Sylvester's arm to that of her uncle, who gravely saluted her late cavalier, the Princess Stella was gone.

A few minutes later, wrapping his cloak around him, Gray left the Quirinal, and, turning to the right instead of to the left, reached the Porta Pia, which he passed in spite of the remonstrance of the sentinel, who warned him that the Campagna was unsafe after nightfall, and struck out across country to be alone with his thoughts.

What they were, it would have been difficult even for himself to say. Of one thing he was certain; he had never been so fascinated, so violently attracted by any woman before. He could not understand her, and, priding himself on an intimate knowledge of the ways of woman, gathered from a wide experience of the sex, he was filled with an unreasoning anger against himself, against her, and against the world at large, at finding himself baffled absolutely and completely by this enigmatical specimen. Honestly, he was at fault. He could not account for her, and for her manner of treating him. He felt, he *knew* that she was attracted by him, and yet she repelled him, at once, by her wilfully transparent misunderstanding of his words, and by the calm dignity with which she seemed to treat him as a spoiled child. Her very frankness was galling to him, and yet she must care for him beyond a mere acquaintanceship or she would not have defied Italian social etiquette by singling him out for a *tête-à-tête* in the midst of the gossiping crowd at the Palazzo Quirinale. If she *didn't*, she was a heartless coquette. At this moment something inside himself said very rudely and distinctly, "You're another."

This was a new aspect of the case. Did he *want* her to care for him more than merely as an acquaintance? Yes, a thousand times, yes! Well, and what then? Was he prepared calmly and deliberately to flirt with her, to make love to her as he had done, and with complete success, to a hundred women before her? No, the idea was revolting. Could he imagine her as his wife? The cold glitter of those wonderful eyes rose before him in the darkness, and he felt something of the terror that one feels for some beautiful wild beast that one longs to caress and to fondle, but which one pets very watchfully, and then carefully locks back in its cage before turning one's attention to something else. As the fever of his imagination increased, he pictured her to himself throwing herself into his arms and looking up into his eyes, and as in his waking dream he bent to kiss them, those wonderful lips, with their delicate, artificial touch of crimson, parted in a little mocking smile, and revealed the clinched white teeth within them, whilst he could almost hear the low soft laugh that rippled from them, as he thrust the beautiful head away from him, repelled by something essentially indefinable, essentially fiendish.

No, certainly, no. He was not in love with her in the ordinary sense of the term. It would have seemed horrid to him if she had been in love with him; there was nothing gross, nothing material in his feeling for her, but he *knew* that to sit near her, to talk to her, to watch the varying expression of her matchless, proud face, to inhale the exquisite fragrance that she spread around her as she moved—all this was a sensuous ecstasy in which there was nothing earthly, nothing sordid. Then he flew into a violent temper with himself for having paid her empty compliments, instead of talking seriously during that little *tête-à-tête*. It was his own cursed folly that had cut their conversation short. Why did he treat her as an ordinary woman, when he had felt that she was unique from the instant he had first laid his eyes upon her?——Great Heavens! It was only this afternoon!

He would see her to-morrow—to-morrow—in the afternoon. Well, he had plenty to do between this and then; the time would fly. (Oh! Sylvester, Sylvester!) How would she receive him? He felt that if she should be as tempting and repellent, kind and sarcastic as she had been to-day, he would be irritated, angry. Diable! he was not a child, was he? Very well then. If she, so to speak, hauled down her colours and came like a lamb to the slaughter, he knew that she would fall forever in his estimation; he would hate her. What did he want? Never mind, he would go there and—

"Carita, signore, per amore di Dio."

A vile-looking *lazzarone* of the Campagna, in filthy *contadino* costume, stood before him with outstretched hand, asking for alms. He passed on, angry at the interruption.

"Carita, signore, carita!"

The beggar was keeping up alongside, and the demand had something of a threat in it. Sylvester Gray looked down at the revolting creature trotting by his side, noted the tremendous muscles of the chest and of the extended arm, the covetous leer in the wicked eyes, and the grin which illuminated his face in the moonlight, as the blackguard eyed the sparkling buttons on Sylvester's court dress and the jewel of the Annunziata hanging at his neck. Gray suddenly awoke to the fact that he was probably a couple of miles beyond the walls of Rome, and that he had carelessly let his cloak swing open, allowing the cut steel facets and the gems of his ornaments to sparkle in the moonlight. He put his hand into his pocket. As is usual under such circumstances and in such costume, he had not a centime with him.

"I have no money," said he shortly, in Italian.

"Oh yes, you have, signore."

"I have not."

"Then give me that," and the *lazzarone* pointed to the order of the Annunziata.

"Take care," cried Sylvester, springing back a couple of yards.

"Take care yourself," said the bandit, and drawing a long stiletto from his sheepskin he sprang forward.

Quick as thought, Sylvester whipped his rapier from its sheath, presenting the point at the bosom of the man, who had not imagined that his opponent was armed, and could not check the impetus with which he had sprung forward.

The sword passed through his body and stuck out at his back. As he fell with a sob to the ground, the narrow blade snapped, and Sylvester stood with the remaining fragment in his hand, looking at the wretch lying at his feet. The blade had passed through his heart—in a moment it was over—he was quite dead.

He lay there in the moonlight, his grey-white face turned up to the sky, and Sylvester, as he looked at him, found himself vaguely wondering what this man's history might be. Had he any relations waiting in some cabin of the Campagna for his return laden with the spoils of the night's work, or was he some solitary drunken vagabond, living alone on the proceeds of his vagabondage?—who could tell? Not Sylvester. At that moment something sparkled in the dust close to the dead man's head. Gray stooped to pick it up; it was simply a common pebble with a drop of dew upon it that had reflected a moonbeam like a gem. He tossed it from him, slightly irritated at having troubled himself to pick it up; then he thrust the broken sword into his scabbard. How queerly the empty lower part of the scabbard wobbled as he shook it, almost like the flexible top of a fishing rod; it felt *dead*. Then be turned and walked back to the Porta Pia and so, down past the Piazza Aldobrandini, to the Via Nazionale and his hotel. Wearied out, he retired at once to bed, and fell asleep almost immediately.

He dreamt that once more he walked down the solitary road leading out onto the Campagna. The Princess Stella walked a few paces in front of him, and despite his most agonized efforts he could not overtake her. At last they came to a kind of *Chapelle Ardente*, in which were ranged three biers, two only of which were occupied by corpses. On the first lay Evelyn Wooster, on the second the *lazzarone* whom he had killed a few hours since, and whom, in the obsession of his mind, he seemed already to have forgotten; the Princess stood at the head of the third, and he at its feet.

"Well, Signor Gray," said she, with her mocking smile, showing her exquisite teeth, "is this for you or for me?"

A wild fury seemed to seize him as he strove to catch her to thrust her down upon the empty bier; but she escaped him, dodging in between and around the two corpses, over which she ran her fingers, as if over the keys of a piano, as she skipped round them. At last, just as he thought to hold her, he caught his foot upon the end trestle of the vacant bier and fell extended upon it. Once there, he was powerless to move a finger, and he lay watching the princess as she advanced towards him; then she stooped still lower—and kissed him—

Sylvester woke, trembling in every limb. It was late, and he rose and dressed himself carefully to go about the occupations of the day.

Four o'clock came, and almost on the stroke of the hour he passed beneath the *porte cochère* of the Palazzo Severi. On the rim of the basin into which the water fell from the faucets of a *Renaissance* fountain, sat two cats, the one snow-white, the other spotlessly black. Both wore golden collars round their necks, and both watched the water with unblinking, emerald eyes. As Sylvester approached, one of them—the white one—rose lazily and stretched himself, closing his eyes luxuriously, so as to enjoy the operation to the utmost, the extended claws of his forefeet giving him a firm hold of the roughened stone. Sylvester Gray passed on; he didn't like cats.

The grave *maître d'hotel* showed him into a gorgeous salon at the top of a flight of massive steps, and a feeling of sacramental gloom came over him at the idea of meeting the princess amid such surroundings. Next moment a smiling Parisian maid entered the salon by a *portière* at the farther end, and summoned him to the presence of her mistress.

The Princess Stella's boudoir was hung with embroidered curtains of a pinkish yellow—of a faded Gloire de Dijon rose-colour; a few cabinets of Venetian Renaissance carving were strewn with gold and silver knick-nacks of all kinds. A brazen candelabrum of Venetian workmanship hung from the ceiling, and the floor was strewn with skins of animals. In one corner, on an easel, stood a small Meissonnier; in another stood a second easel bearing an exquisite Greuze. A book-case of carved ebony occupied the space between the windows, which were filled with the most delicately tinted Murano glass; and on an occasional-table stood a Chinese idol grinning with smug self-satisfaction at his own superlative ugliness. A door, concealed by a *portière*, led into an inner room, and on a low divan covered entirely by a bear-skin of the deepest black, lay the Princess Stella.

She was wrapped, rather than clothed, in the loose folds of a light murrey-coloured cashmere; her feet, clad in striped silk, were thrust carelessly into oriental slippers; and she raised herself upon one arm as she extended the other to shake Sylvester by the hand.

"So you have come—really come, Signor Gray, in spite of all your other engagements?"

"I would, Princesse, that it were possible for me to stay away; but when you have said 'come,' I have no longer any engagements."

"Ah! Ah! Ah! *Voila que ça recommence!* Do not, I beg of you. Let us be sensible; sit down. Seriously, I am glad to see you:—I have looked forward all day to your coming, and now you are here, you must not waste time in *banalités* and compliments. And what have you been doing since we parted last night?"

"Oh! the usual things. I spent the morning in calling and writing, the afternoon in writing and calling. Nothing of any interest disturbs the even current of my life."

"And he is afraid to tell me that he has killed a man with those handsome white hands of his!" This lightly and without looking at him.

"Princesse!"

"You are astonished? That is not right. Emotions do not come well to Signor Sylvester Gray; they cause wrinkles and grey hairs, and are bad. Besides, you must never be astonished at anything I say to you. Ah!" as he was about to interrupt her, "I know many things, and you must not seek to know how."

"But, Princesse, I know I was alone on the Campagna. There were no witnesses to his death but the stars above us."

"Ah! then you *did* kill him?"

"In Heaven's name, what does this mean?"

"It means, Signor Gray, that I saw you, as you left the palace, turn up towards the Porta Pia. I knew the dangers of the Campagna, and I was frightened—yes, frightened for you; and when I arrived here I sent a servant to follow you, but he only heard from a *contadino*, who was entering the gates, that a *lazzarone* had been killed some distance from the city. Oh! my friend, but I was frightened, and have been wretched for fear that you also were hurt."

"And you have taken the pains to inquire about me?"

"Yes. Are you surprised?"

"Surprised! I am overwhelmed. What can I be to you, that you should care what becomes of me?"

"Only this, Signore, that you are the only man that has ever attracted—has ever interested me. Do you think it very wrong that I should indulge myself thus, for the first time in my life?"

"And I—what shall I say to you—what shall I say to you?" He sank upon his knees by her side, and covered her exquisite hands with kisses. "How I love you!" he murmured; "how I love you!"

For a moment she did not stir. He looked up at the grand, dark eyes that were fixed upon his in a gaze of infinite tenderness; and even as he looked, his thoughts wandered, in rebellion against his will, to the other women at whose side he had knelt in just such a manner, and to whom he had spoken just such words oftentimes before. His thought seemed to communicate itself to her. She grew a shade paler, as she bade him rise with a little imperious gesture.

"Do not talk to me like that, I beg of you," she said. "Keep such idle words for the other women. I do not ask them of you.

It is enough for me that I care for you, and that it is a delight for me that you should come and sit here and talk to me. Never tell me that you love me, Signor Gray. I shall not believe it."

"But I tell you it is true, true, true. You must, you *shall* believe it."

She looked at him for a moment almost mournfully, and then, her lips wreathing themselves into the well-known mocking smile that he had learned already to dread, she slowly shook her head and murmured, "No, no, no. It is not true."

Sylvester started to his feet, and began pacing to and fro across the skins strewn upon the floor. He stood still, at last, a few paces from her, and said, in a dry, choking voice,

"God help me! I do not know what to say to you."

"No," she replied, "you have said it all so often that it has become mechanical, a mere theatrical *pose*, a *mise-en-scène*. You cannot think of anything new to say to me, of anything that you have not continually said to your other victims. Ah! my friend, do not imagine that I am going to swell the number, am going to write my name at the foot of the list. No, no!"

"Princesse, *angela mia*, do not be so cruel to me. Look at me as I stand before you. Supposing I confess to you, what you know already, that I have laid my homage at the feet of other women; granted that all this has made me a crawling, abject wretch, not fit to lay my worthless self in the dust before you; can you not believe me when I tell you that I have never known love till *now*, that I adore you?"

"No," said she slowly, "I cannot believe you. You must have said all this to others before me, and much more. Why should I flatter myself that at last you are telling the truth?"

"But if I am not, why should I be here?"

"For two reasons: first, you know that I love you—aye, love you, Signor Gray, but it is a confession of strength and not of weakness—and you are flattered and would willingly add the Princess Stella Pamphila-Severi to your conquests; and secondly, you think it pleases me to hear you say, 'I love you.' But it does not, it does not. I hate to hear you say it. I would give my soul to be able to believe you, but I cannot. You are playing with me as you have always played with women, and always will; and I—well, it is enough for me to know that I value your companionship, your friendship—do not mistake me—above anything else in the world. Oh, how I wish you would be a brother to me! I should not care for what the world would say of us. Is this impossible, think you?"

He paused for a moment, and then, in a half-mocking tone, he replied:

"Not at all, Princesse. I will be a brother to you. I will come and talk to you of my plans, of my pleasures, of my triumphs in the camp of Mars and the court of Venus, and when I marry—*when I marry*, I say—you shall be the first to wish me joy. *Vi piace cosi?*" He laughed a little, hard, dry laugh, and flung himself into a chair at a little distance, watching her as she became white and crimson by turns, and then he added, "You see, Princesse, it is hardly the same thing, is it? hardly the same?"

"No," she said, covering her face with her hands, "it is not the same thing."

"And yet you would fain believe me; tell me *why* you cannot do so."

"Answer me, rather, why can you not *make* me believe you, if it is true, this that you say, that you love me?"

"I do not know. I cannot tell."

And even as he said the words, the reason stood out clearly in his mind. He could not impart a tone of sincerity to the words he had said so often, sincere, agonizingly sincere, though they were at this moment. At last he loved—loved truly, deeply, passionately; but between him and his love there rose the impassable barrier of his past life, that stood like a wall of ice between them.

And so he turned to go, sick at heart, overwhelmed by this calamity with which he knew not how to grapple, how to contend.

"You will come again soon?" she said.

"Whenever you will."

"Then to-morrow?"

"To-morrow," he said, reflectively, searching his mind for the engagements he had made.

She saw his hesitation, and exclaimed, petulantly:

"There, there, go! and come when you have time to spare. I will not burden your mind with thoughts of me. Go, go!"

"To-morrow, then," he exclaimed, recklessly, "to-morrow be it, and so *a rivederla*, Princesse. To-morrow at this time."

He kissed the hand that she extended to him, and then gazed into her eyes, a mute, longing appeal for permission to kiss the lips closed in such rigid determination. She divined his thought and answered:

"No, no; you must leave me."

So he left her; every pulse beating wildly, tumultuously, the blood coursing through his veins like a torrent of flame. The position was new, overwhelming, agonizing. He could hardly think; at every moment he saw the beautiful face before him, and his dream of last night returned to his mind with a vividness that was appalling.

V.

On leaving the Palazzo Severi, Sylvester turned into the Corso, hardly noticing the direction in which his steps were leading him, crossed the Via Nazionale, and reaching the foot of the Capitoline, scaled the steps leading to the Piazza del Campidoglio, and leaning on the parapet, looked out over the Forum. Far away in the twilight he could see the wooded space stretching out beyond the Colosseum and the Arch of Constantine, and crossing the Forum and taking the Via Gregoriana almost unconsciously, he was soon beyond the gates and strolling along the Appian Way in the direction of the catacombs of St. Calixtus. At the catacombs he turned on his footsteps and returned to the city. He reached the Hotel Quirinale at about eight, wearied out with the strain upon his mind, and flung himself into an arm-chair to continue the thread of thought that he had been spinning ever since he had left the Princess Pamphila-Severi.

What was the note missing from the chord he had tried in vain to strike in chaunting his song of worship to the Princess Stella. He had never failed before in persuading women that he loved them; why should the moment of his defeat be postponed until the very moment when the thought of failure was an agony too great to be borne? Something told him that it was for the very reason that he had hitherto been acting a part, that he could not throw his whole soul into his words when at last the curtain fell upon the comedy, and a scene of the drama of real life began to be enacted behind it.

"If I tell her," thought he, "that I love but her, the thought of this woman or that woman who has believed it before this, will come between us like a barrier of brass. I have said all there is to be said so often, so thoughtlessly, so unmeaningly, that now, in her presence, it seems sacrilege even to *think* these worn-out platitudes of experimental love. I *must* find some means of proving my love to her, of laying open before her the truth that lies at the bottom of my soul. The truth! My God! what am I dreaming of? Do I propose to myself to go in cold blood to her and tell her that whole horrible story? No, a thousand times no! I would rather kill myself. But how can I go to her and say: 'I love you; I love you, and I cannot live without you!' with that horrible crime on the soul that I fling at her feet? If I could succeed in convincing her and in making her my own, how could I live with *that* between us? And suppose that, having given me her love, some day she should learn about it? She knows the life, the careless, cruel life that I have led; but she can never guess that it is that terrible fragment of a past, in other respects forgotten, that has prevented my marrying, has till now extinguished even my power to love. To tell her or not to tell her—what shall I do? Surely she will believe me when I have torn out my soul for her in recalling all the ghastly horror of ten years ago, so that she may know how vile a thing it is that grovels in the dust before her; and yet, when it is told—and what greater proof of my love can I offer her than the telling?—what if the horror of it should make her loathe me, and I should never see her again? Oh God! what a punishment is this! what a punishment! How richly I have

71

deserved it all; and yet, had you lived, oh my sweet, first Love, how you would have pardoned me, and spared me the agony of these ten years!"

And as he thought of Evelyn Wooster, the dream-face that he conjured up was obliterated by a reclining figure with laughing black-brown eyes, with crimson lips and teeth of driven snow, which held up a dainty, white hand for him to kiss, and said in a half-regretful tone:

"How I wish I could believe you. Signor Gray; how I wish I could believe you!"

He rose at last, and having changed his dress, issued forth in the direction of the new quarter that has raised its pallid house-fronts against the blue Italian sky, round the precincts of St. John of the Lateran, to call upon the friend with whom I had seen him driving that first day in the Borghese, a prominent member of the American colony that has always kept, and always will keep, things lively in the Eternal City.

As good luck would have it, he found her in and alone, and after the first greetings were over he opened his case with the question:

"Have you read Dostoievski's *Le Crime et le Chatiment*?"

"Yes—what of it?"

"Oh, nothing! only I was thinking of it to-day. It is a book which gives one a good deal of food for thought, does it not?"

"Well, yes. But what particular passage has made so profound an impression upon the placid and unimpressionable Sylvester Gray?"

"Several passages; but particularly the one where Rodia tells Sonia that it was he who murdered the old woman. Do you think he ought to have told her? That it was either his duty, or expedient to do so?"

"Well, the circumstances were peculiar. Sonia being a woman of the town, for whom his feelings were not so much love as an indescribable and almost morbid attraction, he could not

72

expect that his confession would have such an effect upon her as it would on an innocent and pure-minded woman. And again, you see he did not confess to her as a proof of his love, but was rather actuated by the selfish motive of relieving his own mind of half of the burden, and, by confessing to her, of making her carry half of it. It was as necessary for his enfeebled mind to tell somebody his secret as it was for the barber of King Midas; and she, in her degraded condition, was the only creature he felt fit to associate with. It was the sympathy of infamy, not the confidence of love."

"Then you do not think that had they been truly *in love* with one another he would equally have confessed, and that had she been 'an ideal woman,' he ought to have done so?"

"Certainly not! No man has any right to shatter the confidence of a woman by the confession of his previous follies—well, crimes if you will. If the thing is long past and forgotten, it is his duty to die keeping his secret; his wife can never guess it alone, and to confess it to her before or after marriage is purely cowardly. It is not the result of a high-souled honesty, it is simply a selfish horror of paying the penalty of a sin in the past by keeping the secret to oneself and being the only sufferer in the present."

"And supposing there is always a possibility of the man's sin being discovered? Do you not think that the constant dread must dwarf his love, and paralyse his efforts to devote his whole soul to his wife?"

"Not necessarily; but if that were really the case, as might happen in the instance of a super-sensitive man, let him tell her after they are married."

"And lay himself open to the reproach that he has married her under false pretences? My God! how awful!"

"Not at all, my good man. A little 'scene' might follow, it is true; but you men attach far less importance to 'scenes' than we do; you go away to the club and smoke it off. We, on the contrary, have no soothing resource but tears, which, in their soothing effects, are far behind expletives and nicotine. But the scene blows over, and though it should be avoided, if possible—that's why I say *don't* confess, for there is always a little tender spot left behind—a man's crimes, which a woman forgives most easily, are those he has committed against another woman. It sounds odd, doesn't it? but it's the case. At first a young wife fancies that her husband has never loved anyone but her, but this belief soon gives way to another, which is, that he has never loved anyone else *as much* as her. And the latter thought is an excellent substitute for the former, and is more lasting!"

"But, my dear friend, we are straying far from the subject. Rodia's crime was not a prior attachment, it was the treacherous murder of a defenceless old woman. Now supposing a man has done something like that, or even worse—had done something *lache*, *infame*, disgraceful—has he any right to take the love of a pure woman without telling her what she is doing in loving him? Surely not."

"Ethically, ideally, *no*. But actually, practically, *yes*. She loves him and he loves her; that is enough. The crime may never be discovered, may never cloud the horizon of their married happiness; but if it does come out one day, though the woman may be shocked, stunned for a moment, *if he has been a good husband to her*, and more especially if she be a mother, all he has to say to her is, 'Yes, I did this thing, but I loved you so dearly that I could not bring myself to tell you of it, for fear that it would cloud your happiness as it has clouded mine. I prayed that you might never know, and would have guarded the secret from you with my life; but now it's too late, and I have only one excuse; I loved you then, I love you now more dearly still; the purity you have brought into my life has driven the sharper agony of remorse from my soul; can you not look into my eyes and love me only as *you* have known me?'"

"And you don't think that the knowledge that they *know* will rankle in the minds of both, but in hers especially?"

"Not seriously, so long as he behaves himself well; but to a certain extent it must, of course, and for that reason—now I am going to shock you—I consider it a brave and honourable man's duty to sink his own feelings and *lie* boldly if there is no chance of his being found out. He ought, if there are no actual witnesses who can give him the lie, to deny the fact and defy the world

74

to produce its proofs. A loving woman will believe her husband against the world, and if by any chance his lie is discovered he has always the resource I mentioned first, he can plead his love, and I, as a woman of some experience, say that he would have nothing to fear."

Sylvester rose to go.

"I am immensely obliged to you," said he; "I have learnt a most interesting lesson this evening which I shall not easily forget. However, there is one final question which I should like to ask you. Supposing the whilome criminal loves a woman of exceptional intelligence and strength of mind—do you not think that if he were to bare his soul to her, and confess his crime to her before marrying her, actuated thereto by a genuine feeling of honour, she would take his confession to be the most convincing proof of his love, and love him with all the greater strength?"

"She *might*; but I should consider it an exceedingly danger-ous experiment."

VI.

On the following day at four, and on many days after, Sylvester found himself either seated opposite the Princess Stella in the little quaint boudoir, or pacing feverishly up and down the room across the tiger skins, stopping now and then to turn and answer some laughing remark of hers with a little impatient, dramatic gesture.

Their bond of sympathy never ripened into anything closer. When he would implore her to believe in his love for her, she would shake her head half-mournfully, and compliment him on his histrionic talents; and he, alas! could not entirely clear his mind of the suspicion that she spoke what was in a great meas-ure the truth. In the midst of his most impassioned utterances, when he would fall on his knees by her side and beg her to look through his eyes into his soul which was all hers, there would flash across him a pang of memory for his past life, and he would ask himself *why* should this woman believe in him more than the others, and he would suddenly remember having used the same words to others before her. Then these thoughts would seem to communicate themselves to her, and she would push him away with a little contraction of her brows and an expression almost of repulsion, and the next moment their conversation would have resumed its accustomed tone, and they would speak of books, of pictures, and of his travels, but never of himself. Often she used to say to him:

"I wonder if I shall ever know anything about the real *you*, Signor Gray? How I wish you would tell me your real history—I mean *all* that happened before you began to travel—for of course *there* is the story of Sylvester Gray."

"Heaven forbid!" he would reply, and walking to the window would look out into the *cortile* where the Princess's cats remained faithful to their hopes of some-day catching one of the gold-fish that wandered round below them in the basin of the fountain.

"Yes," the Princess used to answer; "the tone and gesture are most dramatic, and would have impressed those other women; but they don't impress me. I want history and not theatricals. Come! why do you not some day throw off that handsome impenetrable mask of yours, and if you really love me as you say you do, do what I ask, and tell me something about yourself?"

"There is nothing to tell, Princesse," he would say half-bitterly. "I have wandered about the world and have acquired the art of impressing the weak-minded by means of what you are pleased to call my histrionic talent; but it is nothing, and need not disturb you so long as you are not deceived by it. Story—God bless you—like Canning's knife-grinder, I have none to tell you."

"Ah! Bah! I am tired of all that. Stop, I beg of you."

And so it would go on. It seemed as if each were matched against the other in a contest of badinage, in which neither would give in, and neither would confess to defeat; and this strange friendship continued until the end—the end which came so tragically, so unexpectedly.

Early one morning Sylvester rose and made his way to St. Peter's to listen to the mass in the Capella del Coro. His heart was full to breaking with his love for the Princess Stella, and his despair of ever convincing her of its existence. Throughout the service he sat revolving in his mind the problem which had led to the conversation I have recorded with his American friend— should he tell her that history of his or no? It was the only thing left, his disease was desperate and required a remedy like unto it. At any rate it would have one of two effects: either she would pity and love him, at last understanding the motive of his strange nomad life; or else the sympathy she felt for him now, would be turned to hate, into despite, and it would all be over—this uncertainty, this heart-breaking struggle to convince her of a love that she would fain, but could not, believe in.

He came to a decision suddenly that afternoon, whilst he stood before her in her dainty boudoir, engaged in the old, hopeless effort.

"Why can't you convince me?" she had said for the hundredth time.

"I will tell you," said he, turning suddenly and standing over her; "I will tell you. It is because my love is pollution to a woman so fair, so pure, as you, and though you cannot tell *why*, you feel it to be so; your womanly *flair* tells you of it. Listen! I—I, Sylvester Gray, the gay, the *insouçiant*, the *debonnair*, am a coward, a scoundrel, a criminal too vile for expression. I told you one day, that I have loved one woman before you, only one, and that was ten years ago. Well, I loved her wildly, passionately; and she trusted me with her very soul. As a return, the trust she reposed in me I betrayed. I shattered her belief in manhood, in honour, in myself, and we parted, not in hatred, but in dull, cold disillusionment on her part, in passionate remorse on mine. She never recovered from the shock; she died soon after, and left me behind to wander through the world, to continue as I had begun, a destroying fiend. And it is the knowledge of this that you instinctively have, that holds you from me; the face of that dead girl stands between us, and it is only your sweet hands that can lay those reproachful eyes at rest."

"Go on, tell me everything—just as it happened."

"So be it."

And he told her of our schoolboy days at Harrow, of his love for Evelyn Wooster, and of her stay at Idlesse; told her the events of that stay which I had only been able to surmise dimly, as some horrible nightmare, and which I never knew till I heard them from the lips of the Princess Stella.

He told his story to the bitter end, extenuating nothing, excusing nothing, told it with a dramatic force that was terrific, with a pathos that was infinite, and at the end sank into a low *fauteuil* before her, watching her to see the effect it had produced upon her.

She had hidden her face in her hands during the recital, and when he became silent, she slowly lowered them and looked up; he was lying before her in one of the old theatrical attitudes she knew so well, a strained look of pleading in his eyes, his hands convulsively clasped before him.

And suddenly, in the midst of her horror, and pity, and grief for the man before her, as she gazed at him, there came over her, like a wave, the revolting thought that even this was all a *pose*, a superb dramatic effort, conjured up as a last resource to impress her and persuade her, against her better judgment that he loved her. As the idea took possession of her mind, her face gradually hardened once more, and at last the lips began to wreath themselves into the little mocking smile. He was watching her;—turning white to the roots of his hair, he started to his feet and exclaimed:

"Well! what do you think of me now?"

"What do I think of you *now*, Signor Gray? Why, as a man, exactly what I did before; but as a *raconteur*, as an *improvisatore* of the most harrowing dramatic narratives, my opinion of you is, if possible, vastly increased."

"Good God! what do you mean?"

"Why—I mean that you have rivetted my attention for a couple of hours with one of the most thrilling romances I have ever heard; but you don't suppose, do you, that I *believe* it? Cielo!

Signor Gray, I know you too well. Ah, *mon ami, mon ami,* how you waste your talents!"

And she rose and turned away, and then walking to the window, looked out into the court-yard.

The brass rings of her *portière* rattled, and she turned suddenly. Sylvester Gray was gone. She turned once more to the window and saw him stride through the *cortile*, and disappear through the *porte-cochère*.

The Princess Pamphila-Severi laughed softly.

"What a boy it is!" said she to herself. "At this time to-morrow he will come and begin all over again. How I love him! and how I wish he loved me as he declares he does!"

✷

Sylvester did not return next day. Early on the following morning I wrote her the following note from the Albergo Quirinale, whither, in the dual capacity of friend and doctor, I had been hastily summoned by Sylvester's body-servant:

> MADAME LA PRINCESSE:—I have a duty to perform by the direction of our friend, Sylvester Gray, in writing to inform you of his death, which occurred during the night. He left instructions that you should be informed immediately, and it is in obedience to those instructions that I hasten to apprise you of this sad intelligence. *Aggredite l'assicuranza,* etc.
>
> JOHN TOMPKINS, M. D.

Half an hour later, as I sat by the side of my poor, dead Sylvester, the Princess arrived. She stooped over and kissed the pale lips, stroking them gently with her fingers, and then, turning to me, she said:

"Tell me the *absolute* truth, doctor; this death was —premeditated?"

"Madame," I replied, "death resulted from an overdose of morphine, which Signor Gray had been taking for some nights to procure sleep. It may have been accidental, or it may have been premeditated; a letter which was delivered to me this morning, containing his last instructions in case at any time he should die suddenly, and evidently written last night before he retired, points with terrible distinctness to the latter hypothesis."

THE STORY OF A YOUNGER SON.

A Commonplace Romance.

I.

GERVASE BRAYCROOKE was a younger son. True; but he did not look it.

To see him scouring the country on his crow-black mare, "Dynamite," both man and beast groomed to perfection, stopping here and there to exchange a few gracious remarks for the greetings of the cottagers and "retainers" of his father's estate, you would have said that he was some benevolent young Russian noble, paying a circular visit of princely patronage among his serfs and other chattels. He was only twenty when I saw him first, but he had already that air of genial command that characterized him in after life, a manner which drew all hearts to him, but forbade the slightest approach to that familiarity which breeds contempt.

Sir Eric Braybrooke's place was in Warwickshire, and I am one of the enthusiastics who declare that Warwickshire is one of the most beautiful of the midland counties of England. Consequently, when my old school and college friend. Sir Eric, wrote to me, pressing me to "sport my oak" in Lincoln's Inn and, leaving the law behind, to come and vegetate in Warwickshire and recuperate my wasted tissues after an unusually hard session, I wrote back and told him that the moment the courts rose at the termination of the great case of Willoughby versus Willoughby (a cause "In Lunacy," which ended by nearly sending all parties concerned to keep the unconscious plaintiff company in his private madhouse), I should bid farewell to Briefs, Cases for Opinion, Special Pleadings, and Drafts, and jump into the first train that left Euston for the Midlands, for Warwickshire, and for Kineton.

In all Warwickshire, rich as it is in historical associations, with the birthplace of William Shakespeare at Stratford-on-Avon and the home of the Washingtons at Sulgrave, few villages are more interesting than Kineton, which is situated within an easy walk of the field of battle at Edgehill, and is the hamlet where his sacred Majesty, King Charles, the martyr, remained for a while before and after that memorable fight. I had explored the whole country round, pretty thoroughly, with Eric Braybrooke, when we were boys at school together, and I had been invited to spend my summer holidays on one never-to-be-forgotten occasion at Braybrooke Hall. I had not been into Warwickshire since, and I looked forward to my visit to the old place every bit as much, now, looking absently out of the window of my chambers in Lincoln's Inn, with polished sconce and silver side whiskers, as I had a quarter of a century before, when Eric and I walked up and down the towing-path at Eton, or discussed the glories of Braybrooke Hall, as we dressed after our matutinal swim at "Athens."

When, therefore, I had at last bidden my clerk "God speed" in starting for our respective holidays—well earned on both sides—and had reached Kineton after a somewhat complicated collection of "changes" on the London and North-Western Railway, it seemed to me on leaving the quaint little station that all the old landmarks were familiar to me; I went back twenty-five years at a bound, and, telling Sir Eric's coachman to take charge of my luggage, I set forth to walk the three miles which intervened between Kineton village and Braybrooke Hall.

About half a mile from the lodge gates of the Hall there was, I remembered, a gate which opened upon a road that wound round among the Braybrooke woods. I determined to pass through it, and reach the Hall by the garden side, a way I remembered of old. As I approached it I heard the sound of a horse's hoofs coming up behind me, and just before I reached it, a solitary horse-man passed me. As he reached the gate, he reined in his animal, a superb black mare, with some difficulty, and turning half round in the road, waited for me to come up with him. Thus I had an excellent opportunity of noting his appearance—which was that of the most prepossessing young man that I had ever seen. He was fair, with a young, boyish face that was singularly frank in its expression. His eyes struck me as being blue. His lithe young figure was shown off to advantage by his tightly-fitting riding suit of dark blue cord, and as he sat on his horse, I could not help feeling proud of him as an English boy, and almost wished that I had married all those years ago when—but never mind.

As I came up he saluted me military-fashion with the butt of his riding whip and said in a soft musical voice:—

"Might I trouble you, sir, to open this gate for me; my mare is having a great game at my expense and won't let me get off and open it for myself."

"Certainly," I replied, and as I did so, I added, "Does not this gate lead through the Braybrooke woods?"

"Yes," replied the boy, "and if you're going to Elverly, you'll find it a short cut and a pretty walk, but bear to the right or you'll not get to the house. Thank you very much; Good day, sir." And with the words he lifted his hat and bowed in his saddle as if to a woman, gripped his mare with his knees, and swept off into the woods. I couldn't help hoping as I walked through the old woods where I had rambled as a boy, that I should find out who the young fellow was. He was good to look at and I was glad I had met him.

Sir Eric Braybrooke was waiting for me on the piazza in front of the drawing-room windows of the Hall. He made me welcome to his old Tudor mansion, and it was with a feeling of the most genuine satisfaction that I sat down with him, in the cosy room that had been set apart for my use, to indulge in a little chat on old times before dinner. We were to be a comparatively small gathering that evening; the majority of the guests were to arrive the next day; at present the house party consisted of Sir Eric and Lady Braybrooke and their sons Eric and Gervase, their daughter

Miss Constance Braybrooke, Miss Rosamund Gilbert (a distant relation of the family, a *protegée* of Sir Eric's who had been educated with his children), Lord George Wilmyngton, and myself. Next day we were to be invaded by half-a-dozen others, so, as Sir Eric grimly remarked, we must make the best of our one quiet evening together. Thus posted, he left me to dress for dinner.

As a bachelor and a hard worker I dress quickly, and when I came downstairs, I found myself alone in the drawing-room with a strange young woman, and a self-possessed withal. She was tall and dark, with the freshest of complexions and the most wonderful wondering eyes. She arose as I came into the room and looked an interrogation point at me. I concluded that she must be Miss Braybrooke, so I remarked:—

"Miss Braybrooke, I presume."

"No," replied she, "my name is Gilbert. I am related to the Braybrookes in a complicated manner which I could explain to you by means of a diagram, but I am afraid hardly without."

"Pray, do not trouble on my account, Miss Gilbert," I rejoined, and in two minutes we were the best friends in the world.

In a word, she was charming, and I was quite sorry when two young men in superlative evening dress entered the room, whom Miss Gilbert introduced as Mr. Gervase Braybrooke and Lord George Wilmyngton. His lordship bowed and dropped into a seat beside Miss Gilbert; in Gervase Braybrooke as he extended his hand, I recognized my young cavalier of the afternoon.

"Surely, we have met before," said he, "and I must apologize for my unconscious discourtesy. Had I dreamt for an instant that you would walk up, instead of driving from the station, I might have guessed your identity, and should have walked up with you. As it was, my mare Dynamite was giving me momentary proof of my discernment in my choice of a name for her, and I was only conscious of having begged a gentleman to act as lodge-keeper for me, and of having ridden on."

I was delighted to find him so soon especially as I found that he would bear a closer inspection. The next moment Lady Braybrooke and her daughter, a beautiful blonde of nineteen, came into the room, followed by Sir Eric and his eldest son, who were apparently engaged in close confabulation on some matter of importance;—and then we filed in to dinner. It did not require much legal discernment to see how matters lay among the party assembled in the oak-panelled dining-room of Braybrooke Hall. Evidently the family were all on the most friendly terms with one another, and from Sir Eric down to Constance, were as lighthearted a crew as could be imagined—with the exception perhaps of the elder son, Eric, who struck me as being reserved almost to the verge of gloom. Miss Rosamund Gilbert was the brightest perhaps of us all, but it was plain from the way she continually flung the ball of conversation into his lap, that Gervase was her favourite, a fact which, not escaping the observation of Lord George Wilmyngton, seemed to cause that gentleman no small annoyance.

After the ladies had left the table, the three young men immediately excused themselves and strolled out through the open windows of the dining-room to smoke a cigarette, with the permission of the ladies, on the verandah. Sir Eric and I remained behind to talk over old times together. From the past, we gradually came to the present, and from generalities we arrived at particulars. It seemed that there had been a boy and girl attachment between Gervase and Rosamund Gilbert all their lives. They had been brought up together, and Sir Eric only awaited the time when Gervase should have hewn out a position for himself in the Indian Civil service, to receive his beautiful *protegée* into even more close relationship with his family. It was not an engagement; oh, no! nothing formal or definite, but an understood thing—an understood thing. But the Braybrooke estates were strictly entailed, and descended with the title to the eldest son, the serious Eric, a young man of whom I am inclined to think his father stood somewhat in awe—anyhow I fancied I detected a regretful ring in the worthy baronet's voice when he told me the time was drawing near when Gervase must join the Civil Service Corps in India and be away from Braybrooke for four or five years.

Somehow *I* felt sorry too, but I was glad that these two young people who had individually created such a favourable impression upon me, were united by a bond so tender as that of the "understanding" that existed between them.

We two old gentlemen did not go out on the verandah, but rejoined the ladies by way of the drawing-room. Eric Braybrooke was sitting by his mother. Lord George Wilmyngton stood by the piano listening to Constance Braybrooke, as she dreamily touched the keys, and crooned snatches of old English ballads. The other two were nowhere to be seen.

"Where are Gervase and Rosamund?" inquired Sir Eric.

"Oh! they're walking round and round as usual," answered Miss Braybrooke from the piano.

The next moment the pair in question appeared arm-in-arm in the open window, the girl's white frock standing out against the blackness of the garden beyond, and the boy rendered the more conspicuous as he stood by her side, his black dress suit thrown up by the whiteness of his waistcoat and shirt-front. What a handsome picture they made, to be sure, as they stood there! She had thrown a white goat-wool shawl, such as the women weave on the Pyrennean slopes, round her shoulders and over her head, and it made a charming framework for her lovely face. They stood there looking in at us, as if they were defying critical examination, and indeed well they might, for it would, I think, have been hard to find in all humanity a more perfectly matched couple. I glanced round the room to see what was the impression that the picture made on the rest of the company. In Lady Braybrooke's expression there was an air of conscious pride, in that of her daughter the most genuine admiration and affection; Lord George Wilmyngton had turned a shade paler, and was nervously biting the end of his moustache; Eric Braybrooke alone looked on as if he was amused by the scene; as for me, I turned and looked at Sir Eric—he caught my glance of enquiry and smiled affirmatively.

I was glad—very glad that it was so.

"Well," said Gervase after a pause, "why don't you ask us to come in? we'll come if we're invited, otherwise we shall continue our promenade and philosophical confab'. We've been discussing a most intricate point; and that is, supposing the existence of two people who are as much in love with one another as Rosa and I are, in the event of the girl going off and marrying some other fellow, can they remain as good friends as ever, afterwards, without making fools of themselves and one another? Now *I* say they could, and Rosa says they couldn't. *I* say that if Rosa goes and marries my hated rival, whoever he is, I shall come and live with them and be just as jolly as ever; and she says she would leave orders with the servants to say "Not at home" whenever I called, and that if I was always about the place, it would end in our falling in love in real earnest. What do you think, Wilmyngton?"

"Well," replied his lordship, "I think there is very little doubt that you would end by falling in love with Miss Gilbert, but I don't see that it need necessarily be reciprocal!"

"But I think," said Lady Braybrooke, "that you might do something better than waste your time talking such nonsense. Anyhow you are *not* going to walk about any more tonight in the damp."

"You, none of you, ask me my opinion, I observe!" said the elder brother, putting down the book he had taken up, "and as you don't seem to want it, here it is: I think that if a man sees too much of a woman he has been in love with before she married some other fellow, either they will fall in love over again, only more so, or else familiarity will breed contempt, and they will come to the conclusion that they can't imagine what they ever saw in one another."

And amid the silence which followed, Eric Braybrooke got up and left the room.

"Your elder boy is no fool," remarked I *sotto voce* to Sir Eric.

"No, indeed!" replied his father drily.

And then the conversation became general on other subjects. Lord George took a seat next to Miss Gilbert, and Gervase came over to persuade his sister to play some favourite tunes for him.

I retired comparatively early that evening, and did not join the rest of the men in the smoking-room; consequently I was down early next morning, and stepping out into the garden, the first object that met my eyes was Gervase dressed in white flannel, superintending the marking out of the tennis court. Close by, in a hammock swung between two trees, lay Rosamund Gilbert, clad also in the whitest and freshest of frocks, swinging lazily to and fro in the morning sun, while she kept up a brisk fire of conversation, chaff, and repartee with Gervase.

As I made my appearance Gervase advanced across the lawn to greet me, and Rosamund cried out across the court:—

"Good morning, Mr. Cornell, do you mind my not scrambling out? It is so ungraceful. Come and be poetical; here you see milk in a tin bowl—only one bowl for the three of us—with the dust and hairs and leaves and things not strained off; gooseberries, peaches, and grapes, with earwigs crawling about them. Peter and I—I always call Gervase, Peter, because he's the only person who carries keys of all the gates about with him—Peter and I always do this, we get so awfully hungry before breakfast. You can sit on the end of the hammock if you think it is safe, but *I* should advise you to take Peter's coat," and so saying, she flung me Gervase's white flannel coat, which she had been using as a pillow, and which I spread out on the grass and sat down upon.

To cut a long story short everything that I saw of this inseparable couple, I liked more and more. Whenever the girl was not with Gervase, Lord George was her devoted cavalier, and it was plain that she only had to say "yes" to become Lady George Wilmyngton; but it was equally plain that she was not going to say "yes," and often when I saw his lordship biting his moustache as he watched the pair go off demurely arm-in-arm to lose themselves in the woods, I used really to pity the young fellow, who loved Rosamund Gilbert so deeply and so hopelessly.

One day I had a talk to Sir Eric about it; he seemed to take it all as a matter of course, and was inclined, as so many country gentlemen seem to be, to bother very little about the affairs of other people so long as they did not directly and personally concern himself.

"Oh!" replied he, in answer to a question of mine, "Gervase and Rosa understand one another perfectly, and when he comes back from India they'll be married—they've plenty of time before them; she's only seventeen—yes, he is twenty—I shall be glad to see them married, for she's a sweet girl, and he's as good as gold, I believe."

I was almost annoyed that the engagement was not formally expressed between them; I had seen so many young hearts separated by a misunderstanding which could not have occurred had they been bound together by a definite promise given and received. Alas! I believe it occurs every day. A boy and girl are thrown together, brought up together, are "the best friends in the world"—the very freedom with which they avow to the world and to themselves their unclouded affection for one another, the matter-of-course nature of their companionship seems to forbid the suggestion of anything deeper, tenderer, warmer. Then, one day, they suddenly discover that there is something unexpressed between them; in a word, that though it is not blazoned forth to the world, they *do love* one another, and then, though, as before, nothing is said on the subject, their friends say, "they understand one another." It is the girl who finds this out first, as a rule, and it is her sudden new consciousness of manner, a word in a conversation that suggests the true state of affairs to the boy, and then—though as before, no actual word of love passes between them—their sympathy becomes more tender, more delicate, more conscious of its own existence; they assume little proprietary airs with regard to one another, and everything seems wrapped in an indolent, treacherous calm.

Whenever I see a little drama of this kind being played between two young people, I am reminded of some verses that were written once under similar circumstances by a young poet of my acquaintance, which are entitled "Sympathy," and which run as follows:—

> Hush! do not speak, lest the spell that enthralls us
> Break like the smouldering spark into flame.
> Still!—Make no sign, lest the small voice that calls us
> Fill this whole planet, for me, with your name.

Absence is death, to be near you is madness,
    Madness or death? which of these will *you* choose
Say, what is death to the anguish, the sadness
    Of finding a life which we find but to lose.

Hush! if you speak, you'll drag down to existence
    A spirit that hovers o'er our twin souls above;
Which will make us its own with a tender persistence,
    That wakes us at last, but to say:—"*This is love.*"

And so it goes on, this deadening, calling thing known as "an understanding," until one of two things happens. Either, something calls the boy or the girl away;—if it is the girl, it is generally another lover, and this brings matters to a head, their love becomes expressed and consummated; if it is the boy, it is generally a call to his work in the world, and too often he goes off with a smile on his lips and words of hope on his tongue, to a life full of incident and occupation, and leaves her to what:—to her own lonely thoughts, and to wonder if he ever really loved her.

Or, the more subtle, the more insidious, the more deadly poison of familiarity—of *custom*,—of *satiety*—creeps into the cup of their contentment, and unless they are separated at once, the sweets of sympathy become changed into the acids of antipathy, and they part coldly, by common consent, with an uneasy feeling of relief which neither can account for, and of which both feel ashamed. "An understanding" is like a pinch of powdered sugar flung into a goblet of champagne—at first it froths up with the excitement of chemical combination, but with each successive pinch the evervescence is less and less pronounced, till at last the surface becomes clear, and the sugar which has been thrown in lies a sticky cloying mass at the bottom of the cup.

Or, again—since we are analysing the matter—let us take another simile which too often illustrates the termination of a boy-and-girl attachment, or of what is miscalled, for want of a better term, a "platonic friendship." Have you ever seen an insulated metal globe, highly charged with *positive* electricity placed close to another charged *negatively* in a locality where the air is dry? So long as the atmosphere remains as it was, the globes remain highly charged with mutually attractive electricities. Presently, however, the air becomes warmer and moister, and, acting inductively upon one another, the globes become gradually "discharged" by one another's proximity. No spark, no report, but imperceptibly each has taken from the other all that it can give, and when the electrician turns his attention to them, he finds them absolutely normal; neither of them attracting or being influenced by the other. And so, alas! too many of these pure boy-and-girl loves come to imperceptible and untimely grief. Let them be brought together, say I! let us hear the "snap!" as the spark flies, let their affection be acknowledged honestly, before God and before man!

Pardon me this digression—but it has been germane to my story, believe me. Thoughts such as these continually occurred to me during the bright summer weeks which I spent at Braybrooke Hall, and one morning, coming down early, I found Gervase standing on the gravel walk throwing pebbles at Rosamund's window to awake her. As I reached him, a white arm waving a handkerchief appeared from behind the curtains. "All right," shouted he, and then turning to me, he said, "That's the signal by which I know that she's not only awake, but out of bed."

"What friends you are!" said I, and he replied enthusiastically:

"Yes—we are. She's the sweetest and the cleverest and the handsomest girl I ever knew, and I don't know what my life would have been without her."

"And when are you going to be married to one another?" I asked.

"Oh! that won't be till I come back from India. Until I'm 'something' over there, I can't afford a wife, you know; but she'll wait for me, Mr. Cornell, she'll wait for me."

"But it is not a definite, absolute, *engagement*, I think I heard your father say?"

"No, because, you see, I'm very young and so is she, and she's never seen any other fellow hardly. I should be very sorry to tie her down by any promise to me, before she's had an opportunity of seeing if she likes another fellow better; but if she's the girl I think and know she is, I don't believe anyone could make her happier than I could, and she knows it."

"Do you ever talk together of your future lives?"

"No; it isn't necessary. The present is so good and lovely, that all we care to know about the future is that it will be just like the present. I haven't a thought in the world, Mr. Cornell, that isn't of her or that she doesn't share, and she knows it; what more can a man want?"

I couldn't help thinking that as a true friend of both of them, I should have wanted a good deal more, but it was unnecessary to say it, and I merely replied:—

"Well, my boy, I agree with you that she's a sweet and a charming girl, and I wish you every happiness for the future. If ever you want any other friend than your father—which Heaven forbid—remember that William Cornell of 50 Old Square, Lincoln's Inn, is ready and willing to do anything he can for you."

"Thank you," replied the boy, "thank you, Mr. Cornell. I hope the only claim I shall ever make on your friendship will be to ask you to rejoice with me in the happiness of my future. Do you see this half-opened rose? It is lovely as it is, is it not? Well that's our present; when it opens fully, it will still be lovely, but in a different way—like this."

And he spread open the unfolding petals with his fingers. A common mishap had befallen the poor rose; a second calyx and set of petals had sprouted inside the first. The rose would bloom, yes, and the inner rose would rival the outer one in sweetness; but neither could ever become perfect, though the imperfection would not become visible until the rose had become mature. A sharp contraction of the features revealed the sudden pang that shot through the boyish heart at my side, as he flung the imperfect flower into a rubbish-basket at his feet.

At that moment Rosamund Gilbert joined us, her freshness and loveliness putting to shame the clematis she had stuck carelessly into her waist-belt. Gervase glanced at me with a curious, almost aged look, and then took the hand I extended to him and shook it silently. Next moment Rosamund had taken me by one arm, and him by the other, and together we strolled down to the stream for a row before breakfast.

II.

"Hullo! Gervase," said Sir Eric, as we took our seats at the breakfast table, "here's an evil-looking letter for you from the Civil Service Commission; it looks suspiciously to me, as if it meant that you've got to go up to town and 'try again' for your examination."

"Indeed," said Rosamund, with quick indignation, "there's no possibility of anything of the kind. It is to say that Peter's come out at the head of the list. Ploughed indeed!—the idea!"

Meanwhile the boy had opened the letter and was reading it. I was not the only person at the table who anxiously watched his face as he did so, and whose heart sunk within him as he noticed the hardening of his features, and the sudden pallor which overspread them. I could see an anxious look come into Sir Eric's and Rosamund's face, as the former said cheerfully:—

"Well lad, what is it? 'pass' or 'plough,' eh?"

"Pass," said the boy drily, and did not add another word as he pocketed the envelope.

Rosamund had turned and was talking at the moment to Lord George Wilmyngton, and without looking round at Gervase who sat on the other side of her, held out her left hand for the letter. She had a little imperious way of demanding his letters when they were interesting, and he always handed them over at once if she wanted them. This morning he did not do so, and with a little impatient contraction of the eyebrows, she half turned her head and said:—

"Give it me directly."

"No,"—quite shortly.

"Peter!" she exclaimed in mock warning, "how dare you?"

"I don't want to show it to you, that's all," he replied.

She turned her lovely eyes full on him, and with almost a tone of annoyance in her voice—for no woman likes a sudden mutiny against her acknowledged authority in public, especially when "the public" means other women—remarked gravely:—

"Peter, I believe that letter says you've been 'ploughed,' and you're ashamed to confess it before everybody;" and with these thoughtless words she turned and continued her conversation with Lord George.

Gervase Braybrooke flushed scarlet, and then turned deathly white. I expect that this was the first time in his life that any one had ever suggested the possibility of his telling a lie. Thoughtless words indeed! but in that second of time the whole drama of Gervase Braybrooke's life in the future was plotted out, and the curtain fell on the first act.

He talked on indifferent subjects for the rest of breakfast time, but I felt that there was something on the boy's mind. After breakfast he and I walked out together, and were immediately joined by his father. As Sir Eric came up, Rosamund and Lord George Wilmyngton passed us and disappeared in the direction of the conservatories.

"Well," said his father, "what is it, my boy?"

"Why, look here, governor; this is rather unexpected; the notice of my qualification is accompanied by a letter from the civil service commission which says that a rather good appointment has suddenly fallen vacant on the vice-regal staff in Bombay. The Duke of Westhampton has asked for it for me, and has got it; they want to know if I will take it up and report for service *at once*. It's a glorious chance, isn't it, but it means leaving you and home—and all of you—so suddenly—what shall I do?"

"Why, my dear boy," replied Sir Eric, as he finished reading the letter, "there can't be two ideas on the subject. You have one of the finest openings any young fellow has ever had. Of course we must accept it, and we will both of us write letters to the Duke, thanking him for his interference on our behalf. I'll just go in and talk to your mother about it." And the worthy baronet went into the house.

At this moment Rosamund came running back to the house;—alone. She was passing us without stopping, when Gervase said to her:—

"Do you want to know what my letter from the Chief said, Rosa?"

"Thank you, I wouldn't pry into your private affairs for the world. Besides, I can't wait now, I want some scissors, and Lord George is waiting for me in the conservatory."

And with that she skipped into the house. A look of intense pain came over Gervase's face as he looked in the direction in which she had disappeared.

"Go after her," said I to him, "and tell her your news."

"No, I don't see why I should; if she doesn't choose to wait, she can't want to know."

"But Gervase," I insisted, "surely she has a *right* to know; you won't let her suffer my boy,—as she will suffer—for any foolish mistake, even if she herself has committed it."

A softer light came into his eyes and he made a half movement as if to turn and go into the house after her, when suddenly she tripped out by another window further down the verandah and disappeared once more in the direction of the conservatories. Gervase's face hardened again as he replied to my remark:—

"No, Mr. Cornell, she has no rights you know we are not engaged formally to one another—she has a loophole of escape;" he added bitterly, "and if she chooses to take advantage of it in favour of Lord George, you don't suppose that I—I, her best *friend*—would seek to stand in her way."

"But, my dear boy," I began, but he stopped me with a little gesture of his hand, and a little proud toss of his head.

"Pardon me," said he, "if I say, Mr. Cornell, that the subject is not one which I am in a position to discuss. Excuse me, will you? I have to spend the day in making arrangements for my departure."

"But goodness me, you are surely not off in such a hurry as that."

"I am afraid so, the Civil Service is a kind of Pool of Bethesda, you know. It is seldom troubled, and when it is, the man who has anyone to help him to take advantage of the opportunity, is the man who reaps the benefit—but he must be on the spot to take his place the moment he has his chance. *Au revoir!*"

And so he left me.

My thoughts were none of the pleasantest as I walked down to the river-side. It was hardly a river, perhaps; more properly speaking, it was a rivulet which wandered through the grounds and disappeared into the Braybrooke woods, to join the Avon somewhere far beyond them. When I reached it, I found Constance Braybrooke and a young artist, who was one of the house-party, making sketches of a bend where the pollard willows bowed down in homage to the Naiads of the stream, as an occasional kingfisher would dart out of the scented rushes in pursuit of the too venturesome minnow.

"Where is everybody?" I demanded comprehensively of Miss Braybrooke.

"Oh!" replied she, "most of them are off to Warwick to see the castle and its peacocks. Eric and Professor Whitridge have started for Edgehill, where the Professor, I believe, fancies he will find Roundhead helmets and Cavalier buckles lying about; Rosa and Lord George have gone off fishing in the boat; and as Gervase isn't with Rosa—for a wonder!—I can't tell you where *he* is."

"I thought Gervase was going fishing with Miss Gilbert," said I.

"So did I," replied the girl; "but they've had a tiff, I think. They're always having them, though the effects are not lasting. I always tell them that one of these days they'll hurt one another in real earnest, and not get over it."

"Heaven forbid!" I ejaculated involuntarily.

And then I wandered away down the side of the stream into the wood, where I lost myself till lunch-time. After lunch I settled myself in the library with Marcus Aurelius, and saw no more of Gervase—or indeed of any of them—till dinner-time.

The party had assembled in the drawing-room, and dinner had been announced, when Lady Braybrooke suddenly said:—

"Why, where are Rosa and Lord George?"

The missing couple answered the question by suddenly appearing in our midst, dressed as we had seen them last at breakfast.

"We just looked in," said Miss Gilbert, "to say 'don't wait dinner'; we'll be down directly; we lost ourselves, or we should have been home hours ago!"

And they disappeared again, leaving us bewildered at their sudden apparition. The fish had hardly been served when the girl appeared "*en toilette*"; and as she took her place by Gervase, with Lord George Wilmyngton's empty seat on the other side of her, broke into a voluble explanation of their truancy. They had sculled down stream, having glorious sport all the way, and it was long past lunch-time before they thought of turning back. Then they had missed their way at a fork of the stream, had taken the wrong side, and had finally landed miles away from home, and had walked across to Braybrooke Hall, hungry, tired, and crowned with piscatorial victory. As the girl finished her recital, Lord George entered and took his seat, and as he did so Gervase broke the silence for the first time by saying:—

"You seem to have had a hard day, Wilmyngton, but I don't pity you, for Rosa keeps one up to the mark and makes the time fly, doesn't she?"

"Yes," replied his lordship, "I congratulate myself on our mistake; for my part I never passed a pleasanter day in my life."

"Nor I either," said Rosamund, a little defiantly, I fancied.

And then the conversation became general. Rosamund and Gervase talked together most of dinner time, but it was not the merry confidential chatter that they usually kept up right through the meal. At dessert, Sir Eric surprised us by tapping the table with the handle of his knife, and saying suddenly:—

"I think we ought to drink Gervase's health—he is on the high road to fame and fortune—but I am sorry to say he leaves us to-morrow."

I saw Rosamund Gilbert turn white for an instant; and I saw too that Gervase, glancing quickly in her direction, also noted her change of colour; but his face did not soften as he nodded all round the table at the various members of the party as they wished him "good luck."

Rosamund alone did not participate in the toast; she merely played with her glass and smiled as if she had been assisting at a little comedy; only I noticed, as she lifted her menu to look at it by way of a diversion, that the leaf of card-board shook as if it had been a living leaf in an autumn breeze. Soon after the ladies had retired, Gervase rose and left the rest of us alone, leaving the dining-room by the window and disappearing across the lawn into the blackness of the night. As soon as Sir Eric made a move, I followed in the direction the boy had taken, and presently seeing the tiny *"phare"* of a lighted cigarette across the rosery, I strolled round the grass walks between the rose-beds to join him. As I turned a corner and approached the seat where I knew Gervase was sitting, there was a sudden *frou-frou* of skirts, and he was joined by Miss Rosamund, who exclaimed:—

"Oh! Peter, why *didn't* you tell me about it?"

"My dear child," replied Gervase, "I don't want to bore you with my private affairs, and you don't care about knowing them—you said so yourself this morning. I thought, of course, you knew by this evening—I should have thought that this would have been part of the brilliant flow of Lord George's conversation during eight hours. He can probably tell you more about it than I can, as it is his father who has cleared me out of the way for his son, by getting me this appointment.—No, my girl, there's nothing more to be said on the subject; do you object to my cigarette?"

There was an instant's pause, and then the girl answered icily: "No, I don't mind tobacco, but it's too cold for me to stay here. No! don't come back to the house with me; I'd rather go alone— as I came—and you must have a good deal to think about. Good-bye for the present."

And so she left him.

I sprang forward and exclaimed: "Go after her, Gervase, re-member what I said this morning—you are making a dreadful mistake which may ruin your whole lives; go after her, my boy."

"No," replied he, with his little proud toss of the head, "I refuse to cringe to any woman that treats me as if I were a child of seven. She has had eight hours of Wilmyngton,—let her get the full particulars from him."

He was immovable, and presently he left me and I returned to the drawing-room. Miss Gilbert, I was told, had retired to her room, as she was tired after her long day in the open air. The rest of the party were sitting around—as country-house parties will do—in groups, chatting and telling stories. Gervase and his father were closeted together, going over papers of one kind and another connected with his appointment, and I did not see them again till they joined us in the smoking-room after the ladies had retired. The conversation not unnaturally turned on Gervase's departure, which was to take place early next day, the nature of his future occupations, and the date of his probable return. It seemed that in all probability four or five years at least must elapse before he saw England again. He spoke of his absence seriously and unreservedly, but with a quick cheerfulness that showed that at any rate he appreciated the opportunity that had been offered him of winning his spurs in the employ of his government.

Bright hopes! Happy future! Ah, it is good to be a man! Who was it that said that the next best thing after not having been born at all, would have been to have been born a woman? He was mad or spoke heedlessly. Gervase Braybrooke was twenty, handsome, and a gentleman to the backbone; he had passed all the examinations which had been his *bêtes noires* throughout his school days, and which had earned for him the pity of his female relations, whose immunity from "exams" he had so heartily en-vied; and now, by the accident of his birth, not being like his elder brother, an independent gentleman, the Duke had interested himself to obtain for the younger son of his old friend, a staff appointment of importance close to the person of Her Majesty's Viceroy. Laurels to win, a position to conquer, a reputation to earn, and glory and renown in the future a visible goal. Ah! it is good to be a man! And Rosamund Gilbert—matchless specimen of womanhood, as he of his own sex, having the same,—nay, on the ground of her prospective motherhood of men as good as he, having *better* claims on humanity at large,—what had she in the immediate future, whilst he was away fighting the battle of life on the stage of government? Nothing! She had only to sit down and wait—to wait, whilst every day her beauty became less fresh, less bright, and her enjoyment of life became less keen and less minute. Ah! it is *good* to be a man. Woman! Woman! we bow before you, and kiss your hands in token of our submission to your will; often—very often—our destinies are moulded by you; sometimes for evil, but more often for good; we strive to please you in all the small things of life, our going-out and our coming-in depend upon your sovereign will and pleasure; the fashion of our cravats and the intonation of our voices; but how is it when the world of men calls us to fill our allotted space in the universe as thinkers and workers?—how is it in the large events of life? the things which mould the destinies not only of ourselves as individuals, but of Humanity? Ah! then!—these things are not for women's thoughts! Get you to your needle-work, to your flower-garden, to your book of fairy tales, and to your instruments of music. Maybe, when we have *settled* the matter, we may speak to you of it again, and tell you *what we have done* for you. Ah! Ah! it is *good* to be a man!

Next morning Rosamund Gilbert did not come down to breakfast. She was not feeling well, Lady Braybrooke told us, but would be down to see Gervase off. This was a ceremony which took place at eleven o'clock; we all assembled in the hall and on the portico, and Gervase walked about seeing to the final embarkation of his luggage and talking to us all in turn. Rosamund was there, and as bright and cheerful as any of us, keeping up a constant ripple of chaff and repartee with "Peter," as he went from group to group. At last the supreme moment arrived. Gervase looked very grey and determined, but got through it manfully. He said "good-bye" to Rosamund last—with the exception of his father, who saw him off at the station—and when he reached her, he took both her hands in his and raised them in turn to his lips. She was deathly pale, but she merely leaned forward and said:—

"Kiss me, Peter."

And putting one hand on her shoulder, he leant over and kissed the white lips that were turned up to his. I believe it was the first time he ever kissed her—and the last. Then, with a sparkle in his eyes and a little husky tone in his voice, he turned, and waving his hat at us as we stood on the steps, he cried out:—

"Good-bye, all of you; good-bye, Braybrooke!" and as the dog-cart started down the drive, he turned and kissed his hand to one of the upper windows where Lady Braybrooke and Constance had probably stationed themselves to see the last of him, and to shed their tears together, unseen by the merry crowd in the hall.

When the dog-cart had disappeared, and I turned back into the hall, Rosamund Gilbert was no longer there, nor did I see her again until after lunch, when she came down looking a trifle pale but as cheerful as ever. It seemed to me that Lord George Wilmyngton was in better spirits this afternoon than I had ever seen him before. He threw himself eagerly into every plan that was proposed, and at last, when his good-humour had communicated itself to the rest of us, and had dissipated, to some extent, the cloud which Gervase's departure had cast over us, it was with a strange sinking of the heart that I saw him and Rosamund stroll away down to the hammock where I had seen her the morning after my arrival, and arrange themselves to chat, she in the hammock and he on the ground, as Gervase had been wont to sit. I felt somehow—stranger though I was—that I had been left guardian of Gervase's interests, and after a while I strolled over in their direction. As I approached, Rosamund cried out:—

"Oh, Mr. Cornell, Lord George says Peter's going to be away for five years at least; it isn't true, is it?"

"Certainly it is true. Did you not know it—did he not tell you?"

"No, he didn't choose to tell me anything about his plans, and *I* didn't choose to ask him—or anybody else."

"I should have thought," remarked Lord George quickly, but meaningly, "that you would have been the first person he would have come to tell *all* about them, Miss Gilbert."

"Gervase had something else to do," said she, flaming up immediately, as a woman always does if any man presumes to agree with her in abusing another of his sex, "than to loaf about all day talking to us girls about things we shouldn't understand. You don't quite see, Lord George, Gervase is not an 'idle man,' and has something to think about and to do in the world besides amuse himself. Help me out of the hammock, please, Mr. Cornell, I'm going to see what all the others are doing."

And with that she walked slowly across the lawn and disappeared into the house. In the drawing-room before dinner, I said to her:—

"Now that Peter's gone, the rest of us have a chance, I suppose. Will you waste half an hour after dinner walking with an old fellow like me?"

"Of course I will," replied she; and accordingly, as soon as I could get away after dessert, I came and found her waiting for me in the drawing-room.

We went out together into the early moonlight and walked slowly round the lawn, talking seriously as we went. I forget the arguments I used in begging her not to think ill of Gervase for having left her thus. I pointed out that the faults had been on both sides, that he had good reasons for not telling her of his departure in the presence of the company assembled at breakfast the morning before, that her refusal to listen when he had offered her his confidence on the verandah must necessarily have hurt him, and that the wound had hardly been healed by her excursion with Lord George, which had occupied the whole of the single, only, day which had elapsed prior to his departure. I told her that I thought he had had fair reason for what he had said in the evening in the rose-garden, and I begged her to write him a letter at once to the India Office, explaining all the circumstances of the case, and asking his forgiveness for her fault whilst she freely pardoned his. She met all my reasoning with a woman's unreasonable but unanswerable objections, and finally, as we drew near the drawing-room windows for the last time, she said:

"No, Mr. Cornell, it is of no use; it is not as if we were engaged to one another. If we had been, he would not have treated me—and possibly I should not have treated him—in such a manner. I had no idea of the contents of his letter, and what I said at breakfast was merely angry chaff at his having mortified me before all the others, I *was* angry, but I would have given anything not to have been so horrid—but then—when I went after him—just fancy my doing such a thing—in the rose-garden, he was cruel and unkind, and it is *he* who ought to ask *me* to forgive him. I will *not* write to him unless he writes to me—and perhaps not then. He has his way to make in the world—he doesn't want to be hampered by me and my feelings. It was all very well when he had nothing to do; I was all very well to amuse an idle hour or two, but you will see how it is—now his life is full, how much shall *I* hear of him? A message in a letter to his mother, a newspaper paragraph if he distinguishes himself—as of course he *will*—and that will be enough for Rosamund Gilbert. Well, I'm not the first woman who has been in my position, Mr. Cornell—don't persuade me any more, my mind is quite made up. You are very good to have interested yourself in my affairs, and now I must go in, so *au revoir* Mr. Cornell, *au revoir.*"

I was at Braybrooke for another fortnight and my visit was drawing to a close.

The evening before my departure I was sitting next to Miss Gilbert at dinner. Gervase Braybrooke had left London for Bombay the day before, and we all felt a little depressed by our sympathy with Sir Eric and Lady Braybrooke. Towards the end of dinner I said to her:—

"Did you write to him?"

"No," replied she.

"He has not written to you?"

"No."

"Nor sent any message?"

"He only asked Lady Braybrooke how I was, and said he hoped that if ever I could find a moment when I was not fishing and going long walks, I would remember his existence and write him a line to tell him what I am doing."

I returned to town next day.

III.

Three years passed during which I often met the Braybrookes and Miss Gilbert in London society. She never asked after Gervase, and it seemed strange to me that she did not, for the boy distinguished himself, as we all expected he would, and many of the daily and society papers spoke periodically of the good service he was doing his government as the right-hand man of the Viceroy, a position he had acquired, notwithstanding his youth, by the charm of his manner and by his moral character, as much as by the energy and enthusiasm with which he entered into his work. Still, Miss Gilbert knew that I corresponded with him, for I told her so. Only once, however, had I led the conversation in the direction of Gervase and his work, and the girl had looked bored and uninterested, and finally had rather pointedly changed the conversation. I did not recur to the subject.

So beautiful a woman as Rosamund Gilbert suffered naturally from a superfluity rather than from a lack of cavaliers, and whether at afternoon receptions, in the Park, at Hurlingham, or at "crushes," the man who principally monopolized the attention of Miss Gilbert was generally a marked individual. Of all her white slaves, however, none was more assiduous in his attentions or more constant in his attendance than Lord George Wilrnyngton; and really, when I think about it calmly, I do not blame Rosamund for her toleration of his unflagging service. Setting aside his title and his wealth, Lord George was an English gentleman in the loftiest acceptation of the term; he was well-built and handsome, not troubled by a superfluity of brains—in fact Rosamund once confessed to me that she found him dull—but then he was supremely "good form," and loved her honestly and humbly. Therefore, though it pained me terribly, for I was really *fond* of Gervase—I was hardly surprised when I read one day in the *Morning Post* that "a marriage had been arranged between Lord George Wilmyngton, third son of the Duke of Westhampton, and Rosamund, daughter of the late Erskine Gilbert, Esquire, and niece of Sir Eric Braybrooke, *Bart*, of Braybrooke Hall, Warwickshire." Three days afterwards the Indian mail brought a letter from Gervase announcing his intention of applying for leave, and of coming home the following summer for a few months.

I wrote back, warmly seconding his proposition, but in the same letter I sent him the cutting from the *Post*, and a little account of the engaged couple which I hoped would soften the blow to him—if blow it was to be. I hoped my letter would get to him before the account that was bound to reach him from home—and I believe it did. Meantime, whilst the preparations for the "Marriage in High Life" proceeded, his answer to my letter came swiftly across the hemisphere that divided us.

The young people had known one another for years, so there was no reason why the marriage should be postponed, and Gervase's answer arrived about a week before it was to take place. It was short and to the point.

His plans had undergone a change since writing last. His Excellency had offered to send him on a mission of importance to Mandalay, and he had accepted the offer. It was a great chance for so young a man, and he had determined to take advantage of it. He proposed to postpone his return for a further period of three years. By the time his letter reached me he was probably on his way to his post—if he was not already there.

And a week after that Rosamund Gilbert became Lady George Wilmyngton.

IV.

What is it that Omar the Persian Tentmaker says of Time?

"The moving finger writes, and having writ, moves on!" A hiatus of four years occurred in my story, and Time, as is his wont, had been quietly at work, making changes in our lives. Personally, I had stepped from the bar to the bench, and exchanged the curly wig of the Queen's Counsel for the fuzzy head-gear of the Judge. Lord and Lady George Wilmyngton in their beautiful house in Picadilly, were among the most prominent members of London society. A terrible tragedy—the simultaneous death in a railway accident of Sir Eric Braybrooke and his eldest son—had caused the baronetcy to devolve on Gervase, and Sir Gervase Braybrooke of Braybrooke Hall, Warwickshire, was one of the most prominent actors on the stage of Indian politics. He had accomplished his mission in Mandalay in a manner which had absolutely astonished the India office. He had been publicly complimented by both Houses of Parliament, and had ascended from the Companionship, to the Knight-Commandership of the Star of India; and even before he became Sir Gervase Braybrooke, Bart, he was already Sir Gervase Braybrooke, K. C. S. I., and England looked forward to a brilliant future career for him, as Her Majesty's Viceroy in India. His sister Constance had married, and was the proud mother of a baby boy and of a not-quite-so-baby girl, and Lady Braybrooke had gone to live permanently in strict retirement in Braybrooke Hall.

One evening I was seated in my study, busy revising the proof-sheets of a new edition of my work on "The Practice of the Court of Appeal," when my servant came and told me that a gentleman wished to see me who had refused to give his name, and was waiting in the drawing-room. I was somewhat annoyed at being disturbed, but came down immediately and found awaiting me a tall, bronzed, and distinguished-looking man, with rather grizzled blond hair, and an erect commanding figure. I bowed, and asked him to be seated.

"What!" exclaimed Gervase—for it was he—"am I so changed in seven years that you don't recognize me?"

Ah! but how glad I was to see him! and how I abused him for not having told me that he was coming. He had arrived the evening before and had determined to surprise me by swooping down upon me without a word of warning. I carried him away up to my *sanctum sanctorum* and after reviling him for having dined alone at the club, set him down in an arm-chair opposite me, and for an hour we chatted and laughed like school-boys, he, the rising young Indian civilian whose habitual gravity was far beyond his years, and I, the grave Lord Justice of Her Majesty's Supreme Court of Judicature, old enough to be his father. I told him all the news that I had not included in my letters to him, and he gave me an outline of his adventures. I told him all I knew of Rosamund Wilmyngton and her husband, and he listened and asked questions in the calm and indifferent manner of a man who is dimly recalling events of his boyhood—events which seemed to him to be of paramount importance when they occurred, and who feels a mild surprise at the recollection of the effect they had upon him in those half-forgotten time's. At last he said, in a reflective and half-amused tone of voice:—

"Well, well, I know that I left Braybrooke, and left England maddened, miserable, and sore at heart, and it took the whole of the first year that I never heard from her, to realize that she had never really cared about me. It took the whole of the second year to accustom myself to the idea that the brilliant exquisite future I had mapped out for myself with her, was nothing but a boyish dream, and even during the third year, when I had applied for leave and was coming home, I knew that my love was not quite dead, and I used sometimes, when I sat in the Gardens at Bombay listening to the band after dinner, to imagine myself back in the old home, riding through the Braybrooke Woods upon Dynamite, with her at my side, touching an almost forgotten chord, and offering her a devotion which was no longer an outcome of the flattered vanity of a school-boy. But then—your letter came;—I knew that it was all over, and that I had only my work out there to fill the remainder of my life, and I gave up my leave when Lord B. offered me the residency at Mandalay, and have stifled the thought of her ever since. But notwithstanding all this. I've sometimes vaguely wondered what she has grown to be—and now that I am in the old country again, I should *like* to see Rosamund Gilbert again. Egad! I wonder whether she would remember me!"

"Why, my dear fellow," I replied, "if you really have left off caring about her, and if you really want to see her again, you can do so this very moment if you like. Mrs. Francis Jeune is giving one of her historic parties tonight, and we can look in for half an hour and then stroll down to the club. Lord George and she are certain to be there; all Diplomacy and all fashionable Bohemia meet there as regularly as clock-work, and though I hadn't intended to go myself. I'll take you there with pleasure, and Mrs. Jeune will be delighted to see you, both on your own account and mine. I'll call at Claridge's for you in half an hour, and we'll go together."

And so it was arranged. When I stopped my cab at Claridge's Hotel for him, I found him ready for me, and certainly a more distinguished-looking man I have never seen, than Sir Gervase Braybrooke, with the Star of India on his dress coat, and the jewel of the order suspended by its ribbon beneath his white cravat.

Our hostess cordially extended to him the welcome that she always had ready for any living creature whose position and attainments rendered him worthy to become a member of the brilliant throng that habitually circulated from room to room in her house in Harley street; and almost the first person I saw as we entered the salon, was Lady George Wilmyngton. She was listening to Oscar Wilde's latest paradoxical axiom when I touched her shoulder and said:—

"Lady George, I have brought an old friend to claim acquaintance with you."

She turned immediately, and, directing one searching look at the tall figure standing by my side, flushed crimson, then turned a shade paler than she had been before, put out both hands and exclaimed in a voice that was almost strangled:—

"Why, Peter!"

After that, a few commonplace words of surprise and satisfaction on both sides, and then Gervase offering her his arm, said:—

"Let us find a comparatively quiet place where we can talk."

As they made their way to one of the smaller rooms, they passed Lord George, who was conversing with a member of the diplomatic corps in the passage. As they went by he turned an enquiring glance on his wife's escort, and she, looking up at him, said:—

"Don't you remember Gervase Braybrooke? Come into the little room with us, we are going to talk about old times."

The two men greeted one another warmly, and half an hour afterwards, as I was gravitating in the direction of sandwiches and sherry with the Persian minister, I saw the three sitting together engaged in an animated confabulation.

Gervase Braybrooke and I left together. We walked almost in silence as far as Oxford street, and then he said:—

"If you'll excuse me, Sir William, I won't come down to the club; I've had a hard day of it, and I think I'll get home and turn in. I'll come and see you again in a day or two."

And so he left me. A few days afterwards he came down to the Royal Courts of Justice late in the afternoon, and when the court rose he drove home with me. I couldn't get him to stay to dinner. He was dining at Wilmyngton House.

V.

Three or four days later I was dining with Lord George Wilmyngton and his wife, a *partie carrée* of which Gervase was the remaining member. He seemed quite at home—quite one of the family—and, knowing as much as I did of the earlier relations of Gervase Braybrooke and Rosamund Wilmyngton, the easy familiarity which appeared to exist between them at this time perplexed me. Knowing Lady George to be a woman of the most exquisite delicacy of mind and of the most unimpeachable refinement, and knowing Sir Gervase to be the very pink and pattern of perfect gentlemanly feeling and honour, I felt no uneasiness on the subject; but it seemed odd, after what he had told me the first evening after his return, that he could fall immediately into so apparently close a friendship—just as of yore—with his old sweetheart. When we left the house on the evening of which I am speaking, I said something to this effect, and asked him if Lady George had referred at all to the past.

"Not a word," replied he; "we talk continually of the old days at Braybrooke, of the place itself, and of our rambles and rides together; but of our parting, never. She does not wish it, nor do I—all that is at an end henceforth and forever. I referred *once* to my last day at Braybrooke, but she silenced me coldly and peremptorily, and I was glad she did so, she evidently does not look upon her conduct in the light that I did, and do, and it is perhaps as well. It need not interfere with our friendship, which is still what it always was. Only those two days are out of our lives, and are as if we had never lived them.

Then he told me that during the day he had finished his official business at the India office for the present, and that early next morning he should start for Warwickshire to see his mother.

At the end of a fortnight he was back in town again. I did not see him for a day or two, and at the end of that time he told me that his plans were uncertain—that he did not know how long he should remain away from his post in India, and that his mother would most probably remain at Braybrooke for the rest of her life. He did not suppose that he would ever marry—the baronetcy was not restricted in its descent, and would devolve upon his cousin. At present—for the season at any rate—he should remain in London.

I knew that there was nothing to feel uneasy about, but there was an uncertainty, a restlessness about Sir Gervase that I did not like. He seemed to be preoccupied, without having anything in particular on his mind, and I began to feel oppressed by an idea that his thoughts were beginning to run—oh! the pity of it!—on the "might have been."

One evening I was sitting at work—as on that other occasion—when he was announced. The moment he came in, I knew that there was something wrong, that something had happened. Appearances were not deceptive.

"I have been with Lady George Wilmyngton this afternoon," began he, "and we have had a talk over those two days."

"Great Heaven!" thought I, "what is he going to tell me?"

"It was all a dreadful mistake. I misunderstood her, and she misunderstood me; she loved me as dearly as I loved her, only she was too proud to confess it, and I was too poor to ask it of her."

"Go on."

"If I had written from London, even from India, it would have been all right, but like an idiot I thought she was in love with Lord George, and she imagined that I thought of nothing but my future—my brilliant future! Good God! how dearly I have bought it!"

"And you have explained these things to one another?"

"Yes."

"Gervase," I said very gravely, "I know you too well for a thought of the possibility of a dishonourable action on your part ever to cross my mind; but with all your knowledge of the world and with an experience of life such as few men have had at your age, you must realize that your position with regard to Lord George Wilmyngton's wife is a very difficult and a very strained one. What are you going to do?"

"Nothing!" said he, raising from his chair to pace backwards and forwards across the room. "Rosamund and I have talked the matter over calmly, deliberately, dispassionately. We are both confident of ourselves and of one another, and you may be sure that no words of mine to her shall ever be such as her husband might not willingly hear. Our lives have been spoilt by a cruel mistake, but though she is Wilmyngton's wife, she shall never cease to be the dearest friend I have ever had, or shall ever have, in the world."

I felt that I was talking to a person very, very different to the boy of seven years ago, and I said but little more that evening. From that time onward Sir Gervase became Lady Wilmyngton's most constant attendant—whether at home or abroad. Lord George knew very well that his honour was in no sense in danger, and upon terms of the most intimate friendship the house in Picadilly became an ideal "*ménage à trois*." It was towards the end of the season that, one evening at a reception at the Foreign Office, I was chatting with one of the Colonial Secretaries of State, when Lady George passed on Gervase's arm.

"Do you know Braybrooke?" asked the Secretary.

"Very intimately," said I.

"Then, if you have any influence with him, get him back to India as fast as you can. That's a most rising young civilian being checked in the last round of a brilliant career. What does he want dangling after Lady George through a London season, when Theebaw is stirring himself up to give us trouble almost within walking distance of his post out there? I'm interested in that young man, Cornell, and I don't like the look of it—I don't like the look of it."

No more did I. And I determined to have a talk with Gervase about it. The end of the season was at hand, the festivities of the gay world were culminating in Goodwood, and already here and there one could see great houses whence the glory was departed until next season, and whose carefully closed and guarded windows announced the absence of "the family." It was in the last days of July that Gervase came to take a little quiet dinner with me in my bachelor house in Eaton Place. During dinner I said to him:

"I suppose you will spend August with her ladyship at Braybrooke?"

"Well, no," he replied, "I shall go there later. I've promised to go down to the Wilmyngtons for August."

"Oh!"

After dinner, when the conversation had taken the confidential tone imparted by arm-chairs and the incense of "Henry Clays," I remarked in the most offhand manner in the world:

"And when do you return to India?"

"Never;" answered he.

"Good God! my dear fellow, what do you mean?"

"Well," said he, "I've thought it all over, and that's my decision. I didn't talk to you about it, Sir William, because I knew you'd argue the matter, and my mind was made up. I sent in my papers some weeks ago, and by this time my successor is on his way out. They raised no end of a dust about it at the India Office; in fact, they refused to gazette my resignation until the other day, and even the Prince had a talk to me about it at Ascot, but I gave him my reasons, and H.R.H. was satisfied and didn't press the point. You see, I should never have gone into the Indian Civil Service if I had not been the governor's younger son; and now that the poor old gentleman and Eric are both gone, throwing the baronetcy on my shoulders, I feel in a manner bound to adopt the life which I should have taken up if I had been born heir to the title and estates;—only that I should have married Rosamund Gilbert. Braybrooke requires a master to look after it, and my mother is an old lady now. Sir William, my father's and brother's awful deaths aged her terribly, and Con's marriage has left her all alone in the world. So I shall keep my rooms at the Albany and spend my time between them and Braybrooke; there's plenty to occupy my time here. Of course I know that I'm giving up a lot out in the Empire, and that many people who don't know my reasons will blame me; but you know them, and you know that they are valid, don't you?"

"Yes," I replied, "I know them, though you have kept silence as to the principal one. Now, don't answer me yet. As a Lord Justice I am accustomed to formulating cases with brutal precision, and your case is this: You—Sir Gervase Braybrooke, Baronet, Knight Commander of the Star of India, Her Majesty's Commissioner for the district of Bowghranee, in the province of Bengal, almost at the head of your profession at the age of eight-and-twenty, prospective Viceroy of the Empire of India, and sure of a peerage—have thrown all this to the winds and relegated yourself to absolute insignificance because you are in love with the wife of an old school "chum," the son of the man to whom you owe your position. I am old enough to be your father, I have watched your career as if you were my son, for I'm very fond of you, my boy, and I have been your father's intimate friend since we were both fourteen and went to Eton together. Therefore I am the only living man who has a right to hold the mirror for you to look at yourself in it. How do you like the picture?"

He rose from his chair and walked to the window. For a few moments he stood there looking out into the late summer twilight, at the people passing underneath in the street, twisting up his slightly grizzled moustache. At last he turned, and coming back, dropped once more into his chair opposite me.

"You have stated the case with startling truth," said he, "but there is nothing more to be said about it. The thing is *done*—finally, irrevocably. But don't imagine that I am going to spoil *her* life with my own. We are as good friends to-day as we were in the old time at Braybrooke. Lord George, thank God, appreciates his wife at her true value, and trusts her as implicitly as she and I trust one another. Don't be uneasy about us, old friend. This is my life. I led off with a terrible mistake, the past has been bitter, but the present makes amends for it all, and I have no fear for the future."

The future! There was a certain grim humour in the way he spoke, but there was nothing to be gained by worrying him about it.

I changed the conversation.

VI.

How unimportant the things which vitally concern ourselves seem to other people! It did not seem in the least to call for comment from the world that wherever Lady George Wilmyngton and her husband were to be seen, Sir Gervase Braybrooke was sure to be found not far off. Few remembered—and they only at rare intervals, when he appeared decorated with the star and collar of the order—that the distinguished-looking young man was the hero of the Bowghranee insurrection. More than a year had passed since the conversation I have just recorded took place in my dining-room, when, one November evening, on my return from Court, I found a note from Gervase asking me if I could spare him the evening, and apologizing for not asking me to come to dinner. I had a vague, uneasy feeling that something was wrong, and I arrived at the Albany at about nine.

Gervase was sitting in a low arm-chair in front of the fire. On a little table beside him stood a pile of letters, which he was reading and burning as he read them one-by-one. A cold spasm of apprehension seized me, as I remarked cheerily:—

"Hullo! boy; burning love letters?"

"Yes; this kind of love letter:—'Dear Peter, Come and dine with us tonight; seven punctually. Yours, Rosamund.' Here's another. 'Dear Peter: George has got a box for "Frou-Frou" to-night; will you come? Yours, Rosa.' Nothing more than that, Sir William, but they are the only kind of love letters I have ever received." And as he spoke he flung the two notes he had read into the flames.

"My dear Gervase, for Heaven's sake what has happened?"

"Oh! Nothing much—nothing much. I'm only burning records of the past, and their ashes are the Ashes of the Future—mine and hers. Ashes—of the Future we look forward to so joyfully together, cantering through the Braybrooke Woods and across the Kineton meadows; I on Dynamite and she on Douchka. It's happened to a good many men before, and will happen to a good many again, to wake up and find that the sacrifices they have made have been in vain, and that all their plans have been based on an initial error. This life is like an astronomical calculation. You reckon the arrival of a comet or the moment of an eclipse, and in stating the problem, start with an unnoticed error of a unit in a logarithm, or an accidental transposition of the ninety-ninth and hundredth decimal places in a fraction. The error is not noticed, and you build your calculation accordingly, and when your phenomenon takes place you find that there is a mistake of a million miles or so.

"But, Gervase, by all that's horrible, please explain yourself."

"Yes!—you of all people in the world have a right to ask for an explanation. What is it that your beloved Persian says:—

"The worldly hope men set their hearts upon
Turn Ashes—or it prospers, and anon
(Like Snow upon the Desert's dusty face)
Lighting a little hour or two—is gone!

115

"Well, well, that's my case. I threw up everything a little more than a year ago, and devoted my life to a pure disinterested friendship for Rosamund Wilmyngton, and for a year I have been, as you know, her almost constant companion—with the full approval of Lord George, who, thank God! has nothing to reproach his wife with. This friendship of ours was enough for me, it was my whole life—but with her it was different, though the difference only began to be dimly discernable at the beginning of last season. Her friendship for *me* raised the tone of my every thought, my friendship for *her* had, alas! the contrary effect. She ceased to require a friend, she wanted a 'tame man;' next she grew tired of the harmless necessary male, and insisted upon a slavery, a serfdom, and then my manhood revolted and I took a higher and more decided tone, and then she came down from the pedestal on which I had placed her, and began to employ all a woman's coquetries to bring me to her feet. I was blind as long as I could be; deaf until the heart-stricken cry of Human Nature reached my ears, dumb until she ceased her silent questioning and paused for a reply, and got it!—a reply such as humbles a woman to the dust. In vain she endeavoured, and I too, to restore the footing of friendship on the even table-land of companionhood; but the conviction grew stronger and more strong that the adamantine polish of our friendship had been worn off by the constant falling of the drop of acid—custom—upon its placid surface. I woke one morning from my peaceful dream to realize the grisly commonplace of the *fact* that I was *bored*. No sooner had I made the discovery than I strove eagerly by renewed attention to my 'duties' to conceal it—but there is nothing, as you know, that a woman's unerring eye is quicker to perceive. It ended in her making 'a scene'—an ordinary vulgar scene, like the heroine of a second-rate novel, or of a transpontine drama.

"In a word, we parted; parted not in anger, but in dull, cold, insurmountable indifference—and this heap of dusty ashes, extinguishing the fire that warms these lonely rooms of mine—the Ashes of our Future—are all that is left to me. I cannot take up my Indian life again, my place is filled, and I cannot *begin* afresh. I go down to Braybrooke to-morrow, and then I shall spend the rest of my days as a plain, quiet country squire, as all the Braybrooke baronets have been. My work in life now is to take care of my dear mother as long as she is spared to me, and to try and forget these wasted years."

So this was the end. I sat with him for a little while, and then left him. Save at rare intervals, when he comes up to town, I have never seen much of him since, and he has never referred to his boyhood and the years he passed by Rosamund Wilmyngton's side; only—when "Violet Fane's" exquisite little volume of poems appeared, he sent me a copy with the corner of the page on which her "May Song" occurs, turned down. It is almost her prettiest poem, and runs:—

> A little while my Love and I,
>   Before the mowing of the hay,
>   Twined daisy-chains and cowslip-balls,
>   And carrolled glees and madrigals.
>   Among the hay, beneath the may,
> My Love (who loved me then!) and I.
>
> For long years now, my Love and I
>   Tread severed paths to different ends;
>   We sometimes meet and sometimes say
>   The trivial things of every day;
>   And meet as comrades, meet as friends,
> My Love (who loved me once) and I.
>
> But never more, my Love and I
>   Will wander forth as once together.
>   Nor sing the songs we used to sing
>   In spring-time in the cloudless weather;
>   Some chord is mute that used to ring.
>   Some word forgot we used to say
>   Among the hay, beneath the may.
> My Love (who loves me not) and I

✳

Lady George Wilmyngton is still one of the most prominent leaders of London society. She is never without one especially attentive and ever-attendant cavalier, but those *who know* say that she never has had again so unflagging and assiduous a servant as her *first*. And that was Sir Gervase Braybrooke.

"By-the-bye—whatever *has* become of him?"

THE SILENCE OF
MRS. CHARITON'S CHILDREN.

A Story with No Middle to It.

PART I. THE END OF THE STORY.

I.

"BUT who *was* their mother, anyhow?"

"My dear! How can I tell you what nobody knows? Of course they say—etc.—etc.—etc."

"But was she really as bad as they say?"

"Well, we don't know. She can't have lasted long, for I never met an Englishman who could tell me anything about her, or him, or them——"

"All I know about it," broke in a fourth lady, who had hitherto kept silence, "is what I've collected from a variety of sources, and it's all that is known by anyone. It seems that when Mr. Cheriton was quite a young man—etc., etc., etc."

"Oh! how dreadful for those two poor children!" was the comment of the chorus.

At this moment a stranger was announced, and a discreet silence fell upon the occupants of Mrs. Van Talkin's drawing-room.

II.

The gaieties of the winter season were in full swing, and New York Society—with a capital S—had for some months past entirely ceased from any endeavour to save the few moments necessary for serious reflection, from the wreck of time amid the rapids of existence. We, that is to say Society—with a capital S—worked hard. We interviewed our tradesmen in the morning, we lunched at Delmonico's or at the Sapphic function known as a "ladies' lunch," we paid three or four calls and "looked in" at two or three receptions in the afternoon; then we dined and went to the opera—not to listen to the music, or to reward the hard-working mothers of families who catered for our amusement under the names of *Mdlle. Des Trois-Etoiles*—or as the case might be—with our perfunctory and inappreciative applause—but to chatter the same irresponsible *banalités* to the same uninteresting people whom we had met in the afternoon three or four times, and whom it was a matter of the completest indifference to us if we never met again!

Day after day we walked or drove on "the Avenue," and passed the same people again, greeting them with the same uninterested smile, or stopping to engage them in that style of conversation which Oscar Wilde has epigrammatically stigmatized as "the last resource of people who have nothing to say!" And, by-the-bye, we called this "Life." It was, I believe, the Bishop of Carlisle who defined life as "a potentiality for action, locomotion, and change, without the assistance of any external cause." This is a definition that has often recurred to me during a "busy" winter's day in New York, and I have often caught myself wondering vaguely whether the learned ecclesiastic founded his definition on an observance of Society in Gotham.

We—that is to say Society (with a capital S)—had attended our dinner-party, and had adjourned to the club for a quiet weed and a meditative pool, whilst our wife had got inside her ball-dress; and we had run together again, like the Athenians of old, in search of some new thing, to meet *chez Delmonico*, and play our parts in the little realistic drama known as "The Patriarch's Ball." I was a stray Englishman, and the exquisite hospitality of the historic eminence known as Murray Hill had provided me with a ticket for the ball, and would have furnished me with a partner, had I desired one, for the cotillon.

Before that somewhat spasmodic dissipation commenced, however, I had, as a result of my recent arrival, been betraying a tendency towards "holding up the doorway," and therefore, when young Æselkopf Van Spook came up and offered to present me to somebody, I almost forgave him the hybrid intensity of his aggressive Manhattan ancestry, and strolled off round the room with him.

Sitting, for the moment alone, against a background of cotillon bouquets, in an angle of the room, I noticed, for the first time that evening, as we pursued our way round the floor, a young girl whose air of innocent enjoyment, and fresh colouring, bespoke, no less surely than the unrelieved snowiness of her costume, "*the ingénue*," the *débutante*, in fact, the Bud." She arrested my attention while we were yet some yards distant from her, and, gripping Van Spook by the elbow, I said to him:

"Who is the fair maiden in white, over there?"

"Oh! that's Miss Daphne Cheriton, and the girl just sitting down by her side is her twin-sister, Miss Josephine, 'of that ilk.' They're both *débutantes* of this year, and this is their second ball. I'll present you; old Cheriton's worth five millions if he's worth a cent, and you see before you his entire family. If you want to call on them, say you've heard of their father over *here*, and would like to make his acquaintance. Whatever you do, don't say a word about *Mrs.* Cheriton, or in any way recognize the possibility of their ever having had a mother."

"Goodness me! why——"

"Hush!—Miss Cheriton, will you allow me to introduce an English friend, Mr. Lyster? Mr. Lyster; Miss Daphne Cheriton;" and he was gone.

The Cheriton twins were dark and fair; of the two I think Miss Josephine was the more interesting. There was something in the calm watchfulness of her grave, gloomy eyes, something about the expression of reserve that she habitually wore, which seemed to intensify the delicate pallor of her face, and produced an effect that was essentially indescribable. I was therefore more than pleased when, at the end of our waltz, she suggested that we should "sit somewhere cool for a moment." We chatted of men and things, general and individual, for a space—indeed time slipped by faster than I knew; and we were interrupted in our conversation by the sudden appearance of Mr. Cheriton, with an inquiry as to his daughter's supper arrangements. I offered myself with that true British promptitude which has been known to the vulgar as "cheek." Miss Josephine Cheriton presented me to her father, and we three went down to supper together.

Eugene Cheriton was a tall, dignified man of perhaps forty-three or four; I should have guessed his age at that from the erectness of his carriage and the quickness of his manner and conversation, a quickness in which there was at times something almost brusque. At the first glance you would have given him another decade at least, for his hair was almost white, and in the lines round his mouth and eyes one could see the indications of acute suffering, mental or physical, or perhaps of dissipation. Still, beneath the affability of his manner and conversation, the cordiality with which he greeted me, and, so to speak, took me to his heart, I fancied I could detect a certain watchfulness, and a suppressed irritation which might be either the nervousness of the hypochondriac or the subdued ferocity of the caged brute. There are men who always impress me thus, and Eugene Cheriton was one of them.

We had been settled only a few moments when Miss Daphne Cheriton, who was seated at a neighbouring table, came over and whispered a few words to her sister. Her father took advantage of the circumstance to say:

"I say, you children, you're not going to stay for the cotillon."

(Chorus) "Oh Papa!!"

"Well, I'm dead tired, and ought to have been in bed hours ago."

"But, Papa," said Miss Josephine, "it's as much as our lives are worth not to stay; we've been engaged for weeks."

"And even girls should meet their engagements," added Miss Daphne.

"But—" began Cheriton.

"There's no 'but' about it," said Miss Daphne. "The Miss Cheritons are just going to stay right here," and she skipped off.

"You see," said Cheriton, turning to me with benign paterfamiliarity, "what a thing it is to be a father."

"I see, on the contrary," said I, totally forgetting Van Spook's injunction, "what a thing it is to have *such* a father—or only a father to deal with. My last partner was taken home before supper by her stern mamma, and I don't think that even Miss Daphne Cheriton would prevail under such circumstances, once the chaperonial mind was made up."

In an instant what I had done flashed across me. Miss Josephine turned a little paler than usual, and looked across at her father in a manner half anxious and—it seemed to me—half contemptuous. Eugene Cheriton had bitten his lip and risen from the table, supporting himself by one hand resting upon it, whilst the other was pressed to his heart. Huskily stammering, "Excuse me," and bowing, in a manner which exhibited an effort of the supremest self-control, he left us; as he disappeared through the doorway, he passed his handkerchief across his forehead, and the play was over. I say "the play," because somehow or other, in the whole scene, it struck me that there was a false note somewhere—that it was too dramatic—not "good form."

Still, it was a very awkward thing to have done, a most unpleasant position to have placed oneself in, and required some spontaneous tact for its solution. The tact of women comes out in rapid initiative, the tact of man lies in inaction; and in cases like the present—the man generally throws the difficulty immediately on to the shoulders of the woman—a tacit recognition of her superior ethical powers. Manlike, on this occasion, I merely looked across at Miss Cheriton interrogatively, and she, rising also, remarked:

"Shall we get back upstairs? It is very close here."

As soon as we had left the elevator I said to her:

"You cannot conceive, Miss Cheriton, how grieved I am that a blunder of mine should have caused this *contretemps*. I have evidently wounded your father deeply, but I hope you will explain to him how innocent I was of any *intention* to wound."

"There is no need to discuss the matter, Mr. Lyster," replied the girl, a faint tinge coming to her cheeks, and the pupils of her eyes slightly contracting. "Of course you are in no way to blame; as a stranger to the city you could not know my father's peculiarity—his idiosyncracy—in this respect. Any suggestion involving my mother always has that effect upon him; it is a subject on which the profoundest silence reigns, not only in our family, but among our friends. I am sorry to have to tell you this myself, but I feel it is better to get over it at once. Now, if you please, we will talk of something else."

We did so, and presently her partner for the cotillon came to claim her, and I went in search of Æselkopf Van Spook and an explanation.

"Well, you see, my dear Mr. Lyster," said the young gentleman in question, in answer to my query as we drew up easy-chairs on either side of an anti-temperance table, in front of the fire that we found blazing in my rooms at the Everett House, "you are asking for information on a subject about which I know as little as anybody else in New York; but what everybody knows I can tell you."

"Eugene Cheriton is an Englishman. He arrived in New York thirteen years ago with his twin daughters, who were then six years old. Immediately on his arrival the nurse who accompanied them from England was sent back, and thus the city was deprived of its only source of definite information. Cheriton seemed well off when he arrived—was so undoubtedly—and since his arrival the business to which he has devoted himself with unflagging

124

enthusiasm has doubled or trebled his capital. Who his wife was or is—for no one knows whether she is alive or dead—is as much of a mystery to-day as it was on the morning of his arrival in the new world. It was understood that he had been the petitioner in a divorce case—not a sensational divorce case, but an ordinary vulgar affair disposed of in four lines by the *Times*, and without any redeeming features, sensational or romantic. Beyond this, thirteen years of assiduous female enquiry have only elicited the shadowy information that Cheriton, when very young, married a beautiful pauper over there: she was not, it appears, duly grateful, and after a couple of years or so, he was separated, leaving her the children in the hope, it is said, that they would reform her. They didn't. She went from bad to worse, and three years afterwards he had finally to sue for a divorce and take the children from her. The tragedy aged him as you see—for he's not much over forty—and from the day he arrived the word 'wife' or 'mother 'upsets him, whilst if you allude to Mrs. Cheriton even indirectly he has a kind of fit. I saw you 'strike a snag,' as we say over here, whilst talking to him in the supper-room. Now you understand the position."

"Yes," I replied, "I understand the position, but I don't understand Cheriton."

"No, I should think not. No one does. He's about as deep as a well, and though the water is pure enough that comes out of it, in consequence of the fact that the bucket never gets far below the surface, I shouldn't be surprised if it were precious muddy down at the bottom."

"Eh!" I exclaimed, astonished principally at discovering in young Van Spook a penetration for which I had not given him credit.

"I mean," said he, "that *entre nous*, I believe that Cheriton is an infernal fraud."

"Shake!" said I, *á l'American*. We understood one another, and changed the conversation.

III.

Calling a few days later at No. 7 West 40th Street, I was fortunate in finding the Miss Cheritons at home; and, improving an acquaintance which had promised, it seemed to me, such a pleasant future at its commencement, I soon became almost an *habitué* in the Cheriton household. Certainly there was no house in which, during my stay in New York, I felt more thoroughly at home; and when I have said that, I have said almost everything a confirmed bachelor of six-and-thirty can say.

Of the twin girls, Miss Josephine was—if one may apply the expression to a twin—the elder. She seemed to be of a stronger fibre than her sister, and gave me the impression of being a charming *woman*, whilst Miss Daphne was nothing more or less than a singularly attractive *girl*. It was with the psychologically-elder twin therefore, that I felt most in sympathy, and I used to hold long, serious conversations with her whenever we found ourselves alone. I fancy that Mr. Cheriton encouraged our intimacy somewhat from a mistaken idea that we should eventually marry one another, though I may confidently say that such an idea never for one fleeting instant entered either of our heads. With Eugene Cheriton I never got below the surface—the undisturbed and apparently undisturbable surface—of his calm social affability. He never alluded in any way to our first unhappy conversation, and during the five months that I frequented the Cheritons' house, I never heard the name of the late (?) Mrs. Cheriton mentioned, or her present or past existence even remotely alluded to. Nothing in the house suggested her—nothing beyond young Van Spook's account, shadowy and unsatisfactory as it was, could I ever learn about the mother of the beautiful twins.

One day, the servant having admitted me in No. 7 W. 40th Street and disappeared incontinently (as had grown to be his wont), I entered the inner drawing-room unannounced, and caught Miss Josephine standing in the bay of a window looking intently at an open miniature-case which she held in her hand. I was coming up behind to surprise her, and discover her tender secret, when suddenly, her sharp ears catching my footfall, she turned, started violently at seeing me, and, blushing crimson from her beautiful throat to the roots of her hair, shut the miniature-case with a snap. I held out my hand as if to take it, saying laughingly,

"Give it up—who is he?"

Quick as thought she put her hand behind her back, exclaiming as she did so: "Oh, Mr. Lyster, how you startled me!"

Her hand struck some piece of furniture, the case flew from it, and opening as it reached the floor, lay thus, face downwards. I stooped to pick it up, and the girl exclaimed rapidly:

"On your honour as a gentleman don't look at that picture, Mr. Lyster!

"Of course I picked up the case, closing it as I did so; but having restored it, I began to chaff the girl about the original, wondering vaguely who the man could be who would risk encountering the expression "No" in those dark, solemn eyes. I saw that my *badinage* pained her, so I desisted, and we turned to other topics.

As I rose to go I saw something white on the floor, and stooping to pick it up, I saw that it was a picture of a woman. A cry of astonishment broke involuntarily from my lips as I stood looking at it, transfixed with amazement; the girl gave one look at it, and snatched it from my hand with an exclamation that seemed to vibrate with agony.

"In God's name," said I, hardly above a whisper, "who is that woman?"

"My mother."

IV.

Nearly fourteen years before the events above recorded, Rex Stanhope, one of the dearest friends I had ever had in the world, an old school-fellow of mine, a gentleman *aux bouts des ongles*, and the soul of honour, went hopelessly, irretrievably, to the devil.

There was a woman in the case, though poor old Rex was as pure from any blame, as far as she was concerned, as an unborn babe. She was an old, old love of his, and had thrown him over to marry another man. Had thrown him over, did I say? Hardly that. She had been forced by her people into an unwilling marriage with an older and richer suitor, and Rex had consecrated his life to a dumb, passionate regret for the "might have been." Five years after her marriage, however, his idol fell, shattered, stained, defiled; and Rex, no longer having any hope in the world, shocked out of all power of reflection, had abandoned every tie that bound him to his fair pure life, and, in trying to drown his grief in the mad dissipations of three capitals, fell from bad to worse, from worse to vilest, and finally died insane, in a garret of the Quartier Latin in Paris.

He had never told me the name of the woman he had loved and lost, but he had often shown me her picture, and this picture I found in the breast-pocket of the tattered coat that was made over to me by the *concierge* of the *maison-meublée*, wither I betook myself, accompanied by his brother, at the request of poor Rex's people, to bring the boy's body home. The portrait was a duplicate of the one I had just returned to Miss Cheriton, the portrait of her mother!

The whole story flashed across me again as we stood in the gathering twilight of the winter's afternoon—that woman's daughter and I. My brain whirled, and I could hardly remember where I was, so vivid was the picture of the past that the miniature had brought up to me. Josephine Cheriton's voice broke the silence, as we stood looking at one another:

"Mr. Lyster," said she calmly, "did you know my mother?"

And as she spoke the light of a great Fear seemed to blaze from her eyes, fear for what my answer might be. Fortunately I had recovered myself sufficiently to reply:

"No, Miss Cheriton, I did not; upon my honour, I never saw her. My astonishment was caused by the startling likeness that your mother's picture bears to that of a woman who crossed the path of a dear friend of mine—before your father was married even. Please think no more about it. I can imagine how painful this accident, and its impression upon you, must have been. I was mistaken in the dim light for a moment; believe me, I shall not refer to it again, and you will favour me very greatly by not doing so either. I shall leave you now; when next we meet I shall have forgotten all about it. You understand, we must have forgotten all about it."

And I left her, shaken for my part to the soul by the sudden revelation of the last act of the tragedy in which I had played a minor part nearly fourteen years before.

A few nights afterwards I was dining with the Cheritons. When the ladies had left the table, the conversation turned on the modern taste for Russian novels, and the analytical, almost morbid romances of the Tolstoï and Dostoievski school. We had been establishing comparisons and contrasts between the Russian novelist and Honoré de Balzac and Emile Zola, and in turn between their realism and psychology and that of Baring Gould and Edgar Saltus. Suddenly a young journalist remarked quite casually:

"It simply comes to this. The merely *narrative* form is practically a thing of the past; and just as the French novelist of the last half century has had but one direction in which to exercise his originality and his imagination, namely, the development and *dénouement* of what has been aptly called *l'etérnel aduterè*, so, the English novel of to-day consists solely of a study of human nature, in which a woman's life is ruined by a man, or a man's life is ruined by a woman."

As I fully expected, this was Eugene Cheriton's cue and he promptly began to go through his artistic histrionic agony of recollection and remorse. I never believed in the genuineness of this performance, and after the revelation of a few days previously I felt disgusted by it, so I remarked out loud and quite distinctly to him:

"As, for instance, in the case of Rex Stanhope."

The effect was electrical. The "performance" ceased abruptly, and for the rest of the evening Cheriton's eyes wandered continually and nervously in my direction. I carefully avoided his glance, however, and as we rose to rejoin the ladies, young Van Spook, who was of the party, whispered to me:

"By Jove! Mr. Lyster, you've harpooned the fishing-frog this time!"

His remark requires explanation. I had, whilst dining with Mr. Van Spook a few weeks previously, elaborated to him my theory of The Fishing-frog and the Flat-Fish," which is a favourite one of mine, and is shortly as follows:

Men who have anything in their past lives or present occupations which, for reasons of their own, they wish to conceal—in a phrase, "men with histories," are, to me, the fishing-frogs and the flatfishes of society.

Both of these fishes are formed by nature to conceal themselves whilst on the war-path for either victims or food, but their plans of campaign are essentially and diametrically different. The flat-fish sinks upon the sand of the ocean-floor, a "flap" or two disturbs enough sand around him to fall back and cover him up, with the exception of the one protruding eye which looks like a tiny pebble on the sand, but which watches for the unwary animalcule, whilst attracting it to its alimentary fate. The fishing-frog, on the other hand, lies upon the mud at the bottom of the water, and when anything approaches it, goes into violent convulsions, which hide him in a nebula of mud. If it is an enemy, the animal escapes under cover of the turgidity it has produced; if it is a fishlet available for food, he throws out a multicoloured "feeler," which the ill-fated creature lays hold of preliminary to being swallowed up; and if it is neither, the fishing-frog—like Brer Rabbit—merely "lays low."

Verb sap; Eugene Cheriton had struck me, the first time I saw him, as one of the fishing-frogs of society, and the discovery of his wife's identity, and the history which he concealed in theatrical mud—the history which I knew so well—confirmed me in my opinion.

On the day following this dinner-party Mr. Cheriton called upon me. It is needless to waste time and space in recording the game of words we played with one another, a game in which Cheriton had much to lose, and in which I held the winning cards. Be it sufficient to say that I closed the confabulation with these words:

"Our position is this, Mr. Cheriton. You have, for very obvious reasons, imposed a silence with regard to their mother upon Mrs. Cheriton's children. It is not improbable that you and I are the only people in America—perhaps in the world—who know the true story of your poor wife's disgrace, and of the circumstances which led to and followed it. I entertain too warm a regard for your daughters, ever by any action or word of mine, to enlighten their happy ignorance of their mother's fall, or to lay bare to the world the deceit which you have practised for so many years. Unfortunately, your lie is not all a lie; but should it ever become so, should your daughters or the world ever come to know anything definitely reflecting on their mother's good name, I give you fair warning that they shall know to its minutest details the story of Eugene Cheriton, of Ethel Fethrestone—and of Rex Stanhope. This question is now at an end between us; pardon me if I refuse to enter into it any further, and now, good-morning."

He saw that my mind was made up, and he took his leave. A week later I started for San Francisco, *en route* for Japan and India and home. I kept myself informed, however, upon the subject of the Cheritons; and, as far as I can learn, Mr. Eugene Cheriton has kept religiously to his part of the bargain.

I never saw either him or his daughters again.

PART II.

THE INTRODUCTION TO THE STORY.

I.

In all Oriel College, there was no greater, no more universal favourite than Rex Stanhope. He was one of the best-looking boys in the university, and one of the most charming and *insouçiant*. Among the wives and daughters of the "Dons" he was a sort

131

of spoiled child, and, when, before the beginning of the long vacation of the year 18—, it became understood and realized that Rex, having taken his degree, was "going down," and that Oxford would know him no more, the expressions of regret that echoed from all sides were eminently sincere.

"Down" he went, however, flushed with his successes in the schools, and with the most exalted anticipations of his entry into the merry, dazzling life in London society, to which, as youngest scion of one of the oldest families in the country, he eagerly looked forward. He knew by hearsay enough of "life" to be unalterably of opinion that the "bitters" thereof were sweet, or at most only mildly pungent, whilst its "sweets" were a matter of course! *Faites votre jeu, messieurs et 'dames; c'est à prendre ou à laisser! Trrrrwi!! Zero!* It's thirty-seven to one against it, but it's surprising how often it comes up in the *roulette* of "life." Pardon this digressive echo from Monte Carlo, and let us proceed.

Rex Stanhope made his entry into "society" at Lady Oswald's ball. Lady Oswald inhabited a beautiful old place in Fulham—I am talking of twenty years ago—hidden among giant elms and surrounded by a carefully-kept, old-fashioned garden, the whole protected by a high red-brick wall, which, at the same time, formed a warm background for the giant hollyhocks and sunflowers, the lupins and the gilly-flowers, which straggled in picturesque confusion over the borders, and protected her lady-ship's old-time refuge from the gaze of the curious, who were at this time just beginning to seek light and air in the direction of West Kensington, of Putney, and of Barnes. Once a year Lady Oswald gave a great ball to which "everybody" went, and thither, panoplied in the magnificence of his newest *toilette*, went the Honourable Rex Stanhope, to make his first appearance in the "world," just ten days after he had bidden farewell as a scholar to his Alma Mater and Oriel College.

As yet his acquaintance was small, and, at the termination of a waltz, he stood, as is the habit of the unknown young man, in the great square hall, watching the long procession of dancers seeking the cool of the conservatories and the solitudes of the garden, to re-appear—or not, as the case might be—in time for the next dance. And as he stood, there appeared in the doorway, leaning on the arm of her late partner, his first love—Ethel Fethreston. He had never seen her before; he had no idea who she was, but it seemed to him that he saw a "woman" for the first time. It was the story of Manon Lescaut and the Chevalier Des Grieux over again, and Rex Stanhope followed "the mistress of his soul" into the garden. For as she passed him their eyes had met; in his, a great wondering confusion, born of the new sensation of a beating heart and a hot, strained feeling at the throat; in hers, the calm triumph of a woman in the knowledge of her own peerless beauty, and the half-uncomfortable triumph of the not altogether heartless flirt—for Ethel Fethreston had been the most accomplished flirt of two seasons, and her victims, whom she thoroughly understood how to manage, were to be found in every drawing-room in London. Rex Stanhope, however, knew nothing of this—how should he, poor boy?—and as she bowed to him in passing, a great wave of joyous triumph came over him, and he followed her into the garden in answer to her bow.

Ethel Fethreston was not very tall, nor had she, in common with many medium-sized women, the trick of holding herself so as to give an impression of dignity, if not of height. Her features were not very regular, but she had great, wondering, violet eyes, of the "*ingenious ingénue*" description, and a grand, passionate mouth and square, strong jaw that were strangely belied by her almost impertinent tip-tilted nose and her almost childishly enthusiastic manner. The whole, framed by her Titian-like burnt-sepia hair, produced an effect of torrid beauty which had turned many a head before Rex's; and there is no denying the fact that, when the beautiful Ethel flirted, she flirted with a will, and in a way peculiarly her own. Rex had every cause therefore to be as proud of his conquest as she of hers, and the novelty of the situation was essentially indescribable, as, when the music of the next dance commenced, he met her returning to the ballroom, and, she transferring her arm to his, they had wandered off together into the discreet gloom of Lady Oswald's pleasaunce, just as if they had known one another for years.

'Twas she who broke the silence. Rex was too "inexperienced" to take up the cue with the *aplomb* which she had given it to him.

"You will think me very rude," said she, "for what I am going to say, but I must confess that though your face is perfectly familiar to me, I can't for the life of me remember where I've met you before."

"I am sorry to say," answered Rex, *gauche*-ly, "that we *never* met before."

"Oh, how dreadful! Please excuse my most stupid mistake. Will you take me back to the house; I suppose I've got a partner for the next dance, looking for me somewhere."

"Ah, no! don't go away. I know I've no right to ask it, and it's awful cheek on my part—but—won't you let me introduce myself. I'm Rex Stanhope; my governor's Lord Lorrimer, you know; and your name is——?"

"Ethel Fethreston; but I ought not to tell you, ought I?"

"Of course you ought. I'm so lonely here; I don't know anybody; won't you take pity on me?"

Miss Ethel Fethreston's partners were always prepared to resign themselves to her non-appearance when they had a right to expect her, but on this eventful night they had a more uniformly bad time than usual. The butterfly was singed at last, and both she and Rex found themselves hopelessly in love with one another when her sister and her brother-in-law found them at last, still strolling round the grounds, and with much sternness of manner and acerbity of countenance, took her home in the small hours of the morning.

Next day, impelled by a desire to revisit the theatre of his joy of the night before, Rex took a hansom and drove down to call on Lady Oswald. Her ladyship greeted him with the words:

"Well, Mr. Stanhope, for a Lothario of your age you are really *du dernier chic*, monopolizing the one unmonopolizable beauty of my ball for the whole evening."

134

"Why, how do you mean. Lady Oswald?"

"Only this, my dear boy, that if Eugene Cheriton hears of your performance of last night, there will probably be trouble."

"And who is Eugene Cheriton?"

"Who is Eugene Cheriton? Why, bless the boy! he's only the man who is to marry Ethel Fethreston this day fortnight!"

Poor Rex! It was his first lesson, but he learnt it with a rapidity that did him credit. "Does she—does she love him?" asked he, a trifle huskily.

"Well, I'm afraid not, poor child!" answered Lady Oswald; "but he's very well off, and the Fethrestons haven't a penny to bless themselves with. Ethel lives with her sister and brother-in-law, and they treat her as a kind of upper servant, and no doubt, have made her accept Mr. Cheriton to get rid of her. It's a cruel thing, perhaps for her at present, but it will be all right in time; these *marriages de convénance* are generally the happiest after all. But I tell you all about it so that you mayn't fall in love with her yourself."

Well, well! He was a younger son, without a chance against his rich rival, and he got back to his rooms almost blind in his agony of mind. He went to a florist's and bought a great bunch of Rucharis lilies, which he sent to her with a note—a little pathetic note—in which he told her he had heard of her engagement, and hoped she would be very, very happy, and would she accept these lilies and remember a fellow who was very grateful to her for the happy hours she had contributed to his life?—and good-bye—he did not think it likely that they would ever meet again.

A couple of hours later his flowers were returned to him, and with them his note, across which, in the handwriting of her brother-in-law, was scribbled a hideous, insulting message.

Flung brutally from the altitude of his new-born hopes, Rex Stanhope for some days went about as one suddenly awakened from a dream half-ecstatic, half-nightmare, striving to distinguish the one from the other, and to recollect whether it had been wholly the one or wholly the other. During those days he tottered on the brink of a precipice, a precipice overhanging a grisly gulf of wanton dissipation, in which to seek to drown the memory of his false first love. Then his resolution was taken. He would become great, he would keep himself unspotted from the world, and make for himself a position that should make her regret him—should make her regret her hurry to marry the first rich man who offered himself, regret the callous cruelty with which she had played with him for an evening, and then flung him from her as a disappointing toy.

II.

And so Rex Stanhope, to whose appearance "in town" more than a few society matrons had looked forward, became a kind of hermit, devoting himself to his books and his manuscripts, travelling with avidity whenever the opportunity presented itself, appearing but seldom in the places where "his world "congregated to amuse itself, and never anywhere where there was the remotest possibility of his meeting Ethel Fethreston. Meanwhile, in the columns of *The Saturday Review* and The *Athenaeum*, in the pages of the *Contemporary Review* and the *Fortnightly*, his name began to appear, until, four years after the evening of Lady Oswald's party, his was one of the names most prominent among those of the younger writers of the day.

Four years had, as I say, elapsed since that eventful night, and during that time he had heard but seldom of Mrs. Cheriton, and what he did hear made his heart ache. Cheriton had not *married* his wife—few men do now-a-days; he had merely *collected* her as he would have collected any other specimen of bric-a-brac which nobody else has got or possibly can get, and having collected her, he was jealous, cold, calculating, cunning. Worse still, he was brutal, unfaithful, cruel to her, developing, one-by-one, all the meaner vices most likely to disgust a sensitive, refined woman; and Ethel Cheriton had ample opportunities of appreciating the magnitude of the crime her relations had committed in forcing her, and of the mistake she had made in allowing herself to be forced, into this unhallowed *marriage de convénance.* During the second year of their marriage she had become the mother of twin daughters; and it was this tender tie alone that kept her at the side of the man to whom she was—already—"something dearer than his dog, a little better than his horse."

For, from a light-hearted—nay, frivolous girl,—Ethel Cheriton had become a high-minded, chivalrous woman. The sudden awakening in her soul of a genuine ideal love for Rex Stanhope, when it was "just too late," had sobered her character, and made her steadfast in her determination to do her duty to this man who had bought the right to become the father of her children—her children, in whom all the wild love of her passionate nature had become concentrated. She knew that Rex was avoiding her, and she bowed her head before her punishment. She had never seen him since the ball. Better so, she thought, for after all what could an explanation have done? None at all; indeed, it might be dangerous; but this she never admitted, even to herself. Meanwhile, her friends, seeing her grow more miserable day-by-day, in spite of her still matchless, developed womanly beauty, urged her to take advantage of her ample cause for the step, and divorce the man who was making her life a hell for her, before her children should be old enough to realize the state of affairs. But no; to their suggestions she turned an ever-deaf ear for her very children's sake; for their sake she listened in dull, cold resignation to the only too well founded scandals that attached themselves to her husband's name; and things were in this state in the winter of the year 18—.

One afternoon in early January, Rex started out to call on a friend in Queen's Gate, started out in the midst of a driving snow-storm, with many imprecations upon the necessity that drove him forth. Unfortunately he had bound himself by a promise to pay this call, which was one of *adieu,* and punctually at the hour he had named, he rang the bell at his friend's house. In answer to his enquiry the grave domestic replied:

"Not at home."

"But," replied Rex, naturally irritated that his comfortless expedition should have been made in vain, "Mrs. —— told me she would be in at this time; will you tell her, if you please, when she returns, that——?"

"Oh!" interrupted the servant, "Mrs. —— is expected home every moment, and left word that if any one called they were to be asked to wait."

Somewhat soothed by this assurance, Rex decided to remain; and he made his way upstairs to the drawing-room. Seated in a low arm-chair before the fire, also evidently waiting for Mrs. ——, sat Ethel Cheriton! How little changed! And yet, how far more dazzlingly beautiful in her mature woman-hood than when he parted from her in those bygone years! After a momentary stupefaction, a rush of blood to the heart, an instant during which neither of them could speak, they had warmly shaken hands, and sitting on either side of the fire-place, found themselves calmly talking the *banalités* of every day as if their meeting was an ordinary matter of daily occurrence.

"So it was *you*, of all people in the world," said Mrs. Cheriton, "whom Mrs. —— was expecting. I came to call, more to shelter from the storm than anything else, and the butler told me that Mrs. had left word that I was to wait. I was surprised, but said nothing, half-glad not to have to go away again, half-curious to find out who the anxiously expected guest *was*. So it is you who are the *cavalière* so *sèrviente* that we leave messages that he is not to be sent away!"

"No, Mrs. Cheriton, mine is merely a conventional visit of *adieu* before starting for Spain. As I am a hardworking son of toil, you know, I only call on people I really want to see, and therefore I let them know when I am coming." He paused slightly, and then continued, "You, of all people on earth, should know that I am never likely to be any woman's *cavalière sèrviente*."

She said nothing for a few moments, but turned a shade paler, as, after what seemed to be a momentary hesitation, she said:

138

"Mr. Stanhope, I am glad we have met at last—after all this time; there has always been something on my mind which I should have been glad to have spoken to you about. Before—before I was married—you were kind enough to send me some flowers one day—at least I heard so afterwards; and—my brother-in-law returned them to you. I couldn't—I couldn't write an apology for his rudeness, and—I always hoped some day to meet you and tell you I was sorry."

"You might have written one word to answer my note, in addition to, or rather, to soften, your brother-in-law's comment on it."

"Your note! What note?"

"Why, the one he returned with the flowers."

"I don't understand you; what do you mean?"

"Do you mean to say that you never knew that I had written you a note with those flowers, conveying to you my wishes for your happiness."

"Never—never! Oh the cruelty of it! Ah; why did I never receive it! I should have prized it so." And she bent her beautiful head forward upon her hands.

Stanhope had risen, and had walked in his agitation to the window. Now he turned and advancing toward her drew his letter-case from his pocket. Taking from it a time-worn and oft-unfolded and refolded letter, he held it out to her, saying:

"Well, here it is."

She took it and said, hardly above a whisper: "And you have kept it ever since!"

"Yes," he replied, in a dry, strained voice, "I have kept it ever since as a lesson—as a punishment for my folly in believing that there was any truth in woman's love. Whenever I have been speaking to any fair young girl, or whenever any friend of mine has married, I have taken it from my pocket-book, and said to myself, 'That is the fruit *your* love has borne; you have pocketed that insult as its reward. Beware! do not sin again!'"

"Oh Rex!"

He seized the poor imploring hands that were held out to him, and gazing deep through her eyes into her soul, he said sternly:

"Do you swear to me that you never knew I had written to you?"

"I swear it."

✳

When Mrs. —— came in ten minutes later, she was quite over-joyed at this strange meeting of old friends, and when it was time to go, she was sure Mr. Stanhope would see Mrs. Cheriton safely home.

Ah Rex! why did you not keep that pitiful token of your great, faithful love hidden away in your pocket-book? Had you done so you would have been now the brilliant man you gave promise of being, and Ethel Cheriton would have been home with her children.

III.

Do not let the reader run away with any evil interpretation of the last paragraph. Specifically, Rex Stanhope had no hand in the fall of Ethel Cheriton; but had they never met she might have gone on in the old painful groove, upheld by her stern sense of duty. But alas! having refound her old—her only *love*, a man of refinement, of cultivation—in a phrase, a scholar and a gentleman, her loathing of the ignorant sensualist to whom she was tied became the more intense, the more violent, by contrast. Her new born, constant intercourse with Rex Stanhope, an intercourse of sympathy in which no word of love was ever breathed, turned her thoughts continually in the direction of the terrible future, as contrasted with the exquisite "might-have-been;" and at last one day she announced to Rex her intention of obtaining from her husband a formal separation—not a divorce; that, said she, would rebound in after years on her children.

But she had quite made up her mind no longer to bear the continued agony of a life which, always revolting to her, had become doubly so since that winter's afternoon. It was useless to attempt to dissuade her; she had the right on her side undoubtedly; and one day, when, in the course of a quarrel on some point concerning the children, Eugene Cheriton had struck her to the ground in his drunken fury, she felt that the last straw had been added to her load, and—separated formally from the man who had "collected" her, she took a little flat in Kensington, and devoted herself thenceforward to her children—her children, on whose account alone she had refrained from obtaining a definitive divorce.

What of Rex Stanhope? He took the only course possible under the circumstances. Sufficiently wise in the ways of the world to know what he would bring upon the woman he loved, if he allowed his intimacy with her to continue, now that she no longer lived beneath her husband's roof, and knowing moreover the weakness of human nature too well to exclude himself and her from its penalties, he announced his intention of travelling; and, in spite of the entreaties of Ethel and the remonstrances of his friends, he started on a tour of the world that should occupy some years at least.

No one knew the cause of his self-imposed exile, for in his horror of compromising Ethel, he had kept their affairs religiously to himself, maintaining before the world merely a footing of ordinary social acquaintanceship. One man alone knew anything at all about it, and even he did not know the name of the woman who had come thus into his friend's life, though Rex told him, step-by-step, the circumstances which had led him to the course he had adopted. This man was myself, Dick Lyster, a school and college friend who was more than a brother to Rex, the only man who was in a position to remonstrate with him on the step he was taking, in severing all his newly-cemented ties to the old country, in giving up his brilliant prospects as a writer and politician, and in expatriating himself at four-and-twenty for the sake of some—to me, the mentor,—unknown woman.

"It's no use arguing, old man," Stanhope had said in answer to my remonstrances; "if I had not come back into her life, if I had not committed the cursed folly of showing her that her image had never left my breast, she would never have left her husband. Now that she has taken the step, unless I efface myself we must be thrown more intimately together than ever, and then—well, we are only human creatures after all! No! I shall go, and you must admit that I am doing right. My memory, and the memory of the sacrifice I have made to her of my life, will be the sheet-anchor of her womanly purity, and in giving her an ideal, an ideal that I know that I could not keep up if I were always by her side, I am making but a very meagre reparation for the wrong I have done her and her children, by causing indirectly this separation."

It was chivalrous, it was Quixotic, it was absurd; but his mind was made up, and Rex disappeared. People asked after him sometimes, and the answer was always:

"Oh, he's still idling round the world. He didn't stick to his ambition long; no doubt there's a woman in it somewhere!"

IV.

How continually, continually we hear women envy the position of men. How often it has occurred to all of us to hear a woman say, "I wish I were a man!" and though we smile and tell them they don't know what they are talking about, if we stop to think for a moment, how absolutely they have reason! And why should we condone, pardon, and, if the truth must be told, rather admire in man, what we loathe and condemn in woman? Is it worse in woman to be impure, than it is in man? Is it worse in her than in him to be unchaste, to be unsexed, to be contemptible? If, as is generally admitted, woman is the weaker vessel, in God's name is it not a thousand-fold more vile in man, whose intellect is the stronger, as a rule, to yield to the weakness of a moment, than it is in woman? If a man and a woman sin equally together, why is it the woman alone who is blamed, on whom *alone* a *lasting* stigma rests? The sin has been born of the superior strength, mental and physical, of the man over the woman. Is it not he that should be chastised rather than she? for his is the initative, and his, as a rule, is the action. In a joint crime of whatever kind, it is always the woman who is commanded and directed by the man; but, in the subsequent record, it is always *he* who had been brought to grief by *her* and not her by him. She is a "fiend," an "adventuress," whilst he is only a weak man! Oh! it is horrible, it is *lâche*, it is *infâme*!

And how infinitely worse than this is the case which occurs every day, the case in which the marital tie has been severed, either by separation or by divorce. Is it not always the woman— to our shame be it said—on whom the blame invariably falls? A man is cruel, brutal, unfaithful, to his wife; she bears it as long as she can, and at last, driven to the step in self-defence, or in defence of her innocent children, she is compelled—with the fullest approval of all who know the circumstances of the case—to sue for a separation, or even for a divorce. For a week— perhaps, if she is lucky, for a month—she is sympathized with and supported, and then people who know nothing at all about it begin to whisper among themselves. "Who is she?" "Oh, that's the beautiful Mrs. ——. Poor thing! you know she had trouble with her husband."

Second stage, "*That!* Oh! that's Mrs. ——; she's separated from her husband, you know." "Oh!"

Third stage, "Ah! Mrs. ——? Yes; *Mr.* —— was a cousin of the So-and-so's; they don't live together. Shall I introduce you?" "Well, thanks, I think not. One has to be so careful now-a-days."

Fourth stage, "Is that the Mrs. —— who was separated from her husband?" "Yes." "How was it?" "Oh, he was a happy-go-lucky sort of a fellow, and they didn't get on. No doubt there were faults on both sides." "Ah!"

Fifth stage, "Who's the man so devoted to Mrs. ——, the one who was divorced, or something, you know?" "Well, I don't know, but a *very* old friend I believe." "Oh!"

Sixth stage, "Well, he couldn't stand it any longer, and had to get rid of her; they say he's never got over it."

Seventh stage, "Why did he let her keep her children with her?" "Well, you know, he thought that they might perhaps keep her straight, but I'm afraid, etc., etc., etc."

And so it goes on, on, on, *vires que acquirit eundo*, like a snowball; and at last the victim, forsaken by all the friends who, greedy of some new sensation, espoused her cause so warmly at the first, finds herself relegated to the society of fast men and *déclassées* women, and in nine cases out of ten takes up willingly the role that is thrust upon her. The end comes in her making a single slip, wearied out and sick at heart at being pointed at as guilty of sins of which she is spotlessly innocent. She sees other women around her leading happy, or apparently happy, and brilliant lives; the "set" into which she has become transplanted, and in which she seems to have taken root, think her unnecessary "principles" rather contemptible than otherwise—like the fox who lost his tail; she finds herself deserted and despised; and one day, maddened by her hopeless yearning for love and friendship——

Such was the history of Ethel Cheriton. Cheriton, after his wife left him, had, with the cunning of the serpent, led a life that was discretion itself, watching her the while with a ceaseless vigilance, and keeping himself informed of her every movement. At last his opportunity came. For the sake of her children she had not divorced *him*; now he turned upon her ruthlessly, and petitioned against her for the divorce, the indignity of which she had spared him; and one day, Rex Stanhope, slowly accomplishing the last stages of his journey round the world, took up the *Times* in the English Club in the Rue de Pera at Constantinople, and read:

PROBATE, DIVORCE AND ADMIRALTY DIVISION.

BEFORE THE PRESIDENT.

Cheriton vs. Cheriton and De Torriano.

"This was a suit by Eugene Cheriton, a gentleman of independent means, for the dissolution of his marriage with Ethel

144

Cheriton, whose maiden name was Fethrestone, on account of her misconduct with Ippolito de Torriano. Dr. Bayard appeared for the Petitioner. *There was no defence.*

"The Petitioner was married to the respondent in 18—, and they lived together up to May, 18—. There are two children of the marriage. Mr. and Mrs. Cheriton lived happily in the earlier portion of their married life, but in 18— he had reason to complain of her conduct and quarrels ensued between them. In May, 18—, they separated, he securing to her by deed an annuity of ——, which he has since paid quarterly. In June last, Mrs. Cheriton and the correspondent, who is a singer, were served with citations in this suit.

"Decree *nisi*, with costs against the correspondent, *the petitioner to have the custody of the children of the marriage.*"

————

This is what Rex Stanhope, after two years, during which he had heard no word about the Cheritons, read in the Club at Pera. That night, for the first time in his life, he played high and drank recklessly. In the early morning he was sent home to his rooms insensible; but for weeks he sank lower and lower, striving in vain to drown his agony in the worst, and to him hitherto absolutely unknown, forms of dissipation. The sudden change shocked and alarmed his friends in the English colony at Constantinople; and at last, though with great difficulty, they persuaded him to turn his face homewards. He stopped in Vienna, where the same thing recommenced, and he had to fly from the Austrian capital at dead of night to escape the consequences of the part he had taken in some drunken riot, and arriving in Paris, he sank rapidly to the nethermost abysses of infamy. All this time we, in England, knew nothing of it, for no one knew his address: we expected him home almost daily, but alas—he never came!

One morning his eldest brother received from Paris a dishevelled package containing an account of poor Rex's last days, and an almost undecipherable letter addressed to me by the dead boy, containing an account of his first and last meeting with

Ethel Cheriton, whom still he did not *name*, bitterly reproaching himself with having caused her fall, remorse for which crime doubtless, had driven him to his terrible end. During a lucid interval at Constantinople, when he had been intending to kill himself, he had made a will leaving what little property he had to the woman,' who, forsaken by the man who had completed her fall, was living in misery abject and shameful in one of the slums of Pimlico. This will, carefully sealed up, he enclosed, that his brother might carry its provisions into operation; and, by the consent of his father, who did not wish to court publicity in the affair by contesting a will made under such circumstances, this was done by the family solicitors.

God help her, poor girl! Without this meagre sustenance I tremble to think what would have become of her.

I went over to Paris with his brother to bring home his body, and there, for the first time, I saw the picture, the duplicate of which I recognized as being that of Mrs. Cheriton, years after, in far away New York. We hushed matters up so far as it was possible; and our task was rendered easier by the fact that Mrs. Cheriton's husband and children had left for America, and the will was made out in her maiden name of Fethrestone, a name which she had now resumed. Thus it happened that, though I alone knew the story of Rex Stanhope's blasted life, I never knew the name of the woman more sinned against than sinning, but whose story is, alas! such a common one.

With all his strength of character, Rex Stanhope committed one folly, and it ruined one of the most promising careers in England: in the midst of all her self devotion and grand forbearance for her children's sake, Ethel Cheriton made one slip, of which her dastardly husband took advantage to found upon it his sham respectability. There was only one way in which to stifle all account of the ruin he had wrought in two lives, each a thousandfold purer and better than his own, and that was to impose a silence like that of the grave upon Mrs. Cheriton's children.

A FATAL FIDDLE

(The Commonplace Tragedy of a Snob)

The instrument on which he played
Was in Cremona's workshop made
By a great master of the past.
            —LONGFELLOW.

A FATAL FIDDLE

I.

IN that terribly ambiguous and elastic neighbourhood, known to the City and Suburban mind as "West Kensington," Botticellian maidens and Fra Angelican youths live, and have lived since West Kensington came into existence, in high-art semi-detachments, or in rows of "villa residences"—I quote the circular of the local estate agent—and call themselves æsthetic. The sun of Oscar Wilde is setting in the West—the Wild West—of London, with all the glory and exaggeration of a sunset seen across the sand-swept deserts of Araby, and the youth and beauty of West Kensington out-Oscar Oscar in the inexpensive picturesqueness of their startlingly original costumes.

Once you have made up your mind that the solid oaken and mahogany furniture suites, beloved of our grandfathers, are relics of barbarism, and that the unassuming, but substantial upholstery of half a century ago is gothic, philistine, and withering to your artistic soul, the trouble and expense of "furnishing" are immediately decimated; and in the West Kensington you can find little houses peculiarly adapted by their construction for garnishing with odds and ends of inexpensive furniture, the main items of which you can pick up at sales, or in the wilds of Upper Tottenham Court Road, and the subordinate items of which you can get presented to you "with every half pound of our best tea;" and in this way, worthy families who, twenty or thirty years ago, would have been compelled to adopt the dingy monstrosities cased in carapaces of woven horsehair, that furnish—save the mark!—the lodging-houses of unknown Bloomsbury, can make for themselves charming little houses of artistic, if undurable, detail, within an hour of the fresh air of Hammersmith, Ealing, Barnes and Chiswick.

Cheap though their surroundings, ambiguous though their locality, eccentric though their costumes may be, strong, true hearts beat behind the unsubstantial walls of the West Kensington "residences" as elsewhere; men are born, and marry and die bravely, notwithstanding their queer ties and velveteen coats; and women soften the hearts of the men, devoting themselves royally to the cares and sorrows of maternity, notwithstanding their peculiar headgear and shapeless frocks; the old story nerves the sons to go forth into the world on the tops of omnibuses, to fight the battle of life, whilst the daughters sit at home and sew—and wait.

At the time that my story opens, Grace and Harold Willoughby lived with their mother in one of the indistinguishable houses of one of the then newest and most eccentrically artistic rows of West Kensington tenements. Mrs. Willoughby possessed a few hundreds a year that enabled her to live—an annuity purchased by her late husband, sometime junior clerk—despite his sixty years—in a department of her Majesty's Waste-Paper and Sealing-Wax Office, but now deceased; and Harold contributed a little to the payment of the household expenses by means of the income of the slender estate his father had left him, and of his salary as a junior clerk in the same department of the same office—a position his father had obtained for him through the influence of his "Chief" a few months before his death.

Willoughby *père* had married as most junior clerks are bound to do,—if they marry at all,—late in life; Mrs. Willoughby was an old woman, and lived only in the life of Harold and of her "one fair daughter who loved her well"—Grace Willoughby, Harold's senior by three of four years, a beautiful maid with auburn hair and deep brown eyes, whose scheme of existence mainly consisted of lightening her mother's declining years with her sunny smile and willing service, and keeping at a distance her army of penniless but picturesque West Kensigtonian adorers.

The little family presented all the features of a middle-class suburban *ménage*—features which though incongruous in themselves, are singularly common under similar circumstances. Mother and daughter were content with their lot in life; mother would die and be buried in Brompton cemetery by the side of the late Harold Willoughby of Her Majesty's Waste-Paper and Sealing-Wax Office, and daughter would marry any unrepulsive male who would give her a home after her mother's death, and make the end of mother's life easier for her should he come in to perform that office.

With Harold, on the other hand, it was different—he prided himself on being a Government Official and a Gentleman,—as he understood the term,—and his ambition soared continually towards the higher grades of permanent government employment, filling his idle hours with day-dreams of the time when he should sit in a room by himself in the "Office," and sign papers brought to him for the purpose by junior clerks such as at present he was himself, and should draw for these services a salary which though inadequate to his services should still entitle him to a position in "Society" as a member of Her Majesty's Government.

There are larger and more pretentious dwellings in West Kensington than those of which one was occupied by the Willoughby *ménage*—dwellings nearer to the Addison Road, dwellings with gardens behind them, and iron railings separating them from the road, and in one of these there dwelt, at the time of which I have constituted myself the *trouvère*, a worthy merchant by name John Baxter, senior partner of the firm Baxter & Co., haberdashers and general linen-drapers of Finsbury Pavement E. C. John Baxter, a highly respectable widower of six-and-thirty or thereabouts, took the Underground Railway every morning at nine o'clock, and having occupied the transit from Uxbridge Road to Moorgate Street in the perusal of the *Daily Telegraph*,—which he gave, on arrival in Finsbury Pavement, to his junior shop-walker and care-taker,—stayed in his counting-house until half-past five, when his employés bade him respectfully "good-evening," and he returned to his house in

West Kensington, where an unmarried sister superintended his household affairs, and the education of his two small children.

Educated, himself, to regular business habits, and to little else, John Baxter seldom took part in the mild dissipations of West Kensington, and if ever he left his comfortable home after dinner,—which he took silently with his sister at seven precisely,—it was to stroll down to the Willoughby's and pay an evening call. Mrs. Willoughby liked him. His regular habits reminded her of Willoughby deceased, and Grace liked him too, for she made it a rule to attach herself to anything or any one dear to her mother. Not so Harold. For his part, he sought the society of people whom he considered entitled to recognition as members of that society into which he so ardently desired to go on his own merits, and he considered that his mother and sister were too good to be on terms of easy familiarity with a haberdasher; and as John Baxter took little trouble to conceal his opinion—which was not far from correct—that Harold was a prig, a snob, and a fool, the latter usually left the house when the former entered it, and betook himself to a house a few doors lower down in the same row where dwelt "*la reine de ses amours*," Mary Warburton—a fair sweet maiden of eighteen summers, who lived with her father, a retired Naval officer on half-pay, and her mother, a good unnecessary soul, who made the best of their reduced means, and spent none of her valuable time regretting the social position she had lost in marrying the handsome lieutenant of Her Majesty's Ship *Excalibur*, whose fortune consisted mainly of his face, a fortune which was now identically that of her lovely and lovable daughter. They were gentlewomen—both mother and daughter—in every sense of the term, and as Harold considered them good enough for him, he soon came to consider himself good enough for Mary Warburton, who, captivated by Harold's handsome face, made no concealment of her affection for him, and loved to listen to his ambitious schemes for his—their—future.

Dick Warburton had married his wife on his pay and his prospects, and they had been very, very happy; and as both he and his wife saw all that was good in Harold, and excused his follies on the plea of his youth, they made no opposition to the match. It was an understood thing that as soon as Harold should have conquered for himself an independent position in his official life, Mary should share it with him; meanwhile they were quite young enough—he was but twenty-two—and they could well afford to wait a little.

So, in the quiet evenings when John Baxter sat with his mother and sister and talked to them of affairs in the city, Harold would sit at one end of the Warburtons' little drawing-room with Mary, and unfold to her his dreams of the—he hoped—proximate future.

"You see, dear," he used to say, "my chief, Sir Edward Carshalton, was a great friend of my father's, and though he never did anything for *him*, except to get me into the office, I know he will do what he can for *me*. Already he makes me to a certain extent his confidential clerk, and looks after me generally, and I look forward to his helping me to get the Permanent Under-secretaryship of the Department, and then—" The rest was eloquent silence, broken only by the gentle susurrus of a kiss. Harold did not know that Sir Edward's interest in him was to a great extent an act of restitution, for the chief owed his elevation to the Permanent Secretaryship and the Knight Commandership of St. Michael and St. George mainly to the unremitting labours of his over-worked and underpaid subordinate—Harold's father.

"And do you think, Harold dear," she would reply, "that Sir Edward will do this for you soon?"

"Yes, as soon as he can. You know there are a great many strings to be pulled in getting these permanent government positions, and society pulls most of them. Now through Sir Edward, and as his protégé, I shall get into the best society in London, and once there, I shall find someone who can help me, and can help Sir Edward to do the same, if I play my cards properly."

"Will the 'someone' be a man—or a woman, Harold?"

"One can never tell. Some of these society women have a great pull with the authorities—and perhaps—but you needn't be jealous, darling, for I shall only have one object in going among them, and that will be getting of my place with a view to marrying you."

And then another similarly interrupted silence would ensue.

John Baxter's opinion of Harold Willoughby, though tending towards correctness, was not wholly founded on fact. With all his West Kensingtonian pretensions, Harold was not by any means a fool in the ordinary acceptation of the term. He had long since realized that in the society in which he wished to move, a state of things existed that was adequately expressed by the Scotch lady who remarked that "In this shop there's naething for naething, and precious little for saxpence," and bearing this in mind, kept constantly before him the problem—what could he give to society in exchange for the patronage he required of it?

He was well educated—with that object his father and mother and sister had denied themselves many a little luxury that would have made life easier for them than it was. He knew that, and regarded it in the light of a debt that he owed them. He was a good talker, a clever conversationalist, even as conversationalist went in those days, but he knew that he could not hope to excel in this respect ninety-nine out of every one hundred men that he would meet in "the gilded saloons of the aristocracy." He must bring other goods than that to the world's market, and it was as an amateur violinist that he proposed to establish his right to cards of invitation dating from addresses aristocratically West and South-west.

He was really a very fair performer on the instrument; it had been his one amusement, his one relief after the toils of the day in Whitehall were at an end,—till he fell in love with Mary Warburton,—and he did all in his power to attain a proficiency in his art that would cause him to be sought after by the wives of gilded dukes and belted earls—and his efforts had been crowned with a very fair measure of success.

It was to a great extent this artistic strain that helped his chief to take an interest in him, for his Sir Edward Carshalton, K.C.M.G., was an amateur in every sense of the term. His rivals, his enemies and some of his subordinates, declared that he was an amateur government official. Into that I do not propose to enter; it was as an art amateur that he figures principally in this story, and it is as such that I wish to present him to my readers.

The friends of the Permanent Secretary were wont to say that life was not worth living if Sir Edward had anything to buy or sell. If anyone possessed any article of *vertu* that Sir Edward wished to add to his collection he had no peace until the said object had changed hands, either in exchange for some uninteresting curio, or some Correggio of doubtful Correggiosity, or for a consideration so inadequate as to be no consideration at all; until which exchange had taken place the whilome owner had to submit to morning, afternoon, and evening calls from the Secretary, or to the horror of Borgia-like *tête-à-tête* dinners, throughout the course and courses of which it was a fate to be glared at as by a vulture who awaited the first signs of death to rend him. But it was worse still, if Sir Edward became possessed of anything he did not want, in a miscellaneous lot, or by purchase or exchange with some collector of more potent immorality than his own, for then Sir Edward wanted to sell! When this happened, those of his friends who could afford it went out of town, and it became a question, as in the time of the plague, among his remaining friends: "Whose turn next?" And within a greater or lesser number of days the piece of bric-a-brac old master, first edition, or instrument of musical torture, had left Sir Edward's collection, and his friends breathed freely once more for a space.

From this slight sketch of the Permanent Secretary for Her Majesty's Waste-Paper and Sealing-Wax Department, it will have been gathered by the reader that Sir Edward was a collector *pur sang* of the omnivorous sort. Nothing escaped him—seals, cigarette-ash, etchings, watch-cases, china, book-plates, musical instruments, fire-arms, postage-stamps, geological, mineralogical, pathological, ethnological, geographic and other curiosities of all sorts filled his house in Prince's Gate, in a word, there existed nothing collectible that remained uncollected by Sir Edward Carshalton, K.C.M.G.

It was owing to this startling idiosyncracy on his part that one morning Harold Willoughby espied under a chair in a corner of his chief's room at the "Office" an antique and worm-eaten leather-covered violin-case, and, always anxious to take an interest in anything that interested the chief, and, moreover, this being something distinctly in his own line, he remarked, as the secretary signed the documents he had submitted to him,

"Ah! I see you have a fiddle there, sir."

"Ye-e-es-'m 'm 'm! A fine instrument—a Joseph Guarnerius of the best period. Take it out and have a look at it. You play, don't you?"

And the secretary went on reading and signing, whilst Harold opened the case, and stripped the instrument of the silk handkerchief by which it was cautiously enwrapped.

Though Harold, and eke the chief, considered themselves connoisseurs, like many connoisseurs erroneously so called, a fiddle became entitled to whatever name a wily dealer liked to give it, and they judged violins by eye—take it whichever way you will. I mean, tell either of them that a fiddle was a "Stradivarius" and they would probably see the work of the "great master of the past" in every gouge mark and arching of its varnished surfaces; and conversely shew them the label "Stradivarius" and the name would blind their eyes to the crudities of the rankest Mirecourt or Mittenwalder toy-fiddle.

In the present instance, however, there was no room for doubt, and Harold's eyes gloated, as memory took him to his own German instrument that lay in his room at home, and he mentally compared it with the gem he held in his hands. A real Joseph Guarnerius del Jesu—with the *croix-patée* and the I. H. S. on the time-stained label inside. The bold arching of the tables, the audacious ugliness of the *f. f.* holes, and the irregular cutting of the head. And above all the glorious Cremonese varnish, the rich crimson on the yellow ground! Ah! this was *the* fiddle of a million—and poor Harold sighed as he carefully encased it again and deposited it beneath the chair.

"Well—what do you think of it?" said his chief as he finished signing his papers.

"Why, sir, there can be no two ideas on the subject. It's the most gorgeous fiddle I ever saw. Where did you find it?"

"I got it in exchange for an original Tintoretto of great value," answered the chief, and a nasty smile flickered at the corners of his mouth.

All that day there was but one object in Harold's mental eye—the matchless "Joseph," and as he drew forth his own instrument that evening to practise a little with Grace, he felt sadly out of conceit with the poor little German fiddle that had been such a companion, such a solace, such a confessional to him for years past. In the middle of his practice John Baxter was announced, and as that worthy never concealed his aversion to the instrument, and habitually made caustic remarks anent the operation of "sawing the bowels of a cat with the tail of a horse, till the defunct pussy squealed for very agony," Harold put away his fiddle and disappeared "down the street" for the evening, to Mr. John Baxter's unconcealed relief.

And he had good cause for his relief, for it was with a high purpose that he had sought the Willoughbys' tiny house that evening, and he was glad that "that young fool, Harold," was well out of the way.

However it suited his purpose to enquire of Mrs. Willoughby how Harold was getting on in his official work, and the good woman told him of Harold's prospects and ambitions, as far as she knew and could understand them.

"Yes," said John Baxter, "I see how it is. He thinks that we're none of us good enough for him and prefers the society of these aristocratic jays who look down on us hard-working folk, and hate us because we put them in the County Court when they don't, can't or won't pay us the bills they owe us. Official life is all very well for a man of independent means, but for a poor man it's everlasting disappointment and heart-ache. If he rises to a decent salary he is at once sought after by a society above his head, that takes all the amusement it can get out of him, and gives him none in return beyond the gratification of his foolish vanity; and makes him live up to the last penny of his income if not beyond it. It is a miserable life, Mrs. Willoughby, and for all your sakes I'd much rather see Harold superintending a department in my shop on Finsbury Pavement than working his heart out for barren honours that exist only in his own imagination, in Whitehall."

"But, Mr. Baxter," replied Grace gently, "Harold is very fond and very proud of his work, and the chief of his department has his interests at heart and will help him."

"Help him to what? To a higher salary which will be utterly inadequate to his disproportionately higher needs! He will never be able to rise beyond a certain level, and on that level, if he reaches it, he will not be able to support more than himself. What is to become of you?"

Grace kept silence, for deep in her heart she knew that there was much solid sense in John Baxter's words. Seeing that she made no reply, he continued,

"I have thought very seriously of all this, Miss Willoughby, and it has caused me many an anxious moment. I hope you will forgive me for what I am going to say—but I am a plain man, thinking neither better nor worse of myself than I have a right to; and since the death of my poor wife—God rest her soul!—I have passed many a cruelly lonely hour. I hardly know how to say it, but it is a far deeper feeling than one of anxiety for your material future that makes me speak. I love you, Grace, and for months this has been the gentlest and best thought in my life—can you—will you be my wife?"

"Oh, Mr. Baxter!"

"Perhaps I have asked you this great blessing too suddenly. If that is so, take time to consider the matter. And if you cannot feel for me the sympathy you should give to a husband, the one thought of whose life will be your welfare and that of your mother, I pray you to believe that my affection for you will be in no sense diminished."

Grace rose from her chair, walked to the window and looked out into the street, and there, covering her face with her hands, thought in silence for a few minutes.

Mrs. Willoughby also rose and left the room, after silently pressing John Baxter's hand as he sat motionless, looking at the woman he had asked to be his wife.

Who shall pry into the secrets of a woman's heart? Who shall say what were Grace Willoughby's thoughts as she decided her fate in those short minutes? What dreams did she suddenly extinguish beneath her duty as she understood it; what hitherto half-considered love woke suddenly and died forever in her heart? Who shall tell? Who can say? Whatever her thoughts had been, her face gave no indication of them as she turned from the window and came towards John Baxter. He rose, pale as death, and advanced to meet her; and then a great wave of colour surged into his face as she extended both her hands to him, and said softly,

"Mr. Baxter—John—I will be your wife."

The grim merchant folded her in his arms, and as she raised her head to his he bent and kissed her lips.

When Mrs. Willoughby returned to the microscopic drawing-room a glance told her the state of affairs even before John Baxter had risen and had come gravely to salute his prospective mother-in-law. He did not remain long this evening; he felt perhaps that Grace might like to be left to think it over; anyhow he took leave early, and mother and daughter were left alone.

"What will Harold say?" was Mrs. Willoughby's first remark.

"I am sure," said Grace, "that Harold will be neither so foolish nor so unkind as to express anything but satisfaction at the prospect before us, mother dear. What Mr. Baxter—I mean John—said about him, is quite true. He has his own way to make in the world, and we must not bar his progress with anxieties on our account. I feel sure that Harold will wish me joy from the bottom of his heart."

"Indeed, I trust so," said Mrs. Willoughby, and a moment later their doubts were dispersed by the entrance of Harold himself.

"Well, good people," said he cheerily, as he put his head into the room, "can I come in? Has the worthy haberdasher gone?"

"Mr. Baxter left a short while ago, Harold," said his mother, feebly.

"Ah, that's good. Well! what's the news in the city? What is calico doing, and is there much stir in buttons?"

"You will oblige us very greatly by not speaking in that tone about Mr. John Baxter," said his mother with as much severity as she could command.

"Good gracious, what's the matter with the pair of you? You look so serious. There's no bad news, I hope?"

"No, Harold, there's no bad news," said Grace.

"Well, then, what has happened? I left you cheery and jolly with the milliner, and I come back and find you attending each other's funerals."

"Harold," said Grace, rising and going to him, "Mr. Baxter has asked me to become his wife."

"He dared!"

"Yes—why not? He has conferred an honour upon us; you have your own future to look after, and must not be hampered by mother and me. John Baxter is a good honest man for whom I have the deepest respect."

"You can respect him as much as you like, Grace, but there must have been something very strange in your manner to him, or he would never have dared to ask you to be his wife. Ah! I see how it is. I ought not to have left him here alone with you always. I forgot that these *parvenus* always presume. Of course you answered him properly."

"Yes."

"And how did he take it?"

"He seemed very gratified, Harold, naturally."

"How naturally?—What do you mean?"

"I mean that I have promised to be John Baxter's wife."

"What!"

Harold rose to his feet and began pacing up and down the room.

"You are going to keep a shop—you—my sister—egad! How proud I shall be! When I am Permanent Under-secretary at the Office, and Mary Warbuton is my wife, how proud I shall be of my brother-in-law, Baxter & Co., of Finsbury Pavement! I think you might have had some consideration for *me*. Here am

160

I, working hard day after day, moving heaven and earth to gain a position to which I may raise you, and in which I may be proud of you, and before I can move an inch or say a word, you throw yourself at the head of a shopkeeper and begin to drag me back. What will the fellows at the office say?"

"Harold," said Grace Willoughby, all her womanly dignity rising beneath her brother's scorn, "before you say another word—and you have said too many already—understand this: mother and I have to look to ourselves; you have your own life to live, we have ours. You have chosen to seek after honours for yourself. I choose to seek after comfort for mother's old age, and an honourable position for myself as the wife of an honest man. I had hoped that you should approve this action of mine—an action which every day of my life I feel sure that I shall have less and less cause to regret. You have elected to do otherwise. All I can say is this—I have done, and shall do, my duty. If you are not pleased, go your way and let me go mine. Some day—mark my words—you will say I have done rightly. All I ask of you is this—John Baxter is to be your brother-in-law; I beg of you to treat him if not with cordiality, at least with courtesy and respect; he may some day prove your best friend. No, don't answer. I have put the case clearly to you; think it over—now I am going to bed—good-night."

She stooped and kissed his forehead, and the next moment she was gone.

In leaving the room, Mrs. Willoughby bent over him and said,

"Try to think the best of it, my boy. I am sure that Grace has acted rightly. Think it over, Harold. I am sure this is what your father would have wished."

Left alone with his thoughts, Harold spent an hour pacing up and down the little drawing-room. So this was the end of the Future he had mapped out for his sister, whom he had pictured to himself being sought in marriage by some "swell" or other as "the beautiful sister of Her Majesty's Permanent Undersecretary for the Waste-Paper and Sealing-Wax Department." Well! there was nothing to be said, nothing to be done; he must make the best of it. In the first silly despair of his ill-regulated mind he felt that he could not ask Mary Warburton, the daughter of an ex-officer of the service, to become the sister-in-law of a haber-dasher's wife; "but with the morning, cool reflection came," and he persuaded himself, as he took the Underground Railway to Westminster, that the brilliancy of his own future would dazzle the world, and blind its eyes to what he already looked upon as his sister's unfortunate *mésalliance*. On this point he was also reassured on the following afternoon when he looked in at the Warburtons, on his way home, to break what he called his "bad news" to them.

With much hesitation and beating about the bush, he finally succeeded in announcing his sister's engagement, to the family assembled.

"What," exclaimed Dick Warburton, "John Baxter? Isn't he 'Baxter & Co.' of Finsbury Pavement?"

"Yes—I regret to say he is—" stammered poor Harold.

"Why regret? It is an excellent match. Major Hibbert lives next to him, and has often spoken of him. An honest man and a reputable citizen, well off materially, and rejoicing in the highest possible character for commercial and private integrity. Harold, my boy, I congratulate your sister."

And so saying, the worthy retired captain got his hat and stick and started off up the street with his future son-in-law.

It is probable that Dick Warburton never knew what a serv-ice he rendered not only the Willoughby family in general, but Harold in particular, by this simple action, prompted by his simple heart. Arrived at the little house, they found John Baxter himself paying his first official visit in the capacity of *fiancé*, and bending over Grace he said,

"Grace, my dear, you must let an old fellow kiss you, and wish you every joy in life that you deserve, and that you are sure to attain. And this is Mr. Baxter? Sir," continued he, grasping the merchant by the hand, "I know you already through mutual friends—accept a full share of the congratulations I have offered Grace. I am proud to know you well, and shall be prouder to know you better."

162

Harold simply "thrown on his beam-ends," as the ex-captain would have said, by the turn things had taken, and advancing in his turn he held out his hand to John Baxter, saying,

"Mr. Baxter, I hope you will excuse me, a day-labourer like yourself, for not having come to express my satisfaction in person before this. I am afraid I have sometimes lacked in courtesy to you. I hope that you will forgive me, and believe that, in letting by-gones be by-gones, I welcome you as the husband Grace has chosen for herself with my dear mother's approval."

"Say no more about it, Harold," replied Baxter, who, if the truth must be confessed, had looked forward with some anxiety to Harold's first reception of him as his sister's "intended." "I know that we shall be friends now that we know one another better, and I hope you will always remember that any assistance of any kind I can ever render you will be rendered most cheer-fully to Grace's brother."

And so the thing was settled. John Baxter remained to dine with the Willoughbys, and after dinner Dick Warburton and his wife and daughter joined them. The evening passed off delight-fully, and as Harold went to bed he said to himself that things did not look so bad after all, that Grace might have done worse, and that, all things considered, his mind would be relieved of one of his principal anxieties.

Six weeks later Grace Willoughby became the wife of John Baxter. His two children attached themselves to her wildly and at once, and whilst Mrs. Willoughby and Harold lived together in the little house that Grace had left, she became the presid-ing angel, *vice* Baxter's sister retired, in Baxter's house,—nearer to the Addison Road, with a garden behind it and iron railings separating it from the road.

II.

More than a year had passed and the month of June had arrived. The London season was what journalists call in "full swing." Save as regards Grace Baxter, little or no change had taken place in the lives of the actors in the little tragedy which seemed at this time to contain so little element of the tragic. Day by day Harold Willoughby sought the classic shades of Whitehall, and already, as far as Sir Edward Carshalton could compel fate, the object of Harold's official ambition seemed getting nearer and nearer within reach. Governmental Secretaries and Ministers had been interviewed and interested; the Willoughbys, the Warburtons, the Baxters, had but one engrossing thought—Harold's appointment, and really it seemed as if he had as good if not a better chance than the half dozen other juniors who were vying with each other to attain the Permanent Under-secretariat of Her Majesty's Waste-Paper and Sealing-Wax Department, and better still, from his point of view, his own symmetrical proportions were becoming obscured, as he gazed at himself in his looking-glass, by polished pasteboards requesting the pleasure of Mr. Harold Willoughby's company at functions given by Mrs. This, Mrs. That, and at rare intervals by Lady The-other. His foot, said he to himself, was on the first rung of that social ladder he desired so ardently to scale, and he trusted to his personality and accomplishments to aid him in the ascent which he felt was so necessarily conducive to his official success.

It was one morning early in June that the beginning of the end arrived. Harold had entered his chief's room with a bundle of papers, as was his wont, and, having obtained thereto a collection of the chief's autographs, was leaving the room when that gentleman suddenly remarked,

"By the bye, Willoughby, here is a thing that may be useful to you: an invitation to the reception next Friday at the Foreign Office. You can go there with me, and I'll present you to my wife's sister-in-law, Lady George Wilmyngton, who, they say, influences the decisions of the Minister in filling the Undersecretaryships very materially. I was speaking to her of you yesterday, and now you had better do what you can with her yourself."

"Oh, sir, how can I thank you sufficiently?" exclaimed Harold, his mental eye instantly obscured, dazed by a picture of himself circulating amid the throng of decorated dukes and diplomats at the F. O. reception. "Do you think I shall be able to enlist her ladyship on my side?"

"Well, Willoughby, I think it rests entirely with you. You are young and somewhat good-looking; she is appreciative, and somewhat romantic, I believe. She has a passion for social and artistic lions of all kinds, and if you can succeed in impressing her with the idea that you are in any way different from the vast majority of young men that wander about the rooms at Wilmyngton House on her reception days, I think you would stand a good chance of gaining her support. Anyhow, go in and win if you can."

The F. O. reception! What a triumph! Indeed he had done well in seeking social distinction, for behold, his efforts were crowned with success. "The Earl and Countess of Blank requested the pleasure of Mr. Harold Willoughby's company, etc., etc.," and *en comble*, he would go to the reception with "his friend Carshalton—Sir Edward Carshalton, you know, of the Waste-Paper and Sealing-Wax Department."

Oh, the joy of bringing the invitation, with a bundle of lesser documents, out of his pocket to exhibit it in a *dégagé* manner to his mother, and to Mary Warburton and to John Baxter. And oh, the joy of contemplating said invitation stuck in his looking-glass! What a shame that it had to be given up at the door, and could not stay stuck in his mirror for all time! Still, it would be there till Friday, and he would see that any friends who came to the house went up to his room and saw it. He even took down and destroyed, to make room for it, two cards of invitation to West Kensington "at homes" of which he had erstwhile been preternaturally proud. It was the last thing he saw as he extinguished the gas at night, the first as he opened his eyes in the morning. What a shame that it had to be given up at the door!

By Wednesday everybody in West Kensington who was honoured by Mr. Harold Willoughby's acquaintance knew that he was going to the F. O. Reception with Sir Edward Carshalton. John Baxter said nothing, but smiled grimly at the pleasure with which Grace announced her brother's good fortune.

And at nine on Friday evening, Harold, spotlessly arrayed, took a hansom to Prince's Gate to call for Sir Edward Carshalton, who kept him waiting for an hour, during which he got hot and uncomfortable, his hands lost their snowy whiteness and got red from very nervousness, and his hair got—he was quite sure of it—untidy.

Arrived in Whitehall, however, his troubles were all forgotten, and wandering among the uniforms and stars, and *grand cordons*, he almost forgot the object of his presence there, till Sir Edward, exceedingly anxious to get rid of him, stopped him before a good-looking woman, *fortement capitonnée*, and not altogether innocent of powder, said in his suavest manner,

"Lady George, let me present to you my young friend and Junior, Mr. Harold Willoughby."

Harold had not forgotten his carefully rehearsed bow, but not a word of his carefully prepared first speech could he remember,—fortunately for him; and her ladyship giving him a sweeping glance through her lorgnette, and seeing that he was good to look upon, took pity on his obvious embarrassment and made room for him to sit by her side, saying as she did so,

"Ah, Mr. Willoughby, I am glad to make your acquaintance; Sir Edward has said the most charming things of you to me. You are young and ambitious, he tells me; the two best things that a man can be. Tell me about yourself."

Started thus on the one subject on which a man can be truly eloquent, Harold, who had a soft musical voice and a pleasant deprecating manner that veiled his conceit admirably, found himself almost immediately quite at ease, and when Lady George Wilmyngton finally rose, and taking his arm, proposed a stroll through the rooms in search of some quiet corner where they could chat at ease without being continually interrupted, Harold felt that this was the golden evening of his life.

From generalities they arrived gradually at personalities, and he told her ladyship all about his aspirations, his pursuits and his accomplishments. Small wonder was there that by the time they parted, Lady George was firmly convinced that, if conceited on the subject, Harold must be a really eminent amateur violinist, and, to his wild but carefully concealed delight, she bound him by a promise to play for her at her reception on the following Friday week. He would cost her nothing, she could announce him all round among her friends as a marvellous amateur fiddler, and make a great feature of him, and as Harold jumped into the last train from Westminster for West Kensington, his heart beat high with hope, and his already exaggerated opinion of himself became more than ever hopelessly hypertrophied.

The whole of the following week was spent by our amateur virtuoso in practising the *morceaux* he was to play at the coming reception, and every day he explored the *criard* tone of the good little German fiddle whose voice was to herald his talent to the noble world he sought to take by storm. On the Monday preceding the eventful Friday, a brilliant idea struck him—happy thought!—why not?

When he took his daily batch of correspondence to his chief for signature, he hesitated before leaving the room, and finally said,

"You know, do you not, sir, that I am to play at Lady George Wilmyngton's reception on Friday?"

"Yes," replied the great man, "I have heard in all directions of her ladyship's new and marvellous amateur. I hope you will do yourself justice."

"I hope so, I'm sure, sir, but I have one terrible difficulty—my violin. It is a German fiddle by Withalm in imitation of Steiner, and is horribly crude and nasal in tone. I feel that I can't do myself or my music justice on it."

"Well, I'm sorry to hear that."

"You could very materially assist me, if you would," hazarded the boy.

"Oh! How?" said Sir Edward, retreating into his official shell at once, and assuming his most request-for-favour-receiving air.

"I've noticed that your Guarnerius has remained under the chair ever since you showed it to me, Sir Edward. As you are not using it, will you lend it me till Saturday? On such an instrument as that I could make and effect that would vastly increase her ladyship's opinion of me, and help me with her influence, joined to yours, to get this position."

"Oh, as for that, she has spoken about you already to Lord Dash, and your appointment is all but secure—and," continued Sir Edward, his nasty smile coming over his face again, "that is a very valuable instrument, and I am just about to sell it."

"But you won't sell it before Saturday, will you, Sir Edward? and you shall have it back the first thing on Saturday morning. Besides," added he, a gleam of intelligent argument lighting up his mind which was momentarily dulled by the chief's remark about the secretariat, "if I play on it till Saturday, restring it, and fit it up generally, it will be in much better and more salable condition than it is at present."

His words seemed to strike the amateur dealer who sat before him, disguised as Sir Edward Carshalton, K. C. M. G., and after a moment's thought he said:

"Well, I'll trust it to you, though, on my soul, I wouldn't trust it to any one else. Mind you take the greatest care of it, and let me have it back on Saturday morning. I shall, of course, hold you responsible for any damage that happens to it."

"Of course, of course," replied Harold delightedly, "but I shall see that no harm *can* come to it. Thank you a thousand times, Sir."

"Oh—all right, not at all—" returned his chief, and when Harold had left him he turned to his papers once more with a queer malicious little chuckle.

Till Friday the week's evenings were spent again in practising—these times with his accompanyist—a West Kensington pianist who was to make his first appearance before "aristocratic society," under the ægis of Harold Willoughby. Ah! but what a fiddle it was, how covetously Harold gloated over it as he took it from his case. What joy to possess such an instrument. He had it refitted and restrung, and by Friday he could have played his two solos on it backwards and standing on his head.

And thus he arrived and played to "the lords and ladies assembled" at the Lady George Wilmyngton's reception.

The word "amateur" covers a multitude of sins—it covered Harold's. Her ladyship and some of her guests were surprised to find that the vaunted amateur didn't play better, but still it was quite a creditable performance, and many and verbose, if unnecessary and insincere, were the felicitations showered upon his hostess by the interested listeners who felt it to be their duty to themselves and their plans to say something nice about her protégé to Lady George. Thus all things worked together for the good of Mr. Harold Willoughby, and as he left the reception that lady whispered a few words to him concerning his success both musical and official that sent the future Under-secretary away, walking as if on air, a jauntier cock to his head, and increased fling to his legs, and he got into the train at Westminster, his head spinning with the tumultuous whirl of his prophetic day-dreams. Indeed so engrossed was he with his thoughts for the future, with his plans for his own aggrandisement,—now that he had triumphed, or as good as triumphed, at all points—that his pleasant reflections carried him on—on—on—till at leaving the station at West Kensington they stopped suddenly and Harold Willoughby was pulled up with a jerk.

He had left Sir Edward Carshalton's Joseph Guarnerius in the train!

I have only once in my life experienced the sensation of pure, unrelieved, grisly, horrible terror, and that was in an earthquake in Asia Minor. I stood on a little hillock on the plains, about twenty miles from Diarbekr, in Koordistan, and my camel, too terrified to stampede, crouched beside me laying his long neck on the ground, and shivering, whilst for three or four eternal minutes the earth billowed and shook, cracking here, rising there, subsiding elsewhere. It was the frightful irresistibility of the cataclysm, the sense of one's utter powerlessness, to resist or protect oneself from the horror going on before one's very eyes, that was terrible, and this it was that Harold Willoughby experienced as he leaned against the station house window, and watched, disappearing into the distance beneath a tunnel the rear lights of the train that was bearing away Sir Edward Carshalton's Guarnerius.

He was aroused from his state of semi-consciousness by a railway porter, who enquired whether he were unwell or intoxicated, aroused to the realization that the fiddle was gone—by this time it was probably a couple of stations away. His first action on recovering his scattered senses was to fly to the railway telegraph office, and have the train searched at the first stopping station that it should reach after his telegram, and then again at the terminus. The answers returned whilst he paced up and down the station in a state of feverish misery—the fiddle had not been found!

Off he started down the line, alighting at every station in turn, interrogating the officials, searching the cloak-rooms and Lost-Property Offices,—the Guarnerius was gone. The ticket-collector at the next station to West Kensington fancied he remembered seeing a man leave the station carrying a violin case—but he was not sure. And that was all.

What was to be done? He could not advertise in the London papers for the instrument; his chief would see the advertisement, and at any cost that was to be avoided—how to conceal the loss from Sir Edward?—that was the question—why! if he came to know of it, even at this last moment, it might jeopardize his appointment to the Under-secretariat; for he knew his chief well, and to lose for him an object that he was on the point of selling, especially an object of such value, meant incurring an enmity bitter as it was everlasting.

He arrived home at midnight, to find his mother in a state of the wildest anxiety about him—Mary Warburton had spent the evening with her, and Grace had come round, but, worn out with waiting they had severally gone home. Where had he been?

Where had he been? Poor wretch—he had spent the evening among the music and pawnbroker's shops of the district, leaving descriptions of the fiddle and offering immeasurable rewards that he could not afford to pay for its recovery. He arrived home worn out and never closed his eyes all night. The day that had opened so gloriously for him had closed most miserably; what would the morrow bring forth?

170

The early morning—nothing. He sent a message down to the office to the effect that he was seriously indisposed. He had advertised for the recovery of the instrument in the local press, but had not dared, for reasons before mentioned, to advertise in the great dailies. Well—now he had Saturday and Sunday in which to work.

Almost without intermission he perambulated London in search of the lost Guarnerius, not a violin-dealer did he leave unvisited: he even spent Sunday ringing up unlucky people whom he thought might possibly be able to assist him, and on Sunday night he flung himself, worn-out, upon his bed—saying to himself that everything that could be done, had been done, and he could do no more.

All this time—for it seemed an eternity to him since Lady George Wilmyngton's reception—he had not said a word to his mother or sister or even to Mary Warburton about the real cause of his troubles; of his perpetual coming and going; of his fever-ishness and misery. Tonight he told his mother the whole story, and the poor old lady, though completely ignorant of the value of a Guarnerius violin, seeing the distress of her son, felt and knew that a great misfortune had fallen upon him.

"What can you do about it, my boy?" said she.

"Nothing. I have only one chance, which is this, desper-ate though it be. Fortunately Sir Edward is a collector, not a player, and his connoisseurship is all nonsense, he wouldn't know a Guarnerius from a Mirecourt toy-fiddle; much less one Guarnerius from another. I must gain a week's time on some pretext or other and get him another fiddle; so long as the real connoisseurs tell him it's a Guarnerius he'll never know that it wasn't the one he lent me. That's what I must do, mother, I must buy another Joseph del Jesu."

"And what will it cost you?"

"Heaven only knows! It depends on the conscience of the dealer I get it from—there may not be one in the market to be had for love or money. If there is I may have to pay three, four, even five hundred pounds for it."

"Harold!"

"Yes, mother, it's true. The finest Cremona fiddles fetch almost any price you like to name. And any price I am asked I've got to pay between this and next Saturday."

"But have you got the money?"

"No—that's the deadly part of it. What money I had, I paid last week as deposit for the rent for the furniture of my rooms in Queen Anne's Gate, and I shall have to raise the price of the fiddle among the Jews."

Alas! poor Harold; it was true. Sure of his position and it's emoluments, he had taken an apartment in Queen Anne's Gate more fitted as he thought to his "Official Position." All his savings had gone in furniture for said rooms, and he looked forward in a few months' time to taking Mary Warburton thither, and installing her as the goddess of the place—alas! poor Harold!

Monday morning saw him down at the office with a pale face and a palpitating heart. He watched the clock miserably, as the hands moved round to the time when he must enter the dreaded presence of his Chief, and at last it came. Nerving himself with a supreme effort, he entered Sir Edward's room with his batch of papers, and the Secretary, looking up said, cheerily:

"Ah! Willoughby, glad to see you back. We want you here on your last days as a Junior—but you're looking pale and worn even now. Well, what was it? the over-excitement at Lady George's reception? I've heard about it of course. How did the fiddle go?—and by the bye—where *is* the fiddle?"

The blow had fallen.

"Why—didn't I tell you about it in my letter on Saturday, sir?"

"No—what is it?" snapped the Chief, his urbanity suddenly disappearing.

"Why, sir—a most unlucky accident happened. The old case you lent me the fiddle in, had no key, and on leaving the station, at West Kensington on Friday, the clasps of the lid flew open and the fiddle dropped out onto the asphalt, and the finger-board and back got jarred. I've sent it to be fixed by the first repairer in Europe, and he promises it to me before the end of the week."

Sir Edward Carshalton turned purple with rage.

"So, sir," he exclaimed, "*this* is the result of my condescension in lending you a fine instrument wherewith to make an effect upon a society you can never enter, because you're not fit for it, sir—not fit for it! *This* is your return for the way I've worked to get you an appointment which you are about as capable of filling as the place you seek in society. This is your gratitude—you repay me by the grossest carelessness with my property which I foolishly entrusted to you. I ought to have known better—to have known *you* better!"

"Really, sir, I—" began poor Harold.

"Don't argue the point, Willoughby, I won't have it—do you hear? I won't have it. Where is my Guarnerius being repaired?"

Harold had prepared for this question, so he answered as calmly as he could:—

"I am sorry to say, sir, that I may not tell you that. I entrusted it, regard being had to the immense value of the instrument, to a celebrated German repairer and fiddle-maker who is visiting a friend in the trade here, and who undertook the task solely on my assurance that I would not betray his presence in London. If it became known that he is in the country he would be deluged with applications to work."

"Well—all I can say is," grunted Sir Edward, "that it's a very queer story, and I shouldn't wonder if there's more beneath it than meets the eye. Oh, don't look at me like that, you can't frighten me. Damme! remember if you please that you're not Permanent Under Secretary yet, and if things hadn't gone so far, I'd see that you didn't get the post. Mind I have that fiddle by the end of the week—if I don't, mark my words, I'll have you out of the Under Secretariat as sure as I've got you in. Now go!"

And the unlucky Harold went—miserably, sheepishly.

Every moment that he could spare during the next two days was spent hunting London for a Guarnerius. Every dealer in turn shook his head at him—there was not a perfect Guarnerius for sale anywhere in the trade. At last on the second day he made known his need to an unprincipled old scoundrel well known to all English Fiddlers of that day, who resided not a hundred miles from Wardour St. and whom we will call—Trichebut.

Guillaume Trichebut's evil eyes gloated as he heard Harold's story and finally he said:—

"Eh bien! M. Willoughby, I tink that I can make for you your *affaire*. Dere is one fiddle by de great Joseph Anthony himself of the date 1730—his best period, but alas! he is in de hand of an amateur who does not particularly want to part wid him. Still he may be inclined; you will give him a good price, *Quoi?*"

"But I can't afford a good price, and still I want the fiddle very much. I might go even as high as four or five hundred pounds."

"Faïve hondred—*mais mon cher monsieur*, dat is notings for a fine Joseph. But nevair mind, you shall come back to-morrow morning and I will give you the answer of my amateur."

Accordingly next morning, nine o'clock, saw Harold Willoughby in the dingy shop of Mons. Trichebut.

"Well," said he, "will he sell?"

"Yes,—I have persuade him—he will sell—but *mon Dieu!* dese amateurs, what prices dey want!"

Harold's heart sank within him.

"How much does he want?" asked he.

"Nine hundred—*cher monsieur!*"

"Nine hundred pounds! why, Trichebut, you must be mad—it's unheard of!"

"No, sair, not unheard of—you want this fiddle you most pay for him. Remember Count Trautmannsdorf who paid Stainer 20,000 florins for an instrument. M. Wieniawski bought M. de Beriot's fiddle for 20,000 francs, and *ce fou* Hay of His Majesty's band refused three hundred pounds and an annuity of one hundred pounds a year for a German instrument. I myself bought a Guarnerius for nearly seven hundred pounds five years ago, and fiddles have gone up! You are not asked so terrible a price after all."

"Well, I won't pay it, and there is an end of it."

"Very well, *mon cher* Monsieur Willoughby—as you say there is an end of the *affaire*. I have no interest in it—*c'est a prendre ou a laisser.*"

"Well—bring the fiddle here and keep it till Thursday and I'll give you a definite answer. Who is this amateur?"

"That I cannot tell you. He desires not to be known. You also desired not to be known as de purchasair, I keep both of your confidence."

And with that Harold had to be content. Then there followed two miserable days, during which he visited every money-lender between Regent Street and Bond Street, humiliating himself before greasy Hebrews with covetous leers and dirty finger nails, begging them to oblige him by robbing him as much as they chose in return for nine hundred pounds sterling, paid down in notes.

On the strength of the position of Under Secretary which was as good as his already, and on the security of his apartment full of furniture which represented an expenditure of close on a thousand hardly earned and carefully saved pounds, he succeeded by Friday in raising the money required by Trichebut's unconscionable amateur, and went home to West Kensington carrying with him a Joseph Guarnerius fiddle, which this time he did not leave in the train, for to get it he had left in Cork Street and Sackville Street and Saville Row, blue slips of paper with stamps upon them, binding him to pay during the course of the next six months close upon two thousand five hundred pounds, to Messrs. Shadrach, Meshech, Abednego & Co. and the other members of the lamb-skinning and stone-sweating fraternity.

Mrs. Willoughby on seeing the fiddle, enjoyed the first moment of peace of mind she had known since the preceding Friday. Poor woman! she little knew what a price her boy had paid for the instrument he was to take to his Chief on the morrow.

Saturday morning came, and immediately on his arrival at the office Harold carried the Guarnerius to his Chief's room.

"Here is your violin, sir," said he, "for the loan of which many thanks. I am sorry for the delay in returning it, but I do not think you will find it has suffered by its fortnight's absence."

"All right, all right. Don't say any more about it. Perhaps I was a little hasty about it last Monday, but then I was very much annoyed. However, put it back under the chair where you took it from—no, I don't want to see it. I expect the man who's to buy it in a few minutes, he can look at it as much as he wants, and he considers himself a connoisseur."

"Then this fiddle will be a treat for him, sir, it is, I am told by the repairer of whom I spoke, a matchless instrument."

"Yes?" replied the Chief, interrogatively. "Well, it's all right now about the accident. Here is something that will salve any wounds that my anger may have inflicted upon you."

And Sir Edward Carshalton handed to Harold Willoughby the Royal Commission which appointed him Permanent Under Secretary for Her Majesty's Waste-Paper and Sealing-Wax Department.

III.

So Harold Willoughby deserted the post of Junior Clerk and became Permanent Under Secretary for Her Majesty's Waste-Paper and Sealing-Wax Department. Grey-headed juniors who had striven in vain for the post, turned up their noses, sniffed and shook their heads, muttering the while about social influence, and boys filling men's places, and uttered to one another grave fears that if the country were not to go the dogs, Her Majesty's Commissioners had better reconsider their decision, and make an appointment more suited to the requirements of the office.

The faces of these old curmudgeons, however, grew longer and longer when they saw Harold throw himself into his new work with a steadfast ardour that promised great things for the future, and they began to fear that they were doomed after all to fill unknown and unofficial graves. Their fears would, however, have been in a great measure allayed had they known the nature of the feelings which prompted Harold Willoughby's industry.

Poor Harold! West Kensington knew him no more; for though at rare intervals he went thither to see his mother and Mary Warburton, more often they came to see him, when his day's work was over, in his pretty rooms in Queen Anne's Gate—but neither his mother nor his *fiancée* had pierced the veil that hid the old Harold from them, and both would sometimes watch him in silence whilst he sat looking into vacancy, taciturn and preoccupied. Harold took no pleasure in life; his position had gained for him the coveted *entrée* into society, but he did not avail himself of half the opportunities that were offered him. The pasteboards of invitation accumulated almost unnoticed upon his table, and often when bidden to parties which erstwhile would have caused him weeks of joyful anticipation he would sit alone, moody and moping, in his rooms. The evil days had come when he said—"I have no pleasure in them."

The cause? It was not far to seek. His income satisfied little more than his needs, and that was mortgaged to the hilt; he had no resources on which to draw, and the days grew into weeks and the weeks into months, and the time drew near when he would have to pay, somehow or other, the price of the Fatal Fiddle, two thousand five hundred pounds! His bills ripened and he renewed them, renewed them with a dull horrible consciousness that the added load of debt was far beyond the wildest possibilities of his paying it, but still he renewed them, clinging to his position as the dying man craves the mercy of another minute's life.

Six months after his appointment to the Under-Secretaryship, men began to look askant upon Harold Willoughby—they fought shy of his invitations to dinner, and avoided him as cordially as possible with their friends, for fear of being left alone with him. Harold Willoughby had begun to borrow money. Poor devil—the interest and costs of his debts had to be paid somehow and he was at his wit's end. His chief heard of it and sent for him one day.

"Willoughby," he said, "I'm afraid you're not going on all right. I don't want to seem to pry into your affairs, especially now that you are no longer a junior, but remember it was through my influence that you gained this position, and I am to a certain extent responsible for you. The income of the Secretaryship should be quite enough for your needs. I hope I shan't hear any more stories of your getting into debt on the strength of the position you hold."

Harold had made no attempt at an explanation and soon after this the blow fell in real earnest. The Jews, imagining that he must be strongly backed to have got into the Under-Secretaryship at his age, thought that if they put on the screw they could squeeze their pound of flesh from the unlucky young civilian.

From the remaining fragments of the capital he could lay his hands upon and with the assistance of what he could borrow from his mother, he managed to pay a fair instalment of interest, and by renewing the bills yet more ruinously, he succeeded in postponing the avalanche for a further period of six months, but beyond that, look forward in what directions he would, he could see no light through the clouds that obscured the future he had so anxiously striven for. He lost interest in life, even the smiles and hopeful prognostications of Mary Warburton were powerless to rouse him from his dull settled apathy.

Meanwhile his *train de vie* required fuel, and he had beggared himself. Harold was beginning to get into debt, not only among the obsequious tradesmen who were only too happy to ensnare the young official in the meshes of their seemingly unlimited credit, but among the friends he now met on all sides; the men who ate his dinners, and sought official influence through him.

Sir Edward Carshalton was not misinformed—Harold Willoughby was no longer "all right."

The second period of six months passed by as only such half-years can, and in his despair he made a sort of half confidence to his mother. Poor old lady, save with her sympathy, she was powerless to assist him—the amount of his indebtedness had become enormous.

"Why don't you ask John Baxter to help you, Harold?"

"Never," he had cried energetically. "This humiliation is bad enough, but to confess to that man that he was right and that I was wrong, is more than the last degradation would ever induce me to do."

It was towards the end of his tether of time that Harold sat down one day in Queen Anne's Gate, and miserably considered his position with regard to Mary Warburton.

One fact stared him relentlessly in the face. In a few weeks he would be a pauper, and then—his obvious course was resignation from the Under-Secretaryship. A bankrupt official seemed a contradiction in terms, and even if the position were tenable, he could not face the sneers and whispers of his colleagues and sub-ordinates. But it was strange that he found himself brave enough to do the hardest thing that man can be called upon to do.

He sent for Dick Warburton, explained his position and told him he must give up all hope of marrying his daughter. The ex-captain was terribly concerned.

"Can't we help you, my boy—is the sum so terrific?"

Harold named it.

"Good God! Harold, it's iniquitous. Do you mean to say that this has grown up out of nine hundred pounds? Why it's illegal! We'll carry it into court and protect you from these thieves."

"Alas! Captain Warburton, that is impossible. The nature of the debt, the purpose for which it was incurred, everything makes it impossible for me to parade it before the world. I've in-jured my position, and compromised myself irrevocably, getting money to keep my head above water as long as I have. There's nothing for me now but abject insignificance and concealment of myself for the rest of my life. If I could have made a clean breast of it to Sir Edward at once, it might have done some good, but more probably it would only have ruined me at once, instead of now. I've made my bed, and I must lie upon it."

There was nothing to be done. That evening he went to West Kensington and had an affecting little scene with Mary Warburton, and they parted from one another broken-hearted.

A few weeks later the end came.

The Jews came down upon him in force—the gentle Israelite who held the bill of sale on his rooms in Queen Anne's Gate acted upon it, and his pretty furniture was sold to that Hebrew himself, and the whilome haunt of the "gay" young official be-came the head office of Mr. Lewis Moss's money-lending estab-lishment. The sending in of his resignation became a matter of course—the junior clerks rubbed their hands in glee, and new cabals started into existence for the refilling of the Permanent Under-secretaryship of Her Majesty's Waste-Paper and Sealing-Wax Department. London society was astonished and interested for three days—of course they had all foreseen it from the first—and Harold Willoughby went to hide his diminished head with his mother in the old home in West Kensington.

And that was all.

⁕

The new order of things had existed for a few days only, when one evening John Baxter came in to see them, and remained closeted with Harold for a couple of hours.

What was the nature of their deliberations not even Mrs. Willoughby knew. At their close, when John Baxter had left, Harold broke out with a eulogy of his brother-in-law which startled his mother as much as it delighted her.

"That man," concluded he, "is of the salt of the earth. If I had taken your advice, mother, and gone to him at once, I should still be in my office in Whitehall. Even now he has saved my life."

It was true. Many times Harold had been within a few seconds of killing himself, and he had only stayed his hand for the sake of his mother and sister, and Mary.

"What are you going to do?" queried Mrs. Willoughby.

"John Baxter has offered to make the superintendent of his house of business on Finsbury Pavement. I shall live there, and be a sort of care-taker on the premises, and during that day I am to give him what help I can in the business—I shall be half secretary, half shop-walker, and what is most important, I shall be hidden, out there in the city, from the world—from the society I loved so much when I knew nothing about it, and which I found such a cold, hollow mockery when I entered it. He will give me a salary as well as a home and a hiding place, and in time I may be able to forget my humiliation and pay off the debts of honour I owe the friends who have helped me to postpone these dark days till now."

Their further conversation was cut short by the entrance of Mary Warburton.

"Harold," she said, "I know it all now—"

"What! Your father has dared—?"

"No, dear, John Baxter has been to see me, and he has told me everything."

"Everything?"

"Yes, Harold, everything."

"Well?"

"Dear, don't think me overbold or unmaidenly. If what I ask you is wrong, put it down to my love for you—our love for one another. May—may I come to Finsbury Pavement with you?"

"My darling," and he folded the girl in his arms.

"Does your father know of this?"

"Yes, and he believes in you, my own boy, and he gives me to you to help you in your new life."

IV.

Twenty-five years have passed since the spruce young Under Secretary handed in his papers and resigned his position in Whitehall when my story reopens.

A quarter of a century! And what changes may take place in such a space. In the lives of our actors the only changes have been such as time works quietly in all our schemes of existence.

John Baxter was a hale old fellow of close upon sixty, his wife was his junior by a decade, and her two boys were already "in the business" which they proposed to carry on, instead of going into the liberal professions, and society. This was the effect of "Uncle Harold's" advice.

Uncle Harold—what of him. Well, his has not been such a bad life after all. The bitterness of his expatriation in the far eastern city was sweetened by the loving care of his wife—from care-taker and shop-superintendent he had gradually risen in the business and became a partner, a new care-taker had been found, and Harold and his wife had come back again to West Kensington, which had by this time become almost the heart of London. Here he lived happily and quietly with Mary, who in the sweet womanhood of her forty-three years was still to him what she had been at eighteen. Mrs. Willoughby had died—but not before she had proclaimed herself the grand-mother of five children, of whom two boys were the proud possession of Grace Baxter, and the other three, two girls and a boy, had been born to Harold.

The first twelve years after his marriage had been a hard struggle. Weighed down by the load of private debt he had incurred to pay up the interests and costs incidental to the transaction of the Fatal Fiddle, he had toiled and slaved, in and out of business hours, till at last every penny was paid off. It was not till the end of these twelve years that the last of his creditors was astonished at receiving the amount he had lent Harold Willoughby all that time before; and during the whole of those twelve years, Mary had encouraged him and never complained of their condition in Finsbury Pavement—for he continued to live there on economical grounds till his last creditor was paid. It was not till then that he returned to West Kensington, and established himself near his brother-in-law in one of the larger houses nearer to the Addison road, houses with gardens behind them and iron railings separating them from the road.

One peculiarity, however, he had preserved for all these twenty-five years. Since the day he left Her Majesty's Waste-Paper and Sealing-Wax Office, he had never been down Whitehall again—he would make any *détour* to avoid it, he had a horror of the scene of his old humiliation—for, prosperous merchant as he was, and highly respected as a partner in Baxter & Co.'s house on Finsbury Pavement, the old wound had never quite closed up.

Time, however, the gentle and imperceptible healer, kept quietly at work, and one morning Harold Willoughby said to his wife,

"Mary dear—I've made up my mind at last to go back and have a look at the old place—I shall leave the city early this afternoon and go down Whitehall, and see what the office looks like after a quarter of a century—it's twenty-five years to-day since I saw it last."

And Mary was glad, for she knew that the old sore had ceased at last to hurt her husband.

That afternoon Harold Willoughby stood in front of the office of H.M.'s W.P. & S.W. Department, and looked at its façade long and searchingly till the gorgeous grenadier mounting sentry for the guard of Her Majesty's Stationery, began to wonder whether he were not an anarchist, a nihilist, or an Irish-American. The sentry was about to question him, when a smart brougham drew up—the soldier presented arms, and "The Chief," an aristocratic looking old gentleman, every inch a diplomat, the Right Honourable the Earl of Carshalton, K. C. B., K. C. M. G., got out and prepared to mount the steps. Harold recognized in the senile peer of the realm, his old executioner, Sir Edward Carshalton, and automatically lifted his hat before he knew what he was doing.

Lord Carshalton had one foible on which he prided himself, and that was affability to his inferiors despite his exalted rank, and instead of entering the office at once, turned, touched his hat, and said,

"G'mornin'."

"Good day, my lord," returned Harold, "I am surprised that your lordship should recognize me, it is so long since we met."

"Recognize you! Why, of course I do. I never forget a face—though, by-the-bye, I fear you will think me very rude for—for the life of me I can't remember your name at this moment."

"Don't you remember Willoughby, my lord, Harold Willoughby, for a year Permanent Under Secretary for this department?"

"God bless my soul! is it really Willoughby?" exclaimed his lordship, drawing up, annoyed with himself to think that his affability had betrayed him into conversing on the office steps with a man who had notoriously gone to the devil, though it was a quarter of a century since his netherward progression.

"I didn't recognize you, 'pon my soul. Well, I can't stop—" and he was just turning away, when his curiosity overcame his exclusiveness, and seeing that Harold was well dressed, and apparently quite unrecognizable, he asked him to step in with him for a moment.

"Now, Mr. Willoughby," said he, when they had seated themselves in the Permanent Chief Secretary's private office, "I should really much obliged if you would tell me how it was you came to grief so suddenly. I see you have recovered from you fall or I shouldn't ask it of you. But this is a question that has often recurred to my mind since you left us under circumstances that it is not necessary to recall. You were quiet, steady, and so careful—such a sno—ahem! such a society man—it was strange that you should go under so suddenly."

"Good God! did it never occur to you, my lord, that you might have had something to do with that fall of mine?"

"Mr. Willoughby! really, my dear sir, you can hardly know what you are saying!"

"But I do know what I am saying, my lord. You remember that Guarnerius violin that you lent me to play upon at Lady George Wilmington's reception? You remember there was some delay in my returning it? I told you it had been damaged. It was a lie. I told it for fear you would withdraw your support from my candidature. I *lost* that violin. I could not trace it, and dared not advertise for it, and I had to buy you another. At that time there was not a Guarnerius in the market, and I had to get one from an amateur through Trichebut, the dealer. They knew I must have it, and between them they made me pay nine hundred pounds. I had to get the money from the Jews. The load of debt that it saddled me with in renewals, interest, and costs, beside my private debts (for it robbed me of every penny of my ready money), dragged me down, down, down, till the end came, as you know. Had it not been for a brother-in-law into whose house of business I went in the city, I should have sunk I know not where. Now you know the story of Harold Willoughby's resignation. What do you think of it?"

"What do I think of—ah! help me!" and the old peer fell forward upon his table.

Harold summoned assistance, and when the chief recovered consciousness was about to take his leave, when Lord Carshalton motioning him to stay, collected himself as best he could, and in disjointed sentences spoke as follows,

"Willoughby! what a tale is this you have told me—what a tragedy! what a tragedy! Forgive me, if you can, my boy, when you have heard it all. I am an old man at the close of a successful official career, but on my soul, I would give up many of these past years of my life to have heard your story twenty-five years ago. Why did you not make a clean breast of it then? Listen—and do not speak till I have done.

"I used always to laugh at your pretensions to connoisseurship in violins, which I knew was no better than mine, and I told you that that instrument was a Guarnerius just to see if you would know the difference. *It was nothing of the kind!* only a clever imitation made by old Trichebut himself, and worth at the outside a five-pound note. Still, you were pleased with it, and I let you take it. When you told me it was damaged I was very angry, because I had a purchaser for it, so I did not undeceive you. The violin you brought back in its place, I sold half an hour afterwards, for seven pounds—but, my God! that is not the worst of it. Listen!

"Trichebut had come to me and told me that a young fool wanted to give any amount for a real Guarnerius—I had one at home at the time—and I let him have it for seven hundred pounds—that—*that* was the violin you brought back to me, and that I sold for seven pounds. How can I forgive myself—what a tragedy—what a tragedy!"

The two men sat looking at one another speechless—the ruined official, and the successful one. Harold could not trust himself to speak, but took his hat and left the office without a word.

That evening he told the whole story to the Baxters and to his wife. Whilst they all sat in silent horror at the conclusion of his story, Mary Willoughby came to his side, and putting her arms round her husband's neck, said to him,

"Harold, dear—has it not perhaps been all for the best? our trials have been sore, but their end is sweet. Without them, who knows how the world would have turned out for us? Let us thank John again, for all he has been to us."

The two men shook hands in silence:—and the silence was only broken by a kiss that made them turn round. The kiss had been given by their boy Dick Willoughby and it had been received by his cousin, Mary Baxter.

And to cover the confusion of the two young lovers who stood confesed in a corner of the drawing-room, Harold's wife quoted:

> "I hold it truth with him who sings
>   To one clear harp in divers tones,
>   That men may rise on stepping stones
> Of their dead selves to higher things."

The Willoughbys and the Baxters are old people now—and whilst they sit in their homes in West Kensington they watch for the Indian Mail that brings them news of Dick Willoughby and his wife, Grace's daughter.

Dick Willoughby is a rising young Indian civilian with brilliant prospects before him. The Right Honourable the Earl of Carshalton G. C. M. G. is dead, but he lived long enough to see his nominee, Richard Harold Willoughby start for the Empire in search of fame in the service of his Government.

It was his father, my friend, Harold Willoughby, who asked me to write the story of the Fatal Fiddle.

186

THE LUTE GIRL'S CHARM.

I.

THE story which follows came to me in a somewhat round-about way, but it is not on that account less accurate in its details than it would have been had it come to me at first hand.

On the death of Sir Clarivaux Faunt, Ffolliott Grange became the property of the Ffolliotts who were descendants of the old stock through a maternal branch of the family. The succession of Sir Clarivaux to the baronetcy eventuated much in the way that the Braybrooke title descended to Sir Gervase Braybrooke. Gervase Braybrooke's sister Constance married Robert Ffolliott of Ffolliott Grange, and perhaps one of the best friends she ever had was Sir William Cornell, Kt, one of Her Majesty's Judges of Appeal. Sir William and Sylvester Gray were dining one evening with me, soon after Sylvester's return from the East. He had been telling us of some of his adventures in the Orient, when Sir William remarked,

"All that you say Mr. Gray has a great interest for me, for one of the strangest stories I ever heard was told me, in con-nection with the places you have been telling us about, by Mrs. Ffolliott."

"Do you mean the story of the Faunt opal?" queried Sylvester.

"Yes—you know it?"

"But imperfectly. Eric Trevanion was speaking of it a few nights ago, I had some idea of writing it up as a romance. I should like to hear the reality of it."

"And I should be glad to hear it also," said I, "especially as I seem to be becoming the historiographer of this circle of people, all so strangely connected with one another."

And Sir William Cornell told us the following history which is handed down from generation to generation at Ffolliott Grange in perfect reverence and implicit faith.

The modern oriental traveller thinks that he visits a new civilization or an old barbarism, when he treads the precipitous and dog-infested streets of what Théophile Gautier called "The Constantinople of To-day." He fancies himself to be in a new, almost an unknown world, and when he has "done," tourist-wise, the Mosque of Muhammad,—the Arsenal at Tophane and the Mosque of Agha Sofia, he regards himself almost in the light of an explorer. If this be the case, how much more adventurous must the traveller have deemed himself to be in the first decennium of the present century, before the reforms of Mahmoud the Second had filled the Bezesten with spruce young Turks in immaculate broad-cloth, pointed patent-leather boots, and the neat tarboush called by the occidental misnomer of "fez;" before the turban, and kaftan and baggy pantaloons had been banished to the darkest corners of the bazaar and the provinces; before the Orient Express had begun to connect the east and west by three days of comfortable railway travelling, when it took more than a month to reach Istamboul, and when the cry "giaour," from the throat of a Constantinopolitan urchin, could make the traveller's life worth less than a moment's purchase?

It is with that period of Ottoman history that my story deals. Young men of good family making "the Grand Tour" with their tutors seldom sought the dominions of the unspeakable Turk, and Asia Minor was practically unknown. The trade with Mosoul and Baghdad and Trebizond, in silks and damascene work and precious stones was in its infancy as far as Europe was concerned, and Ispahan and Teheran occupied the position in traveller's minds which is now yielded to Timbuctoo, Thibet and the cities of the Western Chinese Empire.

Emigration to the United States, that Eldorado of the *mauvais sujet*, and of the younger son, was popular, and even then, in the minds of many, overdone. A few adventurous spirits, and a few victims of the laws relating to entailed estates, were consequently beginning to turn their faces toward the rising, instead of toward the setting sun; were beginning to scan the Oriental horizon for roads to wealth, athwart those almost fabulous longitudes where civilization was frenetically over-developed in centuries when the sites of Paris and London were occupied by the elk and the anthropoid ape, if not by the mammoth and the pterodactyl.

Among the pioneers of the new movement let me introduce my hero, Clarivaux Faunt, the third and youngest son of Sir Lionel Faunt, Baronet, of Ffolliott Grange, Devonshire, one of the most exquisite old Tudor mansions in the South of England. There are no Faunts of the old line now, the place is owned by the Ffolliotts, a maternal branch of the old stock, and save in the picture gallery at Ffolliott the Faunts have left no trace behind them.

That Clarivaux Faunt would ever inherit the estates was beyond the bounds of probability. Ffolliott was strictly entailed, and he was the youngest of the three Faunt boys; the eldest, Lionel, would inherit the place, and in the event of his death without heirs, then Philip his second brother. There was nothing for Clarivaux to do but to seek some sphere in which his usefulness and energies might lead to independent fortune, and he turned a wistful gaze toward the East, whence travellers brought stories of silken and golden embroideries, of sapphires and emeralds and turquoise picked up by the bushel along the muddy banks of the Tigris and Euphrates, of illimitable fortunes to be had for the asking in the territories which had shivered beneath the frown of forgotten Khalifs of Baghdad.

So Clarivaux Faunt found himself costumed—almost disguised—*en Turc*, in the streets of Constantinople, buying camels and hiring men, concealing the amount of his worldly possessions, and learning the language in the crowded streets of the Great Bazaar.

The Fast of Ramadzan was drawing to its weary close; in a week or so the world of Islam would rouse itself from its morbid and fanatical immobility, to run wild in the festival of Bairam. The true believer, for a month past, had gone about his work in silence, neither eating nor drinking, never smiling and scarcely speaking, between sunrise and sunset. For a month past the cry of the Muezzin from the minarets of the mosques of Istamboul had silenced the world at sunrise and permitted it to sustain life but no more, at sunset. During the month of Ramadzan the Turk becomes irritable, revengeful, fanatic; and at the time that I chronicle the Frankish population kept within doors—woe be to the giaour who should expose himself during those weeks to the religious frenzy of the mob.

But in a week all would be changed—illumination and feasting would take the place of darkness and semi-starvation; the Ottoman world would wake to excesses that would bring the blush to the cheek of a later Roman Emperor.

At midday beneath the full glare of the Orient sun the Sultan's mother, the Sultana Walide would come down the steps of Agha Sofia to meet her son, and there before the assembled Osmanlis would present to him a beautiful virgin slave, the most beautiful that had been brought to Istamboul during the year; for whom, during the year, the villages of Circassia, or Georgia, of Cappadocia, and Ararat, famed for the beauty of their women, had been searched by the slave-dealers. The crowning ceremony of the Festival of Bairam would be solemnized in the presence of the Court, the Ottoman world and the High-priest—the Sheik-ul Islam.

Clarivaux Faunt wandered at nightfall amid the tortuous alleys of the Bezesten, and presently—hardly conscious of the direction his footsteps had taken—emerged into the slave-market.

To the musical ear the Bezesten at Samboul is an unwearying delight; the prevailing impression that it gives one, is that of a filled silence. The archings of the roof seem to overwhelm the multitude of life-sounds and blend them together into a wonderful mystic *susurrus*, and in the month of Ramadzan this effect is all the more accentuated by reason of the gloomy spell that appears to have fallen upon the world. It was therefore with a stronger significance that, as Clarivaux Faunt entered the slave-market, a weird, strange, barbaric chaunt struck his ear. Seated amid a group of slaves awaiting purchasers among the Osmanlis released from the arduous hours of the fast, a young Georgian girl plucked the strings of her lute as she crooned some melody of her far eastern home.

Faunt paused, spellbound, mesmerized by the sound of the weird, barbaric chaunt of the girl that seemed to seek his soul amid the silence of the place, and kill the murmurs of the Bazesten, as a strange, faint, Oriental perfume will drown the stronger but less individual odors in a perfumery. The singer was short of stature as the Georgian women are, her deep red-brown hair—rare colouring for an eastern woman—retained only by the fastenings of the *yashmak* or veil, that she had thrown aside, hung in a tawny mass down her back and floated in confusion over the cushions against which she leaned. Her big black eyes stared straight before her into the gathering dusk as she continued her chaunt, and her little perfectly arched mouth hardly stirred to release the melody that escaped into the twilight. The *yashmak* had been laid aside and revealed the beautiful lines of her body clad in a golden gauze *feredje* from beneath which her little bare feet, thrust into brocaded slippers, drew forth a tiny space of the loose silk trousers that complete the national costume. Around her, seated on rugs or reclining against cushions, a dozen other slaves posed in unconscious artistic attitudes, and listened to the Gerogian's song.

And, as she sang, her wild instinct told her of the master-gaze that was bent upon her, and turning her head her eyes plunged into those of Clarivaux Faunt.

Then stopped the music and her lute sank upon her knee. The other slaves raised their heads to discover the cause of the interruption whilst the slave-merchant and the *kizlar-agha*, the black eunuch-guard, "sent to sleep with sound and waked with silence," roused themselves upon their respective rugs, to catch the hurried gestures of the girls who, following an Ottoman woman's first instinct, had hurriedly drawn their *yashmaks* across their faces, all excepting the young Georgian who sat spellbound and steeped in the heinous sin of gazing with uncovered face upon the handsome giaour.

Following the direction of her eyes, the merchant and the eunuch caught sight of Clarivaux as he too stood transfixed by the witchery of the slave-girl's gaze, and springing to their feet the merchants raised the fatal cry—"Giaour!" whilst the ebon eunuch dived among the cushions from which he had risen, for his damascened firelock. It did not require more than an instant's flash of thought to tell Faunt of his danger, and, plunging through the curtains that divided the slave, from the slipper-market, he reached the main *allée* of the Bezesten and mingled with the crowd where, costumed, as he was, his individuality was lost.

The sense of the danger he had escaped, the necessity for increased caution in reaching his *mehana*—the inn where he lodged, and in which, being held by an Armenian, his person was safe—were all forgotten under the spell of the gaze that had sunk from the Georgian's eyes into his soul; and as he traversed the yet comparatively deserted alleys of Stamboul, his brain was filled with a dull, reverberating echo, the echo of the weird barbaric chaunt that he had interrupted.

"What a fool I am," soliloquized the young Englishman as he flung himself upon a divan and watched his servant going through the complicated operation of preparing his *narghile*, "what a fool I am. I must put my mental foot firmly down upon this absurd obsession. Bah! to let myself be absorbed like this by the thought of a girl who is little more than a beautiful wild animal at best—ignorant, probably brutal; come Clarivaux, my boy, get rid of her image; you must think no more about it—or her. What a strange melody that was!"

But the resolution was easier to form than to keep. Throughout the night he tossed sleeplessly among his rugs, falling momentarily asleep, ever and anon, only to start once more into vivid wakefulness, as the weird barbaric chaunt seemed to fill the very room in which he slept—to rub his eyes and persuade himself that he

192

was really alone, and that the image of the young Georgian that he saw before him was but a figment of his excited brain.

The leaden footsteps of night died away amid the grey shadows of approaching dawn, and as Clarivaux lay staring at the ceiling, the muezzin cried aloud that "Allah was Allah, and that Muhammad was his prophet" to greet the arisen day and plunge the Osman world once more into the gloom of Ramadzan until nightfall.

Throughout the day, as throughout the night, Clarivaux Faunt wrestled in spirit with himself; do what he would he could not chase the beautiful Georgian's image from his mind—in a phrase, he was madly in love. Could he marry the slave-girl? Hardly, in her present state of Oriental ignorance—but surely with eyes like that and such a voice she might be educated to become an ornament to any man's household; why not? Yes, his resolution was formed; he would buy this beautiful slave. If he could agree as to price with the slave-merchant, he was assured the latter would overlook the fact of his being a giaour, an infidel! The commercial spirit is the same all the world over. He would commence her education himself; he would have it completed when he had made his fortune and returned to the old country, she should be the glory of his life. Ha! ha! what a Quixotic notion—how supremely absurd! But this aspect of the case did not present itself to him. His one thought was to re-seek the slave-market and negotiate with the Caucasian merchant for the purchase of the houri of his dreams.

His preparations made, and

> As under cover of departing day
> Slunk hunger-stricken Ramadzan away,

he sought once more the corner of the Great Bazaar, where, twenty-four hours before, his wandering footsteps had been arrested by the weird, barbaric chaunt of the beautiful Georgian.

To open his business with the merchant, beneath the cloak of concealment of his faith, was like all business transactions in the East a matter of considerable time, and one requiring the exercise of a vast amount of patience. At last with the help of much *chibouk*, and more Osmanli circumlocution, the merchant came to terms.

"Certainly, *Insha'allah!*" He would sell to his Beyship the Frankish child the prophet. He even went so far as to express a hope that wild jackasses might never so far forget themselves as to bray over the hitherto undefiled grave of Clarivaux Faunt's maternal great grand-uncle.

With the expression of good will, the merchant exposed his wares, descanting with Oriental imagery on their charms and accomplishments. But Faunt turned a deaf ear to his eulogies—the Georgian was not among them. In vain, trying to conceal the fact that his had been the sacrilegious eyes that had looked upon the group the night before, Clarivaux endeavoured to describe the girl he sought. At last the merchant said:

"May the beard of your great-aunt's youngest son never be laughed at by the dogs of Stamboul. From among the pearls that be here before my Bey's eyes, my Bey must make his choice— may Allah's goodwill be upon it. Yesterday a houri such as my Bey describes filled my house with brightness and music; but to-day the *kislar-agha* of her sublimity the Sultana Walide—Allah upon her!—robbed me of this jewel to gladden the eyes of the son of God, his transcendency the Sultan—Allah upon him!—at the Feast of Bairam. My house was unworthy of the honour but my Bey is too late. *Insha' allah.*"

Too late! Making what excuses he could to the Osmanli who received them with true Oriental impassability, Clarivaux Faut, sick at heart, made the *temâm* salutation, and turned to leave the slave-market. He had hardly proceeded a dozen steps before the cry "Giaour" was raised behind him, and it was only by an elaborate combination of dodgings and doublings that he reached his *mehana* with his life, to be alone with his agony of grief. The Georgian was condemned to be immured in the *seraglio*—she was lost to him for ever.

II.

Clarivaux Faunt gave himself over to despair, for he could not hope to see the mistress of his soul again. She had been separated from the other slaves as befitted one upon whom so high an honour had fallen, and was now carefully guarded in the merchant's private *seraglio*, and where that might be he knew not, nor had he any means of ascertaining. Stay! he might see her at the great ceremony of Bairam by mingling with the crowd—but only to see her handed over to the Commander of the Faithful, and condemned to an imprisonment that would be worse than death, in the Imperial Harem. Could he bear such a torture? No; he would leave Stamboul before the feast day. But oh! to see her once more, to hear that divine voice again!

In his misery he confided his sorrow to a young attaché of the French Embassy, and this young gentleman who for some years had aired his dapper person in the city of the Golden Horn, gave him a gleam of hope, though the gleam was faint indeed.

Then, as now, a custom existed in the Imperial Harem which was and is as follows: If for the space of four years from her entry into the *seraglio*, an odalisque conducts herself in such a manner as to merit the esteem of the Sultan, at the expiration of that time she is at liberty, if she so pleases, to leave its walls and choose for herself a husband from among the pachas, and beys, and effendis of his Majesty's household, who are generally only too willing to marry thus at second-hand, by reason of the more or less intimate knowledge of the Sultan's household that the ladies of the harem may be supposed to acquire during their sojourn in the Imperial Seraglio, a knowledge that is of great practical value for the furtherance of the schemes and plots by which the Commander of the Faithful is continually surrounded. Therefore, after four years, the idol of Clarivaux's heart might be released. But how should he find her then? He had never spoken with her—how could he convey to her the knowledge that he was willing, anxious to await her emancipation and carry her off to his home in Baghdad? The *fête* of Bairam grew close at hand, and Clarivaux Faunt wandered the streets of the City of the Crescent, his mind filled with one absorbing thought—how to find her. He had striven in vain to discover the whereabouts of the slave-merchant's *cachette*.

But forty-eight hours remained to elapse before the feast-day, and Faunt, wrapped in the mantle that formed part of his Oriental costume, braved the dangers of the lower parts of Galata, in pursuit of his untiring quest. Far away across the Golden Horn and the Bosphorus the lights of Scutari and Stamboul proper seemed to mock him, and he was on the point of giving up the search when suddenly from the far side of a white wall that concealed he knew not what, there reached his ears the lilt of a weird barbaric chaunt.

It was she!

The street happened at that moment to be deserted, save that the squalid population of mangy curs held their uninterrupted carnival in the dusty roadway. To leap for the coping of the wall and get a hold whereby he could raise himself to the broad top was the work of a single instant, and peering down into the gloom, he distinguished the form of the girl sitting alone upon a rug beneath a palm-firm, the music of her lute arrested by the slight noise that he had made in his escalade, which had drawn her great eyes in his direction.

With a rapid gesture he silenced her exclamation and arrested her movement of terror.

"*Ghiwzellim*, my sweet!" he cried, scarce above a whisper. "It is I—the Frank—do not fear. *Ehvw'allah!* God be praised, I have found thee."

She had recognized him, and coming close beneath the wall, she answered him.

"*Ya, Beyim*—oh, my master, is it indeed you?"

"Yes, yes, I have come to save thee. Oh, that the time were longer! Let us escape. Tell me how thou canst leave this place, that I may come for thee, that we may fly from hence—together."

"Oh, my master," answered the girl in her corrupt Caucasian Turkish, "it may not be—it is too late. Even now I await the footsteps of the slave-master. It is too late; but oh, how good to see thee again—how I have waited for thee!"

"Thy name?"

"Nouronihar, and my master's slave. Nay, descend not, thou art in deadly peril. Should they find thee thou art worse than dead—the torture—the bow-string. Ah, but I am not worthy."

"Fly quickly with me now, my sweet."

"I cannot, the house is guarded; even now I hear footsteps. Oh, save thyself!"

"Nay, unless thou wilt tell me thou shalt be mine; I will wait these weary years for thee."

"With the morrow's dawn I journey to the rising sun. In Mosoul or in Baghdad thou shall find me—nay! I will come myself to bring thee thither. Here take this, and wherever I may be, give it me, and I will redeem my pledge, Nouronihar *ghiuzellim*."

As he spoke, with feverish hands he had sought beneath his kaftan and found a jewel that he wore suspended by a chain about his neck—a family jewel, a charm that had never left him since his mother had placed it there in bygone years; a great opal set round and framed in emeralds. He dropped it into her outstretched palm, saying:

"Bear it with thee till we meet again. Hark, what is that?"

"The guard, the guard! the master comes with the *kislar agha* of the Seraglio. Oh, my lord, they will kill thee!"

"Nay be not afraid, little one," and so saying he flattened himself along the top of the wall. As he drew up his booted legs, the noise attracted a couple of the dogs who had come to the foot of the wall, disturbed by the unwonted murmur of their voices. At the movement they commenced to bark furiously. The slave merchant and his escort passing at the moment halted at the sound, and a great, black slave came to the wall and looked up.

Clarivaux did not stir, hidden by the darkness and by the leaves of a tree-fern that overshadowed him. The slave was about to return, reassured, when as an after thought, and to make more certain, he drew his *kilidj*, or long sword, and struck at the fern canopy. The blow was stopped by the coping, else it had severed Clarivaux's leg. As it was it reached his boot, and cutting through the leather inflicted a gash upon the living flesh. Grinding his teeth and clutching the stone coping, the poor wretch restrained a shriek of agony, and, apparently satisfied, the slave withdrew.

The wounded man raised his head; the party had passed on and were already knocking at the gate; but a servant had remained watching the suspicious movements of the dogs. As Faunt stirred, he raised the old, terrible cry, "Giaour!"

Discovered! Without hesitation he dropped into the garden beside the girl who was almost inanimate from terror. The merchant was entering the house.

"Whither can I flee—where is another road?" he whispered.

"There—there—on the other side. Oh, fly, my lord!" He bent and imprinted an impassioned kiss of pent-up longing on her lips. Then making at full speed across the garden, he gained the opposite wall, scaled it, dropped into the road, and fled in the darkness of the night.

His boot was filled with blood, though, fortunately, the wound was not deep. He reached his lodging in Stamboul; bathed his wound, and next morning before dawn he had crossed the Bosphorus and at the head of his caravan made for the valley of the Tigris.

Meanwhile amid the blare of horns, and the thunder of the drums, beneath a sun that baked the mobs assembled, the Sultana Walide came down the steps of Agha Sofia to meet her son, and there, before the gathered Osmanlis, presented him with a beautiful virgin-slave—the most beautiful that had been brought to Stamboul during the year—Nouronihar!

III.

In four years what changes may take place; civilizations are developed or extinguished, nature herself alters her features so far as often to become unrecognizable. How much more then the ever-changing unstable heart of man! To be faithful to an ideal is woman's prerogative, and to her ideal, won and lost in a few minutes of time, was Nouronihar the Georgian odalisque sublimely constant during the four years that she lay on the rugs of the

Imperial Seraglio: surrounded by her companions of the harem and alone with her thoughts of the handsome Frankish lover to whom she had plighted her troth in the slave-dealer's garden on the last night of the Ramadzan—so long—so long ago.

From the latticed windows and screened terraces of the Seraglio she gazed wistfully out over the Golden Horn and watched the *kaiques*, infinitesimal in the distance, flying to and fro across the turquoise water, or peered after the merchantmen as they spread their sails and dropped over the horizon beyond the mouth of the distant Bosphorus, and wondered vaguely whether their sails were set for Iskenderoon or Trebizond, and whether any among the busy sailors were bound for the cross country routes to Mosoul and Baghdad,—were going to see her love in the far East; and oft times the Commander of Islam himself, as he lounged among the houris of the place, would let his eyes rest on the beautiful Georgian, and rouse himself from his imperial impassibility to ask whether her thoughts were far away with some half-forgotten boy across the Caucasus, or whether like the rest of his odalisques she were but an unconscious chattel, existing only to satisfy the passing caprices of his sluggish mind.

No, Nouronihar had never forgotten, and constant to her love, as she lay upon the silken rugs from Ispahan, to listen to the crooning of the Nubian slaves of the harem, her hand would steal beneath the folds of the *feredje* to seek the charm that lay against her heart,—an opal, set round and framed of emeralds,—and then echoed back the burning words that rang ever in her ears when life seemed emptiest of hope: "Wherever I may be, give it me and I will redeem my pledge, Nouronihar *ghiuzellim*; bear it with thee till we meet again."

And now four years had lived and died, with little or nothing to mark their births and deaths, and the time approached when the Georgian would be free to leave the Seraglio should she so desire. Would her Frankish god be in Stamboul as he had said, to bear her thence?

"Where wilt thou go?" they said to her, and she answered, turning her eyes to the rising sun:

"Yonder."

And so she left the harem, friendless and alone, but glorious still in the developed beauty of her twenty years. Clarivaux Faunt had made no sign. He was not in Stamboul. Well, she would go to him. "Wherever I may be, give it me," he had said. She would find him, even though her life should be claimed by Allah as the penalty of her fidelity.

Her resolution was formed. Aided by an Armenian woman in whose house she had taken refuge on leaving the Seraglio, she equipped herself to perform the journey in the company of a band of Armenian traders who were leaving Stamboul for Mosoul—from Mosoul, if he were not there, she would make her way alone to Baghdad—and so, just as Clarivaux had left Stamboul four years before, Nouronihar set out for the valley of the Tigris.

Slowly and amid a thousand perils the caravan crossed the *vilayets* of Asia Minor, past Angorah and Yuzghat, by way of Diarbekr to Mosoul where the caravan halted to disperse after its six months' march, in a khan outside the city, on the site of Nineveh, that was at that time but beginning to attract the attention of European explorers and scholars.

Had the Frankish merchant been heard of there? No, if Clarivaux has sojourned in Mosoul he had left no trace behind, and Nouronihar, garbed as a wandering lute-girl, accompanied only by a couple of peripatetic *fakirs* commenced the hardest part of her journey—along the banks of the yellow, thundering Tigris—playing her lute from town to town and earning a lute-girls' scant means of existence, enduring the contempt and hard-ships of her trade with a fortitude that put the *fakirs* themselves to shame—and all her love.

So journeyed Nouronihar, and something more than a year since the gates of the palace at Seraglio Point had closed upon her, she arrived, weary and alone in the capital of the Khalifs.

IV.

Baghdad! What dreams the name evokes—what visions of departed glory are conjured up by the word! Built of white marbles and red porphyries on the Tigris where the Euphrates flows nearest to it, Baghdad to-day strikes the traveller as a spot where time has stood still. We are still in the early centuries, and the touch of the European has been powerless to mar its almost prehistoric beauties.

High upon a bluff that shelters the left bank of the river from the desert winds of Persia, stood a house, fashioned like others of the city, out of huge square blocks of quarried stone. Surrounded by a great garden where cactus and tropical ferns broke the force of the blazing eastern sun, it was bounded along the river's edge by a low stone parapet, where lizards basked in the noonday heat, icy cold even in that torrid atmosphere, and here and there beneath the palms were strewn rugs of rare Persian and Arabian embroideries. Evidently the home of some wealthy merchant of the place, a retreat where the Effendi might rest undisturbed by the travails of the outer world.

It was afternoon, and already the sun was beating upon the garden from the west. On the flat roof of the house two or three women lounged, drugged with the lethargy of the hour, beneath a canopy of woven silk; one alone seemed wakeful, and with a golden lizard fastened in a harness of silk threads, amused herself teasing a white angora cat, who blinked her green eyes doubtful whether to close them and relapse into contemplative unconsciousness, or dive with one paw for the wriggling thing that ran so temptingly within reach.

Below in the garden, sheltered by a huge tree-fern, as he lay upon his rugs, puffing lazily at the flexile stem of his *narghile*, lounged Clarivaux Faunt, the merchant. Clarivaux had prospered; he was one of the richest merchants in Baghdad. He had adopted the Turkish habit of life; he had also grown fat. During these five years his life had been full, and he had never bestowed another thought on Nouronihar. If he had, it would have been only to smile at the impetuous folly of his youth, and recall the incident as one of a long series of queer oriental experiences.

He was, essentially, a man.

He lay, revolving lazily in his mind the schemes that filled his life at the moment, the embroideries that had arrived from Hamadan, the turquoises *en route* from Ispahan, the silks from Aleppo, and the wrought silver and gold from Damascus to be shipped to Basrah, the ancient Bussorah, on the Persian gulf, to be consigned thence to Europe and to India; and as he lay a faint sound reached his ear from beyond the cactus hedge, the lilt of a weird barbaric chaunt.

Nothing in the melody struck him as being in any way familiar to his senses.

"Ah, a lute-girl! she will amuse me, *ghel!*" he clapped his hands and a servant appeared. "Summon me the lute-girl that sings beyond the gate," said he, and he sank back again upon his rugs as Nouronihar entered the garden. He cast upon her a rapid look in which there was no recognition, and motioning her to sit upon a smaller rug at some distance from his own, he ejaculated:

"Sing!"

And Nouronihar, seating herself, gazed before her at the man whose image had never left her heart, and—who did not know her again. Faunt repeated his mandate—this time somewhat sharply, and Nouronihar her great fearless eyes fixed on his that did not look at her, commenced. It was the weird barbaric chaunt that had arrested his footsteps in the Bezesten, and by which he had found her in the obscure alley in lower Galata.

This time something in the melody struck him as familiar; it was very distinctive; where had he heard it before? The thoughts that it evoked were not pleasant ones, as the girl's voice, rendered somewhat thin and weary by her year of hardship, rose and fell in the cadences of the chaunt. No, he could not fix it. Well, never mind! it was an irritating, stupid tune after all. He would have no more of it.

"Stop!" he ordered peremptorily. And as the girl became suddenly mute in the middle of a strophe, he closed his eyes and seemed to have forgotten her. A minute later he opened them, and saw her sitting in the same humble posture and his eyes met hers. He could not help seeing the mute agony of that appealing look, and it annoyed him.

"Tell me a story," said he, "I would fain sleep; and when thou art finished, wake me not, but take an hundred piastres from my servant—and go."

He closed his eyes once more, and after a moment's stifled pause, she began. She told a story of a Georgian maid enticed from her home in the Caucasus by the glittering tales of the slave-merchant—of her journey to Stamboul; of the nights waiting in the Bazaar. Of the eyes of a Frankish Bey which had rested on her, and reft her soul from her; of his finding her in a slave-merchant's garden; of his plighted troth, and of his given charm; of his words as he dropped the jewel into her outstretched palm—"Wherever I may be, give it me and I will redeem my pledge, Nouronihar *ghiuzellin*;—bear it with thee till we meet again!"

Clarivaux Faunt's eyes opened wide as he listened to his own story. Sleep was banished far, as this half-forgotten romance came back to him. Fixing upon her a gaze as potent as that with which he had riveted her soul in the dusk of the Great Bazaar, he leaned forward and said:

"Who art thou?"

"I am Nouronihar—and my lord's slave. I have come to thee, and here is thy jewel;" and she drew from the folds of her *feredje* the charm he had given her in Galata, an opal set round and framed of emeralds.

"Art thou indeed Nouronihar?" he said, a great wave of wrath coming over him as he thought of the annoyance that her constancy might cause him, since he had willingly forgotten. Then he added, "And why art thou here?"

"I have come because my lord desired me. Have I done wrong? Has my lord forgotten?"

"Yes," he exclaimed brutally, "years since. Thou also shouldst have forgotten. I want thee not; depart as thou hast come! Thine eyebrows are joined; there are others fairer and more pure in my house; there is no place for thee."[1]

"Oh, my lord, judge me not! To find thee I had to assume the garb of that which—Allah upon my soul—I am not. The sign shall disappear beneath thy smile; turn me not away! Oh, cast me not from thee now!"

"Nay, I have said; depart as thou camest. I will none of thee. Pursue thy trade! Stay, here is money—I know not how much; return to Stamboul and trouble me not."

And as he spoke he took from his girdle the knitted purse in which the merchants of the East carried their gold, and flung it to her.

With a wild hoarse cry, she sprang to her feet, and stamped upon the purse; then clasping the charm in the hand where it lay, she broke stridently into the weird barbaric chaunt with which she had roused him. Turning she fled down the path, and before Faunt could arrest her, she had sprung upon the parapet and plunged headlong into the rocky torrent of the Tigris that bore her mangled body to the sea.

The woman on the roof who had ceased playing with the cat to watch her master with the lute-girl, wakened one of her companions, and said:

"Behold whilst thou wert asleep a lute-girl played to the master. He gave her gold, but she has cast herself from the parapet into the river."

And the black cat who had at last caught the lizard, made a last futile attempt to free its dead body from the silken harness in which it had been bound.

---

1 Women whose characters leave much to be desired, the light-loving members of the community, connect their eyebrows in the East with a touch of antimony, to announce their trade. They are generally Armenians and Georgians.

V.

Ffolliott Grange in the county of Devonshire was once more instinct with life and movement. For a space exceeding two years it had been silent and empty. Philip Faunt had been killed in the hunting field, and Sir Lionel and his eldest son had left England to make the tour of Europe. In Naples, whilst they were there, the cholera had broken out, and before they could fly, both father and son had been stricken down; their bodies had been brought home and interred in the family vault a year before, and then the Grange had been closed. Meanwhile the new baronet, Sir Clarivaux Faunt, who was far away in the East at the time of his triple bereavement, had been notified, and had arrived bronzed and consequential, a month before, and now the Grange was populated by upholsterers and decorators, who were overhauling the old Tudor mansion and disposing around it the contents of the bales of Oriental stuffs and curiosities that its new master had brought with him from Asia Minor. Gradually he installed himself, and bringing with him many of the habits of his Oriental life, Sir Clarivaux caused no small scandal among the country-families by the disregard for conventionalities that characterized his life. His Turkish servants were regarded as heathen and horrible; and the two Turkish ladies who basked in the sun on the ample lawns of Ffolliot Grange were never mentioned in the presence of young persons.

But in the life of every man, whatever may have been his training, there comes at some time or another a desire to settle down and gain respectability—theoretical at any rate—and an heir to perpetuate his name. This time came to Sir Clarivaux Faunt, and presently the Turkish ladies were no more heard of, and the Baronet roused himself to look round the county for a damsel worthy to become the mistress of Ffolliott, and the wife of its master.

His choice fell at last upon the daughter of the deputy lieutenant of the county, and her parents, in consideration of his radical reforms in the matter of character,—and of his reputedly fabulous wealth,—expressed themselves as willing to welcome him as a son-in-law. The engagement of Sir Clarivaux Faunt and Miss Yseult Colberton became an item of fashionable intelligence in the society papers. Again was Ffolliott given over to the decorators; and the preparations for the approaching "marriage in high life" proceeded rapidly.

It was one day, about a week before the date fixed for his marriage, that Sir Clarivaux invited his *fiancée* to come over to the Grange to look at the improvements and make any final suggestions that might occur to her. The visit of inspection having terminated, the bridegroom elect took the fair Yseult into the picture gallery, and began showing her his ancestors that frowned or smiled upon them—as suited the whim of the artist—from the walls.

In the middle of the gallery Sir Clarivaux suddenly stopped. He had heard something. Through the open windows of the gallery there reached his ears the tinkling as of a lute playing an air upon the terrace below; the lilt of a weird barbaric chaunt came to him, and stopping in the middle of his discourse upon his pedigree, he turned and said,

"Yseult, do you hear a sound like a harp—or lute—being played upon the terrace?"

"No, Clarivaux, I hear nothing."

"Surely, yes—I hear it distinctly—now it is in the hall below us. Surely you hear it now?"

"No, I hear nothing."

The girl was becoming alarmed. The man, pale as death, stood as if transfixed. In his ears the lute girl's song reverberated like a challenge from the dead, as it came nearer, nearer, nearer. Now it was on the stairs, coming up—up towards the gallery. Now it was outside the door. He looked at the woman by his side—evidently the song was for him alone; then, like a wave of sound, the chaunt broke into the gallery and seemed to fill it with strange Oriental cadences.

"Do you not hear it?" he cried, "here in the gallery with us?"

"No, Clarivaux," she answered, now as pale as he. "All is still as death. You are ill—let me summon help."

"No," he whispered, "listen!"

The music had advanced to where he stood with his intended bride, and seemed to wrap them in a cloud of melody. Then it passed on to the other end of the gallery, and so out once more into the air. It grew fainter as it was borne away on the breeze, and as the last echo was merged into the outer silence Sir Clarivaux Faunt fell heavily forwards upon his face. Terrified, the girl cried for assistance—it was too late. Clarivaux Faunt was dead.

The cause of his death remains a mystery to this day, but with bated breath and wide-stricken eyes they tell in the county that when they took his body from the gallery they found, tightly clenched in his dead hand, a strange jewel—an opal set round and framed of emeralds.

AN ATLANTIC TRAGEDY.

IT is but a short while ago that I was spending a few weeks at Trthwwsthpllgg Manor with Eric Trevanion and his wife. The only other visitors were an old college friend of Eric's, by name Richard Lyster, and the American doctor, Schuyler Van Boomkamp, with whom Eric had kept up an acquaintance and correspondence ever since the death of Daphne Préault.

Dr. Van Boomkamp was a singularly interesting man, and his stories of his native land were as amusing as they were infinite. Consequently the hours in the smoking-room after Maye Trevanion had gone to bed passed all too quickly.

One night after a contemplative silence of a few minutes, Mr. Richard Lyster remarked:

"Do you know, Dr. Van Boomkamp, your accounts of America recall most vividly to my mind one of the most overwhelming stories I ever heard. It was told me in your country by a resident Englishman, and has always made a great impression upon me."

"Let's have it, Dick," remarked Eric, reaching for the tobacco.

"Yes, tell it us," urged the American; and thus exhorted Dick Lyster cleared his throat and began as follows:—

"I had newly arrived in America. It was only a few days before that I had suffered the indignities of the custom-house, and I had not been asked what were my impressions of America more than a hundred or so times. I had not yet learnt at what streets Broadway crosses the avenues, and still felt nervous about the elevated railways, whether upon, or underneath them. This information is given you merely to point out how newly I had arrived in America.

"But, newcomer as I was, I had learnt two most important facts, and these were Tiffany and Delmonico—especially the latter, where my story opens.

"There was an election of some kind going on in New York, and a queer rabble—or, at any rate, a rabble that was queer from a stranger's point of view—surged about the streets, or congregated outside the Fifth Avenue Hotel, waiting for the state of the polls to be advertised by stereopticon on the opposite corner, and greeting the successive announcements with lively expressions of opinion. Wearied by the atmosphere of excitement, on a subject that I knew nothing, and cared less, about, I turned into the Café at Delmonico's, and found with some difficulty a small table unoccupied, in a corner. Here I seated myself and watched a crowd of *consommateurs*, the like of which I have never seen since, in that classic haunt of anti-temperance *flânerie*.

"I had been seated but a few moments when I became aware of the presence of a man, who seemed to be wandering among the crowded tables in search of rest, and finding none. As he caught my eye, he made a slight gesture in the direction of the chair opposite to me, in which I had deposited my hat and coat, and said, in a low-toned, quiet voice:

"Pardon me, but is this seat reserved?"

"By no means," said I, hastening to remove my impedimenta, and, touching his hat militarywise, the stranger sat down and summoned a waiter to minister to his needs.

"I made some casual remark, on the crowded state of the Café, which he answered with some explanation connected with the elections. Pleading my ignorance, as a stranger only just arrived, I questioned him further, and somehow we drifted into conversation. I have always congratulated myself on my 'newness,' for, had this occurred six months later, I should certainly have taken Claude Radcliffe for a confidence man and not struck up an acquaintance with a casual stranger in Delmonico's on an election night.

"Radcliffe—that was not his name—was tall, well but not heavily built, with a smooth shaven face, steel-grey eyes, and hair of an ashen-blond colour, freely intermingled with white—a rare thing in a blond head—which gave a still stronger individuality to his colourless, ascetic face—a face which, though infinitely calm in its expression, showed traces, in a few deeply-marked lines round the mouth, of a past suffering which must have been intense. After we had parted, strangers still, on this night at Delmonico's, his face haunted me as I returned to the Everett House, and I wondered who this calm stranger might be, and what was the history which had written itself, in a cipher to which I held no key, on those hard, impenetrable features.

"It was not until a week later that I learned his name even. It was then that I met him at a dinner party at Eugene Chariton's on Fifth Avenue, and, being introduced to one another, I learnt that his name was—say—Radcliffe. I asked my fair neighbour at the table if she could tell me anything about him, to which query she replied:

"'No; I can't tell you anything about him, nor can anybody else. He's what you might call "a man with a history," but what that history is, is more than I or anybody else for the matter of that can tell you,' and she talked of something else.

"When the ladies had left us I joined Claude Radcliffe, and we exchanged expressions of mutual satisfaction at our re-encounter.

"'How do you like America?' said he. 'I know it would be justifiable homicide were you to kill me for asking the question, but, as a fellow-countryman, I think I am justified in asking it.'

"'Well, on that plea,' I replied, 'I don't mind telling you that I am charmed with it.'

"'Are you staying long in the country?' he asked.

"'I don't know; I came only for a month or so, but I should not be at all surprised where I to remain a year, if I continue to find life as interesting and amusing here as I have hitherto done.'

"'Ah! then,' he replied, 'your experience would be something like mine, for I came over for six months seventeen years ago, and here I am still.'

"'You came on business, I suppose,' said I.

"'No; I came on my honeymoon,' returned he.

"'Ah! then I suppose "Madame" liked the country,' said I, wondering which of the ladies round the table had been Mrs. Radcliffe.

"'My wife never arrived in America.' A sharp contraction, as if of mental agony, crossed his features as he spoke, and, seeing that the subject was a painful one, I changed it.

"That evening I found myself walking down Fifth Avenue with Claude Radcliffe, on my way home, and as we passed Thirty-Third Street, he said:

"'I live at the apartment house at the end of this street. Won't you come in and chat for half an hour over our national brandy and soda?'

"'Willingly,' I replied; and we reached his rooms, which were charming in every sense of the term. What particularly caught my eye was a picture-frame that occupied the space over the mantel shelf. I say a picture-frame, for the picture, if picture it contained, was carefully hidden behind a crimson silk curtain which was drawn closely over the space that should contain the canvas.

"We parted shortly after midnight, and parted excellent friends. So much so, indeed, that during the two months that I remained in New York, whenever I had an hour to spare, or happend to be passing the corner of Thirty-Third Street and Broadway, I used to look in on Claude Radcliffe, and I looked forward with regret to parting from him.

"It was only a few days before I left the city, that one evening on my way home again from dinner at the Cheritons, I passed the door of the building that contained Radcliffe's rooms and turned in. It was the evening that I confronted Eugene Cheriton with my knowledge of the Rex Stanhope affair, and I was feeling a little fagged by the excitement. I knocked at Radcliffe's door, and, receiving no reply, gently tried the handle. The door opened, and thinking that he must be in an inner room, I went in. He was standing motionless before the fire-place looking up at the picture, the curtain usually concealing which was drawn aside.

"The face of a woman with great violet eyes, and features like a statue by Canova, looked out from amid a mass of blue-black hair. The dress revealed an exquisite neck and throat. The painting was a masterpiece.

"The noise I had made in coming in had roused Claude Radcliffe from his rêverie, and he turned toward me, as perceptible flush rising to his ordinarily white face. I apologised for having come in, explaining the manner of my entrance, and would have gone again but that Radcliffe bade me stay. Then, as my eyes flashed involuntarily in the direction of the picture, he said, briefly:

"'My wife.'

"We seated ourselves and talked of indifferent subjects for awhile, but Radcliffe was obviously oppressed in some indefinable manner. He had not covered the picture again, and the beautiful face seemed to watch us as we talked in the stillness of the night.

"At last my host rose and said: 'I'm afraid you find me dull and distraught tonight. I can't help it, my dear fellow; it's an anniversary with me. Seventeen years ago tonight, I lost my wife.'

"I murmured some conventional expressions of sympathy and regret, but he interrupted me, saying:

"'No doubt the idea will occur to your mind that I am morbidly sensitive with regard to a loss which I suffered so long ago, but the circumstances are such that my wife's death must remain to me an ever-living horror. I have never told the story in America, I would not have my widowhood made the subject of a social sensation (and you know what American journalism is), but you shall hear it, for, in the first place, it is time someone knew it, and in the second, I feel a confidence in you which inspires me to tell you what I think you will say is one of the most terribly tragic stories you ever heard:

"'A few days more than seventeen years ago I was married, at St. Peter's, Eaton Square. Mabel—that was my wife's name—and I had known one another since as children we had played together. The friendship of our childhood ripened into a love that was little short of ideal, and when she was nineteen—I being her senior by four or five years—we were married. I was an orphan, and had spent many years on the continent; her parents were wealthy, and with them she had travelled much; thus, it happened that we were both familiar with the European capitals, watering places, and winter resorts, and determined—as we had neither of us crossed the Atlantic—to spend the winter in New York and Washington, and the summer in the Western States. Thus it happened that, a few days after our wedding, we found ourselves on board the Royal Mail Steamship "Arcadia," our faces turned towards the setting sun, looking forward in joyful anticipation to the novel scenes we were to witness together.

"'The passage began by being a rough one, but we were both excellent sailors, and we enjoyed its opening days. There was only one cloud in the horizon of our happiness, and that—foolish as it may seem—was Mabel's fear of the sea. She declared that she had a horror of death by drowning; and, every night as I climbed into my berth, she would say—half seriously, half laughingly—

"'"Eugene, pray that the ship does not go down in the night."

"'Our stateroom was rather far forward, and almost an isolated one, where we felt the motion of the ship rather badly, though, excepting for the fears with which it inspired my wife, we did not care much about that. I used to laugh at her, and point out the fact that the Royal Mail Steamers of the company never *foundered*, and I used to add:

"'"Don't you see, silly child, that every precaution is taken. Why, suppose the ship were to go down, there are boats enough to take us all off, and even if we were left behind, all these cork jackets and belts that hang round the staterooms insure our safety. Wrapped up in these you would sit quite comfortably in the water till we were picked up. The water is warm at this time of year, and we are in the most frequented track of ocean steamers. And again—I used to conclude convincingly—even if we hadn't these life-preservers in abundance, I'll back myself as a swimmer against most men I know, and I could easily support you in the water for four or five hours, within which time we *must* be rescued. Don't bother your poor, silly little head about it any more."

"'But she would not be quite reassured, and used to repeat:

"'"Well, pray that the ship does not go down in the night!" It was a kind of presentiment—an obsession, with her.

"'One night we had retired as usual, and certainly the sea was awfully rough. It took even me, hardened as I was, some time to get to sleep.

"'I was awakened by Mabel rapping on the side of my berth and crying out:

"'"Eugene! Eugene! what *is* the matter?"

"'I roused myself and listened. Certainly a dull, roaring sound filled the ship—a banging and splashing which drowned the noise of the propeller, if it still revolved. A little alarmed myself, I jumped out of my berth, and, telling Mabel to keep quiet, I went out into the passage.

"'I ran into the arms of a scared, white-faced steward, of whom I inquired the cause of the commotion.

"'"The ship's sinking," he cried; "haven't they roused you? They're manning the boats up the on deck."

"'It was true. Isolated as we were in our stateroom, we had been forgotten.

"'Assuming as careless an air as I could summon up on the moment, I returned to our stateroom, where Mabel lay in an agony of alarm.

"'"Well, little woman," I said, "the curtain is rising on your long-looked-for drama—the ship *is* going down, but there's no particular hurry and no cause whatever for alarm; the worst that can happen to us is a wetting. Dress quickly, as lightly and warmly as you can."

"'I helped her, and dressed myself, putting some papers and valuables into my pockets, and then, fastening the life-preservers round myself and her, we went up on deck. We had indeed been forgotten! The last boat was just preparing to leave the ship with the captain and some of the crew. We hailed them, and jumped in just in time.

"'The boat that had left the ship before us had been swamped by a wave, and its occupants were struggling in the water. Instead of pulling off at once we hovered in the dangerous vicinity of the

214

sinking ship, trying to rescue them. All at once the deck of the "Arcadia" burst up, and the ship settled. Our boat was engulfed in the water; I had only time to seize Mabel by the arms, and we found ourselves struggling for our lives in the eddy.

"'The cork belts supported us well, however, and, holding my wife in my arms, we rode lightly over the crests of the waves. The night was pitch dark. There was no moon, and the stars were hidden behind the heavy masses of the storm clouds. I could not see Mabel's face, but her feverish clutch on my arms reassured me, and I knew that she retained consciousness. After about ten minutes, during a lull in the wind, I said to her:

"'"You see, darling, the night is warm and we are perfectly supported. It cannot be more than three or four hours to daylight, at most, and then we are bound to be picked up immediately. You feel safe with me, do you not?"

"'Her voice came back in the impenetrable darkness: "Yes, Eugene, I feel safe with you; but you have tied this belt too tightly round me—it makes me feel faint; can't you shift it a little?"

"'"Of course I can," I replied; and the moment the sea seemed to get a little calmer I proceeded to do so. She was lying on one of my arms and I was busily readjusting the belt with the other, when, in the darkness, a great wave broke upon us and dashed her out of my grasp. I dived instantly and caught her by the hair just as she slipped under, and, bringing her to the surface, I held her closely to me. The life-belt had been washed out of my grasp, and I had to trust to my own strength, assisted by the belt that was tied round myself.

"'Alas! my wife had lost consciousness and hung a dead weight in my arms. In vain I implored her to speak to me; in vain I strained my eyes in the pitchy darkness to catch a glimpse of the face that was the fairest thing in the world for me. Nothing but a feeble flutter of the heart, over which I kept my free hand fixed, and an occasional twitch of the cold lips which I found with my own, gave me any sign that me precious burden was alive. For hours and hours and hours, it seemed to me, that I bore her up in the blackness of the night, imploring her to speak to me—to open the dear eyes which I could see were tightly closed. It was all in vain; save for the occasional beat of the heart she might have been dead.

"'What a night of agony! Lord, God! how I prayed for morning—for one ray of light by which to see my darling's face. I thought I should go mad! My arms ached, my limbs—my whole body grew numbed and cold; sometimes I almost felt myself dozing off into the sleep of death, waking with a start to cry aloud, "Mabel—Mabel, my darling, speak to me!" and nothing answered but the moaning of the storm as it died away in the distance. Immediately around us it had become comparatively calm. And then I would turn myself in the water, seeking in vain for the east and the rising sun.

"'At last, a faint streak lit the horizon, a flush tinged the edge of a cloud and made it visible in the darkness, a breeze rippled the sullen billows that rose and fell smoothly around us. The day was breaking. I shrieked aloud a prayer of thanksgiving to God, for that night was over, and bent over the motionless, senseless body that I held in my dying arms with a vigour renewed.

"'Little by little the sun uprose, and the dawn came. With the first grey beam that crept across the ocean, I peered into the face that had lain close to mine all night.

"'It was another woman!'"

AN ETERNAL EXPIATION.

A Story of the Royal Mail Steamer "Amalia."

"WELL!" remarked Dr. Schuyler Van Boomkamp, as Mr. Richard Lyster finished his story, "I think that is about as overwhelming a catastrophe as I have ever heard. It puts me in mind of one of the grisliest bogey stories that I ever conceived—I say conceived, because I can find no explanation for my experience, though I think I am fairly posted on the subject of hallucination and aberrations of the brain. I know that I did not *dream* this, and I do not think that I was in any way unconscious, but the impression on my brain was the ghastliest thing that ever occurred to me."

"But what was it," asked Trevanion, "and when did it happen?"

"Well," returned the medico, "it happened on my return to America, after I had completed my studies with Charcot at the Salpêtrière, a few months after—you know, Trevanion."

"Yes, yes; go on!"

"I had taken a passage on board the 'Amalia'; the voyage was pretty rough. Even I was knocked over, but when I came up on deck, a mutual friend introduced me to a girl making the home journey with her mother."

"She was the only person on board who had not been ill. I was only just getting over it, and spent my time lying limply in a folding chair on the deck, and whenever she grew tired of being adored by the rest of the male contingent on board and would anchor herself near me—for I was still motionless and powerless—I would tell her sad stories of the deaths of kings and others of every sort and kind, and this practice continued after I was on my feet. So, during the four days that we wandered about the 'Amalia's' decks together, or sat under the leed of the funnel, getting gradually covered with blacks (which always strike me as the many-times-more-unpleasant substitute for dust at sea), I told her a somewhat vivid collection of stories—echoes of the boulevard, of the Quartier Latin, reminiscences of old student days in Rome, stories of the Balkan Peninsular, and of the torrid East, from grave to gay, from lively to severe. But none of the stories that I told her came up in weirdness to the one that was told *me* before we left the ship, and was told me by a ghost."

"What?"

"You may laugh, perhaps, but what I tell you, or am about to tell you, strange, incomprehensible though it may seem, is the absolute truth, as surely as you sit there.

"We had been walking round the decks one evening, in the little interval between dinner and supper, arm in arm, battling against the wind, periodically passing between the ship's boats to the side to watch the phosphorescence of the waves which gave the sea, as it rushed past us, the appearance of a continuous sheet of living flame—you probably know the Canarde lines and the way the ship's boats stand in rows round the decks, one above the other?

"We had completed our tour of the decks several times when suddenly the prettiest hand in the world tightened its grasp on my arm ever so little, and a voice at my side whispered:

"'Good gracious, look there!'

"I looked in the direction indicated which was that of the upper boat on the starboard side, nearest the bows. The boat, with its tarpaulin cover, looked much as usual, but seated apparently in the stern, and closely muffled in tarpaulins, sat the figure of a man.

"I have been accustomed during times of war and peace to wander about in the dark a good deal, and can generally distinguish things pretty clearly, so that the fantastic shapes which things assume disguised beneath the cloak of dusk no longer scare me as they did once, but I confess that, having stood for an instant to make clear to myself what it was up there, a cold feeling of terror came over me at the sight of this hopelessly lonely creature sitting, as it were, in mid air, looking out to sea. The face was turned away from us, and we were so close underneath that we could only just see the head and shoulders. I am accustomed by my profession to making excuses quickly and giving rapid explanations, and I said at once:

"'Why, don't you see, it is only the two "blocks" by which the boat hangs from the davits, which with their tarpaulin coverings thrown over them, look, in this light, like a man. Isn't it odd?'

"The calmness with which I made this statement reassured my companion, and after looking at it for an instant, we moved on. But tacitly, and, as it were, by common consent, we walked up and down the larboard deck, and did not go around to the side where the lonely boatman kept his solitary watch again. Soon after a man came up with a message from her mother, saying that she was wanted to go down to supper, and she went.

"Immediately I betook myself forward on the starboard side, and took my stand as before underneath the boat where the lonely figure was seated. By this time the moon had risen and was behind me as I stood on the deck, clearly illuminating the figure in the boat.

"'Boat ahoy!' I cried, or rather said.

No notice.

"'Who are you, in God's name?' said I.

"A kind of long-drawn sigh came from the figure above me as it moved and slowly turned its head in my direction.

"What a sight! Had I had the slightest idea of what I was going to see, I think I should have thrown myself overboard amid the phosphorescence of the steamer's wake before I disturbed the lonely watch of this grisly thing. The moon, which, as I have said, was behind me, shone directly into the cape of the boat cloak which shrouded the head and revealed a hardly human face, desiccated, mummied, brown, wrinkled, ghastly. The eyes, half closed, had shrivelled into the head and were fixed in a dull idiotic stare. The parched, dry lips, contracting with the flesh, had receded from the teeth and gave to the face, if such it may be called, the ghastly grin of a skeleton. An old tattered fur cap scarcely restrained the few straggling grey hairs still attached to the shrunken scalp; and all this stood out in startling relief outlined by the moonlight as a dried up hand clutched the side of the boat nearest to me, and the figure leaned over and looked at me. A feeling of sickening repulsion came over me as the teeth unclinched themselves apparently with an effort and a hollow unearthly voice croaked the words:

"'Who are you that have disturbed my watch for the first time in half a century?'

"'I am a living man,' I replied, 'that dares address the dead. Who, and what are you, that you sit there alone, in such hideous vigil?'

"'I,' said he, 'am a poor, damned soul, condemned for my sins to sit up here, through the centuries maybe, until I have expiated the crime of which I reap the eternal punishment.'

"'What is your crime?' said I.

"'Go hence,' replied he; 'I will not answer you.'

"In a moment I had climbed upon the lower boat, and hoisted myself by means of the chains and davits into the upper one, and there I sat, the spectre—shall I call him?—facing me—sat in grim confabulation with this mummied relic of humanity.

"'You say,' said I, 'that I am the first to have disturbed your watch since it began; by the same authority by which I woke you to speech, I command you to tell me what it is that brought you here.'

"'Listen," said he, 'I sit here through everlasting cycles in expiation of a crime so ghastly that even the loathly relics of my poor living self, which you see, are fair to think upon beside its hideous atrocity.

"'This boat, new painted though it be, recaulked and rendered seaworthy as it has been, inscribed with the name "Amalia," as you see it, was one of the boats of the ship "Fingal" which foundered in these waters on the 3d of July, 1830. The ship caught fire at sunset, and I was put at the helm of the first boat that abandoned her, filled with women and children, with a few men

220

to keep her afloat and in the right direction until we should fall in with a passing vessel.

"'Among the passengers was a beautiful French woman, the Countess of G—, who had come up on deck almost first amid the confusion, had flung herself into the boat as I took my seat in the stern sheets to direct the embarkation of the rest of her passengers, and putting a small brass-bound box into the space between me and the helm, crouched down by my side and whispered,

""'This case contains jewels worth ten millions of francs. I must save them, and the captain has ordered that nothing but necessaries shall be put into the boats. Help me save these jewels and I will give you a million of francs as soon as we are picked up."

"'I promised to do so; it was over in a flash. As they lowered some provisions into the boat, I seized hastily two or three cases of preserved foods of various kinds, and placed them in the stern sheets by the side of the countess' jewel case. The whole, ranged side by side, looked in the darkness merely like a projecting compartment of the air cases of the boat, and the bulk of the provisions for the passengers and crew were placed along the bottom as ballast.

"'All night long we kept afloat, and in the morning, having eagerly scanned the horizon and scanned it in vain, in search of a passing vessel, one of the cases of food was opened, and short rations were served out to all of us. This went on for three days, the provisions getting lower and lower, starvation staring us in the face. Periodically, however, I would put my hand behind me where I could feel my own private store, which had escaped the notice of the rest, and it was this knowledge that my reserve was there which I think prevented my feelings the pangs of hunger as much as the rest of them.

"'The beautiful countess suffered horribly.

"'One night I suddenly conceived the grisly notion of letting this boatload of women and children starve slowly before my eyes, of killing those surviving the longest; of supporting myself on my hidden store of provisions, and subsequently of returning into more frequented waters; for as soon as the idea had occurred to me, I, who alone in the boat understood navigation, had commenced to steer the boat in a direction where no vessels were likely to pass and pick us up. Days passed, several gales of wind arose and at last a storm overtook us. How the boat lived through that frightful surging of the waters I cannot tell; but when at last the sea became calm once more, and we were able to relax our efforts, our company was reduced to five women, two sailors, and one child. The countess all the while lay crouched at my side against the seat on which I sat, steering, steering,— steering these unhappy creatures to a ghastly death.

"'The child died first, and then one by one, the women, with the exception of the countess, from inanition, and we flung them overboard.

"'One of the sailors, maddened by hunger, sprang into the sea under the delusion that we had reached the land. The remaining sailor, at the end of the same day, caught sight of the package in the stern, the brass-bound corner of the countess' jewel box, and I saw him, with gloating eyes, creeping toward it. I felled him in the boat with a broken oar, and by this time there was not one to fling him overboard, and he lay there, rotting before my very eyes. I had only looked in the direction of my coveted store once, just before the storm (for I feared its discovery by my famished companions), and had hastily crammed into my pockets a few handfuls of dried raisins. These I had now almost eaten, and I was beginning myself to feel that terrible sinking which precedes the insensibility brought on by starvation. I had only kept up by the knowledge of my hoard and my dreams of what I should do in the future with my boundless wealth.

"'As I was carrying the last raisin to my mouth, the countess, opening her dying eyes, saw me, and nerved suddenly with a feverish spark of life by the sight of the morsel of food, flung herself upon me to drag it from me.

"'I strangled the dying woman as she lay across my knees, and I was alone in a boat in the middle of the Atlantic Ocean with the corpses of the man and woman whom I had murdered, provisions enough to last me three or four days, and jewels worth ten millions of francs.

"'At last, thought I, the end is in sight, and I turned to get food from my *cache*. As I turned round and realized what had befallen I must have become insensible, for when I recovered consciousness I was tossing about in a rising gale, lying at the bottom of the boat. The waves that had broken over us during the storm had washed out of the boat the last atom of the provisions I had concealed. The jewel case alone, by reason of its greater weight, remained where I had put it.

"'Madly, furiously, I rifled the pockets of the dead woman at my feet for the key. I found it at last suspended by a little gold chain around her neck. I flung open the lid of the box, and in my rage cast the shining devilries as far as I could from me into the sea. Handful after handful of diamonds, of rubies, of sapphires, I threw into the waves, and at last sank to the bottom of the boat to die the ghastly death by which I had seen so many perish before my very eyes without stretching out a hand to help them when I might have done it.

"'As morning broke next day (for I never lost consciousness) suddenly the air became filled with a strange, unearthly brightness; a balmy, exquisite breeze seemed to bathe my temples, such as I have felt in the Bay of Naples or off the coast of Greece.

"'I said to myself: "This is death!" and the voice of one who seemed quite close to me seemed to say in accents as distinct as they were severe:

"'"Thou fiend! For this ghastly crime that thou hast committed thou shalt remain in this boat throughout eternity, shalt follow wherever a plank of it remains whole, until, in it, thou shalt be permitted to steer some other shipwrecked crew to safety." The every sense seemed suddenly to be extinguished.

"'I knew that I was dead.

"'A few days afterwards the boat was picked up by a ship, for it had drifted back into the track of vessels crossing the Atlantic. The sailors who came down to examine the floating craft flung overboard the decomposing bodies of the sailor and of the countess and her empty jewel case, *but they never noticed me.* They carried the boat into harbour, where she was refitted and repainted. After a long time a new name, "Amalia," was painted upon her, but through all the years nobody ever noticed me sitting in the stern, waiting throughout eternity for the expiation of my crime. And no one, until your voice aroused me, has ever disturbed my everlasting watch.'

"As he said these last words, the corpse, the spectre (call it what you will), sank back into its old listless attitude and turned its head once more toward the sea. I made a half movement forward to touch it, but the sickening sense of repulsion returned so strongly that I could not do it.

"I climbed down from the boat, and below it I found a man, who greeted me with the information that he had been looking for me.

"'Good heavens!' said he, 'what have you been doing up there? Looking at the water? What folly! It is enough to give you your death of cold. Why, you look as if you had seen a ghost. Come and have something warm to drink.'

"I debated whether to tell him my story or not, but finally I decided to wait until the following morning, when my nerves should have regained their accustomed equilibrium.

"Next day I came up on deck and the first person I saw was my pretty companion of the evening before, who said to me:

"'Oh! Dr. Van Boomkamp, I have been looking at that thing in the boat which startled us so last night—for we were a bit scared,—now, confess it,—weren't we? How stupid it was for us! Come and look at it. You see, it is only two of the round things which they fix the ropes to with coverings over them; but it is odd—even by daylight it looks like a man, doesn't it?'

"There it sat, leaning on the side of the boat away from us, all unheedful of the beautiful eyes that were fixed upon it and the voice which was speaking of it. The outline was perfect. Thank God, from its position she could not see the face—the mask that I had looked into the night before."

MY FIRST LOVE.

THE following little idyll was sent me from America by
Bernard Rawlinson. After that gay bohemian and prince of
good fellows deserted the Holland Street colony of artists and
went to America (it was soon after the death of Miss Daphne
Préault, when the Hawleighs had gone away and Eric Trevanion
had taken Maye Trevethick to Cornwall, and our society was
practically broken up), I was perhaps the only member of the old
set with whom he kept up any communication. The fact that I
had known something of his half-sister, Ethel Cheriton, seemed
to cement a bond of sympathy between us, and sorry to see him
drop out of our lives, I wrote and asked him for an American
story for a magazine that I was editing at the time. He sent me
this little romance, in which I detect a certain touch of reality—
more, perhaps, than he would confess to—and which he entitled
simply "My First Love."

"What an old, worn-out title," I fancy I hear somebody saying
as he or she turns the leaf and reads the heading of my idyll.
Old, I grant you, sir or madam, but worn out, never. Do you
say as you meet the hundredth face in a crowd, "What an old,
worn-out pattern?" No, for though the faces possess the same
features, those features individually and their arrangement are
ever varied, even to the millionth face. So it is with the story of
"My First Love"—there are features in it which you will doubtless recognise as having formed a part of your day dream, gentle

reader, but as you turn the last leaf of the narrative I believe you will feel, with me, that none save this old, pure, sweet phrase has any right to head these lines.

I am an Englishman, brought up in all the traditions of an old Tory family by a dear mother—God rest her soul—of whom her friends used to say: "Ah! but she is of the old school." Very stiff and ceremonious, very punctilious and very polite, but every thought and action fraught with an old-world purity and courtesy that made one think of the pictures of Sir Godfrey Kneller, and of the perfumes of dried lavender and *pot-pourri*. Man, says Herbert Spencer, is formed by his environment, and my environment was my mother, a woman of the world, mark you, *aux bouts des ongles*. You must not imagine that I was brought up to a man's estate in ignorance of the foul gases of the valley and marsh, while breathing the pure air of the mountain-top. The only effect visible of the tender influences which guarded my life until I was twenty-four was a certain reserve of manner and a more than ordinary "English" horror of anything approaching to "bad form," though I was admittedly a thorough bohemian. I tell you all this to show you once more how love laughs at prejudices and calmly ignores preconceived ideas.

My mother died with the tulips of 18—, and some of the fellows at the British Museum persuaded me to come to America, and furthermore, with a view to a thorough distraction of my thoughts, prevailed upon me to give a series of readings in the States of my own and other verses. I have coquetted a little with the muse, and, as would be the case with most young poets—or rather rhymesters—the thought of presenting my work *viva voce* to the people of the United States caused me a strange thrill of delight. I communicated, therefore, with an American Lecture Bureau, and in the early autumn of 18— I sailed for the States and commenced a tour which, I am happy to say, has not been unsuccessful.

The following June found me in Denver, Colorado, and I put up at the Grand Cañon Hotel for a week, during which time I gave a couple of readings and rested amid the gorgeous scenery of the State.

The third day after my arrival I had come down as usual to take my matutinal coffee in the public dining-room, and was hardly seated when a lady, whom candour compels me to describe as "an *old* lady," came into the room, accompanied by a young girl. They took their seats exactly opposite me. A young girl did I say? Nay, she was hardly more than a child, seventeen or eighteen maybe, and her face traced itself upon my soul in a manner that is ineffaceable. It was a round face, with just that slight squareness of jaw which promised to give to it a wonderful strength of personality as the years went on: her colouring was perfect, faintly flushed with the dawn of womanhood, with white temples and throat, and a high, pale forehead, the whole framed in a careless torrent of hair like to liquid gold. A pair of great wondering, but withal perfectly fearless, blue eyes; a finely moulded nose, just the least bit tip-tilted, and a mouth like those of the cherubs in Raphael's "Madonna" of the Sistine Chapel. She was a *little* girl, and her figure was just taking unto itself the sweet sinuous curves of womanhood, which showed themselves as she moved to her seat with all the untaught, unconscious grace of perfect and healthy development. Our eyes met as she sat down. She looked at me with a full, frank gaze, in which there was an undefined "something" of half recognition—she had evidently known someone who resembled me—and then, having satisfied herself of my non-identity, she turned her attention to the older lady and their respective breakfasts. A moment afterward I rose and left the room.

During the next two or three days we met periodically, in the dining-room, in the corridors, in the elevator or on the streets of Denver, and we always threw one another in passing that glance which, though apparently absolutely expressionless, seems to say: "If we knew one another we should be friends." Have you never seen people in the streets, in theatres, in ball-rooms, concerning whom, as your eyes meet for a fractional part of a second, you have said this to yourself almost unconsciously? I have, and I always regret these unknown friends of mine, but I never felt it more strongly than I did with regard to this golden-haired child whom I met 'way out in Denver, Colorado.

227

The last morning of my stay in the city arrived and I was sitting alone in my rooms up-stairs, jotting down on a scrap of music paper the chords of an accompaniment to a little song that I had written for a friend in Baltimore. My task finished, I went down stairs to the parlour, where there was a piano, to try their effect, and finding the room apparently empty, I seated myself on the music stool. As I opened the piano I heard a rustle, and turning round I saw my little unknown friend sitting in a low-chair in the embrasure of a window, her great blue eyes fixed upon me in fearless curiosity. I rose instinctively and said:

"Shall I be disturbing you, mademoiselle, if I play over a few chords?"

"Oh, no," she said. "Please go on."

As I turned to the key-board she added: "Will my presence disturb *you*? shall I go away?"

"By no means," I hastened to reply, "on the contrary. Indeed, I shall take the liberty, if you will allow me, of asking your opinion on a little melody that I will run over."

She looked out of the window for a moment and then turning her eyes full upon me once more, she remarked:

"I came down here because I was so lonesome upstairs. Auntie has gone out of business, and some friends I expected to call and take me for a drive haven't arrived."

"Is it possible?" was my rejoinder, and in ten minutes we were the greatest friends in the world. We sat in the drawing-room of the Grand Cañon Hotel for nearly an hour, chatting gaily of America and England and our hobbies and of ourselves. At the end of that time she rose and said:

"Well, it's a humiliating necessity, but we must eat to keep alive, and if you will excuse me, I'll go down to luncheon."

I rose also and answered: "You are quite right—if there were no prosy side to life we should not appreciate the poetry of it"— and then after a moment's hesitation I added: "I am a foreigner and don't quite understand your rules of conduct over here: but would it be very casual of me to suggest that as I also must live and with that object in view must also lunch, we should lunch together, as you are alone?"

"Why, of course—why shouldn't we?" and then she added, with a look of perplexed inquiry coming over her brows, "I don't quite know who is going to introduce us to one another, Mr.—?"

"Rawlinson," said I, "Bernard Rawlinson, at the service of Mademoiselle—?"

"Tressahar—Pauline Tressahar," said she. "Let me give you a card."

She fumbled for her card case and I for mine, and, standing in the doorway of the hotel parlour, we gravely exchanged cards and bowed formally to one another.

"I live in Nashville, Tennessee," she said, "and if you ever come there it will give papa—Colonel Euclid W. Tressahar—very great pleasure if you will come and see us—you will come, won't you?"

I assured you that I would, and we went down to lunch. The head waiter gave me a menu and a check, and I ordered a tiny little meal with some care, during which operation she watched me with a nervous perplexed look which I perfectly well understood, but which for the life of me I couldn't see any way of softening—unless I told the head waiter to give me two checks and filled up one for her and one for myself—which would have been foolish to my English ideas. As we finished our microscopic repast, however, she said in the most matter-of-fact tone to the waiter:

"The check, please."

The obsequious Italian brought it to me naturally and she looked up and said:

"And mine, too, waiter."

"They are both together, madam."

"Oh! but—no—I want—" she began.

"Really," said I, feeling very uncomfortable, "it is such an absolute nothing that it would be simpler, and would give me a pleasure into the bargain, if you would allow me to sign this, Miss Tressahar."

"Certainly not," she replied, blushing, though her tone was quite decided; "will you hand it to me for a moment?"

I did so, and she gravely calculated what her share of our lunch had been, and then, producing her purse, she counted out the exact amount in silver and handed it over to me with the check.

"Now," said she, "if you will sign it, it will be all right."

I did so without a word, fascinated, but withal feeling a little "mean," and then the child, laying a quarter down beside her plate for the waiter, said:

"Now, let's go back to the parlour for a few minutes, and then I must go out."

We went up-stairs again and sat for a half an hour or so, talking of quite serious matters, and then we bade one another farewell, mutually expressing a hope that in truth it might be not "good-bye," but "*au revoir*." She was leaving Denver in an hour's time; I was leaving the same evening.

And then we parted.

Upstairs in my room I had a somewhat battered copy of my last volume of poems. I put a pen through my name on the fly leaf and wrote thereon a little inscription in verse expressive of the pleasure I took in transferring to her the volume, and sent it down to her by a servant and betook myself to my packing. I was thus employed, talking to a friend who had dropped in to say "good-bye," when a bell-boy brought a crimson rose upon a slaver from the office.

"Miss Tressahar has just left, sir, and sends this, with her compliments; she has received the book and is much obliged, and says she will write and thank you from Nashville."

I laid the rose reverently between the leaves of my Bible and put it into my valise. A week later I was on a ranch at Los Angeles, California, and the post brought me a letter of four pages in a pretty Italian handwriting—it was from Pauline.

She had received my book just before she left Denver, and hoped I had received the rose. She had read my verses, and was pleased to say she liked them—that they touched her. Some of them, written in a cynical, despairing strain, she criticised and regretted. She hoped that some day I should meet someone who would make me think better of life and cure me of my love of solitude. She commended my body to happiness and my soul to God, and remained ever, very sincerely my friend, Pauline Tressahar, P. S.—She hoped I would not forget my promise but come to Nashville.

Yesterday—only yesterday—a friend sent me a Nashville paper containing an article concerning myself; alongside of the criticism on my poems, in a column headed "Personal Intelligence," there appeared as an item of local interest the announcement of the engagement of the "beautiful daughter of our esteemed fellow citizen, Colon Euclid W. Tressahar," to the son of some equally esteemed inhabitant of Nashville, Tennessee.

I cut out the article on myself and my poems with the paragraph attached to its side and, folding up small, opened my Bible to place it with Pauline's gift. The leaves of the book were perfumed by the sweet dry petals—the soul that still lived of her crimson rose. And on the page where it had lain there was a little crimson stain—I had pressed it upon that verse of St. Paul's epistle to the brethren at Philippi: "Whatsoever things are *true*, whatsoever things are *honest*, whatsoever things are of *good report*, if there be any virtue—think of these things."

She was my first love.

AN INDUCED DREAM (?).

IN my youth I was a wild psychologist, or more properly speaking, a rabid ghost-hunter. Had the Society for Psychical Research existed at that period in the lives of my actors of which I am the chronicler, I should have been one of its most enthusiastic supporters; as it was, I had to content myself with attending spiritualistic séances in the capacity of a profound sceptic, and, as often as not, got turned out for my pains. In Eric Trevanion's mediæval manor-house at Trthwwsthpllgg he had a lovely ghost, with a haunted chamber all to itself, but he never allowed it to be mentioned; for, to tell the honest truth, he was extremely sensitive about it. Soon after his marriage with Maye Trevethick he and I devoted an entire month to the investigation of his family spectre, and we arrived at the lamentable conclusion that the family spectre was a fraud of the deepest dye, and had no right to the veneration bestowed upon it by the family. And yet Eric relinquished it with many a pang, and never admitted that his haunted chamber was only a draughty and disused room, over the stable provided for the black cattle of which the lords of Trthwwsthpllgg were so justly proud.

I have related, elsewhere, how, soon after the death of Daphne Préault, Dick Lindsay, married Eva Easton; this took place immediately after the death of his father, which placed our old friend Dick in the pleasantly independent position of the freeholder and squire of Marshmoor in the county of Bedfordshire; and no sooner had he taken possession of his new domain than he found that he was the owner of a manor-house containing an extremely well authenticated "spook" legend of its own.

As soon as he made this discovery, his first idea was to play "the spook" upon me, and accordingly sent me repeated invitations to spend Christmas at Marshmoor, whither in due course—that is to say in the second year of Dick's tenancy—I betook myself one Christmas, somewhat to the chagrin of some old friends with whom I had always hitherto spent this festive season.

Immediately upon my return I committed to paper the subjoined account of my experiences.

I have appended a note of interrogation to the title of my story, in the fear that to some severely scientific minds it may appear to take too much for granted, and that to those who cling after the purely mystic in what—for want of a better name—has been called a "ghost story," it may seem like a blasphemy to try to explain the events here narrated at all.

Belonging to a school of psychology that takes as its axiom, "The unexplainable does not exist," I have endeavoured to account for the event that happened to me, personally, on Christmas morning, in the year of grace 18—, and which I propose to narrate exactly as it occurred to me.

Throughout the month of December I had been harder at work than usual over the concluding sheets and proof-slips of a—to me—important volume, and, consequently, when Dick Lindsay and his wife wrote me a joint invitation to spend Christmas with them, I accepted with joy, regretting deeply, however, that my work would keep me in London until Christmas Eve, when I proposed to pack up my traps and make for Lindsay's place—Marshmoor, in the county of Bedford.

Of all the counties in England, Bedfordshire is perhaps the plainest—and planest—therefore I did not look forward to gorgeous winter scenery. I wanted to rest, pure and simple, and rest I knew I was sure to find in Lindsay's manor-house. I had never been there before, but Dick had often spoken to me about the place. It had been shut up for half a century, the succession thereto having lapsed in the first ten years of the eighteen hundreds to a remote branch of the family to whom originally belonged. For some reason or another the place had acquired a bad name, and was practically tumbling to pieces when Dick's father bought the house and a couple of hundred acres of low-lying land round it for, comparatively, a mere song. The old gentleman never occupied it—he only visited it once, and that was the Christmas after he bought it—he went down alone to find the rafters tumbling about his ears, and myriads of rats holding high carnival in the deserted rooms and passages. He declared, on his return, his unalterable determination never to go near the place again—the rats were too much for him, he said—but there were those among his intimate friends who declared, in timorous whispers, that William Lindsay had "seen something!" in his ramshackle manor-house that had undermined his intellect and planted one foot firmly in the grave, whither it was followed by the other and his body a few years later.

Whatever credence may have been the due of these surmises, certain it is that when Dick came into possession of the property and married Eva Easton who was a strong-hearted and strong-minded English lass of unparalleled health and equanimity, he announced his intention of inhabiting his Bedfordshire demesne, and, proceeding with the assistance of builders, rat-catchers, plumbers, upholsterers, and decorators to carry that intention into effect, straightway Dick instituted a practice of filling his house with choice spirits at Christmas time, and yearly sought in the neighbourhood of Marshmoor a welkin for the purpose of making it ring.

Well, to get to my own story. Christmas Eve arrived, and with it my temporary release from labour, and I found myself on the Midland Railway making the dull, uninteresting journey from St. Pancras to Luton, where they make straw hats and die of malaria. At Luton, Dick's dog-cart waited for me, and in the early winter afternoon I bowled along in the direction of Marshmoor. What a revolting country! I had never seen it before, and profoundly sympathized with the elder Lindsay's disgust for his real estate in Bedfordshire. Eight miles of uniformly hideous and straight moor-road brought us to a half-mile cutting, through which, though the air had hitherto seemed still, a north wind howled and chilled one to the bones. At the end of the cutting the little, God-forsaken village of Barton-by-Ampthill nestled unnecessarily in a hollow, and another mile brought us to a dilapidated looking gate in the winter-stricken hedge, which was opened by a toothless and evil-looking old man, the whiteness of whose sparse locks was thrown into stronger relief by the dirtiness of his wrinkled face. This was the gate leading to Marshmoor. What a horrible approach! The drive lay across black, dank fields, down a slight incline that culminated in another pronounced hollow which—thank Heaven, thought I—seemed filled with trees and evergreen shrubs. To this oasis we were admitted by a second gate, and found ourselves before the main entrance of Marshmoor Manor.

Marshmoor was an oblong building, in the ugly and un-compromising style that spoiled so many landscapes in the last century. In the early dusk its white stuccoed front rose against the purple-grey sky, and had it not been for the broad avenues of light that streamed from the French windows of the *rez-de-chaussée*, might have inspired "The House on the Marsh," or "Wildfell Hall." Such gloomy thoughts as these, however, were dispelled by the jolly face and hearty welcome of Dick Lindsay, who came to meet me at the door, and ushered me into a wide hall, where all was tapestried and rugstrewn, where a great fire blazed, and where half a doyen young people sat chattering over the tea-table.

As usual, Dick had filled his house for Christmas, and a merrier party than that gathered around the hall-fire on the afternoon of that Christmas Eve, it would be difficult to discover or imagine. Still something about *me* seemed to cast a momentary cloud over the group; the conversation suddenly ceased, as it ceases when the subject of a conversation suddenly enters the room, and while Dick presented me to two—the only two—of the party with whom I was not already acquainted, Mrs. Lindsay offered me some tea, and one of the girls remarked that, save for the less picturesque effect, it was lucky there was not snow on the ground to make it difficult for the guests to reach the house that night.

For there was to be a Christmas Eve dinner at Marshmoor that evening—Christmas Day proper fell on Sunday, and the majority of the neighbours proposed to keep the day on Monday, so as not to be arrested in their merry-making by scruples of conscience at midnight. Therefore many had been able to accept Dick's invitation for Christmas Eve; and, besides, Dick told me it was an immemorial custom at Marshmoor—long before his or his father's time—to celebrate the Eve instead of the day itself.

The party round the fire gradually regained its life and spirits, though once or twice a furtive look in my direction confirmed my suspicion that at the moment of my appearance I had been the subject of their conversation. However, this did not trouble me much, and very presently I went up with Dick to inspect the room I was to occupy during my stay at Marshmoor. It was a large room on the first floor, with two large windows looking out over the hills in front of the house. The space between the windows was occupied by a high, carved press; at one end of the room a bright fire blazed in an old-fashioned open grate, and at the other another press and a writing-table were set against the wall. The bed, which stood facing the press and the window, was of the type familiar to us all in the ghost stories of our childhood—a great square machine, with the conventional canopy and curtains at the head, and the conventional canopy and curtains at the head, and the footrail at the foot. But the room was brilliantly lighted, and I felt that I was going to be supremely comfortable as Dick said to me:

"Here you are, old man; we've put you as the guest of honour into the best guest-chamber. The history of the house centres round this room, and former owners have died in it—I hope you appreciate the honour."

"Haunted?" I queried.

"No; I'm sorry to say it isn't. The most nervous and impressionable persons may sleep in this room with perfect impunity—sounds like a house-agent's circular, doesn't it? If we'd had a haunted room we'd have put you in it, so as to give you something to talk about at the next meeting of your ghost-hunting club."

Now this was an antique joke of Dick's. The society of which he spoke, the forerunner of the present S.P.R., had only then lately been started, and we had recently formed ourselves into a committee to perambulate England in search of ghosts, sleeping in haunted rooms and watching o' nights in spook-frequented churchyards. I regret to say that we had failed to discover a single genuine bogey, and by the outer Philistines we had been considerably laughed at for our pains.

Presently Dick left me to my own devices, and I completed my tour of inspection of my new quarters. The windows were rather deeply set, and in the embrasure of each there was a bench seat. I parted the thickly-drawn curtains and looked out into the blackness of the night; there was, as I have said, no snow on the ground, and the heavens were unillumined by a single star. There was also no moon, and consequently nothing broke the dirty gloom but the blurred yellow dabs of the carriage gates that shone at a little distance from the house. I shuddered as I carefully reclosed the curtains, and, turning back into the brightly-lit room, commenced leisurely to dress for dinner, and arrange on my writing-table the books and papers I had brought down to be leisurely worked upon in the moments of *désœuvrement*, which, especially in winter, fall at intervals upon country-house parties.

The at first infrequent, and subsequently almost incessant roll of wheels upon the gravel outside, told me that the guests were mustering in the drawing-room below, and, as the clock pointed to the dinner hour, I went down to find a large country party assembled, with Dick doing the honours of the house as if he were the descendant of a long line of baronial entertainers. Dinner, as all Christmas dinners are, was merry to the verge of riot. When one is ten miles from the nearest railway station one becomes necessarily mediæval, and there being mistletoe artfully disposed in unsuspected coignes, we freely kissed thereunder— we made the most of our time that evening, for the time was short. At 11 o'clock the rector of Higham-Gobion and the vicar of Barton-by-Ampthill gave the signal of departure, and shortly before midnight none but the house-party were left within the hospitable walls of Marshmoor. Some of the ladies went to bed, others clustered round the fire in the hall; some of the men adjourned to talk shop in the smoking-room, while the remainder ensconced themselves among the petticoats in the hall. At Marshmoor one smoked all over the house, and there became apparent a tendency to make a night of it despite the fact that the joy-bells that celebrated the birth of Christ rang in the Sabbath with the Christmas morn.

I had, as I have said, been working very hard during the preceding weeks, and bidding Dick Lindsay and his wife good-night, I took my candle and unostentatiously retired. The fire blazed in my grate, and I stirred it into new activity before seating myself in a cosy arm-chair to cut and read a volume of Christmas stories preparatory to cutting them up in a forthcoming review. It must have been about one o'clock when I tumbled into bed and fell incontinently asleep.

I could not tell how long, but it seemed hours, after this, when I awoke with a start into a sitting position and looked round my room. The fire, which had burned low, lit the room dimly and threw gaunt shadow-shapes upon the almost indistinguishable walls. I was indubitably alone, but my whole being was possessed by the sensation that something weird was happening. I smiled, then frowned at myself, and sank back upon my pillows. As I did so I noticed straight in front of me, and, as it were, upon the carved press between the curtained windows, a tiny point of light.

I lay looking at it lazily, wondering vaguely whence it came— what metal object caught the ray of firelight and reflected it upon the press. And as I looked it seemed to increase in size.

"Good!" thought I. "I am automatically mesmerizing myself, staring at this point of light. It will swell to the size of my fist, and then I shall fall asleep."

But I did not fall asleep. On the contrary, the spot grew larger and larger, and invested by an intense curiosity, I crawled down my bed to the foot, and there, leaning on the foot-rail, I watched this strange phenomenon.

※

238

The circle opened wider and wider till at last it occupied the whole side of the room, showing me a beautiful picture in a wide oval frame. I was looking out over the fields in front of the house, and the ground was covered with a shining layer of snow. The heavens blazed with myriads of stars, the great winter moon rode serenely in the purple-azure vault overhead. It surprised me that such an atmospheric change should have taken place since I looked from my windows earlier in the evening. Set diagonally across the upper-hand corner of the picture was a hedge broken by a stile; from this stile a foot-path trodden in the snow led past a hazel copse in the left foreground and lost itself in the shadows beyond.

And as I looked out upon the snowy landscape, there appeared at the stile the figure of a man. He climbed over the stile and began making his way down the footpath. He staggered slightly from side to side, as though he were drunk, and as he came along, with one hand he pressed down upon his head a three-cornered hat, while the other was engaged wrapping a red muffler about his neck; he seemed to be walking against a strong wind, for the skirts of his long, brown coat flew out behind him as he bent his head. Nearer he came until he reached the copse in the left foreground, and then—a man, the vileness of whose face remains stamped upon my memory to the present day, sprang out, and, seizing the solitary traveller by the hair, that seemed long at the back of his neck, drew his head backward. His hat flew off, and a marvellously handsome face was upturned to the winter moon; then his assailant, drawing from his boot a long knife, cut the wayfarer's throat from ear to ear, the blood sprang forth staining both men as they fell to the ground in the incarnadined snow.

And instantly the whole scene closed in, and all was dark.

I was leaning on the foot-rail of my bed, staring blankly at the press before me, bathed from head to foot in a cold perspiration.

Collecting my dazed senses as best I could, I arose and looked at my watch. It was a quarter-past two. I went to the window, and drawing the curtains, looked out into the night. All was black as it had been before; not even the lamps at the gate pierced the cimmerian darkness of the scene. Wondering at the startling vividness of my dream—for dream I held it to be—I regained my bed. A quarter of an hour later I was fast asleep, and slept till daylight.

The moment I awoke I drew my curtains. There, indeed, was the scenery I had looked out upon in my dream. The field, the hedge, and the pathway leading past the copse. But not a trace of snow; all was black, dank, horrible. I dressed thoughtfully, wondering yet the more.

As I entered the breakfast-room the majority of the party were already assembled. As I took my seat and exchanged the conventional morning greetings, it struck me that the same silence that I had remarked on my arrival seemed to fall on the company.

"Well!" said Dick Lindsay, cheerily, "how did you sleep?"

"Extremely well," I replied, "after I settled down to sleep in earnest; before that, however, I had the most extraordinary dream. I—"

"You dreamed that you looked from your room upon a snow scene," interrupted Dick, amid a dead silence. "As you looked, a drunken man staggered across the home-acre and was assassinated at the hazel copse."

"Good God!" I exclaimed, "that is exactly what I dreamed. What does it mean?"

"I can't tell you what it means, but these are the facts: The man who built this house, in the last century, had two sons. The elder was what was—even then—called 'a bad lot,' and left home before he was of age, travelled to the West Indies, and was there reported to have been killed in a conflict with savages. In course of time the old man died, and the younger son entered into possession of the property. Many years later a rumour reached the then proprietor that his elder brother had returned from the Bermudas and was stopping in the village of Barton-by-Ampthill, waiting to see how matters stood preparatory to dispossessing his younger brother. It was Christmas-time, and the wrongful heir sent a message to the claimant inviting him to join his Christmas Eve gathering, with a view to talking over the position, and subsequently giving up possession of the property should his claim prove to be a just one. He came, and the meeting between the brothers seemed to be in every way fraternal and cordial. It ended by the younger making the elder very drunk, after which he sent him home across the fields. At the copse he had stationed one of his farm hands, who murdered his brother while the tortious owner watched from the window *as you watched last night*. A story was spread in the country to the effect that the two brothers had satisfactorily arranged matters, and that the elder had departed as he came, leaving no trace behind.

"They say that, year after year, whoever occupies the room from which he watched his brother's assassination, sees the whole scene re-enacted. I believe my father saw it, though he never spoke of it. We determined to put you, as a trebly-distilled sceptic and ghost-hunter, into that room, without telling you anything about it. We were all in the secret, and you nearly surprised it when you arrived yesterday afternoon. What do you think about it?"

I did not know what to think, but since then turning the matter over in my mind, I have come to the conclusion that I was, in my tired state, the victim—the agent, if you will—of all those strong young minds, and that with every one in the house thinking of the story and directing their thoughts upon me, they caused me to see in my mind the scene upon which their own were fixed.

That is why I have called it "An Induced Dream."

A DESPERATE REMEDY.

THERE may be among my readers, English and American, a few who have had the curiosity to go through experiences which have led to events such as I am about to relate, but the number will be few, for it is only one of many hundreds of Englishmen even who ever brave the dangers of the remote east end of London.

At the time of which my story speaks George R. Sims had not brought "slumming" into fashion; he had not by his intimate acquaintance with the lower forms of life in London excited the interest in the east which was aroused a few years ago in the drawing-rooms of the west, in a word, as I say, "slumming" had not "come into fashion." The fact that it had not done so was perhaps the main inducement to me to become an inveterate "slummer," and sometimes accompanied by Gerome Markham, when he wanted pictures of low life, or by Bernard Rawlinson when he wanted "copy," but more generally alone, arrayed in the oldest and most terrible of clothes and fortified with a carefully concealed revolver of somewhat heavy calibre and about five shillings as a rule in my pockets in sixpences and coppers, I commenced a series of voyages of exploration in the east end, where the dregs of the population assemble and pickpockets do congregate.

If you take the white omnibus which passes Charing Cross and cling to it until it reaches the end of its allotted route, it will take you along the busy Strand and literary Fleet Street, up classic Ludgate Hill, past St. Paul's, past the Bank and by Cornhill to London Bridge, and there descending you will set your face eastwards, and passing the Monument and Tower, you will reach narrow and treacherous paths, ways that are dark and streets not always too clean, and you will find places with names like Wapping Old Stairs, Shadwell, Radcliff Highway and Tiger Bay; places where a decent coat would be the oriflamme of attack, and where they would sell your hair if they could get a penny a pound for it.

Across the river lies Rotherhithe, pretty, fresh and smiling in the noonday sun, looking as if it had suddenly been evolved out of the inner consciousness of some seventeenth or eighteenth century artist; rows of little whitewashed houses with bright pebbled walks, leading from the rustic portico to the brilliantly green-painted gate, where sweet peas straggle untidily at their own sweet will, and pots of gilly-flowers mingle their heavy sensuous perfume with the tarry and fish-like smells which announce the trade of the inhabitants.

It is here that Walter Besant has laid the scene of "The Captain's Room," and a more beautiful and interesting spot it would be difficult to find; but scarcely anybody ever goes there, because Rotherhithe is, or was at the time of which I write, almost impossible to get at.

It was something of a romance that awoke in me an ambition to explore Rotherhithe, though for reasons which will hereinafter appear I never explored it. I had been in the habit of haunting Ratcliffe Highway in the character of a defaulting bank clerk and had fraternized with my companion outcasts, on strength of a certain skill in amateur legerdemain, which enabled me to amuse the occupants of bar-rooms, whilst I listened to their talk, with a few simple tricks performed with some pennies, a handkerchief and a pack of cards.

I had been thus engaged one night, and was sitting at a dirty table conversing with two of the lowest specimens of the population, when suddenly above the roar of the market outside, there rose from the mews, at the back of the public house we had selected as a resting place, a piercing shriek, the cry of a woman—and of a young woman—in mortal terror. Following the scream rang forth the cry:

"Oh, God! help!"

"Boys!" I exclaimed, jumping up, with a tightened, sickening sensation at my throat, "here's some fun. Don't let miss it! Come and rescue the gal."

"Go an' do it yerself!" answered the apparently elder of the blackguards, and before he had finished his reply I was out in the back-yard.

A scoundrel who may have been a sailor, but who was more probably a dock loafer, had evidently seized a girl, whose outline I could barely distinguish in the darkness as she passed the narrow passage that led from the street to the back of the house and had dragged her into the yard for purposes of robbery or even worse. Such little things as this are of too ordinary occurrence in Ratcliffe Highway to excite remark from the passers by.

The assailant had flung his victim to the ground, and crouching over her was not aware of my approach from behind. I did not dare to shoot, for fear of arousing the neighbourhood—a pistol shot would undoubtedly summon a policeman (though little short of it would in Radcliff Highway), and my identity would be revealed,—so I struck the cowardly ruffian a stunning blow with a Colt butt, on the back of the head. He rolled over without a groan—I think his skull was smashed.

Without bestowing upon him another look I turned my attention to the girl. She had fainted, but was apparently at that moment recovering consciousness.

The moon, that was full that night, ran out from behind a bank of clouds, and shone on as fair as a face as I ever saw. The hair that framed it was of a rich ruddy gold, and had escaped from its confinement as the girl's bonnet had fallen off; the eyes that opened and looked at me were large and soft, and appeared a deep violet in the gloom. An exquisite little mouth opened as I bent over her, apparently to cry out once more, when I whispered:

"Be quiet; you are safe! Don't utter a word—I'll see you safely where you want to go. There's the man show seized you—let's get out of here."

Casting a frightened glance at the motionless prostrate figure by her side, the girl rose, and coming close to me she said in a low tone:

"For God's sake, don't you hurt me too. You talk like a swell—don't let any of these beasts touch me."

I reassured her to the best of my abilities as I led her down the passage to the street, and the next moment we were striding rapidly eastward along the highway.

"Where are we going to?" I asked after we had put a hundred yards between us and the scene of our late encounter.

"To Wapping Old Stairs," she answered. "I live across the river at Rotherhithe with my uncle. I've never been over here before, but uncle was taken ill tonight and I came over to find a doctor who saw after him when he was bad once before. I found that he'd gone away from the old address, and I was hurrying home when that brute seized me as I passed the entry to that passage."

"But, my child!" said I, "you can't go back to Rotherhithe alone at this time of night. How a beautiful thing like you ever got here safely at all I can't make out. However, you're safe with me anyhow—I'll take you back to Rotherhithe."

The girl drew closer to me and looked up into my face.

"Ah!" said she, "I thought you was a swell. Thank you kindly—I shan't be afraid if you come with me."

And so, arm in arm, we reached Wapping Old Stairs, she chattering about herself all the way.

She was seventeen, but she looked twenty. She had lived all her life, she said, as long as she could remember, with her uncle.

That was the alpha and omega of her story.

We reached the ferry landing and found the ferryman making his last round trip for the night, and stepping into his boat we were all too quickly landed upon the opposite shore, and here I held out my hand and said "Good-night."

"Last trip over," shouted the ferryman. I looked from him to the girl—she laid her hands on my arm and looked up into my face.

"Won't you come and see uncle," she repeated, "you'll be able to get a wherryman to scull you across—there's always lots of 'em about—looking for corpses," she explained.

I shuddered a little, but I couldn't resist her appeal. I went with her to her uncle's cottage.

We found the old man sleeping peacefully. From her description of his illness, I concluded that he had been suffering from an unwonted combination of anno domini and alcohol. We decided that it was best not to waken him, and after remaining for a few minutes in conversation with this Rotherhithe Venus I rose to take my departure.

She accompanied me to the gate. As I held out my hand once more to say "good-night" she put up her lips, saying:

"Aren't you going to kiss me?" There was not a shade of coquetry in her voice now; she was merely making a simple inquiry.

"You'll come over again and see me, won't you?" she said, as at last I announced my intention of *really* going away.

"Certainly I will," was my answer, as I held her hand over the garden-gate, "as soon as I can; good-night."

And retracing my steps along the way by which we had come, I reached the ferry stairs. It was a long while now since the ferry had made its last trip, so, after looking around disconsolately for a few minutes, I hailed what I think was the most repulsive looking specimen of humanity that I ever saw in my life, and after some haggling agreed that he should scull me over to Wapping in his dilapidated old wherry for the sum of sixpence.

You, oh, my gentle readers, who have never crossed the Thames, lower perhaps than Vauxhall or the houses of parliament, will perhaps think it is nothing to make this crossing of the river from Rotherhithe to Wapping, but allow me to tell you that though I have walked the streets of Scutari and the blind alleys of Galata, the passages of remoter Paris and the deserted piazze of Rome at all hours of the night, I would infinitely rather patronize all these localities, dressed from head to foot in the gold-embroidered gown of a Chinese mandarin, with a sapphire button on the top of my head, than be rowed across the Thames at dead of night "below bridges."

You shoot out from the stairs where you have stepped into your boat between the black undefined masses of shipping, and from beneath the overhanging attics of the lower river-side tenements, and excepting for the dreadful, lonely "lap, lap, lap," of the water, and the greasy "dip, dip, dip," of the dilapidated oars, everything is in profound silence, save for an occasional volley of oaths indicative of some gambling quarrel or other in the cabin of a hawsered barge, the occasional scream of a woman under the blow of some drunken sailor, or now and again a pistol shot that tells of the rough and ready adjustment of a difference of opinion between a couple of long-shore men.

These sounds grow fainter as the shore recedes into the night, the greasy stream runs past the boat silently and swiftly, and brave man though you may be, you dare not trail your fingers in the water, and you shudder involuntarily as you turn your eyes away from every dark mass which floats past the boat.

On the occasion of which I am speaking, we had got about three-quarters of the way over, when, in the brilliant moonlight, an idea suddenly seemed to strike my wherry-man; possibly the light shining on my face made it look more than ordinarily pale, and he thought I was frightened; anyhow he said:

"Here, you swell, pay me my fare."

I asked him what he meant, and he replied:

"I mean that I am going to be paid before you get out of this boat."

I was wrapped up in a large and rather shabby cloak as I sat in the stern of the boat, my arms crossed upon my knees, and thus we sat looking at one another, whilst, concealed by the folds of my cloak, my right hand sought the revolver which lay upon my right hip. I said to him:

"I shall pay you when I get out and not a moment before." And he said to me:

"I know this, that unless you pay me half a sovereign right this minute, you will never get out of this boat at all, and then what?"

"And then this," I said, "now, look here, you be reasonable; I've told you that I am a broken-down 'sport' and that I haven't got any money at all; I've only about three shillings in the world, and you won't be such a brute as to take that away from me."

"Won't I though?" he said. And then another thought seemed to strike him, and he added, "Is that all the money you have got on you?" And I said, "Yes."

A hideous grin displayed two broken ranks of blackened teeth, and with a chuckle more awful than anything I ever heard before or since, intensified as it was by the surrounding, he said:

"Very well, then; there is three shillings that you have got, and five that I shall get for taking your body to the river police, that will make eight."

"Good God!" I exclaimed; "what do you mean?"

"Why this here," said he; "I am going to chuck you out of this boat, and I am going to see that you drown, and then I shall get five shillings for revering your body and taking it to the police station. Don't you see?"

I don't think I was ever in such a frightful situation in my life; but I knew perfectly well that if I were to shoot the man there and then I should probably fall into worse hands when I landed, heaven knows where, on the other side, so I said to him:

"Now, see here; supposing I lied to you, and that I have got a watch on that is worth some money, and that I would give you that, how long will it take you to reach the other side?"

By this time the moon had hidden herself behind a cloud and the gloom was profound. He said:

"About a minute and a half."

"Very well, then," said I, "if you throw me overboard I shall swim ashore and then you will lose me."

"Oh, ho!" said he; "will you? You could no more get through the barges and shipping alone than you could get to heaven without I sent you there." (Heaven was not the word he used.)

All this time my brain was working pretty actively, and I said to him:

"Now, see, here is another scheme: Admitting that you will get five shillings for my dead body, you would get a sovereign for saving me alive, according to the rules of the river police; now, if you throw me overboard (as I see by your size you are quite capable of doing) you shall jump over also and save me, and I give you my word of honour—I take my dying oath—that I won't say you threw me overboard, only save me and put me safely into a police station."

"That would be very well," said he, "and you speak fairly enough, but I can't swim a stroke."

"Can't you," said I, "then by God! pull to save *your* life."

I had had my hand on my revolver all this time, and drawing it suddenly, I fired two bullets through the bottom of the boat. The water began to gush in, and the wherry-man, seeing possible escape for me and certain death for him, turned the boat's nose to the shore, and in less than two minutes we were safely on dry land with nearly a foot of water in the boat.

Arrived at the other side he disappeared incontinently, and as good luck would have it, at the top of the street in which I had been deposited I found a stray policeman walking his solitary round. He told me where I was and how to get back to London bridge.

I did not go to Rotherhithe again, according to my promise; in fact I have never been there at all since, and I think I am safe in saying that I never shall.

As for the fair one with the golden locks who let me into the scrape, I have never heard of her or seen her from that day to this.

I wonder what was her name.

MY BREACH OF TRUST.

A Story of the Russo-Turkish War.

IN a certain New York drawing-room, in the early Spring of the year 1887, I told a story, and propounded a problem in connection therewith, which elicited strangely varied and strangely interesting solutions, and many ethical discussions upon the point involved. So great was the volume of criticism, *pro* and *con*, brought forth by my confession, that I have determined to state the case with all possible completeness, and leave it, once and for all, to the judgement of the reader of these pages.

I must take him back with me to the spring of 1877, when, in the cheering company of two or three good fellows, all of us war correspondents, I found myself seated in a compartment of what then did duty for the Orient Express, leaving Paris rapidly behind us on our way to the seat of the war in the Balkan Peninsula, which had then been recently declared.

The experiences of a war-correspondent are always exciting, often perilous, and generally unique. To an even greater degree than the officer or soldier actually engaged in the field, he requires to be in the fore-front of the fight, and, on the principle that lookers-on see most of the game, he is often afforded opportunities of witnessing events which escape the observation even of the officers commanding, as, besides watching the actual progress of the strife, he is bound to keep an eye on surrounding circumstances, ethnological or otherwise, and is often required to play a part—important or unimportant, as the case may be—in the little personal dramas of life and death, which go to make up the history of a war.

The experience I am about to relate was one of these. I was called upon to act, almost without premeditation, in the last act of a drama which was touching, pitiful, and full of human interest. Whether I did right or wrong is the problem I am about to propound to you.

We sat together in the train bound eastward, chatting over the *casus belli* and probable result of the war, whilst the long vista of iron rails terminated in nothingness at the point of sight behind us, and landed us towards evening at the German frontier. As I wandered around amid the confusion of the *douane*, looking with objectless curiosity at the names inscribed upon the rummaged portmanteaux and other *impedimenta* of the European traveller, and wondering which of the harried passengers belonged to which pieces of luggage, I observed a young fellow, scarcely more than a boy apparently, standing a little apart from the crowd, and evidently unconcerned in the general haymaking that was officially proceeding. What struck me at once about him was the shadow of a great sadness clouding his fine grey-blue eyes. He was short rather than tall, with curly yellow hair, and was dressed in grey corduroy with a *quasi*-military helmet on his head, a leathern belt about his waist, his legs cased in knee-high soft leather boots. His expression of despair attracted whilst it touched me, and, guessing his nationality to be French, I sauntered up to him and addressed some casual remark in that language, *apropos* of the scene before us. He replied, and we entered into conversation.

"You have got through the infliction of the custom-house," said I.

"I have nothing but a valise," replied he.

"Ah!" I rejoined. "You travel light, like a veteran,—for your costume seems to indicate a long journey."

"I am proceeding to the seat of war," replied he. "I am a Special Correspondent."

"Indeed! Welcome, then, *camarade*," and I handed him my card in exchange for his, whereon was inscribed, "M. Maxime Durand, *Correspondent Spécial du Bulletin Quotidien.*"

I made him transfer his valise into our compartment, presented him to his future *confrères,* and before many leagues had separated us from the frontier, his sadness had apparently worn off to a great degree, and we all became the best friends in the world. Thus we reached Giurgevo on the Danube, and set off thence in search of the Russian staff to which we were attached. By the end of the campaign, most of the boys talked a funny gibberish which they called "Turk" in the party: so I had it all my own way, so to speak, and coralled the soft places in the *arabas*, or carts, that took us to the front. It was this divine right of leadership, I think, combined with the fact that I was the first correspondent to know him as "one of us," that attached Maxime Durand especially to me. Altogether, we correspondents in the Russo-Turkish business were a joyful crew, and kept as close together as we could throughout the campaign; but my especial comrade, and the pet of the whole crowd, was Maxime Durand.

He never lost heart, never complained, though he suffered terribly from the cold, poor boy, and we used to chaff him unmercifully for the care with which he would put on his gloves and wax his moustaches before a triangular bit of looking-glass, before going to the front. He was the life and soul of the party. He was a really remarkable cook, and performed culinary prodigies with half a dozen looted eggs, some hedge-row weeds, and an antique hen, cut off considerably past her prime by a revolver bullet. In the evenings he would sing, or rather croon, echoes of the Champs Elysées, or tell us the most "impossible" stories till we threw things at him.

We used to rout him out with a bayonet, or a lump of ice, in the small hours of the morning, to do the lighter work of the mess, but when it came to his turn to do the heavier work of the community, one of the older men used always to do it for him, assuring him that he would get his hands dirty, or break his eye-glass, or something terrible of that kind, if we suffered him to do his share of the rough work of the camp. In a word, he was our spoilt child, and if ever he happened to be late in returning to quarters in the evening, we used to feel positively sick until he appeared, with probably a string of *Kebabs* in his hand—which he had a knack of trading with confiding Turks, against an old decoration picked-up on the field, or a dilapidated sword—a bunch of looted but homesick carrots, or a handful of apples, no longer "fragrant with the fire of forgotten suns." He attributed his triumph in this direction to his eloquence in the vernacular: Maxime's Turkish consisted of *"Bou issterim"* ("I want this"), *"Vir bana bou"* ("Give me this"), *"Chapuk ol!"* ("Look sharp"), *"Souss ol!"* ("Shut up"), *"Sheitanyah ghit!"* ("Go to the ——"), and *"Shekurler Effendim hazretleri"* ("Thank you, my Mr. Your Excellency"). I taught him the original Turkish of these practical phrases, and more he refused to learn.

Well! well! you must forgive me for digressing in this manner, like an old man babbling about his darling. He was very dear to me, was our gold-curly-headed little *frileux* Maxime, and when he was killed, I saw tough old correspondents weep for him—and I was of them.

The war progressed and dwindled to its culminating point (if I may be allowed the paradox)—the Fall of Plevna. For a month we had been encamped with the Muscovite battalions, waiting for Osman Pacha's superb defence to yield before the omnipotent generals Famine, Frost, and Disease, supported by Skobeleff and Todleben.

Since the 3d of November we had been sitting before the walls inactive, waiting in grim, horrible expectancy for the heroism of the besieged to give out, for since Skobeleff's disastrous storm of the 3d September, known to history as the Lovtcha attack, in which he had lost fully half of his army without impairing the position of Osman, we had learned to respect our foe and to trust to the slow, irresistible weapon of Starvation, rather than to the impetuosity of the Muscovite soldier or the sting of the Berdan rifle. On the 9th of December, however, spies brought us the intelligence that a sortie was imminent, and on the 10th, the Turks having deserted the Krishin redoubt, it was occupied by a Russian battalion.

We knew that the besieging force might expect to be shelled from the fortress at the dawn of the morrow, and as we were ignorant of Osman's resources, we none of us knew for certain that we should be alive to mess together on the following evening, and I for my part wrote a letter, which I felt might be my last, to my paper and scribbled some short notes home under cover to my editor. At ten o'clock I took my despatches to the headquarter lines and having seen them safely *en train de départ*, returned to our tent.

As I approached our canvas shelter, I saw, outlined against the dim light within, a cloaked figure in a *tarboush* (erroneously called a *fez* by the occidental). "A Turk!" thought I, as I crept up behind him and gripped him by the throat. As the starlight shone upon the colourless face I exclaimed, starting back as I did so,

"*Dieu! Maxime, que fais tu là!*"

"Ah! *mon cher*," replied he, "I was waiting for you—I wanted to speak to you." On the pale, drawn features I could see the traces of recent tears, but I rejoined as roughly as I could,

"How dare you rob yourself of your beauty sleep like this? Don't you know we've got to turn out at dawn to-morrow in all probability?"

"Codger!" replied he (a perversion of the Turkish "*Khodja*"—teacher—bestowed upon me as a vocative by "the boys" in deference to my knowledge of the language), "don't laugh at me to-night for I'm quite serious—for once. You are my dearest friend out here—are you not? And I want to talk to you very seriously tonight under these stars which I shall never see again."

"Come, come, *cher ami*," I said, "you mustn't talk like that. In the first place it's ridiculous, and in the second it's unlucky. We knights of the pencil don't get shot, and of all of us, you at any rate are bound to return and make some fair Graziella happy for life."

I had taken him by the arm and we had reached, by a pathway trodden in the snow, the summit of a little earthwork thrown up by Todleben's sappers. He pointed to the distant lights which outlined the fortifications of Plevna and said,

"Behind these walls, old fellow, lies a bullet that will find me in the field in the morning, and I want you to do me a great favour when I'm under the snow in the trenches yonder. Promise me, *mon ancien*, promise me!"

"Well," I replied, seeing that he was bound to relieve his mind, "I promise—the more readily as I know I shan't be called upon to perform—what is it?"

"Thank you. I must tell you—by way of introduction—something about myself. I was born in Douai, where I lived until my parents died and I became a travelling correspondent of the *Bulletin*; and in Douai there lives a child whom I should have married after this campaign had I lived—we have been betrothed for many years. She is Euphrasie, the daughter of old Baptiste Sterelle, one of the most respected citizens of Douai, and we have loved one another ever since we were children—so high. When you spoke to me at the German custom-house on our way out here, you remember that I was almost heart-broken; I will tell you why. I was engaged for the *Bulletin* at Avignon when I received a telegram from Paris ordering me to report myself for service at the seat of war, at ten on the following morning, in Paris. My first thoughts were naturally of Euphrasie whom I had not seen for weeks, and whom I might never see again, and I left for Douai at once, intending to bid Euphrasie farewell and proceed to Paris by the midnight train. I reached Douai faint with hunger and anxiety, and on my way to M. Sterelle's I stopped at the restaurant of Père Larréze to take a glass of wine and a crust to strengthen me for my adieu. Whilst I ate, there entered a man by name Nicolas Dufoure, who for many years had endeavoured to supplant me in Euphrasie's love and who hated me with all the hatred of an unsuccessful rival. I did not want to part—even from him—in anger, so I addressed him, and, on his expressing surprise at seeing me, I told him that I was leaving for the war tonight. He could hardly believe it and I took from my pocket my editor's telegram; as I did so, Euphrasie's last letter to me fell from my pocket-book—I instantly replaced it, but not before he had seen the writing, for he turned white with anger and rose and left me without a word.

"I finished my little meal and proceeded in the direction of Baptiste Sterelle's. It was twilight, and, as I mounted the little narrow street behind the *mairie*, which led to their house, suddenly I received a blow on the head. I remember nothing more. When I came to my senses I was sole occupant of a third-class carriage on a train whirling I knew not whither.

At the first station at which we stopped, the guard opened the door and seeing me recovered, exclaimed:

"'Ah! *mon brave*, that's well. We are better now?'

"'Where am I?' said I.

"'You are in the midnight express on your way to Paris.'

"'And how did I get here?'

"'You were carried into the station at Douai, and put under my charge, by a tall blond man, who gave me your ticket, saying that you had to be in Paris early to-morrow, but had been indulging in a little farewell "jollification" with your old friends at Douai. *Dieu de Dieu!* We all know what it is; sleep on *mon ami*, we are yet some hours from Paris, you will be all right when we arrive.' And so he left me.

"What did it mean? Who was the tall blond man? Certainly not Dufoure, of whom I thought at once, for he is short and dark. A footpad no doubt—for I had been robbed containing Euphrasie's letter and my editor's telegram. It was from the latter, no doubt, that the robber had discovered my identity and the need in which I stood of being in Paris to-morrow, and I felt almost grateful to the unknown giant who had been so far considerate to me though he had robbed me not only of my worldly possessions, but of my last interview with Euphrasie. But besides having been stunned I had also been drugged—it was only twilight when I left the restaurant of Père Larréze and it was nearly one o'clock in the morning when I received the guard's explanation at that unknown station on the road to Paris. What was to be done? How communicate with my darling in Douai? Well, I hoped that I should be able to write from Paris. To telegraph was out of the questions, for, in Douai, the telegraph operator is general retailer of public and private news.

"I reached Paris, worn out, in the early morning, and put in an appearance at the office at ten o'clock. I was closeted with the editor for an hour, and received instructions to leave Paris, by the Orient Express at midday, giving me barely time in which to make my final preparations. And thus I left *la belle France* behind me—now you know the cause of my misery when you met me in the German *douane*.

"I have written two or three times since I have been in the Balkans, but alas, it is such a chance whether private letters get through the lines, and even if they do, it is a still greater chance if they ever arrive, and I have a terrible fear that Euphrasie has never heard anything from me since I left. I had looked forward to telling her all about it on my return, now I shall never see her, or Douai, or France, again. It is only you, *cher ami*, who can help me now, and you will—won't you?

He paused, his utterance choked by a great sob. I felt dangerously near tears myself as I answered: "Yes, yes, *mon garçon*,—come, what is it you want of me?"

"It is this,—I wear round my neck a chain on which I carry her portrait in a locket and a little gold image of *la Sainte Vièrge* that my mother gave me when I was confirmed. When I am killed to-morrow, I implore you to seek my body among the dead. I want you to take these from my neck and carry them back to her, and tell her that I loved her and her alone, to the very end, that Maxime died in harness, with hers, the dream-face before his eyes, that his last thoughts were of her, and tell her not to think hardly of him when you have told her the story of his last visit to Douai. Promise me Codger, promise me."

Of course I promised him, though I repeated my expressions of derision at his "presentiment," and then, the stars being on the wane, I bade him get what sleep he could before the first bass notes of the orchestra should wake us to the fact that the opera had commenced.

The next morning the 11th of December, before dawn, the stir of the camp woke us, and in less than one hour, as the first rays of the sun began to tinge the snow with streaks of transient crimson, that should ere long become permanent, the celebrated sortie of Osman Pacha in the direction of the Sofia road—the Fall of Plevna—had commenced. I had routed out Maxime Durand, who had slept through the opening chords of the cannon's music like a child, and we had ridden to the front together.

To compensate for the dangers that a correspondent has to run, he has one protective axiom—it is his duty to himself and his journal to keep as much out of harm's way as possible, and acting in this sense Maxime and I climbed into a couple of trees on a slight eminence commanding a fine view of the fortress and the trenches where the Siberian regiment lay hidden. There we sat for a couple of hours—I with my horse's reins hooked over my foot so that should the animal take fright and start off, he would jerk me down on to his back. Maxime was similarly posted about twenty yards distant. The incidents of that terrible sortie and Osman Pacha's magnificent dying effort are now historic and need no recapitulation,—suffice it to say that we must have been discovered by telescope from the walls, or by the advancing columns, for suddenly a bullet lodged in the branch on which I was seated, and was immediately followed by a dozen others that whistled unpleasantly near my sacred person. I dropped into my saddle and riding over to Maxime I called out:

"Come down! they're firing at us. Let us find some safer place."

He came down, and seeing me lighting a cigarette he cried: "Ah! Codger, *pour l'amour de Dieu et de moi!* give me a cigarette, my fingers are frozen and I have not got a match."

I rolled him a cigarette and handed it to him with my lighting apparatus, an American invention in which a spring revolves an emery wheel against a steel spike and throws a shower of sparks upon a scrap of tinder. Now, in lighting the tinder I always directed the shower straight before me, between my charger's ears, so that the animal had never seen this miniature firework display, and it was a startling novelty to him when Maxime fired the thing a yard away from his head. He reared, turned and cantered off about thirty yards, and as I returned towards Maxime

258

the keen intelligence of my brute who was an old campaigner, "perceived"—as somehow or other horses do perceive, very often long before their riders—the approaching flight of a shell, and "crouched" as it were. I threw myself along his flank as circus riders do, shouting to Maxime as I did so:

"Shell!"

"Pas pour moi!" I heard him cry airily as he lit his cigarette. They were his last words—almost as he spoke the explosion took place covering my horse with snow and earth. I looked towards Maxime. Good God! shall I ever forget the horror of the sight!

A fragment of the shell had struck him full in the breast and the poor golden-haired boy was literally smashed to pieces. I draw the veil of silence over the horror of my task; it is enough to say that I found the gold chain, the locket and the image and hung them around my own neck, where they remained till the termination of the campaign. We were a saddened and silent group in the correspondent's mess that night.

Plevna had surrendered soon after midday—what a day of carnage it had been—I have been in many such scenes since, but seldom have seen anything approaching it.

The war drew to a close and ended with the treaty of San Stefano. Most of us had mothers, sisters, sweethearts, wives, waiting for us at home—I had none of these, I am alone in the world, so I went straight to Paris, and thence to Douai, where I arrived in the blaze of a warm spring noon. As I made my way from the station, I saw inscribed over the window of a *cabarét* in the main street, *Larréze-Restaurateur.*

"Here," thought I, "is where the boy passed his last conscious hours in Douai!"

I went in, and seating myself before a modest *déjeuner,* soon succeeded in drawing mine host into conversation.

"I have just come from the war in the East," said I by the way of introduction.

"Ah! Monsieur is from the war!" replied the garrulous Frank, rising at once to the bait, "then perhaps he met M. Durand, the correspondent of the *Bulletin Quotidien.*"

"Durand?" said I reflectively—"oh yes, I remember. Did you know him?"

"Do I know him! *Mais oui, le scélérat!* He came from Douai, and I saw him the night before he went to the war. He has stayed out there in the East has he not?"

"Yes—he has stayed out there."

"Ah the wretch! He was betrothed to one of the sweetest young girls in this city, but he didn't appreciate her and has stayed out there, no doubt *living la vie Turque* with its immoralities and horrors."

"How do you mean?" queried I.

"Why, the night before he left, he came to Douai and dined at the very table at which you are sitting, monsieur. And then, instead of going to say 'good-bye' to his loved one, he got into some drunken brawl in the lower parts of the town, and had it not been the goodness of a friend, who also loved Mlle. Sterelle, he would never have reached Paris in time to follow the call of his duty. This friend happened to know that he had to leave, and saw him off to Paris, terribly intoxicated, and naturally the good people of Douai were very indignant."

"And where does Mlle. Sterelle live now?"

"Ah! monsieur! Her father died suddenly, soon after Maxime departed, and left her alone in the world; and then, as she had never received word from Maxime, and heard, moreover, that he had decided to remain out there amid the horribly luxury of the East, she married M. Nicholas Dufoure—the *bon bourgeois* who had loved her long."

"And did she love this M. Dufoure?"

"Not as she loved Maxime, of course, but,—*que voulez vous*—she was alone, deserted, with a business on her hands which she could not manage by herself, and she respects her present husband,—which is, no doubt, far better than loving him,—and she will be happier with him than she would have been with Maxime, who has turned out to be a drunkard and a sensualist."

"Ah! and where does Mme. Dufoure live now?"

"At the top of the street, behind the *mairie* monsieur, where she and her husband carry on the business left behind him by Baptiste Sterelle."

I thanked mine host, and having finished my *déjeuner,* betook myself in the direction of the *mairie.* I found the narrow street Maxime had described to me, and climbing its treacherous cobble-stones, found at its head a well-to-do looking harberdasher's shop, over the window of which was inscribed "Nicolas Dufoure, successor to Baptiste Sterelle." I entered, ostensibly in quest of some cravats, to be served by a comely young woman, who advanced from behind the *comptoir* at the end of the shop. We were alone. Indeed, at this hour Douai seemed to be fast asleep in its entirety, and I had no difficulty in getting into conversation with "Madame," whom I learnt at once to be Mme. Dufoure, *née* Euphrasie Sterelle.

I opened the conversation, as I had done in the case of Père Larréze, with the statement of my recent return from the theatre of war, and, like the worthy *restaurateur* Mme. Dufoure immediately asked me if I had known Maxime, and on my replying in the affirmative, added the question:

"Why did he stay in the East, monsieur?"

"*Parce que c'était plus fort que lui,*" I replied, ambiguously.

"And when he left, he was *fiancé* to me," exclaimed the little woman, indignantly.

"But you also, madame, have married elsewhere," I ventured to suggest.

"And had I not the right—did I not owe it to myself, to do so?" she returned. "Maxime and I were betrothed to one another when we were only 'so high,' and though I had many an offer from some of the best matches in Douai, I remained faithful to my promise to him, for—I love him. Well, m'sieu, when this war broke out, he came to Douai—to see me?—not at all—to join in some drunken orgy in the lowest parts of the town, I know not where. But, fortunately, M. Dufoure, who was there for business purposes, saw him and heard him read aloud to his vile companions my last letter to him. Oh! I know that it was so, for M. Dufoure remembered whole passages from it, which

I recognized as having written. He was naturally indignant, for he had loved me almost as long as Maxime, but he sincerely hoped that Maxime would clear himself by letter, and even went morning after morning himself to the post-office to see whether he had written. But no, he maintained a silence as cold as that of the grave, and when my father died and left me alone in the world, I married M. Dufoure, who offered himself at once as my protector. And now he tells me that Maxime has remained in the East to live *la vie Orientale.* Bah! it is all that he was fit for. I do not regret him." She paused, more to gain breath, I think than anything else, and then added: "When did you see him last, monsieur, and where."

"It was in the month of December, and at the Fall of Plevna, madame," replied I, slowly, and was about to add, "he was shot down within a few yards of me," when a great wave of thought and commiseration surged up within my soul. Thought for the details of the horrible story of treachery and lies that unfolded itself before my mental vision, and commiseration for the little woman before me, and for her lover, our poor dead Maxime.

Obviously it was this self-same Dufoure who had stunned Maxime in the dark on his last visit to Douai, and who had stolen the letter he had seen fall from the boy's pocket—that letter which he had evidently committed to memory and declared he had heard Maxime read aloud. Obviously it was he who had suppressed Maxime's letters if they ever reached Douai, and on this basis of trickery, treachery, and lies, had supplanted the poor gold-headed boy whom I had seen shattered by a shell from the walls of Plevna.

A problem requiring almost instantaneous solution propounded itself to me as I stood in the little shop at Douai on that spring afternoon. It was this—Here was Euphrasie, married, bound irrevocably and for life to this man who had won her by fraud, but for whom she felt a calm, permanent respect, if not a love like that she had given to Maxime; on the other hand, Maxime was dead, and it could do no good, but on the contrary must do a terrible harm, to fill her young life with a ghastly passionate regret for her dead love, combined with a horror, a loathing of the man to whom she had been bound for life by his grisly treachery.

To fulfil my promise to Maxime and shatter the woman's trust in the living out of a sentimental respect for the dead, or not to do so, and by my breach of trust let her continue in the path of her duty as the wife of Nicolas Dufoure, untainted by the knowledge of his crime, for crime it was—that was the question. Whilst I stood deliberating as rapidly as I could upon the problem, a short, sour-faced man entered the shop, and, casting an evil look at me, said to Euphrasie,

"Madame Dufoure! would it not be better to attend to your business instead of chattering with strangers?"—and the little woman, curtesying to me retired with a half-suppressed sigh to her *comptoir*. The man came behind the counter and commenced defiantly wrapping the cravats I had selected in paper for me.

So this was the husband of Euphrasie Sterelle. God help her, poor child! My mind was immediately made up—better thought I, to let her make the best of her life, such as it is, than to mar the whole of it from now henceforward with the knowledge of her husband's baseness. Douai is a queer, primitive little place, and little from the outer world disturbs the placidity of its provincial existence: the chances were that the story of Maxime's death—already ancient history—would never reach the ears of Euphrasie Dufoure.

My mind was made up. I came away without executing my mission, and returned to Paris where I sought Maxime's only living relation—a sister, the wife of a jeweller in the Palais Royal. To her I confided the whole story, and the souvenirs of Maxime, which I had religiously worn ever since I took them from his mangled body.

And Maxime's sister approved of my breach of trust.

THE HERESY OF SPENCER CARLYON.

THE spectacle of a Lord Justice of Appeal telling ghost-stories to a circle of rapt auditors might strike the casual observer as verging on the incongruous, but I think that my readers will agree with me that Sir William Cornell told the story of "The Lute Girl's Charm" with such an appreciation of the artistic touches, and dramatic points of his narration, that I for one determined to get him on the subject again.

Accordingly one evening towards the end of the season of 18— I invited Dr. Tompkins and Sir William to dine at my chambers presumably to say *au revoir* to Dick Lyster, prior to his departure for the United States. After dinner as we sat smoking and chatting, I made some remark about the medico's story, which he had called "On a Roman Balcony," and asked him if he ever expected to hear anything else of that spectral hand. At the word "hand" Sir William pricked up his ears, and at his request I gave him a short outline of the story Tompkins had told Trevanion, Dr. Van Boomkamp, and me at his own rooms.

"Ah!" said Sir William. "That reminds me of one of the most spectral stories I ever heard; it belongs to the Carlyon's of Clough-Iveagh, and was told me by Sir Erule himself. Erule was called to the bar the same term as I was, and we were briefless barristers together, so it wouldn't be worth his while to lie to me."

"Tell us the story, Sir William," I suggested.

And after a little persuasion and hesitation the old judge took a fresh cigar, settled himself in his chair, and said:—

"When, on the death of Sir Willoughby Carlyon, enquiry was made, and it was ascertained that his brother Charlton had died in Rio Janeiro, a bachelor, no one was more surprised by his un-expected accession to the title and estates than Sir Willoughby's orphan nephew, Erule, himself.

"Sir Erule Carlyon, the new baronet, was the only son of the late Sir Willoughby's youngest brother. His father Erule Carlyon had never addressed speech or letter to his eldest broth-er, Sir Willoughby, since he was a lad, and his second brother, Charlton, had betaken himself to Rio Janeiro whilst Erule was still at college—but even supposing him to have remained in the country it is probable that the youngest Carlyon would have been equally isolated from him and from the rest of his family.

"This condition of affairs requires some explanation and the explanation is as follows:

"When His Majesty King James the First instituted the per-petuity of knighthood, by conferring the new title of Baronet, on such gentlemen as were willing to aid his Irish reforms, one of the first to assume the dignities of the new order was Mr. Carlyon of Clough-Iveagh. The Carlyons of Clough-Iveagh were said to be the oldest, proudest, and wealthiest of the Catholic families of the north of Ireland—that they were old, proud, and wealthy there is no doubt, but whether they were entitled to the superlative qualification is a question on which Milesian gene-alogists have been divided.

"Suffice it to say that the Carlyons, who succeeded one an-other in sets of four, as it were, Sir Spencer, Sir Charlton, Sir Willoughby, and Sir Erule, and then back again to Sir Spencer and so on, had one fetiche that was embodied in the blazonment of the family escutcheon. To wit: 'On a field argent, a Crucifix supported dexter and sinister, gules a hand bearing a sword' —with the device 'To the faith, faifhful.' From this it will be gath-ered that the Carlyons were Catholic to the backbone, and every tradition of the family was in some way connected with, or the outcome of, their devotion to the Church. Two of the Carlyons had been Cardinals, whilst the family tree positively bristled with Priors, Monsignores, and Bishops of the Hoy See—more than once the family had been threatened with extinction by the celibacy of these holy men, and had the baronetcy been conferred upon Mr. Carlyon of the Clough-Iveagh in feetail it would have become extinct with the third baronet—as it was, the succession was unhampered and fell from generation to generation on the nearest living male relative of the late baronet. It was thus that Erule Carlyon woke one morning in his chambers in Lincoln's Inn to find himself entitled to the Red Hand upon his armorial bearings, and what was of more importance to a briefless barrister, to the castle and broad acres of Clough-Iveagh in the county of Belfast.

"It was a complete surprise to him, for, from the day he was born he had never held any communication with, and had never seen either of his uncles Sir Willoughby, or Mr. Charlton Carlyon, and for this all-sufficient reason.

"His father Erule Carlyon whilst a lad at Oxford had fallen in love with a fair Protestant maiden, the daughter of the Dean of his College, and had announced to his brother his intention of marrying the lady. The two elders had promptly, with the traditional bigotry of the Carlyons, informed their youngest brother that should he disgrace the family by union with 'the heretic woman' he would be disowned on the spot by the older members of the family, and moreover he was warned that the lady would never be recognized by them as their brother's wife. Wounded to the nethermost depth of his romantic Irish soul, and boiling with all the fury of which the Celtic nature is capable, Erule Carlyon had formally separated from his brothers, who in turn ruled a crimson line through his name on the pedigree that was preserved at Clough-Iveagh.

"Married to the gentle Episcopalian and the father of a baby boy the image of his mother, it is hardly surprising that Erule Carlyon embraced the Protestant faith, and young Erule was duly baptized a Protestant, despite a last strenuous effort made by his uncles, as they said, to save his soul from hell-fire. The breach had been complete and Erule Carlyon had grown to man's estate and had been called to the bar conscious, indeed, that he was the nephew of Sir Willoughby Carlyon of Clough-Iveagh, and that he had an uncle in Brazil, but beyond that knowing naught of family save in the remembrance of his mother who had died when he was a child, and of his father who had followed her, some ten years later, to the grave. Their bodies were at peace in Brompton Cemetery—the idea of claiming for their remains a resting place in the Chapel at Clough-Iveagh had never for one moment entered their son's mind.

"One warm spring afternoon, therefore, of the year of grace eighteen hundred and seventy-nine, Sir Erule Carlyon arrived, a stranger, and in the eyes of his tenantry, a heretic, at Clough-Iveagh, the first avowed Protestant Carlyon who had trodden the ancestral demesne.

"I say, the first 'avowed Protestant,' for there dwelt in the memory of Sir Erule Carlyon a story that had been told him by his father, years ago, of a great-grand-uncle Spencer, who had been pointed to by the family as having heretical tendencies, and as having in some mysterious way come to a bad end in consequence. The details of the narrative he had never been able to gather, but as far as he was able to learn they were as follows:

"Sir Spencer Carlyon had been a bachelor and a student. He lived in Clough-Iveagh Castle a solitary, studious life, unbroken by any companionship save that of his chaplain-confessor, a young priest, distantly connected with the family, and noted, in the Roman Catholic Church, despite his youth, for his exemplary piety and devoted austerity. It was not without an object that His Eminence Cardinal Willoughby Carlyon, principal of the Benedictine confraternity at Monte Cassino, had appointed Monsignore Whiston to the Chaplaincy of Clough-Iveagh. Rumours had reached him in Rome to the effect that the devotion of Sir Spencer Carlyon to the interests of his Church left something to be desired, and he hoped that the propinquity and example of Monsignore Whiston would effectually check the tendency that, according to rumour, Sir Spencer betrayed, to dabble in Occultism, Mediæval Magic, and other studies forbidden to her children by the Church of Rome. Accordingly the young priest had been installed at Clough-Iveagh, as the custodian of Sir Spencer's orthodoxy, and two years later the winter sun shone in upon a ghastly scene in the Castle library.

"The first servant to enter in the morning was greeted by the sight of his master sitting in his accustomed chair, his head lying on the table before him, his brains beaten out. A window behind him was wide open, the shrubs outside were torn and trampled, beneath the casement a blood-bespattered paper-weight was found, which had evidently been the instrument of Sir Spencer's murder, and from that day Monsignore Whiston had never been seen or heard of.

"Sir Spencer having died a bachelor, the baronetcy fell upon his younger brother Charlton, who consequently relinquished his purpose of entering the Church.

"Of all his ancestors 'the heretic Sir Spencer' was the one whose history interested most deeply the young Sir Erule. That his great-grand-uncle had been murdered in a fit of fanatic frenzy by his chaplain he never for one moment doubted. He deeply regretted that he had never been able to discover, inductively or otherwise, the nature of the studies that had been interrupted by his ancestor's death. That he had been engrossed in study at the moment of his murder, there seemed no doubt, but whatever had been the books or papers that had encumbered the desk at which the corpse was found, either they had been taken with him by the murderer, or had been destroyed. The library consisted almost entirely of theological works, and no folio, quarto, octavo, duodecimo, or pamphlet in the shelves, seemed in any way to savour of the forbidden studies which had led to his great-grand-uncle's destruction. Often in the night-watches, whilst Sir Erule sat in that self-same chair at that self-same desk, immersed in his work, he would lean back, lost in thoughts on this subject, his eyes fastened on the darkness before him which his single working lamp was powerless to pierce.

"It was on one of these occasions, a few months after his arrival at Clough-Iveagh, that he was made the victim of a terrifying and wholly inexplicable incident.

"Suddenly, without the slightest shadow of a warning, he was seized with a sensation of deathly sickness and apprehension. In spite of his faintness he was overwhelmed by the feeling that something stood behind his chair, but, paralysed with terror, he was unable to move. At last, with a wrench he turned in his seat, and as he did so, it seemed to him that he caught a momentary glimpse of a tall figure robed in the black cassock of a Benedictine monk standing behind his chair. The face of the figure seemed deathly white, the eyes like flaming jet stood out against its pallor. The right arm was raised above his head in a menacing gesture. That was all he could catch, as the figure faded in the shadows of the heavily curtained window behind his desk.

"But as he stood, petrified, and gazing in the direction of where the apparition had been, he became aware of a spot of pale light in a far corner of the library. As he watched it, it moved, and appeared to wander up and down the book-cases and along the shelves. Pulling himself together with a tremendous effort he advanced towards the light. He reached it.

"There!—within six feet of him, suspended in the air and sharply outlined against the surrounding gloom, was the spectre of a human hand bearing a taper. The taper was alight, but the whole hand and taper seemed to be of themselves luminous as they wandered from shelf to shelf as when one searches for a volume in the dark.

"His brain reeled. His senses left him, and with a stifled groan Sir Erule Carlyon fell heavily to the floor.

"It was thus that the servants found him when they entered the library next morning."

"Sir Erule Carlyon was eight-and-twenty, sound in mind and limb, and of exemplary habits of life. The idea of his being frightened by a ghost was preposterous to his daylight sense—yet the impression of the night before had been too startlingly vivid for him to pass it by without a further thought. Naturally his mind reverted to the fate of 'the heretic Sir Spencer,' and on the following afternoon he sought the chapel of Clough-Iveagh and found the tablet commemorative of Sir Spencer's death. It read simply:

Sacred to the Memory of
Spencer Willoughby Carlyon,
VIIIth Baronet,
who departed this life
on
the 13th August, 1797.
R. I. P.

"Sir Erule started as he read; it was now the 14th of August. The preceding night had been the anniversary of his great-grand-uncle's murder.

"That night, and on many nights after, he watched in the library for the reappearance of the apparition and the searching hand. In vain. No supernatural happening disturbed his labours, and as days formed weeks and the weeks grew into months, the incident became lost amid impressions of the past. More completely was it obliterated by the fact that Sir Erule was on the eve of taking to himself a wife, the daughter of the Protestant rector of a neighbouring village, who had enslaved the fancy of the Lord of Clough-Iveagh, and had been selected by him to found the 'Protestant Succession' in his ancestral halls."

"Once more the 13th of August had arrived. In two days' time the bells would ring and the solitary reign of the master of Clough-Iveagh would be at an end. Sir Erule was reading, as was his wont, in the library, when suddenly he felt creeping over him the same sensation that had terrified him a year ago. In an instant the whole thing came back to him, and he sprang from his chair, turning as he did so.

"There, as in the year gone by, stood the apparition, the spectral form of a Romish priest, whose coal-black eyes seemed to burn into his own. Mastering himself with a supreme effort, he sprang forward, as the spectre raised its arm;—he saw then that the hand held one of the square leaden paper-weights that our forefathers were accustomed to use. As he sprang *into the space occupied by the shade*, a sensation of icy coldness and faintness gripped his whole body; in another second he had recovered from the shock,—and he was alone. Quickly he turned to the point where he had seen the hand on the former occasion—there it was—wandering from shelf to shelf. He came close and watched it as it roamed over the bookcases.

"The books that became visible in turn as the luminosity of the severed hand reached them, were all the most orthodox kind. There were, among others, the *Rationale Divinorum Officiorum* of Gulielmus Durandus, printed at Venice in 1559; Ducange's *Glossarium*; the complete works of the Abbé Fleury in the edition of 1739; the life of the arch Romanist Julien de la Rovère, Pope Julius I., who paved the way for Leo X.; the Amsterdam 1755 edition of the *Testament* of Richelieu. All these details he noted as the ghostly taper passed the volumes, and then, suddenly, even as he looked, a great folio edition of the commentaries of Origen disappeared before his eyes. As the volume vanished the hand holding the taper also disappeared, and Sir Erule, bathed in a cold perspiration, was left in absolute darkness in the corner of the library.

"He had watched too long to be content to abandon his investigation there. He returned to the writing-table, and bringing his chair and the lamp into the corner, deposited the latter upon a stool and seated himself to watch the empty space in the shelves whence the Origen had been rapt by an unseen hand. For an hour he kept his eyes fastened upon the gap, and then, worn out with the fixity of his gaze, and the reaction of his nerves, he fell fast asleep.

"When he awoke it was broad day. The lamp had gone out and—the Origen was back in its place!

"With a stifled exclamation he drew it from the shelves and carried it to the table. There he opened it.

"It was Origen only as to its outer cover. Enclosed in the binding that had once contained the early Christian Commentary was fastened the *Parva Naturalia* of Albert Magnus, the corner stone of mediæval magic.

"This must have been the work in which Sir Spencer Carlyon had been engrossed when the blow, treacherously delivered from behind, had hurried his unshriven soul into the presence of his Maker. Feverishly he turned its leaves to find whether any papers or notes were concealed therein. About half way through two leaves were stuck together: cautiously he began to separate them; they adhered to one another with a clotted sticky brown substance, now dried and hardened by a century of time.

"Sir Erule started back. *This* had been the page at which his ancestor's studies had been interrupted. His brains and blood served the purpose of a ghastly book-marker to identify the place!

"Shuddering, the master of Clough-Iveagh restored the volume,—the silent witness of Sir Spencer's murder, to its place in the dark corner of the library, and rested there awhile in thought.

"What was the outcome of his deliberations I know not. Sir Erule was married on the following day, and his bride, whose senses were sharpened by her love alone, noted the worn, grey look in her husband's eyes.

"But he never told her of his vigil in the library, and to this day she does not know why, at nightfall on the 13th of August in every year, the library is locked up by Sir Erule Carlyon himself, who keeps the key until he re-opens it on the 14th with his own hand."

THE AUTOBIOGRAPHY
OF A DISEMBODIED SPIRIT.

By Cyprienne de Valneas.

WHEN, after the first few days of my stay at Sir John Worlstenholme's, I lost colour and appetite, and betrayed a tendency to mope around nervously all day, I committed the folly of telling Clarice Wolstenholme, the daughter of mamma's old friend Sir John, that I had seen the family ghost, and was thoroughly well laughed at for my pains. I suppose this happens to every one who is honoured by the personal attentions of a family spectre, but I felt it very keenly all the same. On mature reflection I have come to the conclusion that it was pure jealousy on the part of the family—jealousy that I, an American girl, spending the summer in London and the autumn in the country-houses of friends I had made during the season, should be thus favoured with the nocturnal visits of their ancestor, "the bad Sir George," rather than any of the family then in possession of Wolstenhole Grange.

I had, however, the satisfaction afforded to few ghost-seers I believe—in fact I never heard tell of such an occurrence before—of having my assertions verified in a manner which exonerated me forever from the charge of hysteria, and that by no means less a person than "the bad Sir George" himself. Still, the whole thing was so weird and mysterious, that it made an impression upon me that will never be effaced; and as I am continually asked to tell "my ghost story," I suppose I may as well rush into print once and for all and save myself the trouble of telling it viva voce hereafter. So, before the story can get garbled and exaggerated, as ghost stories always do, I set myself to work to record it all as it actually happened.

My father, who was one of the last of the pure old Creoles of Louisiana, and whose ancestors are continually mentioned by G. W. Cable in his historic Creole traditions, died when I was a little thing, and left me alone in the world with mamma, who has been father and mother both to me ever since I was five years old. I hardly remember him, but I have a dim recollection of a handsome soldierly man who called me "little mamma," and who used to croon old-time snatches of melody to me as I sat on his knee on the verandah of our house on the Bayou St. Hilaire.

Catholics, all of us, I was brought up at the Convent of the Sacred Heart on the Hudson, and knew little of aught save our quiet life in the cloisters and school-rooms there, varied with summers spent with mamma in the mountains, until the winter of 1886, when mamma took a house in New York; and after showing myself at an Assembly, and after standing till my feet ached throughout a winter's afternoon, dressed in white, whilst hundreds of people told me I was lovely, which I knew, and said other things that I didn't want to hear, I was officially "in society," and set my weary feet on the tread-mill of continual entertainments, to keep tramping until the season of 18— had come to a timely end, and mamma and I were free to rest from the laborious "pleasures of life"—save the mark!

I had made a great friend of Clarice Wolstenholme, principally, I think, because I had initiated her into the mystery of two famous secrets of mine, upon which I had been living and looking well for eight months, when I started for Wolstenholme. There were Mrs. Smith's "Peerless Paste for the Complexion," and Dr. Jones' "Elixer of Life and Soul Restorer"—two preparations that I swear by, and receive an annual allowance from the proprietors for advertising. She had never heard of them, so you can imagine that she looked upon me as the saviour of her life and complexion—and after all what is the one without the other to *nous autres femmes*?

I don't know whether it was my allegiance to "Peerless Paste" and "Soul-Restorer" that gave her the idea that I was a person of rare strength of mind and exceptional scientific knowledge; anyhow, for some reason or other, the house being full of guests, she had put me into "the haunted room," the room where "the bad Sir George" had been found dead in the winter of the year 17—. I could never quite learn wherein his badness consisted; he seemed from all accounts to have been an awful flirt, and to have made love to every woman he ever came across, which didn't strike me as being so very dreadful after all. But it further seems that he was deeply versed in occult sciences and mesmerism, and, in the company of a mysterious Italian doctor, used to conduct his experiments and concoct his spells in the room that I occupied. Anyhow, one day the Italian having disappeared, they broke down the door of the room and found Sir George lying, apparently dead, in the very chamber in which I was to sleep. I say "apparently dead," because for many days they couldn't make out whether he were really dead or not. There was no life, no soul, nor any sign of them in the body, but the body didn't feel like a dead body, and it was only after days and days and days that they decided to give him his appointed place in the family vault, and lie about his virtues on a marble slab in the village church of Wolstenholme.

Clarice said she had been given to understand that American girls weren't afraid of anything, being especially indifferent to mice, ghosts, spiders, banshees, and earwigs, and though I was not quite so sure about this myself, for the credit of the stars and stripes I wouldn't cast the shadow of a doubt upon her belief; and with a brave heart inspired by the warmth of the summer sun on a glorious August afternoon, and a cup of the most irreproachable English tea, I surveyed the room which was to be my abode for a month, and arranged on my dressing-table my boxes and brushes, my "Peerless Paste" and my "Elixir of Life." It wasn't a bit like a haunted room, it was too comfortable; and though the bed was rather big and bogey, and the walls were panelled with oak squares that suggested sliding aside to give entrance to "spooks," I confess that the thought of "the bad Sir George" didn't trouble me much. But wait a bit!

From Waterloo to Pagbourne, the nearest station to Wolstenholme Grange, is not a long journey—especially for an American; but cooped up in the compartment of the first-class carriage in which we made the transit, mamma and I both managed to get very tired; and had it not been for the assistance of Dr. Jones we could hardly have got down to dinner. Clarice seemed annoyed that I retired so early. "Why don't you sit up with the rest of us?" she said. "Never mind your complexion; no men of any real importance come down till the end of the week."

But I was nearly dead, and half-past nine saw me "snuggled" away between the lavender-scented sheets of that grim old bed—and I never passed a better night in my life. I woke once, fancying mamma had come into my room, but as I could neither see nor hear anything, and had forgotten all about "the bad Sir George," I fell asleep again at once. Next morning I found one of my rings lying on my pillow; how it got there Heaven knows! I came to the conclusion that either mamma or I had walked in our sleep, and fidgeted with the things on the dressing-table; several of them struck me as disarranged—I'm a perfect maniac for tidiness—but after all, most probably I had been too tired to fix my things properly the night before, so I thought no more about it. It was my second night at Wolstenholme that my experience began.

I don't know how long I had been asleep when I woke with a start! The same feeling that some one was in my room took possession of me as on the night before, and though I could see nothing, the story of "the bad Sir George Wolstenholme" suddenly occurred with most unpleasant vividness to my mind.

Surely something moved over by the dressing table? Yes! there was the squeak of a cork! I sat bolt upright in bed, repressing my first intention of hiding myself under the bedclothes, and said in the bravest voice I could summon up,

"Who's there?"

No reply,—but a great sigh echoed through the room and then all was still. At that moment the full August moon "lighting the skirts of a long cloud, ran forth" and brilliantly illuminated every corner of the room. Nothing!

To say that I was awfully frightened is to use a miserably inadequate form of words, and it was broad daylight before I fell asleep again. As soon as I woke "for keeps" I ran into mamma's room—which was next to mine—and told her what had happened. Would you believe it, she laughed at me. She said that probably a mouse had been waltzing about on my dressing-table, and, frightened by my waking movement, had squeaked and fled. Well—it was a reasonable explanation, but it didn't satisfy me, and so I took her advice and said nothing about it to the family. I went to be the next night firmly convinced that "something was going to happen." Something did!

Try as I would I could not get to sleep, and my first moment of easiness arrived when the clock in the hall struck midnight and nothing appeared. The ghost, if ghost there was, had no sense of the ghostly fitness of things, as to the proper time to appear and gibber, if to gibber he felt inclined. But alas! how vainly we take comfort from such trifles; the clock had hardly struck a quarter to one, when I distinctly saw in the corner of the room a tiny point of light, and if England had fire-bugs as we have, I should have said it was a fire-bug; but being fairly well up in natural history I knew this could not be the case and I thought at once of Théophile Gautier's story of "Avatar," and came to the rational conclusion that I was being visited by a soul, with which liberties had been taken by some Dr. Balthazar Cherbonneau of English extraction.

Somehow or other I didn't feel so frightened as I expected to do under the circumstances; it is a different matter I think when one sees a spirit arrive. It is not as if one suddenly wakes and finds it there. My only hope was, that if this particular ghost was going to become visible, he, she, or it, had died with its clothes on—for I had always understood that family spectres are very conservative in their habits in this particular. Indeed I once knew a bashful man who never dared to ask a blushing bride to share his ancestral home, because his ancestral ghost had been drowned whilst bathing; and no entreaties on the part of his descendant could induce him to vary his excessive indumentary désinvolture.

The spark moved to the dressing table, and there expanded into a faintly luminous form, clothed—thank goodness!—in the costume of the last quarter of the preceding century. It was the ghost of a man, but he was far more interested in his own ghostly reflection in the mirror than in me, and contemplated himself with apparently supreme satisfaction. And well he might, for he was exceedingly handsome; and though it was so dark that no colour was visible in the luminosity of his clothes, I could see that from his finely cut face his hair, which was worn long, as was the custom in the preceding century, was tied back in a queue with a knot of ribbon.

The spook—of course it was a spook—seemed very much interested in my belongings. He took up my jewels one by one and examined them with much care. Then he turned his attention to my bottles and things. He took up my pretty little pot of Peerless Paste, opened it, put in his fingers, smelt it, and smiled, put it to his lips, and a puzzled look of distaste crossed his face. Then he took up my bottle of Soul-Restorer and, pulling out the cork, put the phial to his nose. He was about to carry it to his lips when it struck me that even in a ghost it was vulgar to drink out of a bottle, and rather, I think with a view to offering him a glass, I said, valiantly,

"Say! *pst!*"

He put down the bottle, corking it with a jerk, and looked round at me. Seeing me awake, he made me a profound bow, quite *"le grand salut l'on faisait à la dernier Régence;"* and seeing him so polite I asked,

"Who are you?"

He seemed to be trying to speak, but in vain. Whether he would have eventually succeeded or not I cannot tell, for unfortunately a stupid rooster down at the farm, who had either gone to bed ridiculously late, risen ridiculously early, or been dreaming of sunshine and worms, crowed unseasonably. Instantaneously the ghost—who in this respect respected the canons of ghost law—disappeared. Again I saw the spark, and the next moment I knew that I was alone.

This time there was no reason why I should keep my counsel, so I told the whole thing to Clarice Wolstenholme, directly after breakfast. The horrid girl not only laughed at me and declared that I had been dreaming, but told some of the men, who in turn told it all around; and all that day my life was made a burden to me. One of the men—a Mr. Ditcham—had the audacity to say to me at dinner,

"I say, Miss de Valreas, if 'the bad Sir George' would only write a testimonial of his opinion of your cold-cream and your corpse reviver—what a grand advertisement it would be for the proprietors. I expect he would if you asked him, you know. 'The bad Sir George' was an awful masher, and men used to rub themselves with cosmetics to make themselves pretty when he was alive; whilst as for the tonic stuff—Miss Wolstenholme gave me some the other day when I came in dead tired, and it made me feel splendid."

I need hardly say that I didn't deign to answer him, and refused to be led into the discussion. I thought it horrid of Clarice to have said anything about my two patent medicines, but I didn't feel a bit ashamed of it for Mrs. Smith's Paste isn't "make up" and I've a lovely complexion "though I say it as shouldn't," and as for Dr. Jones' Elixir, I attribute to *it* the fact that I didn't look—like all the other girls at the end of the season—as if I'd been kept in a soda for weeks and then had all my bones pulled out of me like a sole at Delmonico's.

But that night I opened my Paste-pot and wrote on a card which I leaned up against it, "You rub this on you and it makes you lovely," and I poured some Soul-restorer into a little glass and wrote on a card which I lay upon it, "You drink this and it makes you feel good—try it and see how you like the sensation for once." And then on a card which I stuck in the mirror where I *knew* he would look I wrote, "If I am asleep wake me up and tell me what you think of things generally." Then, all things being arranged for "the bad Sir George," I tumbled into bed and slept only as one *can* sleep when one has the pleasant consciousness of having done a good action at little personal inconvenience and no expense.

It was therefore with a feeling of peaceful security, and no alarm, that I woke to see the "Avatar" of "the bad Sir George" just expanding itself before my dressing-table. Just as young authors who are misunderstood, or unappreciated, by the world at large, attach themselves in almost filial bond, to the few bright spirits who estimate them at their proper worth—from their own point of view—so did the apparition of the departed Baronet of Wolstenholme seem to attach himself to me, who alone appreciated his existence; and though he chose a somewhat unconventional hour for paying his respects, after all one cannot seriously compromise oneself with a ghost—a "Thing" that, having laid aside humanity, becomes exempt from human social laws—a "Thing" that you can put a parasol through without inconveniencing "It," and which, in moments of the most righteous indignation, you could not possibly slap. It was this sort of kindly affection which shone—I say shone advisedly—from the handsome face of "the bad Sir George" as he turned and bowed politely in reply to my premonitory "Ahem!"

"Have you read my cards?" queried I.

An interrogatory look came into his face as he turned to the dressing table, took up the Peerless Paste and the card attached, and carried them to the window to read my instructions by the moonlight. Depositing the card on the window-sill, he daintily uncovered the little ornamental jar, and delicately inserting one finger rubbed his nose carefully with it. I saw the thus anointed organ shine in the moonbeams, as he returned to the dressing-table and took up the Elixir card. He read it, as before, with some curiosity, and then, lifting the glass, laid one hand on his breast, raised the glass as if "toasting" me, made me a grave bow, and then drank the potion.

"Ah!" he sighed, and then remarked in a very faint, but not unmusical voice—"that gives me life—and voice. Do you know, madame, I have not been able to speak for more than one hundred years?"

"Not madame," corrected I, "*mademoiselle*."

280

A look of almost pained surprise passed over his brow as he bowed once more, and then he positively blushed;—evidently "the bad Sir George" was quite a different sort of person from what tradition made out. But I hastened to reassure him by introducing myself in form.

"Miss Cyprienne de Valreas, I am called—I presume I have the pleasure of addressing Sir George Wolstenholme."

"Exactly," replied he; "'the bad Sir George,' at the service of mademoiselle. I trust I do not inconvenience you by my presence."

"On the contrary," said I, "and after all, it is I who should apologize. I believe it is your room that I am occupying."

"That is nothing," returned he; "in my present condition I can hardly be said to occupy any room. Ahem! mademoiselle is French?"

"No, American."

"Ah! I understand." At this moment he caught sight of the card stuck in the mirror, and leant over to read it. Horror! as he did so that horrible cock crowed again, though with more reason than on the previous occasion, for the dawn was just beginning to give greyness to the mists of night. Instantaneously, as before, he disappeared; the last I saw of him being his Paste-anointed nose which sank onto the dressing-table. I was quite sorry he had to leave so suddenly and anathematized that cock.

But wonder of wonders! Next morning when I rose and went to my table, there, on the white damask of the toilet cover, outlined in Peerless Paste, collapsed and greasy, lay the impression of Sir George's nose. A handsome aquiline nose, and I felt a certain satisfaction that he had left with me the counterfeit presentment of his leading feature. And this, though I carefully eradicated the stain, gave me the cue for my programme of the following night, to which I now almost anxiously looked forward.

I had observed that it was only under the influence of the "Soul-restorer" that the disembodied spirit of "the bad Sir George" found itself endowed with the corporeal attribute of speech. I therefore poured him out a liberal measure before retiring, of what Mr. Ditcham had called "my tonic stuff," and then, as the departed baronet was gradually becoming singularly "human" I arrayed myself in my most becoming wrapper, and dozed off in my arm-chair, instead of seeking the seclusion of my grim old four-poster.

I must have been unusually weary, for I did not wake until I felt a soft, ghostly touch upon my shoulder, and, as the shade bowed me his nightly salutation, I heard a soft, ghostly voice remark:

"Pardon my apparent rudeness, mademoiselle; but my time being short, and not wishing to be deprived of the pleasure of your conscious company, I have taken the liberty of waking you up. Much against the dictates both of my conscience and politeness, believe me."

"Not at all!" I replied, rousing myself. "How are you this ev— tonight, I mean?"

"Why," replied Sir George, "I feel most singularly well. This tonic of yours seems to give me substance as well as voice. You doubtless observed that I took the liberty of touching you, to rouse you from your very becoming slumbers. Now, last week I could not have done that, for I was impalpable—not to say diaphanous—as I have been, much to my annoyance, for more than a century. It is most unpleasant to be impalpable; it robs one of one's sense of dignity, and on windy nights is most draughty. Now if only I could regain some of my original personal appearance—which I was given to understand was not unpleasing—during these brief periods of return to existence, I should have nothing left to desire."

"But I am sure," I replied very politely, " you can not want anything more than you already have in the matter of personality."

"Ah! mademoiselle," replied the poor ghost sadly, "this Cimmerian darkness is a most becoming light for *nous autres revenants*—between ourselves that is why most of us who did not happen to be especially favoured by nature when living in the ordinary way, particularly affect the night for our return to the haunts—I use the word haunts advisedly—of our lifetime. One must have—ahem!—*departed* under singularly favourable circumstances to be able to bear broad daylight."

"Why?" queried I.

"Well, you see, most of us would prevent somewhat the appearance of fireworks by daylight, should we appear at noon. What seems to you a delicate pallor by this unlight, would appear to be an unwholesome *flabbiness* in the sunshine. This soft watery luminosity which you so much admire, would seem to you mere unromantic *dampness* by day. Therefore we take advantage of precedent, and leave as soon as the common or barndoor fowl, created doubtless for the suppression of the supernatural, raises the pibroch of his race, and salutes the unbecoming dawn."

"Alas! poor ghost!" as Hamlet says. I felt for him deeply, and seeing him apparently much upset by the confession he had doubtless felt himself called upon by my hospitality to make, I poured him out another glass of "Soul-Restorer" under the influence of which he seemed to grow so solid, and his voice to become so distinct that I was quite nervous lest mamma might overhear him from the next room. It was therefore with considerable relief that I received his assurance that he could absolutely disappear instantaneously at any moment.

What I most sympathized with were his regrets for his personal appearance, and to change the conversation as much as anything else, I begged him to consider my Peerless Paste entirely at his disposal, assuring him that whatever might have been his personal appearance on earth, the application of this preparation even in his disembodied state could not but be attended by the most beneficial results. He seemed much impressed by my account, and, tentatively at first and then boldly, applied the delicately scented paste to his shadowy but otherwise satisfactory face. Whether it was the Elixir of Life or no, I am not in a position to state, but the apparition of "the bad Sir George" seemed to acquire solidity before my very eyes; this was the more strikingly visible in his face, coated as it was apparently to his supreme satisfaction with Peerless Paste. I remarked this circumstances to him, and he seemed pleased that his effort was not thrown away upon me. He held out his hand, and, save where it bore traces of his recent application to his face, it was, as he had just deprecatingly remarked, damp, not to say *flabby*. He saw my aversion to the undoctored portion of his person, and requested me to observe the effect on his face. So I raised both my hands to his forehead, touching it on either side; he had taken advantage of my offer of liberality with regard to my paste, and it was sticky—*but it was solid.*

At this moment a rap came upon mamma's door and mamma's voice said, "Is that you moving about?"

What I should have done or said in my confusion I really do not know, had not the ghost of "the bad Sir George," with charming discretion and true gentlemanly feeling, instantaneously disappeared. Nothing was left of him spiritually speaking. The tiny firebug spark which heralded his appearance, announced his departure, and I was alone; BUT—modelled in Peerless Paste upon an almost but not quite impalpable basis of Soul-Restorer jelly, I held in my hands a cast of the face of "the bad Sir George." In no wise was Pygmalion more astonished by the sudden statueification of Sir George Wolstenholme!

I deposited the cosmetic impression of the late Baronet's handsome features on a soft cushion, for fear that I might, by rough handling, destroy it, and, having explained my wakefulness ambiguously to mamma, I went to bed, and to sleep.

Next morning my first glance was directed to my "Figure;" alas! it was hardly more than a shapeless mass, a viscid and protoplasmic patch on the cushion where I had placed it; and though it no longer bore a strong likeness to "the bad Sir George," it remained a distinctly human outline on the cushion.

I am but a woman after all, and though I had sworn myself to inviolable secrecy on the subject of the ancestral spook, things had come to that point that I absolutely *had* to confide in some one or die. So I told Clarice Wolstenholme *all* about it that very afternoon, and in confirmation of my, to her doubtless remarkable story, I pointed to the spoilt chair cushion. Would you believe me when I tell you that even in the face of this convincing proof, she refused to believe that I had not dreamt it all? In vain I pointed to the empty bottles of Soul-Restorer, and the diminished Peerless Paste, it was all of no avail. St. Thomas was an easily gulled individual as compared with Clarice Wolstenhome.

"Of course you were dreaming, my dear child," said she. "You put on more paste than usual and fell asleep in this arm-chair—didn't you fall asleep in it?"

I was compelled to own the soft impeachment, but could not confess that I had done so because "I expected company."

"Well, there it is, perfectly explained!" continued she triumphantly, "this mark on the cushion is simply the impressing of your own head, and as for the Paste and the tonic that have gone, I don't wonder at your using all the former quickly in the blazing sun we've been having; and as for the latter, it can't do you any harm. You probably drink it in your sleep!"

What was the use of arguing with such a sceptic? None whatever—so I determined not to mention Sir George, whom I no longer considered to be in any way a *bad* baronet, and it is well that I made this resolve as has been proved by the termination of my story. Only, every one in the house chaffed me about it, and asked me after my own pet bogey in a way which would have been most unpleasant had they known that they were dealing with what was an actual and existing *fact*.

Every night Sir George Wolstenholme made his appearance at one in the morning and disappeared as the earliest cock crowed, and I confess that very often his disappearance in the middle of an interesting conversation made me feel inclined to do as St. Peter did on a similar occasion. Only, as the time wore on, whether it was true, or whether it was merely complimentary, Sir George expressed himself as experiencing an increasing difficulty in disappearing at the conventional moment. After his soul had departed a filmy protoplasmic bodily form would remain lingering about the room for a few minutes before following its "Avatar" or disappearing into a corner, and this caused me an uneasiness which was but a foreshadowing—I use the word advisedly—of what was to come.

Our stay at Wolstenholme was drawing to a close; in three days we were to leave Sir John's hospitable roof, and I began to feel quite *désolée* at the idea of parting from my friendly ghost. It was this which, I think, led me to be more than usually liberal in my nightly libations of Elixir of Life, for which he had acquired

285

a fine and cultured taste. Had I then realized the literal meaning of Dr. Jones' nerve-tonic, "Soul-Restorer," I should probably have hesitated before giving it so freely to a disembodied spirit, for the space of one month. Be it enough to describe the overwhelming result.

Sir George had appeared as was his wont, and I had broken to him the news of my almost immediate departure. The poor shade was, or seemed to be, infinitely depressed and, whether returning to the habits—the unfortunate habits—of the time in which he had "lived," or whether in a fit of pure abstraction, he drank more than usual of the Elixir and I feared more than would be good for him. But wonder of wonders! Instead of becoming intoxicated, or even incoherent, as he replaced his drained glass upon the dressing table, a strong convulsion shook him before my very eyes, his whole body seemed to take substance, its luminosity disappeared, and had it not been that at that moment the moon flooded the room with a soft light, Sir George Wolstenholme would have been invisible—naturally invisible in the darkness. A vague sensation of fear took possession of me, and I recoiled into my arm-chair as he remarked in a perfectly human voice,

"Have you a flint and steel and tinder-box?"

"What for?" said I.

"Why, to strike a light with, of course!"

"No, I don't know what you mean; but there are lucifers on the mantlepiece," said I, growing more and more frightened.

"Ah, of course—I've seen them used; my great grand-nephew, Sir John Wolstenholme, once put my spirit to flight in this very room by 'scratching' one. That is the right expression, is it not?"

He found a lucifer, and after muttering to himself, "Let me see, let me see, how did he do it?" the thought seemed to suddenly strike him, how matches were to be ignited, and crooking one shapely leg he produced a light in the most approved fashion on the ribbed silk of his claret-coloured "smalls," and lit the candle.

At this moment the cock crowed.

I looked for Sir George to disappear, but, horror! he did not do so. I saw him shake himself, and gather himself together and brace his muscles as if with the strain of a violent effort.

"Tut—tut—tut—" he remarked turning to me with a frown of annoyance on his brow, "something has happened; I cannot disappear. I fear that that cock will be very much annoyed if he hears of this," and he made another effort.

Then he caught up my Elixir bottle and held it to the light. As he read the words on the label he turned to me with an expression of horror on his face and said in a stifled tone of voice:

"'Elixir of Life!' 'Soul-Restorer!' Good God! I've got back my body—I'm alive again!"

And in my room at half-past two in the morning!

"Sir George!" I exclaimed, "you must see that the powerful action of this tonic has entirely altered the position of affairs between us, but as you are alive, you must also be alive to the impropriety of your presence here at this very unseasonable hour. As a ghost it was quite *de rigueur*, but as a man it is quite contrary to the laws of social etiquette."

"Perfectly, perfectly," replied the poor baronet, looking extremely confused; "but where shall I go? If the servants find me in the morning, they will take me for a burglar, in spite of my likeness to my portrait in the picture-gallery. Really, mademoiselle, I regret very much to cause you this embarrassment."

"Is there no secret way out of the Grange?" suggested I. "The night is warm and there is a summer-house by the lake into which no one ever goes. Could you not go there for tonight? You really *can't* stay here."

"Of course not, of course not," replied he; "and now I remember, there is a panel in this very room which opens on a stairway leading to the garden, but I positively forget where it is. You know we ghosts are so restricted in our movements." So saying, he walked around the room, lightly touching the panels with his fingers as he went. "Ah," he exclaimed at last, "here it is!" and pressing a spring in the moulding the panel creaked a little and finally opened, and "the bad Sir George," after having made me a profound bow, stepped through.

"Ahem! mademoiselle, I regret to say that when I 'departed'— under circumstances which I will explain to you to-morrow when you come to visit me in the summer-house—I had on neither hat nor gloves. Lest I should catch cold—for I have not left the house for more than one hundred years—would you oblige me with a shawl? And as the air is bitter and bad for the skin, pray oblige me with a little more of your very charming paste before venturing out-of-doors."

I did as he asked, and tying a lace shawl over his head and around his neck, and anointing his face and hands with Peerless Paste the courteous baronet considerately withdrew.

I heard him groping his way down the secret stairs, and when his footsteps died away, I flung myself into bed and thought, and thought, and thought, till I fell asleep. My cogitations had but one termination: Sir George Wolstenholme was the rightful owner of Wolstenholme Grange, and his great grand-nephew was not "Sir John" at all, but plain "Mr. Wolstenholme." And it was indirectly my fault. The thought was horrible, and I lay planning to find some means whereby to avert the catastrophe that hung over the devoted heads of the family at the Grange. By morning an idea had presented itself, and directly after breakfast I escaped from the rest of the house party and gained the summer-house by the lake.

Poor Sir George was sitting huddled up, in a corner, shivering and sneezing by turns. As he rose to bow with his old time courtesy, I saw that his silk stockings and *"autres choses"* were scratched and torn, and that his coat and white satin waistcoat were covered with dust, whilst what I could see of his hair below my shawl was woefully dishevelled.

"Ah! mademoiselle," said he, in reply to my look of annoyed interrogation, "I have passed a terrible night; it would have been, I think, far better not to return to life, than to pass another such an one. It is only the pleasure of having made *your* acquaintance that reconciles me at this moment to existence," and he made me a rheumatically jerky, but intentionally polite bow.

"But explain," said I; "you were quite tidy when you left me last night or rather this morning," and I positively blushed at the recollection.

"It was that abominable staircase. In the first place it was three inches thick with dust, and that almost choked me; in the second, there were some old weapons lying about which I tumbled over, and with which I barked my shins most dreadfully; and in the third, my great-grandnephew had erected against the exit at the foot of the staircase, and infernal tool-shed—pardon me—where I found all kinds of weird instruments of torture, and a dog who made himself unpleasantly free with such parts of my person as he could gain access to. Added to that, a heavy dew was falling, and I have caught the most shocking influenza to herald my return to life. For all these evils the mere fact of being Sir George Wolstenholme, alive, and owner of this place is a miserably inadequate compensation."

"It is of that that I wish to speak to you, Sir George," said I; "what are you going to do about it?"

"Well," replied he, "first I must get some clothes of the present century; then I suppose I must seek an interview with my great-grandnephew and prove my claim to the estate, though I confess it will be a most unpleasant task, and one which I would very gladly avoid, if I could."

His words made my heart beat high with hope.

"Have you any money?" said I.

"Yes, fortunately and curiously, a large sum, nearly one thousand pounds in gold of the last century. I seem to have hidden it in a box behind that panel in my—I beg your pardon—*your* room, and nearly broke my nose tumbling over it last night as I left you."

"Well," said I, "I think I can suggest a way out of all your new-born difficulties. But first of all, will you tell me how you have regained your life with so much ease, with the assistance of Dr. Jones' Soul-restorer? I always knew that it was an astonishing tonic, but I never supposed it would bring the dead to life."

"Nor has it done so."

"Goodness! what do you mean?"

"I mean I have never been dead—ah, mademoiselle, do not be alarmed—I did not intend to tell you, but I feel some explanation of my apparently extraordinary conduct is due both to you, and to Dr. Bones—eh? Jones—yes—thank you."

And with that he commenced:

"The Autobiography of a Disembodied Spirit."

"It has been with the profoundest dissatisfaction," began the baronet, "that I have from time to time overheard myself referred to by my family as 'the bad Sir George.' All barts, are not necessarily 'bold, bad barts,' as I have heard some one quote from a recent drama, and in my days—which are now referred to as the 'bad, wicked days of the Regency,' the term *roué* was hardly one of reproach. I lived with the bloods, the young men of my day, but I was by no means a 'Charley,' or even a 'Macaroni' of the Regency. I dressed, danced, talked, and fought well, and I was given to understand that my personal appearance was not unprepossessing, but as for spending my life in the debauchery which was then so common, and which has been attributed to me, I was rather a studious man than otherwise. The favour shown me by the ladies was, it is true, great; but this was more the result of a certain studious impressiveness, a certain personal magnetism, amounting almost to mesmerism, that I possessed, than of any effort on my part. It was this very attribute that caused my mysterious departure, and has occasioned me a century or more of very serious inconvenience. I was not a ghost—ghosts whom I met on my nocturnal rambles in spirit-land looked upon me as a *parvenu*; and I remember very well how annoyed I was on one occasion when the ghost of a butcher-boy who had been murdered, helped himself to the phosphorus before me, and was most impudent when I claimed social precedence over him. It was the same with the others: elves and junior sprites treated me with familiarity, banshees with contempt, and I have known an entire conversation stopped dead upon my joining a circle of 'spooks' who might have chosen the galleries of Wolstenholme Grange as the temporary scene of their night's spooking. No, I was not a ghost, a bogy, a spook, or a banshee. I was a spirit, departed—but alas! alive! In conversing with you I have referred to myself as a ghost merely to avoid explanation—that explanation is now, however, due to you.

"I have said that I possessed certain mesmeric powers. Those powers gained for me a somewhat evil reputation as a sorcerer in the country round, but at the same time, that power I was most anxious to develop, and with that object in view attached to my service a mysterious Italian, a creature of rare psychic powers with whom I used to closet myself for hours at a time, and try remarkable experiments in electro-biology. There lived with me at the time, my mother, the dowager Lady Wolstenholme, my brother John, his wife and a baby boy, the grandfather of the present baronet as he considers himself—not unnaturally. And these persons watched my proceedings with growing anxiety. My mother dated from the good old days when a prevailing maxim was 'every woman for herself and a man for us all,' and regarded my *belles fortunes* with what was considered even in those days of gallantry a lenient eye; but my brother John, a serious young man, who had in a fit of abstraction got himself married and become a father, highly disapproved of me, and was eternally— as I subsequently discovered—scheming to remove my Italian companion and preceptor from Wolstenholme Grange. I knew nothing of this, and in the solitude of my—I beg your pardon— *your* room, conducted our experiments without interruption.

"We had progressed so far that it had become possible for him to separate my soul from my body, and in the disembodied state, I used to roam about the country and frighten people into fits—much to my personal regret, I assure you—for periods of hours at a time; returning, when I felt inclined, to my body and resuming my daily life. At last we arrived at such perfection that it was possible to separate myself from the more earthly portion of my 'ego' for days—nay *weeks* at a time—and these disappearances caused my friends the greatest alarm though my Italian jealously guarded my body in the temporary absence of my soul and allowed no one to approach it, merely giving as an excuse that I was unwell and could see nobody. Small wonder—now, when one comes to think of it—that they attributed my alleged illnesses to him, and redoubled their efforts to drive him away.

"I have never known how they finally succeeded. Suffice it to say that on one occasion, immediately after my soul had freed itself and gone for a stroll through space, my brother John caused certain information to be conveyed to the Italian which necessitated his immediate return to Italy. So, leaving behind him a letter explaining his departure, for my perusal on my return, he left for the sunny South. He, being no longer by my side, and not being able to elicit any response from me, they battered down my door and found me apparently dead. With regard to the sum of money which I found last night behind the panel, leading to the secret stairs being gone, they concluded that the Italian had possessed himself thereof, and had poisoned me before taking his departure. Hearing that this suspicion had attached itself to him, he did not return and so never learned what had happened. Still, for some days they could not realize that I was dead, for my body seemed supple, and they used every means in their power to bring me to life again. But I—that is my soul—millions of leagues away, was blissfully unconscious of what was occurring in my absence, and consequently after waiting more than the usual time, they buried me in the family vault, credited me in marble with virtues that I did not possess, and in rumour with vices of which I never dreamed; and my brother became Sir John Wolstenholme, great-grandfather of the present baronet.

"I returned the day after my own funeral, a disembodied spirit, with no corporeal form in which to clothe myself. They had destroyed the Italian's letter, so I had no explanation of his, as I thought, treacherous disappearance. I began to revisit the old place whilst the old order gradually changed, giving place to new, and my room became 'the haunted chamber,' whilst I, to my extreme annoyance, not to say disgust, became the ghost of 'the bad Sir George.' Unfortunately I was not dead, and, having no mortal frame to decay and die in the ordinary course of nature, I became immortal; and thus, though born in the year 17—, I am really to day the age at which I died, to-wit: thirty-four.

"My existence since then you can imagine. Though not properly speaking 'a ghost,' I was yet governed by some of the rules of Ghost-dom, and long habit has made me adopt permanently many others, and from time to time, I have very seriously inconvenienced persons sleeping in my room—which has consequently got the reputation of being haunted; though I endeavour as far as possible only to visit it when it is otherwise unoccupied. When you arrived, Miss de Valreas, I had forgotten the circumstance that you were expected, and paid my nightly visit as usual. My delight at finding that you were not scared out of your wits by me, emboldened me to return, and return I did with the result which you know. The moment I tasted your curious tonic, I felt that it was a marvellous life-giving fluid, and a great hope, which I forebore to express, for fear of alarming you, sprang up within my unsubstantial breast, and I continued to trespass upon your hospitality night after night. I felt my body growing in solidity, and substance, and, after my soul had left it, used to conceal it beneath your dressing table or in other places where, as a strong-minded young woman, you were not likely to look. But now I find myself in the very awkward predicament of being alive, and young in spite of my 130 years, unable to claim a place in the world of men, without very seriously incommoding my brother's descendants whom I have observed to be very worthy persons, not in any way inheriting the more unpleasant characteristics of their ancestor, my younger brother. Besides, you have been largely instrumental in my revivification, and regard being had to the circumstances under which I have obtained new life, I am exceedingly loth to place a very charming young lady"—here he bowed—"in a very annoying—not to say false—position. You said you had a plan—what is it?"

"Well, Sir George," I replied to this long and interesting harangue, "what I suggest to you now may seem hard to perform, but regard being had as you say to the circumstances of your reincarnation, it seems to me to be the only way out of our predicament. I am, as I told you, an American. In our country there is an opening for any man who wishes to make a career for himself. You have money enough to last you some considerable time; why not go over there and seek out a lucrative employment for your undoubted talents, a remunerative field for your labours in psychology? There is a great interest taken in such matters, over there at this moment, and what with Christian Science, Faith-healing Chirosophy, Spiritualism and Thought-reading, I am sure that your lectures in Chickering Hall would attract large, fashionable, and paying audiences. If that does not suit you, why not go to New York, and apply to Dr. Jones or to Mrs. Smith?

Such a living testimony to the value and efficiency of their world renowned preparations could not but be of the greatest service to them. I will give you letters of introduction to them, and I feel sure that they can make a comfortable position for you. Setting aside the considerations on this side of the Atlantic to which with true chivalry you have referred, you owe them a debt of gratitude for your revivification which you can hardly pay, save in person. What do you think about it?"

"I think," replied the Baronet, whose teeth chattered as he spoke, "that your idea is an excellent one. But the thing is, what am I to do for clothes in the first place? I cannot stir out in the tattered garments of a past century, and getting others must be a work of time. And that another night in this summer house will kill me in real earnest, for good—or bad,—and all, I am quite sure."

True! These *were* questions to be seriously considered. I thought for a space whilst the chilly creature gibbered and sneezed distressingly in front of me, and finally exclaimed,

"I have it! My stay here terminates as I told you last night. To-morrow after we are gone a certain Mr. Ditcham, an idiotic young man who has rudely made fun of *you*, Sir George, is to take my—I beg your pardon—your room, for a few nights to see if he can 'see the ghost' as he stupidly puts it. Now, until we go, I will tell mamma that I am too nervous to sleep another night in 'the haunted room,' and will go in and sleep with her, whilst you can occupy your own room, stepping into the secret passage whenever anyone approaches. When I am gone, and Mr. Ditcham sleeps there, you can take enough of his clothes in the night to see you up to London, where you can get others, and start at once for New York. It will punish him for his gross incivility to me, which I trust to *you* to resent in this manner for me, and serve *your* purpose. Meanwhile I will have meals served for you in my—your—ahem! excuse me,—*our* room, on some pretext of my own; for now that you have a body, I presume you must grow hungry. What do you say?"

"I say—*atishoo!*" sneezed Sir George, "that your idea is excellent, and I adopt it gladly."

And so it was arranged. On the following afternoon when I had locked myself into "the haunted room" to complete my packing, Sir George stepped through the panel and bade me "good-bye," or rather *"au revoir;"* for we mutually expressed a hope that we should meet in America, and I gave him my letters to Mrs. Smith and Dr. Jones, giving them a short outline of the story—an outline which I left him to fill in.

He was dishevelled, tattered almost to the verge of impropriety, but courtly and reverential to the last, and as he kissed my hand with an old world grace, I hoped that indeed it might be *"au revoir"* and *not* "good-bye." Mamma and I then departed from Wolstenholme, where I left behind me the reputation of being a very nervous and hysterical young woman, a reputation which lasted for exactly the one evening of my departure.

That one evening only, for next morning Mr. Ditcham, I am told, came down to breakfast haggard and pale, his eyes bloodshot and his hair snow white! Interrogated as to the cause of the change, he gasped out, as he sunk into a sofa:

"I've seen the ghost! It was all true! That girl was a plucky one, by Jove!"

Nobody laughed as they had at me, the physical effect was too apparent on the poor man, and they listened with awe, and let the breakfast get cold, as he recounted how he had been awakened to see the figure of a man standing at the foot of his bed. How, speechless and paralyzed with terror, he had watched him whilst he slowly divested himself of the garments of a by-gone century and had deliberately garbed himself in those he, Mr. Ditcham, had relinquished, when he went up on the previous afternoon to dress for dinner. How, at the conclusion of his toilet he had suddenly disappeared, how, he—Mr. Ditcham—could not tell; but in the morning he had found on the floor a coat and breeches of claret-coloured ribbed silk, the worse for wear, a white satin waistcoat, a pair of silk stockings and buckled shoes, a time-stained but fine cambric shirt, profusely ruffled, and a court-sword; whilst on the dressing-table he had found a slip of paper, one of his own unpaid bills, on which was written, "To pay for the clothes," and on it six guineas in gold bearing the date of 17—.

"Don't tell me I dreamt it," said poor Mr. Ditcham in conclusion; "I've got the things up-stairs, and it must have been a malignant spirit or he wouldn't have swapped such an outrageous pair of breeches against mine, which were bran-new."

Clarice Wolstenholme wrote and begged my pardon for having laughed at me, and to this day the entire family declare that "bar none the pluckiest trump of a girl they had ever heard of, and who probably was ever born, was the daughter of the Governor's American friend—Cyprienne de Valreas."

POSTSCRIPT.

A few months ago an exceedingly handsome man called upon me in Wilson Street and presented a letter of introduction from my sweet little friend, Miss Cyprienne de Valreas. I need hardly say that, having read it and heard his own account, I was more than astounded—I was overwhelmed and gladly communicated his story to my present partner. He announced his desire to be employed in my establishment, and as it fortuitously happened at that moment an important post was vacant on my staff, I was charmed to be able to place it at his disposal, and since last August I have been continually asked about my fascinating new employé, especially by susceptible ladies—young, old, rich and poor. I religiously kept his secret however, and no one knows which of my assistants is—or was—Sir George Wolstenholme, Baronet, of Wolstenholme Grange, Wiltshire, England. And it is very fortunate that I did so. He was of a singularly retiring disposition and refused to make acquaintances, especially female acquaintances, and I can hardly say that I was surprised when, about three weeks after the return of Miss de Valreas and her mother from abroad, that young lady came into my office, embraced me, and whispered that she was going to marry Mr. ——! dear me, I nearly mentioned the name under which he served me!

As Miss de Valreas was her father's sole heiress in her own right, Sir George, to give him his *real* name by which he is unknown, was no longer required to work for his living, and the young couple have been quietly married this spring and have gone off West for their honeymoon. I lost a charming clerk, but I have seldom been so satisfied with the preparation that I have put before the public, as I was when I saw Miss Cyprienne de Valreas—really Lady Wolstenholme—and known to the world now by a name I am pledged not to reveal, leave the Church of the Sanctified Pocket-handkerchief a month ago, leaning on the arm of a husband who, under the benign influence of my partner, Mrs. Smith's "Peerless Paste," has regained all his beauty of a hundred years ago, in a body which, though perishable, contains a "Soul Restored," and consecrated only to her worship.

Theophrastus Jones, M. D.

I hereby certify that the above narrative is absolutely veracious in every particular.

Elizabeth Smith.

THE STRANGE PAPERS OF DR. BLAYRE

By
CHRISTOPHER BLAYRE
PH.D., D.LITT.
(Sometime Registrar of the University of Cosmopoli)

ANTESCRIPT.

THE position to which I was appointed in the early years of the twentieth century—that of Registrar in a great University—is in many respects a peculiar one. The Registrar finds himself not only on terms of friendship and equality with the Professorial Staff, but also to a great extent occupying a fiduciary position which brings him into what is very often intimate touch with his Colleagues. It was in virtue of this relationship that, from time to time, Manuscripts were confided to my care which, by reason of their intimate personal nature, were not destined for publication during the lifetime of their Authors, but were confided to me as records of events which appeared at the time to be of too striking and inexplicable a nature to be published by the Recorders. Many years have passed by since I resigned the Registrarship on attaining the age-limit, and I think the time has arrived when I may, without breach of confidence, give a selection of these Papers to the public.

CHRISTOPHER BLAYRE.

THE PURPLE SAPPHIRE.

(Deposited by the Smithsonian Professor of Minerology.)

O N the 24th of June, 18—, a few months after my appointment to the Professorship of Mineralogy in the University of Cosmopoli, I received, as a gift to the Museum from the surviving executor of the late Sir Clement Arkwright, under the most dramatic conditions, the Purple Sapphire. The facts attendant upon its arrival were as follows:—

Sir George Amboyne, the Regius Professor of Medicine came into my room and deposited upon my table a small package.

"This is for you," he said, "a gift to the Mineralogical Department, made under most unfortunate circumstances. An elderly man has been run over by a motor-car just outside; he was brought in, very badly damaged, though not, I hope, fatally. As I was in the building I was sent for, and have done what I can pending his removal to Hospital. When he recovered consciousness, he said with some difficulty, "The packet—where is the packet?" The porter, who had carried him in, produced this parcel, which the man had been carrying when he was run over. When he saw it, he said "For the Museum—Purple Sapphire— give it to them," then he lost consciousness again. You see it is addressed 'To the Mineralogist, University of Cosmopoli.' You had better take charge of it."

"Rather an ill-omened way to receive a presentation, isn't it?" I observed. "Very," replied the Regius Professor. "I suppose we had better open it?

We did so. Beneath the outermost wrapper was an envelope, addressed "To My Executors." It was unsealed and contained a sheet of note-paper upon which was written: "*It is my earnest wish that this packet shall not be opened until twenty-five years after my death. When that time has elapsed, it is to be delivered to my eldest male direct heir. It contains the Purple Sapphire given to me by the younger son of Colonel George Cardew. Whether by that time its power of doing evil to its possessor will have waned or not, I cannot tell, but I earnestly recommend my heir to get rid of it, if he can, at the earliest possible opportunity. —Clement Arkwright, Bart.*"

"This is very queer," remarked Sir George; "the poor old man downstairs was evidently on his way to deposit it, whatever it is, here. Let us have a look at it."

The removal of the inner wrapper disclosed a sandalwood box. Inside that, closely fitting, was another; inside that, another. There were seven of them, one inside the other. In the last and smallest, wrapped in a piece of curious fine muslin was the Purple Sapphire.

It was without exception the finest stone I had ever seen, perfectly cut, of the most brilliant deep amethyst-purple, and the size of a flattened bantam's egg. It was set in a sort of cage; two silver snakes, with their tails in their mouths, ran round it above and below the circumferential edge, and these were connected and held together by twelve small silver "plaques" inscribed with the twelve Signs of the Zodiac. On one side were two silver rings, evidently for suspension, and from these hung, so as to cover and conceal the stone, on one side a circular plaque, evidently of very ancient make, of the kind familiar to students of Occultism and of the rites of the so-called Rosicrucians as the Seal of the Tau—a Greek T, surrounded by a flat band on which were engraved the familiar "mystic" letters ABRACADABRA. This fell over the flat or "table" side of the stone. Over the other, the faceted side, hung a pair of amethyst Scarabs, evidently early Egyptian, threaded upon, and held in place by, thick silver wire.

Whether it was the circumstances in which it had reached us, or for some other and inexplicable reason, as I held it in my hand I felt an overwhelming sensation of nausea and faintness. I handed it to the Regius Professor without a word. He turned it over in his hand, raised the Tau and the Scarabs, and then put it down on my table.

"What a *beastly* thing," he observed. We looked at one another for a few moments in silence, but neither of us gave utterance to the thoughts that were in our minds. Probably we could not have done so if we had wanted to.

I was the first to break the silence—with an effort of which I felt ashamed. I think," said I, "we will take it straight up to the Museum."

"Yes," said Sir George, "for God's sake let's get rid of it." He was quite unconsciously reiterating the advice of Sir Clement Arkwright.

Using one of the lids as a tray, we carried the Purple Sapphire up to the Museum, and placed it in the Table-case by the door, destined to contain "Recent Acquisitions" which had not yet been registered and classified. When we came down again, the elderly gentleman had been removed to the nearest Hospital, and his relations, as indicated by letters and cards in his pocket—his name was also Arkwright—had been notified by telephone.

That afternoon the Mineralogical wing of the University Museum was struck by lightning. The damage done was ghastly. Many priceless exhibits were destroyed, and several weeks elapsed before the room could be opened and used again. The Table-case of "Recent Acquisitions" was untouched.

It was perhaps a year after this that a card was brought to me bearing the name *Sir Gilbert Arkwright.* I had not forgotten the Purple Sapphire, for the romance of its acquisition stuck to it, and students showed it to visitors as "The Unlucky Stone," and invented all kinds of fantastic stories about it. The assistants and even the charwomen hated it. One story went that it glowed at night with an unearthly refulgence—I was foolish enough to go up one winter evening when the lights were turned off to see for myself. I saw nothing—but I confess to having experienced a sensation of—to put it mildly—extreme discomfort. I felt like a child afraid of the dark. Idiotic!

One of the charwomen declared that one evening when she was "cleaning up," a "naked Heathen—and, what's worse, black," had suddenly looked at her over the top of the case she was dusting, and that she would sooner lose her place than ever enter the Mineralogical room again. Idiotic!

Well,—the card of Sir Gilbert Arkwright preceded the appearance of a charming young man of the regulation British athlete type, in the thirties I should say. In answer to my look of enquiry he said, easily:

"I think you have here a Purple Sapphire, which my uncle was bringing here the day he was killed in a street accident."

I was shocked to hear this, and all the circumstances recurred at once to my mind. I murmured some conventional phrases, and the young man replied:

"Oh! that's all right. It was a terrible thing of course, but that was the last of it for us. We were none of us ever allowed to see it, but it was supposed to have been, and was called, "the Curse of the Cardews" in my father and grandfather's time. I only came to bring you this book which turned up the other day in going over a lot of my poor old uncle's papers—we thought you might like to have it."

He laid on my table a small quarto MS. note-book of the cheap American-cloth covered type, the first page of which bore—without more—"THE NAGHPÚR SAPPHIRE," and the date 1885. I was rather "thrilled," and having suitably thanked my visitor, he left me. That night I took the book home with me, and, after dinner, I sat down to read it. There were only a few pages written upon—as is usual with note-books—but the story they contained was so uncomfortably weird that I offer no apology for transcribing them in full. The original MS. is in the library of the Mineralogical Department (M.M.3.b.36).

✳

The MS. of Sir Clement Arkwright.

I hope and believe that I have made such arrangements and pro-visions as shall prevent any of my immediate descendants taking the Naghpúr Sapphire into their custody, possession or control. But as there exists a widely spread impression in my family that it is a Jewel of great value and of exceptional beauty—which is indeed the case—I think that in the future some member of my family may be moved by curiosity or Cupidity to claim posses-sion of it. I will therefore write in this book my reasons for not wishing this to happen.

One of my earliest recollections is that of Colonel George Cardew and his wife. They lived in a poor little cottage—how poor I was then too young to appreciate—on the outskirts of the village nearest to my father's place in Shropshire. The Colonel used to give me pennies, and his wife cake, but the latter gifts were discounted by the fact that she was everlastingly advising my mother to give us castor oil, and periodically insisted upon our being taken to see the dentist. We children resented this interference—if interference it really was—in the placid lives of an otherwise very happy family. The Colonel was an invalid and very lame, the result of a wound received in the Indian Mutiny, which continually gave him trouble; his wife was peevish, con-tinually at war with Fate which held from her the position and wealth of a great lady. In fact, as the saying goes, they had seen better times, and were ill-adapted to worse. They had two sons, Richard and George, who were the constant playfellows of my elder brothers. I was too young for them. These two boys, after they left Haileybury School, cut themselves adrift and set out to make their own way in the world by sheer grit and hard work. Richard became a medical student, and as he was a sharp contrast to the lazy, rowdy class which constituted the medical students in those days—the early seventies—he passed his examinations with distinction, and, having no home prospects or capital, joined the Indian Army Medical Service—he was always known as "Dr. Dick." George won a Cadetship at Sandhurst, and, knowing that he had no one but himself to rely upon, worked hard, did well, and was in due course gazetted to an Indian Regiment, where he rose to be Major and was regarded as a very rising man—he was always known as "Major George."

Their sterling merits carried everything before them. In due course Dr. Dick left the Army Medical Service and became a successful physician in Simla. Major George, promoted to Colonel, became "Resident" to one of the Indian Native Rajahs, and was regarded as one of the really notable Administrators under the Indian Government. Their rare visits home were hailed with delight not only by their old parents but by all of us, for they brought home wonderful things from India as presents, and would talk—how they talked! Thrilling accounts of their lives out there, of dangers from rebels, from snakes, from wild beasts, from plagues—we were never tired of listening to them.

Then old Colonel Cardew died, and within a year his wife followed him to the grave. Though their later years were much ameliorated by handsome remittances from their sons, they were never happy. The Colonel was a terrible sufferer, and they were really unlucky, in small things as in great. If they saved money and invested it the investments went wrong—people always said that if they had wanted to cultivate weeds, or to encourage rats in their little place, the weeds would have refused to grow, or the rats to be encouraged. It was a sorry business when Dr. Dick came home to wind up his parents' affairs, and he returned to India a distressful man. He told us he was afraid to go back for he felt that his luck was gone. This was quite inexplicable to us, but he was a true prophet, unfortunately. An untoward "accident" or two in his practice, one fatal one in the treatment of a great Maharajah, dragged him down from his professional eminence, a bank in which his savings were invested—an "unlimited" concern—failed, and carried with it the whole of his savings, and in the end Dr. Dick, who was fortunately a bachelor, was reduced to living in a suburb of London on an allowance made him by Colonel George. After some ten years of an aimless and unlucky existence he fell out of a railway train and was killed. There were those who did not hesitate to doubt whether his tragic death was accidental.

After his death Fate seemed to turn her malevolent attention to Colonel George. He became unpopular with succeeding Viceroys and lost influence and caste in the Service. Finally, not supported as he should have been by his Government, he came to loggerheads with his Maharajah; an insurrection in his native State was attributed to his management, or mismanagement. He was superseded and sent on a punitive expedition to the borders of Afghanistan. In this affair he failed utterly and unaccountably. The natives, soldiers and civilians alike, seemed to hate him, and of the few faithful Sikhs whom he commanded only one returned with him. The rest had been killed—his other troops had practically deserted him. It was amazing, for until the death of Dr. Dick he was almost worshipped by the natives both civil and military. On his return to Madras he twice escaped assassination by a miracle, and in the end he was "retired" and came home to live on an inadequate pension, with his wife and two children. The change, I suppose it was, preyed upon his wife, and she went mad. His daughter died—apparently of what was not then recognised as appendicitis, and his son, having gone utterly to the dogs, fortunately emigrated to New Zealand and was never heard of again.

It was then that I came into the story. Colonel George was, as I have indicated, some six or eight years my senior, but this did not count so much when I was thirty and living a rather luxurious bachelor life in London. Colonel George often came to my rooms and we used to talk over old times, and, on occasions, to dissipate mildly together. He was always cheerful, and seemed quite resigned to the ill-luck that pursued him—he said that it did him good to be with me, for my "good luck" was proverbial. I had health, wealth enough, and a reliance upon my "lucky star" that never betrayed me—"let me down" is, I believe, the modern expression.

One day when I had made a preposterously lucky "hit" over a horse-race, we were celebrating the occasion at dinner at the now extinct St. James' Restaurant. I said to him, cheerfully:

"Now, why can't you strike a streak of Fool's Luck like that?"

"Well, Clement, my boy, I've a good mind to tell you. I have often thought of telling it to someone."

I rather quailed. Was my ideal Colonel George going to confess some shady episode of the unknown past that was dogging his footsteps, embittering the present, and making the future ominous?

However, he changed the conversation, and after dinner he asked me to go back with him to his rooms—up near Regent's Park, a wretched place—instead of coming back to mine, and I did.

When our pipes were lit, he sat looking at the empty fireplace for a little while, and then got up and went into his bedroom. When he returned he had in his hand the Naghpúr Sapphire—the most splendid stone I had ever seen. I thought it was an amethyst but he told me no, it was a purple Sapphire—jewellers sometimes call them "Oriental Amethysts."

(Here in the MS. follows a long description of the stone and of its setting, practically as the Professor of Mineralogy has given it above. C.B.)

I said to him: "You don't leave this about, do you, in a place like this?"

"Yes; it always lies about on my dressing-table."

"Aren't you afraid of having it stolen?"

"No; it has been stolen three times."

"How did you get it back?"

"I didn't get it back. I didn't want to. It *came* back. It always comes back."

"What do you mean—you didn't want to?"

"I'd give all I possess (it's not much) to get rid of it. Instead of which, I have given all I possess for keeping it. This is 'the Curse of the Cardews.'"

"My dear George," I said, "you are raving!"

"No, I am not; you asked me at dinner about my bad luck. Well, you hold it in your hand. That stone has ruined my whole family in turn."

I protested. "Such things only happen in books."

"Listen to me. You know what a distinguished servant of 'John Company' my old father was. He looted that stone off a statue—an idol if you like—of Vishnú at Naghpúr, a stronghold of the Mutiny. The whole Shrine was razed to the ground by order; not a trace of it left. Next day he got his wound—one of those mysterious wounds that never heal—his never healed—it tortured him to his dying day. A month later he was on his way home—'Invalided out of the Service' they said at home—but do you know what they said at the Secretariat in Calcutta?"

"No; what?"

"'Cashiered for cowardice in face of the enemy.' It was hushed up, first (I hope) on account of his past services, and then on account of the probable effect upon the loyal native troops. On the way home his skull was fractured by a falling block—he was trephined and got over it, but his brain was never really clear again. You know how we lived down there in the little old house—pretty wretched, wasn't it? But what none of you knew was that my mother loathed the sight of my father—they never saw one another excepting in company. He was weak in the brain, as I said, but his nightmares were awful. I didn't know until afterwards that he was haunted by the phantom of a Hindú Yoga."

As he paused, I put in, uneasily, "Of course sick men do invent such things."

"He didn't invent this one. It was the Attendant of the Shrine at Naghpúr, whom he had cut down himself. And my governor knew that it was after the Purple Sapphire."

"Why didn't he get rid of it?"

George Cardew smiled.

"You have a short memory, Clement," he said. "I told you just now we can't get rid of it. The Governor sent it out by post to a man stationed near Naghpúr and told him to restore it to the Temple, or Shrine, and if he couldn't do that, to sell it. It came back with the notification that there was no trace or record of the Shrine, and the jewellers in the bazaars refused to buy, or even to touch it. My father sent it out again to another man, told him to bury it at Naghpúr; six months later it came back

311

by post—the man had buried it just as he received it with my father's letter—whoever dug it up got his address from that."

"Why didn't he send it out without a letter to an imaginary address?"

"He did. It came back through the Dead Letter Office, straight to our village post office, and ofcourse they knew there."

"I'd have got rid of it somehow."

"Would you? I'd like to see you try."

A brilliant idea occurred to me.

"Give it to me," I said, "and I'll undertake to get rid of it."

"You wait till you've heard the rest of it. When the old man died, and then my mother, it came to Dick. Well, you know what happened to *him*. I was at the zenith of my career when Dick died. Good God! Clement, my boy, but I was just on the point of stepping up to goodness knows where. And then I had to take over the Purple Sapphire. On hearing of Dick's death I spent eight pounds on a cablegram telling them to put it away, and on no account to send it out to me. I was too late—it had started. The day after he died—before he was buried—they sent it off. It arrived with his watch and chain and his shirt-studs. The rest of his chattels only just paid for his funeral and a few small bills. Well, you know what happened to *me*. I had the bright idea to present it to my Maharajah, who had millions worth of gems. He refused it, and he began to mistrust and hate me from that day. I offered it to the Government Collection, but they looked upon it as a sort of attempted bribe to cover the mess I was making of things. I can't tell you what plans I made to get rid of it—scores—but it always came back, and there it is."

He paused, and after lighting his pipe again, he smiled and said:

"Do you still want to have the damned thing?"

"Rather!" I said. "You know *my* luck; it's impregnable."

"Don't say that for Heaven's sake; it's an awful thing to say."

"But I mean it," I cried. "I defy ill-luck, and if I can't get the better of a mere stone——"

312

"Nobody ever will," he interrupted, quite gravely.

We argued the matter for some time, and in the end I persuaded him. I took a cab home in the small hours, delighted with my splendid new toy.

Two years passed during which, personally, I was quite unaffected by any malevolent influence attributable to the Purple Sapphire, but I am bound to confess that there was something about it which passed comprehension and defied investigation.

To record an instance or two: I was deeply interested, as a hobby, in the elucidation of a curious text, half Persian and half Urdú (but this has nothing to do with the story) and a young Hindú scholar was sent to me by the Professor of Arabic and Persian in the University of Cosmopoli, with a view to the discussion of some obscure points, and to the augmentation of his income (he was a clerk in an Anglo-Indian House in the city), and he arrived one evening about 8.30. He was called Mr. Something Ghose, I remember. I had the books out on my study table, and we had been at them about half an hour, during which I thought Mr. Ghose the most incompetent and absent-minded fraud I had ever met. At the end of that time he rose and said, with a little bow:

"You will excuse. I cannot work. I do not like this house. I go away."

I was very much astonished, and not a little annoyed, and expressed myself with some succinctness. All he said was, as he made for the door:

"I am sorry—very. I did not know. You must excuse. I go." And he went!

Shortly after this my friend the Professor of Arabic dined with me, always a delightful occasion for me, for he had been for many years Principal of a Muhammadan Madrassah in India, and was a delightful talker. As we sat before the fire smoking after dinner, I noticed that he looked all round the room at intervals, uneasily as it seemed to me. I said:

"Are you looking for anything?"

"No," he replied. "No; I don't think so. Tell me though, do you collect Indian curiosities?"

"No; I think them, as a rule, hideous."

"You haven't got a Tirthankar in the house have you? One of those little squatting alabaster idols one sees in the curiosity shops?"

"No. I've seen hundreds of them and I hate them."

"You are not far wrong," replied the Professor, "they're beastly things."

"How?"

"Oh! they are uncanny things to have about," and he changed the conversation.

Five minutes afterwards he looked round again, rose suddenly, and looking into the dark end of the room he exclaimed:

"I thought so! I felt it! *Kaun hai? Kiyá mangta?* ("Who are you? What do you want?")

"For heaven's sake, what's up?" I said.

"Haven't you seen *That* before! A Hindú squatting on his heels, naked excepting for a loin-cloth, scrabbling at the carpet—there in the corner?"

"My dear fellow," I observed. "I know you are not drunk, nor are you mad. What is it?"

He did not answer me at once, but extending his hand in the direction in which he was looking, he called sharply:

"*Jáó!*" (Go away!)

He sat down again with a short laugh, and relit his pipe with a shaky hand.

"I don't wonder you are surprised," he said. "I'm sorry for this exhibition, but I've been so long in India; these things get into one's blood, I think. It's very stupid. You are *sure* you haven't got any Temple loot about the place? There's a lot of it about."

I thought at once of the Purple Sapphire, and, rising, I took it from the drawer of my writing table and put it into his hand.

"Good Heavens!" he said. "Of course this is it. This is what he is after. It's the pectoral gem of a Hindu God. Where did you get it? And how long have you had it?"

I gave him an outline sketch of the history of the Purple Sapphire—which he had put down on the table by his side—and when I had finished he said:

"Of course that explains it—if anything can be said to explain the inexplicable. My advice to you, my earnest advice, is to get rid of this thing as quickly as you can."

"Why?"

"Because—for goodness sake never tell anyone of this incident or of this conversation—it will hurt you—smash you, sooner or later."

We spent the rest of the evening in a most "gruesely" conversation. The Professor told me a number of stories in point, and if I had been an imaginative or nervous person I should have been very much upset.

But I am not, and I wasn't. That was the last time the Professor dined with me until—afterwards.

There were other such incidents, greater or lesser in degree, but I never saw any Yoga, and suffered no ill effects from being the custodian of the Purple Sapphire, which gradually acquired a romantic and rather fearsome interest among my friends. I pass on to the night when I gave a dinner party which we shall all of us remember to our dying days. We were eight—B. a rising young author; and a charming young actress Miss C., of whom he was the temporary "enamourite," to quote Burton (of the *Anatomy*); his sister (married), and G., a man in the Foreign Office, asked on account of one another; Mrs.—I will call her Smith, as she comes back into the story later on under tragic and unforgettable circumstances; and Mrs. A. and her husband (recently married, after a double divorce). Mrs. A. was a queer woman. It might be said that she had not an enemy in the world, but was rather disliked by all her friends. She dabbled in Occultism and led her rather sheepish husband reluctantly to séances. She liked to flatter herself that she was "a strong Medium." She interested me, but I always regarded her as a fraud—a semi-unconscious fraud perhaps. But we had a jolly dinner, and afterwards congregated in the library. Mrs. A., as usual, forced the conversation upon the Occult. She talked very well, and was always rather "thrilling" to people who had not heard it all before.

B. said suddenly: "I say, Arkwright, haven't *you* got a wonderful jewel or something that evokes spooks, and murders people in their sleep?"

At once there was a chorus of delighted curiosity, and finally I produced the Purple Sapphire, which sparkled with remarkable vividness that night. At that moment one of those things that happen to the electric light happened—it is, I believe, when they change the accumulators or the dynamo at the generating station. At any rate the lights went down to about half their normal candlepower. The Purple Sapphire seemed to flame even more brilliantly in the subdued light.

"Oh! do give it to me," exclaimed Miss C. And with a view to making light of the whole thing I tossed it into her lap. She immediately held her hands up and away from it, as if it had been a spider or a mouse, and shrieked to B., who was sitting beside her: "Take it away! Take it away!"

B. picked it out of her lap and handed it back to me. After this she sat closer to him for the rest of the evening, holding one of his hands in both of hers.

"Give it to me," said Mrs. A. in her most impressive tone, "I am accustomed to these things." I gave it to her and she laid it, with the cover-flaps open, on her knee. She began to yarn about "maleficent talismans," but the evening was spoilt. We were all uneasy. Mrs. Smith alone did not say a word, but sat looking at the Purple Sapphire and at me, in turns. Presently the preliminary murmurs of impending departure arose, and then some amazing things happened. Mrs. A. leaned back in her chair and closed her eyes. Then she cried out:

"Something is coming. Something is here! Everybody except Sir Clement go out of the room."

They all sprang to their feet and scuttled into the hall. Mrs. A. said in a stifled voice: "Oh, God!" and fainted. At that moment the disturbance at the main righted itself and the electric lights blazed up again. I went to the door and called A.

"Your wife has fainted," I said; "come in." He came in, and with him Mrs. Smith, uninvited.

The rest were whispering together in the hall.

Mrs. A's eyes were now open, and she said: "It fell upon me, it fell through me." With one hand she was still holding the Purple Sapphire on her knee. We comforted and re-assured her as best we could, but she declared that something had fallen into her lap and disappeared. "It went through me," she said, over and over again. We got her on to her feet, and to prove to her that she was mistaken we pushed back the low armchair in which she had been sitting.

On the floor beneath it lay a small scarlet disc, faintly luminous in the strong light, about two and a half inches in diameter, on which were figured in black, exactly as on the flat flap of the Purple Sapphire, the Sign and Letters of the Tau! We all gazed at it, horror struck. I was the first to pull myself together. I got the tongs from the fireplace, with a confused idea of picking the Thing up, and flinging it into the fire! But even as we four looked at it, it turned white and clear of markings, and appeared to volatilize.

The others came in—and then they went away. As a newspaper report would say "the meeting broke up in confusion." They did not all go away though; Mrs. Smith remained. I may say at once that round this lady for some time all my thoughts had been concentrated. I shall write of her again. We talked, she and I, long into the night. At 2 a.m. a ring came at the front door and I opened it. It was B. He said:

"What *am* I to do with Marie C.? She won't go home. We have been driving all over London in a hansom. She's there now, outside. She says she dare not go home to her rooms alone. Damn your infernal stone."

I might have remarked that it was he who had insisted on its entry upon the scene. I forbore, however, and in the end Mrs. Smith came out and took Miss C. home to her house to sleep with her. B. walked home, and I went to bed, I confess, rather shaken up. As Mrs. Smith left, she put her hands on my shoulders, and looked into my eyes searchingly. The others had gone outside.

"Didn't *you* see the Indian Man squatting on the floor behind Mrs. A's chair?"

"No, I didn't."

"I swear to you he was there. Please don't go back and sit in the library. Promise me."

I promised her—indeed, I do not think anything would have induced me to do so. As I say, I went to bed.

I was out to lunch next day, and on my return home I found a letter waiting for me, delivered by P.O. Express. It was from A. In it he wrote:—"I feel that I must send you the sequel to last night's extraordinary occurrences. About 3 a.m. my wife woke me, and said that something was burning her where the Jewel had lain upon her knee. I tried to soothe her to sleep but she insisted so strongly that we switched on the light, and turned down the bed clothes. Sure enough, those letters round a capital T were burnt black upon, and through, her night-gown. We cut out the piece and I enclose it herewith—and on her leg, exactly the same thing, bright red, as if done with a hot iron. We dressed it with vaseline, but it is there this morning. We will show it to you when you like."

To avoid returning to this matter I may say that Mrs. A. wears this brand to this day. She makes no bones about showing it to people, and I need hardly say that her account of my dinner party does not lose in the telling. Her enemies say she did it herself with a red hot needle. Her husband says that he always knows, when she puts on her daintiest *lingerie,* that she is going to tell someone the story of the Purple Sapphire—as far as she knows it.

I now reach the dark and terrible part of my record. I have intimated that I was deeply devoted to Mrs. Smith, who was one of the most beautiful, the cleverest, and by virtue of her husband's wealth, one of the most fastidiously luxurious women in London Society—which was literally (as the saying goes) at her feet—which were exquisite!

We had a vast community of interest, and were as inseparable as a decent regard for conventionality permitted us to be. I do not think I flatter myself when I say that I must have been a relief after her husband. As to that gentleman, I was, and am, no doubt, prejudiced, but he combined in himself the millionaire, the lout, the drunkard, and the fool. I was ultra-careful never to compromise Mrs. Smith in any way, for, as I repeatedly warned her, I would not have trusted her husband out of my sight for a moment, and was always prepared for him to lay some dirty trap or other for her. He encouraged our friendship, however, and threw us together continually. *Timeo Danaos!*

It made me therefore very uncomfortable and very unhappy when Cecile, at our next meeting after my dinner-party (next day, in point of fact) implored me to *give* her the Purple Sapphire.

Though I had no fear of the thing for myself, I was frankly horror-struck at the idea of its passing into her possession. She argued with me—how she argued!

"You brag about your invariable luck," she said. "Well, look at me, am I not the luckiest woman in London by common consent—in everything but my marriage. Am I not brave? Then why do you want me to be a coward? I thought *you* were brave. Then why are you a coward now? You do not believe the thing is bewitched. Then why do you behave like this now? I have never asked you for anything since we first met, have I? And now that I do beg a gift of you, you refuse it. Be very sure, my friend, that I shall never under any circumstances ask you for anything again. No, not if I were starving in the gutter."

These words came back to me most bitterly when she *was* starving in the gutter, and when she did come to me for help. But what was I to do? One is only flesh and blood after all, and in certain circumstances *"Ce que femme veut—!"* In the end I gave her the Purple Sapphire.

I will pass as quickly as I can over the miserable history which followed. Men and women of my generation have not forgotten the Splendour and Decadence of Cecile Smith. In a phrase, everything went wrong with her. Her whole nature changed, she became hard, reckless, unsympathetic. She gambled frenetically and lost vast sums; she got money to pay her debts by every means, fair and foul; she bought fabulous jewels, her transactions with which would have landed her in gaol had not her friends accommodated the situations into which she recklessly flung herself. People whispered of lovers of low degree, of orgies, of drink, of drugs, of all the degenerate horrors of a decadent civilization. And meanwhile Smith was on the watch, to jerk the rope when she had had rope enough to hang a score of women.

This was not the affair of a moment—it took two years. All that time, though we seldom met now, for our paths had widely separated, I was continually imploring her to give me back the Purple Sapphire. I believed in it fundamentally at last. But she would not. She clung to it with a superstitious obstinacy. In a letter from St. Petersburg where she had drifted as partner (?) in a gambling enterprise (which failed of course) she wrote:—

> The Stone is the last thing I had when I was Queen of my Race—and I *was* a Queen! It is the only thing I ever asked you for. Nothing shall part me from it.
>
> P.S.—The Yoga is here all right; thank God he costs nothing for railway fares and hotel expenses.

Once, in reply to a passionate appeal for money from Madrid, I offered her £1,000 for it. Same result.

Time went on. We heard of her occasionally—twice that she was in prison. I was very unhappy about her, worn out indeed, but there was nothing to be done. To distract my thoughts I went an aimless voyage round the world, on which I met the lady who is now my wife. I returned to England in the spring of 18—. Passing through Paris I read to my horror that an unknown woman who had shot herself in a tenement house in La Vilette a few weeks before, had now been identified as the once beautiful and notorious Mrs. Smith of London, Paris, Rome, St. Petersburg—and where not? It was a ghastly shock, and in spite of the light that was breaking on my own horizon, I returned to London a sad and distracted man. A huge correspondence awaited me that my Secretary had been incompetent to deal with in my absence. Among the heap was an official packet—it was from our Consul in Paris. The letter said:—

The enclosed packet, sealed up and addressed to you, was found among the effects of the late Mrs. Smith who, as you may have heard, died recently in this city, in tragic circumstances. Kindly acknowledge, etc. etc.

It was the Purple Sapphire. Wrapped round it was a slip of paper on which Cecile had written: "It has downed me—take it back. I have tried to sell it, but no one will buy it. Even thieves won't have it. *Sayonara. Ave atque vale!* CECILE."

And so it came back. A month later when I had settled down, burglars got into my house, and carried off property of great value, including the Purple Sapphire. They left me on the floor of my dining room with a bullet in my neck which all but closed my earthly record.

As soon as I was convalescent—that is to say about six weeks afterwards—I found that the burglars had been apprehended as the result of another burglary, the last of a long series perpetrated by this particular gang, which had hitherto completely baffled the police. Their master-mind had had a serious accident when on a professional tour, and had been arrested; the rest of the gang fell out among themselves, and partly by treachery and partly by mismanagement the burglary for which they were awaiting trial, which had been postponed for my evidence, proved to be their last. It was the only beneficent action which can be laid to the score of the Purple Sapphire.

After these unhappy men had been sentenced, the solicitor in charge of the defence handed me a small packet. I knew, without asking, what it was. He accompanied the restoration with the words:

"My clients instructed me to return this to you. It is the only one of your jewels which they were unable to dispose of. They attribute—you know criminals are notoriously superstitious—solely to it the unfortunate position in which they find themselves to-day. It was, in fact, their unaccountably rash efforts to get rid of it that gave the police the clue they have been seeking for a year past."

And so it came back, and from that moment things began to go wrong all round me. My power to control the Purple Sapphire was gone. My solicitor absconded with a loss to me of several thousands of pounds which he had in his hands for investment. I also broke a leg and a collarbone riding along a simple country path. I spare you the rest of the catalogue of disasters, major and minor. They were many and varied.

I set about the task of getting rid of the Purple Sapphire. I sold it to a second-hand jeweller in Wardour Street who knew me well, but did not the less on that account offer me the value of a common Scotch amethyst of the same size. A week later he brought it back saying that his wife (who was Scotch) to whom he had given it would not have it in the house; she had a "scunner" on it. I pawned it for £2. A month later the pawnbroker failed, and his trustee in bankruptcy sent it back to me "as the sum for which it had been pledged was obviously inadequate, and he felt it his duty," etc., etc.

Finally I took it to the National Museum of Cosmopoli, and offered it as a gift to the Keeper of Jewels. He turned it over and over, looking at me curiously, as I thought, and then said:

"This is a marvellous jewel—we have nothing like it—and you may think it odd, but I don't think we want it."

"For Heaven's sake, why?" I asked.

"You *will* think it odd, but I am a firm believer in the malevolence of certain stones which have been the witnesses or causes of tragedies. I am convinced that this is one of them. Why do you want get rid of it?"

There was no help for it—I was too broken in spirit—I told him.

He listened very attentively and when I had finished, with a suggestion that I should smash it up and scatter the fragments, he said:

"No, don't do that. As it is, you know it, you can recognise it, and can be on your guard; if you smash it, it will come back to you, somehow, in pieces, re-cut, that you will not recognise, and you may unconsciously hurt someone. Now do not think that I am mad—though I admit that my colleagues in the Museum think I am, to say the least of it, eccentric upon this subject—but you must follow the direction of the old books on Magic and Witchcraft; there is much more in them than most people think, or will admit. You must drop this into a tidal river at the exact moment of dead high water; it is the only thing you can do, and I warn you that even that may fail."

I confess I felt extraordinarily relieved at the suggestion; this surely must be final! We got out a Nautical Almanack and calculated the time of dead high water in the Thames on a particular day, and on that day and at that minute I dropped the Purple Sapphire into the river from the middle of Charing Cross Bridge.

All went well with me for about three months. The happiness I had seen approaching on my world tour seemed well on its way to realization. My nerves regained their equilibrium. Life was once more worth living.

Then one day as I was working in my library my parlourmaid announced "A man with a note from Mr. X." This was my jeweller friend in Wardour Street. The note said:—

> The bearer has a curious jewel for sale which was once in your possession. I do not know how he may have come by it, but I send him to you as you may care to re-purchase the article, of which he does not know the value, or to hand him over to the police.

I looked up, and the man, a common working "navvy" produced from a wrapping of dirty rag, the Purple Sapphire.

I was stunned. I sat looking stupidly at the accursed Thing, and it seemed to me as if someone else's voice said to the man:

"Where did you get this from?"

He began a whining rigmarole. It had been in his family from father to son for many generations; they had come down in the world. He had come to London to seek work, had got it—good work, highly paid, but he had lost it, luck had turned against him, one of his children had died, his wife was ill, they were

323

starving. At last, with great reluctance they had decided to sell the old "amethyst"—that's what his father had said it was. Worth lots of money. He had taken it to Mr. X., and Mr. X. had sent him to me as I was a gent who gave good money for curios.

My interruption startled him. I sprang to my feet and shouted at him: "You liar!"

"Come, governor, none of that. Give me back my curio."

"Not till I've got the truth out of you. If you try to get away I give you to the policeman outside. Now then, out with it. How did you get this out of the bed of the Thames?"

He fell into a chair as if he had been shot, stammering.

"Christ! it's witchcraft, that's what it is. Devils and that. It's just bloody witchcraft."

"You see," said I, "I know something. You had better tell me the rest."

It took him several minutes to recover his normal self, and then he told me. It was amazing. The extraordinary network of underground railways—"the Tubes" they came to be called, later—was just then beginning to be constructed. One of them passed under the Thames from Charing Cross to Waterloo Station. This man was employed in the caissons the river mud, pushing forward foot by foot in compressed air chambers, digging out the river bed and passing the débris back to shore. He had caught the glint of this Thing in one of the scoops as it came home, and watching his opportunity, he (to use his own words) "pinched it—and pouched it."

"I give you my word, governor," the wretch went on, "I've never had a good since. It's the first thing ever I pinched, and it's got back on me. I've to sell it—no one will buy it from the likes of me. I've tried to lose it—it's brought back to me. I believe the police is after me on account of it. For Gawd's sake Mister take it off my hands."

My heart went out to the poor devil.

"I know the stone," I said. "I lost it. I'll take it back. Here's a fiver for you. Go home and good luck to you. You'll get along better now."

His gratitude was pathetic.

"I *feel* better already, governor," he said. "Gawd knows it'll be a lesson to me." And so it came back.

I knew now that any effort of mine to get rid of it would be in vain, and I decided that after all it would be better to know where it was, than to dispose of it and feel that any day or hour it might turn up again. So I wrapped it up in the piece of Indian muslin in which George Cardew had given it to me and put it into its nest of boxes. I have forgotten, in writing this, to record that shortly after Colonel George made it over to me, he sent me a "nest" of seven sandal-wood boxes of Indian make, fitting closely inside one another, the smallest and innermost of which exactly held the Purple Sapphire. Whether he, or his father, or Dr. Dick had them made I never knew, or if I did, I have forgotten. I then wrote a note of instruction to the executors of my will directing that the Purple Sapphire should not see the light of day until twenty-five years had elapsed after my death. I little supposed that by that time its power for evil would have, so to speak, evaporated, but at any rate I could make sure that it should not fall into the hands of my children (if I had any) until they were old enough to have read this manuscript and to judge for themselves what was the next thing to be done with it. *(The Professor of Mineralogy has transcribed this letter of instructions in the early sheets of his record, so it is not necessary to repeat it here.— C.B.)* With a view to enforcing the performance of my wish I set aside by my will a sum of £10,000, the income of which followed my residuary estate, with a provision that, in the event of the parcel having been opened before the prescribed time, the capital sum was to be transferred at once to one of our larger hospitals. I felt that the Governors of that Hospital would keep an eye upon the parcel and see from time to time that it was intact. At the end of the twenty-five years the £10,000 is to fall into residue. I wrapped up and sealed the parcel and took it to my bankers, where I deposited it for safe custody in their vaults. The manager, a charming man and a personal friend of mine, received it in the ordinary way, and I need hardly say that I did not give him any inkling of its contents or of my motives for the deposit. Whether it was a coincidence, *or otherwise,* I cannot tell, but from that moment the affairs of that branch of my bank went wrong in many ways. One of the cashiers absconded with a large sum of money, loans which the bank had made went wrong, commercial houses which they had financed failed and involved them in heavy losses, and of course the manager got the blame, and he was forced into retirement on a small pension, a broken and disappointed man. I had my own uncomfortable ideas on the subject, but it is obvious that I could not go to the head office and say it was all my fault for having deposited in the vaults a parcel containing the Purple Sapphire. They would rightly have assumed that my brain was softening.

And there it lies to this day. I am happily married and I have two charming children, a girl and a boy. I sometimes wonder whether it will be he, or his son, upon whom will devolve the awful responsibility of taking the Purple Sapphire from its resting place.

CLEMENT ARKWRIGHT.
31st December, 18—.

The manuscript of Sir Clement Arkwright stopped here. He lived for many years after the date which he appended. There follows in the notebook a further entry in another hand which reads:—

"*1st January*, 1920. The twenty-five years since the death of my brother expired yesterday, and I went to the bank and claimed the parcel, which we found—the manager and I—dusty but intact. I opened it in his presence and read the letter of instructions, but I did not open the sandal-wood boxes. I am not superstitious, but somehow I—well, at any rate I did not open them. We wrapped up and re-sealed the parcel and left it again where it had lain for over forty years. I must record, by way of postscript to my brother's account, a curious, and to me very ominous, circumstance. During the Great War the staff of the bank, those of military age that is to say, had been largely replaced by women, several of whom are still in the employ of the bank. As the manager was seeing me to the door I said to him:

"'I suppose you will be gradually getting rid of these young ladies?'

"'Yes,' replied he, 'and I shall be very glad when we see the last of them. One can never rely upon their work, their hearts are not in it for they know that it is not their life's work and that they can never rise to the administrative grades in the service. They make the most annoying mistakes, and one has to have their work continually checked by the men. And as a culminating touch, what do you think? There is a mad idea among them that makes them absolutely refuse to go down into the vaults when we want to send for anything. They say the vaults are haunted! Two of them (we have got rid of them) declared that they had seen an apparition of a naked Indian who grinned and gibbered at them down there. Did you ever hear of such hysterical idiocy? Oh! I shall be glad to get rid of them.'

"I said nothing beyond what might be conventionally expected of me, but I drove home feeling very uncomfortable.

"Is this horrible Thing, after lying quiet for forty years, going to wake into renewed activity? I suppose I ought to deliver it to my nephew and god-son Sir Gilbert Arkwright, but frankly *I am afraid to do so.* Fortunately he is still abroad, in the Army of Occupation in Germany. I shall let matters rest as they are until he comes home.

GILBERT ARKWRIGHT."

Following upon this was a further entry in the same hand which reads as follows:—

"*23rd June*, 1920. My nephew Gilbert has returned home, and I have made him read this record in his father's hand. He is a splendid fellow and he laughs, of course, at the whole thing. 'At any rate,' he said, 'let us take it out and have a look at it.' I begged him not to insist upon anything of the kind, and at last, after many long arguments, which I fear have convinced him that I am suffering from senile decay, he has consented to the plan which I have proposed. This is, that I should take the parcel just as it is to the Professor of Mineralogy in the University of Cosmopoli and present it to the university Museum. It may be presumed—or at least hoped—that, placed among a large collection, many specimens in which may possibly have histories no less mysterious than that of the Purple Sapphire, its evil powers may be as it were diluted, if not dissipated. In any case, I take it to the University to-morrow, and there I sincerely trust that, so far as our family is concerned, the history of the Purple Sapphire is at an end.

GILBERT ARKWRIGHT."

✳

It was very late when I had finished reading through the pages of the black note-book. The handwriting of the main record left much to be desired in places, having evidently been written under the influence of strong emotion. And no wonder! I felt that the writer was compelling himself to a violent effort all the time, omitting much, passing lightly over incidents which it must have been very painful for him to record. I pitied him from the bottom of my heart.

Next day I went up into the Museum and looked at the Purple Sapphire. There it lay, appropriately labelled:

"Sapphire (Purple) Alumina. Corundum. Refraction, 86°4''. Hardness, 9. Sp.gr. 3.9.—4.16." A bald description of what is perhaps the most remarkable stone in the collection.

There is no reason why any student should ever refer to the little black notebook, but I do sometimes wonder whether anyone, browsing among the shelves of the library, will ever take it down and read these records. And then I wonder many things.

THE HOUSE ON THE WAY TO HELL.

(Deposited by the University Librarian.)

I was sitting in my office, checking some term-lists, one afternoon, when Glenardagh, the University Librarian, came in with a sheaf of papers in his hand

"Are you busy?" said he.

"No—I am never busy," I replied, "the duties of Registrar in this University consist solely in the enjoyment of conversation, confidences, and complaints of the Professorial Staff."

"That being so, I will bide a wee, and have a crack."

Alexander Glenardagh, M.A. and Doctor of Literature of Aberdeen University, was in appearance, habits and vernacular a typical Scot. Books were his whole life and his only love, and when Collinson his predecessor had been found dead in his cubby-hole adjoining the library, the Senate had accepted Glenardagh's application for the post *nem-con*, almost by telegram. He was a man of Encyclopaedic information, few words, sandy appearance, and much nicotine.

He took the chair on the other side of my table, placed for the convenience of inquisitors and complainants; he put a sheaf of papers on the table, also his elbows, and observed interrogatively:

"You remember the Purple Sapphire?"

"Good God! I should think I did. You haven't got another, I hope?"

"No—that was before my time, but I have often thought about it."

"So does everyone else who ever had anything to do with the beastly thing."

Glenardagh sat looking at me in silence for a full minute or so, watching the smoke from his pipe mingling across the table with mine, and then he said:

"Have you ever heard of Spirit-writing?"

"Oh! yes," I replied, "messages from the deceased Aunt Jane, written in a cataleptic scrawl and appalling grammar inside a sealed-up slate in the dark. You can buy the apparatus at Hamley's."

"It's not that. I mean what they call Automatic Writing. You hold the pencil and the Spirit of the Just Departed does the rest."

"I've heard of that too. That is done, as I rule, by a small green-grocer's Lady, employed by the hour for a fee proportional to the credulity of the 'Sitters.' That is the Lady through whom the spirit of Cardinal Newman greets the company with the magic formula '*Pax verboscum.*'"

"Well, wait a minute and tell me when your fount of humour is dried up."

Glenardagh looked so serious—and so entirely sober—that I composed my features (that is, I believe, the correct expression), and said:

"Get on with it."

He looked at me very seriously as it were to make sure I was seriously attending, and then he said:

"I've been doing it myself."

"Is it a habit of yours?" I queried.

"No, it never happened before, and I hope it'll never happen again, but it did happen this morning, and here," touching his papers, "is the result."

"Go on."

"I had set a writing-block in front of me to start a list of Missing Volumes to be hunted down or replaced, and I suddenly had the very uncomfortable sensation that Collinson—whom I never saw—was looking over my shoulder."

330

"Collinson! my *dear* Glenardagh. It was in the *morning*?" I asked meaningly.

"Yes, as sober as I am—or you are—now."

"Well?"

"I put my pencil on the first line of the sheet in front of me, determined to shake off what was really a very uncanny obsession, and my hand began to write of its own accord. It wrote: 'This is what happened.'"

"Good gracious! What did you do—"

"Nothing. I left my hand where it was and it went on writing. It wrote all this. It has only just left off. I haven't had any lunch. I thought I would bring it to you."

"What is it all about?"

"I don't know."

"What?"

"It's the simple truth. My eyes were shut most of the time, but I was conscious enough to tear off each sheet as it was filled, and to go on with the next."

"Let's have a look at it."

"That's what I brought it for," said Glenardagh, and he handed me the Manuscript; "read it aloud."

Fortunately his handwriting, though small, is extraordinarily clear, and this is what I read:—

This is what happened—nothing of any importance had ever happened to me before: I was looking through a Quaritch Catalogue when, all of a sudden, I died and went to Hell. I had always felt a stronger inclination towards Hell as a place of permanent residence than Heaven, because if there were any foundation for the existence of either, I felt that the company of the Great Pagan of Antiquity, and of "Tinker," my Irish Terrier, would be more congenial than that of the Just Men made Perfect, and my Aunt Amerlia's Pug. I never had either taste or talent for Biblical Exegesis.

I left my body sitting in the accustomed chair, without any regret, for it was always a bore to me. The finishing touches put to my anatomy by my parents left much to be desired. Fortunately my incorporeal self gathered a kind of modified consistency as it struck the fresh air in the Quad, rather like a saucer of warm varnish or glue when one puts it out on a windowsill. No one noticed me as I walked up the High and out into the fields beyond St. Simeon's, and I made instinctively for the gap in the Chankbury Cliff known as Hell's Gate. There I found a charming-looking young man, sitting on a rock, who rose as I reached him. He was obviously waiting for me.

"Welcome," said he, "we have been waiting for you for a long time. Though rather an imperfect specimen of humanity, you led too careful a life to get ill, so we decided to give you the Progressive Touch and get you at once. I may tell you that that is a great compliment to you, Dr. Collinson."

"Thank you," I replied, "you evidently know me. May I enquire——?"

"Certainly, I am the Authorized Guide. I suppose that if I were alive I should wear a cap with gold letters on it. As it is, come along."

We entered the gap, and almost immediately stopped at a natural opening in the rock which I had never noticed before, and no wonder, for, as we passed through, the rock face closed behind us, and I found myself at the top of a gentle incline, a broad and easy road paved with what appeared to be octagonal stone plaques, fitting closely together, and stretching downwards before us to an apparently limitless distance.

"What a very fine paving this is," I observed.

"Yes, these plaques are Good Resolutions. If you look at them closely you will see what I mean."

I stooped, and then became aware that each plaque was inscribed. The inscriptions were in all languages except the Oriental. I saw no Arabic, Turkish, Persian, or Sanscrit inscriptions. The others were clearly legible. The group upon which I was standing were progressively inscribed: "I will never drink again. I will drink much less. I will only drink at meals. I will eschew spirits, wine, beer," and so on. Here and there I read: "I have smashed my hypodermic and will never buy another," and again: "I will never touch, kiss, look at a woman again." The variety was infinite. "I will never strike my wife again." "I will be respectful to my parents. "I will never owe money again," and so on *ad infinitum*. I looked enquiringly at the Authorized Guide. In answer to my unspoken query he said:

"Of course you must understand that all these Good Resolutions are excessively thin. They are super-imposed upon one another as they come in. There!" he went on, as the writing seemed to change, but not the inscription, upon a plaque at our feet which read: "I will never believe in another woman,"—"you see, another of those has just been added. The leaves or layers of the plaques are only about 0.0001 millimeters thick; there is not much wear in them, but they do not have time to get worn before a new one is added at the top. That particular column— they are in columns like the Giant's Causeway at Staffa—goes down about a hundred and fifty miles."

I wondered how deep the Drink group went; superficially they seemed to pave about an acre of the road. Presently we came to a part that seemed less solid. "These," explained the Guide, "are more or less scarce and isolated resolutions. See here: 'I will not kick Jane's Pom again;' you see, the animal died as a result of the next kick. Here is one that should interest you: 'I will not go to sleep when the Vice-Chancellor is preaching,' and here is another: 'I will not pull that old fool Blayre's leg any more.'" These I observed to be inscribed with my own initials. Close by was another: "I *will* ask that ass Collinson to dinner"—this had the Vice-Chancellor's initials appended.

And so on, and so on, and so on. This broad and easy way extended, descended, for what seemed to be several miles, and the end was not in sight when the Authorized Guide stopped me and said: "You do not go any further, your job is here now."

I then saw an enormous building, several storeys high and extending in broad wings to right and left, standing back a little distance from the road, in front of it a grass plot with a circular path leading round it to the main entrance. In the middle of the grass plot a number of uncanny-looking creatures were raising into a perpendicular position an immensely long monolith of red granite. In front of it, between us and it, with his back towards us, stood a man of majestic proportions, apparently directing the operations. His legs were well apart, and his hands were clasped behind his back. He wore shepherds'-plaid trousers, and a short alpaca coat, and a rather bad top-hat was crammed on the back of his head.

"Goodness me!" I exclaimed, "that is Collis Ridge."

"Yes," explained the Guide, "he is superintending the erection of what was the Unfinished Obelisk from the quarry at Assouan."

"But," I remonstrated, "it is *not* finished. I have seen it."

"Oh yes it is. Everything that has been left unfinished comes here finished. This is the Library and Museum of projected and unfinished Books, and projected and unfinished Works of Art, Science and Manufacture. You will see when you get inside. You have been appointed Librarian and Curator: that is what we wanted you for."

"But look here," said I, "Collis Ridge! He isn't dead."

"Oh yes he is," replied the Authorized Guide, "but he doesn't know it yet."

"But surely he cannot be in two places at once?"

"It is a condition peculiarly reserved for High Government Officials. At an age regulated by Statute they attain the Nirvana of perfect and pensioned peace, and in that state they wait quietly to enter the Pari-nirvana of physical annihilation."

The *causa causans* of many letters published in the *Times* began to dawn on me.

We went inside. One side of the Atrium or Hall was hung with an enormous frame containing an inexplicably complex geometrical design.

"What is that?" I asked.

"Oh! those are the Architect's Completed Plans for the Tower of Babel."

From this Hall, vistas of rooms leading into one another departed in all directions, as far as one could see; shelves reaching to the ceilings were filled with books of all sizes. The Authorized Guide led me into the first series, or vista, of rooms. The shelves were filled with small volumes, some rather worn and dilapidated, some apparently almost new; the bindings were of every material from paper, via leather, shagreen, mother-of-pearl, fancy wood, even to silver and other precious metals—the latter were *duo decimos*.

"These are Diaries," said my Mentor; "in this room, and several following, the entries stop in January, in the next series in February, and so on through the months. They extend for some miles and end in a small room where the entries are continued into December; but they are all finished—in red ink—before they are brought here. A large staff of assistants is engaged night and day making the entries which the original Diarists ceased to make."

I took one down, a beautifully Morocco-bound Diary with gilt clasps, and opened it. It stopped in May, but there was no red ink continuation. I turned to the Guide with a question which he anticipated.

"She was killed in a railway accident the morning after she made the last entry," said he.

I took down another. It stopped in June, and the leaves that were written upon were charred black, but the writing had been restored in white ink. I looked at the guide again.

"She was married next day," said he. "You will find that there are more additions to this section every year, than to all the rest of the Library put together."

"I notice that, with the exception of the Tower of Babel Plans in the Entrance, you have nothing on the walls but books. Surely there must have been unfinished pictures——"

The Authorized Guide made a gesture of comic despair. "My good Doctor," said he, "if we took unfinished pictures, not only this Library, but all Hell, which, so far as we know, is fortunately limitless and bottomless, would be entirely filled, even if we super-imposed them as we do the Good Resolutions. Any true artist will tell you that no picture has ever been finished; they can set a sort of time-limit and reach a point when they decide 'not to do any more to it,' but no picture has ever reached finality. The Managing Director——"

"I beg your pardon?"

"Yes, that is what we call him—he prefers it. Poor Devil! he rather fancied himself when he was a Fallen Angel—and put up with it when he became the Spirit of Evil—but since the Christian Church forced upon him the universally accepted and recognized position of the lowest grade of Detective Policeman, the *Agent-Provocateur* of the French, he has bowed to the commercialism of the age, and is now Managing Director of an Unlimited Company in which he holds all the Founders' Shares."

"I see. But you were saying——"

"Oh yes! The question of finality arose with regard to later Architects' plans of buildings never erected, but it became immediately obvious that millions of people have plans made of buildings that they have no real intention of ever erecting, and the architects, when work is slack, make plans—finished plans—'on spec.' Ninety-nine out of every hundred, to use an inadequate expression, never get beyond the plan stage, and so they must be regarded as finished works, and are therefore ineligible for our collections."

I began to feel a certain relief in the reflection that I should be allowed to use a reasonable amount of discretion in accepting or rejecting proposed contributions. My thoughts flitted momentarily to the countless newspapers and magazines that never got beyond their first, or their first few numbers. I said:

"Then you have no newspaper department?"

"No, thank goodness. There was some idea of collecting the prospectuses of projected newspapers, but it became immediately apparent that a large proportion of these were only composed for the purposes of blackmail. They are efficiently dealt with a long way further down the Road. A vast number of Company Prospectuses are dealt with in that department, and you will not be bothered with them."

By this time we had reached the December room—quite a small one, not occupying more than about an acre of space—and a lift took us up to the first floor. And here, at once, my emotion and delight as a librarian may perhaps be conceived.

The first volume that I took down was Coleridge's *Kubla Khan*, London, 1816. It was complete!

"I thought," said the Guide, "that you would pick that out at once. You will remember that Coleridge was interrupted by a 'person from Porlock on business.' And he never touched it again. Some day, with the limitless time at your disposal, you must read it. The conclusion of the work will astonish you."

In the centre of the room we had reached was a table-case in which were exhibited a few yards of a light, diaphanous material, exquisitely embroidered with a design that I recognized at once as being similar to those that decorate the gold vessels and pottery of Mycenae and Hissarlik. I turned to the Guide.

"Surely this is——"

"Yes, it is the web of Penelope. I have often wondered what the National Art Collections people would give for that with a view to exhibition at South Kensington."

Some strange marbles were disposed on pedestals in some of the windows. The Guide, observing that my attention was directed to them, remarked:

"We had some discussion about those, but the late Librarian——"

"Ah! I was going to ask whether I had had a predecessor, and what had become of him."

"That is rather a painful matter. It came to the knowledge of the Managing Director that he was trying to 'operate' in some of our greatest treasures through the Society for Psychological Research, with a view to 'acquiring merit,' as the Buddhists say, and getting transferred—er—elsewhere. Of course it was disgraceful; he came here from London, and he was sent down the Road. I hope nothing of that kind will ever happen to you. But you interrupted me. About those marbles—the question was whether Rodin and Epstein ever intended to finish them, and we decided no great artist—and they were that—could possibly have intended to leave them like that for ever."

I still had *Kubla Khan* in my hand.

"You had better put that back for the present," observed the Guide, "if you cling to what you propose to read you will soon require a wheel-barrow. You can always send for what you want from your room. The Card Index is always complete. It is printed by Dictaphone by the Reception Clerk as the books finished by our staff come in; and each card finds its place at once by a mechanical contrivance—American, of course—and stays there, and returns there by itself if it is left out."

My mind flew back to hours wasted in our Library, looking for misplaced cards and to infuriated searches among the "waiting for Catalogue" shelves.

As I replaced *Kubla Khan* my eye fell upon *Edwin Drood*.

"We are not a Lending Library," observed the Guide; "if we were, that volume would never be in its place. Of course the real simple ending has been told over and over again, but it is quite confused and obscured by the many unreal ingenious ones."

"What about Card Indexes?" I asked.

"That comes under the same rule as Pictures—they are always complete as far as they go—and they are never finished. The same applies to 'Registers of Books Read.' The late Librarian wanted to start a section of 'Books to be Read,' but the Managing Director pointed out that this would mean a vast list comprising almost every book in every library in the world. Though, thank goodness, we have no Office of Works here, we cannot extend our buildings to infinity."

His next few comments were lost upon me. I was searching the shelves with feverish intensity.

"What are you looking for?" asked the Guide.

"I am looking for the one book which I have perhaps longed to read more than any other, Mr. Pickwick's *Speculations on the Sources of the Hampstead Ponds, with some observations on the Theory of Tittlebats.*"

"That has a place by itself in the next wing—books that were never written at all. It is almost unique, owing to the fact that there exists considerable historic doubt whether Mr. Pickwick ever really existed—one can hardly imagine that he did not—but Official Records are still waiting. He certainly did not come here. On the same shelf as Mr. Pickwick's *Speculations* you will find the play with which Dr. Johnson commanded Fanny Burney in 1778 to begin her dramatic career, *Streatham: a Farce.* And, speaking of Fanny Burney, you will find here all her earlier works, including *The History of Caroline Evelyn*, rescued by our fire-proof agents from the bonfire in St. Martin's Street. In this section we have only Books which were really begun. Here is Racine's Tragedy, *Iphigenia*, which he laid aside at the request of Mlle de Treves. Here is Xavier de Maistre's *La Prisonnièrre de Pignerol*; he speaks of it in his celebrated *Voyage autour de ma Chambre*, and Vineuil's *Vie de Turenne*, mentioned by Mme de Sévigné; but the whole of this Section is occupied by such Commencements."

"There must be a vast accumulation of unfinished collaborations."

My companion laughed.

"Rooms full of them, wings overflowing with them. The Managing Director loves them and makes a special hobby of them. They have played into his hands perhaps as much as any other human weakness. Think of the millions of devoted friends who have become bitter enemies simply as a result of entering upon a collaboration in a book—or more especially a play! Lower down the Road there is a vast 'Home' for people who have murdered their Collaborators."

"Yes," I replied, "I suppose that does happen pretty often." I was thinking of the *History of the University of Cosmopoli*, which I began, in collaboration with the Dean. He still lives, but we had not returned to being on speaking terms when I started upon this immemorable journey.

"Speaking of collaborations, here is one which would make the fortunes of a German publishing firm. Goethe's *Commentary* to Tischbein's Engravings of the Pictures made on their Italian Journey. What there was of it was left here by the Girl on her way—lower down."

"The Girl?"

"Ah! I suppose that is not so well known as it might be. They had an awful row over a Girl in Rome, and Tischbein went home. The ostensible cause of the rupture was that Tischbein said Goethe's verses were rotten, Goethe said it was all because Tischbein's pictures were rotten, and it was because Tischbein would not paint the Girl into the Pictures, and expressed his views about her in good, sound early eighteenth-century German. We finished both the Book and the Pictures, of course, when we got them. The Pictures are rather hard on Goethe when he comes into them—and the portrait at the beginning! Well, you shall see it."

We wandered on—a wonder-voyage among treasures indescribable. We reached the Poets.

"I want to see the Poems of Sappho," I said.

"They were not unfinished, they were only lost. To our knowledge there are two perfect copies at Herculaneum. There were two in Athens, but they were completely destroyed by expert excavators."

"I always had an idea that she left some of her lines unfinished, like Virgil."

"Not she! Whatever Sappho set out to do she did thoroughly. Even her suicide. Had she left her work unfinished we should have had Wharton down here long ago."

"Then I suppose it is no use looking for the lost books of Ovid's *Fasti*, or the lost plays of Euripides?"

"Not the slightest. Hundreds of visitors have asked for the *Famous Historie of the Virtuous and Godly Woman Judith*, of which only a title-page, dated London, 1565, is known to exist. The same thing happens with regard to books of which all traces have disappeared, such as Skelton's *Nigramansir*, of which the Poet Laureate, Thomas Wharton, *saw* a copy in the middle of the eighteenth century. Seventeen books described by Herbert at the end of that century have utterly disappeared. We know, from the confession of John Skot, the printer, that seven hundred copies of the treatise concerning Elizabeth Barton, the Maid of Kent, who was burnt at Tyburn in 1534, were printed, but no copy is known to exist. Horace's *Art of Poetry*, translated by Ben Jonson and published in 1640, is likewise lost. There are scores of others, but they would not be allowed in here. If they were, Froggy Dibdin would have cut his throat and come here—literally hot-foot—years ago."

"What about Dr. Burney's *Poetical History of Astronomy*, parts of which he read to Herschel?"

"Well, that *is* here, but under reservation for no one—not even Mme d'Arblay ever *saw* it finished.

"But you mentioned Virgil. Here is the complete Aeneid. You know that his dying request was that it should be destroyed. That was because there are not only unfinished lines in it, but the Character of Aeneas was left practically a sketch—he intended to elaborate it, but had not time. As for the unfinished lines, some Protagonists have tried to make out that he left them like that on purpose—intentional irregularities—the classic precursor of the *vers libre*, that refuge of the Incompetent Rhymster; bur Virgil was not that. Anyhow, all the lines are complete in our copy, and as for the Character of the pious Aeneas!—one can imagine the row there would have been in Rome if that had been published! Talk of Voltaire on Joan of Arc! Phew!"

We reached a vast hall, the shelves of which were entirely filled with thick, fat volumes, all stoutly bound in leather.

"Are these liturgical works, left unfinished as usual, because unfinishable?"

"No—these are Interleaved books. When Quaritch passed through——"

"Quaritch? B.Q.? You surely don't mean to say that he——"

"Why should he be an exception? I do not know of any authenticated instance of a real bookman going anywhere else. A very few publishers perhaps—but they died in extreme poverty, if not in disgrace. There is an immense colony of book collectors lower down. We love them. They bring with them an Odour of Sanctity which is extremely pleasing to the Managing Director, and provides our other inhabitants with much harmless amusement—especially the Calvinist and Supra-lapsarian kind."

I thought of our University Press, whose Director was prosecuted for—but, however,—I said, "What about Quaritch?"

"He told me," replied the Guide, "that he had had thousands of interleaved books through is hands, but that he could count on the fingers of one hand the instances in which more than twenty pages of rhat 'interleaf' had anything on them at all, and they were Author's Copies of Local Guides, which never reach a second edition. We have millions of them."

341

"Tell me," I said after a deeply thoughtful pause, "is there a Music Section?"

"Oh! of course. Operas, the endings of which would delight those who began them. They are really interesting, and will repay you if you are a Musician" (which I am) "for many years—even Centuries of Study. You have all the time there is, you know. A large majority of them are brilliant—the works of real Geniuses, or Genii—who either died at their work or gave up to despair at ever being able to realize their aspirations."

"Books too?"

"Yes, you will find de Beriot's *History of the Violin*. Also Fayolle's, announced in 1810, and Chanot's, promised in 1882. You will also find Dr. Burney's *Fourth Volume*—hundreds of others. It seems impossible for one human being to finish a History of Music—it grows and grows to the Vanishing Point. Our Musicians almost hate Fuller Maitland for completing Groves' *Dictionary*, so that we cannot have a copy here for reference. The nearest thing we have to that is the *Biographie Universel* of Fetis, with the unfinished Supplements."

"The first thing I shall look for will be Beethoven's *Unfinished Symphony*."

"I expected that—it is worth coming here for, alone."

"I think," said I, "that I shall be the most interested in the Books that were never written at all. They must afford a marvellous scope for your Finishers—though in those cases they can hardly be called 'Finishers'."

"No—we have a special staff for them—they are called Realizators. You will find Lord Acton's *History of Liberty* and Gibbon's *Lives of all the Most Eminent Britons from the time of Henry VIII to the Present Time*. He was full of it when he wrote to Lord Sheffield from Lausanne the year before his death. Here too are all the Books adumbrated by Samuel Butler in his *Note Books*, his *Character of the Compete Drunkard*, and especially his *Penitential Psalm as David would have written it if he had been reading Herbert Spencer*. Here you may read Robert Louis Stevenson's *The Young Chevalier* and *Sophia Scarlet*, his 'improper' novel *Canon Mills* and the 'proper' one, *The Rising Sun*.

I recommend to you Thackeray's sequel to *The Newcomes*, and his three projected novels concerning *Simon Fraser*, Lord Lovat. Prescott's *Conquest of Mexico* prevented Washington Irving from writing his; but you will find it here. It is vastly different to Prescott's. One could go on *ad lib.*, but I must leave you to find them out. Burke's *History of England*, and his *Life of Jane Austen*. What a loss for those who go—elsewhere—if they have a Library—elsewhere. We are not in communication—it is a pity from their point of view. Here is Lally Tolendal's five-act Tragedy, *Tuathal Tamar, ou La Retauration de la Monarchie en Irlande*. Our Irish visitors fortunately arrive here unarmed, or there would be bloodshed——"

At this moment a messenger appeared with a note for the Guide.

"I must leave you," he said, "but I have given you a fair idea of your duties and their infinite possibilities. But before I do so I will give you a volume which I feel sure will interest you." And he handed me a ponderous tome.

It was my *History of the University of Cosmopoli*.

AALILA.

(Deposited by the Professor of Psychology.)

THERE is not—or at any rate there should not be—any romance in *"Nature."* You will observe the italics and the inverted commas, which indicate that I refer to the Journal and not to the Dame. *"Nullius in verba"* is the inexorable motto of the Royal Society of London, which means that you must not state a fact unless you can table, or screen, the evidence which supports and proves it. It will be difficult, indeed impossible, to observe this rule in recording the story of Aalila, but I will do my best.

Among the "Notes" which supply to the Curious the scientific news of the week in *"Nature"* of the—well, perhaps it may be better to refer the Curious to his file of that admirable journal for the exact date, for I am writing face to face with the gorgeous panorama of the Pyrenees as seen from the Hotel de France at Pau, and I have only the paragraph—cut out—with me. It reads:

"We regret to announce the death of Professor Alured Markwand, which took place suddenly in his Observatory at Piping Pebworth on the 14th instant. The cause and manner of his death is unknown, the coroner's jury having, as directed, returned an open verdict. It seems probable that Professor Markwand met his death by electrocution, as his body, strangely scarred, was found beside a powerful dynamo which generated the electric current of an arc light in the Observatory. It is well known that he was engaged in researches upon the development of photo-telephony, and his Observatory was fitted with an arc-light apparatus of exceptionally high voltage." Then follow biographical details for which the Curious may be referred to the columns of *Who's Who*.

I have given anxious thought to the question whether I should record the manner of his death, or allow the "open verdict" of the coroner's jury to stand as the only (and official) account of the matter. My own reputation for veracity, for reliability as an observer, for scientific method of record—nay, I may say for sanity itself—is at stake. In any case this record cannot be published in my life-time; my position as Professor of Psychology in the University of Cosmopoli would be seriously compromised, and though, as I believe myself to be, not lacking in physical or moral courage, I should shrink from facing the genial gathering of my colleagues in the tea-room of the Royal Society on Thursday afternoons, and probably feeling that I am relegated to that small coterie of eminent men of science who have flown—and unhappily have published an account of their flights—into the cloudy atmosphere of metaphysical—research? experiment? self-delusion?—call it what you will. Thus much by way of apologia. But I feel myself compelled to record, to enregister, the most amazing and overwhelming experience of my life.

In the reports of the inquest, it will be remembered that it appeared that it was I who gave evidence as to the discovery of Alured Markwand's body. It was stated in those reports, that entering his Observatory at 8 a.m. on the day in question—I had been spending a month with him in Warwickshire—I found his body lying against the dynamo as described. This is not true. I dragged it there—it was the only thing to do—an explanation of some kind had to be forthcoming. *I was there when he died.*

It has been noted in *"Nature" (ut suprâ)* that Markwand was actively engaged in the study of photo-telephony. Those who were privileged to be present at the Soirée of the Royal Society in 1919 will remember the demonstration given by Dr. A. O.

Rankine of this remarkable method of sound-transmission. The beam of light that extended above the heads of the assembled guests from the Council Chamber to the furthest of the library, the telephones attached to the mirror which caught the beam, and the delicate apparatus of Selenium cells, which enabled people to hear in the library what Dr. Rankine's assistant spoke into the receiver in the Council Chamber, and how the speech was interrupted when a sheet of card was interposed, cutting off the beam from the receiving mirror, will be within the memory of all who were present. I remember one exquisitely pretty red-haired girl who—but, however, she has nothing to do with this record. Markwand was explaining, or trying to explain, it to me—I knew he had an installation of his own—and, intimate as I was with him, as the result of a friendship that dated from boyhood and had persisted through Eton and Trinity until we found ourselves colleagues on the Professorial Staff at the University of Cosmopoli, I was vaguely distressed at the nervous absorption with which he discussed the matter.

"It is extraordinarily interesting," said I.

"Interesting!" he exclaimed, in the tone he might have adopted to the Yankee girl who, on seeing the Falls of Niagara for the first time and by moonlight, remarked "Well—well, *ain't that cunning!*" "Interesting!" he said. "Good God! it's overwhelming—it's terrible!"

I looked at him in some disquiet; it had not struck me in that light. His face was ashy, and his lips, like his hands, trembled. I knew he had been overworking. I felt very uneasy. I had been trying to persuade him to go down to his cottage and Observatory at Piping Febworth for a real rest, and he had promised to go as soon as the term was over, on condition that I would go with him. Meanwhile I succeeded in getting him back early that evening to his rooms, where, over a pipe and a whiskey and soda, he made half-confidences. It seemed to me he was on the verge of a serious breakdown, if not of actual insanity. I felt called upon to remonstrate with him, gently, as one would humour a patient suffering from acute neurasthenia.

346

"Come, Markwand," I said, "what is all this about? You are overstraining the cord. It will snap if you are not careful. A Professor of Astronomy—a mathematician—should, of all people, keep a level head. Remember our motto *"Nullius in verba."* If you didn't seem to be in such deadly earnest I should say you are simply talking tosh."

"I *am* in deadly earnest," he replied quietly. "This *is "Nullius in verba,"* I know what I'm talking about—and it's too much to know. You think I'm going mad? Well—if I don't talk about it pretty soon to somebody I *shall* go mad. And I've made up my mind to talk to *you.*"

"Fire ahead."

"Not now. I'm too tired. And there's still something more to be done. I'll tell you all about it when we get down there. Meanwhile, think, man! Try to realise what photo-telephony means—the carrying power of a beam of light; the illimitable spaces of æther, across which beams of light are still reaching us from planets that became extinct thousands of years ago. Think of the lines of light that are connecting us at this moment with the other planets—Mars, Jupiter, Venus. Venus!" he repeated, reaching for his tumbler, and I saw that his hand shook like a contact-breaker. "Think of it! Has it never occurred to you that between talking from one end to the other of the Society's rooms, and talking from here to, say, Venus, is only a question of degree? Why not?" And he looked at me as if challenging me to express an unbelief—as who should say, "Can I go on? Are you safe? Do you think it is worth while to listen?"

I was extremely uncomfortable. I hated to leave him, wrought up as he was, but on the other hand I was afraid to let him go on—then. I decided rapidly.

"Anyhow, it is frightfully suggestive—extraordinarily interesting—but it's too big a subject to go into now. I'm off home. See you at lunch to-morrow."

And so we parted for that time. Next day, as we smoked in the Common Room after lunch there was no trace visible of his agitation of the night before. Indeed he appeared to be so entirely his normal self that I felt emboldened to revert to Rankine's demonstration.

"Oh, yes," he said. "A delightful entertainment for an evening party. I quite envied Rankine's assistant, fitting the receivers over the prettiest possible ears of the prettiest possible people, and listening to their delighted squeals of astonishment. But you know," and he became graver, "our friend has hardly touched the fringe of the subject. Wait till you get to Piping Pebworth and see what I can do. I'll astonish you! And by the way, do you remember years ago, the talk there was of transmitting designs—drawings, portraits—by wire? There were pictures of it on the back sheet of the *Daily Mail*. Well, if by wire, why not by wireless? If by wireless, why not by light? Think it over. I must get back. I've got a lecture. See you later." And he was gone with a jovial nod and a quaint expression as of one who pulls the leg.

Though I saw a good deal of him both in college and out, until the end of term, we never referred to the subject again, and when the University closed for the summer vacation we found ourselves "by divers mesne assignments," as the lawyers say, at his adorable little cottage in Warwickshire, where he had his private observatory and did his own work, uninterrupted by the need of imparting such knowledge as might be necessary to enable his students to proceed to a science degree.

I am to assume that you, who read this, know all that is necessary to be known about the equipment of a stargazer's observatory. Markwand's observatory was like any other in all essentials. The noticeable feature was an extremely powerful arc-light apparatus, to which the current was supplied by a powerful dynamo. This he used for his experiments in photo-telephony, and I quickly realised that he had made no idle boast when he said the subject was yet in its infancy. From his observatory he could throw a beam of light some four hundred yards into his den at the house, where, caught by the mirror and the Selenium cell apparatus, you could carry on a conversation as comfortably as if the conversant had been in the room. He could "ring up" along his beam before switching in the voice receiver, and by the same means could transmit written words, drawings, and even his own features to the receiving screen. It was positively uncanny to me who am in no sense a Physicist—it was as a Psychologist that the state of exaltation in which Markwand lived interested, and, I am bound to confess, sometimes alarmed me.

He showed me many beautiful experiments and results, but at his own research work he would never allow me to be present. He would laugh and say:

"You are too inquisitive, my dear fellow. You would fidget about and make me nervous. I should always be afraid of your monkeying with the dynamo, or touching a live wire somehow. I don't want to have you on my hands as a horrid little burnt corpse."

And so it went on. I was genuinely resting, but whatever may have been the nature of Markwand's holiday researches, he certainly was not. All that I could get out of him was that he was observing certain phenomena connected with the planet Venus. He would come over from the observatory sometimes in a state of almost wild elation, at others utterly worn out and dejected, but always shrouded in a mantle, as it were, of absorbed introspection. One day when for forty-eight hours he had been more abstracted and "nervy" than usual, he startled me by saying:

"You remember my chaff about you and the dynamo? Look here, if anything of that kind were to happen to me you will know how it happened, if any enquiry should be made. But before anything of that kind happens, and people—executors, all that sort of rot you know—come messing about, take this key off my watch-chain. It opens this writing case. Take the case and pack it up in your luggage, and take it away. You can read the papers yourself afterwards, but not until I am buried."

I was very much shocked, and begged him to relax in his work, to accept my help in so far as it might be of any avail, but he only laughed queerly and said:

"I am only putting a very unlikely and hypothetical case. I'm all right. But a research worker should always be prepared for the most unlikely eventualities. As for help, my work is purely personal, no one can help."

"When shall you publish?"

"Never."

"Why not?"

He thought for a moment, and then he said: "I have gone too far. The world is not yet fit to know what I know. Don't think I am mad, I am not. I'm deadly sane. Some day someone else will happen on the same results, and who knows what may happen then? I won't be responsible. It's too much." By this time he was apparently talking to himself. He had forgotten all about me.

By the way, I don't think I have mentioned that Markwand was a bachelor.

I had been with him about a fortnight, and every day it had seemed to me that he was becoming more exalted—a stupid word, but I can think of no other. He spent the days as it were in a dream, seldom speaking except upon the most conventional subjects, rather impatient if I referred to our work at the University.

"Don't talk shop for goodness sake, old man. That's our work-a-day world, this is something different. Another world? Hardly, but perhaps the threshold."

I didn't like this. "The Threshold" is one of the cant terms in the Jargon of the Spiritualist, the Esoteric Buddhist, the Rosicrucian, and it turned me cold.

"I say, old fellow," I said, "you know I'm broad minded, and I don't sneer at poor old A, B, and C, who believe in spooks, and commune with those who have 'passed over'; I look upon it as a mental disease, exploited by quacks (who are, I understand, generally charwomen when not doing the Prospero act), just as some physical diseases are exploited by the quacks of a different walk in life. But I do think the result is the same. The incurable is the quarry of the quack. But that you should have any truck with that kind of thing is unthinkable. Threshold of what?" I concluded rather inconsequently.

"Oh, don't be afraid. I'm not disturbing the sainted spirit of my Aunt Jemima. When I said 'threshold,' I meant a real Threshold, like a flight of steps, or a plank. Difficult to find a word. But I can't explain. I'm sorry."

I thought seriously of writing in confidence to Sir George Amboyne, our Regius Professor of Medicine to ask him to invite himself down for a day or two to have a look at Markwand.

However, I didn't, and I am glad now that I didn't. One night I woke up in his den, where I used to read, and smoke, and wait for him to come over to bed. It was just day-break, and, gadzooks, I *was* stiff! He hadn't come in, so I risked his displeasure and walked over to the observatory. The east was just reddening, and the plantation was full of the little sounds that animals and birds make when they shake themselves to start the day's work. I could see that the arc-light was burning, and I could hear the purring of the dynamo. Thinking he must be asleep I reached my hand towards the door and was just about to turn the handle when the light went out and a wild cry came from beyond it—a word? A name? An exclamation? What?

"Aalila!"

Drawn out on the first syllable "A-a-lila!" I opened the door. Markwand was standing by his telescope, his arms extended over his head, looking at me. He blinked like an owl in daytime, though the struggling dawn made light hardly visible. He looked at me stupidly for a moment and then looked at the Sidereal clock.

"Good heavens," he said quite calmly. "I *am* sorry. It's daylight. I had forgotten the time, and you, and everything else. I don't wonder either. Haven't *you* been to bed? I'm a rotten host. Come and have a bath."

And we walked back to the house as if nothing at all had happened. Markwand was in splendid form. We bathed, made coffee, fried bacon and potatoes, and went down to the stream to fish.

"You're overdoing it, Markwand," I said, after a rather long silence.

"Am I?" he replied laughing, and landing a trout. "Do I look like it? I've had a splendid night. Do I look the worn-out scientist?"

He certainly did not.

Later in the day we were lazing in two chairs on the lawn under a tree. I caught Markwand looking at me in the manner which is described by story-writers as "whimsical." I fell to an irresistible temptation.

"What is Aalila?" I said.

"If you only knew!" he replied. "Well, you shall; I'm going to tell you."

Then he plunged into it. Later I verified every detail of his marvellous story, and was able to fill in a mass of others which he left out or slurred over.

✳

"I was observing Venus—conscientiously from full-Venus to no-Venus—last year. You will find all the notes in the Observatory Record; all that matter to the star-gazers. I shall communicate them very shortly. The rest is in that writing case. You know the one I mean.

"One night, at about half-Venus, I was lying in the chair, watching and making notes, when on the dark part, near the outer edge, I saw a bright spot. I couldn't make out what it was of course, but as I watched, it flickered, went out. And look here, don't laugh or say a word or I shall dry up. It flashed S.O.S: . . . — — — . . . Morse, you know. I assumed that I was dreaming, or that my eyes were tired or playing me a trick. It went out, and then it came again. Then it made a lot of letters, all higgledy-piggledy, but I swear to you that every group was a perfect letter. It went on for over an hour, and as each letter was made I wrote it down. You know I was a signaller in the regiment during the war? Then it stopped dead. I tried to make sense of the jumble of letters; of course there was nothing in it, but the last two letters were Vick

E: . . . — . The Signaller—don't laugh, I warn you—knew how to end a message anyhow.

"The next night, the same performance over again. I had read a lot of what I regard as tosh about "signalling from Mars"; it's a hardy perennial, but I was as certain as I am that you are sitting there, that Venus was signalling to Earth and signalling in mad hysterical Morse at that. I found that night, and verified by references to the transcript of the night before, that before every pause in the flashes came the regulation full stop Ack-Ack-Ack . — . — . — Lord, man! can you imagine what I felt! I'll tell you what I did. I trained the mirror of my arc-light on to the spot as near as I could make it out, aiming by the telescope, and next night the moment it began—as usual, with S.O.S.—I flashed it back, cutting the ray with a sheet of tin plate. Venus 'went out' for a minute, and then repeated S.O.S. Same reply from me. Then came other letters, in no kind of sequence, but I repeated each one religiously. When this had gone on for an hour, I took the initiative in a pause and flashed 'Vick E.' Venus understood; she flashed it back, and then Ack-Ack-Ack. That was all that night.

"I won't weary you with what followed during months, whenever Venus was observable, but you'll find it all there. I took the initiative again, and flashed the whole alphabet from A to Z, and got every letter back; and at last the whole alphabet came back to me in its proper order. Venus was profiting by its lessons. And then came the climax. I can't think why it had not occurred to me before. I switched in the Selenium cells and put on the receiver. Instantly I heard a noise, sounds, linguals and labials. 'Mu, ma, mu, la, lo, la' and vowel sounds. It was, at least, clear that Venus had a photo-telephone in circuit, ready for me in case we had got so far as that on Earth. After listening for a minute or so I flashed 'Ack-Ack-Ack.' Venus knew that that was a stop, but not the 'very end'—Vick E. I connected the transmitter. I flashed Ack, and *said* the letter A. It came back—both flash and sound! So on through the alphabet.

"After this I began teaching Venus to spell—like a child with a spelling-book—AB—ab, BO—bo, and so on, and after a

353

time—you understand I am condensing weeks into words—the 'conversation,' if you can call it one, always began 'Aa-li-la' and after 'Vick E.' again, always 'Aa-li-la.' Man! I realised that this was the name of the Thing that was signalling. I tell you one thing and that is that Venus, the Thing, was much cleverer than I; it tried to make *me* understand sounds, but I couldn't make head or tail of one, and meanwhile It was beginning to say English words. And what is more it had an apparatus which repeated perfectly, and improved upon, everything that mine did.

"For nights I tried to get an impression upon a photo-transmission plate, but for at least a week there was no result whatever. Then one night I said 'Aalila' and tried to transmit the letters, in Morse of course, but in dots and dashes on the plate. I only found out later what happened up there—I say 'up' for the sake of definition—but my plate went mad and got covered with scratches in all directions. Aalila had caught on to the idea, and was doing her—I was certain somehow it was 'her'—best, and at last one night after weeks of patient scratching I got Aalila's face. Lord, man! it was lovely. Just imagine to yourself a—but what's the good? She was—she is—indescribable!

Markwand paused and looked away with that strange exalted air that had puzzled me so often. "Is?" I queried softly. I was afraid of, as he said, drying him up.

"Yes, *is.*"

"You see her picture then?"

"I see *her.*"

To say that I was flabbergasted is to use a miserably inadequate expression. What was all this about? Was I talking to a madman? But if it was a delusion, as of course it must be, it was the sanest and most deliberately nurtured delusion that ever a man originated.

That was all Markwand told me that day. I think his idea was to let me so far into his amazing secret, and to let what he had told me sink in, so as to judge by my manner how I took it, and whether I were worthy of further confidence. But it was evidently a great relief to him to be able to talk at all about it. He often set little traps for me, to see if I would laugh, or doubt, or sneer, but as time went on and I always listened with a keen interest which required no simulation, he arrived at telling me the progress of his adventure, step by step, and as I have said, what he left out then, I could supply from his journal of the affair—afterwards.

It would take far too long; it would indeed fill a volume of no mean size, were I to set down here the gradual "anastomosis" (to borrow a term from the Physiologists) of Markwand and Aalila, how they arrived at the meanings of words, and how, out of the chaos of incomprehensible sounds, they arrived at conversation. It is not enough, but it must be taken as enough, to record that Markwand little by little arrived at knowing all about Aalila, and about life on the planet Venus, where the Physical Sciences had reached a development which would stagger the imagination of a Jules Verne produced to the power of n. What is really most important was the stunning fact that Markwand was in love with Aalila as only a bachelor of his age can be, when he makes his first acquaintance with the grand passion.

It will be observed that I have not hitherto touched upon a very important point. You will not unnaturally have been asking yourself how on earth—or rather in Venus—had Aalila learned the Morse Alphabet? As soon as I felt that I could safely ask questions without "drying him up" I put this to Markwand.

"Oh," he replied, "of course I ought to have told you that. She learnt from our Fleet Signallers during the War."

"What?"

"It takes some believing, doesn't it? The question of interplanetary signalling has always been a burning one up there. They signal to many other planets already, but they had never 'picked up' Earth, which, by the way, they call Waluma. Aalila, you will not be surprised to hear, is a great astronomical 'nut' up there, and she has been searching Waluma for a sign for years. In August, 1914, and onwards, she observed that our seas were constantly starred with intermittent flashes—of course their telescopes are to ours what Big Bertha was to a pop-gun—and after puzzling over them for months she found that there was a regular sequence in them, that certain groups of dots and dashes continually recurred, especially 'ringing up' with a series of 'E's,' and that a single 'E' at a short distance always stopped it. She got on to the full stop 'Ack-Ack-Ack,' and the 'Vick E' at the end of a message, almost directly. And from this she gradually worked out all our letters, not in their order of course. One of her first questions when we could talk was to enquire what were 'Toc,' and 'E'—T and E, our commonest letters. She had got a lot of common words pat— 'and, the, it' and so on."

"What did she make of it?"

"Why—the inference was obvious to her—we were signalling to Venus!"

"Good heavens!"

"What confused her most were the constant and reiterated 'E's' on land. Those were the flashes of the great guns."

It made one's brain reel. I seldom had to ask questions after that.

And here it becomes very difficult for me to write at all about it. I have been so shocked by the death of Markwand and all that it meant and conveyed to *me,* the terrible proof, as it would seem, that this amazing adventure was no delusion at all, but drew to its inevitable and tragic end, irresistibly, that I cannot think with equanimity of anyone even smiling at details which would readily lend themselves to humorous treatment, but which were in themselves the very essence of the tragedy. In the foremost place there stood the fact that Aalila had, conformably with the customs of her planet, seven husbands—a multiple fact that did not in any way appear to militate against her full reciprocation of Markwand's passion. Husbands in Venus appear to be of a singularly easy-going disposition, to our mundane intelligence, but an exception would appear to occur at intervals, and one of these loomed large in Aalila's cosmogony in the shape of an infuriated and jealous male. Highly intellectual as Aalila was, and occupying an exalted position in the scientific world of the planet, this husband, Illuha by name, was to Aalila what an ignorant woman (only one of course) would be to a Regius Professor in one of our own Universities—a woman who sets her own personal gratification and feelings far above the career and the life-interests of her husband. And so in her "affair" with Markwand, Aalila had to be very careful—in certain mundane circles her attitude would probably be described as "wily."

It was all very well for Aalila to shut herself up in her observatory and communicate with her Terrestrial Lover. Illuha, who was of course not ignorant of the vast potentiality of Astral physics in Venus, was, it appeared, far from easy in his mind as to the scope and extent of Aalila's researches, and—well, as I have said, Aalila had to be very careful. Very frequently the nightly communion would be intercepted by unreasonably uxorious reproaches, not to mention physical interruptions, which scared Aalila intempestatively from the photo-telephone; and it seems from a note of Markwand's that Aalila had in a moment of relaxed vigilance allowed Illuha to catch sight of sundry telephotographs of Markwand, and, to put it perhaps somewhat crudely, Illuha was on the prowl.

All might, however, have been well had it not been for the high quality of Aalila's scientific knowledge, attainments and ambitions. From transmitting very remarkable, and I am bound to say often highly compromising pictures of herself, she soared to the ambition of, and devoted much research to, the accomplishment of transmitting *herself*; that is to say a replica, an astral body of herself, perfect in every essential detail, and of a bodily consistency adequate to all practical purposes. Of the development and ultimate success of this crowning triumph of Aalila's scientific career I can only gather the broad outlines, for Markwand himself seems to have grown shy of his record in this matter, and the scientific accuracy of his register is marred from this point by a doubtless proper and laudable discretion, which leaves certain details, but not many, to the imagination, and tends therefore to the detriment of scientific knowledge. It must remain enough to say that the semi- but not too-æthereal Aalila came to Earth and visited Markwand in his observatory, whenever she could get away, whilst her physical body remained on guard, as it were, in her observatory in Venus. And it must be recorded to her credit that she never attempted to conceal from Markwand the paramount, the terrible danger of these astral excursions. Though her physical body remained behind, she brought her intellect to Earth with her, and this it was that in fullness of time brought her and Markwand to grief. For the physical body, temporarily bereft of its directing mind, was not up to controlling the apparatus, and the romance of her interviews with Markwand must have been seriously hampered by the necessity of keeping an eye on the screen, and an ear at the photo-telephone.

Consequently these amazing interviews had to be arranged for occasions when Illuha could be counted upon to be absent from home, or at any rate not likely to come bothering after her at the observatory. From what one could gather, the position of husbands in Venus is—setting aside, of course, their plurality—much the same as that of wives in the so-called civilized portions of the Earth, and, perhaps, vice versa.

Markwand was, as I have indicated, reticent as to the details of his interviews with Aalila in conversation with me, and *a fortiori* recorded in his scientific journal only political, economical, and sometimes ethnological details of life on the planet, and looking over the record, it may be said that the personal equation must have bulked largely in their communion, for lengthy meetings with Aalila frequently furnished but a few lines in either his private or scientific journals. He tried to explain to me, however, the nature of the risks they ran, but the explanation was largely beyond my powers of comprehension—Hertzian waves—Potential—Amperage, and other technical terms bristled in his exposition, and I gave up trying to become an expert in the matter. I only knew that the physical Aalila left behind had mechanical control of the projection apparatus, and if disturbed, or damaged, might work irretrievable disaster. It was clear that the interference of any unauthorized or inexperienced person in the observatory might, and probably would, divert the full force of Aalila's generating plant along the communicating beam. Upon what would happen in that event Markwand did not care to speculate.

"The physical Aalila," he said, "would almost certainly be destroyed, and what would happen here it is difficult to conjecture. I should imagine some form of instantaneous annihilation—volatilization—I don't know. But we take all necessary and possible precautions."

I hazarded a question.

"Is the replica-Aalila of sufficient substance to suffer physical hurt?"

He thought for a moment—and I am not sure that he did not blush a little. Then he replied: "Oh, yes. There is little doubt about that."

"Take another postulate," I said. "Supposing some unauthorized person" (we seldom or never mentioned Illuha by name, from motives of delicacy no doubt) "were to get at the apparatus in her replica-absence, and supposing that person found himself—or herself" (I hastily added), "projected along the ray in some way? What then?"

Markwand, I am sorry to say, shrugged his shoulders and laughed; yes, he positively laughed, and instead of answering he turned away, chaunting under his breath a line of an old plantation song which ran:

"The congregation all stand up, and sing—Hallelujah!"

My stay with Markwand was drawing to its close, but I lingered on, obsessed with a vague feeling of apprehension. Though in no way regarding myself in any degree in the light of a chaperon, I did not think it quite safe, or quite proper, to leave him alone with Aalila. I hinted at a visit elsewhere, accompanied by him; I would have liked to see him safely back to town, but he would not hear of it. Markwand was lovelorn. And he was very happy. I grew more and more apprehensive, and, I will admit it, more and more curious. I endeavoured to convey to him that I would like to be present at one of their interviews, and then it was Markwand's turn to be shocked. I felt at once that I had been guilty of a most indelicate indiscretion, so there was nothing for it but to wait, on the chance of being of some use should an emergency arise.

We come therefore to the night, or rather the early morning of the 14th. For some days Markwand had been preoccupied, nervy, and I gathered that things were not going as pleasantly as they might. In a word, Illuha was giving trouble, and it became an increasing strain to keep in touch, so to speak, with the observatory in Venus, whilst occupied in the researches and instructive discourse which should, from their point of view, have exclusively occupied their periods of companionship.

"It's rather difficult sometimes," he admitted, "to keep the necessary amount of attention fixed upon what is going on up there. For instance, only the other day——" then he broke off, and I never knew (nor was there any record among his private memoranda) what had disturbed the primrose path of scientific research on this occasion.

I was sitting in the den waiting for Markwand as usual. I never liked to go to bed till he returned and I knew that Aalila had been safely packed off "home;" and I had been to sleep, also as usual.

Suddenly the beam from the observatory swung into the den, and the gong sounded furiously. I snatched up the receiver but nothing came excepting confused sounds and a violent crackling like that of a radiogram transmitter. I flung it down and rushed over to the observatory and burst in. It was full of a brilliant violet light, independently of the arc-light, and a smell of burning.

Markwand was standing as I entered, and whether my overwrought senses deceived me or not I cannot tell now, but it seemed to me that a female form—overwhelmingly comely, I must admit—was kneeling on the floor at his feet, her arms encircling his waist, and her head turned towards the complicated mirrors and cells which constituted Markwand's end of the apparatus. Terror was in the beautiful dark face, and she seemed to be trying to shield him, to protect him from something invisible to me. But the whole vision only lasted a second or two. Then a sort of seismic cataclysm took place; all the lights went out and the observatory was in pitch darkness, save that on the floor appeared a circle about a yard in diameter, not exactly luminous, but scintillating. I fumbled for the lighting switch. I got no light, but I got a shock that I shall remember to my dying day. It made me violently sick. After a delay, which seemed to me to be like an age in length, I got at my matches and struck a light and lit a couple of candles which always stood on the table in case of the current failing at any time.

The photo-telephone apparatus was wrecked, it looked like the debris of a spring mattress in a marine storekeeper's back yard. The telescope was twisted off its massive base and was hanging nearly to the floor; there was a rent in the dome beside the observation slit. I was vividly aware of an uncanny silence, and then I saw that the Sidereal clock and the Heliostat had both stopped—their sonorous tick would have been such a comfort.

I was alone with Markwand.

He was lying on the floor, where I had seen him standing, quite motionless, and quite normal, save that his lips were drawn back showing both rows of teeth in a ghastly grin.

Recollection of "first-aid" classes came to me. Electric shock, artificial respiration, and so on. I loosened his waistcoat, trousers-band, and shirt-collar, and began to apply my inadequate knowledge. There was a sickening smell as I gradually got him undressed. Then I knew he was dead. I made a violent effort to retain my presence of mind, my sanity, to think. There would be doctors, an inquest, people prying about, viewing the body. Horrible! I felt that at all hazards *I must view it first*. I undressed Markwand very carefully. The instantaneous blanching of death had made his fair skin look whiter, and he was physically uninjured, externally at any rate.

But round his waist, where I had seen the arms of Aalila, was a deep brown and blistered band. He had been girt in a zone of fire, fire which had burnt deeply beyond the skin into his body, but his clothes were not even singed. A detail: in the small of his back was the burnt impress of a small right hand, deepest at the finger tips. All I could think about was "I wonder where her other hand was?"

I sat and looked at Markwand, I don't know how long, but suddenly through the rent in the dome I saw it was dawn. I dressed him carefully. I wonder if you have any idea of how difficult it is to dress a dead body? He was also growing stiff.

I made myself *think* with a mighty effort. How did he die? The newspapers, the obituary notices, the coroner. Of course— the dynamo! I dragged Markwand over to the dynamo which was apparently wrecked too. I forced up his stiff arm so that the hand rested on the commutator. I took the key off his watch-chain.

Where I had seen the scintillating circle in the darkness lay a ring of pale grey dust. This struck me, and taking a small ordinary collector's corked tube from Markwand's laboratory bench I filled it with the dust and put it into my waistcoat pocket.

Then I crept back, like a murderer, to the study, found the writing-case, and put it into my portmanteau.

Then I roused the house.

THE MIRROR THAT REMEMBERED.

(Deposited by the Professor of Pure Mathematics.)

WE—that is to say, several members of the Professorial Staff—were taking wine in the rooms of our esteemed colleague, the Wetherell Professor of Physics, and the conversation ran upon the remarkable dynamic properties of Light, which, starting from the mysterious Radiometer of Crookes, had recently culminated in the delicate experiments of an eminent Physicist, in which the dynamic action of the human eye upon an ingenious apparatus had been demonstrated to the amazement of the scientific world.

"We are far from knowing," observed the Professor of Physics, "what is the ultimate, the permanent action of reflections—as in an ordinary looking-glass, for instance."

"It would appear," said Markwand, the Professor of Astronomy, "that our knowledge of the ultimate possibilities of the Selenium cell is in its infancy. Photo-telephony is only at the beginning of its development."

"True," replied Erichsen—the Professor of Physics, our host—"now that what has been regarded as a mere phenomenon of vision has been shown to possess a dynamic force, the question must naturally arise, what, regard being had to the conservation of force, becomes of the energy imparted to the mirror when we look into it?"

"If it comes to that," said Markwand, "where is the picture that we see in a mirror?"

"Explain," said someone.

"I mean exactly what I say. If you stand in front of a mirror, at a distance of six feet, you see yourself apparently twelve feet away—so that the picture cannot be further than that. Where is that further six feet?"

"Good heavens," said the Professor of Psychology. "It seems to me that you have there an inexplicable problem."

"Not so inexplicable," said Erichsen, "as the further problem of what becomes of the picture when you have moved away? What becomes of all the pictures which have been impressed upon the mirror since the moment when the reflecting amalgam was laid on to its back? Remember that in the light of these new discoveries every picture has its own energy, its own dynamic force—a force that cannot perish."

A silence fell upon us. Erichsen was sitting in his accustomed armchair by the side of the fire, the rest of us in a semi-circle extending to the other side. He, with his head resting upon his hand, was looking into the fire with an expression which would be described by a popular novelist as "haunted."

"Are you going to suggest," said Markwand, "that the recurrent images reflected in a mirror either dissipate themselves in the form of force—or, worse still, that they are accumulated—superimposed—in, or upon, the reflecting surface or substance?"

"That," replied Erichsen, rousing himself with an obvious effort, "is precisely what—I do not suggest—I postulate."

A murmur of astonished incredulity flickered around the circle.

"What an awful idea," exclaimed Magley, the Physiologist, "it makes one's brain reel. Imagine a mirror suddenly running amuck and reproducing, as in a Cinematograph, everything it has ever seen."

"It strikes me," said Sir George Amboyne, our Regius Professor of Medicine, "that if ever such a thing become possible, some of us would be running round the world with a hammer, smashing mirrors whose reminiscences we should regard—with reason—as potentially indiscreet."

"It may come to that," replied Erichsen.

"What?" A chorus.

"The revolving powers of vacuum tubes," pursued Erichsen, "are being developed every day. Look at the revelations of invisible light—the infra-red and the ultra-violet rays. Remember the beginning of it all—the prints of a hand upon a whole unopened packet of dry plates which had been unconsciously exposed to the action of a Crookes tube. How can we tell to what a point this may be developed—accidentally. Accidentally," he repeated, looking back into the fire.

"Well," said Markwand—uneasily it seemed to me, "let us be thankful that we are so far away from *that*, that we are justified in saying that it is utterly impossible." What he meant by "*that*" did not require definition.

"And suppose," said Erichsen, looking round with that same "haunted" look, "I were to show you a Mirror that *remembered?*"

"Erichsen," said Amboyne quietly, "you have been overworking. You want rest. Take a holiday."

"I don't think that I shall ever rest again. It might happen again at any moment."

"Again?" Once more a chorus.

Erichsen seemed to sink for a moment into a profound abstraction, and then pulled himself together with a violent effort. Then he said: "I've got to tell someone. If I don't I shall go mad. You see that Amboyne has grave doubts on the matter already. It may as well be you fellows—and now."

We all looked at one another uncomfortably, and at Erichsen. He, with a grim look on his fine handsome face, stood up.

"Come with me," he said, and we all moved towards the door, which he opened, showing us into the passage. Erichsen had fine rooms, occupying the whole first floor of a large house. He was a bachelor of ample private means—at once the hope and despair of the University Matrons with daughters. The room we had left communicated with another, which was his dining-room. In front of us, across the passage, were two doors.

"That," he said, pointing to the left-hand door, "is my private laboratory. This," pointing to the right-hand door, "is my bedroom. Come in here."

We went in, and when we were all inside he followed us and switched on the lights. The centre of the room, behind the door and against the wall, was occupied by his bed, a large one. Against the wall on the left was a tall mirror, four feet wide and rising six feet from the floor.

This had been smashed into a thousand atoms. From a great hole in the centre radiating fractures extended in all directions to the sides.

"Hullo," exclaimed Markwand, "you seem to have had an accident."

"It wasn't an accident," replied Erichsen grimly, "it was a woman."

We looked at him in uncomfortable consternation. The Professor of Psychology looked shocked.

"This is no place for you," said Markwand, nudging him.

"Now come into the lab.," said Erichsen.

We followed him. Standing against the wall on the right, so as to be immediately behind the smashed mirror, was what appeared to be an ordinary X-ray apparatus. The wires connecting the induction-coil were torn away and lay in untidy spirals on the bench—the sockets for holding the tube were empty, and the spaces between them were strewn with the finely comminuted fragments which arise from the implosion of a large vacuum tube.

This time no one said a word.

"Come back to the sitting-room," said Erichsen, and we followed him again.

When we were settled round the fire once more, he served out drinks, and most of us lit our pipes again in silence. Some of the hands shook a little. Erichsen remained standing, his back to the fire. He began, without introduction:

"You know my lectures this term have dealt principally with the infra- and ultra-spectrum. I have had many tubes made by various instrument makers; some have been entirely successful, some have been complete failures. A short while ago I had one made to a new formula. I shall not tell you what it was—or who made it. It was made abroad. I set it up where you saw the fragments, for, according to my computations it should have

366

made the mirror, on the other side of the wall, glow in the dark. It struck me that it would make a weird—romantic—fantastic light—in certain circumstances. I set it up in the afternoon, for I wanted to try the effect in the dark—next night."

He paused and looked round the circle of listeners, keenly—critically—as if he were trying to detect any marks of incredulity, or levity on our faces. I think we all kept our eyes fixed on the fire—I know we did not look at Erichsen. Then he went on:

"I had a friend to dinner that evening—a woman."

Then we looked at one another. I have sufficiently described Erichsen.

"It was later on, that night, that I wanted to try the effect of the new tube. I took her into my bedroom and left her there for a few minutes whilst I went into the lab., connected the wires, and switched on the coil. As I entered the bedroom on my return she quickly switched off the light—and then—in the dark, she uttered a low cry and clung to me with all her strength. The Mirror was glowing—but it did not reflect *us*. One does not often see nowadays what used to be popular years ago—dissolving views. Well, we were looking at a confused, distorted, jerky series of dissolving views, a veritable cinematograph. At first, workshops, streets, darkness with patches of railway station—where the protecting straw had shifted.

"At last the pictures settled down to an even continuity—the Mirror was in my room. We saw me dress for dinner, go to bed, get up. Evening came again and I dressed for dinner again. The Mirror was catching up. It was within three weeks of us—and then *she* came into the room.

"We looked—petrified—for a few seconds longer, and then she—the living woman—sprang from my arms, caught up one of a pair of dumb-bells which lay on the floor by the fireplace, and hurled it through the centre of the Mirror. In an instant it was as you saw it just now. I lost my head. I rushed from the room and into the lab., and instead of cutting out the coil, I seized a steel ruler and smashed the Tube.

"After that I don't quite know what happened. When I returned to my room, she was gone."

PURPURA LAPILLUS.

(Deposited by the Regius Professor of History.)

"WHILKS!" The Merchant hardly raised his voice. It was only when a passer-by slackened his pace before the Establishment, and looked in the direction of the Stock-in-trade with an expression of interest (which expression the Merchant had learned by long experience to gauge with surprising accuracy) that he ejaculated on a note of interrogation his everlasting monosyllable: "Whilks?"

The Establishment occupied by prescriptive right some eight feet of the roadway against the kerb. It was of semi-nocturnal habit, arriving at its post—known as its "pitch"—late in the afternoons. At each corner sooty flames struggled through greasy lamp chimneys to irradiate the Stock-in-trade. A few yards away a constant procession of omnibuses punctuated the throbbing life of the Edgware Road. The Stock-in-trade, piled high against the back of the barrow, a pale yellow heap of shells, diffused a marine aroma which fought for supremacy with the more pungent perfume that spurted continuously from a little pipe projecting from the façade of the Sausage and Mashed Emporium on the landward side of the pavement. The roadway below the barrow was strewn with empty whelk-shells, the lately-evicted inhabitants of which lay coiled in small circular plates of doubtful cleanliness, disposed along the front of the Establishment.

"Two penn'orth, Daddy, and fat ones, ladies for choice," said Albert. Albert was a wag, and also a regular customer. Daddy looked up in nervous greeting—he knew Albert and prayed to

Neptune that he might be in his good mood. Albert's bad mood was recognisable by a tendency to critical sarcasm that had been known to blight trade for half an hour at a time.

"Pick 'em out where you like, Albert, you're a judge." Thus Daddy, slavishly obsequious. "Whilks!" The word formed a full stop to his every utterance. His lips once unsealed by the necessities of commerce, it seemed a pity not to include his trade-announcement, as a recurrent termination. "Whilks!"

The Professor was returning home, dog-tired after a day of research culminating in a lecture. With the semi-unconscious habit of the Systematic Zoologist, he murmured to himself as he reached the Establishment, "*Buccinum umdatum.*" He paused and cast a rapid glance over the heaped-up shells. The Whelk Barrow, like its aristocratic rival the Oyster Stall, is often a happy hunting-ground for the Professor. At both Establishments an infinite world of marine life may be found encrusting the shells—Polyzoa—Ascidians—Annelids—you never know what you may find. He paused.

"Whilks?" said Daddy. A new customer perhaps. A cut above his usual clientele no doubt—but who knows what strange cravings may suddenly develop even in a Toff whose normal tastes would lead him to Whitstable natives and Champagne wine? Daddy had once sold a plate of "Whulks" to one whom he identified from the picture-postcards as a Cabinet Minister.

The Merchant kept an anxious eye upon Albert. This patron, the small plate poised upon his left finger tips, was detaining the vinegar which he grasped in his right hand. A Lady wanted it, and was on the verge of becoming articulate. Daddy trembled. Albert's small eyes were fixed in what Daddy could not but realise was a baleful glare upon the Stock-in-trade. Bad luck! Albert was evidently in his bad mood. Slowly he replaced the plate upon the barrow and handed the vinegar to the Lady, with the deadly observation, "You be careful what you're eating, Marm!" A ripple of disquiet visibly ran over the clientele. It was, I believe, Dr. Johnson who observed that the only requisite for the perfect enjoyment of Sausages is implicit confidence. It is the same with

Shell-fish. They share with the Egg, and Caesar's wife, the imperative necessity of being above suspicion.

"Now then, Albert, what's wrong with you? Over-eaten yourself at the oysters?" Thus Daddy anxiously, and with ill-concealed alarm, hoping to carry the war into the enemy's country with a rapid thrust of wit. But Albert was not to be disarmed. He had *facts* to go upon. The Storm broke.

"'Ere! what yer givin' us? Whilks! I don't think. What's this?—and this?—and this?" With unerring eyes and dirty fingers he rapidly picked from the heap three smaller univalves, thicker in texture, whiter in colour, which he exhibited to the clientele in the palm of his hand. From one of them as it rolled over, a small stream of yellowish purple fluid oozed.

"'Strewth!" cried the Patron as he dropped the shells among the plates already decked with the red and white blobs which had once inhabited the discarded shells, "they're poisonous—and that's the poison."

The stricken business came to a standstill, but the crowd immediately increased in density. Daddy became active and vocal in distress. "They're all right," he said loudly, "they're only Dogwhilks—a smaller size—just as good, but I don't serve them, not never—'cause why? Not that they're *bad*, mind you, but because they're small, and I always give my customers good measure—full portions—you know that, Albert"—this despairingly, in a last effort to propitiate the foe.

"Oh, yes! we know all about that—don't we?"

The Lady chimed in: "My sister's 'usband 'ad a niece what ate a wrong whilk. She 'ad spots—orful—and she doied."

The crowd became murmurous. Half a dozen hideous reminiscences sprang to the lips of the bolder cognoscenti. The Professor picked up the damning evidence. *"Purpura lapillus,"* he observed, the habit of a lifetime over-mastering appreciation of his audience.

"There! the gentleman says they're poisonous—'e knows." Thus Albert springing to greet a heaven-sent witness for the prosecution.

370

"Not at all," said the Professor. Then, catching sight of the agony depicted on Daddy's features, he went on: "They are only a smaller whelk, but as the man says, they are not eaten, for the dye in them makes them unattractive." The Merchant threw him a glance which was a Benediction, and the Professor had an inspiration.

"I will take these," said he. "Have you any more?" In the manner of nervous conspirators he and Daddy picked out another three from the heap. "I am glad to have them." And with a look of infinite comprehension he put sixpence into Daddy's hand—ostentatiously—and disappeared into the Edgware Road.

"'E's dotty," said Albert. The crowd was confused by the multitude of testimony, and dissolved, divided between admiration of the knowledgeable Albert's heroic defence of the public, and sympathy for the mad Toff who was doubtless on his way home to commit suicide.

Business did not recover that evening. The "windy crowd" were not allowed to forget that a great and learned Toff had convicted Daddy of selling a poisonous winkle called "Purple bilious" as whelks. The Office of this Propaganda was the Establishment of the Oyster Merchant a little farther down the street.

After his solitary meal the Professor returned to his study to put in a few hours' work on his Monograph of the British Mollusca. He was, as previously recorded, dog-tired. On his blotting-pad lay the half-dozen Dog-whelks which he had put down when he came in. Where they lay, the white paper had absorbed a patch of the fluid which, upon exposure to light, becomes a deep purple stain. The Professor looked at it with weary eyes. *"Purpura lapillus,"* he murmured again, "and this is Tyrian Purple."

It seemed such an anachronism. The animal that yielded its marvellous colour to the dyers of Tyre and Tarsus, fifteen hundred years before the Augustan age, to become later the distinguishing mark of the Officials and Nobility of the Roman Empire, sold on a barrow in a side street, and the subject of a costermonger's quarrel with a 24-carat cad! And then an echo of his early schooling came down the dream-vista of Time—"for no man buyeth their merchandise any more, the merchandise of gold of purple"—and he smiled wanly over the later Revelation. And again, "the soldiers put on Him a purple robe, and said Hail! King of the Jews." A world of thoughts crowded in upon him.

The Professor stretched himself and stared at the ceiling. Evidently he was in no mood for Systematic Zoology. His eyes fell upon the purple patch again—wondered whether it was not exactly the breadth of the purple border of the *toga praetexta;* as a professor he would have come under the *jus togae praetextae habendae.* He would have been indistinguishable in the Forum from the Consuls, the Praetors, the Augurs, the Ædiles, so far as his apparel went. Perhaps as an Augur he would have worn his purple in stripes on the *trabea* in the Dawn of Science. And—as the picture became clearer, the scene more actual—the Professor rose, drew his toga more closely round him, gathered the flowing end over his left arm, and stepped forth from his house to join the groups converging upon the Colosseum.

It was a *première*—he must hurry, for the application for seats from the would-be "first-nighters" had been Overwhelming. Titus had completed the Monument which his father, Vespasian, had not lived to see perfected. The widowed Domitilla, and her daughter and namesake, would be there. A new denarius had been struck with the Colosseum on its reverse as a souvenir of the occasion for the tourists who had flocked to Rome from all parts of the Empire. His seat was in the podium, level with the Emperor and the Senators. Beyond him the Vestal Virgins were early-comers, and their views upon the fashions prevailing at court and their speculations upon the coming show forced a treble note upon the great chord of sounds that filled the air imprisoned under the velarium. The gradus had been filled to overflowing since the night before, especially the popularia—which reeked to heaven.

Strangely enough the experience was almost a new one to the Professor. He had once been taken to a contest at the National

Sporting Club, and it had made him feel sick; this, and a rat-hunt at Oxford, constituted the limits of his experience of *circenses.* The afternoon wore on. He looked anxiously towards the seats of the Vestal Virgins when the Star-Retiarius disembowelled a really most deserving Secutor—but no one fainted. Then he pulled himself together, reflecting that the Virgins seldom or never faint in the Operating Theatres of our Hospitals. The two spectacles had much in common.

The chariot-races appealed most vividly to his London-bred senses. Some of the observations and epigrams exchanged between the competitors reached his ears with startling distinctness. A shocked memory of the current vernacular of competing omnibus drivers in the Edgware Road came over him like the echo of a song. At first he did not like to look at the Empress Marcia and her ladies, but when at last a constant repetition and unlimited application of the same word had dulled its primary significance he looked towards the Imperial Box. The ladies were much amused.

It seemed a terrible thing to the Professor that the Keepers should have allowed the Council of the Zoological Society to sacrifice no less than four magnificent African lions, merely to make this opening performance a success. He was on the Council himself, and could not remember the matter ever having been brought before them—clearly the Secretary and Curator were taking too much upon themselves—but then he reflected suddenly that Africa is much nearer to Rome than to Regent's Park, and that the settlement of strikes among the Transport Workers was conducted in the Imperial City with a hatchet. He felt indeed a certain shamefaced satisfaction when the last lion successfully ate most of a rival Professor of Zoology before he could be induced (with red-hot irons) to return to his cage beneath the podium. The rival Professor owed his unfortunate experience to a rash suggestion that man—including the Emperor—was derived from the apes. He so far forgot himself as to shout "Bravo Toro!"

Nevertheless he had a sick headache when he walked home with the Professor of Applied Mathematics in the evening. A dreary dog this Professor. He had lately been allowing himself a relaxation in Pure Mathematics, and had, after four months' assiduous work, proved that there was no possible solution to a problem which he had himself invented. He had talked of nothing else for four months and the mood was still on him. The Professor shook him off in the vestibulum of his house. He would have liked to come in and cadge a drink—the Professor's Falernian was justly celebrated—and go on talking. But the Professor was firm. At the ostium he picked up his letters and reached the atrium dog-tired—still.

Seated at his desk, his head fell forward on to his blotting-pad from very weariness. A sharply pointed object dented his forehead and he raised himself again to a sitting position with a start. The six Dog-whelks were still there—fishermen call them "Stinkers." It occurred to the Professor that like many phrases in common use among seafaring folk the name was amply justified. He was clearly in no mood for Systematic Zoology.

He went to bed.

MANO PANTEA.

(Deposited by the Hunterian Professor of Fine Art.)

ONE of the peculiarities—or perhaps one should say, the survivals, or anachronisms that gave distinction to the costume—for it amounted to that—of Casimir Autrive, Hunterian Professor of Fine Art in the University of Cosmopoli, was the heavy, snaffle-pattern gold chain that wandered from his right-hand to his left-hand waistcoat pocket, the weight of which was supported by a cross-bar that passed through a button-hole. From the ring, through which the chain passed, there hung a "charm," as it was called in the 'seventies and 'eighties of the nineteenth century. This "charm" was a little Silver Hand—about an inch long—which seemed so incongruous to its environment that it arrested one's attention, though no one—not even Magley—would ever have dreamed of alluding to it in a spirit of idle curiosity. Professor Autrive, though, as may become a Professor of Fine Art, he showed traces of what used to be called the Higher Bohemianism—as opposed to the modern meretricious variety—was, beyond a clearly defined limit, an unapproachable kind of person. And he may be said to have "dressed the part."

He was on the point of being made "Emeritus," but he still lectured, and he met his assembled pupils in the frock-coat that he habitually wore on occasions of ceremony; his "mufti" was a black or brown velvet coat and waistcoat, and when not crowned by the somewhat *rapin* felt hat and loose collar and tie of his youth, "sported" the Gladstonian collar, the black bow, and the curly-brimmed tall-hat of the 'eighties. A remarkable personality, and, at that time, quite the most striking figure in Cosmopoli, was the Hunterian Professor of Fine Art.

The Silver Hand, therefore, did not seem to be an eccentricity. Its third and fourth fingers were flexed into the palm, as they are in the Episcopal Blessing, and it bore certain Signs in relief, as to whose signification, however, no one had ever had the temerity to enquire.

History—it was more than mere tradition—related that, descended from one of the aristocratic families of the Emigration—his great-grandfather had been one of the *côterie* at Jupiter Hall—his name was originally d'Hautrive, but, whether shrinking from its anglicized pronunciation, or, as some averred, because certain of his earliest pupils had affectionately, but, in his opinion, too familiarly, converted d'Hautrive into "Dotty," he had adopted the form of his name by which, for longer than any of the professorial staff could remember, we all knew him.

One evening, in Common Room, the conversation had turned upon Hand-superstitions, and Wentworth, the Bakerian Professor of Ancient History, had held forth at some length, from his inexhaustible store of early superstitions, religious and profane, and his prodigious memory. Then, quite suddenly, Autrive detached from its ring the Silver Hand, held it out to Wentworth without a word, and from him it passed round the circle, which remained silently expectant. Then he spoke:

"It has no history, and, as far as I know, no especial significance. I bought it for one *lira* in a small and dirty jeweller's shop in Genoa about 1880. I hung it then on my watch-chain because in those days people wore such 'Charms,' but later it became connected with what is certainly the most remarkable occurrence that ever happened to me, and so I have worn it ever since. Would you like to hear about it?"

A murmur of polite attention and anticipation.

He began, and he held us spellbound—for he was an accomplished *raconteur*—for a space of time that seemed all too short to his audience. Later I walked back with him to his rooms in the Quad of St. Simeon's, and on the way I begged him to write the story and let me have it for preservation among the Archives from which the incidents recorded in this volume have been selected.

A few weeks later he came into my office, and, putting a small sheaf of manuscript on my table, said: "Here is the story connected with the Silver Hand for which you asked me." And with that he left the office. Here follows the narration.

C. B.

There are three forms of Hand-Charm (they are made of silver, gold, coral, ivory and so on), sold all over Italy—the most familiar is that with the first and fourth fingers extended, the others and the thumb being folded into the palm; this is identical with the Indian *mudrá* called "Karana," which protects the wearer, like the Italian examples, from the Evil Eye. It came, like the Swastika, from the prehistoric East. That with the whole fist clenched and the thumb protruding between the first and the second fingers is more rare—this is without doubt of phallic origin; and that of which mine is an example, reproduces the *mudrá* of the Episcopal Blessing. But mine is, so far as I know, unique, in that it bears upon it symbols in relief of a pair of Scales, a figure of the Virgin and Child, a Turtle and a Lizard. The girl who sold it to me told me that it was a copy in miniature of one of life-size, known as the '*Mano pantea*' the Pantheistic Hand—which had been in the Museum of Gian Pietro Bellori in Rome, but that the original had disappeared and no one knew where it was in 1880. But she was fervently earnest about it: as she pointed out: "I simboli che la ricoprono formano un gruppo di simboli che, uniti insieme, si credevano essere potenti a respingere gli effetti del fascino." Personally, I have no superstitions, but I bought it as a *ricordo* of a week spent in Genoa, the city of Columbus and Paganini.

At that time I never dreamed that I should ever lecture upon Art to successive generations of undergraduates at a University. I practiced it, however, and spoilt much good canvas in the hope of some day making a career, and, incidentally, a living, as an Artist. A few years later I drifted to Rome, the inevitable Mecca of all budding—and other—Artists, in those days, and lived for a time in a charming "apartment" in the Tempietta, a conical house at the apical juncture of the Via Sistina and the Via Gregoriana, overlooking the Piazza of the Trinita de' Monti, at the top of the steps leading down to the Piazza di Spagna. One of its chief attractions for me was the crowd of picturesque tatterdemalions who, in those days, were to be found at all hours at the top and at the bottom of the steps, waiting to be hired as artists' models, and I frequently spent idle hours chatting with them. Peasant girls from the Campagna whose stormy beauty had justified them in forsaking the manual labours of the country for the coffee and cigarettes and the *dolce far niente* and other allurements of the studios; handsome, dirty shepherds from Orvieto, and beautiful child-ragamuffins of both sexes, willing at any moment to loll about on an estrade and be painted in exchange for a packet of sweetmeats and a few *lire*.

But of all the picturesque, run-to-seed and characteristic blackguards who haunted this classic spot, the patriarch Ippolito was *facile princeps*: he was an old *contadino* of somewhere between sixty and seventy years of age, maybe, but who looked as if the crimes of centuries had concentrated themselves within his decidedly unclean person, and he was interesting with all the crass ignorance of the most elementary type of Italian peasant. He was in great demand as a model for God-the-father, St. Peter and the more robust Saints, as well as on account of his own dilapidated personality and unbridled conversation. It is not surprising that he was a great favourite among the Artists and Students, whose ears he would regale with weird legends of the Campagna, told in the vilest Orvieto dialect, or with folk-songs, often more curious than polite, chanted in the cracked monotone of the Maremma; and from many a studio wall in London and Paris, no less than in Rome itself, even to the present day old Ippolito's face, in more or less finished condition, has leered at me alike from gilded frames, dusty canvas, and tattered millboard.

I had made friends with a very intelligent and charming young Italian, one Domenico Correr—Venetian, of course, as his name indicates—a doctor by profession, but a painter by predilection, who lived in the Via Margutta, and with whom I used to dine, whenever I had no other engagement, at the Café Greco, a queer Bohemian resort of cloistral and subterranean character close to the Piazza di Spagna where, in those days, a cosmopolitan crowd of artists and writers used to congregate for the midday and evening meals, or for the afternoon "*Vermouth e chino*," a mixture of vermouth and quinine—they call it *Vermouth amaro* nowadays—supposed to be a protection against malaria. I sought the Greco last time I was in Rome, but the glory had departed, it had become a teashop infested by tourists. Correr spent many hours with me in the Tempietta, where we talked, as young men were then wont to do, "of the glory that was Greece"—and of every other subject under the sun—and moon. One evening I broke it to him that my tenure of the "apartment" was drawing to a close, and he hailed the news with glee.

"Come and join the throng in the Via Margutta," said he. "The man who has the studio at the top of the house above me, an American artist, is going home for six months—perhaps longer, and I know he would be glad to under-let his place to a respectable and responsible tenant."

The idea appealed to me, and next day we inspected the *locale* together. The Via Margutta is a queer little street. You leave the Piazza di Spagna by the Via Babuino, and, after proceeding a few yards only, you turn into a little alley, which takes you into the Via Margutta, a narrow street, one-sided as it were, with north-west exposure, and running parallel to the Via Babuino, a street, on this account, especially affected by artists. The north side of the street was principally occupied by stables—low, two-storied buildings, which allowed the soft Italian light to pour without interruption into the studios on the south side, especially in the mornings. These had no "front doors," no staircases; built one over another, as it were, against the backs of the houses which overlooked the Villa Medici. The studios were reached by a series of balconies, connected by iron-staircases, which led from one balcony to the next. Their white-washed "fronts" were covered with trailing boughs of wistaria, and the ironwork of the balconies was almost hidden by straggling masses of clambering roses, which, at the time of which I am writing, filled the air with fragrance, in defiance, or challenge, so to speak, of the gilly-flowers, which, flourishing in pots on the window-sills, mournfully let their blossoms hang down over the copings as if in silent reproach for the laziness which prevented us tying them up to sticks.

By the time we reached the second balcony—there were three of them—the distant view was unobstructed—we were on a level with the slopes of the Monte Pincio, and could see far out over the roofs of Rome, ancient and modern. Higher still, from Vansittart—the American's—balcony, the view expanded further, and forming, as it were, a foreground for the disappearing Campagna, one could see the Castle of St. Angelo, and St. Peter's, and, looking to the left, the tops of the arches of Constantine and Septimus Severus in the Forum which was hidden by the Capitoline—further still the Colosseum and the Arch of Hadrian.

A fortnight later I was installed in the topmost *piano*. There were two rooms, one, whose doorway opened on to the balcony, was the studio, a queer place, filled—strewn, I might say—to confusion and repletion, with the heterogeneous mass of bric-à-brac which an artist gathers around him in an incredibly short time if he makes a practice of wandering about the less beaten tracks of the Eternal City on foot, or haunts the Campo de' Fiori on Fridays. Here lay a fragment of fifteenth-century tapestry, in which only the foresight of the craftsman in weaving it enabled one to differentiate Adam from Julius Caesar, and Mother Eve from Queen Elizabeth—their names being embroidered above them so that you should make no mistake. There, odd leaves of an illustrated Missal, grimy with age and showing prayers in Gothic script, and to me, unintelligible *canto fermo* music. In the fireplace a Venetian screen of marvellous ironwork: on the walls more fragments of tapestry, scraps of brocade and dilapidated ecclesiastical vestments of wonderful, worn embroidery. An ivory lute, and an inlaid mandolin; a hideous but imposing *Serpe* hung high on the wall, and in the gloom of a far corner the gaunt head and neck of a dismantled Arch-lute, or Theorbo, rose in the shadow. Chiselled plaques and brass *lucerne* all around one, evidences of Vansittart's omnivorous taste in artistic antiques, and finished and unfinished canvasses, covered—more or less—with landscape and architecture, sable-haired *contadine* and bronzed *contadini*, sketches of shepherds from the Campagna, and studies of still life. In the other room, whose window looked out similarly on the balcony and over it to the far north-west, I slept, and it was here that the grisly story I have to tell you is staged; this was the stage upon which the mysterious drama was enacted with which the Roman papers were filled in the spring of 1880.

Old Ippolito and I had become great friends. When I gave him the chance he would sit in my studio for hours at a time, entertaining me whilst I worked with his varied and eccentric gifts as a *raconteur*, and prospecting around in search of any portable and unconsidered trifles that might appear to his *contadino*-brigand mind as being worthy of more than a passing regard on his part. On such occasions Correr would often join us, for the young doctor knew his Campagna well, and when Ippolito became more than ordinarily unintelligible he would translate him into decent Italian for my benefit.

One day he had been telling us a more "spooky" kind of story than usual, when suddenly he caught sight of the Silver Hand dangling from my watch-chain. He seemed struck dumb for a moment, and then, rapidly crossing himself, he flung his arms into the air and exclaimed:

"Ah! *per amore d'Iddio*, Signore—why do you wear that?"

"*Perche mi piace*—because I like to," I replied.

He came, or rather crawled up close to me, and looking around as if in fear of being overheard, he whispered:

"Are you afraid that it will kill you if you let it get loose?"

Now, emotions of any kind were, in the case of Ippolito, invariably the manifestations of an extra fit of craziness—he was acknowledged to be slightly mad at times—or of conscientiously acquired intoxication. I examined him closely and decided that it was the former, and, as his emotion seemed to prelude some new story, I answered carelessly:

"No—why should I be?"

"Do not wear it, Signore, do not wear it. Suppose it should get loose from its chain!—it would surely kill you. Take it off and shut it away before it is too late. See!" he continued, fumbling feverishly beneath his sheepskin *contadino* jacket and coarse linen shirt, from whose recesses he dragged a dirty silk bag, apparently hung round his neck by a black silk cord. He opened it, and produced a small brown, dried-up hand. A woman's?—a child's?—it was impossible to tell—but it was human. "I wear this," he continued, "holding it to me always. If I were to let it get loose it would kill me—*kill* me, Signore. I fear it, but I dare not be without it, day and night, on the week-day and on the blessed Sunday. Always—always."

I looked at the gruesome object more closely. It was completely desiccated—mummied—and the third and fourth fingers were broken off short.

"Nonsense, *mio vecchio*," I replied, "you got this in some *antichita* shop—it is probably Egyptian. How could it hurt you, and why should it?"

"Oh, Signore! I broke off those two fingers and ever since then this hand has sought to revenge itself upon me. It will not rest until its *vendetta* is accomplished. I shall be killed. And you too—you will be killed by that," and he pointed with a shaking hand to my *Mano pantea*.

I unhooked it and showed it to him, pointing out the fact that no fingers were wanting, but that the final two were bent down upon the palm. But he refused to be satisfied or reassured. He sat as if mesmerized, looking at it with the mad light of terror in his eyes, periodically crossing himself and invoking his patron saints and the Virgin Mother on our joint behalf. At last, as I realised that my toy was tying Ippolito's tongue and spoiling our symposium, I removed the disturbing influence and concealed it. After that Ippolito's mind regained such equilibrium as it was capable of, and thenceforward I made it a practice to pocket the Mano pantea whenever he was in the studio—to his unconcealed relief.

There is no doubt about it that—as I have intimated—Ippolito was more than half crazy. Had it been otherwise I should not have humoured him, or permitted him his thousand and one eccentric familiarities in the way I did, and now—God rest his soul!—I look back upon them with something like regret.

Living, as I did, a thoroughly bohemian life, my knowledge of Rome soon became like that of Mr. Sam Weller with regard to London, "intimate and peculiar," and friends from England and elsewhere, who knew that I was there, used to come and see me, as a rule immediately upon their arrival in the Eternal City, with a view to being "put up" to the things to be seen, eaten, drunken and avoided, or, when I was amiably inclined, to be "shown round."

It was at the end of the month of May—and growing hot—that some New York acquaintances found me out, having arrived with the stern American purpose of "doing Rome" in three days.

I told them what to do during the hours immediately following, and made an appointment to meet them in the Colosseum in the evening, then shew them that monument and the Forum by moonlight. When the appointed time came it was drizzling with rain, but nevertheless I wrapped myself up in a cloak, cursing my genial altruism, and proceeded to the trysting place. I waited half an hour, and then, as, very wisely, they did not put in an appearance, I commenced, with a clear conscience and some relief of mind, to retrace my steps across the Forum and to proceed via the Capitol homewards.

In those days there were no palisades round the Forum; no turn-stiles where they mulcted one of *lire* before being allowed into it; no brigands in brass-bound caps insisting upon shewing you what is plainly visible; or covering matters of interest that were not, with little heaps of saw-dust, to be swept away, disclosing the mosaic, or whatever it might be, fore ready *lire*. The Forum was open to all, and it had a bad reputation after nightfall: one crossed it prepared for eventualities and sufficiently armed—if only with a large stick. All the approaching streets ended at the edge of the circumferent slope, and one just scrambled down and wandered about at large, Baedeker in hand.

As I passed along the south-west side of the Forum, where the excavations were just beginning which were to disclose the Palace and Gardens of the Caesars on the Palatine—then surmounted by a large modern house—and keeping as much as possible in the open and away from the *scavi*, a queer, gurgling, choking sound fell on my ears, coming, as it were, out of the Palatine Hill itself. At this moment the moon "brightening the skirts of a long cloud ran forth," and revealed a kind of cave or recess, from the excavations and recent rains. Always ready to practice what I could remember of an "Ambulance Course" if necessary, I stepped into the recess, and striking a match—there were no electric torches then—there, lying on the damp earth, I saw poor old Ippolito, writhing and groaning, evidently in some kind of a fit.

Fortunately I made a practice of always carrying a brandy-flask as a safeguard against malaria on any nocturnal rambles through miasmatic Rome, and, kneeling by his side, I loosened his shirt, brought him, in a measure, to himself, and, getting him on his legs, I bade him "good-night" and told him to go home—wherever that might be—remonstrating with him, as a last resource, for giving way to a weakness that, if it did nothing else, imperilled the safety of the mummified hand which lay, as I saw, in its bag on his shaggy chest. This argument appeared to bear weight, and clutching his "fetish" in his hand, he shambled away.

So, over the deserted Capitoline and down the steps of the Campidoglio and along the wet and shining flagstones of the Corso, I made my way back to the Via Margutta and settled myself down to write letters until a little after midnight, when I went to bed.

I had been asleep about a couple of hours when I woke suddenly into a condition of the most vivid attention, my heart beating in the manner which is described as "almost audible," my brain dazed by its sudden return to startled consciousness, and hideously possessed by the familiar sensation that Something was looking at me. The moonlight, streaming into my room through the great uncurtained north window, flooded everything with its soft light, making every object in the room distinctly visible. I looked round in something approaching panic—I was quite alone—no sound was audible.

But, as I lay, raised up on my left elbow to listen in the dead quiet of the night, I heard a footfall in the street below. Someone had passed through the narrow alley leading from the Via Babuino, and had reached the foot of the iron stairways—a shuffling, vacillating footstep, as of one intoxicated.

"Some belated tenant," thought I, but in spite of my attempts to reason calmly I felt an uncanny nervousness, an uncomfortable "presentiment" that the nocturnal visitant was *for me*. As the steps came from balcony to balcony, reaching at last Correr's, this idea became a horrible, meaningless, nameless fear; and as the steps came further up to my balcony I broke into a cold sweat, and was absolutely paralysed. I tried in vain to spring from my bed. I could not move. I just lay, supported by my elbow, staring out into the moonlight.

As I lay there, as I stared, a dark form intercepted the moonlight, throwing a gigantic shadow into my room. A man in the *contadino* costume had laid hold of the bars which protected my window, and *hung* rather than stood there, his white convulsed face turned up to the sky. The moonlight, striking upon the glass of the window, was reflected upon his face. It was the face of Ippolito, livid, ghastly, rigid, as he hung by his bony hands, clutching the window-bars.

And now came the horror which even in remembering and recording it turns me cold. As I lay, paralysed by terror, within a few feet of this ominous figure, a withered hand—*and nothing more!*—a hand severed at the wrist with no arm belonging to it, appeared from below, *crawling*, spider-like, as it were, up his chest. *And the hand had lost its two last fingers.* The remaining three crept up over Ippolito's sheepskin jacket on to his linen shirt, and at last, finding his throat, seized it with a sudden convulsive grip. I was still paralysed, still powerless to move—and it took a good deal to terrify me in those days. But then, of course, my nerves were all unstrung, and I suppose that accounts for it.

Slowly, and, as it were, by little jerks, this mutilated paw tightened its grip on the old *contadino's* throat, and at length the face became violet, the bony fingers which clutched the window-bars relaxed their agonized grasp, and with a dull thud the strangled *contadino* fell upon the balcony.

The spell was broken. I sprang from my bed and out through the studio into the warm night air, out upon the balcony barefooted and in my pyjamas, to find Ippolito lying there on his back, his face hideously distorted and turned up to the moonlight. Without waiting an instant I sprang over his body, down the iron stairway and, reaching Correr's balcony, I hammered on his window with my fists and woke him up.

"Correr—come up!" I cried. "A ghastly thing has happened on my balcony."

He came at once, in the same unconventional costume as my own, supplemented by a medical student's First-Aid case, and together we lifted the old man into my studio.

Correr knelt by his side and began making his examination, whilst I turned to prepare hot water, and other matters of which we might stand in need. I had hardly applied the match to my brazier when Correr, rising to his feet, said:

"Do not trouble, *caro mio*, he is dead. This is a most unfortunate occurrence—I mean, there will be an enquiry, for Ippolito has been strangled on your balcony."

I stood there motionless and inarticulate with horror. Correr, guessing, in part, the cause of my perturbation, hastened to add:

"Do not worry unnecessarily, for the murderer has left an unmistakable impress of his personality upon his victim, and, if he is above ground in Italy, the police will have no difficulty in laying their hands upon him."

"What do you mean?"

"Why," answered he tranquilly, "Ippolito has been murdered by a man who had only three fingers upon the hand with which he strangled him."

"Good God!" I exclaimed, flinging myself on my knees at the dead man's side; but it was not to look at the marks upon his throat. Correr had opened his shirt—I tore it still further down.

The dead hand was gone!

All Rome rang with the tragedy of the Via Margutta. I was even formally arrested, but on the evidence of the medical experts was immediately released.

The murderer of Ippolito was never discovered, and a few days after the enquiry had been "*classificato*"—abandoned—I left the city.

Was it a vendetta? I do not know, and I never shall; but it seems as if old Ippolito's superstition had communicated itself to me.

I am never without the *Mano pantea*.

THE THING THAT SMELT.

(Deposited by the Professor of Zoology.)

TO the Zoologists of twenty-five years ago the name of Augustine Black—Austin Black he called himself—was uncomfortably familiar. He was a patient and keen observer of animal life, and his photographs of beasts and birds made under all kinds of critical conditions were greatly and justly admired. But there was another and an extraordinary side to the man. He was a semi-professional spiritualist, and reaped a rich harvest, it was said, from that curiously constituted segment of humanity whose vanity leads them to seek for evidence of a personal life after death, who "sit" with obscurely disreputable "mediums" in lower middle-class parlours in doubtful neighbourhoods, and accept the suggestions of the managers of such séances that the raucous cacklings of uneducated persons through tubes of brown paper are "communications" from their dear ones who, in the cant phrase of the profession, "have passed over." They even welcome the futile familiarities of "John King," whose Arab face glowers over the "circle"—and incidentally may be bought for a few shillings from any reputable purveyor of conjurors' accessories.

Austin Black's success in this branch of industry resulted from the fact that he ran his séances in his studio at Tulse Hill on more highly sophisticated lines. He had an admirable chamber-organ and employed a professional string-quartet to play behind impermeable curtains, what time "materializations" took place, of High Church Dignitaries whose Latin would disgrace a fourth form schoolboy, and of eminent Scientists whose scientific observations were startling in their puerility and ignorance.

At the same time it must be confessed that there were occasions upon which the phenomena exhibited in return for the guineas of his "sitters" (for his were not the normal five-shilling entertainments) were, though futile, quite inexplicable to an ordinary observer—and a new patron had to be introduced by a convinced dupe, and the keen scrutiny of Austin Black, and his few well-chosen remarks and questions to the new-corner, made it clear that none but ordinary observers were privileged to get their money's worth. If Black was not satisfied as to gullibility, or suspected a plot to expose the *modus operandi,* the spirits "lay doggo" and would not perform. He would explain that there was "an inimical Influence" present, and when the séance was given up the habitués regarded and treated the stranger in such a manner as to convey to him that they considered that he had not only spoilt their evening, but had meanly swindled them out of the fees for that séance—and that stranger was never introduced again.

I frequently met Austin Black at the scientific meetings of the Zoological Society, and in spite of his over-florid courtesy he was to me as Dr. Fell of pious memory. It was therefore with mixed feelings that I yielded to my friend Mark Shelton's pressing invitation to assist at one of Black's séances in company with him and his friend George Carver.

"No doubt he does help out his séances with tricks," explained Mark, "but things do happen there that I cannot explain in any way whatever. I do wish you would come, once at least."

"What sort of things?" I asked.

"Oh! little things—generally of no importance, which have little or nothing to do with the 'show.' But at least twice there has been a sort of snarling in the room, and when this happens Black stops the séance—says the Controls are getting angry, or out of hand; and then, when the lights go up, he is a sight to see. Horrible! He seems to have worked himself up to such a pitch that he is white and sweating with terror. He bundles us all out as quickly as he can."

I confess that this interested me. Shelton was an extraordinarily prosaic and clear-minded man, an idle man-about-town, with ample means and a beautiful apartment in the Albany. He did not believe in "spiritualism" as such, but confessed that the manifestations interested and, on occasion, thrilled him. He never missed a good conjuring show at a Variety Theatre, and admitted that he loved to be taken in, and to see tricks and "phenomena" that passed his comprehension.

Well—I went. Black had small piercing dark eyes and a little waxed moustache, and I found him a very different person from the obsequious Black I had avoided becoming accustomed to. He put me through a short but highly efficient cross-examination as to my experience of séances, and my object in assisting at this one; but I managed to convey an impression of imbecility, and to place in his hands my guilty secret that, in spite of my position as Professor of Zoology in the University of Cosmopoli, I was a dabbler in metaphysics, and prepared to admit the existence of super-physical forces which I did not understand but viewed with respect.

The solidity of my introduction, however, it was, that secured my admission to the "Circle"; but Black was obviously on his guard, and nothing called for astonishment or remark in the performance—unless it was a "materialization" of Pope Innocent the Third, who welcomed and blessed us in a mixture of elementary school Latin and atrocious modern Italian. A Cardinal was in attendance upon him who wore a long beard. I commented, foolishly, upon this, and Black quickly explained that he was a Franciscan Cardinal, which entirely satisfied the "Circle" but put our ecclesiastical visitors to flight.

"What did you think of it?" asked Shelton as we walked down to the main road.

"I didn't think of it," I replied. "But I can't help thinking of Black—poor chap."

"Why 'poor chap'?"

"Don't you see how it has got hold of him? He is clearly a charlatan, *but he is afraid of himself.* Have you never seen a child who is afraid of the dark experimenting with mock-bravery? Going into a dark cupboard of which he controls the door handle—he is not *really* in the dark. Black's tricks are the dark cupboard of which he holds the door handle. I'll bet you he doesn't hold séances by himself."

"I wonder!" replied Shelton. He was curiously silent all the way back to town.

A few weeks later I noticed casually in the *Daily Telegraph* the announcement of the death of Augustine Black, F.Z.S., at his house on Tulse Hill.

※

It was about three weeks or a month after this that Mark Shelton rang me up on the telephone. The telephone was not then the universal blessing (or curse) that it is now, and installations were few and far between, a sort of scientific toy for the chosen few, and I could have counted on my fingers the friends who had them in their houses. Shelton's voice sounded grave and subdued, in answer to my cheery greeting.

"I want you to dine with me tonight," he said.

"Can't possibly—I am dining out."

"Oh! but you must," he answered; "I want you particularly. It's most important."

"But I tell you I can't. Who else is coming?

"No one—I want *you,* and you must come. Put your other party off. Tell them it's a matter of life and death."

"But, I say——"

"Don't say anything," he interrupted. "I'm telling you the truth. I've got something to tell you, which must be told here; and it *is* a matter of life and death. If you don't come, I shall not be alive in the morning."

By this time his voice was quivering, and I realized that something very serious was the matter. So I answered curtly:

"Oh! all right. I'll come, but don't talk bosh; and buck up. What have you been doing with yourself?"

"Nothing. I haven't left my rooms for three weeks."

"All right," I replied; "I'll come and dig you out."

I got to the Albany at half-past seven, and was let in by his man, the imperturbable Bates.

"How is Mr. Shelton?" I asked him casually, as I put down my hat and coat.

"I don't know, sir," replied Bates; "I can't make him out. Seems to be brooding all the time. Never goes out, and doesn't eat anything to speak of."

I went into Shelton's sitting-room, which was stiflingly hot. Though it was a fine May day he had a large fire, and all the curtains were closely drawn. Mark was sitting before the fire in his day clothes, doing nothing.

"Good heavens!" I said. "What an atmosphere! No wonder you are nervy. Got any windows open?"

"No—and don't open them. I've a reason. Is the air very beastly?"

"Not beastly," I said; "but intolerably hot."

"Not foul and stuffy?"

"No."

"Don't you notice a queer smell?"

"No—what sort of smell?"

"Well"—he hesitated a moment, and then said—"like the Small Cat House at the Zoo."

"Not in the least," I replied. "What ever is the matter with you?"

"I don't know. I want you to tell me."

I looked at him critically. Was he—the sane and athletic Shelton—going mad? The phrase "olfactory delusions" came into my mind.

"Tell me all you can about it," I said.

"Presently," he replied, "after dinner." So with that, for the moment, I had to be content. We went in to dinner. As usual it was exquisite. Shelton could, and did, afford a perfect cook, and on this occasion she had surpassed herself. Shelton tasted everything and sent his plate away practically untouched. At every dish he said:

"Pah! beastly. Don't you notice a filthy taste in this?"

"No—it's excellent. What kind of taste?"

"Well"—and again the hesitation—"like the Small Cat House at the Zoo."

It seemed to be a mania. I told him he should consult X., the great nose and ear specialist. He only shook his head wearily.

After dinner he consented to have a window open, and to let the fire die down. He told me he had "got up a frowst" so that I should get *It* in all its force—but he accepted, doubtfully, my assurance that the air was perfectly clean.

He brought me a volume of Japanese engravings he wanted me to see, and as he leaned over me, he said:

"Don't you mind my leaning over you?" and he looked searchingly into my eyes.

"Not in the least. Why on earth should I?"

"Good God, man! don't you notice that I *stink*?"

"Not at all. What do you imagine you stink of? The Small Cat House again?"

"Yes—that's it. It's ghastly. I can never get away from it."

"Tell me," I said quietly. "When and how did this begin?"

And he told me a most amazing and horrible story.

"You remember Austin Black—the Spiritualist Zoologist? Yes, we took you, Carver and I, to one of his séances. You may have seen that he is dead. Carver and I were there when he died; there was no inquest, for his domestic G.P. certified the ever-ready heart disease of long standing.

"There was a séance, only four of us and Black and his Medium. Black was awfully strung up that night—he told us the conditions could not be more favourable. It wasn't a 'show night,' and there was no music and no tricks—but queer, uncomfortable things happened. A spreading light over the table—and a leg of my chair suddenly snapped off. We turned up the lights—it seemed to have been bitten through. I wanted to stop, but Black, though he looked ghastly, wouldn't hear of it. He said: 'I want to see this thing through—I want to "down" it'—and we started the séance again. Almost immediately I heard that snarling I told you about, and Black, who was on my right, got up in the dark and left the table. We heard a sort of scuffling, and then a choking noise in the corner of the room. We switched on the light and saw Black lying on his back by the wall, his tongue out, and blue in the face, struggling violently with *nothing*. We rushed at him and tried to pick him up. There was Something that we could not see, between us and him, pinning him down. We could feel it though—it was soft and pulpy, with a surface not furry, but like a mouse or a mole—and huge! And it stank like the Small Cat House at the Zoo. We could not free him of it, and we saw him die; choked before our eyes, whilst we clawed at that soft pulpy Nothing. We could not move it. When he was quite still, the Thing got up of its own accord. Carver and I were crouched close together, and the Thing forced its way between us, and so away. How it stank! It seemed to leave a greasy smear of smell all over us. We called his wife—a queer woman—she did not seem badly shocked, or to care much. Carver said afterwards that she seemed to him to be intensely relieved at something. All she said was: 'I expected this—it has happened before'—she evidently did not realize that he was dead—'please go away at once. I will send for his doctor—he is close by.' We went. The other two—strangers—and the Medium had bolted directly we turned up the lights. As Carver and I walked down the hill he said: 'It's awful—it's awful. How it stank! and I can't get rid of the stink.' No more could I. Carver and I parted at Vauxhall. I never saw him again. I enquired a day or two later and heard he was ill; a week later I heard he had had a stroke, and was in a private mad-house. I had baths—Turkish baths—I changed my clothes half a dozen times a day—I always smelt of that Thing—I do still—I can't bear it. I shall go mad like Carver. Everything I touch smells of it, everything I try to eat tastes of it. I've tried to get over it and I can't. That's why at last I sent for you, and closed up everything and lit a fire, to give you the fullest chance.

"Now I know that I can't do anything. It's in me and part of me—I shall never be free of it. That Thing is here with me! It's prowling round all the time, but only I can smell it. God help me!"

To say that I was horrified is to use a miserably inadequate term; but before I left Mark Shelton that night I had arranged with him to go in three days to Norway, fishing. We settled everything—when to start, where to go, and what to take. I left him, still rather dazed, but much easier in my mind.

That night at about 1 a.m. Mark Shelton blew out his brains.

THE BLUE COCKROACH.

(Deposited by the Professor of Applied Chemistry.)

DORA was responsible—the Dora who punctuated her name after the manner of the plural of Mouse as affected by Civil Engineers. D.O.R.A. Primarily responsible that is to say; for this is a story of one of the very few instances of that *Ersatz,* which devastated Germany during the Late Unpleasantness, but of which our more favoured Nation suffered but few aggressions.

From another point of view perhaps the responsibility lies with Itha and Armorel. They are the imperious nieces of the Professor of Applied Chemistry in the University of Cosmopoli. Itha was twelve at the time, and Armorel eight, but, having no wife to rule him with a rod of iron, the Professor had, by the dire progression of a process for which he was unable to account, gradually become as a slave beneath their ferule, and in the most meagre days of Dora's sumptuary regulations Itha and Armorel had demanded Bananas.

Well, Bananas were at that moment as Snakes in Iceland— apparently, and many a rebuff did the Professor endure from "proud young Porters" at Stores whence of old he had been accustomed to supply his nieces' demands.

Of course the Professor ought to have been married. So ought Pamela, but the youth of the Professor had been spent, not only in consuming the midnight oil and other illuminants, but in abstract researches into their nature, composition, and adaptations. He was an acknowledged authority on Coal-tar Products, Inverted Sugars, and their derivatives commercial and prophylactic. Pamela had waited; and she had waited too long. By the time the Professor had become a Member of Council of the Chemical, and a Fellow of the Royal Societies he was a confirmed bachelor, and Pamela had reached the age which used to be labelled in their series of photographs of Celebrities (female) by the *Strand Magazine* as "Present Day." They corresponded at long, and met at longer, intervals, when Pamela, growing fragrant with the fire of forgotten suns, like a Winter Pear, came up from Wiltshire in a spirit of revolt against the limitations of the Provincial Milliner.

In the meagre days above referred to, Pamela was in town, and the Professor, rather grudging the expenditure of time involved, had bidden her to lunch with him at the Imperial. A visit to Kings-way, in search of chemical glass, had the result that his way back to the Imperial lay through Covent Garden Market, at that time a dreary vista of empty windows and derelict packing cases, where erstwhile the fruits of distant lands had been wont to overflow in polychromatic luxuriance. But in one of the windows lay a small bunch—a "hand" they call it—of homesick and weary Bananas, and the Professor remembered the grey reproachful eyes of Itha and Armorel, who could never believe that he could possibly fail them if he really made an effort.

He went in. An adolescent representative of an Ancient Race—who had escaped conscription—received him with scarcely inquisitive apathy.

"Are those the only Bananas you have?" asked the Professor.

"And all we are likely to," replied the Merchant elliptically.

"I am in trouble," said the Professor. "I have a little niece who is eagerly desirous of Bananas—and she is very delicate," he added as a mendacious afterthought, blushing as he thought of Itha in a dilapidated Scout uniform perched in the highest branches of a tree, or careering along the sands "bareback" on a repatriated Army remount. "Do you think you could help me?"

The Adolescent Oriental looked him over with a scrutiny which became, in the end, sympathetic. Perhaps he had a niece—or something—and understood.

"Bill!"

A subterranean noise as though the dirty floor were in labour, and from a square hole in the planks at their feet half a human being emerged. This was evidently part of Bill—a sinister figure, mid-way between Phil Squod and Quilp. A vision of strabismus and a fustian cap.

"Could you find this gentleman a hand or two of Bananas out of that case?—you know."

Disappearance of the upper half of Bill, a sound of rending timbers, and presently his reappearance with two "hands"— beautiful golden Bananas, and the nether portion of his person.

"Beauties," remarked Bill, "come yesterday."

"How much?" inquired the Professor.

When he recovered he saw himself, mentally, a poorer, but a better man. The Merchant was delivering a lecture upon the economics of War, and the iniquities of Dora. And as he turned the "hand" over, that its excellence might act as an anaesthetic to the operation of extraction, there ran out upon the counter the Blue Cockroach.

Unconsciously the Professor—like the Poet in the Den of the Scarabee—recoiled, but no Scarabee was there to murmur without emotion "*Blatta.*" But Bill was there.

"Ah!" said he, "I've seen *him* before—queer things we get sometimes in the cases—lizards—snakes—and whatnot. Once I found a Monkey. Jolly little beggar—he was all right, lived on the fruit. We used to take them to the live-beast place at the end. Shut up now."

"Don't you ever get bitten—or stung?"

"No—we're careful. This fellow's harmless."

It was a most lovely beast. In shape and size identical with the cockroaches which stray among one's brushes on board ship, and architecturally indistinguishable from the larger members of the Kitchen family, the Blue Cockroach was clad in a pure, pale azure, as if a cunning artificer in enamels had fashioned it, and had given to its surface a texture of the finest smooth velvet. Its long antennæ waved inquiringly back and forth, its tiny eyes sparkled black with crimson points, and then it began to run.

The Professor caught it in his hand as it toppled from the edge of the counter.

It bit him.

A curious sickening little puncture like the nip of an earwig. A sensation of heat, and then of cold that ran all over him, and Bill and the Merchant grew nebulous—and waved about. The Professor had never fainted in his life, but he said to himself: "This is how they must feel." In a moment it was over. He had shaken off the insect, and true to the scientific instinct he took out of his pocket one of the corked tubes he had just acquired, and drove the Blue Cockroach into it.

"One of the fellows at the Museum may like to have it," he said.

The Merchant shrugged his shoulders. A boot-heel, not a corked tube, seemed to him to be the appropriate climax to the Odyssey of the Blue Cockroach. For some inexplicable reason, however, he reduced the price he had quoted from the limits of Chimaera to within the bounds of Extravagance, and the Professor went upon his way, the Bananas in his hand and the Blue Cockroach in his pocket.

A tiny point on his right palm showed where the insect had attacked him, but beyond that the incident was closed.

As he proceeded along Coventry Street, the Professor became aware of a great calm—an undefined happiness. He had regarded his appointment with Pamela more in the light of a kindly duty than as an occasion for pleasurable anticipation, but now he suddenly found himself looking forward to their meeting with a keen sense of curiosity and satisfaction. It was too long since they met last. He felt sure she would have come to town sooner had he expressed a wish in that direction in his letters. What a handsome creature she had been when he was a student! What a shame it was that she had never married. The Professor found himself quietly wondering why—if—whether?

"I am fifty-four," said he to himself. But he smiled frowningly— or frowned smilingly.

❊

"She's a wonderful woman!" was his first thought as she rose to greet him from the big chair in the vestibule. Indeed Pamela seemed younger than he remembered her to have looked a year ago. She seemed to radiate that impression of delicate strength and ultra-feminine self-reliance which constitutes the undefinable charm of many middle-aged spinsters.

Their lunch was delightful. Pamela seemed as though she were starting fresh. The Professor seemed to have shed his professorial armour, and to have become once more a human being. He entertained her with descriptions of his war activities, no longer as of yore skimming over the subject, but letting her into the secret chamber of his ambitions, his aspirations, his work. When a man of the Professor's intellectual eminence exerts himself to charm, the charm is dangerously subtle. An element of flattery pervades the exercise, which is—or should be—irresistible. Pamela did not resist—she had never been called upon to resist, and was not going to begin now. Thirty years fell away, as time wasted in sleep. It is not a disagreeable admission—indeed there is a curious emotional joy predominant, when two people who should have been lovers find themselves saying in their hearts, "What fools we have been!"

By the time that the arrival of coffee and cigarettes had cleared away the last barriers which had erected themselves upon their voyage of re-discovery, the Professor was virtually identifying Pamela with his life-work.

"It is not all explosives and bacteriology," he confided to her. "I have been at work upon substitutes for sugar, and I have found one which will be a god-send to the people who properly detest saccharine. I have brought here a little tube of my finished article. It has all the sweetening properties of the finest cane sugar. Will you try it?"

Of course she would. If it had been a dangerous poison she would have gladly offered herself as a martyr to Science—his Science.

"You need not be afraid of it. It is not only a wonderful sweetener—it is also a powerful prophylactic. It acts like an atoxyl that would kill with extraordinary rapidity any pathogenic organisms in the system. I look forward to trying it as a remedy for Sleeping Sickness, Yellow Fever—any of the tropical diseases carried by insects which inject death-dealing bacteria—trypanosomes—into our blood by their bites. My dear"—she quivered—"I believe I hold here one of the greatest discoveries that has ever been made in prophylactic medicine!"

They sweetened their coffee—each with a tiny pellucid crystal.

"It is just like real sugar," she said dreamily, "not harsh like saccharine. My dear"—his eyes grew narrower—"I do believe you are right. I am so proud of you." She ended with a little contented sigh which was half a laugh, and looked round the restaurant, which was by this time gradually becoming empty, and wondered whether anyone else there looked out upon their worlds with so supreme a sensation of satisfaction and fulfilment as she. What fools they had been!

The Professor also finished his coffee and leaned back in his chair, looking round the room with a sudden sensation of discomfort. He had just thought again of the Blue Cockroach—the reason he had thought of it was that he had suddenly experienced, as it were, a return of the sensation which came over him at the moment it bit him. It was, however, only momentary, though, casually glancing at his hand, it seemed as if the little puncture were more visible than it had been.

And then a remarkable thing happened. He turned again to Pamela and saw her with new—or rather with old—eyes. He found her eyes fastened upon him with a mingled expression of apprehension and curiosity—and as he returned her gaze—she blushed vividly. He felt strangely uncomfortable, and without any conscious volition on his part he found himself going rapidly over in his mind their conversation of the previous hour. It was surely a waste of time to orate for an hour to this dull but worthy person, upon a subject which could have no interest for her and of which she could not possibly understand a single word. He

400

was dissatisfied with himself, and naturally blamed her vaguely for his dissatisfaction and discomfort.

"Well!" he said, "it has been very pleasant seeing you again, Pamela. We must—er—not let it be so long again—before—" His stereotyped phrases lost themselves in embarrassed silence.

He asked for the bill. It seemed to him rather excessive. However, just for once . . .

Pamela had not ceased looking at him. She was puzzled; it seemed to her as if a newly opened door had been quietly but relentlessly shut in her face. The Professor certainly had aged a good deal since she saw him last; she had not noticed it before. An uncomfortable sensation crept over her that she had been expansive beyond warrantable limits with this grave grey man, and she felt a little hot under an impression that she had allowed the conversation to stray beyond what was quite seemly and decorous—at her age. She was rather relieved that he seemed in a hurry to get away. She had all an intelligent woman's horror of an anti-climax.

An hour later she was in the train. At that moment the Professor laid down his pen in his study and looked before him out of the window. The same thought struck both of them simultaneously.

"What fools we were!"

"Now whether there be truth or no in that which the native Priests do aver, I know not, nor may I make more curious enquiry, but if it be indeed the fact that the sting of divers of their Flyes do engender Passions as of Love, Hate, and the like, then the matter is curious and worthy of enquiry, but such as I did make enquiry of did postpone me with shrewd cunning and avoiding answer, nor would they be come at to speak further upon it at that or any other time."[1]

1 *The True Accompt of the Travels into Distant Lands of the learned Doctor Franzelius Bott, wherein many curious Customs and Wisdom of the Inhabitants are truly set down.* (Leyden: 1614, p. 117.)

THE MAN WHO KILLED THE JEW.

(*Deposited by Myself.*)

"There be some of them that stand here that in no wise
taste of death till they see the son of Man
coming in his Kingdom."
—Matthew XVI. 28.

"And as he went forth Khartophilus struck him and said:
'Go quicker, Man,' and Jesus replied: 'I, indeed go
quickly but thou shalt tarry till I come again.'"
—Roger of Wendover, 1216-36.

SIR GEORGE AMBOYNE, Regius Professor of Medicine in
the University of Cosmopoli, came into the Senior Common
Room, a portentous frown on his normally placid brow, nodded
curtly to the fellows present, sat himself down in a remote arm-
chair, and buried himself without speaking in the *British Medical
Journal.*

"Something has worried our Regius Professor," observed
Magley, the Professor of Psychology to me. "What has he been
up to, I wonder?"

"You can ask him," I replied. "I know that *noli me tangere* air
of his. I'll leave the touching to somebody else."

Magley, who afterwards came to such horrible grief, was no
respecter of persons, but even he sat tight and waited for the
atmosphere to clear.

402

Several fellows happened in, but those who greeted the Professor cheerily got but a grunt in answer to their greeting.

Half an hour passed by, and then Sir George rose, flung the *B.M.J.* on to the table and observed: "Damn the titular courtesies of our profession."

Magley, without taking up the direct challenge, turned to Peterson, the Professor of Geology, and said: "You will observe, my dear Watson, that our Regius Professor of Medicine has been out in the rain without an overcoat—also he has not wiped his boots. What is your deduction from this?"

"I should say, my dear Holmes," replied Peterson, "that he has been called into consultation by one of the General Practitioners of this town, and has expressed his opinion that 'Our friend has done all that could be done in the circumstances, and we must hope for the best. Should any change take place, you will let me know at once'—that is the classic formula, I believe."

"Very clever are you not?" snapped the Regius Professor. "But let me tell you, it's not a thing to joke about. Talk about something you understand, if such thing there be."

"This," continued Peterson, still addressing Magley, "is one of those courtesies of the medical profession to which he alluded so feelingly just now."

"As a matter of fact," pursued the Professor, "you have made one of those brilliant deductions which show that your proper place is Scotland Yard and not a University Chair."

"Sir, you flatter me. I have always felt that I was fit for a higher position than that of explaining uncomfortable strata to young men who do not care twopence about them. May we ask, O Pandit, what has forced this Eternal Verity upon you?"

"The usual thing," replied Sir George, wearily, "an S.O.S. message, life or death, you know, just as I was starting out for my eleven o'clock lecture. Just an hour too late, the patient bleeding to death."

A shocked silence ensued, and then someone said: "I suppose you get a good deal of that sort of thing?"

"We all do. These chaps, who are usually the sons of equally incompetent fathers, go to London, or to an University, with a view to qualifying for the hereditary practice, doing as little work as they can, idling through the course. Sit for their M.B., get spun, and then go somewhere up north, sit for God knows what kind of examination—they all 'pass' and are entitled 'M.R.C.S. Steeple Bumstead.' They leave out 'Steeple Bumstead' on their plates, however, and 'by courtesy of the profession' are allowed to call themselves 'Dr. So-and-So'; and their victims, when they succeed to, or barge into the paternal practice in provincial towns, have no means of distinguishing between them and Bachelors of Medicine of recognized Schools! Well, I suppose the death-rate must be kept up. But it's hellish when one is 'called in' at the last moment and dare not say, 'This incompetent fool evidently does not know the difference between cancer and a broken leg, but he does not dare admit it; he has chanced it, but if he had called in someone who knows his job earlier the chances would have been in the patient's favour.' Surgeons have a great advantage over physicians—*their* mistakes are buried."

"A bad case, evidently," observed Magley.

"Rotten—imperfect sterilization, if any at all. Sepsis. Prognosis—Death."

"Is there no remedy?"

"Of course not—the courtesy of the profession forbids it. Did you never hear of the Man who killed the Jew?"

"? ? ?"

"The thriving seaside village of Mudbury-on-Slush boasted two 'Medical Men.' One *was* an M.B.—Guy's and Oxford. He had come and put up his plate when the village was only a collection of fishermen's huts and a couple of boarding houses and a shop—the kind of shop that in Germany is called Gemischtwarenhandlung—a General store. He hoped that with the erection of bungalows and, later, the building of better residential houses, he would establish a practice. It didn't happen, and after a while he devoted himself mainly to collecting postage stamps and the local Lepidoptera.

"Meanwhile, a shocking thing happened. This was the arrival of Jones, M.R.C.S. Steeple Bumstead—also L.S.A. He was a large and sporting Welshman, with loud clothes and a still

404

louder manner. This was a blessing very much in disguise for the simple villagers, for when the Guy's man sent in a bill, they could turn indignantly to Jones, whose staple prescription was Epsom Salts, dispensed by himself, until he found that by paying a reasonable commission to the local chemist—who was also a Beauty Specialist—he could collar most of the practice among the Summer Visitors.

"Jones' 'bag' was phenomenal. Enjoying a kind of terrifying popularity among the villagers and fishermen, his death certificates were as leaves in Vallombrosa. 'Indigestion' was his magic diagnosis. Cancer, phthisis, pneumonia, pernicious anaemia were all diagnosed as Indigestion—Dyspepsia *pour ces dames*—and invalids, sufficiently ill to be shepherded into his Surgery by the Chemist (who did all the prescribing for simple ailments) died like flies, full of Epsom Salts. A tolerable billiard player and a Champion at Bowls, not to mention a truly Welsh capacity for drinking level with any or all of the patrons of the local Pub., he was always in the eye of the public, and there were few accidents at which he was not well to the fore; his manner of giving evidence at Inquests stifled enquiry and appealed to the most inexperienced reporter. The coroner of the nearest town was his solicitor. Jones came to be regarded as an Act of God.

"Well, so much for Jones, by way of introduction to my story. You may want to know how I became acquainted with the facts I am about to relate. I shall not satisfy your curiosity—you may take it that they were revealed to me in a dream.

"Most—probably all of you—have heard of Khartophilus, the Wandering Jew. To the few he is known from Roger of Wendover's *Chronicle of St. Albans*; to the many he is best known by Mr. Matheson Lang's remarkable performance of the character in the world-famous film. You have perhaps read various accounts of how this wretched man became condemned, as the result of an unseasonable levity or brutality on an historic occasion, to be immortal—and how, down the centuries, he wandered from place to place, never growing any older, impervious to accident or mortal disease, an Accursed Thing that nothing could kill.

"In the course of his wanderings, on one occasion—even God cannot provide against all contingencies, as you shall see—he turned up as an ordinary summer visitor at Mudbury-on-Slush. There, as the result of an indiscreet paddling, he developed a nasty cold in the head. Calling upon the local chemist for a 'bottle of stuff,' that worthy, eyeing him with professional gravity and scenting a 'case,' told him he must immediately see a doctor—and that Jones was his man. Khartophilus, the only amusement of whose eternally wandering existence was to study the progress of medical science in his own person—he knew that he was quite safe, however many doctors he consulted—thanked the astute Pharmaceutist and called upon Jones.

"The scene of the story now shifts—you will be properly astonished to hear this—to Heaven. The Heavenly Choir was enjoying a rest during the usual Saturday choir-practice. Gabriel, who was conducting, was rather irritated; the strings (and especially the Harps) were always a little 'difficult,' for they considered that he devoted too much attention to the brass (he had been First Trumpet before he became Conductor). He had joined Michael and Raphael, who had been sitting in front, listening to the rehearsal, and he was complaining of the usual preponderance of Harps, when they became aware of a concourse and commotion at the Golden Gate. St. Peter was engaged in what seemed to be a robust argument with a gentleman of Semitic appearance who was insisting upon admission.

"'Look—look!' cried Raphael, 'do you see who is trying to get in?'

"The other two concentrated their gaze upon the group at the Gate, and finally Gabriel said: 'Why! it is Khartophilus—the Wandering Jew!'

"'Impossible!' replied Michael; 'he was expressly forbidden to die or to try to come here till Gabriel plays his final solo.'

"Raphael shrugged his shoulders. 'What chance have *we*,' said he, 'against Jones?'"

And with that the Regius Professor of Medicine stalked out of the Common Room.

THE DEMON.

(Deposited by Myself.)

DR-R-R-R-R! Dr-r-r-r-r! and so on.

"Bless the Telephone!" said the Regius Professor of Medicine.

I make use of a conventional euphuism—it was not a blessing that the Regius Professor invoked in favour of the National Telephone Company, the mention of which dates the events which I am about to relate—it was before a Paternal Government had assumed that Control, which enabled it to provide the last straw, which gave the hump to that patient animal, the British Public.

Dr-r-r-r-r! Dr-r-r-r-r!

"Yes—Yes—Hullo!—Hullo!" Sir George Amboyne was in the middle of writing an important paragraph in an important paper, and he felt as if someone had suddenly thrust a marling-spike between the spokes of the fly-wheel of his mind, and had brought the machinery of thought to a crashing and dislocating stop. It was a law, both written and unwritten, that he was not to be "rung up" by his friends during the working hours of the morning. He was prepared to be nasty.

"Is that you, Reggie?"

A guttural laugh rattled the microphone.

"Who do you want?" asked the Professor, with that lapse from grammar which is universal in the circumstances.

A contralto voice replied, "I want Sir George Amboyne, Bart., F.R.S., etcetera. Don't you know me, Reggie? It's me, Cynthia." Again the grammar of telephonic speech.

A wave of disgust and disquiet surged over the Professor. "Reggie!" There was only one person in the world—the most unexpected person in the world—who had, on the last occasion on which he had seen her, suggested that this would be a humorous and affectionate name for him, an echo—or contraction—of his title "Regius Professor of Medicine." It had made him shudder with disgust, the more so as the authoress of this solecism had been for long years his most dainty, refined and delicate friend— Cynthia Carlyon. He had hoped that the manner in which he had received the suggestion had made the occasion unique—a "joke" never to be repeated.

"I am George Amboyne," he replied, with as much severity as one can assume over the telephone wire.

"That's all right, Reggie dear. I know you don't like it but you've got to put up with it."

"I *don't* like it, Cynthia. What do you want? I am very much occupied."

"I know you are—that's why I thought it would be fun to ring you up." Again the guttural laugh. It seemed a pity that the laugher could not see his face as he heard it.

"Will you *please* tell me what you want?"

"I'm feeling dissipated and devilish—I want you to come and play with me. You might take me out to lunch."

"I am sorry, but it is quite impossible."

"Oh! damn!"

"Please—*please, Cynthia—don't.* It's horrible. If you want to see me particularly I will come to you after four."

"No good to-day, old chap, I've got a bran-new Johnnie coming to tea, and I want him all to myself."

He went back to his desk and sat down, but he could not go on with his work. He sat staring out of the window. It was horrible. That this vulgar, slangy creature could possibly be Cynthia, absolutely stunned his senses. The most dainty—the most delicate—the flowerlike—. He gave it up, and leaning his forehead upon his hands, he groaned aloud.

※

Some years—less than a decade before the date of this unpleasant incident—Cynthia Canyon occupied the position of Queen of a Cult. She stood out in the literary, the artistic, and the scientific society of Cosmopoli, as it were, an object of reverent and affectionate worship. She was beautiful in the manner of a Titian Madonna, a reddish-gold woman of infinite grace and perfect taste. A poetess, an essayist, a musician, a painter, she met the men of literature, science and art on their own ground. As a bachelor-girl (to use a phrase which was invented, I think, long afterwards) of independent means, she had a real "Salon," where one met everybody worth meeting from an intellectual point of view. She was popularly supposed to have refused to marry every man who had ever come under the spell of her curious crooked smile—it was the probationary stage through which he who would join her charmed and charming circle had to pass. This formality satisfactorily accomplished, and the period of convalescence—or quarantine—safely negotiated, you settled down into your place in her studio. No one ever resumed the Quest of Cynthia—he merely adopted the Cult.

And then, to the horror of all of us, she came back from Florence one fatal spring day, married to Max Carlyon.

Carlyon was a blackguard; he was an adventurer of the subtle type, not the flamboyant—he had tried that and it had proved a miss. He also drank. And—as Herodotus would put it—this is all that we shall say about Max Carlyon; excepting that he curdled the coterie, and Cynthia's salon was reduced to the faithful few who put up with him when he was present, rejoiced when he was absent, and melted away when he came home drunk.

Among these Sir George Amboyne (who was appointed to the Regius Professorship of Medicine in the University of Cosmopoli about two years later) was one of the most faithful. In the events which followed he was also the last. But this is to anticipate.

About two years after her disastrous marriage Cynthia faded; indeed she obviously became very ill. Her condition became so alarming that Amboyne insisted that he should merge the friend in the surgeon, and he, with a no less eminent colleague, after a careful and heart-breaking examination, pronounced upon Cynthia Carlyon sentence of death—humanly speaking. She underwent a terrible operation, and took up her abode in a charming nursing home, a little way outside the town. And so we waited for the end.

But whether by reason of some hidden force of vitality, or of her determination not to give up, the end did not come. A year passed, and "The Death-bed of Cynthia" became an institution—indeed it may be said to have become a social function. Her friends rallied round her, and each of them had his or her appointed hour, when they met round the bed, where she lay like a bright and cheerful Madonna, told her the news, brought her their books and pictures, played to her (she had a "baby grand" in her room), and by degrees, a new and highly selective Salon gathered again by her bed-side.

During the second year of this strange existence, the disease woke up again. Since that time the scourge of cancer has surrendered to the besieging forces of Science, and now we know what to do to eradicate it, but in those days, the cure, persistently sought, had eluded the vigilance of its untiring pursuers. I walked away from her bed-side one day with George Amboyne, through the as yet undesecrated lanes of Bromley, and I asked him:

"Is this the end?

"Humanly speaking," he replied, "yes. Unless a miracle were to happen. And miracles do not happen in the clinics of cancer."

"How long will she live?"

"Perhaps a month—possibly longer—but I hope not."

Two days after this I was astonished to receive a note from the Matron of the nursing home, couched in the following terms:

Sir,—I am instructed by Mrs. Carlyon's medical attendant to request you to discontinue your visits until further notice. He hopes that in a week or two you will be able to resume them.

Mrs. Carlyon's medical attendant—George Amboyne!—what the——!

I jumped into a hansom cab and was at Amboyne's house in less than a quarter of an hour. I found him at breakfast. I had not breakfasted.

"What is the meaning of this?" I said, putting the Matron's letter before him.

"What it says," he replied.

"But you——?"

"I am no longer 'Mrs. Carlyon's medical attendant.'"

"For heaven's sake, explain!" said I.

"Canyon called upon me yesterday morning——"

"Was he sober?"

"Partially. He asked me what hope I had of his wife's life. I told him none. He said: 'Then you will not be surprised if I call in another opinion.' I said, 'Not at all—I shall be happy to meet any other medical man that you may call in.' He smiled his beastly unctuous smile and said, 'I don't think you will be troubled.' And so he left me."

"Well—what next?"

Amboyne handed me a letter which had been lying open by his plate. It read:

DEAR DR. AMBOYNE:—Mr. Carlyon's visit to you will have prepared you to hear that at his request I have taken over the treatment of his wife. I shall be happy to meet you on the case, if you can time your visit to coincide with mine.

Yours faithfully,
ERASMUS QUAYLE.

"? ? ?"

"Erasmus Quayle is a quack. He advertises in provincial and clerical papers 'Cancer cured by an infallible treatment. Payment by results. No cure, no charge.' "

"Good God! and are you going to meet him?"

"On a first impulse, no—of course not. And yet, Cynthia! I don't know what to do—I don't know what to say."

"He'll kill her."

"No—that is predestined—but this man—(he is an Honorary M.D. of some Middle West American Institution which sells Degrees)—keeps his patients alive for a bit by some preparation of his own—sometimes for months. He announces a cure, gets paid—enormously—and then clears out. The patient then dies."

"What's to be done?"

"I don't know. Excuse me; there's the telephone."

In a few minutes he returned, very pale and obviously very much distressed.

"Well—that settles it," he said quietly. "Carlyon on the telephone. He says that Dr. (Doctor!) Quayle thinks it unnecessary to trouble me, and that his wife would rather I did not call until I hear from her."

"There's only one gleam of light in the murk," I said. "I hear that the Matron exercises her authority, and does not let Carlyon see his wife when he is too drunk."

"Yes—that's something," replied Amboyne.

Two years passed by. Three weeks after the conversation I have recorded with George (now Sir George) Amboyne, I, in common with others of her "intimates," received a letter from Cynthia asking me to come and see her. I went, of course, at once. Frankly, I was amazed.

"Come in, dear man," she called out, as I opened the door. "Come in! what do you think of me? I am cured!"

I cannot describe what I felt. The room seemed to spin round me. All I could say was, "Thank God, dear Cynthia."

"And Dr. Quayle," replied she, rather wistfully, "I know I must not say too much about him to you people. Fortunately he refuses to meet any of my friends. But look at the result!"

I could only murmur commonplaces. The foundations of my belief in medical science were being shaken. But there it was. Cynthia seemed to be quite her old self. Amboyne came in whilst I was there. It was not a very comfortable meeting—indeed we were both relieved when Cynthia told us that for a few weeks she must cut her interviews shorter than she would like; and we left her.

We went into the Matron's sanctum, and after the ordinary greetings, Amboyne said to her: "This is very remarkable, Matron. What does it all mean?"

"I don't know," she replied, with an air of visible distress. "It passes everyone's comprehension. This Mr. Quayle—"

"Yes?" said Amboyne, encouragingly; "can you tell me?"

"No," she replied, "it's all mysterious. He cooks things in a little pot behind a screen—he brings the materials, and takes them away again."

"We merely give his medicines as he directs. It is most extraordinary—and unsatisfactory."

And with that we left her. Amboyne was silent all the way back to town. Like the parrot of folk-lore.

And then the two years went by. Cynthia received her friends as before, Carlyon kept in the background, but I gathered indirectly from the Matron that at intervals he made scenes about money. Cynthia spoke of moving to a less expensive room. I remembered grimly the legend in gold on some of the fancy mugs at Schwalbach *"Mann ärgere deine Frau nicht; das Kur kostet viel Geld."*

At the end of the two years, I went one day to the home for my bi-weekly visit, and met Amboyne in the hall.

"You can't go in," he said. "Cynthia is dying."

"Dying?"

"Yes—Quayle has given up the case—made all he can, I suppose. Says she grew over-confident and disobeyed orders. I was sent for this morning. She is quite unconscious—she will not regain consciousness. It is the end."

We came away. Outside, Carlyon, speechlessly drunk, was being led firmly away by a policeman.

✳

But Cynthia did not die. I called next morning and the Matron told me that after being dead as they all supposed for two hours, her eyelids suddenly flickered and she regained consciousness. In the morning she seemed much stronger and asked for food.

"You had better not see her," said the good woman; "she is very fretful, and uneasy. So unlike herself—quite disagreeable. I am very worried over it all. I rang up Mr. Quayle and he refused to come—so this morning I sent for Sir George Amboyne. He seemed very shocked."

For several weeks there was no fresh development in this astonishing case. I had a note from Cynthia merely saying, "Don't come till I let you know. I'm growing stronger every day."

I saw Amboyne. He could give me no news, beyond that she seemed to gain strength every day, according to the report of the nurses—he had not seen her since the first day. He had received the same note as I had. He hesitated a moment and then said:

"I am afraid that you will experience—and so shall I—a shock, when we see her again. From what the Matron tells me she is woefully changed—for the worse. They say she is 'a trying patient' and they will be glad to get rid of her."

"Get *rid* of her?"

"Yes—she talks of leaving the home in about a fortnight."

"Leaving the home?"

He shrugged his shoulders. "Yes—that's it. All we can do is to wait."

✳

We waited three weeks, and then, on the morning of an unforgettable day, I received a letter from Cynthia, dated from a second-rate hotel in the S.W. district, asking me to call upon her! She told me not to call till the afternoon "as I am going on a jamboree

414

to a music hall tonight, and don't get up very early anyhow. I've been here ten days, but didn't tell any of you good, serious old fogies. I wanted to have a fling around before I encounter your solemn mugs, and high-flown ideas, and have to become serious and respectable again, after all these wasted years."

I took the note round to Harley Street, and thence to the University where Amboyne was lecturing, and I waited for him. I showed him the note, and for all reply he took another from his pocket and handed it to me. It said:

> Here I am, you see, in spite of your determina-tion to kill me. What price "Infallibility" for the Mortuary Stakes? But come along and see your little Cynthia and make up for a lot of lost time. You have become no end of a swell since I "took ill" as the servants say. "Regius Professor"—I bow! But what a mouthful! I think I shall call you "Reggie" in future.

I handed it back and looked at him, speechless.

"Isn't it horrible?" he said in a low tone. "What do you make of it?"

"Let us go and see," I replied.

We went that afternoon, and were shown into a tawdry sitting room, which smelt of dust and patchouli. Cynthia was lolling on a green "rep" sofa—smoking a cigarette. Carlyon was sitting by her side, and got up sheepishly as we entered.

"Well, so long, old girl," he said huskily; "I'll leave you with your intellectual friends." He gave a short laugh as he turned to us and said, "You'll find the old girl a bit different to what she was, and a jolly good thing too. She's woken up—fine!"

We sat down and for a moment we simply could not utter a sound. *Was* this Cynthia. Yes—it was the same willowy figure, the brown eyes, the fine long hands and feet—but her hair! In place of her red-gold aureole was a short thick crop of black curly stubble. The expression in her eyes was that of an animal gathering itself together to spring. She was the first to break the silence.

"Good Lord, how glum you both look. You look as if you had never seen me before. Have a cigarette, or a drink—or both—and let's be jolly."

"Are you sure," said Amboyne, "that you are not overtaxing your strength? I should hardly——"

"Oh! for heavens' sake, don't preach at me, Reggie——"

"I beg your pardon!"

"Yes—Reggie—don't you think it's rather nice for a Regius Professor? Much nicer than George—a dull, solemn name. But don't be dull and solemn with me, I've kicked free and I'm going to have a good time. Be jolly—or stop away. If you are going to look at me like that, I prefer Max—he's a sportsman."

The interview was a short one. To this day I don't know how we got through it. She was dreadful—when we got up to go she did not try to detain us, nor did she ask when we would come again. We got into the street somehow.

I found that I could hardly speak above a whisper. But I said: "What is it?"

"I don't know—I don't know—but I *think* it is a Demon."

"Amboyne!—pull yourself together."

"Do it yourself!—you are shaking all over—it's difficult. But"—and he stopped dead and looked straight at me—"didn't you see IT lurking behind the eyes that used to be Cynthia's, watching us to see whether we recognised It?"

"Yes—I did." (But I was glad that the Regius Professor of Medicine had mentioned it first.)

And this brings us to the morning with which I opened this record, when Cynthia Carlyon rang up the Regius Professor—for fun.

He got through the routine of the day—consultations, a lecture at the University, a committee at the Royal Society, and arrived home exhausted with work which had been made painful and difficult by a suppressed emotion of horror. He was just sitting down to the simulacrum of dinner when the telephone rang again. A woman's voice, in a flutter of excitement.

"Is that Dr. Reginald Burgoyne?"

"Amboyne is my name, Sir George Amboyne."

"Beg pardon, I didn't know whether to say George or Reginald. You are the doctor?"

"Yes."

"Please come at once to the Hotel ———. A lady, Mrs. Carlyon is calling out for you something awful."

"What has happened?"

"I don't know, sir, I'm the manageress. The lady had a gent to tea, and when he had gone I heard a screech and went in to her. She was in a fit seemingly. Screaming something awful. I got her to bed and called in the doctor. She keeps calling for you, he says. I thought he said the name of Burgoyne. She called out 'Reggie' and 'George.' Will you come, sir? Please do, the doctor says so."

"At once," replied Amboyne.

In the tawdry sitting room he met a harassed looking young practitioner, obviously paralysed at finding himself face to face with the world-renowned Regius Professor.

"Epilepsy, I suppose, sir—with submission—but I don't know. I never saw anything like it before. And her language, it is frightful. Like sometimes—in puerpural fever. Will you see her?"

They went in. Cynthia—the old placid Cynthia, save for the short black hair, was lying in bed, as the woman of the house had left her. The old tender half-humorous eyes were open, and as Amboyne leaned over her she said softly: "It was good of you to come, George. Don't let them take me away again."

"Of course not, dear. I'll look after you."

"Can you, do you think? I have been in Hell."

But as she spoke the Demon flashed into her eyes, and she sprang to a sitting position with a wild cry—like an animal in pain.

The Regius Professor put his arm round her, and she clawed at his face. But only for a moment. Then she sank in his arm, and he laid her gently back upon the bed.

That was all.

THE BOOK.

(Deposited by the Late University Librarian.)

I happened to be in our Registrar's room one day, and quite unconsciously I produced "an effect." I had some letters in my hand, and when I had finished with Blayre, I referred casually to one of them. I said:

"Do you know anything of a man called Max Carlyon?"

He sprang to his feet and almost shouted:

"Do I?—what do you know about him?—ask Amboyne! Where is he?"

To this singularly confused address I had no direct answer to make. What I said was:

"I don't know anything about him? Preserve your capillary decoration against the time when age shall commit indiscretions regarding your bumps. There is a letter from him—he appears to have dropped very unexpectedly into a Baronetcy and some books. Whatever may be his views about the Baronetcy, it is clear he does not care a hang about the books. He wants to sell them, so as to repair his house, which would appear to be mouldy. That's all. Now *you* tell me about him."

The Registrar had re-seated himself, and looked rather ashamed of his demonstration. He said rather wearily:

"Oh! nothing in particular—but what a small place the world is! Amboyne and I came across Max Carlyon years ago, under very painful and unpleasant circumstances. Fancy *him* a Baronet! I thought he must have died of alcoholic poisoning by now. I hope he hasn't got any children."

"Sir," said I, "you interest and excite me. Shall I ask him to call? You might gather up the threads of what appears to have been a very pleasant acquaintance."

"Don't play the fool—it isn't a matter to laugh about. What are you going to do about it?"

"Well—I shall put the matter before the Council, and then—I hope—I shall go and see the books. He says there are hundreds of volumes of early Medicine and Science—especially Occult Science. It sounds like a very interesting lot."

"Whatever you do, don't have him here, I couldn't stand the sight of him," thus the Registrar, uneasily.

To pass over the preliminary and intermediate stages, I went in due course to Clough-Iveagh in the North of Ireland, where I met the new Baronet. I have never learned what were his relations with our Registrar and the Regius Professor of Medicine, but I agreed with every word they had not said. He was an appalling Beast. Fortunately for me, after the day of my arrival I saw no more of him. The house was empty save for the books, and was in wrack and ruin. Sir Max Carlyon left next morning for an unknown destination, and I put up at the village Inn, which was unpretentious and comfortable. Still more fortunately for me I found that the pastor of the parish was an old college friend, Fergus MacDermott, of whom I had lost sight for years. I spent my evenings with him, and he told me—in sections—the amazing story which I am going to write down.

The Library, which was kept partially clean by an old Irishman and his wife who lived in the Lodge, was a Bookman's Paradise. The books were wonderful. I found the *editiones principes* of all the rarest works of 16th and 17th Century Science and Medicine, but what made my inspection lengthy and tedious was the remarkable fact that, though they were all in contemporary bindings, they were all lettered on the backs as Theological Works, Lives of the Saints, Commentaries, Biblical Exegesis and the like, and every volume had to be taken down and examined separately. It puzzled me extremely until I heard the "story" from MacDermott.

I asked him if he knew anything about the Beast.

"Divil a word," he replied, "and don't want to, but his great-uncle married my great-aunt. You know"—course I didn't—"my father and grand-father were parsons here before me—that's how it is I'm here."

Mac did not appear to be much impressed by the advantages of his hereditary cure of souls—but he had a friendly parish, an efficient stable, and an excellent cellar.

"You know," said he—of course I didn't—"this man is an unexpected arrival from Heaven knows where. He wasn't on speaking terms with any of the family—that's why he has only got the place, strictly entailed. The Carlyon title seems never to pass direct from father to son; it spurts about like a firework cracker, you never know whom it will hit next. By the way, you ought to spend the night in that library."

"Not for the wealth of the Indies!"

"Don't interrupt—in that library on the 13th of August. You'd see the Family Ghost, and, with luck, might have your brains bashed out."

"Thanks—no. But tell me about it."

And he told me. The following is the gist of it, extracted from Mac under the influence of much tobacco and the generous wine of the country. I seldom had to interrupt him, excepting for the verification of genealogical details, which in his discourse had a tendency to become confused.

"Way back in the early 19th century the then Sir Willoughby Carlyon died without male heirs, and it was ascertained that his brother Charlton had died in Rio de Janeiro, years before, leaving a son, Erule, who was a briefless barrister in London, and than whom no one was more surprised at his unexpected accession to the title and estate. His father had never addressed speech or letter to his elder brother since, as a lad, he had betaken himself to Brazil; but even if he had remained in England it is probable that the surviving Carlyon would have been equally isolated from the rest of his family.

"This condition of affairs requires some explanation, and the explanation is as follows: When His Majesty King James the First instituted the perpetuity of Knighthood by conferring the new title of Baronet upon such gentlemen as were willing to aid him in his Irish "reforms," one of the first to assume the dignity of the new Order was Mr. Carlyon of Clough-Iveagh. The Carlyons of Clough-Iveagh were said to be the oldest, proudest, and wealthiest of the Catholic families in the north of Ireland—that they were old, and proud, and wealthy, there is no doubt, but whether they were entitled to the superlative is a question upon which Milesian genealogists have been divided.

"Anyhow, the Canyons who succeeded one another had one fetich which was embodied in the emblazonment of the family escutcheon; to wit: 'On a field argent, a crucifix proper, supported dexter and sinister by a hand gules, bearing a sword,' with the motto 'To the Faith, faithful.' From this it may be gathered that the Carlyons were Catholic to the backbone, and every tradition of the family was in some way connected with, or the outcome of, their devotion to the Church. Two of the Canlyons had been Cardinals, and the family tree positively bristled with Priors, Monsignores and Bishops of the Holy See—more than once the family had been threatened with extinction by the celibacy of these holy men, and had the baronetcy been conferred upon Mr. Carlyon of Clough-Iveagh in fee-tail it would have become extinct in the third generation. As it was, the succession was unhampered, and fell from generation to generation upon the nearest living male heir of the late baronet. It was thus that one morning Erule Carlyon woke in his chambers in Lincoln's Inn to find himself entitled to the Red Hand of Ulster upon his armorial bearings, and, what was of more importance to a brief-less barrister, to the house and estate of Clough-Iveagh.

It was a complete surprise to him, for, from the day he was born in Rio de Janeiro, he had never held any communication with, and had never seen, his uncle, Sir Willoughby, and for this—to them—all-sufficient reason. His father whilst a lad at Oxford had fallen in love with a Protestant maiden, the daughter of the Dean of his College, and had announced to his brother his intention of marrying the lady. The elder brother had promptly, with the traditional bigotry of the Carlyons, informed his younger brother that, should he disgrace the family by union with 'the heretic woman,' he would be disowned on the spot by all other members of the family; and moreover lie was warned that the lady would never be recognised by them, or by the Church, as his wife. Deeply wounded, and boiling with fury, young Carlyon formally cut himself adrift from his brother, who, in turn, ruled a crimson line through his name on the pedigree that was preserved at Clough-Iveagh.

"Married to his 'sweet heretic,' and, in due course, father of a baby boy, the image of his mother, it is hardly surprising that Carlyon embraced the Protestant faith; and young Erule was duly baptized a Protestant, in defiance of a last strenuous effort on the part of his uncle and sundry ecclesiastical 'collaterals' to save his young soul from inevitable hell-fire. The breach had been complete, and Erule Carlyon had grown to man's estate, and had been called to the Bar, conscious indeed of the fact that he was the nephew of Sir Willoughby Carlyon of Clough-Iveagh, but beyond that knowing nothing of his family, save in the remembrance of his mother who had died when he was a child, and of his father who had followed her some ten years later to the grave.

"One warm spring afternoon, therefore, in the year of grace 18— Sir Erule Carlyon arrived, a stranger, and, in the eyes of his tenantry, a heretic, at Clough-Iveagh, the first avowed Protestant Carlyon who had trodden the ancestral halls. I say the first 'avowed Protestant,' for there dwelt in the memory of Sir Erule a story that had been told him, years ago, by his father, of a great-grand-uncle Spencer, who had been regarded by the family as having heretical tendencies, and as having in some mysterious way come to a bad end in consequence. So far as he could gather the details of the story were as follows:

"Sir Spencer Carlyon had been a student. He lived at Clough-Iveagh a solitary life, unbroken by any companionships save that of his chaplain-confessor, a young priest, distantly connected with the family, and noted in the Roman Catholic Church, despite his youth, for his exemplary piety and fanatic austerity. It was not without an object that His Eminence Cardinal Willoughby Carlyon, principal of the Benedictine confraternity at Monte

Cassino, had appointed Monsignore Whiston to the Chaplaincy of Clough-Iveagh. Rumours had reached him in Rome to the effect that the devotion of Sir Spencer Carlyon to the interests of his Church left much to be desired, and he hoped that the propinquity and example of Monsignore Whiston would effectually check the tendency that, according to rumour, Sir Spencer betrayed to dabble in the Occult Sciences, Mediaeval Magic, and other studies forbidden to her children by the Church of Rome. It was even whispered that he had leanings towards the doctrines of Luther and Calvin! Accordingly the young priest had been installed at Clough-Iveagh as the custodian of Sir Spencer's orthodoxy, and, two years later, the winter sun shone in upon a ghastly scene in the Library.

"The first servant to enter in the morning was greeted by the spectacle of his master sitting in his accustomed chair, his head lying on the table before him, his brains beaten out. A window behind him was wide open, the shrubs outside were torn and trampled, beneath the casement a blood-bespattered paperweight was found, which had evidently been the instrument of Sir Spencer's murder, and from that day Monsignore Whiston had never been seen or heard of.

"Sir Spencer having died a bachelor, the baronetcy descended to his younger brother Charlton, who consequently relinquished his purpose of entering the Church.

"Of all his ancestors 'the heretic Sir Spencer' was the one whose history interested most deeply the young Sir Erule on his accession to the title. That his great-grand-uncle had been murdered in a fit of fanatic frenzy by his Chaplain, he never for one moment doubted. He deeply regretted that he had never been able to discover, indirectly or otherwise, the nature of the studies that had been brought to a close by his ancestor's death. That he had been engrossed in study at the moment of his murder there seemed no doubt, but whatever had been the books or papers that had cumbered the desk at which the corpse was found, either they had been taken away with him by the murderer, or had been destroyed. The library consisted almost entirely of Theological Works, and no folio, quarto, octavo, duodecimo or pamphlet on the shelves seemed in any way to savour of the forbidden studies which had led to his ancestor's destruction. Often, late at night, whilst Sir Erule sat in that same chair at that same desk, immersed in his literary work, he would lean back, lost in thought on this subject, his eyes fastened upon the darkness before him, which his single working lamp was powerless to pierce.

"It was on one of these occasions, a few months after his arrival at Clough-Iveagh, that he was made the victim of a terrifying and wholly inexplicable incident.

"Quite suddenly, without the slightest shadow of warning, he was seized with a sensation of deathly sickness and apprehension. He was overwhelmed with a conviction that *Something* stood behind his chair, but, paralysed with terror, he seemed unable to move. At last, by a strong effort of will, he turned in his chair, and, as he did so, it seemed to him that he caught a momentary glimpse of a tall figure, robed in the black cassock of a Benedictine Monk, standing behind his chair. The face of the Apparition was deathly white, the eyes, like flaming jet, stood out against its pallor. The right arm was raised above its head in a menacing gesture. That was all he could catch, as the Figure faded in the shadows of the heavily curtained window behind his desk.

"To put it mildly he was severely shaken up, and turning back to the desk he became aware of a spot of pale light in a far corner of the Library. As he watched it, fascinated, and frankly terrified, it moved, and appeared to wander up and down the book-cases and along the shelves. He pulled himself together with a violent effort and advanced towards the wandering light. He reached it.

"There—within a few feet of him, suspended in the air and sharply outlined against the surrounding gloom—was the Spectre of a Human Hand, bearing a taper. The taper was alight, but the whole hand and the taper seemed to be, of themselves, luminous, as they wandered from shelf to shelf as when one searches for a volume in the dark.

"His brain reeled. It was dawn when he found himself awaking from unconsciousness in one of the deep chairs of the Library, and crept away to bed.

※

"Sir Erule Carlyon was eight and twenty, sound in mind and limb, and of exemplary habits of life. The idea of his being frightened by a ghost was preposterous to his daylight senses—yet, the impression of the preceding night had been too startlingly vivid for him to pass it by without a further thought. Naturally his mind reverted to the fate of 'the heretic Sir Spencer,' and on the following afternoon he sought the Chapel of Clough-Iveagh and found the tablet commemorative of Sir Spencer's death. It read simply:

Sacred to the Memory of
SPENCER WILLOUGHBY CARLYON,
VIIth Baronet,
who departed this life
on
the 13th August, 1787.
R.I.P.

"He started as he read: it was now the 14th August. The preceding night had been the anniversary of his great-grand-uncle's murder!

"That night, and on many nights after, he watched in the Library for the re-appearance of the Apparition and of the Searching Hand. In vain. No supernatural happening disturbed his work, and as days formed weeks, and weeks grew into months, the incident became blurred amid later impressions. More completely was it obliterated by the fact that Sir Erule was on the eve of taking to himself a wife, the daughter of the Protestant rector of the neighbouring village.

"My grand-aunt," commented Mac, as he paused to refill his pipe—and eke his glass. "That was the foundation of the 'Protestant succession' at Clough-Iveagh."

After a moment or two Mac went on.

"They were married on the 15th of August that year. On the 13th Carlyon was sitting, reading, in the Library, not thinking at all about the Ghost, as you may suppose, when suddenly he felt creeping over him the same sensation that had terrified him a year ago. The date flashed into his mind, and in an instant the whole thing came back to him, and he sprang from his chair, turning as he did so.

"There, as in the year gone by, stood the Apparition—the spectral form of a Romish Priest, whose coal-black eyes seemed to burn into his own. Mastering himself with a supreme effort, he sprang forward as the Spectre raised his arm. Then he saw that the hand held one of the square leaden paper-weights that our fore-fathers were accustomed to use. As he sprang *into the space occupied by the Apparition,* a sensation of icy coldness and faintness gripped his whole body—in another second he had recovered from the shock—and he was alone.

"Quickly he turned towards the point where he had seen the Hand on the former occasion: there it was—wandering from shelf to shelf. He came close and watched it as it roamed over the bookcases.

"The books that became visible in turn as the luminosity of the Severed Hand reached them, were all of the most orthodox kind. Carlyon noted some of the titles lettered on the backs. There were the *Rationale Divinorum Officiorum* of Gulielmus Durandus, printed at Venice in 1559; Ducange's *Glossarium;* the complete works of the Abbé Fleury in the edition of 1739; the Life of the Arch-Romanist Julien de la Rovére, Pope Julius I., who paved the way for Leo X.; the Amsterdam, 1755, edition of the *Testament* of Richelieu. All these details he noted as the ghostly taper passed the volumes, and then, suddenly—even as he looked—a great folio edition of the *Commentaries* of Origen disappeared before his eyes! As the volume vanished, the hand holding the taper also disappeared, and Sir Erule, bathed in a cold perspiration, was left in absolute darkness in the corner of the Library.

"He had watched too long to be content to abandon his investigation there. He returned to his former place, and, bringing his chair and the lamp into the corner, he deposited the latter upon a stool and seated himself to watch the empty space in the shelf whence the Origen had been rapt by an unseen hand. For an hour he kept his eyes fastened upon the gap, and then, hypnotised by the fixity of his gaze, and worn out by the reaction of his nerves, he fell fast asleep."

※

"When he awoke it was broad day. The lamp had gone out, and—the Origen was back in its place!

"With a stifled exclamation he drew it from the shelves and carried it to the table. There he opened it.

"It was Origen only as to its outer cover. Enclosed in the binding that might once have contained the early Christian Commentary, was the *Parva Naturalia* of Albertus Magnus, the corner-stone of Mediæval Magic.

"*This* must have been the work in which Sir Spencer Carlyon had been engrossed when the blow, treacherously delivered from behind, had hurried his unshriven soul into the presence of his Maker. Feverishly he turned its leaves to find whether any papers or notes were concealed within. About half-way through, two leaves were stuck together: cautiously he began to separate them; they adhered to one another with a clotted, sticky, brown substance, now dried and hardened by the lapse of time.

"Sir Erule started back. *This* had been the page at which his ancestor's studies had been brought to a termination. His brains and blood served the purpose of a ghastly book-marker to identify the place!

"Shuddering, the Master of Clough-Iveagh restored the volume—the silent witness of Sir Spencer's murder—to its place in the dark corner of the Library, and stood there wrapped in thought.

※

"Well," concluded Mac, "he married my great-aunt the following day, and my father says she wondered for years why he seemed so grave and grey on that important occasion.

"But he never told her of his vigil in the Library; and to the day of her death she never knew why, at night-fall on the 13th of August in every year, the Library was locked up by her husband, who kept the key himself until he re-opened it on the morning of the 14th."

We bought the books. I did not think it essential to point out in my report that the majority of them would require to have the backs re-lettered. There was an awful row over the expense of this.

(Note.—Reading over this Record after the lapse of many years, I think it proper to add here that Sir Max Carlyon died some years after the sale of the Library at Clough-Iveagh, childless, and as there appeared to be no living representative of the family, the property, in a shameful condition of decay, escheated to the Crown.—C.B.)

THE COSMIC DUST.

(Deposited by the Clarkian Professor of Chemistry.)

MANY years ago Mr. Kipling related a remarkable incident in the lives of certain journalists who had what is known in the newspaper world as a "scoop." They were present at the capture of a sea serpent. And, having written an account of the capture—each according to his lights and personal idiosyncrasies—they agreed that the "story" was too overwhelming for publication, and, by common consent, suppressed their narrations and wrote nothing at all. I have found myself in the same position, but I am impelled, after a considerable lapse of time, to set down the following account of the matter. It may be that the time will arrive when what I have to say may be rescued from the scattered archives of dead records and brought to life as an anticipation—like Roger Bacon's and Leonardo da Vinci's adumbration and invention of the aeroplane.

There are those still living and at work who will remember the account given by the Professor of Psychology—not the present occupant of the chair, but his predecessor, Chalmers—of the death of Alured Markwand, and of his commerce with Aalila, which account may see the light contemporaneously with that upon which I am now embarking. It will be remembered that he recorded, without laying any particular stress upon the matter, that on the spot where he caught his momentary glimpse of Aalila there was a circle of scintillating dust, a small quantity of which he collected and preserved in a tube which he carried away in his pocket.

The scientific instinct which led him to preserve this specimen was the cause of his death—a horrible death. A short time after the incidents which he related, much in the spirit of the present record, he found himself to be suffering from a painful blister on the right breast. As it refused to yield to ordinary treatment, and, enlarging, became deeper and more malignant, in point of fact a rodent ulcer, he confided the trouble to his friend the Regius Professor of Medicine.

The Regius Professor took a very grave view of the matter.

"Are you sure," said he, "that you have not been exposed to the direct action of radium?"

"Not that I am aware of," replied the patient. "Why?"

"Because if I know anything about it, this took its origin in a radium burn."

My late colleague knew enough to realise the gravity of this pronouncement.

"Then this flaky, corn-like, granulation of the sore and of the skin round it, you think may be—" and he hesitated.

"Yes—I am afraid so," replied the Professor of Medicine.

The early history of the discovery of radium is punctuated with the names of its victims, martyrs to science, who, in the dawn of knowledge of this terrible element, and before the methods of protection and their vital necessity were understood, paid with their lives for the knowledge which they gave to the scientific world. Visitors to the gruesome galleries of the Museum of the Royal College of Surgeons in London have been appalled by the exhibits illustrating the progress and results of that unconquerable scourge Exfoliative Dermatitis—the gradual and irresistible flaking away of the tissues, which precedes a lingering and irresistible death.

The Professor of Psychology was a brave man, but the verdict of the Regius Professor was one to make the bravest man on earth quail. It was sentence of death.

It was not till some weeks afterwards, when the disease had reached its maximum force, that my colleague suddenly remembered the tube of scintillating dust which he had tucked into his upper right-hand waistcoat pocket, and had carried there until his return to town, when he transferred it with other relics of Markwand to the case containing his private journal and papers. It was then that I came into the story, for he sent the tube to me with a request that I should give him my views on the contents.

It was only recently that I had been appointed Professor of Chemistry in the University of Cosmopoli, and to tell the truth I had not yet quite settled into the position and got "my bearings," either among my colleagues, or with the students, and I confess to a feeling of satisfaction which I experienced when this ordinary "collector's tube" was brought to me by the Regius Professor of Medicine, with my dying colleague's message, to which he added his own earnest instance. He brought it to me wrapped in a piece of lead foil out of a tea-chest, late in the short afternoon of a dull December day. After his short explanation of the circumstances—he made no allusion to the death of Professor Markwand—we took the tube into the dark room of the laboratory, and there unwrapped it. The display of scintillations was staggering. Imagine a Super-Spinthariscope! I hastily wrapped up the tube again, and placed it in the "safe" where our microscopic store of bromide of radium was kept, and we returned to my study.

"How long," said I, "has this deadly thing been in existence—and where has it been kept?"

"Chalmers has had it for months, in a writing case, which he has kept in an iron safe in his cellar. But for two days he carried it about, naked, in his waistcoat pocket."

"Good God!—and Chalmers?"

"He is doomed—rodent ulcer, and Exfoliative Dermatitis."

✳

And thus it came about that the Chemical Laboratory of the University of Cosmopoli possesses the largest and purest specimen of the element radium in the world.

Whether the dust, which consisted of quite fifty per cent. of pure radium, was shed upon the floor of Markwaud's observatory in a scintillating circle from the draperies of Aalila, or whether it arrived independently of her during many weeks, by radiation pressure, remains an open question. We shall return to this later on. Let me attempt, at least, to marshal the facts as they unfolded themselves in the months that followed—though, like the journalists to whom I referred at the commencement of this record, I can never—nor can the colleagues who took part in their unfolding—publish them. All I can do is to transcribe them from my laboratory note-books, and leave them for the information of later research-workers.

After we had, with infinite care and taking every possible—every known—and some new, precautions against radium burns, separated out the pure elements, we had left remaining about three cubic centimetres of a pale grey dust. I divided this into four parts, one of which I confided to the Professor of Botany, one to the Professor of Zoology, one I retained for myself, and the fourth remains as it reached me, in the cabinet of the Chemical Laboratory. My successors, if they think fit, may repeat our observations.

It resisted all known methods of chemical analysis; all that I could show was that it was largely organic—that is to say, I proved by negative methods that it contained no inorganic element, excepting perhaps a trace of iron, and of the mineral olivine. The work of my colleagues, however, was rewarded by results that, even now, I feel a considerable hesitancy in setting down.

The Professors of Botany and of Zoology conducted their researches together and concurrently—the methods they employed are familiar in the textbooks, and to these were added some blind and empiric processes of which, no doubt, they have preserved records. It is only the results with which I am at this moment concerned. It was after the lapse of some six months that I was sent for to the Botanical Laboratory, where I found my two colleagues in a state as nearly approaching excitement as is permitted to a University Professor. The dust had yielded no results under ordinary conditions of atmosphere and temperature, and the final cultivation had been made in slightly saline water at a temperature of 100° centigrade—in fact boiling point. They laid great stress upon this.

"May one ask why?" I said.

They looked at one another, and then one of them—I forget which—laughed nervously, and said:

"That would appear to be the temperature on this planet, within a very few years of the consolidation of its crust—the *consistentior status.*"

I was startled. The reply seemed to open up illimitable fields of conjecture. I stammered: "But—the Cambrian Period—azoic rocks?"

"Why azoic?" replied the Professor of Zoology. "But you are thinking of the Archaean series—Pre-Cambrian. With the earliest sedimentary rocks we get life without question—perhaps before."

"My good man," said the Professor of Botany, watching for my recovery, "we are going to show you some things so entirely inexplicable, that the mind flies at once to the only possible explanation—which is an impossible one."

"That is rather confusing," I suggested.

"Yes—confusion worse confounded, beyond the dreams of Milton. In this pressure chamber you see the culture of your dust, actively proceeding. Here are some mounted microscope slides—in balsam you have Protozoa, Algae, Mosses, Bacteria—in dry cells you have microscopic shells, baby Lamellibranchs."

"And they came?" I was almost afraid to ask.

"From the material you submitted to us."

"Then you think?"

"We don't think. We dare not think. Here is a tiny thing—we dare not give it a name—but we know it."

They showed me their preparations. To the Botanist I said: "What are they?"

He replied: "These things do not inhabit the earth to-day—excepting in that boiling tank."

To the Zoologist I said:

"What are they?"

He replied: "These things do not inhabit the earth to-day—unless represented by one little bivalve shell—excepting in that boiling tank."

My brain reeled. "What are you going to do next?"

The Professor of Zoology replied:

"We are going to call in the Professor of Geology and Palaeontology."

We made an appointment with him for the following day.

My esteemed colleague the Professor of Geology was one of the most remarkable men of his time—or of any other. He presented, to the astonished student of human nature, the almost unheard-of combination of a distinguished man of science and a prig. In the earlier days of his career it had been confidently asserted by Cosmogonists—on the metaphysical side—that in the beginning the Almighty created the Professor of Geology, and that having rested awhile after this stupendous effort, He set about the creation of a World which might, in some respects at least, be a place worthy to be the habitation of the Professor of Geology. The latter, it may be said at once, was far from convinced that the second effort of the Almighty had been altogether a success. He inspired a wholesome fear and respect not unmingled with dislike.

He duly attended the conference in the Botanical Laboratory, explaining that the utmost limit of time he could spare was twenty minutes. He remained two hours, at the end of which he was visibly annoyed. For the first time in his professional life he was unable to annihilate his colleagues with a few disagreeably-worded ex-cathedral sentences of doom.

"I may assume," said he, "that you are not seeking to make me the victim of some futile practical joke, but if you are, I am free to confess that the means you have adopted to that end are utterly beyond me. You tell me that these organisms have been cultivated—bred—from a few cubic centimetres of dust, found on the floor of Markwand's observatory, after freeing it from a notable proportion of the element radium."

"That is so," replied Cantrell, the Zoologist.

"That is so," replied Warham, the Botanist.

"Well, all I can say is that I—I, Peterson—tell you that we are looking at immature living specimens of Upper and Lower Cambrian flora. This Lamellibranch is Lingulella, indistinguishable from the specimens found in the Lingula flags of Dolgelly, but this is fully represented by a living species. Similarly these microorganisms are the same Foraminifera as have been identified by Chapman in the Upper Cambrian beds of Malvern, *Lagena, Nodosaria, Cristellaria, Spirillina,* but these genera are represented almost unaltered in modern seas. If it went no farther I should be inclined to revert to the practical joke theory, *but,"* and he paused for a moment before he went on, "here are juvenile Trilobites, *Paradoxides, Agnostus Sao;* here, burrowing in the mud is the worm *Histioderma;* here is the Alga *Oldhamia* of Edward Forbes. In any other circumstances I should say that my brain was affected, but if I know anything at all of Cambrian Palaeontology, this minute thing swimming about in practically boiling water is the Phyllopod crustacean—the Shrimp *Hymenocaris."*

He stopped abruptly, and in the dead silence which followed we all looked at one another, and from one another to the tanks, and the slides which lay strewn around the microscope.

Cantrell was the first to speak.

"Then you think," said he, "that the material under examination is——"

"I don't think," replied Peterson, explosively, "I can't think—I dare not think—but if I allow myself to think anything, I think the material is Cosmic Dust."

Cosmic Dust! Moved by one impulse we all leapt to our feet and crowded once more together at the laboratory bench—but none of us said a word. All our minds, I undertake to swear, reverted on the spot to a memorable meeting of the Geological Society, at which Professor Peterson had risen to his greatest height, pulverising the Planetesimal Theory of Svante Arrhenius. The whole frantic and interminable controversy between the mechanists and the vitalists, almost the dead issue between the catastrophists and the uniformitarians, sprang into our thoughts. That Peterson—Peterson of all men in the world—should admit the introduction into a scientific discussion (though he had done practically all the talking—as usual) of the mere phrase "Cosmic Dust!" It was as if Cantrell had suddenly taken up his parable in defence of the discredited Bathybius!

"We will not carry the matter further now," said Peterson, in his best lecture-theatre manner. "I will look in from time to time and watch the development of these observations. You will all of you please meet in my room, after four, this day week."

And with that he left us—leaving the door open.

True to his word Peterson haunted the Botanical Laboratory all that week, and obedient to his summons, we met in his room on the appointed day. We sat round like good little first-year students whilst he lectured us.

"I will not go back to the theory of Nordenskiôld that by the fall of meteorites and cosmic dust the weight of the earth is annually increased by at least ten million tons. I shall advance no new theory of my own. I have here Svante Arrhenius' book *Worlds in the Making*—I will merely refer to some passages which I marked for criticism on an occasion which you doubtless all remember."

We shared between us the flicker of a faint smile—which seemed to accentuate the portentous gravity of Peterson.

"I have heard incomplete accounts of the phenomena alleged to have taken place prior to the death of Markwand. I have supposed, pardonably, that Chalmers was temporarily insane. I have reconsidered that opinion. The presence—the person, if you will—which he has recorded, apparently arrived upon this planet from Venus by radiation pressure. The mean temperature of Venus has been calculated at 40° centigrade, a temperature clearly favourable to organic life—the same may be said of Mars. But the time required for particles to reach here from Venus—forty days as calculated by Arrhenius—is clearly open to revision. Upon the theory of the organic nature of these particles much has been written—the theory of pan-spermia suggested by de Montlivaut, by Richter, by Flammarion—others. I have come to look with respect upon Kelvin's remarkable views on this subject expressed in his presidential address before the British Association in 1871. I will read you Arrhenius's statement of the theory, which is as follows: 'It is probable that there are organisms so small that the radiation pressure of a sun would push them out into space, where they might give rise to life on planets, provided they met with favourable conditions for their development.' I recall your minds to the culture processes you have severally adopted."

He continued to read extracts from the work of Arrhenius.

"Who shall say that such germs are not continually being carried away from this earth? Most of these spores thus carried away, will no doubt meet death in the cold infinite space of the Universe, about -220° C. Yet a small number of spores will fall upon some other world and may thus be able to spread life if the conditions are suitable. You will remember that at the Jenner Institute, in London, micro-organisms have lived for twenty-four hours in liquid hydrogen at a temperature of -252° C. It may take one million, or several millions of years from the age at which a planet could possibly begin to sustain life to the time when the first seed falls upon it and germinates, and when organic life is thus originated. This period is of little significance in comparison with the time during which life will afterwards flourish on the planet.

"It may be objected that the powerful light from the sun during transit would kill these germs—the experiments of Roux have shown us that spores that are readily killed by light when the air has access, remain alive when the air is excluded—no one can assert with certainty that spores would be killed by the light rays in wandering through infinite space. The germs are propelled by the radiation pressure, attached to grains of dust which serve both as carriers and protectors.

"Why have the experiments you have made not been made before? Arrhenius terminates his book with the answer: 'The number of germs which reach us from other worlds will be extremely limited—not more perhaps than a few within a year all over the earth's surface.' The dust precipitated in Markwand's observatory was a concentrated precipitation. Nothing like it has ever been suggested—much less demonstrated—before. Therefore, gentlemen, I am of the opinion—and I express it with a full sense of the responsibility which I incur in expressing it—that the material under consideration is Cosmic Dust—similar to that which was falling in Cambrian times—a thousand million years ago, which germinated when the conditions became favourable, and produced the Cambrian Fauna and Flora—exactly as you have produced them in Warham's laboratory."

Peterson sat down, and dried his forehead with his hand-kerchief. I was the first to break the silence, and my voice was husky.

"What shall we do about it—publish?"

"No! A thousand times no," cried Peterson. "What is the use? We should be laughed to scorn in every Scientific Society of the world. We should go down to posterity as hoaxed—or mad. There is only one thing to be done—we must destroy all traces of the cultures—and we must hold our tongues."

And upon that we parted.

THE CHEETAH-GIRL

DEPOSITED BY
THE PROFESSOR OF PHYSIOLOGY
IN THE UNIVERSITY OF COSMOPOLI

NOTE OF EXPLANATION.

THE note by my Publishers on page 211 requires an explanation which circumstances rendered it both difficult and desirable to offer in that place. The seven published MSS. were selected by me from among a large number of which I had become custodian, as explained in my Ante-script to "The Purple Sapphire" and at the same time I brought away with me from the safe in the University library, for re-perusal, the MS. of "*The Cheetah-Girl.*" This MS., though setting forth the principles of an enquiry, and experiments, in a branch of Biological research the importance of which it would be impossible to over-estimate, contains matters of record of such a nature that it could not possibly be published in a volume destined for public circulation. The table of contents was, however, compiled from the Title covers of the MSS. by my Secretary, who, I may mention parenthetically, made the mistake of writing "Deposited by the Professor of Biology" instead of "Of Physiology"—there is no chair of general Biology in the University of Cosmopoli. This "table" went to the Printers after my departure from England on a protracted holiday, and was "set-up" with the rest of what is technically called "the preliminary matter". When, on my return, my Publishers asked for this MS. I considered that I was justified in showing it to them in confidence, and they at once agreed with me that it could not be printed. Hence the "Note" which Reviewers have regarded, some in the light of a joke (!), and some as a touch of intentional sensationalism.

CHRISTOPHER BLAYRE.

THE CHEETAH-GIRL.

I have spent a long and very tiring day in London, and I have come home, worn out physically and mentally. But I have settled all my worldly affairs, and am, I think, prepared for any eventuality. I am now ready therefore to kill my wife on the first opportunity that offers.

I have written that deliberately; so as to see and to realise how terrible it looks, written down to "stiffen myself" so to speak, for, if it be possible, I admire my wife even more to-day than I did when we set out upon our wonderful honeymoon, just over three months ago. But, terrible as it is to contemplate, she must die as soon as possible; the welfare of the Race demands her death. There is bound to be an inquest, and I dread, even now, what the Post-mortem examination of her beautiful body may reveal. The manner of her death I have thought out and decided upon, and there is not, I believe, the slightest possibility of my being connected in the remotest degree with the tragedy, but I have deemed it expedient to make such arrangements as regards my affairs as may become necessary in the event of my being hung for murder. For I should not offer any defence or explanation of my act—I owe that to her, to her mother, to my predecessor in the chair of Physiology in the University, and to the memory of three months of the most passionate happiness which have ever fallen to the lot of man. And even if I did explain my action, would my explanation be believed? Perhaps it might, in the light of proofs I could bring forward, but would life be possible for me among human beings afterwards? A thousand times *No*. But I owe it to Science to record the circumstances which have led to the step

I am henceforth seeking the opportunity to take. I shall deposit this record with the Registrar of the University, with precautions that it shall not be read until many years have elapsed after my death—I have no near relations, and I shall not marry again—therefore no one living can be hurt. And in any case the facts I have to record, whilst of paramount importance to Physiologists in the future, can never be given any wide publicity—if indeed they can be imparted to anyone at all, excepting under the seal of professional secrecy.

Thus much by way of introduction. My record must commence with the year 19—, when, having taken my degrees of Doctor of Medicine had Doctor of Science, I was appointed Assistant and Demonstrator to Professor Paul Barrowdale, F.R.S., Professor of Psychology in the University of Cosmopoli. With our academic duties I am not concerned now, and the records, so far as they could be published, of the research work done in the laboratory of that daring and brilliant Physiologist are to be found scattered among pages of the contemporary journals of Science. It is with our personal relations that I am constrained to deal. These became, almost from their inception, of the most intimate nature; in our work in the University, I recognised in him a brilliant master; he recognised in me a devoted and assiduous pupil; outside our professional connection our tastes, our views, were strangely identical. He was no narrow-minded or ascetic Scientist, and, away from the University, his appreciation of the pleasures of life, of "wine, woman and song," of travel, literature and art found a ready response in me, and we became confidential friends and companions, to a degree which is very rare between a Professor and his Assistant.

There was only one subject upon which he never touched even in our moments of closest intimacy and confidence and in regard to which I never attempted to break the seal of silence which he had imposed upon himself, and tacitly upon me. This subject was Mrs. Clayton. As regards this lady, though the gossip which is indigenous to a University town no doubt from time to time formulated theories (for Barrowdale was a very free-living bachelor, was, as such, looked askant upon by many of the

444

Professorial Staff and their wives) no one would ever "come out into the open," so to speak, for the all-sufficient reason that any scandal openly promulgated would have to be rapidly sterilised, should Barrowdale have shown any signs of wanting to marry any daughter of the University, and much will be tacitly ignored in a bachelor professor of more than ample private means.

Mrs. Clayton lived in a charming little house about three miles out of the town. It was understood that Barrowdale was her trustee and had charge of her business-affairs. There was a child, a girl, whom no one ever saw, but whether the child was born after Mrs. Clayton's arrival in the neighbourhood, or before that event, no one was in a position to say. One Academic lady (with daughters) had gone so far as to ascertain that the child, whose curious name was "Uniqua," was not registered at birth in the District Registry. Beyond this nothing was known; Barrowdale never afforded any intelligence, and if, as was whispered from time to time with bated breath, "*à quatres yeux*" she was his daughter, there was nothing on record to convey the slightest indication or *a priori* evidence of the fact.

I saw her once—I was walking with Barrowdale and we met Mrs. Clayton and the child, an ugly, sallow, swarthy little thing, who struck me as singularly repellent and uninteresting. Mrs. Clayton was a nervous, faded person, gentle in manner and appearance, but quite unnoticeable. She went nowhere and knew no one. Neither mother nor daughter interested me in the least. Now and then I believe an undergraduate would refer contemptuously to "old Barrowdale's woman," but there was no "talk," in the Unversity sense of the word. Several years passed by during which our work in the Laboratory and Schools, and our pleasures in companionship, grew more and more intimately connected, so much so that I refused the offer of a Professorship in a Northern University rather than be separated from Barrowdale—for the work we were engaged upon was of the highest Physiological importance. He was grateful to me for this, and I know that he never lost an opportunity of impressing upon the Authorities that I was his natural and indicated successor in the Chair of Physiology on his death or retirement. This came about one day

445

with appalling suddenness. Barrowdale had been seedy, nervy "off colour," for several days. He had been out more than once to see Mrs. Clayton, as I knew, and one evening came home tired to death and drenched to the skin. The next day he was in a high fever, in the evening sceptic pneumonia of a most virulent type set in, and in twenty-four hours he was dead.

I found that he had made me, together with his solicitor, a worthy old man in London, his Executor and Trustee. He provided an annuity of £600 a year for Mrs. Clayton, which on her death devolved to Uniqua. The rest of his property, he being apparently alone in the world, was bequeathed to the University. The good woman, who seemed absolutely paralysed by the death of Barrowdale, came into Cosmopoli to see me whenever her affairs required an interview, always the same nervous uninteresting creature. I confess I hoped she would be led on some occasion to speak of Uniqua's father, but in spite of one or two "leads" she never "followed," and, being really quite uninterested in the matter, I never tried to press the subject.

In due course, almost mechanically, I succeeded Barrowdale in the chair of Physiology, and I had neither time nor inclination to concern myself about my two "*cestuis que trustent.*"

We come then by effluxion of time to the end of last term. The men were due to go down for the Long Vacation next day, and I had made all arrangements for a protracted tour down the Loire and through the Midi of France. I may mention that Barrowdale left me by his will the comfortable and comforting legacy of £10,000. Some paper came to me on this memorable day from my co-trustee, connected with a change of investment, which required Mrs. Clayton's signature. There was no time to communicate by post, so I jumped into my two-seater and ran out to her house. I rang the bell and the door was opened by the most Beautiful Being that I had ever seen in my life—and I had seen a good many.

"Mrs. Clayton—?" I began.

"Mother is out," she replied, "you are Professor Magley? Please come in."

446

She held out her hand, which I took, and without letting go of mine, she drew me into their sitting-room, a cosy little place furnished with great taste (Barrowdale's taste) and strewn with fur rugs which gave off a warm sensuous perfume. The touch of the girl's hand was electrical, it sent a thrill of intense desire up my arm to my brain, and when she dropped my hand and stood before me, her lips parted in a smile more provoking than anything of the kind I had ever seen, I was simply struck dumb, and stood looking at her, my heart beating violently.

She was a lithe creature of rather more than average stature, draped, rather than dressed, in a kind of dull red silk wrapper, confined at the waist by a suede leather belt. It folded across her breasts (one of which, perfect in form, almost escaped from the folds) and came down to just below her knees—her legs were bare, and her feet were shod in fur-lined slippers. I verily believe that, save for this garment, she was naked. Her face was indescribable, a mass of purple-black hair gathered into a loose bunch on the top of her head, thick dark eyebrows shadowing long lazy eyes which seemed to me to be enormous, her complexion a tawny russet brown, with a suspicion of down on the cheeks and more than a suspicion of it at the corners of her upper lip. She had let her hands fall by her sides, and as she looked at me with that marvellous smile, the tip of a crimson tongue passed slowly across her lower lip from one side to the other. I was struck, even at that wonderful moment, by the comparative prominence of her little canine teeth, which gave an indescribable and characteristic charm to her smile.

Without saying a word, and, I declare, without any conscious volition of my own, I held out my arms, and she stepped forward into them. I crushed her body to me and our lips joined. I thought until then that I knew what it was to be kissed. I did not. The lingering passion of Uniqua's kiss was unlike anything I had ever dreamed of as possible. Her tongue which sought mine was strangely long and firm, and even in the delirium of the moment it seemed to me that her lingual papillae were accentuated almost to the point of roughness, but the exquisite power of it defies words. Her arms were round me, her legs were twisted

447

into mine, and I think I should have fallen had she not gently disengaged herself and, still holding me by one arm she drew me towards a low divan covered with fine skins from which I had evidently aroused her. As she reached it she flung herself down upon the skins, and as she fell one beautifully modelled leg, bare to mid-thigh, escaped from the folds of her wrapper. She raised her arms to me in a gesture of divine invitation—and at that moment the door opened and Mrs. Clayton came in.

I do not know what was to be read from my face as I turned towards her, but if it was a reflection of Uniqua's, Mrs. Clayton must have been blind indeed if she did not take in the situation at a glance. I began, very haltingly, to utter apologies and to explain my visit. She was obviously very much upset and distressed, but all she said was—in short, disjointed sentences:—

"I see, I see. I could not have expected—no one comes here—I should not have gone out—I never do. Please bring the papers in here"—and she led me into the dining room, where there were pens and so on.

All this time Uniqua had not moved or uttered a sound, but just lay curled up luxuriously on the divan, watching me with her huge eyes, and, as it were, "swaying" her beautiful smile from side to side—I cannot describe it otherwise. The slipper had fallen from the foot of the leg which still lay unconcernedly outside her "sarong," and here was the only movement that she made. The toes opened and shut and curled inwards towards the palm of her foot with a regulated movement which seemed to me to be indicative of extreme and perfect luxury.

Mrs. Clayton signed the papers, with a shaky hand it is true, but said nothing about Uniqua. The silence becoming oppressive, I thought it obvious and tactful to say:—

"Your daughter has grown into a very striking young woman."

"Yes—very," replied the poor woman nervously, "very. I never leave her if I can help it—but expecting no one, I went in next door for something—the servant is out—and so," she tailed off incoherently, and I saw that I was distressing her, so I took my leave as casually as I could, with my blood boiling in my veins and my heart throbbing.

When I got outside I took a deep breath, but I seemed saturated with the tense, sensuous perfume of Uniqua's room and of Uniqua herself, for, whether it was contact with her divan or what, her whole body gave off a perfume for which there was only one word—it was intoxicating—slightly savage. It clung to me all the way back to my rooms, and even afterwards when I had opened all the windows. I need hardly say that I could not get her out of my thoughts all day—nor did I want to—and I dreamed a dream!

Next morning, as I went on with my packing, and the College was rapidly emptying of the men off on Long Vacation, I said to myself:—

"Look here, my son, you are that girl's guardian. Barrowdale has entrusted her to you. It's a damned good thing that you are off to-morrow for three months—and when you get back again, keep clear of it"—Thus I apostrophized myself, and I knew that I wanted Uniqua more than anything else in the world.

By the afternoon the College was practically empty, and I had finished my packing, and was trying to read an abstruse German treatise on Cytology—but I couldn't. My senses were on edge—unnaturally keen—hypertrophied as it were. I heard a step in the Quad, it "slithered" up my stair—a rap on the door—I knew who it was before the door was flung open. In an instant we were in one another's arms. The long witchery of her kiss, the invitation of her magical tongue, everything was my dream come true. I had in my rooms a divan no less vivid with willing complicity than the one at the cottage; we fell upon it without a word, and in spite of the fact that Uniqua was in a physical condition in which it is customary for young women to withhold themselves from active caress, we gave ourselves up to one another, naturally, unthinkingly, in a whirl-wind orgy of exquisite possession and ecstasy.

Presently, when we were able to talk—for until then not a word had been uttered on either side—I asked her how she had got away.

"Mother's had a sleepless night," she said, "and this afternoon she locked the front and back doors and went to bed. I got out of the window. I wanted you so frightfully."

An hour passed in a delirium of sensuous delight which cannot be hinted at—not from motives of reticence, for I am determined to record here the absolute facts as they occurred, without any periphrasis, but because the marvel that was Uniqua simply beggars and defies description. I thought I had known passion—fool! I had never even touched its fringe.

If Uniqua was wonderful to behold in her dull red sarong, what was she naked! No painter or sculptor ever imagined, much less reproduced, so perfect a body; her beautiful breasts stood out in perfect proportion, the nipples prominent and surrounded with a silky aureole of tiny purple curls, tender and fascinating. Her axillary hair was phenomenally thick and I speedily found that to be kissed and petted under her arms drove her frantic with delight. I have had reason to remember and be thankful for this, as will be seen later. The whole of her body was covered with the light soft down such as is seen upon many fair women, but upon Uniqua it was deeper in shade than usual, and it was punctuated here and there with little streaks, and sometimes almost circles of a still deeper tone. From her navel downwards it increased into a glorious mass of pubic hair which extended from hip to hip, and though so dense, was of the most amazingly soft texture, covering the Whole of the lower stomach and intercrural space with a veritable "*fourrure*"—it was wonderful, and, to repeat the only adjective which describes any of Uniqua's esoteric attributes—intoxicating. Her forearms and legs were deliciously hirsute, and even up and down her spine a narrow furry band invited one's most ingenious caresses. Whoever gave her the name of Uniqua knew what he was about—prophetically.

We were lying in one another's arms, whispering passionate secrets to one another, I in a silk bath-robe, and she clad only in her wonderful skin and hair, when the door—which we had never thought of locking—was flung open, and Mrs. Clayton stood before us—frankly petrified and aghast.

I sprang to my feet and burst into words:

"Do not misjudge us," I cried, "we love one another as I never dreamed it possible to love. We shall be married at once—I will get a licence to-morrow, and next day Uniqua will be my wife. Forgive us the passion that has made us irresistible to one another—you will understand, I am sure—you are a woman who has loved, and you are her mother. Now you will have a devoted son as well as a daughter."

I paused. Mrs. Clayton had not said a word, she had fallen into a chair and, ashy-white, looked back and forth from me to Uniqua, who, utterly unconscious of her exquisite nakedness, lay on the divan, looking at us—with the same wonderful smile that had overwhelmed and held me, her crimson tongue passing to and fro across her lower lip. Then Mrs. Clayton got up—apparently with an effort—and she said:—

"No—no—*no*. It cannot, it can never be. You don't know. Oh! I am a wicked woman! At these times she is not responsible for what she does—and besides, she knows nothing. I never let her out of my sight until the time—the danger is over. Let me take her away!"

"But my dear lady," I said, "reflect a moment. We *must* be married now. We are both—I comparatively—young, and for a University Professor I am rich. I will be the best of husbands to her—the best of sons to you. Our old friend Barrowdale would have wished it, I am sure. I was his favourite—his only intimate friend."

At Barrowdale's name the poor woman started as if she had been stung.

"No, no, no," she cried again, "he would not—he would have killed himself and her rather. It has all been so sudden—I have not had time—forgive me for God's sake, and let me take her away."

"Well then, let us be engaged for a short while," I said ineptly.

"No, never. She must never marry. She can't. Oh, don't torture me!"

There was no reasoning with her. She was like a mad woman. Uniqua stood up in all her glorious statuesque nudity and allowed her mother to dress her with shaking hands whilst I looked on. I cut a poor figure. When she was dressed Mrs. Clayton took her away. She went without casting a look in my direction.

I was simply stunned.

I can give no description of the phantasmagoria of my thoughts for the rest of the afternoon and evening. One thing was certain: I could not leave England without having this matter cleared up and placed upon a proper, the only possible, basis. I thought and thought. What mad idea could the woman have? I tried to reason it out—I racked my brains for an explanation but found none. The girl was alive with passion, she was predestined to fall into the hands of some casual sensualist—what better solution, if her passion was in part, or in any way, pathological, than to give her to a husband who would look after her? I wearied myself with thoughts, and tumbled into bed at midnight.

At 3 a.m. I was awakened by a rapping at my door. I started into vivid wakefulness—It could only be Uniqua. It was. I subsequently learned that she had got past the Porter with a statement that her mother had sent her with a message of vital urgency—and with other inducement.

"I have got away again, sweet lover of mine," she said, as I took her in my arms. "Mother is mad, I think. Hide me—and take me away with you. Marry me or not, I don't care, I love you and want you so frightfully that I could kill anyone who stood between us."

What was I to do? I wanted her just as badly as she wanted me. She wanted to be loved—had, there and then—but I, with that practical good sense which I flatter myself distinguishes me, made coffee and toast and an omelette, and made her eat with me. Then we stole down and got past the heavily bribed Porter (remember Term was over, and he was once more a human being, and I no longer a Professor) reached the garage, carrying my bags which were already packed, got out the car and made a bee-line for London, where we put up at a quiet west-central hotel. Next day, I visited my co-trustee early, whilst Uniqua went shopping. She had of course come away wholly unprovided with any sort of *trousseau*. I confided the facts, in outline, to my co-trustee (who was horribly shocked!) got a Special Licence at Doctor's

Commons, and in the shortest possible time we were married at a Registry and fled—yes, we absolutely fled—to Paris. From Paris we both wrote to Mrs. Clayton announcing the inevitable, irredeemable event, but we gave her no address, merely saying that we should be away for at least three months, and would send an address for her to write to and forgive us. The only person to whom I confided my whereabouts was the horrified lawyer.

I could, in normal circumstances, take a vivid pleasure in recalling and recording the amazement and delight of the most wonderful honeymoon that was ever granted to mortal man. Uniqua who, to my surprise, I found had never been further from her home than Cosmopoli, was delighted, not childishly, but wonderingly, with everything she saw. The beauty of nature, of art, of architecture, of antiquity filled her with deep happiness, which, oddly enough was merged with her in a deep sensual enjoyment of life. Keenly intelligent and interested in everything she saw, whenever she found herself in surroundings of exceptional beauty, a thrill of passion would come over her which rapidly communicated itself to me, and the wayside scenery of Le Vendée and the Bocage, the ruins of departed civilization, a hundred spots in Western and Southern France where we stopped the car to roam at will, come back to my mind as scenes beautified to memory by the most exquisite physical delights. The natural disturbance of her system in which we made our flight from Cosmopoli, seemed to ripen her physical and mental faculties to the highest point, but whenever this was past, she displayed a power of response to emotional stimuli which I sometimes almost feared would wear her out, but we were determined, "not to climb mountains until we reached them," and lived long days and marvellous nights, unimagined by the most poetic and fantastic dreamers of the East.

It was at Avignon one morning as she was lying in my arms, watching the sun rise through our open window, that she said with her lips on mine:—

"Rex—we are going to have a child."

It needed but that to complete our happiness, though from that moment the joy we had in one another became more reasonable, perhaps a little less passionate. I could always rouse her to an ecstasy of desire by caressing and playing with the wonderful masses of hair under her arms, and, her desire appeased, could always soothe her to sleep by the same means. But her passion for me, as a male, had to some extent given place in her to a fierce maternity. As soon as she knew that she was pregnant—she never had any doubt about it—she wrote announcing her news to her mother, and we anxiously awaited her reply, for we felt that this would put the finishing touch to her mother's forgiveness, and reconcile her to the marriage she had so strenuously opposed. A week passed by, and then I received a telegram from my co-trustee. It said:—

"Mrs. Clayton has died suddenly under distressing circumstances. Please return at once."

I was horrified, and wondered how I should break the news to Uniqua. We were sitting in the Palace of the Caesars, quite alone that afternoon, and I thought it a good opportunity. I began:—

"Darling—I have had bad news to-day."

"Have we got to go back?—I shan't mind much, I've got my baby"—she always talked of it as if it were already born.

"No darling," I replied, "it's about your mother."

She looked at me quite gravely, and said:

"Is she dead?"

I could not help feeling a little shocked. She might have been asking if lunch was ready. I began:—

"You must not take it too much to heart. You have got me—"

"And I've got my baby, what does anything else matter? When do we go home?"

I was chilled, but in the circumstances it was better that she should take it like this, than that she should suffer paroxysms of grief. She accepted the situation quite calmly. When I told her she should now have £600 a year of her own, she said:—

454

"I shall not have to spend any of it, shall I? You are quite rich. I shall save it all for my baby." She never said "our baby".

Then she said: "Do you think Professor Barrowdale was my father?"

This was a blow between the eyes, and I said rather lamely:—

"Well, I have often wondered about it myself, but he never told me anything about it. Did your mother never say anything about your father?" I was curious that we had never touched upon this subject before.

"No," she answered. "I never asked her but once, and then she seemed dreadfully upset, and said I must never speak to her about my father. She could not bear to think about it." After a pause she added, "I don't think Professor Barrowdale was my father—I never felt like it, and I don't think I should have, if—. He seemed more interested in me, and how I got on with lessons and things, and how I was growing up, than really fond of me. Sometimes I fancied that he disliked me—that I 'repugged' him," (one of her words), "but anyhow he must have been an awfully good man. See how he looked after us."

"He *was* a good man," I answered stoutly, "no one ever knew what a lot of fine things he did. Especially for women—the sort of women you have never heard of, women who had come to grief, and were down and out."

"Do you mean prostitutes?"

I was ceasing to be amazed at my wife's sudden remarks, which from time to time showed an esoteric knowledge of the world, gathered I am at a loss to know how or whence.

"Well," I said, "that is about it."

"I don't wonder he was so good to them. It seems awful for men to be so down upon girls who are what I should have been—and proud of it—if you hadn't married me. After all, they are responsible, aren't they?"

"Perhaps."

"And yet I don't know. I wanted you so frightfully the moment I saw you, that you could not have helped having me. No one can say you seduced *me*!"

455

And thereupon this amazing girl turned to other subjects as if this had been an ordinary dinner-party conversation. But I never loved her more than I did then, or, for that matter, more than I do now. In truth I could reply when, as she often did, she asked me, "How much do you love me, Rex?"

"A little more than I did yesterday, but not so much as I shall to-morrow."

And then by a three days' journey, for I was anxious in the circumstances that she should travel easily, we came back to London, and the world crashed into ruins around me, and the light went out of my life for ever. *Ich habe geliebt und gelebt.*

We arrived one evening of the late summer, and put up at the same hotel as that which sheltered us when we fled from Cosmopoli, and next morning I called upon my co-trustee, who received me with grave and forbidding formality. It was clear from his manner that he regarded me as a perverter of youth, and incidentally as a murderer. I tried to open the conversation upon conventional lines.

"This is a most unfortunate circumstance," I began.

He interrupted me. "It is more than unfortunate, it is deeply tragic."

"You mean?"

"Professor Magley," he replied, "it is not my duty, nor have I the inclination, to sit in judgement upon your actions, or even to express an opinion, though, of course, I hold an opinion which I should be loath to express. I will confine myself to the facts. When you—eloped is, I believe, the technical expression—with Mrs. Clayton's daughter, she came up to town and saw me. She was quite dazed—stunned—by what she termed the catastrophe. I will admit that she seemed to regard your action with a horror which, bad as it was, appeared to me exaggerated, seeing that you had repaired your fault, as far as it could be repaired, by rapid marriage. She bitterly blames herself for having so far relaxed her vigilance as to make the meeting between yourself and our ward possible, but the extraordinary, if I may say so, the indecent rapidity with which these events took place made it impossible for her to 'do her duty' as she expressed it. What may have been that duty, and what the views entertained by herself, and by the late Professor Barrowdale as to her daughter's future may be, I cannot conjecture, nor did she enlighten me, but I gathered that she had solemnly sworn to prevent her daughter's marriage if it were possible, by the revelation of certain facts known only to herself and the late Professor. Of what these may have been I have no idea, but I gather that they are contained in a written statement which it becomes my duty to deliver to you. I saw her no more after this interview, but I went down to Cosmopoli to see after her affairs and to attend the inquest."

"The inquest!"

"Yes—you have not seen the papers this morning?"

"No—I arrived last night, and came straight here this morning."

"It took place yesterday, and her remains were buried in the Parish Churchyard yesterday afternoon. It was her wish that neither you nor her daughter should see her again—she was right—it was no sight for a young woman who expects to become a mother."

"Then you know?"

"Yes. One moment. I learned from her servant that on receipt of a letter from our ward in which she announced her condition Mrs. Clayton spent two days without moving from her chair, refusing to eat, or to see such neighbours as she had admitted to a slight acquaintance. On the morning of the third day the servant entering the sitting-room which this unhappy lady had not left, found her lying upon the divan which was soaked in her blood. She had cut her throat—inexpertly—with a common penknife; she must have bled slowly to death, the windpipe was not severed, and the jugular vein only just sufficiently wounded to allow the blood to escape—comparatively slowly. She had left a letter for me which you had better read."

He handed me a sheet of paper scrawled over with incoherent sentences. It said:—

I cannot face it, I am a coward—I knew I should be when the time came. I ought to have—but I had no chance. I am going to kill myself. I cannot face Uniqua, she must never know. I promised Paul B. that when a man wanted to marry her I would give him the papers. I had no time—if I had had time I know I could not. Mr. Magley must see them, no one else, not even you. You have them, the packet I gave you when Paul B. died. He will understand. What he will do—I forgive him, it wasn't his fault, it was my fault, he will understand when he reads. God help him—and her. *It must not be.*

URSULA CLAYTON.

"What does it mean?" I asked in a voice which I hardly recognized as my own.

"I do not know. But, Professor Magley, I own that I am terrified, and that I am deeply sorry for you. Paul Barrowdale was a strange man. There were episodes in his earlier life that no one knew about—and what I could guess from collateral evidence and an occasional hint which he dropped, appalled me, hardened as I am by a long professional career to the wilder aberrations of the human mind. Not that Paul Barrowdale was mentally affected—no one was ever more sane, but—he indulged what seemed to me to be terrible and morbid curiosities. Though my views as to your conduct remain unaltered, believe me, I am deeply sorry for you, for I fear that the punishment of your crime—I put it as high as that—may be almost more than any human being should be called upon to bear. Mind! I know nothing, I can only guess, and my brain reels when I allow myself to wander into conjecture. I will now give you the packet of papers to which Mrs. Clayton refers in her letter. I had some difficulty in keeping them from the Coroner on the grounds of professional confidence, and that the papers were not hers but Barrowdale's, and consequently the property of yourself and me as his Executors."

458

And with that the lawyer handed me a large square envelope sealed at every flap with Paul Barrowdale's private seal.

"If I may add a word of advice," continued he, "I would earnestly beg you not to open this envelope until you and your wife are settled in whatever house you have provided, or will provide, for her. Until that is done you will require all your presence and concentration of mind. I will not hide from you the fact that these incidents are likely to have a significant influence upon your career and position in the University."

My mouth was dry as a morphinomaniac's—I felt deathly cold to the tips of my fingers and toes. I felt that my world was collapsing and that I was being buried in the wreck and ruin of forces of which I was utterly ignorant.

I hardly know how I got back to Uniqua. Fortunately she was quite calm, and showed no curiosity as to my co-trustee. A few days passed during which I went down to Cosmopoli and took a small furnished house in the town, and instinctively I engaged the girl who had been in Mrs. Clayton's service to come and attend to us. Whether it was an effect of the nervous tension in which I was living, the sense of impending horror—conscience if you will—I do not know, but it seemed to me as if the few acquaintances whom I met looked curiously, and askant upon me, avoided me rather. My one object now was to get settled, and to know the worst.

I brought Uniqua down to Cosmopoli, where she took to her new abode like a cat to a new and comfortable basket. She never mentioned her mother—my precautionary warning to the servant not to go into details with the ineradicable gusto of her class was unnecessary. Uniqua did not go out at all, she lay most of the day on the divan which I had installed in conformity with what I knew to be her inclination, and did not appear to notice that in these days passion was utterly dead within me. At night she curled up by my side with her arms and legs wound round me as if I had been a sister to her, and slept peacefully whilst I lay awake listening to the University clocks and praying for daylight.

I put off the opening of Paul Barrowdale's envelope from day to day—*I was afraid!* I told myself that I must get my nerves into stable condition before I undertook the perusal of—what?

The time came however when I pulled myself together and determined to solve the mystery, and one evening—it was about a month ago—when Uniqua had gone to bed I broke the seals. I read. And all the time—continuously it seemed to me, the University clocks cut off and flung into 'the rag-bag of the past, section after section of my life.

The Manuscript of Paul Barrowdale.

This must be written. Some day a man may want to marry Uniqua, *and he must know.* I am sorry for him, whoever he may be, but he must know. With an introduction setting forth the physiological researches which have led to the terrible position of affairs here recorded, I will set down the facts in narrative form.

The study of the physiological phenomena of gestation and reproduction, and the evolution of genera and species has occupied my mind almost exclusively during the whole of my career. Closely connected with this question are the remarkable experiments (and their results) upon the artificial fertilization of parthenogenetic—or to use Lankester's preferable "impaternate"—eggs, carried out by Jacques Loeb, Bataillon, Deslages, and others. The outcome of their researches has seemed to prove incontestably that the function of the male spermatozoön in the fertilization of the female ovum is, in the first place, purely mechanical. They have fertilized and brought up to a pronounced stage of development the larva, and even to relative maturity, parthenogenetic (impaternate) eggs of Echinoderms and Batrachians, by means of artificial stimuli, such as hypertonic solutions, pricking with a fine needle, brushing with camel-hair brushes, to cite in a generalized form only a few of the methods employed in the laboratories of Science. Those who would know more of this are referred to the many papers published on the subject in scientific journals, and of late in the text-books. We start therefore from the conclusion that the action of the spermatozoön is primarily mechanical; it merely perforates and excites the ovum, and "sets it going," so to speak, and may therefore be replaced by artificial and mechanical means.

This being so, we may turn to the theory which deeply occupied the mind of Alphonse Milne-Edwards during the later years of his life. The question arises, why should there be any limits to the possibility of miscegenation? We know that, within a genus, allied species can breed together, as for example a horse with a donkey, a tiger with a jaguar, a fox with a dog—instances might be largely multiplied. But genera cannot breed with genera, as for example a dog with a cat, a horse with a hyena, or an elephant with a rhinoceros—to carry it to the highest point, a man with a mare, a woman with a dog. Why not? If the action of the male spermatozoön is mainly mechanical, why not? This was the problem which occupied the mind of Milne-Edwards and he discussed it with Ray Lankester shortly before his death, and Lankester has recorded his impressions of the discussion in one of his later volumes of collected scientific essays. I will transcribe here his account of the matter. He says:—

"He (Milne-Edwards) held it to be probable, as many physiologists would agree, that the fertilization of the egg of one species by the sperm of another, even a remotely related one, is ultimately prevented by a chemical incompatibility—chemical in the sense that the highly complex molecular constitution of such bodies as the anti-toxins and serums with which physiologists are beginning to deal is 'chemical'—and that all the other and secondary obstacles to fertilization can be overcome or evaded in the course of experiment. He proposed to inject one species with 'serums' extracted from the other, in such a way as seemed most likely to bring the chemical state of their reproductive elements into harmony, that is to say, into a condition in which they should not be actively antagonistic but admit of fusion and union. He proposed, by the exchange of living and highly organised fluids (by means of injection or transfusion) between and male and a female of separate species, to assimilate the chemical constitution of one to that of the other, and thus probably so to affect their reproductive elements that the one tolerate and fertilize the other."

In this case, observe that the influence of the male spermatozoön would be more than merely mechanical, the male would transmit his physical characteristics to the zygote—the embryothus called into existence. When the Sea-urchin's (*Echinus*) eggs to which I have referred above, are pierced (as is done in laboratory experiments), by the sperm filaments of Feather-star (*Comatula*) introduced for the purpose in another series of experiments, the sperm filaments pierce the egg-coat but contribute no substance to the embryo into which the egg develops. They merely "stimulate" it and set changes going. But if physiological technique could be perfected to such a point as to harmonize the fluids of the Feather-star with those of the Sea-urchin we should, or might, get a hybrid between Comatula and Echinus.

To adumbrate is at once an ultimate result to be aimed at. How often we find a splendid young woman married to a physically perfect young man, keenly anxious to have babies and carrying out to the full their privileges towards that end—but they remain childless. It is clear that their serums are toxic to one another. The man has a passing affair with a servant-girl or shop-assistant, and she immediately has a baby; the woman gives herself sporadically to a lover and immediately conceives: they have found their natural "affinity." There is in my opinion a great future in store for the bold surgeon or physiologist who will rectify matters in these "sterile" marriages, by bringing the husband and wife into a condition of mutual equilibrium by injection, inoculation or transfusion as suggested by Milne-Edwards.

How is this to be done, and how are the facts to be established? The answer comes to us from the Physiologist's Laboratory, and from the clinic. How often one reads in the newspapers, and even in novels, of devoted friends who have offered themselves, when a comrade is suffering from severe hæmorrhage (and in

462

other circumstances), for transfusion of blood. Sometimes we are told that in spite of the heroism of the friend, the patient has died—in nine cases out of ten it is, or was, because of that heroic gift of the friend; the patient has been killed, as surely as if the operating surgeon had blown out his brains. The War-hospitals of 1914-18 afforded us, first examples, then experiments, and at last lessons, which, once learned, have abolished the grave danger attending transfusion of blood from one human being to another. It has been established that in this matter the human subject is divided into four classes, between which phenomena are varied. If a drop of blood from the donor and recipient are mixed upon a microscope slide, the corpuscles either swim about freely together in the mixed serum—in which case the operation may be safely performed—or, haemolysis (agglutination) takes place. The corpuscles "clot" together, and we know that, if the operation is proceeded with, the recipient will be almost immediately killed. Before the dawn of this knowledge, how many patients may have fallen victims to the "heroism" of a toxic friend? To make this matter clearer, if you are not already familiar with it, I will reproduce here the diagram from Back and Edward's *Textbook of Surgery* (p.79):—

	Serum			
	1	2	3	4
Corpuscules 1	o	+	+	+
2	o	o	+	+
3	o	+	o	+
4	o	o	o	o

In the case marked "+" agglutination takes place. In the cases marked "o" no agglutination takes place. Thus it will be seen that the blood of group 4 may safely be given to *any* recipient—they are the "universal donors." The serum of group 1 does not agglutinate when mixed with that of any of the others—they are the "universal recipients." But give the blood (say) of group 3 to a patient of group 2 and you will kill the patient.

In the case of the sterile marriages a simple blood test of this kind will establish the facts upon which the surgeon may safely proceed.

You will wonder—whoever you are, who is destined to read this manuscript—why I have delayed my narrative by this long scientific introduction. It is in the nature of an "*apologia*," in the classical sense of the word, for what follows.

As a young man, and beyond that time, I made many experiments to prove the truth of this theory—many of which were entirely successful. I produced hybrids between widely separated genera, which often shocked even myself. I did not dare to publish my researches to the world, the time was not ripe—the scientific outlook was not yet sufficiently broad. Negligent as I was, almost to the point of fearlessness, of public opinion, I shrank from the howls of ignorant rage which would have greeted the publication of my results. The anti-vivisection mania was at its height. Foul libels upon the earnest workers at physiological research found ready publication in the Press, and it was tacitly understood among physiologists that our experiments must for the most part be kept to ourselves. University authorities looked ever with an anxious eye upon the biological laboratories, ever anticipating the eruption of some sensational scandal or subversive theory, which would rouse a storm of ill-informed invective against the scientific teaching of the Universities. But in my private laboratory—which became a veritable zoological garden—I never relaxed my efforts.

You will not be surprised—even though you be shocked—at what I am going to say next. I looked forward, as the crowning experiment of my career, to the production of a hybrid between one of the higher forms of the Animal world—and Man. You must realise my position. The sexual union of human beings and animals is, no doubt properly, shuddered at, as perhaps the foulest form of unnatural crime. It figures in our books of jurisprudence under the name of "Bestiality," a felony punishable until comparatively recent years with death, and actually with penal servitude for life. How could a man in my position put himself into the power of a man who would lend himself to so "filthy" an experiment? The widely varying forms of Sodomy were looked upon as "aberrations," but were none the less punished by long terms of imprisonment, but Bestiality was regarded as an even lower and more revolting form of vice. The accomplice would necessarily be of the lowest order of criminal, and one would have laid himself open to everlasting blackmail. The suggestion is obvious that I might have been an active participator in the "experiment." I will only say that my whole soul revolted from the idea with shuddering disgust, and I should—to put it on no higher grounds—have been physically impotent in approaching the subject from a personal point of view. I read the horrible treatise on the subject of Dubois-Dessaules published in 1705, and my gorge rose at the long catalogue of horrors he had resuscitated from the Morgue of forgotten criminal records.

Bestiality, as a crime, dates from the highest antiquity. In the more outspoken early editions of our Bible it is indicated, *haud incerta voce*, as rife among the Jews both male and female, and the references to it in Exodus and Leviticus are explicit.[1] In Mythology it appears as a common ruse among Gods, who appear to have found it easier to seduce the daughters of men metamorphosed as animals, than clothed in their normal and god-like attributes; the legends of Phoebus and the Lesbian Issa, of Pasiphaë, of Leda, of Io, are prominent examples among the Metamorphoses of Ovid. In the Middle Ages the Devil is constantly taking the form of a goat for the purposes of sexual connexion with reputed Witches. The work of Boguet upon the Sorcerers (1607) teems with examples, and gives categoric instances of women who have been fecundated by dogs, whilst the laborious compilation of Dubois-Dessaules runs to 450 pages of revolting record. The works of Voltaire bristle with instances on record of the resultant birth of the monsters. In India, sculptures on the Temples of Shiva, especially at Orissa, represent continually the sexual conjugation of women with apes, dogs and other animals. The Criminal Codes of Prussia, Germany

---

1 Exodus, XXII. 19. Leviticus XVIII. 24 and XX. 15, 16.

and the United States recognise the crime, that of Pope John XIII provided for its "accommodation" but a fine of 250 livres. The historians Aelian and Athenaeus cite numerous instances as a mere matter of record, and as lately as 1882 Lacassagne has produced a work *La Criminalité chez les Animaux*. As active or passive agents, human beings form a long procession down the records of Jurisprudence, and the work upon the subject of Tardieu is well-known to Pathologists, Alienists and Jurists. As a rule the crime was included under the general heading of "Sodomy," but the earlier jurists drew a sharp distinction, e.g. A. de Liguori who gives the definition "*Sodomia, i.e. cum persona ejusdem sexus; et Bestialitas, i.e. concubitus cum bestia.*"

Bestiality as a deliberate inclination is classed by Krafft-Ebing with Sadism, Flagellation, Exhibitionism, Necrophily, and Homosexuality under the general heading of Paresthesia, and the scientific attitude towards these aberrations may be summed up as follows:—Too many different factors concur to produce races for it to be possible to unify, to codify, human morality. Heredity, climate, education, social conditions, riches or poverty, each of these contributes a different factor. The Human Creature is not always master of his functions, his existence depends upon inimical or allied factors against which it is sometimes impossible for him to re-act. Therefore, in the face of the worst turpitudes of human nature, known to us as crime or vice, the Scientist does not protest, he merely seeks for the causes and tabulates the effects.

Undoubtedly the dominating factor is heredity, and Tardieu goes even further than this in ascribing such aberrations to atavism, and we find the records of such factors in every corpus of legend and tradition from the Golden Ass of Apuleius down to the bestialities of the Arabian Nights; from the references of Nicolas de Venette to those of Montaigne, and of Balzac, of Armand Charpentier and others. Among savage races we have the amazing records of Paul du Chaillu dating from comparatively modern times. With loathsome "romances" of de Musset (Gamiani), Bishops and of other Pornographers we have not to

466

concern ourselves. This rapid historic review has seemed to be necessary as an indication of the lines along which this horrible subject may be pursued and studied, should it be required to do so.

There have been many cases recorded of Bestiality in which women have been the passive human participants—they in fact constitute the majority of recorded instances, obviously by reason of the fact that, in such cases, the reasoning human participant is not called upon for action. These are no less horrifying than the others, but it was clear that to find such a woman one would have to ply a muck-rake among the ranks of the lowest, most abandoned, and depraved members of the prostitute class—one had heard of such things in the brothels of Paris, Berlin and Naples. I shrank from the bare idea of encountering such creatures. I had experimented successfully in artificial fecundation with the lower animals—but when I considered the possibility of carrying this higher, I found myself confronted with the same insuperable feeling of horror and repulsion. But none the less, theoretically, the thing became an *idée fixe* in my mind—an *ultima ratio* probably never destined to get beyond the theoretical stage.

This brings me down to a moment—now fourteen years ago—which, in the success of achievement, has cast a shadow over the whole of my remaining life.

I had read so far in Barrowdale's manuscript, and at this point I sprang to my feet, overcome with a hideous nausea; I felt that I was fainting from sheer terror and apprehension. What was I going to read? I put down the MS., took a stiff dose of brandy and walked out into the night air, to think, to recover my senses, to overcome the horror that was gripping me. I had almost determined to read no further, when a fearful thought crossed my mind. It will probably have crossed the reader's. I tried to put it from me in vain—it simply tortured me physically—*but I knew I must read on*. After an hour I returned home. I crept up to our bedroom. Uniqua was sleeping peacefully, her delicious smile just parting her perfect lips. I reassured myself for a moment, and then fell back again into my previous mood of terror and consternation. Whatever I was to read, I had brought it upon myself, and I went back to the damned MS.

※

(The MS. Continued.)

I used to get the animals which served me for my research work down at the Docks—from the successors of the renowned Jamrach. They thought, and I did not undeceive them, that I was an agent of the Zoological Society. One day I visited my purveyor in answer to a note informing me that he had a remarkable splendid specimen of *Felis jubata*, the Indian Hunting Leopard or Cheetah, an animal I had long desired to possess, on account of its curious capacity for being domesticated and kept as a pet. It was a most beautiful beast, a male about a year old which had been bred in captivity, and was already as docile and as responsive to caress as any ordinary cat. I bought him and made arrangements for his transfer to my house in the country where I kept my creatures. The few colleagues who were admitted to a knowledge of my experiments called it my "Island of Dr. Moreau"—from the late H.G. Wells's dreadful book of that title. Not, however, that my work had anything even remotely in common with the horrors suggested in that remarkable work. By the use of general and local anaesthetics my animals were never alarmed, or indeed conscious that they were what the Anti-Vivisectionists would have called "Martyrs to Science"—they were a very happy family, and, in point of fact, when they had spent their allotted time with me and had bred the desired hybrid, or failed to do so, in ease and comfort, I transferred them to Regent's Park. No animal ever died under my care or treatment, except from pneumonia or some other disease incidental to our climate, or to the artificial conditions of its existence.

468

I was returning late in the afternoon up Ratcliffe Highway, speculating upon the motley crowd of seafaring folk of all nations that throng that historic thoroughfare, and the degraded types of harlot who ply their wretched trade among them, when one of these, giving my arm a gentle nip as she passed me, said, in a half-whisper:—

"D'you want a naughty girl?"

I looked at her as I shrugged her off. She was a finely made, bold-looking strumpet, younger in years and it seemed to me of a higher racial type than the generality of the local consorority. Very fair, neatly though shabbily dressed, with large wistful grey eyes, and teeth that were both clean and regular. Her appearance surprised me. My short scrutiny encouraged her and she said rapidly:

"I'm the naughtiest girl in the Highway, and I like old gentlemen. I'll do anything, show you anything you like. Don't you want to come with me? I'll astonish you."

"Go to the devil," I said brutally, "or I'll give you in charge."

"All right, Governor," she replied. "I'm going. *Au revoir, mon ami*," and before I could recover from my surprise at her accent, which was perfect, she flung herself on the rails in front of a rapidly approaching tram-car.

Deeply shocked, and responding to an irresistible instinct, I flung myself after her, caught her by one ankle, and jerked her free of the lines. The driver had applied his brakes, but the front wheels crushed her hat. It was the nearest thing possible. I hauled her on to the pavement and immediately a dense crowd of loafers, seafarers and street-walkers collected round us. She had fainted.

"Give us a little room," I said, "I am a doctor. Does anybody know anything about her?"

"Know anything?" ejaculated a sailor, "yes we all know all there is to know, and that's too much—the dirty bitch."

"Oh lor!" chimed in a loathsome and pustular female who had forced her way to the centre of the crowd, "the gent's in luck, ain't he? He's got Menagerie Sal!"

"Whatever she is," I replied hotly, "she can't be left here. Where does she live?"

"Anywhere you like to take her," said another Brute. "Here, get up Sal!" and he kicked her in the side.

I sprang up and would have collared the beast but, perhaps fortunately, the invariable and imperturbable policeman appeared among us, and the crowd fell back.

"Who—what is she?" I asked the man in blue.

"One of the worst, sir, about the worst I reckon." The woman was coming round. "Here, get up Sal," continued the constable, "and go home, if you've got one—or I'll take you."

"I am a doctor," I said quickly, and gave him my card. "Whatever she is, I can't leave her alone in this state—Help me to take her in here."

There was an eating-house just where this occurrence had taken place, and, aided by the constable, I got the woman inside and sat her down in a corner box. The crowd dispersed. As they did so, a draggled harlot called out:—

"The old gent's in for it all right—good luck to him!" And the strange sobriquet was bandied from foul mouth to foul mouth—"Menagerie Sal—Menagerie Sal!"

I sent for some brandy and sat, looking at her as she gradually recovered her self-possession, without saying a word. At last she gave utterance to a short hoarse laugh, and said:—

"What the hell did you do it for? You told me to go there, and I tried to. Yer don't *want* me; what did yer stop me for?"

"True," I said, "I don't want you, but I couldn't let you kill yourself before my eyes. I'm a man, not a brute."

"All men are brutes," she said defiantly.

There was a most extraordinary struggle of accents in her speech. She spoke the low cockney vernacular with fluency and emphasis, but occasional words, intonations, seemed to jar against the vulgarity of the rest of it.

"Not all," I replied. "Myself for instance. Now look here. I'll turn your own question on you—what did *you* do it for?"

"What's that to you?"

"It is a good deal. You are too young and healthy to want to die, however beastly your life may be. Whilst there's life there's hope. You are worth saving."

"Saving! My Gawd! let me up and out of this. You're a bloody gospeller, that's what you are. You're going to talk about the Temple of my Body, and Gawd and that. I ain't a Temple, it's a Cesspool, and there ain't no Gawd. Let me go!"

"I am not a gospeller, and I don't want to preach to you; but I'm a doctor and I want to know what it all means."

"It means that I'm down and out—I've stuck it long enough. You heard what they call me 'Menagerie Sal' (she pronounced 'Menagerie' perfectly) I'm too low down for any self-respecting whore to speak to—I can't get a lodging except in a Chinks' Dive, and I can't get a man unless he's a stranger in these parts—that's why I clawed you—or a right down utter beast of a heathen."

"You are in a wildly hysterical state—that's evident. Now look here, I've saved your life and you belong to me until I've done with you." The wretched creature turned on a 'professional' smile. "Don't misunderstand me—I'm not going to have you, but I'm going to make you eat something—hungry?"

"I don't know—I ought to be. I know I've been empty as a drum for two days. I wonder what you re getting at?"

"Nothing in particular," I replied, "but you are going to have some food. We can't sit here and do nothing for the good of the house."

I ordered some food, which arrived, coarse, but plain and good, and she ate sparingly—and with a strange refinement contrasting remarkably with her vocabulary. When she would eat no more, I lit a pipe and gave her a cigarette. She had calmed down.

"Now look here," I said again; "do you feel anything like gratitude to me for what I've done!"

"No, I don't," she replied; "but that doesn't matter. There are other ways. I'll do it when there's no interfering Toff around."

"No you won't. You are going to promise me not to do it again."

She looked me straight in the face without speaking, her chin resting on her hand, puffing cigarette smoke quietly, so as not to reach me. At last I said, "Well?" She replied, "Shut up! I'm thinking."

"A penny for your thoughts!"

"I'll take the penny. I want one. You couldn't make it a shilling, I suppose?"

I laid a sovereign on the table. "Will that help you out a bit?" I asked.

"Haven't seen one for years. Ta, Governor." And she deftly slipped the coin into her stocking and resumed her scrutiny of my face.

"You haven't told me your thoughts—and I've paid," I suggested.

And then I experienced the shock which Balaam must have felt when his Ass addressed him. She took her cigarette from her lips and said quite slowly and without a trace of cockney accent:—

"You look like an intelligent man—I should say a scientist of sorts—not many doctors are scientists down this way. How can you be such an idiot as to ask me to promise you not to do it again? Do you remember what that girl, Wade, in 'Little Dorrit' said to the champion ass Clennam? (by the way I've often wondered if Dickens knew he was describing a Lesbian)—you know—about people who are all the time coming to meet us from strange places along strange roads, and what they'll do to us, and we to them will all be done? Whether I do it again or not has nothing to do with me, it depends at the moment upon you, or rather upon the puny little part you happen to be playing in the inexorable progress of inevitable consequences."

I was dumbfounded! It was my turn to sit and gaze at her. "This way and that, dividing the swift mind"—and she, taking up my case from the table where I had laid it, took a new cigarette, lit it, said "Thank you", and resumed her position, her chin on her hands, looking at me.

At last I said: "How in God's name have you come to this?— you are too good—"

"Oh! Don't begin that—that's what that the Missioners to Fallen Women begin with. And don't bring in God—unless you feel the need of him for conversational emphasis—or conven-ience, like Xerxes at the end of a rhyming alphabet."

"Let's put it on the lowest grounds then. You are a woman of some education evidently—and, permit me to say—of some refinement. You are too good for Ratcliffe Highway. If prostitu-tion is your vocation in life, why not practise in the West End? Why not the Empire or the Alhambra?" (The "promenades" at these places had not been closed in those days).

"Never mind when or where I started—that's none of your business. I came to grief on a P. and O. steamer—I'd had lots of men—some of the best; but coming home once from China I fell madly in love with a Lascar. A common ship's hand—a bronze god. I wanted him—and I seduced him, it didn't take much doing—I had some money then—but I was ashamed (I was capable of it then) to take him up West. I joined him down here. I used to go up West myself sometimes—no one here knew it—when I was just longing for love—real love—a woman."

"A woman?"

"Yes—for a real lover, or mistress. Oh! don't look shocked; if you're a doctor you know women can love a woman better than any man on earth."

"Then—among other things—you are a—"

"Lesbian—don't be afraid to say it."

"But I don't understand how you—"

"It's easy enough. Men don't hear of the brothels where women can have anything they want and can pay for, from a vicious flapper of fifteen to an insatiable Messalina of fifty. The only difference between those, and—the others—is that all the 'staff' are amateurs; some shop-girls and clerks, but mostly gen-tlewomen. You've never heard of No. 100, Canterbury Square have you?—no, it's kept pretty quiet—but I didn't go there, I preferred to find my own romances."

"Romances!"

"Yes—can't you imagine the delight, after the brutes down here, of meeting eyes in an omnibus, of a thigh pressed against yours, of a foot that touches yours as if by accident? Of see-ing a pretty shop-girl go scarlet when you squeeze her hand as she hands you a parcel? A few ordinary words—a suggestion of meeting again, and then tea together somewhere, and, later, dinner and a night spent in love that leaves you shattered and sleepy and dreaming for days?"

"It seems horrible to me."

"That's because you are a man and don't know what love—really exquisite love—means. Very few men do—but when they do they're divine!"

"But did you not horrify them—at first?"

"Never. We know one another in a flash. The most wonderful love I ever had was a girl of nineteen—the daughter of a peer—Oh! She had been to a good school—a finishing school—it finished her, I can tell you. I got to know her people. Oh! yes, I can be a gentlewoman when I like, and I took her away into the country for a week. I bet you she remembers it, as I do. And then—back to my brute. He'd have been after me otherwise (he thought I'd gone to get more money), and then there would have been hell—and blackmail. So long as my money lasted we lived in a fairly decent set of rooms, and we had a wonderful time, but my God! he was a brute; he thrashed me sometimes—I loved it. And vicious!—I don't want to make your hair stand on end. I'd read a lot of filthy books here and abroad and I thought I knew what vice was. The things he did to me—and that he made me do! I tell you the Five Cities of the Plain rolled into one were a Trappist Monastery compared to our flat. And his friends that he brought to me—and their animals—you people west of Chancery Lane can't dream what are the vices among the Lascars, Chinamen, Malays, half-breed Spanish-Americans, Niggers, Mulattos of all kinds. One didn't know at the end of an orgy whether one was a girl, or a boy, or a beast. Lucky animals can't breed with humans."

A strange, bitter smile flickered over her lips.

"Now my friend," she continued recklessly, "you know what you've 'saved'. You heard what they called me—Ménagerie Sal."

Literally my hair did stand on end. At least, I felt a cold contraction of the scalp, and my sight vacillated.

"This is too horrible. How could you—why did you—stand it?"

"I liked it."

"What?"

"I don't want you to take home any illusions about a repentant sinner. And I've paid for it—my God! I have paid for it. When my money was gone—I had quite a good deal and it lasted a longish time, I sank, if one could sink below that—but one is always comparatively up, when one can pay; I sank lower and lower, the most vicious of the Scum knew of me all over the world, and came to me like filings to a magnet. It was too late to get away. I was 'Ménagerie Sal'—the Darling of the Beasts—human and otherwise—and that's where I am now. I told you the truth just now when I said that no self-respecting whore would be seen speaking to me—and if any clean white man showed any signs of wanting me, they are all round me and on to him—at once—telling him things—mostly true—and what's more, none of them would go with a man if they knew he'd been with me. You know there are grades of respectability even among harlots—I am afraid I am shockingly *mal vue* in the oldest profession in the world, even as practiced in Ratcliffe Highway! It is not often that I have enough to eat—I shouldn't be allowed in here if you hadn't brought me. Now you know why I am going to kill myself. If I don't, one of the brutes will kill me some day. See this scar?" and she pulled her blouse away upon her shoulder, "that was done by a sort of Gorilla—I was trying to get away from him. So I am going to 'out it'—don't you think I'm right?"

I could not answer. I was paralysed with horror, especially by the calm manner with which she spoke of these unspeakable atrocities. I harked back, and repeated in an undertone:—

"You like it!"

"Yes—sometimes—that's the truth. But I'm afraid of the end of it—afraid!" and she covered her face with her hands and shuddered.

I sat looking at her—at last, as though she were a curious pathological case in a mental Hospital. And then a horrible but irresistible thought came into my mind. The Cheetah!

＊

I began, my heart beating violently, to feel my way.

"What a life!" I said, "but I confess you interest me dreadfully."

"Do I?" she said suddenly looking up; "Aren't you disgusted?" Then she gave a short laugh and said: "I wonder! Well—I expect you'd be as bad as any of them if you had a chance—if the truth were only known—"

"And suppose I were?"

"Oh! I shouldn't mind—I've been through too much. But I *am* surprised—you with your solemn learned old air."

I thought rapidly, and then, to my eternal misery, I made up my mind. Such a chance could never occur again. I said:—

"Supposing I *were* a worn out old rake, with un-nameable curiosities? Jaded with all ordinary vices? And supposing I said to you, 'Come away from here, come and live in the country. I'll settle a sum of money upon you which will keep you from want in the event of my death. I *am* a Scientist—a vicious one, if you like. I should want to try all kinds of experiments on you.' What would you say?"

"I'd say, as the Yanks do: 'Put it there, Governor.' You can't do anything worse to me than I've had done to me already. And I'd love to be away from all this mob. When do we start?"

We talked on for half-an-hour and then I left her. She gave me an address to write to—at a *Poste Restante*.

A month later she was installed in a cottage in the village where I then had my Research Laboratory. She had no desire to mix with the people of the place, but for the information of the public and the parson, she gave herself out to be a young widow. The name she adopted was Mrs. Clayton. Of course it was immediately observed that she had come there at my instigation, and that when I was at the Laboratory she was constantly at my house. They drew their own—the inevitable—conclusions, but, as I had steadily repelled any attempt on the part of the aborigines to establish social relations with me of any kind, this did not trouble us.

Ursula Clayton left behind her in the parlieus of the Docks every trace of her "professional" career, accent, vocabulary and manner. When my solicitor (who with my assistant Rex Magley will be trustees of my will) had proved to her that a certain income was settled upon her in any event, she abandoned all reserve with me; hitherto our relations had been a trifle strained; she seemed unable to realize that I was determined to act in her permanent interest, and was not merely amusing myself with her for a time. She became a really delightful companion; I was a bachelor, and never at any time an Anchorite, and the society of Ursula Clayton was interesting—and satisfying in every respect. I gradually came to know her history, which, though it does not concern this narrative, is illuminating as an explanation of her abnormal sexuality.

In the eighties of the last century, there are still people old enough to remember, a hot wave of what are known as Unnatural Vices almost openly and unblushingly practiced, swept over our English Society. It was the outcome of the Æsthetic Craze, intimately associated with the name of Oscar Wilde, who ultimately, in the nineties, paid for everyone, and subsequently died overwhelmed with public infamy, and the private admiration of the few. It became a matter of ordinary conversation to discuss homosexual love affairs of men and women prominent in Society—especially of the latter. In a word, Sodomy and Lesbianism were—*sub rosâ*—fashionable. Pre-eminent among the male "perverts" was a well-known Peer of artistic taste and enormous wealth, at whose house in the county homosexualists of both sexes congregated, and where, as was averred, "orgies" took place that were spoken about with bated breath in the most fashionable boudoirs. Prominent in this society was a very high born dame indeed, in whose hands, or arms, no woman was safe, and she formed the centre of a Lesbian *côterie* which spread like a rodent ulcer into almost every class of society. It was in the unnatural order of things that the masculinity of the Lady, and the femininity of the Lord X—, should bring them closely together,

477

so closely indeed that, to the astonishment of the inverted world, Lady Z—gave birth to a child who was christened Ursula. This child was sent abroad, to be brought up in Italy. A respectable sum of money was "settled" for her maintenance and education which became hers absolutely on attaining her majority. With such an heredity it is not surprising that Ursula developed, early, a sexual precocity and *désinvolture*, which the settlement made upon her by her parents enabled her to gratify to the fullest extent of her inclination. She told me her early sexual history, which was amazing, but does not concern us, beyond what she told me in Ratcliffe Highway, and which I have already recorded. By the time she came to "our village" her fires were burning low, her sexuality was to a great extent satiated, and she showed no trace in her manner or proclivities of the storms which had disturbed her youth. She was a charming companion, an intelligent and well-educated friend, and a charming mistress.

And the Cheetah? We called him "Kumar". He settled down in our two houses as a great affectionate domestic pet. Sometimes, in passage between the two, led on a chain by Ursula, he terrified the inhabitants of the village, human and animal, but this was very seldom, and the villagers had grown accustomed to what was known as "the Professor's Zoo." The attachment between "Kumar" and Ursula became very close, and indeed I sometimes feared a precipitation of events, but Ursula was too keenly interested in my work to endanger the results by premature action. I conducted my experiment on the lines suggested by Milne-Edwards; it was nothing to inoculate Kumar under a local anæsthetic—he would never have dreamed of the possibility of being hurt by either of us.

The day arrived when the blood tests were wholly satisfactory. The serum of the one accommodated the corpuscles of the other without any trace of hæmolysis—and I left the rest to Ursula.

I do not know what I expected to be the outcome of this experiment. It was impossible to anticipate. As a practising surgeon

I was skilled in obstetrics and had no fear for the result, only an intense curiosity. If I expected anything, it was a queer little "monster," which I should allow to live long enough to be perfectly formed, and then "prepare" as a specimen, explaining its presence as an arrival from a native collector in India. At the end of only six months anticipation Ursula gave birth to one of the most perfectly formed little female children it has ever been my lot to look upon. She was remarkably furry, but new-born babies are often thus, and, as in the case of this child, they lose it in a month or two. I should mention, though it is not material, that I took a house on the South Coast for Ursula to await the event. I delivered her myself, and she brought the child, whom we had registered as of illegitimate birth under another name, and had baptized Uniqua—the only apposite name, it seemed to me—back to our village. There could not be any question of destroying so perfect a little specimen of humanity, and when Ursula returned with her, she "explained" her, when necessary as a foundling she had adopted from a workhouse on her travels.

(I will not try to set down here what were my thoughts as I read this frightful record. They are indescribable—it was all I could do to prevent myself burning the MS. and taking five grains of morphine on the spot. But I dared not do it. I had to read on, though it was now broad daylight.)

The child grew in beauty and charm, developing with a rapidity which amazed me. When she was two years old, Ursula Clayton left her cottage and came to live in the house near Cosmopoli where she now inhabits. After the birth of Uniqua I ceased my physiological experiments in this direction—I had been too successful—and dispersed my collection of animals. I was frankly terrified—and still am—at the success of my culminating effort. Uniqua is entirely human physically, but I constantly recognize the feline influence in little actions, tastes—in her whole mentality. *What will happen when she grows up?*—when her sexual life begins, when puberty asserts itself? I tremble to think. One thing is abundantly manifest, she must never be allowed to marry. What response would she make to the Mendelian Law? Her children—*would* they be children? The thought turns me cold. The one thing I can think of is that as soon as she reaches puberty she must be drastically operated upon—ovariotomy, hysterectomy—the whole thing. But how explain the necessity? Would any surgeon in the world consent to "spay"—to sterilise—a perfectly healthy, apparently normal and beautiful young girl? I doubt it very much. There is only one course to be pursued, but it is one which will shatter and ruin my life and Ursula's. So long as we two, and we alone, know the awful secret of Uniqua's birth, our minds may remain easy, and we can face the world with nothing more against us than the tittle-tattle of our neighbours, who may look upon Ursula as the faithful mistress of a faithful bachelor Professor. Indeed I often regret that I did not marry Ursula before I brought her to Cosmopoli—I should then have been able to keep closer watch over Uniqua, and carry out myself what I now set down. If any man ever desires to marry Uniqua, *he must be told the whole truth*. It will be a frightful thing to do and it might have to be done over and over again! It would end by all coming out. But if, in spite of this stunning revelation, any man is bold enough to persist in his desire to marry her, he must be warned to take every possible and known precaution against having children by her.

I may die before this happens, and then—God help her—this awful duty will devolve upon Ursula Clayton. It is with this in view that I have written out this MS. in all its revolting details, concealing nothing, glossing over nothing. Ursula shall do all she can to discourage suitors, but should one present himself persistently, *he must be told*.

I have told him.

PAUL BARROWDALE.
August 19—.

480

✳

(Following upon this apparent termination of his MS. came another entry dated ten years later.)

✳

I reopen this Record which I ardently hoped I should never peruse again. But it is imperatively necessary. At the age of eleven Uniqua has passed the arrival of puberty and is a fully developed and very beautiful girl, having passed through a stage in which, though beautifully formed, she was a sallow, swarthy, repellent little girl. Her whole body is classically perfect, and as far as showing it to her mother and me is concerned, quite unashamed of her perfect nakedness. She is covered with the light "peach-bloom" down which makes many fair women so intensely attractive, but the down is a light tawny-orange colour, recalling the coat of poor Kumar (who died by my hand, deeply as I regretted the necessity, after her birth). The down is punctuated here and there, at more or less regular intervals, by small imperfect rings of a darker colour (that of her normal hair, though not so dark), which, to our instructed eyes, recall vividly the markings of Kumar's coat. The only idiosyncrasy which she exhibits beyond this is the extraordinary luxuriance of her axillary and pubic hair, which is beautifully grown, but phenomenal in such a young girl. She has another peculiarity which one cannot but recognise as hereditary. If she is unhappy, which is rare, or annoyed, which is rarer still, or if she is afflicted with any passing fit of childish naughtiness, all that is necessary is to insinuate our fingers into the thick curls under her arms and tickle and caress her like an animal. Her mood becomes serene at once, I hate to use the word (knowing what we do), but she positively "purrs" with contentment, and if the caress is gently prolonged she goes fast asleep.

The primary object of this post-scriptum is, however, to call attention to what is really a very serious matter. It is that at her

481

times of periodic disturbance, which take place, not monthly, but at intervals of three to four months, she is subject to what may rightly be called *oestrum*, a frenzy of sexual desire. Though she is technically quite ignorant of sexual matters, it appears in many ways, her beauty is greatly enhanced, her eyes become even finer than usual, her lips more crimson, and her nipples are in a constant state of erection and intense sensitiveness. She is restless and unsatisfied, and wants to go out and mix with people for no reason that she is aware of. As a rule she is self-contained and utterly indifferent to companionship, even to that of her mother. At these times, which are remarkably prolonged—often to a fortnight or three weeks—she must be very carefully watched, above all things she must not be allowed to get into contact with men; I am convinced, poor child, that it would be disastrous to her, and the terrible results I have hinted at in the record would almost certainly ensue. Ursula Clayton is alive to this, and I can rely upon her never to leave her alone in these circumstances. Her husband, should she ever have one, must also be warned of this danger.

I have warned him.

PAUL BARROWDALE.

May, 19—.

✳

It is as impossible for you, who read this, to imagine, as it is for me to describe, what I felt when I at last terminated the perusal of Barrowdale's MS. One amazing fact, one concerning which I had curiously enough evinced no curiosity, was that of her age. Comparing the dates of Barrowdale's Record and its postscript, it became clear, Uniqua was only thirteen years old. It was broad day when I went up to our bedroom. Uniqua had not moved, she lay with her head resting on her right arm, which had drawn her nightdress free of her right breast, which stood up inviting caress. I put my lips to it, and closed them in a long kiss—the delicate intoxicating perfume which I now could explain struck me more persistently than usual. Under my caress she awoke for a moment, and said, "Oh, you darling! then it wasn't a dream. Go on." And so fell asleep in my arms as she rolled over on to me, and slept until the servant brought our morning tea.

After breakfast I told her I had worked until morning and must go for a long walk to get the cobwebs out of my head. She said:—

"All right, so long as you don't ask me to go with you. I shall curl up on the divan and think about my baby."

I went out. Her baby! What would it be? Barrowdale and I had carried out a long series of Mendelian experiments—I could not blind myself to the probability; the inheritance of characteristics transmitted through the female line. That she would "throw back" (I shuddered at the thought) was practically a certainty—a foregone conclusion. There was nothing else for it—abortion is a hideous word, *but this child must not be born.* It must be got rid of at once—she was almost two months pregnant already—I shuddered at the thought of what even a miscarriage might bring to light. I knew that I had a terrible task before me, but I had to face it. How terrible it was I fortunately could not foresee, or what an effect my decision was to have upon both of us.

I tried to prepare the way by calling upon the doctor whom I had had in my mind as our "Family Physician", a good worthy soul and thoroughly conversant, as a result of long practise, with his job, which was to see people safely into and out of the world, instil common sense into their mothers in dealing with their childish ailments, and to comfort his adult patients by an assumption of knowledge of their "cases" which he was far from pretending, in ordinary conversation, to posses. I had been on terms of friendly social intercourse with him ever since my arrival in Cosmopoli, and I thought that I could count upon him to help me deal with my fearful problem with sympathy and tact. This was the one mistake that I have made throughout my trouble, a mistake which has rendered it necessary for me to be prepared for the worst—for scandal—for exposure, and possibly worse.

I had not realized and appreciated, though I had perceived unmistakable indications of, the feeling that existed in Cosmopoli with regard to my "abduction" of Uniqua and the suicide of Ursula Clayton, which was—in the absence of any possible explanation—the direct result of my action. Dr. Fisher received me with a demeanour which was distant, severe, and almost embarrassed, but though I felt this "in my bones" I persuaded myself that my condition of nervous strain led me to exaggerate the peculiar aloofness of his manner. I hastened to put our interview upon a semi-professional basis.

"I want to have a word with you," I said, "about my wife."

"Yes?" It should have been obvious to me that he was on his guard, and had no intention of meeting me half-way.

"She is very young—much younger indeed than I had any idea of when I married her."

"And yet, you, as Barrowdale's intimate friend, should have known. How old is she?"

I passed this question by, and said:—

"He never spoke to me of his relations with Mrs. Clayton, I only saw the child once before we met accidentally—and fell in love with one another."

He shrugged his shoulders slightly and looked away out of the window. I ought to have seen that he did not believe me.

"I am not satisfied about her health," I went on, blindly, "I have reason to suspect an endometrititis. Until this has been dealt with-surgically—I feel that she ought not to bear children."

He remained quite silent, and I proceeded.

"I do not know whether she would readily submit to examination, but I should like you to make it."

"You have reason to believe she is pregnant." It was a statement rather than a question.

"Yes. And if I am right I think that the pregnancy should be—avoided—for this time at least."

He rose from his chair and Walked to the window, where he remained silent for a minute or so—which seemed to me an eternity—and then turning round but not coming back to his seat, he said:—

"Professor Magley, I will be quite candid with you. You know—or should know if you do not, that there is a very strong feeling prevalent in this town with regard to your action in

484

taking this young girl away from her mother, a feeling which was greatly exacerbated by the terrible sequel which your action brought about. It is not my intention or inclination to sit in judgement upon you, your own conscience is probably dealing with the matter, and I do not envy you your reflections. But now you come to me, and in practically so many words you suggest that I should relieve you of immediate consequences and inconvenience by procuring abortion for you. Please understand me once and for all that I absolutely refuse to have any hand in the matter whatever. If your wife consults me I shall do my utmost to protect her by any means in my power from any attempt of the kind. And before we either of us say anything more—which we might subsequently regret—I think it better that this interview should come to an end. I advise you to forget it, but bear in mind that I shall not."

And he moved to the door which he opened. I can only say that I "slunk" out.

※

Well—I realized the colossal mistake I had made, and that if anything was to be done, I must depend solely upon myself—and upon Uniqua.

That evening she was lying in my arms on the divan, and, by the familiar resource of caressing her amid her wonderful axillary hair, I had got her into a condition of luxurious and almost passionate happiness. I opened the subject by saying:—

"Are you very keen to have this baby of yours?"

"Indeed, yes, how can you ask it? Imagine what it will be?"

Alas! my imagination was only too active, too precise, and too terrific. I went on:—

"I have been thinking, darling, that we are so intensely happy with one another, that it seems a pity to put a stop to it by having a child at once. Would it not be better for both of us if we waited a little—say a year, during which we can have one another all to ourselves? I am a little jealous of your baby, just at present, though in a year or so—"

"What do you mean?" she said, drawing a little away from me and looking at me, her beautiful eyes wide open, the pupils fully dilated, "We haven't waited—the baby is here."

"Well, hardly," I replied, trying to convey an impression that we were merely discussing a possibility of no great importance. "These things are easily rectified—avoided. Remember, I am a surgeon as well as a doctor of medicine and of science. I could put you right without any difficulty or danger, and practically without discomfort or disturbance to yourself."

She sprang to her feet. "What do you mean?" she repeated.

"Oh, a very simple matter. A drug, perhaps a very slight operation, and we should be as we were before, and could take our own time about having a child. This one—if it can be called a child yet—is, as it were, an unexpected, a premature, accident."

She stood looking at me, with an expression of savage loathing and horror. Her breasts heaved tumultuously, her lips were parted, not in a smile, tumultuously, but in a ghastly rictus, showing her prominent little canine teeth in an evil indescribable grin. Her fingers clawed at the joining of her wrapper which she pulled free from her breasts as if to give herself air, and then she said in a voice I had never heard before, a kind of hissing growl:—

"You—propose—to—me—to—kill—my—baby?"

"Oh! don't put it like that. I only mean—"

"You mean—you mean?—Oh! You brute—you beast—you devil!"

"Darling!" I sprang up and advanced towards her. She flung out her hands, catching me on the chest with such force that I lost my balance, and fell back on the divan. She took a step forward and stood over me.

"Don't touch me—don't come near me—never again—you murderer!"

And she fled from the room. I sprang up and followed her, but I was too late—she had gained our bedroom, slammed the door and locked it, and I heard her rush to the door of my dressing room and lock that also.

486

"Darling—listen!" I said as loud as I dared—on account of the servants—through the door, "It's all right. I didn't mean it. I promise not to speak of it again. Only come out—or let me in. I *must* speak to you. You have misunderstood me." I was in agony.

After a few minutes, during which I implored her to open the door, I heard her say, still in the raucous voice which had filled me with horror downstairs:—

"If I open the door for a moment and say something, will you promise me upon your honour as a man not to force your way into the room?"

There was no help for it. I promised. Then she opened the door. She had flung off her wrapper and stood, holding the door, clad only in a short *crêpe de chine* chemise, which had slipped down to her waist on one side, being held on the other by a shoulder ribbon. I had never seen her look so superb. And she said, hardly above a whisper:—

"If you force your way in here tonight, I will tear you with my nails. I will bite you—some way or other I will kill you. Perhaps to-morrow I may be able to bear to look at you. Now I must think—leave me alone with my baby."

And she closed the door again and locked it. I went downstairs. The whole horror of the situation burst upon me. *Uniqua had reverted to type.* She was no longer a girl—she was a Cheetah! The animal instinct fiercely awakened in defence of her young was aroused to its highest point. I did not attempt to blind myself to the fact—she had become dangerous. I foresaw a condition of things fraught with all the possibilities of appalling tragedy. To protect her unborn offspring, she was capable of anything—even of killing me. For a moment I wished she would, it would be a happy release for me, but afterwards? Regard being had to her "parentage" it was impossible to tell how long she would carry her young within her; would the period of her gestation be human, or feline? It depended, I felt, upon what was to be born. My scalp contracted with horror at the thought. One thing, and one thing only was clear to me—I must not allow the monster I anticipated to see the light—I must be no party to the perpetuation of a race of hybrid monsters, that might be frightful. And it came to this—I must take precautions that she did not kill me—*I must kill her*. And I loved her as no man has ever loved a woman before—utterly—blindly—and even at that supremely awful moment I desired her beautiful body. I was thirsty to caress—to have her.

I tried to sleep on the divan—worn out as I was—but sleep would not come. I tossed about all night, sometimes going out into the summer night to cool the fever which raged in every limb. I drank. I thought for a moment again of a hypodermic injection of morphia to dull my tortured senses—to forget for a while—but I feared what Uniqua might do if she found me insensible in her present mood. No—I must go through with it and keep my brain clear—my presence of mind at its highest pitch.

Next day Uniqua came down after lunchtime. She recoiled when I would have taken her in my arms.

"Sit down," she said, fortunately in her natural, low, musical voice, "I have something to say to you!"

I sat down and waited. She paced up and down the room—with a curious soft padding step—the Cheetah was dominant. After a while she said:—

"I have thought all night. I know what is in your mind—it's no use to try and reassure me—I have a new instinct—like an animal—a new knowledge—and I can protect myself and my baby. Until it is born—perhaps for always—I will never let you touch me or sleep with me again. I will never be off my guard in your presence. I will take no food which you have had the remotest chance of touching. I will live with you in broad daylight——unless I find it impossible. If I do—I will go away and live upon my annuity where you shall never find me. But you have your work to do here, and I don't want to ruin your career."

Poor child! She little knew how utterly it was ruined already—I hardly knew myself.

It was no use protesting. Her instinct was infallible. For her I was the Enemy, seeking to destroy her and her baby—*and it was true*.

Some weeks have passed since that awful night. As to my own position, I know that my University career is ended, I have only anticipated matters by intimating to the authorities that I retire from the Professorship of Physiology at the end of this term, and already they are looking for my successor.

There are moments when a wave of her old love for me comes over her, and she allows me to caress her lightly—in broad daylight. At the slightest attempt on my part to become demonstratively affectionate she withdraws herself, as cats do when they are bored with the attention of their human companions. I sleep in my dressing room, where I have added interior bolts to the doors. It is a period of armed strain.

But there are times when she allows me to raise one of her arms and play as of yore with her axillary curls, and at these times she is almost off her guard. If my hands wander to her lovely body she comes to herself and flings me off, but it has given me the clue to the ultimate solution. Time is getting on and I must act. I have a hypodermic filled with Aconitine—one day when she is hypnotized by the only caress she allows me, I shall thrust the needle among the roots of the hair under her arm. It will be instantaneous—and undiscoverable. There will be a post-mortem of course. If the opening of the uterus reveals what I fear, professional etiquette will keep knowledge of the discovery from the world. What I shall do then remains to be seen. I now know that Paul Barrowdale was—I cannot call him a coward for I know what he bore through long years—but I know that he inoculated himself with a pure culture of septic pneumonia—and died an apparently natural death.

The scientific importance of the facts which have led to these multiplied tragedies is too great for them to be utterly lost to future Physiologists. I shall deposit this record with Blayre, our Registrar, sealed up with instructions that it is not to be opened until twenty-five years after my death, when a new generation will have forgotten Rex Magley and the scandals which surrounded the closing months of his life.

✳

Note.—More than twenty-five—nearly thirty, in fact—years have elapsed since Rex Magley deposited this MS. with me. It was obvious, when he deposited it, that he was suffering from severe mental strain. I knew, of course, of the "scandal" which was busy with his name and could not but approve of his determination to resign his Chair in the University. He told me that he was shortly taking his wife abroad and would look out for some place in the South or West of France (where they had spent their honeymoon) to settle down in. Within a week, returning from a dinner of one of the University Societies, where he had ceased to be a welcome companion, he found his wife dead upon the divan in their sitting room. At the Inquest he informed the Coroner that he had left her in apparently good health and spirits when he left the house early in the morning. Two days later he was himself taken seriously ill. A virulent form of septic double pneumonia set in almost at once, and in thirty-six hours he was dead. All these tragic happenings formed the almost exclusive topic of conversation in the town and University for a few weeks, and then Magley, his wife and Mrs. Clayton were forgotten. I have pondered deeply whether or not I should destroy this MS. and have more than once been on the point of doing so, but at the critical moment it has seemed to me that I have no right to destroy so astounding a record of research-work in a most obscure field of knowledge. What I think I shall do will be to seal it up again, to be opened long after my death. One thing alone is fortunate, and that is, that neither Paul Barrowdale nor Rex Magley left any ascertainable relations behind them. Barrowdale's fortune reverted, under his Will, to the University; Magley's was escheated to the Crown.

CHRYSTOPHER BLAYRE.

SOME WOMEN OF THE UNIVERSITY

Being a Last Selection from the Strange Papers of
CHRISTOPHER BLAYRE
PH.D., D.LITT.
(Sometime Registrar of the University of Cosmopoli)

"ZUM WILDBAD."

(Deposited by the Registrar.)

I had been detained on the way to my office and was arriving about a quarter of an hour late. I found Wollaston, the Professor of Biochemistry, Walking up and down, Waiting for me, in a state of visible agitation.

"What brings you here, away from your horrible avocations?" I said, as I entered with him. "What are your people doing? Are you not afraid that they will get messing about with your '*cuisine du diable*' as la tante Dide called it? You know your 'Dr. Pascal' of course?"

I was merely chattering, as I hung up my hat and coat and got into my working jacket. As I came to my table, however, and looked at Wollaston more attentively, I saw that his agitation must have some serious origin.

"What can I do for you?" I asked.

"You remember Johanssen, my Lecturer?"

"Remember? You talk as if he were dead."

"He is."

"What! the Finn?"

"He was not a Finn—he was a Swede—at least his grandfather was. I went into the lab before it opened this morning to get something I wanted for my eleven o'clock lecture and there I found him, sitting at his bench, his head on his hands, quite dead."

"But—good heavens——"

"He was in evening dress. He was dining in Hall last night and he must have gone from there into the lab for some reason or other on his way home."

"What was it?—heart—or—or—?"

"Impossible to say at present. His body has been taken to the mortuary, and I have sent over for Amboyne. There will be an inquest of course. Then I came on to you, I thought you ought to know at once."

"Of course, of course," I said, deeply shocked, for, though my acquaintance with Johanssen was little more than official, I had known him as a quiet, rather shy, and at times almost sinister creature, as people of Nordic origin frequently are. Such a happening must necessarily react unpleasantly throughout the little world of the University, in which I exercised the functions of Registrar, and, in a way, of Historiographer.

I closed my office, and accompanied Wollaston on the grim errands of interviewing the proper authorities—and the Police—and the Coroner. He was naturally a good deal shaken, and I took him home with me. In my study, despite the hour, we had a brandy and soda—and we spoke of Johanssen.

We knew very little of him, for he kept to himself. He had come to Cosmopoli as Junior Demonstrator some years before, and had risen to be a Lecturer and Wollaston's right-hand man. A brilliant chemist, and a completely reliable technician—added to which he was a clear and interesting lecturer—he took Wollaston's classes on occasion, and people liked him and his lectures: as one of his students once observed: "He is old Woolley served up as an inspired Chef." It had been quite understood that when "Woolley" retired, Johanssen would succeed him in the Chair of Biochemistry. He never let his imagination run away with him, but he kept in view as the ultimate goal of his work the elusory objective of nearly all biological work, the nature of Protoplasm, and thence the origin of Life.

He never talked about himself, but it was known—probably from something let drop by some visitor who had known him longer than we did—that his personality was founded upon tragedy and it was understood that this tragedy lay in the cir-

494

cumstances in which he had become a widower. Years before, no one knew how many, he had lost his wife, a young English girl—beautiful, according to rumour—within a few weeks of their marriage. He neither made nor invited confidences. Wollaston was the only member of the professorial staff with whom he ever conversed or foregathered of his own initiative. Their life-work, apart from the teaching side, was the chemistry of living things and especially of human life—the inter-relations of the blood of human beings, and the mysterious products of decomposition, the Cadaveric Alkaloids.

"I hope," said Wollaston, "that the post-mortem—at which, of course, I shall assist—will reveal some organic lesion or defect, otherwise"—and the Professor of Biochemistry hesitated,—he was evidently embarrassed—"if we have to assume—I hate to suggest it—suicide—Johanssen had all the material at hand to destroy himself by means of poisons, the presence of which no known technique could ever discover, or separate, in a dead body."

The conversation was taking an uncomfortable, an ominous, turn, and we got away from it.

The last dreadful formalities were eventually carried through. The postmortem examination revealed nothing. Every organ was perfectly healthy. There were no indications of any poison, organic or inorganic. The only noteworthy feature of the case was the extraordinary rapidity with which decomposition had set in. A solicitor, to whom Wollaston had found an envelope addressed in Johanssen's desk, arrived on the scene. He knew nothing of Johanssen's family or affairs excepting that he possessed relatively ample means, which he had devoted to his scientific researches and to the enrichment of his library, and the whole of which he had bequeathed to the University, by a will which he had executed some time after his first arrival in Cosmopoli. The solicitor told us that, originally, he had left everything he possessed to Paul Barrowdale, sometime Professor of Biology in the University, but after the death of Barrowdale, and the subsequent ghastly end of his successor, Magley, in circumstances of which a few people still whisper with horror, he made the will bequeathing everything to the University, to enlarge and finance the usefulness of the Chair, and the equipment of the laboratories of Biochemistry.

A week later Wollaston asked me to go to his rooms with him after dinner at High Table. There he handed to me the large envelope addressed to him which had been found among Johanssen's papers, and brought to Wollaston by his solicitor. It contained a letter and a manuscript.

"You shall put this among your uncanny Records of this University," said Wollaston. "Whether you ever allow it to see the daylight, will be for you to judge. It explains Johanssen."

A sufficient number of years have now elapsed, since the death of Johanssen, for the time to have arrived when this utterly incomprehensible and incredible story may be given to the world.

(The Letter.)

My dear Wollaston,

I forgot who it was who said "*cui non placet vivere licet mori.*" Zeno, I think. Do not imagine that, like many men—especially young men—I have ever allowed myself to be led away by the so-called Gospel, or Doctrine of Pessimism as expressed in the works of Schopenhauer, but he did enunciate some Eternal Verities. For example, here is one: "It is quite obvious that there is nothing in the world to which man has a more assailable title that to his own life and person." And here again: "Great mental suffering makes us insensible to bodily pain. It is this pain which makes suicide easy; for the bodily pain which accompanies it loses all significance in the eyes of one who is tortured by an excess of mental suffering." The young French girl who, before lighting the brazier, pinned a paper to her bosom on which was written, "The pleasure of dying without pain is preferable to the

496

pain of living without pleasure," was a worthy, if unconscious, disciple of Schopenhauer.

Is it not amazing that, in the eyes of the Law, suicide should rank as a Felony? The form of the Indictment stops just short of being comic. I was once on a Jury at the Assizes, and a young girl was in the dock for attempted suicide—for which, as it turned out, she had ample excuse and justification—and the solemn Ass who sits below the Judge, gravely informed the Jury that "the Prisoner at the Bar given them in charge was indicted for that she did wickedly and feloniously attempt to kill and murder herself, against the Peace of our Lord the King, his Crown and Dignity"!

Suicide is first and last, and all the time, one of the incidents attendant upon superior intelligence and education. Morselli, who, I suppose, made a deeper study of the matter than anyone else, observed that it is those countries which possess a higher standard of general culture, which furnish the largest contingent of voluntary deaths, and many years ago Brouc asserted that it was possible to deduce the average of voluntary deaths in a given country from the number of pupils in the public schools. Morselli summed the matter up in one pregnant sentence: "Suicide increases amongst people according to their degree of civilization." You remember the philosophical attitude of the Utopians, which regard to *felo de se*? They were officially advised by the Priests to starve themselves to death or take opium if, and when, life had become unbearable. It is observed, in this connection, that "a voluntary death when it is chosen upon such authority is very honourable."

Who shall presume to dictate to me upon such a matter? I am not, at present, contemplating, but if any time I were to contemplate this felony against the Crown and Dignity of our Lord the King, surely I should have only one thing to bear in mind—its effect upon those who survive me. A clumsy "killing and murdering of oneself " causes pain, disturbance and scandal—in a word, it is anti-social and consequently "bad form." But should you or I, my dear Wollaston, find that, in the words of the Proverbialist, "There's a deal to be said for being dead," do we not know that in a dead body there are immediately to be found, as part of the process of decomposition, poisons essential and efficient to this purpose, and in perfect taste as regards their effects upon survivors—I refer to the Cadaveric Alkaloids. And such alkaloids are easily to be extracted from any dead animal by any Biochemist of your experience. Very well then!

I am, very faithfully yours.

SIGISMUND JOHANSSEN.

✳

(The Manuscript.)

You know that after I had taken my degree—I believe I may say with some distinction—I was appointed to the post of the demonstrator in Biochemistry at another University. It was some time later that I came to be your demonstrator in Cosmopoli, after an interval during which there happened to me the incredible tragedy that wrecked my whole life, leaving me nothing to live for, apart from the researches which you gave me the opportunity of renewing, in collaboration with yourself. You have never shown any desire to probe into my previous history, but I think it is due to you that I should write an account of that tragedy which you may read should life become, as it well may become, unendurable for me.

In the College to which I was appointed, the Professor of German Language and Literature was the most remarkable woman that I ever met. Her name was Paula Kardany, graduate of a well-known German University, speaking English as German women frequently do, with no trace of a foreign accent, and possessing a knowledge of German, and of English Literature as well, which I can only describe as phenomenal. She was a woman of overwhelming personality, and of almost fabulous beauty—raven-black hair which she wore short (at that time a very rare coiffure among women), immense grey eyes, with heavy lids which appeared never to "blink," surmounted by strong, straight eyebrows, the eyebrows which command

and direct, as opposed to the arched eyebrows which enquire or implore. Her nose straight—almost Grecian—a short upper lip, defining a mouth curved like those with which we are familiar in the finest classic statuary. The jaw and forehead square, giving to the outline of her face the contour shewn as characteristic of the Criminal Type in Lombroso's book *La donna dilinquente.*

Her personality impressed itself upon men and women alike, with the invariable distinction that, whilst men regarded her with a feeling akin to fear, discomfort—even dislike—women, from professors down to the most newly-joined "fresher," seemed fascinated, it often seemed to me, hypnotized by her. In her professorial capacity she was impartial, patient and extraordinarily efficient; in her private life she made and encouraged violent friendships, often resulting in bitter jealousies, and often the cause of hopeless and almost hysterical affection, which, excepting in the case of the favoured few, was mercilessly unrequited and even repelled.

When I had occupied my post for a couple of terms, there came to our Department, as junior demonstrator, a girl, twenty-three years of age, who had taken her degree in natural Science with honours in a northern university. I was never what is called a "ladies' man," and had taken no personal interest in any women, save in so far as they looked to me for instruction, and this, I think, was what attracted—if one may use so significant a term—Paula Kardany to me. She often visited the laboratory when I was at work upon my own specialised lines of research, and showed an interest in, and grasp of, the subjects which were engrossing my attention that impressed me very much. Often when we were thus together, one of her devoted students, or even a member of the Staff, would come and try to tempt her forth to some distraction or other, only to be repulsed with what seemed to me unnecessary harshness. Once or twice, when I remonstrated mildly with her upon her repellent manner, she would say:

"*Was wünshen Sie?* She is sweet,—but this is not her hour."

All this was modified, indeed, I might say completely changed, when Barbara Maverick arrived in the University, at the commencement of one Easter Term, as junior demonstrator in our Department. I will not attempt to describe her, my heart and brain are, even to-day, unequal to the task. I will only say that she was of the perfect English type of blonde loveliness. A stronger contrast to the overwhelming dark beauty of Paula Kardany it would be impossible to imagine.

I can never forget their first meeting. A few days after the beginning of term, Barbara was with me, learning her way about, and preparing for the term's work. I was showing her one of the preliminary stages in the preparation of a serum suggested by Barrowdale, one of those which afterwards played so terrible a part in his serum experiments. (I have often wondered whether, had I known what it was leading to, I should have assisted in their preparation—but I suppose that if I had not, some other Biochemist would have been led to them by the awful fascination of the subject.) Barbara had the tube in her hand and was holding it up to the light, when suddenly she seemed to stiffen—she put the tube carefully back into the rack, and turned very pale. I thought she was going to faint and I remember thinking to myself: : "Good Lord! is this the sensitive plant I am to work with?" But she stood quite firm and still, staring over my shoulder.

I turned round to see what had rivetted her attention. Framed in the doorway—I had not heard the door open—stood Paula Kardany, quite motionless, her hands hanging loosely clasped in front of her. She was staring straight at Barbara, and, as I looked, her wonderful mouth developed into the most magnificent smile that I ever saw on a woman's face.

She stepped forward into the laboratory and said: "This is your new demonstrator, Johanssen? Introduce us to one another." As she advanced, I murmured the usual formalities; she came towards us with her hand extended and Barbara put hers into it. She just held it still for a second or two and then said, simply and softly:

"Barbara Maverick."

That was all. Paula joined in the conversation, perfectly cool and collected. Barbara was evidently deeply impressed, for her colour came and went, and at times it seemed to me that she spoke, as it were, at random. From time to time, as if to emphasize a remark, Paula laid her hand upon the girl's arm, and then Barbara flushed and looked at her with a puzzled, troubled expression on her face.

Presently Paula said: "Well, I must be going," and turning to Barbara she said: "We must get to know one another. Will you come to tea with me one afternoon?"

And Barbara, looking at her as if she could not withdraw her eyes from the wonderful face, said, quite simply:

"This afternoon?"

Paula hesitated for a moment and then replied: "Yes," and so she turned and left the laboratory.

I saw that Barbara was disturbed and distracted, and I brought our tour of inspection to an end. The spell of Paula Kardany had fallen, as usual, upon her.

"Another of them," I said to myself. That was the beginning of it.

I was, for the first and only time in my life, deeply, incurably, in love. It would be false modesty to doubt or to deny that Barbara had felt for me the answering thrill that no girl, however inexperienced, can mistake. But I had a terrific force to contend against. She knew her work thoroughly, and was an assiduous and conscientious worker. The students, both men and women, loved her, and would always do their very best for her. They seemed to feel that they must do all that they could to help her gain the confidence and esteem of the Professor and his lecturers. And they certainly succeeded. But none of them ever got beyond a sort of affectionate acquaintance with her. Anything deeper of which she was capable seemed to be wholly absorbed in Paula Kardany. She worked splendidly always, until just before closing time, when she became nervous and rather distracted, and very often I would say: "There, that will do. You run along. I have one or two things to finish. I will wash up, count the platinum and lock it away." She was junior demonstrator, and this was, in our laboratory, her "job".

Away from the laboratory, and when Paula was not lecturing, they were quite inseparable. The students talked and laughed among themselves, as students always will in such cases, and there were not lacking some who were bitterly malevolent, and made no concealment of their wrath against Paula and their resulting dislike of Barbara—*spretae injuria formae.*

My love for Barbara pursued a normal course. I made no concealment about it, and she accepted it. I was content to wait, and, though nothing was actually said, she knew that I was there—waiting and at times she seemed relieved to be with me, to come to me for comfort and advice, to regard me as a sort of ultimate refuge from the malice and jealousy of women whom Paula had ostentatiously dropped.

The day before we "went down" for the Easter Vac. we were clearing up in the laboratory. Barbara was restless, excited, and she seemed wanting, and at the same time fearing to hear what she thought was, as story-tellers put it, "trembling upon my lips." At last I said:

"What are you going to do in Vac.? Going home?"

"Only for a day or two. After that"—and she hesitated—"I am joining Paula Kardany in Paris, and we are going to do a tour in Spain."

My heart missed a beat, and then I said—with admirable composure (though I say it): "I wonder she does not take you to her native Austria."

"I did suggest it," she replied, "but Paula amazed me. She has a perfect horror of 'going home,' as she calls it. She said a queer thing. She said: 'I have no "home" as you would understand it. My only "home" is Hell; there I die gradually in torture—what you would call "home" is for me'—" and she hesitated, and, I think, coloured a little, and then went on "'for me it is where you are. As a snail its house, so, as long as I have you, I carry my Heaven with me.' Is it not curious? Sometimes I am almost a little frightened. You do not think it wicked for people to love one another as we do?"

"Not wicked," I said bravely, "but I think it is bad for you. You should have a holiday away from one another. You should live in a new atmosphere, I think, for a while, until you come back to work—and to me."

She was not startled—you see, she knew. Then, after a pause, she said: "Yes—there is always you. You will be here always, will you not?" she added wistfully. I knew what she meant. I said:

" I will always be here—or there, wherever you want me. But must you go away with Paula Kardany?"

"Yes—I must."

I took her quietly in my arms and kissed her. And so we parted for that time.

When we went up again for the summer term, on the first day I went into the laboratory and found my fellow-lecturer putting his bench in order.

"Seen Barbara yet? " he asked.

"No—have you?"

"Yes, last night. I came up yesterday—so did they."

"They?"

"Barbara and Kardany. They have rooms together this term. Did you not know?"

I took it, standing up, all right. Presently Barbara came in. She came up to me and shook hands. She looked pale and tired. I said:

"Had a good time? You look as if you had travelled too hard—tried to do too much in the time—people do that in the Easter Vac."

"Yes,—I think that's it," she replied.

Life went on without any outward change. But—perhaps it was my Nordic blood—there seemed to be an uncomfortable undercurrent—an atmosphere—call it what you will—in more than one department. To be more precise, that of German Language and Literature seemed to be in a state of suppressed excitement. Then things were whispered—vague rumours of impending changes began to circulate. One day Barbara, who was working alone with me in the laboratory, laid down her scalpel and said:

"Life is jolly complicated, isn't it, Johanssen?"

"I know," I replied, rather irrelevantly. "But I am always here, you know."

"Yes—thank the Lord," she said. Then suddenly: "We know that we—love one another. Why do you never ask questions?"

"Because I know," I replied.

"I am so glad," she said simply, and sighed like a comforted child.

About a week before the end of term she said to me:

"Have you heard that Paula has resigned her Professorship—is going down for good?"

"Yes," I replied, "as your immediate chief I have heard all the rumours." And so I had, and, deep down, I had felt an indefinable terror of what this last week might bring forth or how it might end. What might Paula Kardany do at the end? It would seem that certain students, some said relations too, had made observations to the Principal, and he, good man, had expressed an opinion that students got a more robust grounding in foreign languages and literature from male professors than from female ones—and so, a good, worthy and bearded father of a family from Bonn University was to take the place of Paula Kardany among us.

"They will not learn so much, or so quickly, from him as from her," my fellow-lecturer had observed cryptically.

"What shall I do?" asked Barbara, rather uncertainly, a little later, when we had been working in silence.

"Will you do what I tell you?" I asked.

"Yes—anything."

"Well then—pack your things and go home this afternoon. Get a certificate from Dr. Polly and leave it behind you." (Mary Caslon, M.D., Resident Medical Officer of the Women's Hotel, was a splendid thing, and could be implicitly relied upon in cases like this.) "When the 'Varsity goes down next week, I shall come down to your village." (Barbara's "village" was a large manufacturing town in the Midlands). "We will then discuss the date of

504

our marriage with your mother. We can give her about ten days to get accustomed to the idea, and then we shall have the whole Long Vac. before us, and return here to a new and lovely life. *Stimmt?*"

"*Stimmt!*" she replied, and for a space she was in my arms, and we filled in gaps which had punctuated many of our antecedent conversations.

"Good for her!—and for you!" said my Professor, when I told him the news next morning.

Like jewels in a setting of rocky mountains, in the long range that reaches from the Dolomites to Lake Konstanz, dividing Austria from Southern Germany, are many very beautiful lakes, some very small, some of considerable extent, but all quite lovely. Two of them belong to this story. One is highly sophisticated, for on its shore is the terminus of a railway at a populous little town from which the lake takes its name, or vice versa; the other an isolated jewel in a cluster of mountains separated from the larger lake by twenty miles of luxuriant valley, of precipitous gorges, and of vast pine forests. This has no chief town properly so to be called, but has small hamlets consisting of a few *Land-häuse* and the inevitable *Gasthaus,* dotted at intervals around its shores. Another railway system occurs again ten miles further on, and two thousand feet lower down. A funicular line connects the smaller lake with a town in the valley, which provides this railway with a fairly busy station—a junction. One of the hamlets assumes pride of population and position as being principal among them. It boats several Hotels, and it was here that Barbara and I "washed up" on our honeymoon—the only perfectly happy period of my life that I have ever known.

From the railhead on the larger lake a service of Mail-coaches runs to, and past, the smaller lake, and down to the station in the valley, and back and these being the only means of communication between the railways, are used by tourists for visiting the intermediate points in the districts. At the time of which

I am writing, the horse-drawn old-fashioned "diligences" had just been replaced by motor charabancs and omnibuses—in those days motor-cars were the rare luxury of the wealthy, and the roads were not overrun with large and small cars as they are now. The new motor-service gave a great impetus to the development of the district as a tourist centre, the terminal towns and intermediate villages began to sprout villas along the road, and visitors spending their holidays around the small lake—which I will call "X"—made excursions to the town on the larger lake—which I will call "Z"—and upon this excursion my wife and I embarked one hot autumn day when we had been at "X" about a fortnight.

There was a half-way Posting House on the road, where the cars halted for half an hour, the road at this point running through a vast, dense pine-forest. A little further on, a narrow road diverged to the right and lost itself almost at once among the trees; at the turning was a signpost on which one read "*Zum Wildbad.*" I asked our driver what it meant, and he told me that it led to a "sort of hotel," a *Logier-und-Kosthaus* or Pension, with a thermal spring, where families came and spent the summer months. We lunched at "Z" in a Restaurant overlooking the lake, proposing to return to "X" by the *Post-wagen* which started back in the afternoon.

When the time arrived for the return journey, we found that there were apparently two *Post-wagen*, one almost filled up, the other almost empty. We secured seats in the latter. The driver tried to persuade us to take the other, for various reasons: it was more comfortable; it started sooner; it made the journey quicker; and he gave other reasons which I failed to grasp owing to the strange local dialect in which he spoke. We started off, and took up and deposited various peasants and work-people with their impedimenta along the route.

I should have mentioned that, before we started, our driver had an apparently unpleasant colloquy with an ominous-looking man, to whom I had shown our tickets, and who was evidently annoyed with him for suggesting that we should shift to the other charabanc.

506

"What a horrible-looking man!" said Barbara. "He looks like an Ogre in a Fairy-tale. I should not like to meet him on a lonely road."

"Nonsense!" I replied. "He is probably a part proprietor of this—the rival car. Anyhow we are very well where we are."

As we started off I looked round. The "Ogre" was looking at us, and especially at Barbara, with a foul, leering grin. There was something about it—I know not what—or—why—that seemed unpleasantly familiar. I looked at our man. He was evidently uncomfortable. I asked him who the "Ogre" was, and he murmured something unintelligible to me. The only words I distinguished were "*verwünscht*" and "*gottlos*"—and being, as I knew, in a very religious country, I was merely interested to observe that he "crossed" himself piously.

Just before we reached the half-way house, our car turned off the main road, down that with the signpost "*Zum Wildbad.*"

"Good!" said I, "we are returning by another road. That makes a change, and shows us some more of the country."

"It's a dreadful-looking forest," observed Barbara, "anything might happen in it."

I laughed, but Barbara was obviously and curiously nervy, glancing all the time from right to left, into the impenetrable gloom.

After about half an hour we ran through large open gates, into a wide and evidently artificial clearing, and, a minute later, drew up in a sort of courtyard in the middle of what seemed to be a group of large two-storied, pale buildings. A woman with baskets—we had not seen her get in—alighted and disappeared through a doorway, looking back at us as she did so and calling out something in dialect to our driver, who had got down from his seat. He shrugged his shoulders with a movement of his arms which clearly indicated, "It is nothing to do with me."

We sat tight, looking around at the buildings. There was not a soul to be seen anywhere. The driver came and opened the door at our side and said:

"*Aussteigen!*"

"No," I said, "we are going all the way."

"This is all the way."

"But we are going to 'X.'"

"Not tonight," he replied, and, in his turn, disappeared into what looked like a huge garage.

"I don't like this," said Barbara.

I did not feel altogether comfortable myself, but I said: "It is bound to be all right. Get down, and we will go and explore."

We wandered out of the yard into what seemed to be an ordinary Summer settlement—lawns, tennis courts, odd buildings here and there, even a small chapel. Not a living thing excepting a large Toad, that sat against a wall, looking at us.

Barbara stooped and picked it up. "This, I suppose, is the Guardian Spirit of the Enchanted Castle," she said. "I hope he will hurry up and turn into a Prince, or at any rate a Waiter—which would be more useful."

As she spoke the Toad did with its eyes what toads do when disturbed. It let down pellucid eyelids over them, and after a moment lifted them again. Its eyes, which had been the usual bright, metallic sienna colour, had changed to a grey blue. They were the eyes of the "Ogre."

I did not say a word—nor did Barbara. She merely ejaculated "Oh!" and put the Toad back where it came from. It walked a few inches in the fat, leisurely manner peculiar to toads, and disappeared into what looked like a ventilator-hole in the wall.

We pursued our way along the front (if it was the front) of the building—the whole of it was faced with a huge verandah, two or three wooden steps up to a level boarded space about ten feet broad, then two more steps leading up to glass panels and doors which reached up to the verandah eaves. Quite deserted. It was growing uncanny.

"There must be a Reception Office somewhere," I said. "Come inside."

We opened one of the glass verandah doors, and crossed what looked like an immense Winter Garden. Small tables everywhere with two or three chairs to each. At the far end, a sort of bar with a serving hatch behind it. I thought I saw someone standing behind the counter, but when I came nearer there was no one. The whole place smelt fusty—like damp flannel. We went through a door by the bar, and down a passage into a hall, and there, sure enough, was the ordinary Hotel Bureau. Inside, a large fair man was writing at a desk; he took no notice of me until I was close up to him, and then he turned and looked at me. He was fair—reddish—immensely broad shoulders—and as he looked at me his eyes, which were dark, veiled themselves and became the dead blue—like the Ogre's. And he smiled—that haunting, uncanny smile.

I felt Barbara's hand tighten on my arm. I said to the Reception Clerk (?):

"We have come here by mistake. We had return tickets to Z from X, and we wish to go on back to X at once."

"You cannot do so," he replied. "You must take the auto-car back to Z in the morning if you wish to—and can—and start again from there."

"But I absolutely refuse to do so—your man brought us here, and he must take us back—or rather on to X."

"That is impossible—he has gone home. You should have got into the *Post-wagen* which goes back to X. You came in our private *Wagen* which only brings our own visitors, and a few passengers who may join it, to come here or to alight on the road."

"Why were we not told?"

"Did you ask?"

"No, but I showed our tickets to a man at Z who seemed to be in charge, and he allowed us to get into the car."

He smiled—by this time my nerves were beginning to jump, and I already hated his smile. He touched a bell and there appeared, from apparently nowhere, a little figure dressed like a Hall Porter. He was about five feet high, with a quite square body and a square face, at least the upper part was square, the lower half being hidden by a long, black beard. He was exactly like one of those painted terra-cotta Gnomes—Kobbolds—that one sees sold as garden ornaments—or in children's books.

"Shew the Herrschaften Number—" began the tall man.

"I will not be shown anywhere," I almost shouted. "I want a car at once, and I am going back to X."

"We have not car," replied he, slowly—"you must stay the night."

"No—no—no—!" this from Barbara, who was trembling violently.

The Kobbold-Porter's face came in half. That dreadful smile parted his beard horizontally, and shewed a scarlet lower lip and a row of white sharp teeth. He seemed to shake with silent laughter.

"You will take some refreshment," said the tall man—a command rather than an invitation.

"We will have coffee in the Verandah Saal," I said. I wanted to get away, anywhere, and think out our next procedure.

"The Head-waiter will show you," and I became aware that a thin, elderly man was standing behind us. He was in the conventional evening-dress of a head-waiter—a wolfish face, quite white hair beard and a military moustache. A rosette in his coat lapel. And as he motioned us to follow him, he too smiled—the Wildbad smile—and his eyes veiled themselves and cleared to a dull blue. The Toad—the Ogre . . .

He motioned us to a table in the huge glassed-in verandah, and I ordered coffee.

"Are there no other visitors?" I asked.

"Oh, yes."

"Where are they?"

"Oh! around" ("*Rings herum*"), he replied.

"Something has just passed me," whispered Barbara. I had felt it too—it had passed between us. A horrible sensation, as if a suit of damp flannel had brushed between us, with no "body" in it.

We waited, conversing in whispers, as if we feared to be overheard, until the coffee was brought by a very handsome girl in the national costume—she had a perfectly white face and very red lips.

"Where are the other visitors?" asked Barbara.

"Oh! *rings herum*," she replied, with a short laugh, as she strolled leisurely away. The Head-waiter, looking like a distinguished French nobleman, was walking up and down the outer verandah, looking in sometimes as he passed us.

"You must wait here a few minutes," I said to Barbara. "I am going to enquire about a car."

"For heaven's sake don't be long," she whispered.

I went out at one of the glass doors, and started to retrace my steps by the way we had come, to the yard where we had been landed. I passed the Head-Waiter-Marquis at the end of the verandah as I was reaching the steps down into the grounds. He did not appear to see me. The Toad was back where we had first seen him. I hated him.

I reached the yard, and began knocking at the doors which opened into it—no answer anywhere. Then, remembering the garage into which our driver had disappeared and whose door was still ajar, I pushed my way into it. Coming in from the light, it seemed quite dark.

"Is anybody here?" I said aloud. A voice answered me.

"Yes—I am here, *mein Herr*. I was waiting for you."

"What is this place we have got to?" I said, lowering my voice—I hardly knew why.

"It is Wildbad," the man replied. "What are you going to do?" A queer question in the circumstances!

"What the Hell is the Wildbad?" I asked furiously, and trying to sound very bold.

"A good place to leave," was the reply.

"Well—you must help us to leave it—you brought us here."

"I am not the master," said he.

"Who is?"

"One does not ask questions." A pause, and then I said:

"Can you get hold of a car to take us to X?"

"No—I belong here—for a while. But one might get a car from Z."

"From Z?—that is two hours away!"

"Yes—but there is no other way—and that way is difficult—and costly—perhaps dangerous."

"I do not care what it costs."

"*Also!*" said he, "two hundred schillings?" I was rather staggered, but I said: "Go on, I will pay anything that is asked." He seemed impressed by this, and, after a short pause, he said:

"Return to Madame and behave as if you were remaining the night. I have a friend with a garage in Z—I may be able to telephone to him to send a car—to come and take you away. It will be difficult."

"Good—and then?"

"It will be two hours at least before it can be here," he said. "Stay in the verandah, and when you see me outside again, come and speak to me. Go back to the verandah the other way— through the house is better."

There was nothing else to be done. I found my way round to the other side, apparently the front, of the house—it was rambling and enormous. I entered by the main door and was received by the Kobbold-Porter.

"Where have you been?" he rapped out.

"What is that to you?" I replied. "Is this a hotel—or what?"

"It is what you see—and perhaps what you do not see," and with that he retired by a side door into the office, grinning—the Wildbad smile again.

I found Barbara sitting at our table, almost in a state of collapse.

"I thought you were dead," she said hysterically.

I assumed a calm which I was far from feeling, and I said airily: "What nonsense! I have only been ordering a car—it will be here presently."

"You have ordered——? Oh! where is it? Let us go to it."

"It is some distance off, darling. You must be patient. Let us explore the place a little, it seems interesting," I said bravely.

"I dare not move," she almost wailed. "Don't you feel it? This place—where we are now—is full of *people*."

"People?"

"Yes, invisible, soft people, all dressed in damp flannel—can you not smell it?"

The ghastly thing was that I could not merely *smell* it, but *feel* it, but I pulled myself together and said: "Come along, let us move about anyhow." And I almost had to pull her up from the chair. She clung to my arm, and seemed to stagger now and then, as we walked to one of a range of inner glass doors which led into a vast hall—evidently the ballroom—recreation hall —anything—of this uncanny "Hotel". Once inside, it was no use pretending to one another any more. We proceeded down the room, almost elbowing our way through slowly moving, but invisible, groups of—the Flannel People. The damp, close smell was terrifying, and the touch of them repulsive. At the farther end was a stage or platform, probably for Concert or other Entertainment purposes. There was a grand piano—a Steinway, as I noticed—upon it.

"Come up," I said cheerily. "I will give you a tune."

We mounted the steps to the platform. The piano had a loose brown holland cover thrown over it. As I took hold of one corner to pull it off—Crash!

A full chord—I have what is called a "true pitch"—the chord of F minor, rang out from the instrument.

"God!" cried Barbara.

Determined to "act" for all I was worth, I pulled off the cover and sat down on the broad music-bench. There was one— perhaps two—of the Flannel People there already. Pretending to be "nothing daunted," I, too, struck a chord of F minor—and invisible hands played a true "descant" to it, between my right and left hands—a weird gregorian effect.

It was the last straw, it seemed to me. I caught hold of Barbara and we jumped off the platform, and literally fought our way to the door leading into the main building, pushing between the invisible Flannel People. Outside it stood one of the serving women—the pale, scarlet-lipped servant. She said:

"I was looking for the *gnädige Frau*. Perhaps she would like to go to her room?"

"She has no room, I have no room, we have no rooms," I cried, and I laughed idiotically as I heard myself reciting what sounded like a bit out of a German Grammar. But there were two hours to wait—at least—and I had to sit in the verandah—among the Flannel People, watching for our friend the carman—our only hope—for I was at the end of my tether. I produced a ten-schilling note and gave it to the girl—if it *was* a girl—and said: "There must be a Manageress or Housekeeper (*Haus-hälterin*) in this place. Madame is not well. Take us to her room. Madame will rest there until our car comes back for us."

"Comes back for you?" she said slowly.

"Yes," I shouted—I had lost all control of my voice. "My *Chofför* has had to run back to Z for something I left—at the Police Headquarters," I added recklessly. "He will not be long now."

The girl smiled. I knew it was the Wildbad smile; I dared not look at her eyes. I knew what they were doing. I knew too that she did not believe a word of what I was saying.

She said: "Yes, there is a Housekeeper. I will take you to her. Follow me."

We went along apparently endless corridors. We brushed past several of the dreadful Flannel People on the way—and faces—the faces of the Kobbold-Porter and of the Head-waiter—and of the Toad, seemed to me to catch fleeting glances of us from round corners and from behind softly closing doors. At last, at the extreme end of a wing, which ended in a glass door leading down into the grounds, our guide stopped at a door on the right and knocked. The door opened and a woman stood framed in the opening. The proud carriage, the superb beauty, the curved scarlet mouth——!

It was Paula Kardany.

I stood rooted to the spot. Paula smiled—I knew now why the Wildbad smile had seemed familiar—and bowed slightly to me. But Barbara stepped forward, crying: "Oh, Paula! You!" They were clasped in each other's arms, and, as the door closed upon them, their lips met.

The serving woman was still standing there. "What does it all mean? We must get away," I said helplessly.

"You came here of your own accord—it is for you to leave, if you can."

I held out another note, but she put her hands behind her back.

"Help me," I whispered.

"No——" she said—and then, after a moment's pause, she added: "Yes—if I can—it is not my fault, and it may not be too late."

"What can I do?" I whispered again.

"Nothing now," she replied, "but if you *can* get a car, come round to this garden door—perhaps I——" and without ending the sentence she walked rapidly away.

I simply *had* to be back in the Verandah-Sall, lest I should miss our man, but, before going, I threw open the door again through which Barbara had disappeared. She was lying on a couch, her eyes closed, apparently senseless. Paula Kardany was kneeling on the floor by her side, her arms around her, her head on Barbara's shoulder, her face hidden in my darling's neck. She turned her head, not moving otherwise, and said: "You had better go away."

"Will you look after her?" I said weakly.

"Yes—I will look after her. You had better go away—go away—now."

I lost my way more than once in the gloomy and intricate passages before I found the great Hall, and, crossing it, reached the Verandah-Saal. Several times I ran into—brushed past—one, or more, of the Flannel People—the cold, empty dampness of their touch made me feel physically sick. I took a seat at a table, close to the glass door nearest to the steps leading down from the end of the outer verandah. After a few moments I felt that the other chair at my table was occupied by one of the Flannel People. I rapped on the table, and another of the scarlet-lipped serving women appeared. I ordered a large glass of brandy. There was nothing uncanny about that. And it helped—a little. The Head-Waiter-Marquis came down the Saal and stood looking at me.

"Have you all you want?" he said.

"Everything, thank you."

"*Also, gut,*" he replied, and went back to the Bar, where he disappeared.

How I got through the next two hours I have never known. It was a vague indefinable nightmare, which has visited me a hundred times since. It was becoming dusk when suddenly I saw our driver standing on the path below.

I stepped out to the outer-rail, and he said quickly: "The car is at the main door—go out boldly through the house and step in," and he disappeared. On the way—I knew it by now—I met the serving-woman who had led us to the housekeeper's room. I was about to stop and speak, when she laid her finger to her lips, and as I passed she whispered:

"The end door."

Passing the Bureau, I said to the Head-waiter, who was in conversation with the big clerk and the Kobbold-Porter: " I have left the reckoning on the table—you can keep the change—I am in a hurry."

As I passed them they drew together, and a fierce interchange of whispers took place. Outside, on the drive, stood a powerful open car, with a man in the national costume in the driving seat. Our man was standing, holding the door open. I sprang in, and he mounted the running board and held on.

" *Wohin?*"("Where to?"), he whispered.

"Go round to the end door," I said, rather to the driver. He started at once, and as he did so, the Kobbold-Porter came running out.

"Go on," I cried. We reached the end door, which was standing open. There stood the serving-wench, supporting Barbara, whose head lay upon the girl's shoulder. I sprang out and up the steps.

"I cannot lift her," said the girl.

My driver was at my heels. "Together!" I said. And we lifted Barbara down the steps and into the car. As we did so, I saw the big man and Paula hurrying down the corridor towards us. I sprang in beside Barbara and cried: "Forward!" and the car went off with a bound. Our man jumped on to the running-board again, and clung there. The driver did not wait to turn the car, but swept right round the building, past the verandah, through the yard, and so into the private road. As we passed the verandah, the Head-waiter leapt to the balustrade and shouted to us. The Toad was in the middle of the path—we ran it over.

"Forward!" cried our man.

As we left the yard I looked round. The Kobbold-Porter was running at us from the main entrance, waving something in his hand and shouting something.

"Forward!" cried the man.

The main gates were open—luckily—as they had been when we arrived, and—we were out on the forest-road, running at a good eighty kilometres. Then at last I could occupy myself with Barbara. She was quite unconscious—deathly pale. I thought for a moment that she was dead. But she was not. Her eyes opened for a moment, met mine—she smiled—and relapsed into unconsciousness again. I would have given all that I possessed then for a brandy flask.

Oh! the terror of that drive—two hours through the gathering darkness! Our man—richly rewarded—had jumped off as we slowed down at the half-way house. Barbara was deadly cold, but I could feel her heart beating feebly from time to time.

We reached our hotel at X in pitch darkness. Aided by our Hall Porter and the Proprietor, I carried Barbara up to our rooms, and, with the help of the old chambermaid, we put her to bed.

As luck would have it, the only other English visitor in the hotel was a notable London physician, Sir Malcolm G——, and I sought him and brought him to Barbara. She was still unconscious, and he made a thorough examination.

"It is an extraordinary case," he said. "There is no organic lesion of any kind, and she certainly has not been poisoned. If we were in the Tropics, I should say she had been stung by a scorpion. How, and when, did she get those two little punctures on her neck? They are exactly like the marks made by the nip of a fair-sized scorpion—the African *Pandinus*—before it stings—but there is no sign of any sting."

We sat by her side for a couple of hours. Once Sir Malcolm said: "I never saw a more terrible case of anæmia. I would give a thousand pounds for a transfusion apparatus."

He left me at about two o'clock in the morning. Barbara seemed to grow weaker every minute. She never recovered consciousness. She died at about four o'clock.

———————

The manuscript ended here. At the foot of the last sheet was written in Johanssen's later handwriting:

"This is the story of my life and death. Tonight I dined in Hall, and, during dinner, Cranston, who was sitting next to me, was called away. He had not been gone for more than a few minutes when one of the Flannel People came and sat in the chair which he had vacated.

"It may have been Barbara."

———————

This was dated at 11.30 p.m. on the night that Johanssen died.

THE BOOTS.

(Deposited by Carol Patullo, Linacre Scholar (Natural Science).)

I adore Claudia, quietly and contentedly, and she me. Unlike most passionate friendships, ours does not illustrate Balzac's celebrated axiom: *"Entre deux amants il y'a toujours l'un qui baise et l'autre qui tend la joue."* She came up as a "fresher" at the beginning of my second year at Cosmopoli, and I who, although I had made many friends in what we self-righteously considered to be "the best set" at St. Lewinna's—that is to say, the girls who really "read" seriously and specialised in at least one game—had never been strongly attracted by any one of them, but I fell in love with Claudia Verschoyle the moment I set eyes upon her. I am thankful, too, to say that she felt the same about me, and told me so at once. We became inseparable, and the others christened us "the Deep C's"—I am Carol—and smiled indulgently upon us.

I have often tried to analyse what it is that makes people smile at a close friendship between two girls. The smile is at once friendly and mysterious, slightly pitying and slightly sarcastic, rather defiant and rather envious; I suppose it is that we know one another so well. One does not encounter this attitude with regards to a close friendship between two men. They can "chum up" together, live together, travel together, and no one ever regards their friendship as otherwise than permanent and unremarkable. I suppose it is that there are such an awful lot of us and comparatively so few men, and their friendship is not fraught with the dangers that threaten that of two girls. For instance, if a girl comes along and tries to get away with one of the men, the other is not worried about it; that sort of instinctive jealousy does not exist between them, their friendship is unimpaired—unless, of course, the girl marries one of them—then she instinctively, and as a rule, unconsciously, separates them. This does not appear to happen on the man's side; he can adopt his wife's friend and like her, and encourage their friendship. I suppose it is that men are so beastly sure of themselves. They know, though when the time comes they will not admit it, that when a girl gives herself to a man, it is invariably and entirely his own fault if he cannot keep her in love with him, and so he can sit securely upon his throne or pedestal, so long as his devotion to her does not waver; so long, in fact, as he practises unconsciously, or even consciously, the science of being a husband. Love is an art; marriage is a science—an absorbingly interesting one—one is born an artist, but one can acquire a science—the lover is born, the husband is made, and unfortunately few men realise that what may be a lovable eccentricity in a lover can become an irritating peculiarity in a husband. I do not know why I am writing all this; I did not intend to do so, and it has nothing to do with the story of the Boots. I was led into it by the reflection upon the difference in the attitude which people adopt to a great friendship between two men and that between two women. The one is fool-proof, the other is as vulnerable as a most delicate scientific instrument—say a wireless receiver or a Seismograph. I think that these comparisons are apt.

Either of us might—and may—marry at any moment. I know that the only attitude adopted by the other would be a severely critical analysis of the elected man, lest the beloved might be hurt or even disappointed. For my own part I have never yet met a man for whose love or society I would forego that of Claudia. I have been a good deal troubled by the species, mainly, I think (for I am quite unconscious of ever having been attracted by, or having sought to attract a male), by reason of the fact that I have no near relations, and am what used to be called in Georgian times "a fortune," and I have never been tempted to put faith in the protestations of males, attracted, as I am humble enough to suspect, by "*les beaux yeux de ma cassette.*"

At the end of the summer term—in the Long Vac.—we wandered about France, Brittany, the Loire and Provence, staying as long as we liked wherever we liked. It was very delightful, but when we got back I determined to have a house of my own in some unsophisticated country district, where we could carry out all those ideas of comfort, in a rural existence, that simmer in the minds of every normal man or woman, and we spent all our spare time that autumn inspecting "country residences" described with fantastic and luxurious imagination by house agents, devoid alike of æsthetic comprehension, and of the most rudimentary ideas of the meaning of the word "veracity." We inspected "premises" varying architecturally from mud-huts to mansions, and solaced our evenings in country inns, tempering our weariness with amazed and homeric laughter. It was finally one of the innkeepers in a small town in Sussex, a few miles north of Horsham, where we had "washed up" after a day of indignant disappointments, who suggested that we might look at Stippleworth Hall. The grandiloquent name filled us with misgiving, but as the house—a farm-house our Bardolph called it—was distant but about ten miles, we thought we might inspect it before returning to Cosmopoli.

"It is very old and more than a bit tumble-down," said our Amphitryon, "but if you ladies feel like doing some repairs it might suit you. There are the remains of what used to be a fine garden, there is a wood and some pasture, and a stream running through it that runs into the Arun a few miles lower down."

Somehow this sounded promising, and I said:

"To whom does it belong, and is it for sale?"

"It has been for sale for years, but no one has bought it. It is miles from any railway station, and to tell the truth" (this gave us a shock—after our recent experience—of rather pleasurable surprise) "it would cost a good deal of money to make it habitable. There is a village post office about a mile away—and there is a well—and that is all."

Claudia's eyes glistened. "What fun!" she said.

"And it belongs to—?" I prompted him.

"Gaffer Girrady—French, they say, his forebears was. He's very old, and about as badly in want of repair as his house. He lives there with a woman, his sister says he—she's a queer one too. I saw him about two years gone by—came in to get off the Jury List—he can't read or write—no more can she. He said then that he'd like to go and live in Horsham if he could sell the place."

And then he added in a burst of truthfulness that excited our admiration: "He told me that if I could persuade any silly fool to take it off his hands, he'd give me a bit—a good bit."

This decided us. We had a sort of governess-cart to take us around, which we had hired complete with a sort of horse, and a sort of driver, at Chiddingfold, and next morning we set out in search of Stippleworth Hall. It took some finding, and we lost ourselves more than once in a labyrinth of lanes, bordered by high hedges which made it impossible to see where we were going. At last, by constant reference to a sheet of the Ordnance map and a compass, we reached the entrance to a narrower lane than ever, which I calculated must be near our objective.

Fortunately a native happened along, and, in answer to our inquiry, said:

"Stilworth, yes—up this road. It a'nt a very good road."

"Euphuist!" I said to Claudia. And we plunged—literally, and in spite of the remonstrances of our "driver"—up (and down) "the road."

At the end of about half a mile of moraine and bog, "this road" ended at a gap, which had once been occupied by a gate, in what had once been a stone wall about four feet high. Inside it there was real jungle into which a path, which may once have been a drive, leading to a low stone-built house, half hidden by trees and bushes run wild, disappeared.

We got out and walked up to the house.

Anything more derelict and yet inhabited I had never seen, and I could see that even Claudia's unconquerable spirit of adventure was damped. Only two windows, and those on the ground floor, had glass in them, one on each side of the dilapidated "front door."

"The Chateau Girrady," said Claudia, in a hushed voice. "Not been inhabited since the Murder."

There was no sign of a bell, so we hammered on the door with our sticks. As this turned out to be wasted effort, we pushed open the door and walked in. A narrow stone-paved passage ran from the front to the back door. The only sign of human habitation was a row of Boots—about a dozen pairs, of all shapes and sizes, and in every stage of decrepitude—that stood on the floor against the wall.

To the right and left of us, close to the "front door," were two other doors. From behind that on the right there came sounds. We rapped on that without result.

"Behind this door," whispered Claudia, clutching my arm, "M. le Baron de Girrady lies in wait for the adventurous wayfarer. Let us brave him."

We pushed open the door, whose fastening had long since ceased to function, and found ourselves in a large stone-flagged room fitted in the centre of the further wall with a stone-built fireplace, which had evidently been added to the room, for it was fitted into what was left of what must, at one time, have been a fine mantel-piece, on which the remains of carving and a coat of arms were still recognisable. Standing at this, with her back towards us, and evidently engaged in cooking operations, was a large woman in rusty black, with the grandmother of bonnets on her head. We coughed, and I said politely, "Good morning."

The woman neither moved nor replied.

"She's deaf," said Claudia. This seemed to be obvious and accurate, so I went up to her and touched her on the shoulder. She did not start, or drop a saucepan, or anything of that kind, but just turned round slowly, looked at both of us in turn, and said:

"Lor!"

I began to feel nervous—and apologetic.

"We have been told," I began, "that this house is for sale, and that——"

The woman emitted no further sound, but walked heavily to a window which stood open at the back of the house, and cried in a raucous voice:

"Gaffer!"

She was a tall female of grim, and even repellent, appearance. Broad of shoulder, heavily bosomed, with thick legs and large feet thrust into unfastened and deplorable boots, which shuffled as she walked. Iron-grey hair straying from beneath the ancestral bonnet; apparently toothless, and of any age between fifty and seventy. She remained standing at the window with her back towards us as it would seem waiting for "Gaffer" to react to her call.

"I notice," said Claudia, with an assumption of easy bravery, "that neither this door nor the 'front' can be fastened."

After what seemed to be an interminable two minutes of uncomfortable silence, we heard the back door pushed open, screeching upon the flags of the passage, and footsteps approaching. Then "Gaffer" appeared, and stood waiting in the doorway. He was a tall but slightly bent man of the same hypothetical age as the woman, with the same iron-grey hair, and a beard which, somewhat surprisingly, seemed to be carefully trimmed. He was also clean. In his hand he carried a long spud, upon which he leaned, looking at us. Then he removed his hat—borrowed, no doubt, from an obliging scarecrow—and, with a little courtly half bow, he said:

"Yes?"

"Chatty people!" whispered Claudia, who was by this time clinging to me. And I took up the conversation, which rippled along as follows.

"I understand that you wish to dispose of this property?"

"Yes?"

"We might like to buy it."

"Yes?"

"Perhaps we might look over it."

"Yes?"

"Have you an objection?"

"No."

"Will you tell me what price you are asking for it?"

"Two thousand pounds."

I do not know at this interval of time what surprised me most, the price asked or the length of the speech in which it was announced. The conversation then resumed its normal character.

"You said we might look over it?"

"Yes."

"Will you accompany us?"

"No."

"Then we can wander about alone?"

"Yes."

"Shall we find you here when we come back, or——"

"Yes."

"Come on!" said Claudia, "or I shall scream."

We got back into the passage and heaved deep sighs of relief. Then Claudia laughed—her laugh resembles the much overrated noise made by a nightingale, and is terribly infectious. I laughed too. Claudia, who specialises in sudden transitions, suddenly became Clerk to a Local Land Agent—showing the property.

"The property," she observed, "is, as you see, somewhat out of repair, but it is peculiarly adapted for development as an English gentleman's county establishment. This door on the left leads into—er—(she opened it)—a room of similar proportions to that which we have just left. It is the dining-room—or—er—drawing-room. At present it is used as a bedroom—you will observe the carving of the mantelpiece and the oak panelling, which dates from—er—some time back. Beyond it, through this door (she opened it), we have a smaller room, the boudoir of the lady of the house—or the study of the master—at present in use as a *chambre de débarras*—or, as we say in England, a lumber-room. It is now primarily used as a chicken-house—the poultry is fortuitous, using the window, which, as you see, is conveniently unglazed, for purposes of ingress and egress. From here another door leads into (she opened it) the scullery, wash-house, and unusual offices. For God's sake let us go upstairs!"

We got back into the passage. "Whew!" ejaculated Claudia, and then, in her earlier manner, "Will you please to follow me upstairs, keeping as close as you conveniently can to the wall, which, as you see, is oak panelled, or to the balusters, which, as you see, are dilapidated—but easily to be repaired. I am not in a position to guarantee the central portions of the staircase. At the top, on the left, we have (she opened a door)—er—a room—probably used as a bedroom before the invasion of the rats—Shoo!!—beyond it a smaller room, as on the ground floor. We will take it as seen. Across the landing we see two rooms occupying the depth of the house; in the corner of the back room you see a capacious cupboard. Hullo! look here." The narrow door, which she opened, showed a spiral staircase leading down—where?

"I will go down and explore," said I, bravely.

"No—darling, if you are killed there will be no one to buy the house, let alone pay the hotel bill. I will be the Horatius of this adventure," and before I could stop her she was half way down. Almost immediately she called up the shaft, "It is all right—come down." I followed her.

We found ourselves in a room the size of the one we had first entered. Windows at both ends were shuttered, and when we had groped, past obstacles unknown, to the back window, the fastenings came away from the rotten wood, and revealed a lumber of old furniture and other rubbish—and there was a scuttering, which we pretended was not terrifying. At the front window the shutters hung, so to speak, by a thread, and came down with a rumble like a stage accident—"off."

There seemed to be no communication with the rest of the house other than the spiral staircase. Behind a mound of dilapidated furniture a door led—as we ascertained when we went outside—into the garden. We had seen enough, regained the upper floor by the way we had left it, and so down to the entrance hall, where the Boots were. We re-entered the living room and found Gaffer Girrady sitting patiently at the table in the centre—the woman was still cooking. I said:

"What land—garden—goes with the house?"

"The garden—perhaps an acre. Then the wood—and a field—as far as the brook—together, perhaps fifty acres."

I gasped, and Claudia clutched my arm and said "Oh!"

Turning to Mr. Girrady, I said, "Do I deal—arrange—discuss with you, or——?"

"My advocate—man of law—is Mr. Crayshaw, of Horsham. He will tell you"—and he handed me a scrap of paper—a letter-heading, bearing the address of a firm of solicitors.

"Thank you. I will see him—I do not think I need trouble you any further."

He rose, without replying, and led the way to the front door and so down the pathway to the gate where our barouche awaited us, leaning upon his spud. As we drove away I looked round. Gaffer Girrady was returning to the house; as he did so he stooped and picked up a pair of Boots which I had not noticed as we made for the gate-gap. He was carrying them back to the house.

There was something exciting—weirdly interesting about the place—and it was obvious that, given fairly extensive expenditure, it had great "possibilities." We sat up late that evening talking about it, Claudia characteristically full of wild conjectures and plans of reconstruction, and next morning we drove into Horsham and interviewed Mr. Crayshaw.

He received us with a measure of apathetic reserve—he had evidently been interviewed about Stippleworth (in the vernacular "Stilworth") Hall before, but when he found that we really meant business he told us a remarkable story.

It appeared that at the first rumbling of the storm in Paris, the fall of the Bastille in July, 1789, without waiting for the *sauve qui peut* which followed on the Constitution of 1791, the Marquis Louis-Adhémar-Marie d'Aubry de la Giroday, one of the Fermiers Généraux, realised his property and led the Emigration. He bought the Stippleworth Estate, and enlarged the existing farm house into a small country residence, which would shelter him and his family for the two, or perhaps three years which they feared might elapse before things were settled in France by the wholesale execution of the rising revolutionary party. He thought that, in this forgotten corner of England, he would be beyond the reach and importunities of his fellow-aristocrats, who would, he foresaw, arrive later homeless and penniless. It was not long, however, before the isolation on which he had laid store palled upon him, and he became one of the shining lights of the entourage of H.R.H. the Prince Regent. At one with him in his views upon country life was Mme. la Marquise Marie-Françoise-Gabrielle de Longueville de la Giroday, who, like her husband, found a wide opening for her talents, and for the exploitation of the charms which had been of outstanding merit, even in the *côterie* of Marie Antoinette and the Comte d'Artois at the Petit Trianon. It was rumoured in the Chronique Scandaleuse of the Regency that the happy pair startled even the courageous society of Leicester House—he by the fabulous scale of his play, and she by the splendour both of her toilettes and her *affaires d'amour*.

As a meteorite consumes itself in its passage through our atmosphere, either worn to nothingness by the trail of combustion that it leaves behind it, or ending in explosion and dispersion, so vanished in an almost incredibly short space of time the accumulated wealth wrung by the ci-devant Fermier-Général from the peasants and proletariat of France. I will not burden this story with any account of the decadence and final degradation of this family, represented at the time of which I am writing by the last of the de la Girodays—Gaffer Girrady and the gaunt female—whether related to him or not, no one can say. It is strange that the property should never have been alienated during the century and a quarter since M. le Marquis re-built the house, and doubtless laid out the ground in its immediate vicinity. In the week-end following our visit we made our way there and explored "the property." Traces of a garden laid out in the manner familiar to anyone who has visited a French Chateau of the latter part of the eighteenth century. Remains of stone seats, basins, no doubt at one time furnished with fountains, lay hidden in the jungle of shrubs that had run to riot and destruction, even the ruins—the foundations rather—of a pavilion such as we read about in French romances, on the border of "our stream," which disappeared on its way to the Arun river in a matted forest that might well have surrounded and overgrown the palace of the Sleeping Beauty. As Claudia had said, it was "full of possibilities"—but oh! the work to be done and the money to be spent, and especially on "this road," which would have to be reconstructed. Fortunately I had no relations or, by that time, trustees to deliver lectures upon what might well have been, and later was, called "Carol's Folly." The title was simple and the extreme—the property had descended from father to son, and the muniments of title consisted only of a sequence of records of the Court of Probate. Gaffer Girrady himself had been in possession for over thirty years, and no one knew what he lived upon, other than his own garden produce and that of his poultry, which seemed to live anyhow and anywhere, inside and outside the house. We frequently ran down to see how the army of workmen and gardeners were getting on. Just before they entered upon their labour of Hercules—for it amounted to that—we met our landscape gardener on the premises, and found Gaffer Girrady and the female of his species in the act of removing their "bits of sticks" in a farm wagon. They had not cleared out the stuff stored in what we called the Secret Room, and they seemed averse to talking about it. I asked Gaffer about the Boots, and all he said was:

"They have been there all my time, and, I know, all my father's, and they will be there all yours." More than this he would not say—if he had anything to say.

"Oh! will they?" said Claudia, "we will see about that!"

On our next visit we tied them all up in pairs and distributed them among the workmen, especially among the local "hands" employed in converting the jungle into a garden round the house. And then a curious thing happened. On our next visit half a dozen of the pairs were back in the house passage. When we made inquiries about this, we were met with various explanations. One man said his wife would not have them in the house; another that they did not fit any of his family; another that they were too "old-fashioned"—a common Sussex term for anything queer or inexplicable; another, that he did not want them; another, merely that "he just did not like them." It struck us as odd, and we gave instructions that they were to be cleared out with the other rubbish, of which a considerable pile was accumulating in the forecourt. On our next visit, as this had not been done, we superintended the jettisoning of the Boots upon the pile. On our next, we found them back in the passage, though by that time the builder's men were busy in the house; we asked for an explanation, and were told that "Someone had put them back," but we could not ascertain who had done this, so we left them there until the last rubbish had been cleared out, and then Claudia and I threw them once more on to the pyre (*Anglice* bonfire), set light to it, and watched it burn, which it did fiercely and thoroughly.

Then we went abroad for the Easter Vac. and remained away until the builders had finished, and we could set to work on the fittings and decorations of our country mansion. I need not go into details of our rebuilding, but it was a very charming and convenient house that we had to decorate and furnish.

I refused—and I still refuse—to allow that, on general principles, I committed wild extravagances in the restoration and fitting up of Stippleworth Hall. I met my critics with the arguments that (*a*) I was absolute mistress of my fate and fortune; (*b*) that there were really fantastic accumulations of income which were at my sole mercy when I came of age and bade a graceful farewell to the trustees of my father's and uncle's wills, who, after keeping me supplied with an ample allowance, had invested the surplus in terribly sound government securities; (*c*) that so lovely a part of the country must, sooner or later, but inevitably, be "opened up" (I believe that that is the correct expression) by a branch line of the railway, and that then the Stippleworth Estate would be worth millions; and (*d*) that, married or single, we should always want a country house or houses. We had already considered the probability that we should build another—a sort of Dower house—for Claudia if and when she should marry— and had even fixed upon the site. I had thousands of pounds to play with.

But now I do confess that I allowed myself to get loose upon one very expensive fad—or hobby—call it what you will, that I had never had space to indulge in. We had arranged for ourselves two large rooms, to the right on the upper floor, and cut a communicating door between them. These were our bedrooms; Claudia had the one of the front of the house, I the one at the back, the one from which a new oak stairway let down into the Secret Room, but we generally used the back one—mine— for sleeping in. The Secret Room was, as I have pointed out, not otherwise connected with the house itself, but had a door which led out into the garden. On that side of the house we constructed a flagged terrace, with a pent-house roof over it, a delightful place facing south-west, which could be converted, when the autumn grew chilly, into a sort of winter garden by the fitting in of removable glass panels between the pillars which supported the roof.

I had a pet furniture dealer and repairer, a learned and delightful man who had a little shop in the hinterland of Kensington High Street, and whose chief occupation was the repair and restoration of old furniture for the princes of the trade in Bond Street and St. James's. He had become a great friend of mine, and I had collected from him many charming bits of "Period" furniture for my rooms at Cosmopoli and for my bachelor flat in town. We took him down to Stippleworth Hall and spent and exciting and marvellous day inspecting and sorting out the accumulated ruins of furniture heaped away in the Secret Room. We found what had been wonderful specimens of Louis XV. and XVI. furniture, all in more or less accentuated stages of dilapidation. We had practically the whole lot removed to his place in town, and gave him carte-blanche to clean up and "restore" it, regardless of cost.

For him it was a labour of love—apart from the profits of his work—and in the end we had a perfectly harmonious Louis XVI. room, which could only be reached—excepting for the garden door which was kept religiously fastened—by an open oaken stairway, with which we had replaced the original spiral staircase. When it was finished, it might have been a "specimen" period room in the Victoria and Albert Museum, and we decided that only the very elect should ever be allowed to penetrate to this holy of holies. It was an appalling extravagance, but, as I pointed out to Claudia, a more sensible and satisfactory one than the collection of postage stamps, or coins, or lace, upon which collectors expend vast sums, and have very little to show for their outlay.

"Anyhow," said Claudia, "if the ghosts of the departed la Girodays should feel inclined to 're-visit the glimpses of the moon,' they will find their own room ready for them, furnished as it was when they left it."

Claudia, who is nothing if not "thorough," clothed herself—in every sense of the word—in the atmosphere of the century. She had some dresses made—not fancy dresses, as she contended, but as part of the *décor* of the room—in which she looked like a naughty little French marquise who had stepped from the frame of a picture by Boucher or Baudoin, or from a fan by Fragonard. She had rummaged in second-hand music shops and collected a quantity of airs of the schools of Rameau, Monsigny and Paisiello, which she played upon, or sang to a beautiful and perfectly "restored" Spinet which I had picked up in Paris.

At intervals she would turn to me and say:

"Do you think that *They* liked that?"

She always referred to the departed la Girodays as *"They,"* and really, at times, it was difficult to rid oneself of the impression that *"They"* were in the room with us, listening to Claudia's eighteenth century "Recitals." We loved to feel them about the place.

She came near to tears, sometimes, about her beautiful hair, which she had had "bobbed"—she wanted to be able to dress it high upon her pretty little head in little curls, but she camouflaged her "bob"—lest it should offend *Them*—beneath a lace cap such as one sees in the more *negligée* pictures of Moreau le jeune, and of Schall. She industriously studied the earlier volumes of the Memoirs of Mme. de Genlis, and I had great difficulty in preventing her from buying a harp!

But this is anticipating. This all came later, but it belongs essentially to our lovely room, so I record it here.

At the time of which I am writing, we used to run down whenever we could to watch the re-building, and to discuss the decoration and furnishing of the house, and the restoration, or rebirth, of the garden, which very soon became very beautiful and full of promise for the near future. We took food with us, and had delightful picnics—on packing cases and work benches, in any room in which we could find a clear space.

On one of these occasions, after a long day of measuring and scheming, we were leaving the house at nightfall, when Claudia suddenly clutched my arm and said:

"My holy aunt—look there!"

The whole row of Boots was back in its place—apparently. I say "apparently" because, when we went back into the passage, which had been enlarged into a fairly spacious hall, and looked more closely, there were no Boots, actually speaking, but a row of shadows—I hate to use the word "ghosts"—where they had stood against the wall, which had been moved back.

"Hooray!" said Claudia, rather nervously, "we have got a haunted house. I have always longed to live in one, but just fancy being haunted by Boots!"

"It is some weird effect of the half-light," I said, "we will see what they look like by daylight." And so we left Stippleworth Hall for that time, and though we neither of us said any more about it, each of us knew that we were—to use a mild term—puzzled over the Boots.

We were there again next morning to deal with gardeners. There was no sign or simulacrum of the Boots.

In all our subsequent visits, superintending the decorations and the placing of the furniture, we saw the Boots as soon as it was dark enough to make them visible. This seems an odd thing to say, for the Ghost-boots, as we came to call them, were in no way incandescent—or fluorescent—there was no "weird ghostly light" inherent in or emanating from them—they just grew into visibility as the darkness deepened. Claudia, who had dabbled in Optics before she settled down to Botany, talked learnedly about "the dark-adapted eye," and one evening she exclaimed joyously:

"I have it! We are—so far as the Boots are concerned—nyctalopes"—she was fond of digging up words like that—"we can only see *Them* in the dark. I have always wanted to meet one—and here I am—we are!"

We grew quite fond of them—they became, as it were, secret pets, and we should have missed them—or thought there was something wrong with us—if we had not seen them. We arrived at distinguishing them, and we gave them names. There were M. le Marquis and two brothers, the Vicomte and the Chevalier; there were Madame la Marquise and two female friends or relations—quaint little shoes, square toed with remains of laces which must, when they were perfect, have criss-crossed over the instep and fastened round the ankle. There was a pair that we could not quite "place"—a man's boots, with heels that had been, at some time, red. They were larger than those of "the Family," a visitor perhaps—he had left behind him also a pair of riding-boots—rather dainty and showing wear where the spurs had been buckled on—we called him the Baron. There was another pair of riding boots, of inferior leather, very stout; we decided that these had belonged to the Baron's servant.

"Visitors," said Claudia, "another *émigré* evidently—after all, Juniper Hall is only about fourteen miles away, an easy ride."

"This is all very well—and romantic," said I, "but why did they leave their Boots behind them?"

"Give it up," said Claudia.

The house was finished, and furnished, just before Long Vac., and, full of excitement and enthusiasm, we came down and took possession. How we loved it! A week or two of "settling in" and exploration of our domain and its surroundings, and we felt as if we had lived there all our lives. We ceased to take much notice of the Boots, but Claudia and I never went up to bed, but she dropped a little curtsey to them, and said politely:

"*Á domain alors—bonsoir, Messieurs et Dames.*"

"The least they could do," said she, "would be to make a little movement, as if 'making a leg' in reply." But they did not. They just appeared at dusk and disappeared at dawn, and we rather lost interest in them as the queerness and novelty wore off. Then an extraordinary thing happened.

It was one day in August. We had driven over the Burford Bridge and climbed Box Hill, and we had made a sort of pilgrimage to Juniper Hall—not much altered since Dibden made his

534

sketch of it in 1844, and surrounded by the cedars that must have witnessed the wooing of Fanny Burney and Lafayette's Adjutant-General Alexandre d'Arblay. We boldly invaded it, interviewed the owner and inspected the beautifully decorated "Adams" drawing-room, where we could imagine the gathering of the *émigrés*, Narbonne, Jacourt and all the rest of them encouraging one another with talk of the better times to come when the Comte d'Artois should mount the throne that should have been occupied by the ill-fated child, Louis XVII.

We were very tired and went to bed early.

It was a little after midnight when Claudia, who had been sleeping peacefully in my arms, woke up suddenly and woke me in turn.

"Carol!" she whispered.

"What is it, darling?"

"*They* are dancing!"

I started up, fully awake. I could distinctly hear a kind of shuffling in the Secret Room below us. We got up and, as we were, stepped through the door which led to the stairway which had taken the place of the spiral one. We leaned over the balustrade of the little "landing" at the top and looked down. The Boots were *there* and all moving, rhythmically, as it were, in one of the stately dances of the eighteenth century—or a Pavane perhaps, or a Minuet. We could distinguish six pairs in a curious and, to us, quite inexplicable half light—it was not altogether the moon. We watched them petrified, but in no sense alarmed, until the dance concluded; the dancers, that is to say, their shoes, separated towards the walls, and M. le Baron and Mm. la Marquise—represented by their foot-gear—made for the door leading into the garden. They were intercepted by the shoes of M. le Marquis, and a noiseless "scuffle" seemed to take place. Then the shoes of M. le Baron separated a little and turned over on their sides. And then the whole scene "closed in," as they say in film parlance, and we were left looking at nothing but the Boots, lying about haphazard, as it were, in the moonlight which now streamed through the front windows.

We crept back into our room, and got into bed again, without a word. After a few minutes Claudia shivered violently and clutched me a little more tightly.

"What is it, darling?" I said.

"Carol! I have had a most amazing dream."

"So have I."

"Did you see *Them*—dancing?"

"Yes. You made me dream the same thing. It is telepathy."

After a pause, she said: "I *must* go down to the hall and look—will you come?"

"Of course, darling."

We went out on to the gallery, which now ran round the hall, and upon which all the bedrooms in the house opened, and looked over. The moon had passed behind a cloud, and we could see nothing. We slipped our feet into *mules* and crept downstairs in the dark. As we entered the hall the moon "brightening the skirts of a long cloud ran forth" and illuminated the scene.

The Boots were aligned as usual in their accustomed row across the floor.

We often spoke of our "dream." Claudia had diligently reconstructed the whole story. M. le Baron and Mme. la Marquise were lovers, and M. le Marquis, though tolerant like most French husbands of the eighteenth century to the verge of complaisance, had suddenly reached the end of his tolerance, realising that his wife was burning her boats that night. It was a moment of what Carlyle, in his History of the Epoch, called "murders, rapes, and such sudden sincerities,"—he had intercepted and provoked the lover and killed him. That was all.

"It accounts," said Claudia, conclusively, "for M. le Baron leaving his riding-boots behind."

Then we gave a house-warming. We invited our professor, Dr. Pamela Strachan (who had succeeded Warham as Edelstein Professor of Botanical Research after his awful death in the Amazonian jungle); Wrammsbothame, her lecturer; Cantrell, the Professor of Zoology; and Clodagh Ganthony, a *protegée* of mine, of whom Claudia was inclined to be jealous—which was good for her.

They all arrived in time for lunch one Friday, and warmed our hearts (and incidentally justified me to myself with regard to what my lawyer called my wanton and criminal extravagance) with their enthusiastic admiration and appreciation of Stippleworth Hall—"Carol's Folly," in the unsympathetic vernacular of the envious. And at tea-time we told them all about the la Girodays and the Boots. We—especially Claudia—made the most of it—we became lyrical, and Claudia (though she strenuously denies it) got a little beyond lyrics and strayed somewhat among the flowery shadows of Romance. Our house party listened politely impressed—but I think that "Wrammy" was the only one of them who really believed us.

We sat on a terrace in the Italian Garden until it grew dark, and then Claudia got up and said:

"Now come and see the Boots of the la Girodays."

We trooped into the hall and stood around—Claudia and I on tiptoe with expectation—we hardly knew of what. It came in the measured and judicial tones of Professor Cantrell.

"I do not see the slightest indication of anything of this kind," he said. The others, divided between polite respect for their hostesses and academic respect for the Professor of Zoology, murmured with non-committal incoherence.

"Dispense refreshment," said I to Claudia.

And we told ghost-stories till midnight.

As we dispersed around the gallery, "Wrammy," the last to bid us good-night on the way to his room, whispered to me:

"I *saw* the Boots, Carol."

ANOTHER SQUAW?

(Deposited by the Professor of Zoology.)

FROM *the Times* of the 4th November, 19—

On November 2nd, 19—, at the Marine Biology
Station, Baxmouth, the result of an accident,
Jennifer Sidonia Pendeen, B.Sc., in her twenty-sixth
year. Funeral at Polperro, Cornwall, on Monday,
November 5th, at 2 p.m.

In the concluding years of the 19th century, Bram Stoker, the
efficient and justly celebrated manager of the Lyceum Theatre
in the palmy days of Sir Henry Irving, and the author of many
works of fiction, the best known of which at the present day is
his Vampire novel, *Dracula*, published a short story entitled "The
Squaw," a horrible story, only redeemed by its utter impossibility
and extravagantly exaggerated anthropomorphism. In this story
an American tourist, leaning over the battlements, or parapet, of
the Schloss at Nuremberg, dislodges a large stone, which, falling
into the moat below, strikes and kills the single kitten of a cat
which happened to be lying at the foot of the keep. The frantic
efforts of the mother cat to scale the wall and get at the murderer
of her kitten are vividly described. Later in the day, when the
tourist and his friends are visiting the museum of Instruments of
Torture, the cat has gained admission with them, after the manner of cats, and is malevolently prowling round the turret-room
in which the "Iron Maiden" (recently discovered to be a fraud)

is exhibited by the attendant, who, by pulling a lever, opens the "Maiden," revealing the huge spikes which, when the "Maiden" is closed upon the victim forced into it, stabs him in a score of vital spots. On this occasion, the lever having been pulled and the "doors" being thus held open for the inspection of the inside by visitors, the tourist in Stoker's story, questioning whether a full-grown man could be forced inside, insists upon entering the "Maiden." At that moment the cat, who has been watching her opportunity for revenge, springs at the attendant and claws at his eyes. The wretched man, maddened with pain, lets go the lever, the doors clang to upon the tourist, and he meets with a hideous death. As I have said, the impossible anthropomorphism of the cat robs the story of its ghastliness, and it was received (as it was intended to be) as an ingeniously gruesome effort at sensationalism.

The circumstances which I am about to record recalled this story to my mind; I record them as they happened, and must leave the reader of these lines to form his own conclusions.

One of my most brilliant pupils, and later my assistant in the Zoological Department of the University of Cosmopoli, was Miss Jennifer Pendeen, a Cornish girl, who, having taken her science degree, became in turn demonstrator in my department, and, in due course, my assistant lecturer. Her special subject was fishes, and she was engaged, at the time of which I write, upon an intensive study of the oceanic angler-fishes, the Ceratioids, who inhabit the open ocean, living generally from about 500 to 2,000 metres (250 to 1,000 fathoms) below the surface. These fishes are, for the most part, uniformly blackish in colour, and their "bait," or "lure," is a luminous bulb, which attracts their prey to within a catching distance. Their teeth, which are long, slender and very sharp, can be sloped inwards at will, with the result that when a fish gets caught between them it cannot get back, but must proceed into the stomach—after the manner of an awn of creeping grass. The angler-fish is fortunately (for itself)

extremely distensible, and it can swallow and "accommodate" fishes several times its own length and weight. Once seized by the teeth of the angler, the victim cannot escape, nor can the angler cast itself loose and reject its prey.

A salient and remarkable peculiarity of the angler is that all the free-swimming fish are females, the males being little parasitic dwarves, which live indissolubly attached to the females. As soon as the male is hatched, it seeks a female, to which it attaches itself—anywhere where it can lay hold. In a short while the lips, tongue and teeth of the male "fuse" with the skin of the female, and the two are thenceforth inseparably united. The toothless mouth, being closed by the skin of the female, and, in due course, absorbed, the male can no longer feed himself, but is nourished by the blood-stream of the female, which reaches him through an anastomosis of the blood system, which thus becomes continuous and common to both male and female—indeed, the alimentary canal of the male becomes vestigial and his stomach rudimentary, and he becomes a mere appendage of the female, receiving nourishment through capillary veins in what used to be his snout. This condition of things is unique in the vertebrate animal kingdom. Instances are known of females three feet six inches in length whose parasitic husbands are no more than three inches long, and of females having two or more "husbands" welded into, and parasitic upon them. They "stick" where they first strike, anywhere—on the head, on the abdomen or by the tail, and live happily ever after with a wife who may be a thousand times as large as they are.

The reproduction of these fishes would appear to be brought about by an "urge" at spawning time, effected by some *hormone* which causes the female to discharge her ova, which are immediately fertilised by the parasitic male—this is the only incident and object of his existence. Females have been caught without parasitic males, but the males have never been caught separately, which is not remarkable, seeing that they live in perpetual darkness, mostly at very low temperatures, and would seldom be retained by any net of large enough and strong enough mesh to capture the female.

It was to this remarkable group of fishes that Jennifer Pendeen was devoting her attention and studies at the time of which I am writing. Her Monograph upon the group, which it was my somewhat melancholy task to prepare for, and see through the press, after her tragic and mysterious death, is the outstanding and most notable contribution to the literature of the subject. Her great ambition, which, as we shall see, was ultimately realised, was to obtain a living specimen and to study its life-history.

The difficulties in the way of this seemed to be insurmountable, for it must be remembered that these fish swim about at depths of from 250 to 1,000 fathoms. Now, taking the pressure of the atmosphere at sea-level to be 15 pounds to the square inch and 33 feet of seawater being equal to 30 inches of mercury, at a depth of 33 feet in the sea, the pressure would be two atmospheres, or 15 pounds; at 99 feet, 3 atmospheres, or 45 pounds to the square inch—and so on as one goes deeper. So, at 2,000 fathoms, the pressure is of 360 atmospheres, i.e., 5,400 pounds or (or 2.4 tons) to the square inch. The effect of decrease of pressure upon deep sea fish is well known. As the fish is drawn to the surface the decrease of pressure causes their swim bladders to expand, and after rising a certain distance they go on, as Sir John Murray put it, "tumbling upwards," and they are killed by the distension of their organs as the pressure becomes less and less. It has been found, however, that fishes brought up from moderate depths, to all appearances dead, can be revived by keeping them in "compressing chambers," in which the pressure is not much less than that at which they were caught, and on gradually diminishing the pressure. Their intercellular fluids have time to get into equilibrium, and the fish gradually recovers its normal functions and powers of movement.

This was the problem with which Jennifer Pendeen was confronted, and to it she devoted long-protracted and ingenious experiments, at first with fish from moderate depths and gradually with specimens from deeper ocean strata, which she caused to be caught in copper cylinders, which could be hermetically closed by a "messenger" (as it is called) sent down the line when the delicate instruments used in the experiments announced that a fish had entered the cylinder.

The opportunity, of which during the few years of her working life she had had a "Pisgah-view," came at last when the "Deep Sea Exploration Expedition" was organised by the University of Cosmopoli, under the leadership of Captain John Slatterley, R.N., who presented the rare phenomena of a naval officer of distinguished service record, who was not only an expert hydrographer (which might, at a stretch, have been expected), but also a keen marine biologist. He had even put in six months, when home on leave, at the Baxmouth Marine Biological Station, and the Lords of the Admiralty "seconded" him for service with the Cosmopoli University Expedition at the request of the Senate. A Cornishman himself, and Jennifer Pendeen being the child of an old friend, though at first taking a somewhat humoristic view of her "study," he gradually came round to an earnest interest in it.

Under their joint supervision a copper cylinder was constructed, tested for implosive and explosive pressure up to 90 atmospheres, open at both ends, save for hinged coverings—"lids"—of fine wire netting. This could be lowered to any depth, and the desired depth attained, with wire covers could be withdrawn, and at a given moment their place could be taken by copper covers, which closed the cylinder to all intents and purposes hermetically. The interior was heavily chromium-plated to withstand the action of sea water. An electrical appliance indicated on deck when any object above a certain size entered the cylinder, by weight and oscillation.

This cylinder trap was sent down "baited" with a quantity of small fish, which, of course, were killed by the increasing pressure, but remained in the cylinder. These, it was anticipated, might attract larger "denizens of the deep" when the wire ends were removed or opened. Time and again the cylinder was "down" for various lengths of time and was hauled up again, nothing whatever having happened. Glass panels in the sides, protected by a slipping collar or band, enabled the observers to see whether any fish was inside, and frequently fishes (not *Ceratias*) came up in the cylinder, which were released, and exploded on the spot. A detailed account of their "results" would not be germane to our subject, but they did fish up some very queer creatures.

At last the long-looked-for moment arrived—the presence of a large fish in the cylinder was indicated, and, as usual, the ends were closed and the cylinder hauled on deck. Inside it was a *Ceratias* some four feet long, and the cylinder was hurried home and placed in a large narrow tank filled with sea water kept at an appropriate temperature, in the Marine Biological Laboratory at Baxmouth, where Jennifer Pendeen was waiting to receive it. By means of an ingenious apparatus in the nature of a pressure gauge, attachable to the cylinder, the *Ceratias* was carefully and gradually "decompressed," and, as good luck would have it, it had kept and did keep itself alive with the corpses of the "martyrs to science," which had been sent down in the cylinder as bait. In a much shorter time than Jennifer had anticipated, the *Ceratias* got into equilibrium with its surroundings and was let out into the tank, not, apparently, any the worse for the radical change in its environment.

It became known in the laboratory as Jennifer's "pet." She had sole charge of it, and—a true Cornishwoman—she christened it "Ysolde." Attached immediately below its right pectoral fin was a perfectly formed and apparently happy—though undemonstrative—parasitic male. Him she christened "Tristan."

Remarkable testimony to the care, attention and efficiency, primarily of Jennifer Pendeen and generally of the staff of the Baxmouth Marine Laboratory, is afforded by the fact that this curious *ménage* settled down, lived and flourished in the tank that it inhabited. At the end of a month Jennifer began to consider in all its bearings the biological experiment that she had in view; this was neither more nor less than to separate them: to excise Tristan, and, by an ingenious system of artificial feeding—if such a term may be permissible in the case of a fish whose mouth-parts and alimentary system have become vestigial—to keep him alive. The interest taken in the affair by the Zoological Department of the University was keen, and it was fully shared by the Director and staff of the Zoological Gardens and Aquarium of the town of Cosmopoli. Jennifer held with Sir George Amboyne, the Regius Professor of Medicine, and Michelson, the Prosector of the Zoo, both of whom, it may be said at once, were of the opinion that the idea was fantastic, and its execution impossible, but Sir George went so far as to interest an eminent surgeon in the matter, who undertook to perform the operation under the direction and supervision of Michelson. Jennifer's theory was, that if skilfully performed, so as not to injure and vital part of either fish, Ysolde would not suffer from the operation, and that Tristan might be kept alive—*ein toller Eienfall*, as Burger, the Reader in German, put it.

The conditions and formalities imposed by the Vivisection Act of 1876 were scrupulously carried out and the necessary licence obtained, and one morning, when Tristan and Ysolde had inhabited their tank for about two months, the operation was performed in the circumstances above indicated. Ysolde was carefully "repaired" and returned to her tank, and after a few hours of restlessness seemed none the worse for her divorce. The only change apparent in her was that she developed a nervousness that she had not hitherto exhibited, and seemed averse to allowing Jennifer to touch and "tickle" her as she had been wont to do. As Jennifer put it: "She does not trust me any more, and when I feed her I think she would like to snap at me—it would be rather awful if she got those recurved teeth of hers into my hand!"

With Tristan I regret to say that it was a different matter. For about twenty-four hours he showed signs, unmistakable, of life, lying on his side at the bottom of his little tank, but next day he equally unmistakably died, and received the decent interment due to another martyr to science.

Any student or biologist who is working at Baxmouth Laboratory is given, on his (or her) arrival, a latch-key to the building, so that he can visit his work and observe its progress at any hour of the night as well as by day. By this means any biological experiments of great importance have been facilitated, the workers in many well-known instances spending their nights in the laboratory. Jennifer, who was at this time the guest of the Director and his wife, made it her practice, at least once in the night, to come down and see how Ysolde was getting on.

It was about three weeks after the *Ehescheidung* that the maid who brought her matutinal tea found that she was not in her room. An hour later she had not returned, though her clothes were as she had left them overnight, and so the matter was reported to the Director. He assumed that Jennifer was in the tank-room as usual, but when she did not put in an appearance at breakfast time he went to look for her.

The spectacle that met his eyes was terrible. Clad in her pyjamas and a thin silk wrapper, Jennifer was lying huddled together at the bottom of the tank on the top of Ysolde. Summoning assistance, he lifted her out, and Ysolde came with her, very much alive and lashing out furiously. She had caught Jennifer by the forearm, as, evidently, she had leaned over the edge of the tank, and reached down to touch her. The formidable recurved teeth had met in Jennifer's arm; Ysolde could not have let go, *had she wished or striven to do so*, and Jennifer, encumbered and entangled in her wrapper, could not have struggled to the surface owing to the narrowness of the tank, and the fact that she was on the top of her captor. In the opinion of the doctor, who was summoned, she had been dead about five hours.

Another Squaw?

PASSIFLORA VINDICTA.

Wrammsbothame.

(Deposited by the Professor of Botanical Research.)

WHEN Cynthia Carwardine (pronounced "Cardeen," s.v.p.), the loveliest daughter of the notoriously impoverished Duke of Caversham (pronounced "Carsham," *s.v.p.*), married little Solly Edelstein, her world—that is, the Leaders of Society—shrugged its shoulders and said "Good God!" and his—that is, the Authorities of the Synagogue—was gravely disturbed. It was a crashing *schikser* for Solomon Edelstein to marry an aristocratic *goy*, doubtless of extravagant tastes and spendthrift habits, for Solly was many times a millionaire. Lady Cynthia had no idea of this when, having met him in a distant Colony, at a meeting of the British Association (which was extended to a return journey the other way round the world for those who could afford the time and money), she rapidly got over—and past—his personal appearance, and fell very seriously in love with him. She had, in the preceding summer term, taken, from St. Lewinna's, First-class Honours in the Nat. Sci. Tripos (Pt. I. Special Subject, Pt. II. Botany) and took him to be a Professor of Botany from some provincial University. She was not, however, a young fool in love with Love, and when she realised her own parlous condition and had had opportunities of observing that he had "got it" quite as badly, she made discreet enquiries as to the stipend of a University Professor. When she learnt that the "screw" was a thousand a year, the cloud that was gathering over her soul at the thought of her coming interview with the Duke—and the Duchess—was very noticeably dispelled. It was something of a shock to her when they landed at Tilbury, and he offered, and she accepted, a lift home in his barouche—it was before the days of motor-cars—(owing to some stupidity or misunderstanding the ducal brougham was nowhere to be found), to learn that he was the Edelstein, the one and only Edelstein, all the others having turned into "Jewells" in a single night. Like the well-conducted maiden that she undoubtedly was, her first thought was for her parents—she no longer feared the interview with the Duke; all that was left of her dutiful and filial anxieties was the thought of how they would feel—and look—when they saw him. For there was nothing *sephardi* about Solly; the *tedesco* of the Frankfurt Ghetto was stamped all over him—what there was of him, for he only came up to Cynthia's shoulder—but his eyes were splendid, his voice quite beautiful and his manners orientally perfect.

Many years after his death Lady Cynthia Edelstein said to Pamela Strachan when they were planning the Warham-Edelstein Amazon Expedition: "My dear, I have had the good fortune to meet three Great Gentlemen in my long life, and Solomon Edelstein was one of them. If ever you write my Obituary Notice, you can say that—and mind you put capital G's."

And this is, I think, all that is necessary to be said about the personalities of Solomon Edelstein and Lady Cynthia, his wife.

Of his scientific activities it is only necessary to record that he had contributed some valuable papers to the Transactions and Proceedings of the Linnean Society (which will be found recorded in the *Index of Scientific Papers*) and was the author of a sumptuous volume on *The Plants of Palestine*, and that he died quite genuinely regretted, not only by his wife, but also by several friends who had never had occasion to benefit by his too ready generosity.

The earliest years of her widowhood were spent by Lady Cynthia in the planning and addition of an "Edelstein" wing to the Science Schools and Museums of the University of Cosmopoli, to contain the Edelstein Herbaria and Collections, and the laboratories and workrooms attached to the newly founded Edelstein Professorship of Botanical Research, a Chair so bountifully endowed that Warham, the Savilian Professor of Botany, moved the academic heaven and earth to obtain it in exchange for his existing chair, and succeeded in doing so. It carried with it the appointment of an Assistant Lecturer and Keeper of the collections, with a salary of five hundred pounds a year, and this is how Pamela Strachan came to Cosmopoli. The post was, of course, advertised in *Nature* according to the Statutes, but Pamela had practically a "walk-over," for she had applied with a flaming testimonial from the Professor of Botany under whom she had worked as a Demostrator at Oxbridge, coupled with a warm letter of recommendation on personal grounds from Lady Cynthia herself, and the glamour of a quite remarkable Thesis upon the "Bionomics of Tropical Saprophytes" which had secured her a D.Sc. degree. Add to this that she was twenty-eight years old and amazingly lovely to look upon, and you see Pamela Strachan installed in the post as "advertised." In connection with, and in addition to, these Edelstein endowments, there was also an equipment and "expeditionary" fund, which was the envy of every School of Natural Science in the empire. The whole business cost Lady Cynthia a sum just short of half a million pounds sterling.

The youth and professional career of Philip Warham, late Savilian Professor of Botany and first occupant of the Edelstein Chair of Botanical Research, presented features in common with those of many men who, by sheer force of industry and significant personality, have risen to the highest attainable position in science, a professorship in a great University. Of comparatively humble social origin, a scholarship had taken him to a provincial University where, by singleness of purpose and unremitting industry, he had won through the period of penury and struggle that is inevitable for young men who devote themselves, in the face of social and financial difficulties, to science as a profession. Somewhat after the manner of the industrious apprentice of the stories told us in our childhood, who eventually marries his master's daughter, Philip Warham had solved one of the major difficulties of his early career by marrying his landlady's pretty but wholly unintellectual daughter. She made him a good wife, and their union, though, fortunately or unfortunately, childless, was not, in its inception, an unhappy one, though, as time went on, her complete inability to take any interest in his work, and his career as such, brought the inevitable and insurmountable disillusion and a readjustment of his outlook. On the one side his work, and on the other his home life; and as he rose successively to a Demonstratorship and to the position of Assistant Lecturer, his wife was perforce left behind, and, as in the case of many men in his position, it was generally accepted as a fact that his wife was in many respects a clog upon his career, and though treated with every kindness and consideration by his colleagues and their wives, she never "fitted in" to the social side of the University. So when the Savilian Professorship of Botany was offered to him, he accepted it—as who would not—gladly, but particularly in the hope that in new surroundings his wife would pull herself together and fall into her recognised position in the society of Cosmopoli. This is a somewhat cryptic statement, but it is necessary to indicate that Mrs. Warham was subject to periods increasingly recurrent, in which she exhibited symptoms akin to those of alcoholic poisoning. In a word, the Savilian professor, though his trouble was tactfully ignored as far as possible, lived, as it were, on the brink of a volcano, whose eruptions were as difficult to foresee as they were impossible to obviate. He became a careworn and an unhappy man, and it was only his passionate devotion to his professorial work that enabled him to bear up against the worries and trials of his private life.

The appointment of Pamela Strachan as Assistant Lecturer and Keeper was, to Philip Warham, as the breaking of a new dawn of sympathy and interest in his work, upon which the new and vivifying condition of things had an immediate and marked effect. His domestic affliction faded almost imperceptibly into the background, and in the constant and assiduous work of the new Department he found oblivion, and as Chalmers, the Professor of Psychology, an expert in such matters, put it: Warham seemed endowed with a new soul; and Magley, the physiologist, who was no respecter of persons or phraseology, is reported to have said: "The Assistant Lecturer plays Erda to the weary Wotan: he has presumably touched her, and his youth is renewed." The Department of Botanical Research developed and flourished with healthy rapidity, and within a year was completely organised and established in full and steady working order.

It was in this fertile ground and propitious atmosphere that the seed of "The Warham-Edelstein Amazon Expedition" was sown and germinated, and went ahead like the giant bamboos of the East, which, in the proper season, grow twenty inches in a single night.

Algot Lange's book on the Amazon Jungle was, of course, not yet in existence—the revelations of Sir Roger Casement and of Hardenburg upon the atrocities of the Putumayo District were as yet undreamed of, but no scientific library was without the classic work of H. W. Bates, *The Naturalist on the Amazon* (1864), and the rapidly growing indiarubber industry was attracting the attention of the world to the upper reaches of this almost inconceivable river—inconceivable when one realises that the district we are about to deal with only begins at that ominously named town, at the junction of the Javary and Itecuahy Rivers, 2,200 miles west of Para on the Atlantic Coast—Remate de Males—"Culmination of Evils."

There is little doubt but that the expedition owed its inception largely to the initiative of Pamela Strachan. We have mentioned her Thesis on the Bionomics of Tropical Saprophytes; and it was this branch of Botany and particularly the Insectivorous Plants that had always engaged her most concentrated attention. As a side-line, or lighter side to her professional work, she was steeped in the legendary lore of plant life, and it amused her leisure to seek in such legends any original germ of truth that had led to their growth.

In her professor she had an "*advocatus diaboli*" worthy of her steel! Warham confessed to a sneaking interest in the matter, but was always ready to enter the lists against her, and they had, in their leisure hours which they grew imperceptibly to spend together, in experiments and field-work, waged furious battles over an imaginary work to be entitled (according to Warham)

"Metaphysical Botany by Pamela Strachan, D.Sc., F.L.S.," which grew in their battles ever more and more phantastic, and gradually became an intellectual hobby. Their point of departure was the Insectivorous Plants first noticed by Dr. Roth in 1782, which became the subject of Charles Darwin's historic work upon this branch of botany, starting from the observations of Bunett in 1829 on Drosera rotundifolia, which figures so largely in Darwin's book. Pamela always carried Warham back in their discussions to Darwin's illustrious grandfather (Erasmus Darwin)'s extraordinary book, *The Botanical Garden*, Part II. of which, "The Loves of the Plants," supplied her with texts for the wildest excursions into the theme. The dioecious plants, which are either male or female as opposed to the monoecius, in which the sexes are combined, fascinated her; and she wound brilliant hypotheses around them, creating a fairyland of her own. She cultivated in her rooms the *Vallisneria*, whose female flowers float, and whose male flowers, developed under water, rise in due course to seek the females. She gleefully quoted Erasums Darwin's observation that "amongst Sir Brooke Boothby's valuable collection of plants at Ashbourn the manifest adultery of several females of the plant *Collinsia*, who had bent themselves into contact with males of other flowers of the same plant in their vicinity, neglectful of their own." Among her "pets" in her conservatory she grew the Sundew (*Droser rotundifolia*); "Venus' Flytrap" (*Dioanaea muscipula*), *Aldrovanda*, the rootless water-plant which catches and absorbs the little crustacean; *Cypris*, and whose Australian varieties capture large beetles; the Portuguese Fly-catcher, *Drosophyllum*, and the British Pinguicula, which enfolds insects in its leaves, and the *Utricularia*, the bladder pond-plant, which catches and absorbs water-worms and fleas, and the ubiquitous *Cypris* that flourishes in our bird-basins. And a host of others. Warham called it her "Menagerie of Murderous Vegetables."

She professed to believe implicitly in the personality of trees, taking for her text the mutterings of the country maiden in George Macdonald's *Phantastes*.

"Trust the Oak and the Elm and the great Beech. Take care of the Birch, for though she is honest, she is too young not to be changeable. But shun the Ash and the Alder; for the Ash is an Ogre—you will know him by his thick fingers; and the Alder will smother you with her web of hair if you let her near you at night."

But especially she was attracted by the idea of the plants which are noxious or fatal to man, the *Jatrophaurens*, which, when grown at Kew, almost caused the death of a Curator who touched it, stopping the circulation of his heart and causing him to lose consciousness; after which no gardener could be persuaded to approach it, and both it and other specimens subsequently acquired all mysteriously died or disappeared.

Above all, she was convinced that there must have been some truth in the stories in Erasmus Darwin's book of the Upas tree of Java, appended as a note to his lines:

> Fierce in dread silence on the blasted heath Fell
> Upas sits, the hydra tree of death.

The account given by the Dutch surgeon, Foersch, who relates "simple unadorned facts of which I have been an eye-witness," at Samarang in 1773, was, she was convinced, founded on fact, and certainly on reading his account, as published in the *London Magazine* in 1783 and reproduced in extenso in his "Note" by Darwin, it is difficult to conceive "the whole narrative to be an ingenious fiction." Pamela pointed triumphantly to the "confirmation" of Foersch's account by Christian Aejmelaeus in his essay on the *Boa-Upas tree of Macasser* (sic), approved by Professor Thunberg of Upsala (an abstract of which is to be found in *Dr. Duncan's Medical Commentaries for the year 1790*, Decade II., Vol. V.), and they wrangled pleasantly over the whole range of the subject.

I ought perhaps, at this point, to explain how it is that I come to be writing this account from the fullest available knowledge of the facts. I was, at the time of which I am now writing, junior Demonstrator in Warham's Laboratory, and knew both him and Pamela Strachan intimately. It was indeed owing to their encouragement and support that I subsequently became lecturer in the department, and after the retirement of Professor Strachan, came into possession of the documents from which I have written this account, having succeeded her as Edelstein Professor of Botanical Research, a sequence of events which will be unfolded in its due course.

The preparations for the Expedition proceeded rapidly. Funds were, of course, ample, and no expense was spared to make it, from every point of view, successful. A fine steamship was chartered and fully equipped for the carrying out of the scientific programme. Besides Warham and Pamela Strachan, Magley, who was then Paul Barrodale's assistant, went as physiologist and Cantrell as zoologist, the former somewhat to Pamela's uneasiness, for Magley made no concealment of his admiration for her, and she regarded him with defensive dislike and disapproval. A doctor, nominated by Sir George Amboyne, our Regius Professor of Medecine, a meteorologist, Askew, and a geographer, Clissold, completed the scientific staff, and the expedition started in the late autumn of the year 18—.

Our Registrar, Dr. Christopher Blayre, received letters from them from Lisbon and from Madeira, and in due course from Para, from which point of departure the systematic work of the Expedition was inaugurated. Several members of the professorial staff also received letters from members of the Expedition, many of which came later into my hands. As is almost inevitable in such groups of people, there were, from time to time, indicated elements of possible discord. In a letter to Barrowdale, Magley wrote: "We do not get much converse with the Director. He and the fascinating Pamela keep themselves a good deal to themselves, one would almost think they were on their honeymoon. Tell me when you write, if you can, how Mrs. Warham is bearing up under the enforced separation from her devoted lord and master—and who is looking after her?"

What Barrowdale may have replied I cannot tell, but one thing is very painfully certain, and that is that Mrs. Warham was not taking it well. One afternoon, late, and fortunately just as I was shutting up for the night, she came to the lab.—bursting in, one might almost say. She was not at all well, and she exhibited signs of these distressing symptoms to which I have already alluded. Her conversational opening was decidedly embarrassing. Dropping into the chair at the professor's locked desk, she said:

"Well, Wrammy, how are you getting on now that your fascinating fairy has taken my husband away with her?" I may explain that being burdened with the rather awkward name of Wrammsbothhame, my colleagues soon shortened it to "Wram," or "Wrammy," and I have reason to believe that this euphuism still obtains among my students.

"You should not express yourself like that, Mrs. Warham," I replied. "The professor and his assistant are engaged upon important scientific work for the University, and to say that kind of thing might convey a very wrong and injurious impression."

"Scientific work be jiggered," retorted the lady inelegantly. "You know, as everyone else in the 'varsity knows, that that red-headed slut has been trying to get away alone with him ever since she got in here. I am certain that her coming here was a put-up job—and you know it."

Hereupon the lady became lachrymose and I extremely nervous.

"You really must not say such things," I said. "Everyone knows that Dr. Strachan came here, selected from many candidates, solely on her merits, when the post was advertised."

"Selected—advertised—," replied she, her tears suddenly giving way to termagance, "don't talk such (qualified) tosh. You know perfectly well that all that muck about advertising and selecting is just eye-wash, and that if a man wants a particular girl here, it's all cut and dried long before the saturatory—statutory formalities are set going. He'd seen her at that old (woman), Lady What's-her-name's, got stuck on her—or at one of those blasted Brirish—British Association Meetings, where all the Professors and people go for a week's picnic, to see what they can pick up in the way of fun—and skirt."

I grieve to be compelled to reproduce Mrs. Warham's somewhat confused and wholly slanderous statements—and to tell the truth, a lurking conviction that there was a modicum of truth in her views on the subject of staff appointments put me in a position of some embarrassment.

"But I assure you——" I began.

"Of course you do," she interrupted, "that's what you are left behind to do. But I know better! Why, Dr. Magley——"

"I do not want to hear Dr. Magley's views," I said. "He is a man for whose opinions, apart from his professional work, I have the utmost contempt."

And here I made a mistake, for by letting her "liberate her mind" I might have gained some useful information.

"All right," she replied, getting up rather uncertainly. "I know what I know, and I have means, thank God, of finding out a great deal more than you will ever admit—and when they get back—if they ever to get back—you will see what you will see. I'll learn them!"

And on this pregnant exit-speech, she left the lab, and me very perturbed.

A few days later Dr. Blayre sent for me to speak of some departmental matters, and, these disposed of, he said:

"By the way, Wrammsbothame, have you heard whether Professor Magley has been writing home any tittle-tattle about the scientific staff out there?"

"Nothing very precise," I replied cautiously, "but you know what Magley's reputation and tongue are. No one pays any attention to him. He has always preferred his worst epigram to his best friend."

"His best friend? Are you sure that you would rightly describe Professor Warham as such?"

I really had no answer to make, and was relieved, and at the same time a little startled when Dr. Blayre concluded irrelevantly:

"I wonder if anyone knows anything about Mrs. Wahrham's people? I cannot help thinking that it would be well if she had some relation with her, or could visit her family whilst the expedition is away."

Again I was unable to make any comment or suggestion, and I left our Registrar full of rather indigestible food for reflection.

The next thing that happened was the arrival of some voluminous notes from the expedition, accompanied by a considerable mass of material for arrangement, classification and preservation, which kept me and my assistants very fully occupied. A professor from another University came over at stated intervals and lectured to the students. Our own Professor of Botany (who had succeeded Warham) did all he could to help, but most of the spade-work fell to my lot, and I was a bit overworked; but I realise now that it was this that led to my ultimately occupying the position that I hold at present.

The following mail brought the rather disturbing news that the Expedition had halted and made its headquarters at Manaos, where they were working up their results to date, and that Warham and Pamela Strachan had left them to explore the upper reaches of the river in a canoe with four Indian guides and paddlers—*seringuieros* (rubber collectors)—proposing to collect on the Javary River, and might be away from the base for some weeks.

And then—three weeks later—the truly awful thing happened.

It was a Monday morning. I had been to town for the weekend, and, entering the lab, at about eleven o'clock, I found a note from Dr. Blayre asking me to come over to his office. The moment I saw him my heart "missed a beat," as they say. Without a word he handed me a cablegram. It was from Manaos, sent by Cantrell, and it read:

> Messenger from Esperança brings news of death of Warham by accident in jungle on Itecuahy River. Stop. Strachan returning down river. Stop. Have assumed command. Stop. Cable authorising and confirming. —Cantrell.

We looked at one another for a full minute in silence. Then old Blayre, the kindly, imperturbable and sweet-tempered old Blayre, said an amazing thing.

He said: "I wish it had been Magley."

I will not delay this narrative by describing, even in general terms, the consternation that literally overwhelmed the University. It fell to my lot to break the news to Mrs. Warham. The first thing she did was to burst into a peal of laughter. Then:

"Dead!" she cried. "Bosh! they have skipped to Bunnus Airs—or Rio. I've looked it up in the atlas. What did I tell you, you silly fool?" And then she collapsed in raging hysterics. I sent for Sir George Amboyne, and he got her away somewhere. I never set eyes on her again.

I called on Paul Barrowdale.

"Have you heard from Magley?" I asked.

He thought for a minute or so, and then replied: "Yes—by the last mail. Whether anyone else will ever see his letter will depend on many things. *De mortuis nil nisi bonum.* But I have cabled—and written—to Magley."

And so we awaited the return of the expedition.

I can hardly say what we anticipated, but we—that is to say, Blayre, Barrowdale and the departments of Botany and Botanical Research, and the people who were in any way intimate with Warham and Pamela Strachan—were obsessed with an indefinable sense of uneasiness; so much so that, on a hint from the Registrar, I went up to Liverpool to meet the ship. When it arrived and made the dock, I saw at first glance that our forebodings were all without any foundation whatever.

They were all in splendid health, and though the unspoken thought of the tragedy of Warham's death could not but cast a cloud over our greetings, they were in their normal good spirits. Cantrell, genial, capable and a trifle stern, as is his wont; Rex Magley, cool, cynical and amusing as ever; and Pamela, tanned, thinner, and with a "set" expression that was new to her, but keen, bright and efficient as ever. She carried a rather large botanical case, a *vasculum*, with her, from which she refused to be parted. They chaffed her a little about it.

"It is Pamela's week-end case," said Cantrell. "She never knows what invitations we may have to accept at a moment's notice."

"No," said Magley, for my enlightenment, "that is where Pamela keeps her 'scoops'—new genera and species of plants that none of us have seen." And then the implied significance of his careless words flowed around us, and for a few moments there was a painful silence. What secrets might she have brought with her from the jungles of the Itecuahy River where Warham had met with death?

For, in Cosmopoli, we had received no details of the tragedy. Only one mail had preceded the expedition on its homeward journey, and all that we had learnt from that was that Warham had wounded his foot with some jungle thorn, or been bitten by the giant centipede *Scolopendra;* Pamela could not tell which, as Warham had been delirious when she returned to their *tambo* from a short expedition up a tributary stream; the wound had festered with the ghastly rapidity common in that fever-stricken land, and before morning he was dead, and was buried in the heart of the jungle by some Mangeroma Indians, who, cannibals though they were, had served the explorers faithfully, and had brought Pamela back safely to Esperança, the last civilised point on the Upper Amazon.

Arrived back in Cosmopoli, the members of the Expedition settled down into their original places, each of them fully occupied with the sorting and classification of the collections in his charge, and, of course, regard being had to the primary objects of the Expedition, being botanical, the bulk of the work fell upon Pamela and myself. After the usual formalities had been observed, Dr. Pamela Strachan was appointed to the Chair left vacant by the death of Warham, and I succeeded to her late position as Assistant Lecturer; and we had to take in two more assistants to help us, for the Expedition had been absent for six months, and the collections were vast and of the highest scientific importance.

She neither courted nor avoided the subject of Warham and his end, and between us, to my great relief, his wife was never mentioned. I know that she had a long conference with Sir George Amboyne, the Regius Professor of Medicine, but she never spoke of it to anyone, so far as I am aware, excepting to our Registrar, Dr. Blayre, and he, the repository of most of the secret histories of the University, was always "emblematically silent"—as Magley put it, comparing him to the Greek emblem of Silence—"a toasted fish with its mouth sewn up." Only one who knew her as intimately as I did would have noticed any change in her—always dignified and reserved, her manner took on a deeper shade of austerity, and it was only I who could observe her unremitting care in completing such work and research as Warham had left unfinished. She brought back the keys of his private desk, and went through his papers with an almost religious diligence and exactitude. He had made a will before leaving England, leaving all his private collections and scientific papers and books to her, and the rest of his estate, which was comparatively ample, to his wife. What became of it and her I never knew—his sole executor was Christopher Blayre.

It was not until a year or more after this that she revealed to me the mystery of her *vasculum*. It contained nothing but a complete series of specimens of a monœcious plant of the Passion-flower family. Every part of the plants, both male and female, was mounted and preserved with a perfection of technique that only so experienced and skilled a botanist as Pamela Strachan could have displayed. To this day they constitute one of the most perfect, and perfectly preserved, series of specimens in the world-renowned herbarium of the University of Cosmopoli. During her lifetime she kept this case invariably locked, only, at intervals, adding a new "preparation" or a new sheet of manuscript to the portfolio of notes kept in it.

My emotions as a botanist may be imagined when at last she opened the case for my inspection; here was not only a new plant, a new species, but—as it seemed to me—a new genus. In answer to my natural enquiry she shook her head, whose red gold was now here and there showing silver threads, and said, with her slow characteristic smile:

"I shall never describe or publish it—but when the appointed time comes, and you will know when that is—*you* will describe it and publish it in the Phil. Trans., giving due acknowledgement to the original observations of the late Dr. Pamela Strachan, and it will go into the *Index Kewensis* as *Passiflora vindicta*. Wrammsbothame."

I started to protest, but she put her hand on my shoulder, looked me straight in the eyes, and said:

"I lay this upon you as a sacred charge, Wrammy. You will do as I say. Promise me."

And for the first and last time during the years that we worked together, idled together, and even travelled together, I saw her zygomatic muscles twitch and stiffen, and her strange greenish eyes glisten with tears.

I promised.

The work of completing and publishing the Reports went on actively and strenuously. The members of the Expedition constantly met in our room in the research wing, and discussed their work, Pamela and I being, by tacit agreement, general Editors, of course in collaboration with Cantrell, who had succeeded Warham as Director. There was, at first, a certain "shyness" in discussing the Upper Amazon work that Pamela and Warham had done on their ill-fated extension of the field of research, but this entirely wore off as it became apparent that Pamela was quite ready, indeed anxious, to give us the results, discussing each man's special line with him, and explaining and amplifying the voluminous notes she had brought back. They were really remarkable, especially considering the almost appalling conditions under which they had worked. As Askew, the meteorologist, observed one day, somewhat to her embarrassment: "If Strachan could have split herself into ten, it seems to me that she could have run the whole show on her own." She seemed to know exactly what each man wanted, and had brought it back with full notes made on the spot, which she was able to amplify from memory—a remarkable feat considering that they travelled in a native craft called *igariti*, on which was a kind of cabin, constructed of woven liana, a wicker-work frame thatched with palm leaves. A smaller canoe (called *montaria*) was taken in tow for exploring the smaller creeks and tributary streams. It was obvious that their Indian crew were entirely devoted to them, and concentrated their allegiance upon Pamela after the death of Warham. She discussed and described with calm detachment every step of their dreadful journey, and it was only I, who knew her so well, that could detect at times the strain that she frequently felt in telling us all about it.

It took nearly four years to complete the work, and when the last part of *Sophia Amazonica* was published, I reaped vicariously the rich reward of election to the Fellowship of the Royal Society. I say "vicariously," for had the Fellowship been open to women, it would undoubtedly have been upon Pamela that this honour should have been conferred.

When the "selection" by the Council was published, I went earlier than was my wont into the lab., and was astonished—and pained—to see Pamela sitting at Warham's private desk, her head bowed upon her hands. She looked up with a weary—almost dead—expression on her still very beautiful face, and said:

"Hullo, Wrammy! I see you have had the great news. May you live long and prosper with your Fellowship. I have only waited for this, as I knew it was bound to come, and now I can utter my '*nunc dimittis.*' I have sent in my resignation to the Senate, and you will follow me in the Chair—no—do not protest, and do not try to dissuade me. I am *tired*, Wrammy, oh so tired!—sometimes I have marvelled at myself for having kept up so long. And do not try to deny, Wrammy dear, that you have seen it—but I am sure no one else has. I shall retire into obscurity with my memories, and devoutly thank whatever gods there be that I have them. As Plantin said at the end of his Sonnet: '*c'est attendre bien doucement la mort.*' The mainspring is worn out, if not broken, Wrammy, and the clock is running down. Do not jaw at me, there's a good chap, and run along now. I am lecturing in half an hour."

And that was our last "professional" interview. As she had foreshadowed, I was appointed to the vacant professorship. Pamela went to live in a little house in Cornwall that she had bought some years before "as a refuge for her old age," as she put it; I visited her there twice, and once she came to a Botanical Congress at Cosmopoli, and I was shocked to see how lassitude grew upon her, in a word, how she aged. She was only forty-four when she died quietly of no specific illness—she was just tired. I do not think that I was ever "in love" with Pamela, but I know that from the first moment that I met her I never took the slightest personal interest in any other woman—save as a pupil or as a colleague.

The preparations of and notes upon *Passiflora vindicta* were still in their special case, untouched as she had arranged them there.

A week after her funeral, which Blayre, Cantrell and I attended, I received from her executor, a solicitor at Taunton, a small packet containing a manuscript which she had sealed up and addressed to me. It is many years since Professor Pamela Strachan died, and I am nearing the time when I shall make way for a younger man. My Monograph upon *Passiflora vindicta* is respectably entombed in the Phil. Trans. (Ser. B), and is still frequently quoted and referred to by botanists studying the monœcious plants; and I have written the above account of the Warham-Edelstein Expedition to be deposited with Pamela's manuscript among Dr. Christopher Blayre's remarkable *corpus* of the personal Archives of the University.

(Here follows the Manuscript of Pamela Strachan.)

"Let me tell you at once, dear Wrammy (this may be the last time that I shall ever write the dear old familiar name), that you never-failing and beautiful loyalty to me, your pure affection for me so very near to perfect love, has been, apart from the one great glory of my life, the most wonderful thing I have ever known; without it, I could never have carried on; without it, I should have given up and succumbed both physically and mentally years ago. For your sake—and I feel that it is due to you—I have made up my mind to tell you the story which has haunted, and even comforted me ever since the things that I am going to tell you happened.

"I loved Philip Warham all my life—that is to say, ever since life really meant anything to me. I met him first at Lady Cynthia's at an evening party, when I was nineteen, just after I had gone up to Oxbridge. His wife was there—he did not even notice my existence. The thought of him and my constant study of his splendid work in Botany were my lode-star all the years that I was at the 'varsity, and when I was up for finals, to my mingled joy and terror, he was the External Examiner. I can never forget my *'viva';* he inspired me and 'though I says it as shouldn't,' I *was* brilliant. I knew about his wife, and my heart bled for him. I was so frightfully sorry for him. He 'passed' me, as you know, and said some gloriously encouraging things to me, but I know that he never noticed whether or not I was hump-backed or squinted. You can imagine the fever of hope and anxiety in which I 'put in' for the assistant lecturership and keepership at Cosmopoli.

"Often in the years that followed my appointment I was sorely tempted to ask him if he had the slightest recollection of the girl he had missed the opportunity of ploughing—or at any rate of 'gulfing' at Oxbridge—but I never dared, or did. Once, when we had been working together for a long time, he said to me, suddenly:

"'Do you know, Strachan, I sometimes have a queer feeling that I have seen you somewhere before you came here.'

"I replied: 'You must have seen so many carrotty-headed girls in your nefarious career as an examiner,' and he said:

"'Of course—dozens—but somehow——' He did not finish the sentence.

"On another occasion, when his wife had been peculiarly beastly, in one of her bad attacks, and had, I know (somebody told me, very kindly) said some beastly things about me, he was going through some sections I had made for him, and he suddenly said, quite irrelevantly to all appearance, but I could not help knowing what was in his mind:

"'You will never let anything outside the work drive you away from Cosmopoli, will you?' and I replied:

"'I shall never go away unless you sack me, and then it will be to creep into a corner and die.' I jolly nearly gave myself away that time, but I had the presence of mind to spill some picrocarmine over a heap of slides that I knew we were going to throw into the bucket, and, like a frightened Squid, I got away in the mess and confusion.

"Two people working together day in and day out cannot be in love with one another without knowing it—and we did know it, but neither of us gave the least sign of it—until the Expedition was organised, and it was settled that I should accompany it. When we came back from the Council meeting into the lab., he turned round and looked me straight in the face, and said:

"'Pamela! Great God, how wonderful it will be!'

"The next morning I was in his arms. In my thoughts, waking or sleeping, I have been there ever since, and I pray that I may rest there so long as I live.

"Of course you know that I had trouble with Magley. He has an uncanny instinct, that man, the servant of a foul mind. There are men who are convinced that if a woman is another man's mistress she is fair game, and only requires the appropriate invitation to become theirs. Magley is one of them. I always wondered how it was that Barrowdale, who was a white man if ever there was one, stuck so faithfully to Magley and shielded him in so many adventures which might have done for him so far as his University career was concerned. If what people hinted at when Magley killed himself is founded on fact, hideous though it may be, the thing is more or less explained, and whatever he may have done, and whatever one might have against him, was fully expiated, and one even pities him. Did Dr. Blayre ever tell you about '*The Cheetah-Girl*'? He told Philip, and Philip told me, later. But at the time I was rather horrified when I found that Magley was coming with us as physiologist. He soon gave up trying to 'collect' me. I disposed of his principal argument, which was that a bachelor has 'in the last ditch' an advantage over and a weapon against a married man, in a way that inflicted an incurable wound upon his vanity, which was, as you know, colossal. After that he was always more or less on our track, and never lost an opportunity to make us uncomfortable. I know that he wrote subtle innuendoes back to Cosmopoli—to Barrowdale, and indirectly, I believe, to Mrs. Warham. We drew his fire–and his teeth–to some extent, by planning the extension of our journey to the Upper Amazon, which would have been quite impossible for the whole expedition. And now I will tell you about that.

"You will smile, Wrammy,—I know that smile of yours,— when I tell you a silly little romantic secret of ours—lovers do have such secrets, you know, even when they are Doctors of Science! Philip and I secretly specialised in the Passifloreœ—the Passion-flowers—they seemed to have a hidden meaning for us, though it was really rather a blasphemous one, for, as you know, the original name, given to it by Jacomo Bosio in 1610 in his book, *The Cross of Calvary, Fior della Passione* speaks for itself. The Spaniards, who first found *Passiflora cerulea* in the South American forests, called it *'Flor de las cinca llagas'*—'the flower of the five wounds,' for they saw in its several parts the Emblems of the Passion of Christ—the Crown of Thorns, the Nails, the Column of the Flagellation, the Scourge, the Lance-headed leaves, the Thirty pieces of Silver, and the Five Wounds—they are all represented diagrammatically in the extraordinary plate given in Bosio's book, *Crux triumphans et gloriosa*, Antwerp, 1617 (and also in Zahn's *Specula Physico-Mathematico-Historica*, Nuremberg, 1696). It was a Mexican Augustinian, Emanuel da Villegas, who had arrived in Rome with a drawing which he gave to Bosio, who found it 'so stupendously marvellous that he hesitated to mention it.' But the marvel was confirmed by drawings sent from new Spain to the Mexican Jesuits in Rome, and the Dominicans at Bologna caused drawings of it to be engraved, which they circulated, accompanied by descriptive poems and essays. So Bosio felt justified in publishing it to the world as '*Flos Passionis*,' 'the most wondrous example of the *Croce trionfante* discovered in forest or field,' and the Spaniards announced that 'it had been created by the Almighty and caused to be discovered in order that it might assist in the conversion of the heathen among whom it grows.'

"Plants of it were soon brought to Italy, and were established in the garden of Cardinal Odoardo Farnese in 1625, and his gardener, Aldinus, described it minutely, comparing its several parts with the Emblems of the Passion. The passion which it suggested to Philip and me was of a more mundane variety, and we had even a sneaking affection for its 'poor relations,' the *Tacsonias* and the common white bryony (*Bryonia dioica*, Jacquin), though these have now been banished by systematists from the society of the South American aristocrats.

"You will think that this is a fond and foolish digression from our story, but you will see, when I have finished, that this historical interlude is really quite pertinent to it.

"Well—as you know—we started off up the river—(you know that the name Amazon (Amassona) comes from an Indian word meaning 'the Destroyer'—not from the female warriors of the Caucasus in Greek legends, or spoken of by early travellers in South America)—at the end of April, when the river is at its fullest, and the tributaries were most likely to be navigable—from Manaos, where we had established our laboratories on land, and from whence we could send out 'trips' to collect further and other material if required.

"Our kit and apparatus was as compact and small as was consistent with ordinary field-efficiency, and our first stop was at the place with the awful name—Remate de Males—'Culmination of Evils'—had we but known it, there was something prophetic about this. There we transhipped to a smaller steamer, and in course of time reached Esperança, the official frontier of Brazil, and the last civilised point on the Upper Amazon—opposite, across the river, in Peru, lies the equally decrepit town of Nazareth. Here we 'descended,' as the French say, at the Hotel Agosto—as a matter of fact, we 'ascended,' for, like all the other houses in the so-called 'town,' it is built on piles or poles thirty feet high, so as to be above high-water mark when the river is in flood. The 'hotel' was indescribable—the mosquitoes, the ants, the huge centipedes, avicularian spiders six inches long—horrible—but to Philip and me it was an annexe of Paradise—you see, we loved one another—there it is in four words. The Spanish Agent, who superintended the collection of rubber for shipment to Manaos and Para, quoted a pretty proverb: *'Amor tiene disculpa en sus efectos con solo su amor'* ('Love has the one excuse for all the ills it works—that it is love.') No woman in the world, he said, was as passionate as the Spaniard, but no Spanish woman could ever love to the point of accompanying her husband to Esperança. Spaniards cannot converse excepting in proverbs, and his proverb on this point was: *'Mujer apasionada no peregrina para amor'* (A passionate woman does not go on pilgrimage with her lover—or for love').

"He was kindness and courtesy itself, and saw to the selection and fitting out of our big canoe—called *igariti*—with its 'living' cabin—which Philip called our 'state-room' on it, and the smaller one the *montaria*—which Philip called 'the Launch'.

"I must hurry on, not attempting to describe our journey up the Javary River—the sting-rays *(A raya)*, the alligators, and the awful fish *Piranha*, a fierce monster (*Serraselmus piraya*), the size of a herring, that attacks every other kind of fish, that bit our paddles, and that, if in sufficient numbers, will attack a man and leave his skeleton clean in an hour. But the greater part of the collecting was done from our 'stations' on the banks of the river, where our Indians (Mandurucus) built us substantial huts (*tambo*)—a frame of saplings (mostly rubber) covered with bark and leaves of the murumani palm. The nights in the jungle, where it came down to the river—the strip of sky above us full of stars—and the sounds! The cries of the howling monkeys and of the owl, which the Indians call 'the Mother of the Moon'—every now and then the screams of some animal caught by an anaconda or boa constrictor (*Succuruja*), which may reach a length of anything from forty to fifty feet or more. We used to lie awake for hours, talking in whispers, listening to the cries of love and slaughter, and fall asleep the world forgetting (but not, I fear, by the world forgot) in one another's arms. Wrammy, it was heaven!

"And after the wonder of the night, the wonder of the day—the herons on the rivers, the macaws, the humming-birds—and the everlasting watchfulness for snakes and, what was worse, the fire-ants (*'formiga de fogo'*), which have been known to drive away the entire populations of villages that they have attacked.

"We were happy, for we seized upon happiness as it came and arrested its flight as it passed us. We lived in an ever-lovely present. Never postpone a moment of happiness till 'next time,' Wrammy. There is no such thing as *'next* time'—it would have happened anyhow, and *this* time would have been lost for ever.

"I have not said anything, nor do I intend to say anything about the botanical booty of our journey. No one—excepting myself—knows the wealth of it better than you do—see our reports! When you have read what I am writing for you now, your information will be as complete as mine, and you will describe and publish *Passiflora vindicta*. Wrammsbothame.

"We made many excursions into and along *estradas* of the jungle, which wind their way from the Javary River towards the Itecuahy, and filled our *vascula* with strange and wonderful Orchidaceæ and Saprophytes of all kinds, when suddenly one day Philip stopped and pulled upon a stem that had trailed across the *estrada*. An *estrada* is a sort of narrow track or path, worn through the jungle by the passage of animals, and generally in the direction of a clearing or spring, difficult to find, for the entrance is generally masked by palm or fern fronds. He pulled until the flower came to our hands—it was a huge Passion-flower, the most beautiful that I have ever seen, the petals a deep blue, shading off at the ends into mauve, and finally into pink. We stared at it in enthusiastic delight.

"'Look!' cried Philip. 'I ask you—just *look*. See this remarkable pistil—there are no stamens—this is a diœcious plant—and this is the female. We must find the male.'

"We retraced our steps a short way, Philip carrying the 'trailer.' After half an hour we gave up the search, for night, the sudden tropical night, was at hand. We came back to the spot we had started back from, and traced the remainder of the plant to its root, which we dug up and carried back to our *tambo*. We 'prepared' it for preservation, and retired for the night. Queerly enough, in the mile or so that Philip carried the plant, it had would itself two or three times round his wrist and fore-arm. It seemed rather uncanny.

"Next morning we rose, as usual, at dawn, left our plant in our temporary travelling 'press', and re-entered the *estrada* we had penetrated the day before, and went in search of the male plant of our *Passiflora*. We searched all day in vain, and at nightfall returned rather disheartened to our *tambo*. There a weird surprise awaited us. A stalk some four feet in length, had sprouted from the ground outside our *tambo*, and was creeping up the wall of matted palmfronds and liana. We concluded that a seed that had escaped our notice had fallen to the ground as we reached 'home' in the dark, and had germinated with the inexplicable and terrifying rapidity that is not uncommon in jungle plants. As we looked at it, Philip remarked, not altogether in jest:

"'Supposing that this is the male plant come in search of its mate!'

"Wrammy—it was! In the morning we found that a long tendril had come through the frond-wall and was lying across our 'press'—this is horribly difficult to believe, but it is really true. A huge flower was just opening from a bud. It was full of stamens—with no trace of a pistil.

"'Good God!' said Philip, 'it *is* the male. What luck!' We sort of laughed, but I confess that we felt uncannily uncomfortable. We did odd jobs—'chores' near the *tambo* by unspoken agreement all that day, unwilling to go far from the phenomenon. By midday the tendril had grown another foot, and the flower was fully expanded, filling the *tambo* with a sickly, rather nauseous perfume. We cut a hole in the frond-wall, and got the whole plant, which we 'prepared' and put into the 'press' with the female. The flower was a dull greenish brown, not nearly so beautiful as the female.

"'If we can find another pair,' said Philip, 'we will try to get some seed and send it home by the next mail, after we get back to Manaos, for cultivation.'

"And so we went on with our routine work—feeling half excited and half uncomfortable—we could not have said why. I could see that Philip was uneasy about me—I caught him watching me at times.

"'Feeling all right and chipper?' he said once.

"'Splendid!' I replied—but I did not feel very splendid. I wondered if I was in for a touch of malaria—in spite of our inoculations.

"We searched all round the *tambo* within a radius of twenty feet on various pretexts. But there was no sign of another plant.

"That night I was nervy and restless, and Philip came across from his bunk and took me in his arms. And presently, as usual, I fell asleep.

"Towards morning I was wakened by a sudden movement of Philip's—and a muttered word—'Damn!'

"'Don't move,' he whispered, as he felt me waken, 'open your lantern and give it me—mine is over there. I believe there is a snake around my ankle. Or better—prize yourself up without moving your legs and see if you can see anything.'

"With the help of his hand behind my back, I sat up and opened up the light—there were no electric torches in those days. A trail of the uncanny *Passiflora* had crept in along the ground and was wound round his ankle. We pretended to laugh at our 'scare,' and Philip cut the trailer and unwound the beastly thing.

"We traced the plant as soon as it was daylight—dug up the root and burnt it. Some days passed and we got quite accustomed to our 'intruder.' It turned up in all sorts of places, always growing rapidly in the night, and, as Philip put it, 'lying doggo' during the day. We collected several specimens of both sexes in various stages of growth. I filled a *vasculum* with dried examples, and sacrificed a quart of alcohol for a young plant, and specimens of both the male and the female flowers, and we got some seeds, some of which we put into the jar of alcohol and some of which we dried. You have got all these.

"I get on to the 24th of June, when we had been away from the base at Manaos nearly two months, and were thinking regretfully of retracing our steps. Very often, if I was restless, Philip would come across in the dark, and, kneeling silently by my bunk, would soothe me to sleep by the touch of his hands, which always had a sort of mesmeric effect upon me, and sometimes he would fall asleep, kneeling there, with his arm round me or his hand on my breast. Oh! Wrammy, it was wonderful to love as we loved. He was as tender and as cleverly knowledgeable as a woman when necessary. On that night I half woke and felt his hand upon me, caressing me gently. It came to rest on my shoulder, up against my neck, and he had passed his other arm round my waist. I fell back into sleep, perfectly happy.

"Contrary to my wont, I did not wake again till it was broad daylight, and I woke with a sensation of indescribable oppression and constriction—a nightmare, I said to myself. The next moment I shrieked aloud. Round my waist, and all up over my breast and lying on my neck, were thick tendrils of the plant. Philip was not there—and he did not wake. Terrified, I struggled into a sitting position and tore the beastly tendrils away, and then I staggered across to Philip's bunk. He, too, was covered with tendrils—on his chest a male flower was fully expanded, its stamens thick with sticky pollen. And round his neck three turns of a strong tendril were closely wound—and his face was horribly discoloured.

"Philip was dead!—strangled by a tendril of the male plant of our *Passiflora*. Mechanically I turned to the fragments I had torn from my own body, and picked up a magnificent flower, which had opened on my breast as the male flower had opened on his—it was a female plant that had caressed and lulled me to sleep.

"My cry had brought our head-man to the opening of our *tambo*. As his eyes fell upon Philip, he yelled and fell on his face, giving utterance to a flood of jargon—and the rest of our Indians crowded up behind him.

"I will not re-live or write down the horrors of that day. Strangely enough, I felt no fear at being left alone among those savages—they seemed to be inspired with a reverential awe for me. But they would not remain for a moment longer than was necessary.

"After a strange ceremony of perambulation of our camp, they loaded into our *igariti* all our collections and specimens, and every portable trace of our expedition. Then, moving with curious dancing steps and chanting something almost in a whisper, they laid Philip on the ground in the centre of our *tambo* and covered him with dry palm-fronds. Next they piled over him everything that was not embarked on the *igariti* and the fragments of their own huts which they had pulled down in feverish haste, and then, as they crowded in a circle round the *tambo*, the Headman set fire to this pyre and stood off at a little distance—

chanting—till the whole was reduced to a heap of white ash, which they collected and scattered in the middle of the river.

"And so we fled from that now accursed spot as fast as they could paddle, never stopping, night or day, until we reached Exsperança where at last I collapsed and remained stunned for three days.

"It was the Brazilian 'Agent' who invented, and sent down to Manaos ahead of me, the story of the poisonous thorn, or the bite of the *Scolopendra*. When I was sufficiently myself again to travel, our Indians had disappeared—paid off—and until I was setting foot upon the steamer that was to take me and our collections to Remate de Males, Senor Aguarravilla never mentioned Philip—and then the moment of farewell, with a flourish of his *sombrero*, was:

"'No man, Señora, has ever aroused the jealousy or incurred the vengeance of the Devils of the Jungle and lived to tell the story—*valga con Dios*.'"

A FEW WORDS IN EXPLANATION OF
"THE CHEETAH-GIRL."

A MANUSCRIPT bearing this title is recorded at the end of the "List of Selected Papers," in the first selection of these Papers, published in 1921. The half-title, p. 211 of that volume, bore a "Note" to the effect that my publishers regretted that they were unable to print this MS. So many references have been made in reviews of the volume to this MS., and I have received so many inquiries concerning it, that I think the time has arrived when the Note requires an explanation which circumstances rendered it both difficult and undesirable to offer in that place. The eight MSS. published in that volume were selected by me for publication as explained in the antescript, and at the same time I brought away with me from my safe in the University Library, for re-perusal, the MS. of "*The Cheetah-Girl.*" This MS., though setting forth the principles of an enquiry, and the result of experiments in a branch of biological research conducted by Professor Barrowdale, the importance of which it would be impossible to over-estimate, contains matters of record of such a nature that it could not possibly be published in a volume destined for general circulation. It relates also the circumstances that led to the subsequent social and professional annihilation of Professor Rex Magley, his successor in the Chair of Physiology, whose name has been mentioned in various connections in other MSS. preserved in the archives of the University, not, I fear, as a rule, in a manner redounding to his credit as a member of our University society. The "List of Selected Papers" was, however, copied from the title-covers of the MSS. by my secretary, who, I may mention parenthetically, made the mistake of writing "Deposited by the Professor of Biology," instead of "of Physiology"—there is no Chair of General Biology in the University of Cosmopoli. This "List" went to the printers after my departure from England on a protracted holiday, and was "set up" with the rest of what is technically called "the preliminary matter." When, on my return, my publishers asked about this MS., I considered that I was justified in showing it to them in confidence, and they at once agreed with me that it could not be printed. Hence the "Note," which reviewers have regarded, some in the light of a joke (!) and some as a touch of intentional sensationalism.

Some doubts were even expressed as to the actual existence of the MS., which has, however, been established in a manner recalling the publication of the infamous work of the Prince de Conti and de Bussy Rabutin: *Histoire Amoureuse des Gaules*, the MS. of which was lent for twenty-four hours to a friend, who copied it and caused a small edition to be printed by the Elzevir Press, with the *locus* "Liège," but without date, in 1665. (See the *Memoirs* of de Bussy Rabutin, Paris, 1704, Vol. III., p. 270). This treachery was the ostensible cause of Bussy's life-long banishment from the Court of Louis XIV., though, of course, the real reason was his connection, in his earlier years, with the "Fronde." The Prince de Conti, who was the brother of Madame de Montespan, incurred no penalty or disgrace in the matter. The MS. of "*The Cheetah-Girl*," similarly lent in confidence (by a friend to a friend of hers) was similarly "Printed as manuscript for private circulation" in 1923, and at least ten, if not more, copies are known to exist. The printer was never discovered, the work being such that, in the present state of the law, he would undoubtedly have incurred severe penalties.

C.B.

Lightning Source UK Ltd.
Milton Keynes UK
UKHW041305041019
351005UK00002B/439/P